The author is a Senior Scholar of Peterhouse and graduated from Cambridge University with a First Class Degree in English. He went on to study law, specializing in Commercial Litigation, and applied his creative skills in legal practice for his many grateful clients, prior to taking up fiction. His cases are in the law books and on the syllabus. He is now Senior Partner Litigation for a Worldwide law firm. He lives in London and Cadaqués in Spanish Catalonia.

The Gate of the Burnt One

By the same author: INFINITI

Philip G Cohen

AUSTIN MACAULEY PUBLISHERS™
LONDON · CAMBRIDGE · NEW YORK · SHARJAH

Copyright © Philip G Cohen 2024

The right of **Philip G Cohen** to be identified as author of this work has been asserted by the author in accordance with sections 77 and 78 of the Copyright, Designs and Patents Act 1988.

All rights reserved. No part of this publication may be reproduced, stored in a retrieval system, or transmitted in any form or by any means, electronic, mechanical, photocopying, recording, or otherwise, without the prior permission of the publishers.

Any person who commits any unauthorised act in relation to this publication may be liable to criminal prosecution and civil claims for damages.

A CIP catalogue record for this title is available from the British Library.

ISBN 9781035819379 (Paperback)
ISBN 9781035819386 (Hardback)
ISBN 9781035819409 (ePub e-book)
ISBN 9781035819393 (Audiobook)

www.austinmacauley.com

First Published 2024
Austin Macauley Publishers Ltd®
1 Canada Square
Canary Wharf
London
E14 5AA

To Letitia.

Thanks again to my editors, Jack Pine and Justine Cohen, and a special mention for Bob Kerpner who complained that *INFINITI* was based upon his time at Peterhouse, a fact that went unacknowledged.

Table of Contents

Working Title: Knights of the Ream	16
A Pathetic Demonstration	19
Diva	20
Toureg	24
Albanian George	28
Parking Space	35
The Anal Retentive	36
Cancelled	38
All Hung Up	40
Stainless Steel Crab Cracker Seafood Tool Set	41
Interview	43
Twins	52
Making Virtue of a Necessity	54
Another Desert	58
Presley on the Payroll	59
Salvator Mundi	62
La Mamounia	67
Point Break	69
Split Focus Diopter	74
To Hold Infinity in the Palm of Your Hand	77
Another Desert	81
Designed to Fail	84
The Unsdorfer Twins	87
Agent Elena Troy's Exegesis on Immaterial Assets	89
Aït Benhaddou	92

Blue Phantom	96
A Teams Call	98
The Tao of Ying and Yang	104
A Tour of Atlas Corporation Studios, Ouarzazate	107
Ring Tones	110
A Jineta Sword	114
The Agency Accountant	118
Bvsh Ho	122
RPG-7	128
HMRC Rewrite European History	129
The Relic	138
Frogs	141
Baby Grand	143
Gazelle D'or	148
Ambiguity	157
A Berber on a Bicycle	158
Death in Venice	161
An Email from a Law Firm	163
A Sonnet with 13 Lines	165
Catafalque	168
Billet Doux	170
To His Mistress Going to Bed	173
Preserving the Environment in a V12 Off-Roader	175
After Yoga	176
Oscietra	178
Horizontal Pin Stripes	181
Nomad	183
A Symbiotic Relationship	185
Fires in the Desert	188

Turntable	192
A Nocturnal Visit	195
Shit Happens	197
An Unexpected Visit	202
Rigmarole	204
The Gate of the Burnt One	210
The Director's Cut	215
Ossuary	217
Pretzel Logic	220
Day Off	222
Printers	223
Deep Fake	226
Hannibal	228
Shooting the US 5M Sex Scene	230
A Case of Mistaken Identity	234
When You've Eliminated All Which Is Impossible, Whatever Remains, However Improbable, Must Be the Truth	235
The Tailor of Gloucester	239
Vertigo	240
Elephantine	243
Phoenix	245
A Piece of Advice	249
The Omnibus	250
Moulin Rouge	251
Another Urchin	252
Casablanca	253
An Outage	255
Marfa Lights	257

The Threatened Assassin	259
Ouroboros	261
Man Down	262
Two Men Down	263
Scrapbook	265
An Arse with Three Cheeks	267
Organogram	272
Quiz Master	275
A Dance of Seven Veils	277
OpenSea	279
The New Prometheans	282
The Plot Thickens	288
Teaser Trailer Trash	292
The Smile on the Face of the Sphinx	294
Tamazight	297
Smoking	300
Excel	302
Mint Tea	305
Kasbah Toubkal	311
Rodrigo	314
Death Hath Ten Thousand Several Doors	317
The Man in the Suit Carrier Comes Round	324
Beyond Good and Evil	327
Laocoön	334
Hammam	337
Work Done	341
Tongue Lashing	344
Anfa	347
Scheherazade	348

Brunswick Holt's Airstream	**351**
The Lady's Dressing Room	**352**
Economics	**358**
Celia Quits	**360**
Celia Quits	**361**
El Zogoibi	**363**
Frock Horror	**366**
Coil	**368**
Set Your Turban to Stun, Mr Spock	**370**
The Battle of Algeciras	**373**
An Abundance of Caution	**376**
The Mosque de Notre Dame de Paris	**378**
Suffragette	**380**
The Mosque of St Paul's, City of London	**382**
Argan Oil	**383**
Holt's Writ	**385**
The Argan Farm	**386**
The Book of Andrew	**389**
Celia Makes a Counter-Offer	**391**
The Triplet's Ransom Note	**407**
The Dynamic Status Quo	**411**
Holy Sonnet; John Donne	**415**
CCTV	**417**
Remains	**419**
First You Kill Yourself; Then You Bury Yourself	**420**
Deep Fake	**424**
The Wild West	**425**
Three Card Monté	**429**
Detective Benyaacoub Bencheckroun	**430**

The Art of the Deal	433
Discretion	435
Gmail	438
Colman Hunt Negotiates His Own Ransom	440
Social Media	449
San Pedro Manrique, Soria, Spain	452
L'Heure Bleue	455
Wally Receives Another Female Visitor	459
More Nomads	461
Ay de Mi Alhama	465
Crossbow Purchase	469
The Third Crusade	471
Fee-Fi-Fo-Fum	474
Riyadh Chay	475
The Horniman Museum	481
Indigolin Debriefed	484
A Gentlemen's Agreement	489
WMD	491
A Price Reduction	493
New Kid on the Block	495
The Umbrella Bar	496
Silk Threads	500
The Gate of the Burnt One	504
Satellite Phone	510
Bvsh Ho 2	512
Blow Job	513
Deep Blue Rif	514
Aftermath	524
Probably the Best Beer in the World	526

Aderfi Has a Brainwave	**527**
A Price Reduction	**528**
The Perfume	**531**
The Book of Andrew	**534**
Burnt Pavilions	**535**
Edgar Allen Poe	**540**
Consequences	**543**
Patio De Los Leones an Exhumation Is Followed by Two Weddings	**548**
Two Epilogues of Fire and Water	**554**
Further Reading	**563**

"...so doth a good life here flow into an eternal life, without any consideration what so manner of death we die. But whether the gate of my prison be opened with an oiled key (by a gentle and preparing sickness), or the gate be hewn down by a violent death, or the gate be burnt down by a raging and frantic fever, a gate into heaven I shall have, for from the Lord is the cause of my life, and with God the Lord are the issues of death."

Death's Duel, John Donne, 1630

"My first visit to Epsom was in the May of 1856—Blink Bonnie's year. My first Derby had no interest for me as a race, but as giving me the opportunity of studying life and character it is ever to be gratefully remembered. Gambling-tents and thimble-rigging, prick in the garter and the three-card trick, had not then been stopped by the police. So convinced was I that I could find the pea under the thimble that I was on the point of backing my guess rather heavily, when I was stopped by Augustus Egg, whose interference was resented by a clerical-looking personage, in language much opposed to what would have been anticipated from one of his cloth.

'You,' said Egg, addressing the divine, 'you are a confederate, you know; my friend is not to be taken in.'

'Look here,' said the clergyman, 'don't you call names, and don't call me names, or I shall knock your d---d head off.'

'Will you?' Egg said, his courage rising as he saw two policemen approaching. 'Then I call the lot of you—the Quaker there, no more a Quaker than I am, and that fellow that thinks he looks like a farmer—you are a parcel of thieves!'

'So they are, sir,' said a meek-looking lad who joined us; 'they have cleaned me out.'

'Now move off; clear out of this!' The police said; and the gang walked away, the clergyman turning and extending his arms in the act of blessing me and Egg."

My Autobiography and Reminiscences, William Powell Frith, 1895

Upon the bed, before the whole company, there lay a nearly liquid mass of loathsome—of detestable putridity.

The Facts in the Case of M Valdemar, Edgar Allan Poe, 1845.

Working Title: Knights of the Ream

As Colman Hunt withdrew from his stunt double during a short break in shooting *Knights of the Ream* at Ouarzazate, in the Kingdom of Morocco, he couldn't help reflecting that he had just taken Onanism to a new low. It just didn't float his boat anymore.

"Again, Col?" suggested Patrick, the stunt double.

"Go fuck yourself, Paddy! I think I'm going to become—what's the opposite of one of those Incels?"

"A monk?"

"Yeah, a monk. I'm suffering from post-coital fatigue. I'm like that Greta woman."

"Thunberg?"

"No, Garbo. I want to be alone."

Temporarily unwanted, Patrick Oculus slipped on the silk harem pants that he liked to wear on set, blending in with his Moroccan location, and used his battered backside to push open the door of his colleague's chromium Airstream, because his hands were cradling an empty earthenware tagine.

The first time he had worn those pants, Colman had taken the piss out of him, told him that they reminded him of the crazy costume he had worn when playing Don Adriano de Armado, the fantastical Spaniard in Love's Labour Lost. First a child star, then a matinee idol, then a failed Shakespearean B-actor. Colman Hunt had been a cuddly baby and a charming grown up; but he'd also been a gawky adolescent in between.

Patrick smiled at the memories as the dry desert heat replaced the air-conditioned environment inside the Airstream. He descended the steps barefoot onto the sand and padded up and down. At the same time, Edgar Ash (similarly unshod) emerged from his trailer opposite, came down the steps and jumped straight back up them again.

"Jesus!" Ash screamed. "How can you do that? The sand must be 100 degrees Celsius."

"Walk in the park!" Oculus explained. "We're New Prometheans in here."

Ash prodded his pedicured feet into the curly toed babouches he'd haggled over in the Essaouira souk, and gingerly ventured onto the blazing arena again. Oculus was clutching his empty tagine, taking it for an outing to Aka Akinyola's hospitality tent for a refill. He could check out how the kitchen garden of their charcoal-curating chef was progressing now she had the irrigation system working.

"Fucking sand!" Ash cursed, as though he hadn't noticed before that they were working in the middle of the Sahara Desert.

"With a name like Ash," observed Oculus, "you should join the New Prometheans."

"And good afternoon to you too, Colman!"

"Not Colman," said Pat. "I'm his better-looking stand-in!" He said this with some wry humour, but unfortunately, every passing year, his joke took on a closer resemblance to reality. From a child star to a matinee idol, Colman Hunt's features betrayed an entire life of excess, whereas Paddy's less extravagant emoluments had only enabled him to abuse himself to a more moderate degree.

"Yeah, I know," said Ash. "Just teasing. You wouldn't be the great Colman Hunt, because the whole crew knows that Hunt is sulking inside his Airstream and won't come out. In fact, I thought you were both sulking inside the Airstream. Has there been some rift, Oculus?"

"No," said Patrick, firing up a Lucky Strike. "Just Colman don't approve me smoke in the Airstream." He sat on the bottom step of the caravan with his tagine cradled in between his knees like a hernia and exhaled.

"I still don't get it," said Oculus, "why the director had to bring us to this fucking hell hole."

"Not the director, Paddy. It's the new producer, this Mr Blue Molecule Man; he negotiated a four-picture deal with the studio," Ash informed him.

"Yeah, yeah, I get all that for *Moses*, the remake of *Lawrence of Arabia's Seven Pillars of Wisdom* and *Abbott & Costello meet the Mujahedeen*, but we're supposed to be shooting a Scandi noir."

"We are indeed. Isn't it time you got into your cable-knit polo-necked sweater, or are you waiting until the sun gets even higher in the sky?"

"But why on earth did they bring us here?"

"You're playing the understudy for the fucking detective, Oculus. You tell me."

Despite having an entire desert at his disposal to use as his ashtray, Paddy's house-training was such that he removed the lid from his empty tagine with one hand, and flicked the ash from his smoke into it with the other, an instinctive gesture that he instantly regretted, as he had been on his way to Aka's chow tent to fill the tagine with nourishment, before this chance encounter with his fellow thespian.

"From what I understand," Paddy began, "this Mr Molecule doesn't know squat about making pictures. He's a Berkeley Square bitcoin blagger that's awash with investors for his fucking molecule, and he diversified into producing films as part of some tax scheme. Because the studio quickly twigged that he was an ingénue, they sold him an inappropriate film package, so the scriptwriters are now busy rewriting everything. *Ergo* the Scandi noir is unfolding in Morocco.

"Before they hit on the Scandi noir, it was a soft core gay thing provisionally entitled *Knights of the Ream*. They're just making it up as they go along, but Colman's not going to put his seal of approval to any of them, so he's sulking in his Airstream. Plus I just heard the director's been blown out anyway; contractually what we term a *Very Bad Leaver*, and the search is on to find a half decent replacement who's 'between jobs' and hanging up on the back of the door available at a moment's notice to join us in Ouarzazate for the next 12 months.

"Every day we're sitting here doing nothing is costing the Blue Molecule guy a fortune. The only thing amongst all these moving parts that is fixed, the only item that is absolutely sacrosanct and not going to change, is that the leading lady has contracted to get all her kit off for US $5m, which sum has already been paid."

"Up front?"

"Up full frontal, as far as I can make out! So the US $5m sex scene is screwed straight into the script, but what else gets written in is entirely in the lap of the gods. Don't matter if it's Knights of the Ream, Scandi Noir meets the Sahara, or What Have You. Make it, as they say, and they shall come. The leading lady is getting naked, and that is the *raison d'etre* of the film. The likes of you and me, we're just supererogatory also-rans. I mean to say, for crying out loud, I'm a professional, fully trained stuntman, not a fucking extra!"

"When you put it that way, I guess I can see why Colman Hunt is sulking in his caravan."

"You mean 'cos since the leading lady is his ex-wife in a marriage that never got consummated, and now the whole world is going to be tossing themselves off to what he never enjoyed himself. Yeah, it does kind of stick in the craw, doesn't it?"

A Pathetic Demonstration

Tinctorio Indigolin's driver pulled up on the double yellow line on Mayfair's Albemarle Street outside the Royal Society where Indigolin was due to deliver his tutorial.

A shabby rabble of unwashed scum trawled from the lowest gutters of the Internet were attempting to organise themselves into a credible demonstration. They were all wearing Tinctorio Indigolin facemasks and the same luminous blue suits that were Indigolin's trademark, in an attempt to mock the speaker.

However, the uniformed constabulary, also in blue suits, had spotted their activity early on social media with the result that the police were out in greater force than the handful of demonstrators. Those demonstrators were attempting to unfurl a banner, but they were fighting a losing battle against a Hyperborean wind that was blowing it inside out.

"What's it say, shill?" Indigolin asked.

The driver glanced at the pennant. "I think it says 'FUCK PHARMA!'" He answered.

"Dimwits!" Indigolin pronounced, brushing the lapels of his signature blue legume suit. "I'm not Big Pharma. I'm the only viable alternative. I spy with my little eye a disabled parking space over there."

Indigolin's disabled chauffeur edged the Rolls forward, making for the blue badge holder's reserved space, where he parked up.

Brian Bellweather, a retired Anglican clergyman who had fomented the demonstration on social media, had spotted the speaker's car and his Myrmidons were now crowding Indigolin in menacingly. Undeterred, Indigolin flung the passenger door of the Rolls open with such force it upended two of the demonstrators who went arse over apex, their banner landing on top of them. They'd come from the gutter and now they were back in it again. *'Being lower class,'* thought Indigolin, *'they hadn't appreciated that the doors of a Rolls Royce opened backwards.'*

Diva

Celia Broadsword, waiting for her lift to take her to the airport, sat on her Belsize Park piano stool, smoking an oval Passing Cloud. On a whim, she balanced the cigarette in the cut glass ashtray on the Steinway, lifted the lid and played a few bars of Erik Satie's *Gymnopédies*.

Of course, smoking was just a habit, but it was a habit that didn't give her any pleasure any more. And it was a bad habit. But what was the point of quitting now? She'd be eighty-five years old at her next birthday. If she'd cheated lung cancer for this long, she'd get away with it until the day she died. And if she quit now, what would happen to her voice, the husky, sexy, syrupy modulation that the Sunday Times film critic had described as 'two baritones beneath Fenella Fielding'?

She hadn't been born with that voice. She'd striven to achieve it with thirty cigarettes a day since the age of sixteen. And the pretty pink carton the Passing Clouds were packaged in was a statement in itself. It was almost as good as a new handbag.

She patted her luxurious silver hair. She dyed it silver. Underneath it was as white as snow. But still as thick as ever. At least, it was for real. Not like Joan Collins in her wigs. Stars of the silver screen.

She'd no more than glanced at the latest iteration of her script. Her heart wasn't in it. What was the point in learning her lines when the director would have required the scriptwriters to do it all over again before she'd reached the bottom of the page? And what was it this time? A Scandi Noir in the Sahara desert! This time round the Blue Dude had not only replaced the team of scriptwriters, but he'd sacked the director for good measure.

It was well and truly back to the drawing board. The outgoing director had been replaced by Wallace Pfister. That was a good choice. Very fortuitous that he'd been available at short notice. Maybe the film's luck was finally about to change. Maybe the Blue Molecule dude wasn't such a philistine after all. People assumed he was some kind of Essex oligarch; but he was quite well educated and just donned an East End antic disposition to give him the common touch.

Celia had always wanted to be directed by Wally Pfister. He'd done some amazing stuff. He was whatever the highest thing up was in yoga. He'd have the whole crew on parade at sunrise doing Ashtanga on their mats before shooting started each day. But how was he going to make sense out of the film he'd inherited? It had all been done back to front.

The only fixed point in the film was that Celia Broadsword, at the age of almost eighty-five, would be doing her first nude scene, shot in broad daylight and UHD 8K, something that her fans (if any of them were still alive) had been dreaming of for the last sixty years at least. And she had received US $5M upfront for the planned sixty seconds. The rest of the script was an irrelevance.

Joan had stripped off at the age of fifty in those Brent Walker films where her sister, Jackie, had been the writer. Joan had showed the way. But Joan had only done topless. Celia was contracted to do full frontal, and she'd left it a bit later than Joan.

She wanted to do the scene. She felt like she'd been waiting for it for the last six decades, denied by her agent. Or maybe it was just that no-one had written the right part for an eighty-five-year-old woman before. Come to think of it, it still seemed to be eluding the scriptwriters. But shooting it alongside Colman Hunt, her ex-husband from their unconsummated marriage? She had very mixed feelings about that aspect. He'd never been able to get it up during their otherwise happy espousal. How was he going to act his way out of this one?

Her agent, Manny Wallenberger, had managed her career for more than six decades, but had passed away last year at the age of ninety. Sclerosis of the liver. He had always been very protective of her. He would never have condoned anything smutty. He wouldn't even have used a smutty word like smutty. He would have said 'vulgar' or 'prurient'. But Manny, alas, was no more. She was a free woman now. What was the joke people made about Manny? That he was ninety years old, but had never used glasses. Always drank out of the bottle!

She got a kick out of the fact that none of the scene's promoters had bothered with any pretence that the nude scene was essential to the film. That's what tickled her about it: it was gratuitously gratuitous, flagrantly *in flagrante delicto*. The scene *was* the film, and the rest of the film was merely incidental, an afterthought, an appendix. That's why they kept rewriting the rest of the screenplay.

Who knows? One day they might even come up with something that made it marginally relevant. Working title: *Knights of the Ream*, my fanny! Paddy Oculus had come up with that title as a joke, and it had stuck. It was like starring in one of those *Carry On* films or Frankie Howerd's *Up Pompeii*.

She thought that a woman's entitlement to be paid for stripping off and revealing her charms ought to be constitutionally enshrined in English law some way, like the American Second Amendment: the Right to Bare Charms.

She didn't know why they didn't just do another series of Ferdinand and Isabella's *Book of Hours*, the long running historical soap about the Unification of the Iberian Peninsula that had shot her and her ex-husband, Colman Hunt, to fame. Well, she did know the answer to that one, really. They'd done God knows how many series; but it was a historical drama and history finally got the better of the cast.

Queen Isabella of Castile had died at the age of fifty-four. It seemed like the series had been running for more years than that. She'd still been playing Isabella into her seventies. They had covered everything. Of course, there was the Unification of the Iberian Peninsula; but there were also pirate skirmishes with swaggering English buccaneers.

There was Christopher Columbus, Boabdil the Moor and his overbearing mother; there was war with Islam, the fall of Granada. And the sets had been amazing: France, Spain, medieval England, Oman, Persia, Carcassonne, Cordoba, Granada, and the Royal Alcazar in Seville, the city that smelled of bitter oranges all year round. But her favourite was the Court of the Twelve Marble Lions in the Alhambra Palace.

When they shot there, she stayed for weeks on end in the Parador San Francisco. Happiest days of her life. Maybe she could come back for a final series as Isabella's mother. Conveniently, the mother was also an Isabella, Queen Isabella of Portugal.

She had to act to keep her brain firing on all cylinders. It was either Acting or Alzheimer's.

She looked up at the wall above the piano, the wall completely obscured by framed photographs of her in so many title roles, alongside so many famous leading men, so few of them sadly still alive. But this was the first time she'd ever done a nude scene.

Maybe this would be her last starring role. Go out with a bang!

Still, her ex did have his redeeming features. The fact that he had never been able to give her children meant that she still had the figure of a well-kept forty-year-old.

And she was old-school hourglass, all curves and no hard edges, not like those stick insect size zero models and actresses who didn't go in and out in the middle. That was one of his redeeming features. The other was surely his defining role in *Ordeal by Fire*. Everyone assumed that scene in *Ordeal by Fire* had been faked, but Morty did it for real. New Prometheans!

When she thought of him, it was still by his real name, Mortimer, not his screen name, Colman. She didn't even know Colman Hunt wasn't his real name until he signed the marriage register. But the guy who had signed the marriage register turned out not to have been her husband anyway. Sometimes it seemed as if her personal life as well as her professional life was just one long work of fiction.

She had never wanted to try another marriage, but to this day she maintained a stable of younger lovers, and secretly subscribed to the belief that ingesting all that juvenile juice kept her young. Long ago, she had put away the pre-nuptial agreement, and her weapon of choice these days was the NDA. You didn't get to sleep with Celia Broadsword unless you had signed a watertight confidentiality agreement.

She closed the lid of the piano and took a last drag on her Passing Cloud before stubbing it out. She was the donor. The rest of the film was just a vehicle for her sixty seconds dance of the seven veils. Maybe that's what they should call the film: Sixty Seconds, like a precis of Jackie Chan's *Rush Hour*.

She rose to answer the doorbell. Her driver had arrived. She felt like Dorothy Lamour with Bing Crosby and Bob Hope. It was *The Road to Morocco* for her. Seven veils; seven 'Road To—' films. Lamour had starred alongside Bing Crosby and Bob Hope in the first six, but in the seventh, *The Road to Hong Kong*, the poor woman had been side-lined, and she was replaced by none other than Joan Collins, because Crosby thought that Lamour was too old at forty-eight.

Bob Hope had done the decent thing, and refused to play in the film unless Lamour made an appearance, so they gave her a half-hearted cameo at the very end, singing *Warmer than a Whisper*.

Celia had appeared in so many films, and all the critics loved her voice, *earthier than Eartha*, one had said, referring to Eartha Kitt. But she had never been asked to sing.

Fancy being washed up in films at forty-eight. Joan had risen to the challenge. She had accepted the baton from Dorothy Lamour, and she had gone on to strip off at the previously unheard-of age of fifty. Now Celia Broadsword was about to raise the game to an entirely different level.

Toureg

Tinctorio Indigolin, known to his handful of friends and many hangers-on and online followers as Ti (pronounced so as to rhyme with Shy) and to the media alternately as Mr Molecule or the runt who bore the brunt of the junta against Non-Fungible Tokenism, robed in his trademark suit of legume blue Kano cotton with the spotless Egyptian cotton kerchief blossoming from his breast pocket, held the vial of violet liquid aloft and called out: "Hands up!"

A number of heads turned in confusion. They were an audience, not participants to be picked on in this fashion. If they raised their hands, what exactly would they be volunteering for?

"Hands up for what?" Queried one of the congregation in the Royal Society in Albemarle Street, Mayfair.

Indigolin knotted his brow at the interrupter, who couldn't have been more than eighteen years old. "What's your name, please?"

He was going to say, "What's your name, girl?" but thought better of it as the last word was about to leave his lips. He didn't want to find out she identified differently and get himself cancelled for not being woke enough.

"Cecilia Hope," came the answer.

"Well, Ms Hope, I have only three words for you."

But the three words were addressed in a bark, not to Ms Hope, but to the amanuensis in matching legume blue Kano cotton threads harvested from ancient Nigerian dye pits in Africa's Sahel belt, who was driving the PowerPoint presentation from a fruitwood credenza in front of Indigolin's lectern: "Next slide, please!"

The next slide, projected onto at least twenty-one hundred-inch flat screens lining the circular cockpit as well as the grotesquely huge one behind Indigolin himself, depicted the horrifically ravaged face of an elderly Indian male patient, blistered with advanced and inoperable melanomas.

The audience, which consisted not of medical students, but of a wide cross-section of disciplines seeking enlightenment and possible financial gain at the feet of the cryptocurrency celebrity tycoon turned molecular pharmacist, drew back in horror at the image and one could hear the sharp intake of more than a hundred breaths at once.

"Hands up," he clarified, "whoever thinks he or she has the steadiest hand."

With nothing further to lose in her fall from grace, having already stuck her head above the parapet, Cecilia Hope raised hers.

"Ah, Ms Hope," purred Indigolin, "step forward, if you will. Approach the rostrum."

As she passed amongst those gathered there, Indigolin continued. "Does anyone else here know Ms Cecilia Hope, because you are about to bear witness to the impossible, and I wouldn't want anyone to think that I was a mountebank or snake oil purveyor, and that Ms Hope was my shill in some cheap party trick."

A number of voices confirmed they knew Ms Hope and appreciated she was not a shill. By this time, Indigolin had moved round to the front of the lectern and Cecilia had mounted the three small steps to the wooden rostrum so that they were standing face to face.

"Stretch out your arm, please, Ms Hope. Do I call you Ms Hope, or Cecilia?"

"Ms Hope is fine."

Not the answer he'd been probing for, but no matter.

"Fully extended please. With your palm completely flat and open, like you were feeding a sugar cube to a horse. Is that comfortable? You will probably have to hold that pose for no more than a minute, or a minute and a half, depending on the width of your hand. I am delighted to note that you are wearing a sleeveless blouse, so no-one can suggest there is anything concealed up there."

Indigolin unfastened the stopper on the small vial of dark blue liquid. Inside was a straight-headed one millilitre glass dropper pipette. He drew some of the liquid up into the pipette by depressing the rubber bulb at its end.

"Ready?" He asked.

Ms Hope nodded. She had no idea what she was expected to be ready for.

With a theatrical flourish, Tinctorio expelled six drops of the blue liquid one by one out of the pipette and into the palm of her open hand where they formed a minute reservoir. One of the cameras mounted on the gurney moved in for a close-up of the open hand that was projected by the amanuensis onto the screens in substitution for the gruesome image of the melanoma-ridden Indian, whilst Indigolin assured the young lady that the liquid was inert and perfectly sterile and safe, and that no harm whatsoever would befall her.

He asked her to stare at the 100" wide projections of her palm, punctuated as it was by its blue pool. He asked her to imagine that the blue dot, hugely magnified on the screen monitors around the auditorium, was an Alpine lake. He asked her to imagine that she was standing at the teak and brass helm of a highly polished *Riva* motor launch, cutting a course across Lake Garda on its way to rendezvous with George Clooney.

"What now?" She queried.

"We wait, Ms Hope. We wait."

After thirty seconds. Tinctorio Indigolin, like the true showman he was, withdrew the large spotlessly white handkerchief from the breast pocket of his double-breasted blue legume suit with an expansive gesture as though he were a Cossack drawing a sabre from its scabbard before slicing the top off a champagne cork. He proceeded to fold the white cloth over and over until it was an oblong A4 size which he then placed on the parquet floor directly beneath Ms Hope's outstretched hand, replete with its blue payload.

Another camera came in for a close-up of the snotrag and the amanuensis then bifurcated the screens so that half of each monitor showed the handkerchief and the other half the small reservoir in the palm of Ms Hope's hand, which, inexplicably appeared almost imperceptibly, to be growing smaller by the second. Then, seemingly unhappy at the orientation of the bandana, Indigolin hitched up his signature blue legume slacks, so as not to crease them, bent down, and rearranged the bandana on the floorboards, but this time in landscape.

"Shall we recite some Shakespeare to pass the time whilst we wait?" He asked rhetorically. Without waiting for an answer, he proceeded to intone:

"That handkerchief,
Did an Egyptian to my mother give,
She was a charmer and could almost read
The thoughts of people..."

The screens revealed that the liquid was apparently disappearing from Ms Hope's hand as he spoke. But where was it going? It couldn't evaporate so quickly. Without trauma, it was disappearing *into* her skin.

"...She, dying gave it to me,
And bid me when my fate would have me wive
To give it her. I did so, and take heed on't
Make it a darling like your precious eye
To lose't or to give't away were such perdition
As nothing else could match."

The intake of breath at the sight of the melanoma man was as nothing compared to the confused exclamation that went up from the assembly as they saw, both before their very eyes, and magnified on the huge screens, one by one, the six blue drops, having passed through the skin, fat, bone and sinew of Ms Hope's palm, drip out from her knuckles on the back of her hand, and deposit their unmistakeable indigo stain on the white bandana spread out on the parquet beneath. The liquid had woven its way completely through her flesh, through her epidermis, dermis and hypodermis.

Through her nerves, nerve endings, follicles, glands and blood vessels; down into the very architecture of her column-shaped basal cells as they constantly divided and pushed the lower cells ever upwards, like plants within a rainforest canopy striving for the sun. The blue secretion had passed clean through her hand and come out the other side.

Ms Hope, everyone in the cockpit, and the two billion people who scrutinised the presentation afterwards on YouTube, knew that they had been present, in person or remotely, at the witnessing of a physical impossibility.

Albanian George

Albanian George hated his soubriquet. Although he was born in Tirana, he was a member of the Mayfair Mafiosi now, and he believed that, amongst the cognoscenti of that clique, Albanians had a reputation for being loutish halfwits, whereas George regarded himself as the apogee of sophistication. If anyone asked him, he told them he was Athenian. He had donned an Attic disposition.

Albanian George wasn't even a real gangster. He was self-educated from watching old Ray Winstone films. In his world, you had to behave like a gangster, or people would walk all over you. They wouldn't take you seriously. But he must have had a soft spot when he lent almost a million pounds totally unsecured, and moreover, totally unsolicited, to the Blue Molecule guy on an impulse at the HR Owen showroom in Berkeley Square. Which was now very much overdue, because the Blue Dude insisted on keeping too many CFD positions open at the same time. Dedicated gambler.

George had only suggested the loan, because the Molecule Man seemed so affluent that it should not have been a problem getting it repaid; and he thought that it would be a feather in George's cap for having offered it. A case of casting one's bread on the water.

However, if the Blue Dude was so opulent, it made no sense him being short for a crappy mil in the first place. It was just like they said: money goes to money. If someone had actually needed that million; if some high roller had tapped George up for a stack, George would have due-diligenced him to distraction. But because the Blue Jew Molecule Dude was supposed to be one of the best-heeled dragons in Christendom, and because the Blue Dude had never actually asked him for a dime, George had been practically falling over himself to press the wedge onto him; as if it had been a test, an initiation ceremony that George had to pass before he could get really close to the billionaire.

To hell with it! George was only a millionaire! What was a billionaire doing borrowing money off a lousy millionaire? But the Dude had never asked for it. George had walked right into that one. '*The saying was true,*' George thought to himself. There was no-one so easy to sell to as a salesman, and he'd fallen for his own blarney this time.

The friends you make at HR Owen will last you a fucking lifetime!

Talking of blarney, George was keeping the white-haired Irishman, Hugh Webb, waiting in his meeting room. Tucking his shirt into the waistband of his trousers so that the gaps between the buttons didn't gape open revealing glimpses of his hairy tummy, George decided it was time to meet the guy. George believed that the way to look slimmer was to buy his shirts too small.

George used to have a six pack when he was a teenager, but now he had a pot belly, a barrel chest, and his arms were too short. If you had to describe his appearance in one word, you'd probably say that he was stocky. How did the old song go?

Mr five by five; he's five foot tall and he's five foot wide.

When he drove his supercars, which he very much liked doing, he had to adopt a comical upright driving position right up close to the steering wheel, with his short arms extended in front of him. The overall effect was as if that animated meerkat had given up on trying to sell car insurance and was now driving the actual car. Pressed up against the wheel, he looked like he was trying to gaze into a horizontal wishing well on the far side of his dashboard.

Or stare into the abyss.

His Barbour was draped on the back of his chair. He could never remember if the right word was Barbour or Berber. When he donned it, he felt like he was donning a little bit of Daniel Craig: both Bond and Layer Cake Daniel Craig at the same time. Barbours were where town and country met, equally at home in Grosvenor Square or grouse moor. If he heard a nightingale singing in Grosvenor Square, he'd aim his Beretta at it and take a shot. Try to bring it down plumb in the middle of the hat on the head of Annabel's doorman.

He slipped his waxed Barbour jacket on and tapped the breast pocket to make sure that the deposit money was still sitting there in its envelope with Mr Webb's name scrawled on it in black felt marker pen. *Rough Hugh Webb*. If the Molecule Man's trademark colour was blue, George's would be black. Like his Vantablacked Bentayga Bentley. If he was ever invited onto *Desert Island Discs* and had to name his favourite song, he would say *Paint it Black* by the Rolling Stones.

Albanian George seldom went anywhere without an envelope of what the Spaniards called *effectivo* (or ready cash) in his Barbour pocket. Credit cards were for the wimps who had embraced the contactless culture come Coronavirus, in dread of catching a sniffle. Real wedge was for heroes. Patting himself down so as to feel the reassuring bulge of the wad in his breast pocket, before stuffing his shirt tails back into his trousers, had become part of his regime, like brushing his teeth or combing his hair.

It was a cross between a nervous habit, and calling the register of himself to check that all of his constituent parts were present and correctly accounted for. Lastly, he tugged at the ponderous links of the heavy gold chain round his neck with the crucifix dangling at the end.

In order to give himself more credibility, he had himself started a rumour about himself, to the effect that the big cross he wore round his neck was in memory of all the crosses the widows of the men who had crossed him had put by their husband's graves. Having completed this diagnostic verification of self, and satisfied that he was firing on all cylinders, he then opened the door of the meeting room.

Waiting inside the meeting room was someone who had no need to start false rumours about his fatal body count. Inside the room, the white-haired assassin was keeping himself amused by playing solitaire on the round, glass conference room table. '*This was an interesting development,*' thought George. Most people, kept waiting, pretended that they had found something immensely important that demanded their attention on their telephones, but this guy had brought a pack of cards to the meeting.

George had decided to keep him waiting a full twenty minutes just to let him know who was in charge. When George entered the room, the guy scooped the cards back up into a pack and tapped them on the table, getting them in a nice, uniform block.

The hoary-headed card sharp glanced up, quickly assessing Albanian George as he entered the meeting room. As though there was some unwritten law that dictated that the more ungodly one was the larger the gold cross one should wear on a chain round one's neck, George's was XXXXL. The thought traversed the assassin's mind that if the cross was any larger, George could actually be nailed to it himself and crucified.

"George Georgiou," said George.

"Cut?" His guest said.

George cut the pack. The guy turned the card over. It was the Queen of Hearts.

"Queen," said George. "Are we even allowed to say that these days?"

"Lucky card," said the guy, and then: "How do you do, Mr George. I'm Hugh Webb."

Mr Webb drew two more cards from the pack, namely an Ace of Spades and a Jack of Diamonds. He let Albanian George get a good look at them and then he turned the three cards over and moved them around on the glass table. He was quick, as if the cards were greased, but George could keep track of the Queen easily.

"I guess you've come for your deposit for teaching the Blue Jew a lesson he won't forget in a hurry," deduced George. The guy continued to shuffle the three cards around.

George pretended to crack his knuckles. He had discovered that he could snap the back of his fingers against the palm of his hand and it sounded and looked just like he was cracking his knuckles, but didn't hurt so much. Then he reached in his Barbour jacket and pulled out the envelope stuffed with fifties. As he did so, his left shirt sleeve rode up revealing his Hublot Big Bang quarter-pounder in all its glory.

It caught the light and dazzled Mr Webb, making it look to any onlooker as if his white hair was on fire. He resembled one of those Renaissance religious paintings where the composition was lit by the halo round the angel's head. George noticed that the guy was sporting one of those old rocker pony tails, like he was wearing a Davy Crocket coonskin cap, but with the tail made out of ermine instead of racoon.

"My Hublot's given you the Halo Effect!" George declared. "Good watches keep their value, Mr Webb," he continued, seeing his guest seemingly mesmerised by the huge bauble. "If you've ever got your back up against the wall, you can always count on a Hublot or Audemar Piguet not to let you down." No-one had told George that the t at the end of Hublot was silent.

"An Audemar Piguet's just a fancy wristwatch," replied Webb, speaking in his easy, non-rhotic Dublin drawl, so that the *Audemar* in Audemar Piguet ended on a high note. "Good guns also keep their value. In addition, they can pay for themselves in between buying and selling them, so long as you know how to use them properly; and if my back was ever up against the wall, Mr George, I'd rather rely on my Pump Action Remington, than my Rolex."

Hugh Webb observed that the envelope full of cash had his name written on it with one of those big, black, indelible laundry pens. The kind of pens that mums marked their boys' PE shorts with so that another mother's kid didn't nick them. No-one would have dared nick Mr Webb's shorts when he had been a schoolboy at St Brigid's, Dublin.

His nickname had been Rough Hugh, because he was a complete ruffian. He would gleefully beat his fellow pupils to a pulp regardless of the possible consequences. After all, it was only fear of retribution that moderated human behaviour. Take that out of the equation and everybody would happily be murdering everybody else all day long.

Rough Hugh stared at the envelope with his name inked upon it with genuine disappointment. He frowned at such carelessness. He took the money out of the marked envelope, counted it and re-inserted it into a blank white envelope he'd brought with him that self-sealed. He then pointedly screwed up the old envelope with his personal data written on it, like he was teaching a child a lesson, and tossed it into the waste bin on the far side of the room.

"Hole in one!" George cried.

"Double or nothing?" Mr Webb enquired, nodding down at the three cards.

"Do I look to you like I fell off the top of the Christmas tree this morning?" Albanian George asked.

"You look to me like a man who likes a little flutter," said Webb. "We know you took a punt on the Blue Molecule dude, so now you want me to slap his wrist."

"No slappie wristie, Mr Webb. None of that *Ché Sierra Nevada* shit. I want you to put that Yid oven-dodger down, and then it'll all be Bravo Zulu! Fuck it! Are we even allowed to say that anymore?"

"Yid oven-dodger?"

"Zulu."

"When I say *Slap,* it's a figure of speech called litotes, Mr George. Or even a euphemism. When Hugh Webb slaps someone, he doesn't get up again. Are you familiar with Turgenev's description of Death as a fisherman, Mr George? He catches you early on in his net, but he leaves you in the water flapping ignorantly around, whilst all the time the net is tightening. He'll pluck you out in his own time, or you can employ someone like me to hasten the process. As the Bard says," intoned Rough Hugh Webb, "be absolute for death."

Leaving Albanian George to conjure with that quotation, Mr Webb inclined his head in the direction of the three cards he had spread out on the table.

"You guess the card right; I keep the deposit and do the whole job for the deposit. You guess wrong, you lose the deposit and you still owe me for the whole job."

"Don't you think you might be getting a bit long in the tooth for this game, buddy?" George asked.

"What, playing Three Card Monté, or assassinating people, Mr George?"

"OK," said George. "That's the lady! Are we even allowed to say that these days? Does the Queen of Hearts have to have a cervix?"

He held Webb's left hand, the hand he'd been using to jumble the cards around with, by the wrist, so that he couldn't do any funny stuff on him, like pretending to pick up one card when he really had two in his hand, or crimp the corner of the card. George then moved Webb's left arm away from the game with his right hand, and turned his chosen card over himself with his right hand. It was the Jack of Diamonds. How the fuck had Webb done that? George hadn't taken his eyes off the Queen card since Webb turned it over.

When George looked up from the court cards on the glass table, still holding Webb's left hand by the wrist, he saw that he was staring into the black oxide muzzle of a 9 mm Springfield XD-2 Sub-Compact handgun that had somehow found its way into Webb's right hand in the split second that George's gaze had dropped to the card game.

"You lose your stake," said Mr Webb. He picked up the white envelope into which he had stashed the deposit that had started its life off in the brown envelope with his name inked on it, and put it in his inside jacket pocket. "So you still owe me the full contract price. Want to go again?"

George shook his head. Webb placed the handgun on the table. "Or we could spin the Springfield and see who it's pointing at," suggested Webb.

"Like in *The Deerstalker*?" George enquired, referring to the sort of hat Sherlock Holmes wore. Webb realised he meant The Deer Hunter.

"I wouldn't recommend it, Mr George," mused Webb. "In The Deer Hunter, they can play Russian Roulette because the handgun's a revolver with only one round in the chamber. This gun uses a magazine with sixteen rounds. Every time you pull the trigger, a shell comes out the muzzle. So the odds wouldn't be very good for you."

"Talking of Russian Roulette: you know the one about the three Ruskies?" George asked. "Am I even allowed to call them that these days? I assume that someone with a name like Turgenev must have been a Ruskie? Three Ruskies go into a sauna, each one carrying a crate of vodka. Each one drinks his entire crate of vodka; then one of them leaves the sauna, and the other two have to guess which one it was."

If Webb got George's joke, there was no sign of that on his face. But then again, no-one had really been talking about Russian Roulette to begin with, so the segue was self-serving.

"*Zapiski ohotnika,*" pronounced Webb.

"Meaning the chick called Zapiski's got hot knickers!" George laughed.

'The man was incorrigible,' thought Webb. "*Zapiski ohotnika,* translates as Sketches from a Hunter's Album. It was the book that brought Turgenev to fame; and it's all about killing things."

"OK, polka face," said George. "That's enough gambling for the day. I guess when a man reaches your great age; he has to practise being a card sharp so as to home up his responses in the field."

Mr Webb didn't correct George's latest malapropisms. He just said: "I see you've been perusing my *curriculum vitae*, Mr George."

"Don't know about no fucking *curriculum vitae*. I think the white hair's a bit of a giveaway, my friend."

"As you can see, the hand's still steady enough," said Mr Webb. "Not many people have a CV like mine, stretching from the Troubles to the Good Friday Agreement. Sinn Fein, IRA, Neutral IRA, Real IRA, Continuity IRA."

"Yeah, yeah, yeah! And now you're free-lance Peaky Blinders. Just make sure someone gets it all on social media! I may want to use this guy as an example. Part of my own what-you-call it? *Curriculum Vitae.* Are we even allowed to speak Latin anymore? Health and Safety gone fucking mad! Be Absolut for death, as the Bartender said."

Parking Space

Indigolin had just left the Royal Society and was casting his eyes up and down Albemarle Street, looking for his blue Rolls, when a guy sporting a Tinctorio Indigolin full-face mask and blue legume suit, shot him point blank in the chest. The quarry was temporarily transfixed by the comforting red winking LED of his assailant's bodycam, before realising what had just happened to him. As he weaved his way down into the gutter where he had earlier sent the demonstrators, it occurred to Tinctorio Indigolin that this was what it must feel like to be assassinated by one's own hologram.

The Anal Retentive

The assassin melted into the melee of demonstrators before fading entirely from the scene. He recycled his face mask in a waste bin in Heddon Street, shook free his snowy pony tail, and then entered a dark Moroccan restaurant known as Momo for a late lunch. Inside, his device discovered the restaurant's Wi-Fi, and he uploaded the menu from the Q-Code at the same time as he updated his CV with the addition of his latest assassination.

Maybe he was a bit anally retentive. That's what people said about him. And that he was a mad Irishman. Having his own website on the Dark Web, where he meticulously catalogued all the unspeakable services he could offer, was perhaps a bit anal in its own right.

He paired his bodycam with the app on his phone, uploaded the footage to his website, and then emailed a link to Mr George.

That morning Mr Webb had deliberated long and hard over his choice of PDW. The very few people who were still alive who knew the mad Irishman said he was a finical anal retentive, because the one thing he liked doing was constantly organising and cataloguing his large collection of illegal firearms. Today they were all sorted by Country of Origin. Last week it had been by Calibre.

The week before that by length in mm, and before that by Rate of Fire. Never by name of Manufacturer. That would be too easy. Doing it this way kept Mr Webb sharp for his age. Like doing the crossword, or tricking gullible Greeks at Three Card Monté.

Today he'd selected the 9mm Parabellum 'Red 9' Mauser c96 without the stock. The silencer took some of the kick out of it, but he figured he'd be using it at point blank range.

It had taken him about twenty minutes to choose the right gun that wouldn't spoil the hang of his Tinctorio Indigolin tribute act blue legume suit too much. He had come up with the neat idea of using the Red 9 to shoot the Blue Dude. That's what you call 'colour co-ordinated'.

Choosing which suit to wear for the job had been much quicker, because he had to blend in with the other arseholes due to be at the demonstration: blue legume lookalike and an Indigolin face pack.

Then, on an impulse, he had put the Red 9 back on his gun wall and selected the little 22 Mag 2 shot Derringer, no bigger than the palm of his hand, and you could fold back the barrel so that, doubled up, it was completely obscured within your duke. Rough Hugh Webb had looked down at his hands. Navvy's hands. *'There were jobs,'* he thought, *'that required huge stopping power, and there were jobs where concealment was the priority.'* As he would be working in a crowd and using it at close range, what the 22Mag lost in firepower, it would make up for in concealment.

What the hell had he been thinking earlier, he asked himself, when he was about to select his murder weapon as if it was an accessory to be colour-co-ordinated? The 22 couldn't take an acoustic adjuster, but no-one would be able to pinpoint the bang to him in the middle of a noisy demonstration.

His food arrived: seafood tagine. From what he could see of it in the half darkness, it looked pretty good. The waiter set a terracotta plate of lemons down on the table and said he'd be right back with some implements to eat the shellfish with. Before he'd even taken a mouthful, Mr Webb became aware of a stabbing pain in his gut. He attempted to half rise to inspect what was going on just above his trouser line, but that just made the pain more acute, causing him involuntarily to sit straight down again.

Seated, his attention was caught by his phone pinging. Consulting the phone, it said *You have a New Memory*. It showed him a stitched together movie of Tinctorio Indigolin, the Blue Molecule Man, being murdered on the streets of Mayfair to the accompaniment of some of that atrocious no-copyright background music that you were allowed to upload without being sued by Warner or Sony.

Cancelled

The clocks had gone forward and by 16.00 it was already dark in Mayfair. A ruffled Tinctorio Indigolin raised himself from prone to perpendicular, sitting upright on the kerbstone. The uniformed police were facing the other direction, interviewing the masked demonstrators whilst they waited for the ambulance to arrive and take the cadaver of the Blue Molecule Man away.

If they'd known it was going to play out this way, the demonstrators would have run off long ago, but they'd glued themselves to the building before things turned nasty. Unnoticed, Indigolin pushed aside his own incident tape and stumbled towards his driver. The driver stubbed out his cigarette and opened the door for his miraculously resurrected boss. Backwards. There had to be a reason they were known as Suicide Doors.

The driver wasn't supposed to smoke. He'd had a heart attack last year. There were two plus sides to the heart attack, however. Firstly, it enabled Indigolin's UK company, Flyover Life Sciences, to fulfil its quota of disabled employees. Secondly, it entitled the driver to a badge in his employer's favourite colour, blue, that enabled him to park in disabled parking bays.

Indigolin threw the blue legume jacket across the back seat, and rubbed the sore spot on his chest. He took an aerosol the size of a breath freshener from the rear glove compartment and spritzed his oesophagus with a mist of blue nanobots. They penetrated straight to the submucosa, giving him a pleasant kind of a high, whilst also lubricating the wheels of elocution.

"Your molecule works okay then, boss?" The driver enquired.

"Sure does, shill! It combined with the electromagnetic Kevlar weave in the suit to form a web so fine you couldn't get a flea's fart through it. Good job I picked the double-breasted jacket out of the wardrobe this morning! And a good job my assassin didn't bring a Colt Magnum to the party. That gunshot still packs a punch though. I think I'm more winded than wounded. Must have been taking that tumble on the pavement. I feel halfway between humbled and humiliated."

"Least, you're still alive, boss."

"I've been well and truly cancelled this time, shill."

Well, Tinctorio Indigolin thought to himself that was two impossible things that had happened in the space of two hours.

All Hung Up

"Wait up!" The demonstrator screamed. "You can't just leave us here!"

"Why not?" The policeman asked.

"Why not? I'll give you two good reasons why not. (1), because there's a madman with a gun still on the loose out there, and (B), because your corpse seems to have been stolen."

"You glued yourself to the wall, Swampy. You can leave when you're ready. My shift's done."

With those words, the last remaining uniformed bobby left the scene of the crime and strode back towards Saville Row Police Station for a hot cup of Brooke Bond Tea with six cubes of sugar.

It was dark. It was cold. The protestors' blue nylon lookalike suits didn't benefit from a Kevlar weave or a Blue Molecule. The easterly wind, that had played havoc with their banner earlier, was bitingly cold, and it was now beginning to drizzle. They had been a motley crew to start with, but now, pinned against the wall with their arms and legs splayed out in all different positions, they looked like a sink estate washing line on a windy day.

When they had glued themselves to the wall, they had done so in the confidence that they could rely on the police to unglue them with solvents blended to a secret recipe and pop them in the back of a warm, cosy jam wagon. But the police had been distracted by the more important priorities of a contract killing in Albemarle Street, followed by the disappearance of the corpse.

Now the demonstrators were going to have to live with their own poor choices. Their ringleader, a retired Anglican clergyman by the name of Brian Bellweather, was beginning to wish he hadn't downed that third pint at The Running Footman before joining the protest.

Stainless Steel Crab Cracker Seafood Tool Set

When he had ducked into *Momo*, looking for somewhere dark to hide out until the brouhaha died down, Mr Webb had been pleased at the tenebracity of the joint, but when it came to trying to read the menu with the help of a clip-on head torch and some guttering wax candles, the novelty had worn off. Then the waiter must have spilled something on him in the dark, because it felt like his stomach was on fire through his shirt just above the waistband.

You could tell this was a good restaurant, because the table was littered with those cloven lemons in hair nets, so that the customers didn't accidentally get citrus pips in their food in the profound darkness. He couldn't remember if it was Scott's Restaurant in Mount Street or Led Zeppelin that claimed to have invented that method of squeezing a lemon.

Webb cursed the waiter for spilling boiling tagine down his shirt. The waiter had no idea what he was supposed to have done wrong, but automatically apologised on the principle that the customer was always right. When the hot tagine was still burning his flesh minutes later after his first attempt to stand up, Webb turned on the Flashlight app on his phone to inspect what the damage was down there. To his amazement, there was no spilt tagine, but blood was seeping through his shirt just above the belt.

Pulling his shirt up for a closer look, he was dumfounded to see that he'd been shot. He called back the same waiter he'd cussed out minutes earlier and asked him to get a move on with bringing the implements. He was referring to the tool set for digging the meat out of lobster's claws that the waiter had promised to fetch minutes ago. Pleased with a chance to redeem himself and maybe still earn a tip, the waiter reappeared with an entire toolbox of seafood utensils.

Webb asked the servitor to hold the Flashlight steady on him whilst he performed a delicate operation on himself. The waiter was accustomed to being passed patron's phones and being asked to snap photos. In fact, the most common thing the customers in the restaurant asked for wasn't food, but the password for the Wi-Fi. But he'd never been asked to perform this service before.

With a Lobster Crab Claw Cracker in one hand and a Stainless Steel Seafood Shellfish Fork in the other, Webb dug into the flab round his stomach, using the Cracker as a set of pliers, and extracted the a .22 magnum bullet. He tossed the cartridge onto the plate, soaked his napkin in lemon juice, and sterilised the wound, before thanking the waiter and reclaiming his phone.

How the fuck had he managed to shoot himself in the stomach with his own bullet, and how the fuck had the bullet ended up in him and not in Indigolin, was all he could think as he quit the restaurant. He took the receipt for his expenses, and left behind a bloodied Seafood Cutlery set and a .22 magnum shell on the terracotta dish.

He totally forgot to tip the waiter.

Using the napkin as compression against the wound, he retraced his steps to Albemarle Street, where the demonstrators were still stuck to the building.

"Are you super-glued?" He asked the one that seemed to be their ringleader.

"We are," pronounced Brian Bellweather, proudly, admiring his interrogator's white pony tail, and wondering how long it would take him to grow one like it. "Are you the press?"

"Where is it?" Webb asked.

"Where's what?" Bellweather enquired.

"The super-glue."

"Left hand coat pocket," answered Bellweather. "Do you know how to get us down?"

Webb thrust his hand into Bellweather's coat and extracted the small tube. Bellweather watched in amazement as the guy unscrewed the cap and squirted the adhesive onto his stomach, suturing the wound. He then screwed the cap back on and returned the tube to the guy's pocket.

"Yes," Webb replied. "But you'd have to be prepared to leave your epidermis on the wall."

Interview

Millicent Marcuson, the reporter from Good Morning Britain, had arrived at the headquarters of Flyover Life Sciences with her cameraman, Ynes, where they were carrying out some sound and visual checks whilst awaiting the appearance of their interviewee, the Blue Molecule Man. It was known as Flyover because the roof of Indigolin's laboratory was the Westway motorway into Central London. Like everything about the blue bitcoin blagger, it was edgy.

Above the constant hum and purr of Indigolin's laboratory machines, there was a bass continuous thrum of the moving traffic overhead. The cameraman was going to need a very directional microphone. It was like doing an interview from inside one of Dante's Circles of Hell. The walls were tiled with glowing, cobalt, sap-filled panels that gave her the feeling she was inhabiting a lava lamp of moving blue secretions, or that the blood bank had just delivered multiple sacs of blue-blooded plasma *en route* to Buckingham Palace. Everything about the place was restless, busy. She could have been witnessing the void seconds before Big Bang.

"This is quite a scoop for us," Millie whispered to her photographer. "Tinctorio Indigolin specialises in mass rallies. Doesn't usually do one-to-one interviews."

The photographer, Ynes, rearranged his Bronze Harris Tweed Baker's Boy cap on his head and said: "Think we'll get a chance to view his art collection?"

"He collects NFT's," explained Marcuson. "There's nothing physical to inspect."

"Huh? I thought he had a big collection."

"He does, but what matters is what it's a collection of. He sponges up Non-Fungible Tokens, so all he gets is a certificate of ownership; nothing tangible to hang on the wall. It was like a logical progression from his cornering the market in blockchain. The NFT's legally come into the category of what the lawyers call *choses in action*, so they're trade-able, like cryptocurrency, but they're not divisible like satoshis."

"You seem to know a lot about this stuff, Millie."

"Well, Ynes, I originally wanted to be let loose to grill him about blockchain; then I wanted to face him down over NFT's, but the moving caravan has moved on, and now what our viewers really want to know about is this cerulean molecule thing. You just can't keep up with this guy, and it comes as no surprise to find that he operates out of a place that never stands still. Have you noticed how everything here is constantly undergoing miniscule, random fluctuations?"

"Yeah, like Brownian motion."

"Except for the fact, it's all blue!"

Tinctorio Indigolin was approaching them, crossing the laboratory *en route* to his private office. "Pleasure to meet you, Millie." He shook her hand, and frowned at the cameraman.

"Does he think we're in synagogue?" Indigolin enquired.

"Oh!" She said after making the connection. "He never takes the cap off. Thinks it makes him look highly strung. You know, what with everyone being an amateur cameraman on their phones these days, he has to set himself apart somehow or other."

"By keeping his hat on indoors?" Indigolin pursued. "A Baker's Boy Cap with a button on top?"

"We'll do the questions first and put the noddies in later if that's okay with you?" Ynes said, seeking to assert some sort of authority.

"As you please," Indigolin beamed.

"You know, Mr Indigolin, I was half expecting your PA to cancel our meeting today."

"And why would she do that, Millie?"

"Because we all understood that you were shot dead yesterday afternoon, Mr Indigolin. It's all over social media."

"I was healed by my molecule, Millie. I am whole again."

"Mr Indigolin, does this molecule you've invented have a name yet?"

"But of course!"

He pushed open a door off the laboratory and they passed into his private office, a monastic space shorn of all adornment, save a brutalised desk, his chair, and a glass wall behind the chair. At present, the space behind the glass was in darkness, so that the glass reflected the three occupants who had just entered the room. The contrast in mood to the swarming mobility of the laboratory was breath-taking.

Indigolin seated himself at his desk. He made an inclusive gesture with his hand, as though inviting them to be seated, but there were no other seats in the room. It seemed this office was a very private space for Indigolin's innermost reflections. Or maybe his panic room. Or his bomb shelter.

On the opposite wall, facing the desk, hung maybe fifty or sixty A4 sized identically-framed barcodes, being the ownership receipts for his prized NFT collection. '*So this is where he comes to be with all his invisible art,*' thought Millie. Maybe it wasn't such a bad idea, being able to contemplate all that wealth without the distraction of having to look at what it represented. No-one would ever be able to question his taste.

"Because of its colour, I named it after the blue men of the Sahara. In the patent application, it's called Rif."

"Rif?"

"Rif, Riff, Arif: it's Berber, Ms Marcuson. It's the name of the mountain range in Morocco that runs from Cape Spartel and Tangier to the Ouergha River and the Mediterranean Sea; and the nomadic Berber tribes who inhabit the Rif, all wear blue robes, the dye of which penetrates their skin and turns them blue, the same way that my Blue Molecule penetrates the skin. So they're known as the Blue Men of the Desert."

He rose from the one seat in the office and switched on the light illuminating what lay hidden behind the glass.

In a genuinely unrehearsed moment, the reporter gasped and exclaimed: "It's the biggest terrarium I've ever seen!"

The work desk at which Indigolin sat with his back to the triple-glazed wall was a huge butcher's block table unornamented save for his PC with a DataTraveler plugged into the USB port. Behind him, inside the sheer glass wall, grew all manner of hothouse plants. There were plantains with tiers of pendant bananas, prickly pomegranate trees in fruit, dates, aubergines, and almonds. Millicent Marcuson wouldn't have been the least bit surprised if Mr Molecule told her he had the Tree of Good and Evil growing in there. The guy was full of surprises.

"More of a vivarium," he corrected. "It's not the plants I'm interested in. I just introduced the plants as context—for the reptiles and amphibians."

As she focussed carefully, she became aware that, despite an absence of convection in the enclosed glasshouse, everything was in motion, just the same as in the laboratory, but in the laboratory the impression of motion was synthetic, man-made. In the terrarium, it was natural. From the green reflecting pools embellished with lily pads to the tops of the Tasmanian tree fronds, everything was busy with almost imperceptible twitchings; small, random fluctuations, as if some unseen hand was constantly making minor corrections to an unknown design.

What she had thought to be a rotting leaf revealed itself as the leg of a Burmese Star tortoise; ripples spread out from multiple points in the reflecting bassin, setting up interference patterns with one another; and then, like minute performers in an exercise of synchronised swimming, four frogs jumped up at the same instant, swapping lily pads with one another, before all disappearing back out of sight beneath the heaving vegetation, leaving one wondering if one had seen or imagined them.

"Reptiles?" She queried.

"None of the nasty sort," he assured her. "I was tempted to put some exotic birds in amongst all the trees, but it would have been cruel. However, we do have a large variety of fish; we also have toads, terrapins, tortoises, but principally we have frogs. They lay their eggs by the thousands and, in nature, most of them would get eaten by predators, but here, I am the only predator, so most of them survive."

He turned on his dazzling smile, just In case she didn't know it was a joke. He was quite distinguished and good looking. *'If he didn't insist on wearing those ridiculous blue legume suits, he'd be quite a catch,'* she thought. Forty years old and still single. In the media, he had never been romantically linked with anyone.

"They lay their eggs in the water," he continued, still eulogising his frogs. "But, unlike other reptiles, the eggs have no shells. This is because everything about frogs is designed to prevent water-loss and a shell would represent a barrier between the frog's skin and the water. I took my inspiration for my unique Rif molecule from them. Because the skin of a frog is permeable: they absorb the medium they inhabit.

"You know, they're the most endangered species on the planet, specifically because their skins are so porous, so they're highly sensitive to any sort of environmental degradation. They bruise like bananas. We can use them as indicators of climate change, because, if the biosphere is threatened, it's absorbed straight through the frog's skin to its vital organs, and they'll fall sick, like canaries down coal mines. And also, like canaries, they sing to me."

"You use them in scientific experiments? I'm not sure the BBC approve of that."

"Ms Marcuson, frogs have always been used in scientific experiments. Those that don't die a hero's death in the lab, are either run over by motorists, carried off by birds, or eaten by Frenchmen. The world's first electric battery was built from a frog's leg. Without frogs, there would have been no mobile phones, no Tesla cars. They are intelligent, magical creatures. In there, it's very hot and humid. Sometimes I take my blue legume suit off and just sit in there, motionless as another gecko.

"Always listening and watching; and as they sang to me, I came to understand what they were trying to tell me. I worked out how their skins could transmit liquid, and that was the beginning of the Rif molecule I developed. Starting as a miniscule thought in my head, no bigger than a molecule itself; I patented something that wasn't even in the periodic table before I defined it, a molecule that is so rarefied, so refined, that it passes right through the human body. I had to kiss a lot of frogs, Ms Marcuson, but I got my princess in the end."

"So you've patented a party trick, but what use is it in life science?"

"Ms Marcuson, I unveiled this epoch-shattering discovery before an audience of five hundred random people at the Royal Society in Albemarle Street yesterday morning. If I was Houdini, or even David Copperfield or Dynamo, I could forgive you for referring to it as a party trick. But you're talking to Tinctorio Indigolin, not some prestidigitator or mountebank, no matter how accomplished."

"I repeat, where does your liquid fit in with Flyover Life Science?"

"One has to have vision, Millie. Tip top! This isn't a party trick. It shouldn't even be regarded as a liquid, Ms Marcuson. It's a *delivery mechanism*. We already have medicines that can treat cancerous tumours, but in order to get the treatment to the tumour, we have to hack the patient open. My delivery mechanism combines with other medicines, such as bleomycin, and passes straight through the basal layer of the epidermis and gets to work on the tumour.

"It can even penetrate to previously inoperable brain tumours. Just a question of time. It takes about forty-five seconds to pass through a hand. Penetrating a cranium may take forty-five minutes, unless the patient has what the lawyers call an egg-shell skull, in which case it goes through a lot quicker. But, sooner or later, it hits its target, and delivers its payload. My frogs and I have developed a cure for cancer. They're like my Oompa Loompas!"

He did a little jig then murmured under his breath '*Fee-fi-fo-fum*', then continued: "If we have another pandemic tomorrow, it won't take months to vaccinate the population. I'll just have them all queuing up in their swimming costumes and process thousands an hour through a nationwide network of spray booths. I could substitute brown for the blue tint and give the population a glossy Mediterranean tan at the same time. Just like going to the carwash. Top shelf!

"At Blue Rif Industries, we do a lot of work with frogs. They have remarkable properties. Everything is unique in nature, but frogs are particularly so. Is that an oxymoron? Everybody knows that if you pull a gecko's tail off, it simply grows another one. We don't know if that is because of some special ability in geckoes, or maybe it's just that a tail is an easier thing to grow than, say a jointed arm terminating in a prehensile hand with opposable thumbs.

"In Canada, at Algoma University in Toronto, a group of scientists have been experimenting with frogs. I'm afraid the experiments were rather cruel. They amputated the legs of 115 frogs and treated the wounds with a cocktail of cell-regenerative chemicals. They then put the frogs inside a device called a BioDome, which sounds a bit Star Wars, but is actually something you could knock up yourself at home.

"The frogs' amputated limbs grew back. Unlike geckoes, frogs, in common with humans, cannot naturally regrow lost limbs. But treated under the BioDome with the cell regenerators, it seems they can. Now, I don't pretend that the legs they re-grew were perfect in every respect or identical with the ones they lost. But they were good enough to enable them to go about their daily business. They won't be enrolling to join the Bolshoi, but they could swim, walk and jump perfectly comfortably.

"So I have been building on the findings of the Canadian scientists. I asked myself, what is it that, at a certain point when the human embryo is in the mother's womb, sends out the signal that makes a human's limbs start growing in the first place? Or is it easier to work the other way round, and look at the unfortunate cases when the limbs have not grown correctly, and seek to analyse what went wrong? How can we duplicate the conditions that told the embryo that it was time to start growing limbs?

"Women have been using cell regenerators for years in make-up and moisturisers. It's not a trick or a gimmick, the products are very expensive, because they genuinely make skin cells grow. Some of the products are based on chemicals used by surgeons to transport organs and tissues from recent donor cadavers to the recipient, so that they do not degenerate on the demise of the donor. Skin cells are dropping off by the thousand every minute and regenerate naturally. The products I mentioned just now promote the process of regeneration.

"So, like the relatively simple gecko's tail, we know it can be done. There seems no reason why we shouldn't be able to trick a human being who has suffered the loss of a limb into thinking that the conditions are right for him to grow it back again. We have to make his brain send out that signal to his body once more. If he could do it before when he was an embryo, somewhere within him must lay the ability to repeat the exercise. We just have to find the switch and turn it on again.

"It's not just the loss of a limb. Why can a teenage woman grow breasts at puberty, but never be able to grow them again if she needs to later on in her life? If a woman has suffered a mastectomy and faces years of reconstructive surgery, wouldn't it be an altogether better solution if we could just fool her brain into flicking the switch that could make her grow another breast for herself? I see my research as complementary to my Blue Molecule delivery mechanism.

"The molecule enables us to treat or cure cancers, but the work with the frogs may enable those who have lost limbs or breasts or organs to cancers or diabetes, to grow them back, or at least grow enough of them back to give the patient a decent quality of life. Like the frogs, they might not be dancing in the Bolshoi ballet, or running the quarter mile, but they should be able to walk to the shops.

"I'm sorry. I have been rambling on. But I'm passionate about all this. Tip top! I make the mistake of thinking other people find this stuff as interesting as I do. No doubt part of the reason why I've never married! I'm a crashing bore. Now, if you'll excuse me, I have a meeting with my investors. Ms Marcuson, there is one great favour that you could do for me, if you please. When you air this, kindly make it clear that this morning's interview was recorded yesterday morning before I was assassinated. I would very much like to remain dead, at least until my assailant has been brought to justice."

"I was about to ask you," she said, "how you pulled that one off?"

"What do they say in *Kingsman*, Ms Marcuson? *Clothes Maketh Man*. Let's just say that if I'd put the single-breasted suit on this morning instead of the double-breasted one, you'd be interviewing a cadaver. The pin-stripes in the suit are electro-magnetised filament of Blue Rif. They repelled the bullet. My life was saved by my molecule!"

"Mr Indigolin, if we do you a favour and sit on this interview for a few days, that's bad news for us, because we're current affairs, not yesterday's affairs, you know."

"Yes, I understand."

"And no-one wants to be reading about material where the caravan has moved on. I've already been there when I wanted to interview you about cryptocurrencies and then NFT's. We can't keep up with you, Mr Indigolin. If we don't put this out now, it's just going to be newspaper used for wrapping up someone's fish and chips tomorrow."

"How can I compensate you?"

"You could let me publish the Triumvirate Interview."

"Millicent, that would put you in contempt of Court. You must know there's a Gagging Order on that."

"More than a Gagging Order," corrected Ynes. "It was a super-injunction. No-one's even supposed to know Mr Indigolin ever went to Court."

"Mr Indigolin, I know that you got the Court Order," Millicent resumed, "although no-one has been able to figure out what you were attempting to keep away from the public by doing so. But seeing as how you managed to secure the order in the first place, I presume you can make it go away again."

"Not possible, Millie. As your cameraman pointed out, it's a super-injunction. How can I make an order go away that never existed in the first place?"

"Can you at least let us watch the Triumvirate Interview, Mr Indigolin?"

"Watch it," he reflected. "You mean for personal research and educational purposes?"

"You could put it that way."

"Very well. It's a large file. I'll have my lawyers Mimecast it to you."

"God bless you, sir!" Said the cameraman in sarcastic Cockney, doffing his cap.

"Quite the Purly King and Queen, aren't you?" Indigolin smiled. "Top shelf!"

He killed the light in his vivarium, stuck his PC, with the DataTraveler still inserted, under the arm of his blue legume suit, and left them staring at an empty butcher's block desk, a darkened glass wall, and a gallery of impenetrable certificates.

"Wow! Did you believe a word of what that Molecule Man just said?" Millie asked her cameraman.

"I didn't like the sound of his pandemic spray booths. For me, it had overtones of the Nazis asking you to get in line for a nice shower," said Ynes.

"Except you come out both vaccinated and vagazzled!"

"Yeah. He said he didn't have any birds in his vivarium."

"But he didn't say nothing about bats."

"And he referred to a patent for his molecule. But, as I understand it, the whole point about this molecule is that he hasn't applied for a patent."

"Because, if he did, he'd have to disclose how it works."

"Exactly! But, to give him the benefit of the doubt, it's possible he could have patented it in another jurisdiction that we don't know about yet."

"What was that stuff about the triumvirate?" The cameraman asked.

"I was trying to get a trade-off," explained Millicent. The BBC's Panorama program did an exclusive interview with Indigolin just as his career was beginning to take off. He used to have two partners, which is why it came to be known as the Triumvirate Interview, and I think that was also the working title for the Panorama program, and it came to be the citation for the legal case that followed, because as part of the gagging injunction, one wasn't even allowed to mention the name Tinctorio Indigolin as Claimant, so the legal case couldn't be referred to or cited or listed by reference to the names of the protagonists in the usual way."

"You mean like *Jarndyce versus Jarndyce*?"

"Exactly. It's not just a gagging order as to the content, but the very fact of the parties bringing proceedings in the first place is anonymised."

"And we're going to find out why."

"For personal research and educational purposes only, of course!"

As they quit his office and left the building beneath the Westway, they passed by the inevitable huge, flat screen television in reception where Sky News was playing the assassination of Tinctorio Indigolin on a loop. The ribbon at the bottom of the picture promised that at nine pm tonight they would be assessing the man and his legacy.

Was he an environmental Messiah, a philanthropist or just a con artist on a scale never before known? As if in answer to that question, the display cut to a clip of Indigolin doing his Jewish shrug and saying, "Don't ask me, shill!" Then he got shot. Then he said, "Tip top!" And the loop started again.

"Think what that loop's going to look like when they add the next episode in," remarked Millicent.

"You mean when they show him being resurrected after his execution?"

"Exactly. You realise," continued Marcuson to her cameraman, "that he just did a monologue about frogs and cell regeneration, and we never asked him any of the things we set out to ask him."

"Yes," replied the cameraman, with one eye on the TV. "But a consultation with a corpse has to be a first, no matter how short."

Twins

Indigolin was displeased to discover that the person waiting for him in Meeting Room 2 was not the expected investor but the leading man in the film that seemed destined never to get made, the film that his staff were attempting to shoot in Ouarzazate under the preposterous working title, *Knights of the Ream*.

"What on earth are you doing here in Maida Vale, Colman? Aren't you supposed to be on a tight schedule in the Sahara?"

"Mr Indigolin, sir, I'm not Colman Hunt. What you're looking at is his twin brother, Presley Unsdorfer. But I got past security because everyone always mistakes me for my brother."

"If you're his twin brother, how come you've got different names, shill?"

"You don't think Colman Hunt is his real name, do you? He was born, Mortimer Unsdorferbaum, but we started off by dropping the Baum when we were at primary school because it sounded too much like Bum, and Morty used to do this thing teasing us about '*Fee-fi-fo-fum, I spell my name Unsdorferbum;*' so at school we were Unsdorfer. You know, we believed we'd made a huge step towards acceptability when we dropped the Baum, but turned out we remained objects of ridicule as Unsdorfers. Colman Hunt is his stage name, his *nom de plume*."

"So we're all Children of Israel together, eh shill?"

"Yes, Yids!"

"And why did he go '*Fee-fi-fo-fum*'"?

"He says that when he does that he can track his twins no matter where we're hiding."

"And can he?"

"Seems like he can."

"OK, Presley. And what are you doing here today, apart from insulting your own religion?"

"On the Sky News, I was watching in your reception just now, it says you might be a con man."

"No, it didn't, shill. It said I might be a con *artist*. Important difference in the value hierarchy."

"Gotcha!"

"You can't believe everything you see on Sky News."

"Apparently not."

"I repeat, what are you doing here, Presley?"

"I'm here with a grievance. I've been culturally misappropriated, Mr Indigolin. I've been fraternally misappropriated. Why have you hired a body double for my brother when I'm his identical twin? I'm going to bring a law suit down on you of biblical proportions. You won't be able to see the sun for writs."

"Oh fuck, here we go, shill! Shot yesterday. Sued today! What a shit week I'm having!"

Making Virtue of a Necessity

"Boss," ventured Noah.

"What you got there, Noah?" Indigolin asked, peering into the screen of Noah's PC over his shoulder.

"It's our Excel, boss. We've got lots of tabs, because there's a tab for everything to do with the film."

"Tip top! Except we got no script and we're in between directors, shill."

"That too, but this tab's our shooting schedule, and we're weeks behind, because of this thing with Colman Hunt sulking in his caravan."

"I figured that out for myself without a spreadsheet, Noah. But I also figured that, seeing as how we don't have a script to shoot, the fact that the leading man is ligging it, didn't make much difference to the schedule in the great scheme of things."

"Of course, with respect, you're right, boss. But here's how we make virtue out of a necessity. We use that twin brother of his and shoot with him. No-one will know the difference."

"Yeah, we have to work with the tools we've been given, and that Presley is certainly a tool, but not the sharpest tool in the box. Noah that would be a Top Shelf idea if we had something to shoot. Tip Top!"

"That's it, Mr Indigolin. That's exactly it, you see. We do. We got the nude scene. I say we get the US $5M nude scene that you've already paid for in the can straight off before Celia Broadsword changes her mind."

"Or dies."

"I think she's pretty spry, boss. I mean, it was always going to be challenging, to say the least, shooting the sex scene with her ex-husband, who happens to be a raging queen."

"Noah, you're not going to give me the sexual misappropriation shit, are you? I've already had the cultural and fraternal misappropriation thing with that *kvetcher*, Presley?"

"Huh?"

"Are you about to tell me that only heterosexuals should be allowed to act sex scenes with members of the opposite sex?"

"No, boss. I wasn't going to give you any of that shit. But I'm saying it was always going to be a very tense scene to get in the can, Celia having sex with her ex. I mean, the point is that the sex scene is totally gratuitous and nothing to do with the rest of the film, so the fact that we ain't got diddly script don't make any difference. You get the twin off your case, and we get the sex scene in the can before Celia tells us she's got her period or something."

"Noah, she's eighty-five years old. I don't think she still has periods."

"I wouldn't know, boss. I've never had an eighty-five-year-old woman."

"But Presley's going to! Top Shelf, Noah. Tip Top! Let's get that Presley Unsdorferbaum over here and iron out the inside leg measurements in his contract."

"Hmmm," mused Noah.

"Now what's up, shill?"

Noah was peering at his spreadsheets again.

"It's that item down there with all the brackets around it, boss. When I look at a set of accounts, I don't like to see items with brackets round them. I mean, I try to look at the positives, but when I look at this balance sheet I see too many negatives. I see no ships, only hardships."

"That's what happens if your parents christen you Noah, shill!"

"But look at these parentheses, boss."

"What, the great big one?"

"We know about the great big one. That's your Deep Blue legacy item in the Seychelles. We know about that. But what's all the brackets round this one?"

"That's the Argan Farm project, Noah. It's supposed to have brackets round it because it doesn't open to the public for a couple of weeks. So at the moment, it's all investment flowing outwards, but when we open our doors to the public, those brackets are going to drop away, just the same as the pounds disappear from an obese *schlunter* after his gastric band comes off. It's a brilliant idea, shill, even if I do say so myself. A real educational family holiday. They stay in luxury tented accommodation at the Argan Farm with every amenity laid on."

"Glamping?"

"If you have to shoehorn everything into a cliché in order to come to terms with it, shill, sure. Dead simple: if the idea takes off and we find we're fully booked, we just put up another hundred tents. Don't have to worry about planning permission or messy construction projects closing off the entire resort for ten year-long refurbs and refreshers. We manufacture the fancy wigwams off site and deliver them in flat packs. Not so much Tip Top as Big Top, Noah!

"The parents stay in the 5-star tents, only emerging to gorge themselves in the Michelin-starred restaurant and pamper themselves in the spa, whilst the children engage in educational projects, not realising that we are actually using them as free labour, getting the harvest in for us. We teach them how to make candles and soap and how to press olive oil. They reap the Argans, they tend the goats, they tread the grapes, they gather the strawberries, and they brine the olives that they've just picked. Then we sell the crap back to their parents in the farm shop. This one washes its own face, Noah."

"So, no sooner has the west finally succeeded in doing away with child labour—"

"—Than I re-introduce it, masquerading as a family holiday. If the tents had chimneys, I'd have the little buggers up the chimneys like Benjamin Britten's Sweep. Kids should make themselves useful, not idle away their youth staring at their telephones."

"What about the weedy kids who don't want to do back-breaking toil at half-term, boss?"

"Some of them will be mucking out the petting zoo and the others will be boutique attendants, working in the gift shop. The older ones can drive the guests around in the electric buggies. You know, pick them up from the restaurant, and take them back to their pavilions. Hump the luggage. Staff would regard that as menial, manual labour, but a teenager regards it as his chance to get his hands on a set of wheels. It's all a matter of perspective."

"So the mothers and fathers take the kids away on holiday—"

"And they end up having a wonderful time as hotel porters. That's right, shill."

"Won't the parents be up in arms?"

"Nope. For the teenagers, it's an Argan Farm. For their parents, it's an Argon Farm, get it, shill? They spend a fortnight being *inert*. The parents will be making love in peace and quiet in their air-conditioned yurts, without having to worry about being disturbed by the little bleeders, because we've got them all gainfully employed, running around doing useful stuff.

"If you tell an adolescent that he or she's got to spend his holiday in the Kiddies Club with a bunch of six-year-old wankers face-painting and dressing up as pirates, he or she would be chronically pissed-off. But if you tell them they're going to be driving their own buggies around like stars of Grand Theft Auto, they think that is the height of cool."

"I still think it's exploitative, boss."

"Shill, there you go with the clichés again. In a world where one's fellow man is put on this planet to be exploited, some forms of exploitation are more acceptable than others. Being unpaid chauffeurs in the Argan Farm is a better occupation for kids than doing county lines! If I was running the country, they'd all be doing National Service, not cutting each other with zombie knives. But I'm not running the country. I'm working on the microcosm. Once I've got the Argan Farm functioning properly, I'll sort the country out, don't you worry."

Another Desert

The Empty Quarter stretches across 650,000 square kilometres of the Arabian Peninsula. That is to say, this unbroken expanse of intensely inhospitable desert is 40,000 square miles larger than the entire country of France. It receives 1.2 inches of rain a year. That is half as much as Death Valley. The man had driven his passenger along the E11 motorway from Dubai and crossed the border at Abu Dhabi. He continued for another 30 miles into the area the locals referred to as Rub'al Khali before checking in his rear view and wing mirrors that all was clear. Then he drove his Range Rover off the side of the tarmac, and continued a further ten miles into the Empty Quarter in off-road mode.

When he considered he'd driven far enough into the barren wilderness to ensure his passenger wouldn't attempt to follow him back to Dubai, the man got out of the driver's door, walked round the back of the car and opened the passenger door.

"Get out Andrew!" He ordered. "Andrew, get out of the fucking car!"

Seeing his words had no effect, he goaded, pulled and prodded his passenger, and ultimately swatted him straight off the seat, and clean out of the vehicle onto the hyper-arid sand of the Empty Quarter.

"Fucking well stay there, Andrew!" He shouted. He closed the passenger door, got back into the driver's seat and roared back in the direction of Downtown Dubai. He had gone far, far out of his way to dump Andrew and make sure he didn't turn up on his doorstep again; but gas was cheap. After all, Napier Ransom was driving on top of the largest oil field in the world.

His brief sortie from the air-conditioned cocoon of his car had him perspiring. What did they say? *Horses sweat; men perspire, and ladies glow.* He was positively running like clarified butter. He pulled his omnipresent bottle of *Eau Savage* out of the glove compartment, and liberally hosed himself down.

Presley on the Payroll

"So, here we are again, back in Meeting Room 2, Mr Indigolin," said Presley Unsdorferbaum.

Meeting Room 1 was for big meetings. In fact, they referred to it as Conference Room 1. Room 2, on the other hand, wouldn't comfortably accommodate a meeting of more than four attendees, so it had seemed presumptuous to Indigolin to refer to it as a conference room at all. By way of compromise, they called it a meeting room.

Colman and his brother, Presley, were both well over six feet in height. Presley looked like a caged animal in the small meeting room, and kept crossing and uncrossing his denim-clad legs, trying to get comfortable. Indigolin was musing at the uncanny resemblance.

Obviously when they were little children, the brothers would have been indistinguishable; but what was fascinating Indigolin just now was the fact that they had led completely separate lives for more than half a century; they had presumably taken different amounts of exercise, and put different amounts of food and drink into their bodies. But they were still identical. It was one of those nurture and nature, debates. It seemed like it didn't make any difference.

"Yeah, seems like old times, doesn't it, shill?"

"And who's the Kiwi?"

"I'm Aussie, not Kiwi," Noah informed him.

"That's Noah Nguyen," said Indigolin.

"Nguyen?" Queried Presley. "That's a gook name."

Apparently, tiring of striving to find a comfortable seated position, or maybe just to intimidate the shorter Noah, Presley stood up and hitched his trousers by the belt. Indigolin gave him a straight look and he sat straight down again, but continued to rearrange his tackle, seated.

"In Australia," explained Noah, "after Smith and Jones, it's one of the most common surnames in the phone book."

"Noah's my right hand man," said Indigolin.

"Even though I'm left-handed," smiled Noah.

"As in a left-handed Kiwi queer?" Presley provoked.

"Not all left-handed people are queer," corrected Noah.

"In the southern hemisphere," elucidated Presley, "you go down the plug hole the other way."

Leaving Noah to work that one out, Presley turned back to Indigolin. "Do I take it that you have considered my little proposition?" He asked him.

"Not in the least, shill. We don't bend the knee to blackmail, and we don't welcome any form of discrimination or homophobia; but we do have a little proposition of our own that should kill two birds with one stone. In fact, thinking of our eighty-five-year-old, Celia Broadsword, we might end up unintentionally killing three birds."

"Alright, you've got my full attention."

"If you could just stop rearranging your junk for five minutes, I'd believe you, shill."

Presley composed himself and placed his palms flat down on the meeting room table. Indigolin had succeeded in domesticating him.

"Thank you, Presley," Indigolin continued. "You're officially going on the payroll."

"So you came round to my way of thinking, Mr Indigolin?"

"Where you see obstacles, I see opportunities. Presley, you got a passport?"

"Sure I got a passport."

"Has it got at least six months left before its Eat By date?"

"Sure."

"OK, you're coming in the PJ with me and Noah to Morocco tomorrow. You good with that?"

"Double good."

"Top Shelf, shill! Tip top! My driver will collect you from this very spot at eight o'clock in the morning. Now, here's the deal. When we get on location, you keep your head down and only move when I say so. Point is, no-one must see you and your brother, Colman, at the same time. You're never in the same frame. *Verstehen?* So we have to keep checking the coast is clear."

"How come?"

"Because we aren't so much going to be using you as Colman's understudy, which is what you asked for. Understand? We are going to be using you *as* Colman. Colman's jerking us around. He's gone all monastic on us. Won't come out of his trailer. So we're going to teach him a little lesson in good manners. As I understand it, there's no love lost between you and Colman?"

"That would be an understatement!"

"We're going to get on with the filming, but you're going to be Colman, and we're going to pay you what we would have paid Colman, which is a shed of a lot. And if Colman doesn't like it, he can do the other thing. But this little duplicity has to stay between you and me, shill. The director, Wallace Pfister, has to think that you're Colman, because he's a man who's very troubled by ethics and propriety, not to mention image rights; so if he knew what was going on, well, he'd be doing the other thing.

"That's why you and Colman can't both be in the same frame at the same time. Even the director's got to believe you're Colman. And Colman's ex-wife, Celia Broadsword, has to think you're Colman. As of tomorrow, from the time we touch down, you answer to the name of Colman Hunt. Anybody say *Colman*, you stand up. You good with that, shill?"

"I'm good. What we filming? I got to learn any lines?"

"That's the other thing. We're going straight into the gratuitous sex scene with Celia Broadsword, Colman's ex-wife. We're going to pay you to have simulated sex with Celia Broadsword. You still good with this?"

"Mr Indigolin, that woman is in for the fuck of her life!"

Salvator Mundi

The blue tail-finned Bombardier Global Express was still flying above Andalusia. The two pilots, one male, one female, in their starched white, short-sleeved shirts, ferried their live cargo at breakneck speed. The passengers were Indigolin, Noah and Presley.

"How long till we get to Ouarzazate?" Ti asked.

"We gotta land at Marrakesh first, boss," said Noah. "Two legs: Madrid and then Marrakesh," explained the amanuensis, "and then it's a four-hour drive."

"Two legs good. Four legs bad, huh, like in *Animal Farm*?"

"They're technical stops, boss. We could've landed at Casablanca, but then it's still a four-hour drive. Everything in Morocco takes at least four hours on the ground, because the state of the roads is so bad. We could take a chopper, but you wouldn't feel safe in a Moroccan chopper unless it was your own!"

"I'd never own a helicopter, Noah. They're so vulgar."

"But I hear your new director, Wally Pfister, flies one."

"He's welcome to it, but I find it a noisy, environmentally unfriendly and dangerous form of transport."

"Except," interrupted Presley, "when he puts it down, he won't have to get into the car for another four hours on the road."

"Why do you think the protester shot you, boss?" Noah Nguyen asked.

"It wasn't a protester, shill. It was a gun hired by Albanian George."

"George Georgiou?"

"Yeah, but we call him Albanian George to distinguish him from the other George Georgiou who's a good guy, and I put the double-breasted blue legume suit on that morning, because Albanian George had WhatsApped me and told me that if I didn't get his money back to him he was going to have me seen to."

"Why didn't you just give him his money back?"

"Because I've got too many CFD's open at the moment, shill. If I leave them open, I stand to quadruple my stake, but if I close them down early, just to appease Albanian George, I lose the ranch instead."

"So you thought it was a better option to get shot?"

"Look, when we break the story that I was shot at point blank range in the chest and saved by my Blue Rif Molecule, our shares will go through the roof; I'll dump a few on the market, and pay George off, shill. Top Shelf! Tip Top! It's going to be mega!"

"And in the meantime, you're better off dead."

"Right. We're leaking money all over the place. That was poor advice we received when we bought all those dirhams to make the payments we had to make in local currency during the life of the shoot. I'm paying a washed-up matinee idol over the odds to sulk inside his tent, and then we inherited this Celia Broadsword situation. Her agent snuffed it, so my predecessor found himself negotiating for the first time with the principal instead of the agent.

"The good news was that the principal, Celia, was perfectly happy to do something the agent would have drawn the line at. The bad news was that Celia was a far better negotiator than her agent, so when I took over, I walked into a situation where I had to pay her five million dollars in advance for the nude scene, being dollars I could have used to get Albanian George off my back.

"I mean, which Gerontophiliac's smart idea was it to do a nude love scene with an eighty-five-year-old woman? When I bought into this project I inherited a contractual obligation to pay big potatoes to a superannuated leading lady to perform a nude scene in a script that's not even been written yet. The script, if it ever does get written, is just going to be the vehicle for the devoted fans that she's built up, in a movie career spanning six decades, to find out what she's like in her birthday suit, but I think they're going to find that they've arrived at the scene of a horrible accident about fifty years after her best-by date. Excuse the mixed metaphor, Noah. Sorry, but the situation's so unique, I couldn't even find a cliché to enliven it for you."

"I'm told she's still pretty fit, boss. Did they even have movies sixty years ago? I think she may be older than eighty-five."

"God help us! Anyway, we've got a new director coming on board: Wallace Pfister. Everything's riding on him now. He's supposed to be old school. He shoots everything on celluloid film stock and then he edits it the traditional way with a pair of scissors. Then, only after he's done all that, does he digitise it and put all the M & E tracks on."

"Is that just a retro gimmick?" Presley asked. "Like wanting to play vinyls? Nostalgia ain't what it used to be. All that shit."

"As far as I can make out," elucidated Noah, "he's never done it any other way. Old school."

"Sounds like a slow process that we need to speed up, Noah," said Indigolin.

"Boss, we've got CFD's, we've got investors who are equity, and we've got lenders, like Albanian George. Then we've got our national institution, the NHS. The *crème de la* thing about 'our glorious NHS' is that they never even asked for any shares. Everybody else is on the graft for shares in your Blue Molecule company. But the NHS coughed up millions for a straight option."

"Yeah, it's like a first refusal for when it hits the market. After safety tests, that's still years away. They didn't want another shemozzle like they had with the Pfizer and Astra Zeneca jabs, being held to ransom by the EEC."

"You know that lobbyist was worth his weight in rare earths."

"And the £50,000.00 donation we made to the Conservative party yielded £50m in contracts. That's what I call a good return."

"Yes, shame the Labour party were too incompetent to get themselves elected, or we'd have got £100m of contracts in return for the same thing. And a seat for you the House of Lords, boss."

"If I was running things, Noah, there wouldn't be a House of Lords, nor House of Commons. The only legitimate way that you can run a country without corruption is to have government by blockchain, and if I ever run for parliament, it would have to be on a ticket to burn that august and bicameral body to the ground!"

The idea of an arson attack on parliament animated Presley, who had previously contributed little to the conversation. "Like having Guy Fucking Fawkes for Prime Minister!" He said.

Ignoring him, Indigolin continued. "I could pay Albanian George tomorrow, Noah. But it would cost me money and face. Am I going to tell all my five thousand staff that they're not being paid on time because I've decided to prioritise Albanian George? I could sell this PJ tomorrow, but am I going to fly premium economy just so that Albanian George can get paid on the nail and drive his blacked-out Bentley Bentayga around Berkeley Square with a broad beam on his boat?"

"I heard about that motor, boss. He got Bentley to paint it with Vantablack paint. He had to buy the paint in from Anish Kapoor."

"Yes, the Vantablack absorbs 99.99% of all light in the spectrum. So the car is basically as good as invisible."

"How cool is that?" Presley said.

"The answer is *Not very cool at all*, shill. Because the Vantablack absorbs so much light, the interior of the car is like a fiery furnace. George had to have the air conditioning configured at the factory in Crewe to pump out so much cold that the car only does about one mile to the gallon, and has a usable range of about ten kilometres, before it needs filling up with petrol again."

"Why does a man want to drive around in a black hole, boss?"

"More arse hole than black hole, if you ask me shill. George's original idea had been to put the paint job on an Aston Martin Vantage. Then he could say that he had a Vantablacked Vantage, and roar up and down Park Lane like James Bond. But the car was too low on the ground for him to tuck his portly lunch pack behind the wheel. When he tried it for size, it was like he was climbing into a hip bath, and he'd need a Stannah stair-lift to help him out again. So he went for the Bentley, because you climb up into that. Whereas he had to enter the Aston like a supplicant crawling into a cave on his hands and knees, he could mount the Bentayga like he was a fat priest ascending the steps of his raised pulpit."

"And you're not going to repay this fat priest what you owe him, boss?"

"Heaven sake, shill! George is a moneylender, so the longer he doesn't get paid back, the more profitable his business model is for him."

"So, you're doing him a favour by defaulting?" Presley declared.

"All the greedy *schnorers*, all they want is put n' calls and share options. But you know something, shill? Except, of course to management, I never grant share options, because share options degrade the company. Stands to reason, the *schnorer* who holds the option is never going to exercise it unless the value is more than he paid for it, so it just dilutes the value for all the other subscribers who paid the right price for their shares. I mean, even if the company is worthless, I still don't believe in scattering equity like confetti."

"Company's not valueless. It's valued at £40.6 billion and you still hold 80%, Mr Indigolin."

"Yes, but I mean. As Oscar Wilde nearly said, there's valuations and there's value. The company's got no underlying assets whatsoever to support that value. It's just another dotcom bubble about to burst. What have we actually got here? We've got a laboratory under a motorway on a 5 year lease from TFL; we've got some plant and equipment inside the lab, that we're depreciating at 50% a year; we've got some supercars for the directors on 3 year leases. The jet's in the name of the BVI company, and we're borrowing to invest in loss-making films shot in some shit hole in the Sahara as a tax dodge. Oh, and let's not forget, we've got a helluva lot of frogs. How are we writing them down on the books?"

"It's them that makes the share price so jumpy, boss!"

"We're like the Emperor's New Clothes. I mean, what do we actually have?"

"A molecule, boss."

"How can something that measures 0.14 of a nanometre be worth £40.6 billion?" Presley asked.

"Well, look at that Salvator Mundi painting that got knocked down to the Fake Sheikh for US $450.3 million," pointed out Noah. "That's 45 centimetres in size: $10 million per centimetre."

"And that was a fucking out-of-focus fake too!" Presley responded.

"Should've stuck to NFT's!" commented Indigolin.

"Yeah," mused Noah, "but the fake Sheikh's brain was so broiled with PTSD's, NSU's, and NFT's that he didn't understand you don't have to get fucked to get STD's!"

"Which Emirate was that iron the king of?" Presley asked of Noah.

"Fuck knows! Just another non-fungible cunt!"

La Mamounia

Indigolin's blue jet had landed at Marrakesh, and the three occupants had decided to acclimatise themselves at La Mamounia hotel for a couple of nights, particularly, so as to allow Presley to adjust himself to being Colman Hunt. Indigolin and Noah didn't know that Presley was already fully acclimatised to that. Indigolin was always happy for an excuse to stay at La Mamounia.

Apart from all the other things it had going for itself, it had a gigantic resident population of frogs. Indigolin had booked out one of the three-bedroom Riyadhs in the middle of the walled gardens that were usually reserved for oligarchs. It was a nice change for the maître d' to be receiving calls for room service and flowers instead of hookers. Presley had wandered off to the Haman, enabling Indigolin and Noah to talk about him behind his back.

"Can this Unsdorfer guy act?" The question was being posed by Tinctorio Indigolin to Noah.

"Presley? Who knows? Does the part call for any acting, boss? Apart from the sex scene, I thought he spends most of his time getting thrown out of windows, and that's presently done by the stunt double, Pat Oculus."

"Noah, do we even know what's in today's script? As far as I can gather, the last director went native. Got into this Marrakesh Express thing too much; spent his time reclining on divans and sending out for more and more kif. I wouldn't have minded if it was a man's drug like coke or even cannabis resin; but for Pete's sake, that kif is a drug for guys who roll their own."

"Yes, boss. He got too close to the staff. You know the thing, when you want to convince the hired help that you're one of them, that you're their mate, not their boss."

"Yeah, yeah, like the Sussexes; worst management decision since Nero made his horse a consul. You can't have the lunatics running the asylum. As far as I can gather the actors were telling the director that they thought that it would be really cool if they did this or that, you know, their favourite party pieces; doesn't matter if they're not there in the script, which I believe was bovine anyway. You know if an actor got a good write-up for doing something in the school nativity play twenty years ago, they just wanted to keep repeating it, like a dog returning to its vomit, and the old director was too lazy to restrain them."

"Little Donkey! Little Donkey! I get you! But with this Wallace Pfister coming on stream, I think it's all going to change, boss. The new headmaster is arriving. And I believe he's arriving in some style, choppers himself around in his own Eurocopter."

"Well, you already know what I think of that, Noah."

"Right now, the players may be immured in their caravans, taking their mutinous lead from Hunt. Pfister's going to have to tease them out of their tents like a little winkle picker."

"We've got to turn it round, Noah. All the bad joss you're talking is about the old script; that is about to fall into desuetude as soon as we get ourselves a new one. First thing we have to fix is this little fit of petulance; no-one's doing any acting at the moment, because Hunt is sulking inside his Airstream. But if this Presley pulls it off, that's another obstacle we've surmounted."

"Could almost be the title of the film, *Presley Pulls it Off*. Do we know why Colman Hunt's sulking, boss?"

"Says he's sick of Ouarzazate. The heat and humidity makes the Grecian 2000 hair dye run down his face; he's got gut rot, foot rot, crotch rot, and the food gives his catamite IBS."

"We could give him a shot of loperamide."

"What that, Noah?"

"Like Imodium, but it's generic, so it's cheaper."

"Do we administer it to Hunt or to his catamite?"

"Don't matter; all their bodily fluids get shared anyway. We could give him a shot of whatever's going, but it's not gonna make the problem go away."

"Well, Tinctorio Indigolin doesn't like being held back by things called problems. We've already decided we're covertly going to use this twin. Play one off against the other. Resolves the threatened legal suit about cultural misappropriation. Mashes two potatoes with one fork. Top shelf! Does the twin need an equity card or anything?"

"In Ouarzazate, boss? You gotta be kidding. All he needs is a tetanus inoculation, some cous-cous and Entero-vioform."

Point Break

As Diego's dive boat approached the buoy, Diego unclipped the extendable barge pole from under his captain's seat and passed it to Napier Ransom to catch up the small float that the big buoy was attached to. Ransom missed it the first time and said, "Fuck it!" After having cursed his own incompetence, he then blamed Diego: "You weren't near enough, Diego!"

After Diego took the boat round the block for a second attempt and Napier missed it again, Diego grabbed the barge pole off Napier, went in for a third attempt, lined the boat up, cut the engines, walked up to the bow, caught the small float himself with ease and hauled up the two knotted guy ropes attached to the big buoy that was in turn attached to the ocean bed. He pulled the knots through the front cleats, secured his boat, collapsed his barge pole and tucked it back under his captain's seat onto the clips that held it in place. Everything was ship shape again.

Diego liked to give the crew members little jobs to do, so both the weak and the strong felt that they were making some sort of useful contribution, but he had neither the *paciència*, nor the gas to keep circling his craft round the buoy all afternoon. Besides, he had to consider the wishes of the other divers on the boat.

Agent Elena Troy snapped off her wet suit and tossed it onto the deck of the dive boat. She sat down on the transom and patted her hair dry with a towel. She'd been diving at Cap de Creus all summer and her skin was glowing Mediterranean bronze in a white bikini. Her blonde hair had been bleached almost platinum. She had the toned abdominal musculature and legs of an Olympic athlete. She looked stunning.

Her neighbour, a diver from Croatia, was sitting on the swim deck, counting the number of urchins he'd harvested into a Tupperware box. The divers were all working in their summer holidays on a project to restore the lost red coral reefs for which the area had been famous until the turn of the twentieth century. Elena liked the idea of putting something back into the environment at the same time as taking her holiday. It was described on her CV as 'volunteering'.

At the turn of the twentieth century, the region had suffered a double blow. Pirates had finally plundered the last traces of the red coral from which the town divers had made a living for centuries, and the phylloxera blight from France had wiped out the area's vine stocks at the same time. In a matter of weeks, the previously wealthy region had nothing with which to sustain itself except a trade in tinning anchovies.

The process of harvesting the red coral had been very perilous, leading to the deaths of countless divers. In an attempt to fix that problem, Narcis Monturiol had invented the submarine in this very bay where Napier Ransom had shown himself incapable of even catching the buoy.

The Croatian guy asked Elena if she'd like him to open one of the urchins up for her with his glove and his knife and she nodded. It tasted like the sea, the consistency of an oyster but slightly less viscous. The swim deck was covered in everyone's fins and masks. Other divers were sitting around the gunwales, inspecting how much battery life they had left in their Go Pros. A girl popped up out of the sea on a 40 mph electric Seabob, and tied it up on one of the cleats.

The girl was from America, and appropriately was named Bobi herself. She was like a mermaid. No-one had seen her out of the water. She just scooted around being dragged at high speed by the Seabob. With considerable upper body strength, she heaved herself up, so that her arms were folded on the swim deck, like she was working at a desk, but the rest of her body tapered into the sea.

"Delicious!" Elena said.

"You want another?" The Croatian asked.

"No thanks. Don't want to spoil my appetite. I've booked a 2 pm lunch up there, and I'm looking forward to it." She nodded her head in the direction of the former custom house that was now the Hotel Cap de Creus, where the Scottish proprietor, Chris Little, in addition to local specialities, served amazing curries.

"So what's your day job?" The guy asked her.

"Don't laugh."

"Promise."

"I'm a forensic accountant working for Her Majesty's Revenue and Customs."

"So, you're like a taxman?"

"Woman."

"You identify as a tax woman?"

"I *am* a tax woman."

"You nail tax dodgers?"

"My team does."

"I didn't know tax investigators came in so many shapes and sizes. I mean, you could be working here right now, undercover, conducting an investigation into Diego."

Diego was the Lothario owner of the dive boat. Having secured it to his buoy, he was now busy, keeping himself out of the sun under the Bimini cover by the helm, and constantly in hiding from ex-wives seeking provision for his offspring. Sooner or later the taxi RIB would materialise and take his divers onto the quay four at a time.

"I bet he's never paid any tax in his life," the guy continued.

"You can't wind me up. I'm on holiday," she said.

"I bet you're never off duty," the Croatian said, "you could be like Keanu Reeves in Point Break, just masquerading as a scuba diver."

"Good film, but (a) I work for HMRC, not the Catalan Tax Agency, and (b) I don't subscribe to the HMRC culture of being consumed with a burning desire to haul in all tax dodgers. I look at the bigger picture. The worst tax dodgers and money launderers in the country are the people sitting in government in the Houses of Parliament. I audit them. If Diego skims his tax, I don't give a toss. I only go fishing for the biggest sharks."

Napier Ransom was seated on the other side of the boat. He was an investment banker based in Dubai, who had figured that the best way to break the ice with women and get them in the sack was to sign up for volunteer work helping the planet. That way you'd have something in common, and that was like getting your foot in the door. Rohypnol also had its uses. He'd looked into helping to clear landmines in Angola for the HALO trust. Despite the possibility of a useful networking experience with the Duke of Sussex, he'd decided that particular line of volunteering looked a bit hazardous. He'd considered helping clear plastic shit from beaches in the Maldives, but that looked too ball-breaking. Spending the summer in the Mediterranean however, when it would be an unbearable 45 degrees centigrade in Dubai, swimming around and helping to build a red coral reef, surrounded by gorgeous chicks, topless or in bikinis, seemed to tick all his boxes.

Previously, in Dubai, he'd tried to break the ice with a Rhodesian Ridgeback dog, so that the totty could ask him what sort of a dog that was and what was his name, before he asked the totty out to dinner. But the fucking dog just grew bigger and bigger every day until it was bigger than Napier, and Nap couldn't be arsed walking around behind the hound, picking up its poo in a plastic bag. One day, he put the dog in his car, drove him out to the Empty Quarter, and chucked him out.

He'd tried dogs. He'd also tried being married as a means of having hot and cold running pussy on tap each day. He had courted a Greek prick teaser called Andrea. Her father was Andrew. The daughter doled her body out in portions date by date. It was like entering a tontine. But she wouldn't let him enter her outside of marriage. So he married her.

On their honeymoon, he swiftly came to the conclusion that the reason she had held back was because she was a very unimaginative lay, and, to the eternal rage of her father, Andrew, Napier filed for divorce on their return. The father now regarded her as soiled goods, and she spent the rest of her days living with her mother and father.

"Nap Ransom," said Napier, giving Elena a dazzling smile. "Do you mind if I join you on this transom? If anybody else sits on this side, I think the boat's going to tip over!"

"Go ahead. Be my guest."

Ransom gave up his place on the starboard side and sat cross-legged on the transom beside Elena, who shifted sideways to accommodate him. At close quarters, Elena was aware of his very persistent citrus-based aftershave. She marvelled how it could still be exuding olfactory offence after he'd been underwater for so long. But now she thought about it, she couldn't remember seeing him beneath the surface. Maybe he was just a hanger-on, a camp follower.

"I couldn't help overhearing you talking about the locals not paying their taxes," he began. Napier's tried and tested tactic was, not only to break the ice with an ecologically sound, planet-saving, worthy, shared pursuit, but to let the Croatian guy engage his target in conversation first. That way, Napier could just muscle in on the conversation himself after the Croatian had softened her up and hopefully established she wasn't a fucking dyke, without Napier having to waste valuable shagging time on the small talk stage.

"I mean," he continued, "it's like the Wild West out here! The people in Cadaqués, they've been pirates for three hundred years and waiters for thirty years; I don't think *anyone* in Catalonia pays any tax. Isn't that what they invented Andorra for?"

She smiled.

Just then an experienced diver called Paco pulled himself up the ladder onto the swim platform. From the dry bag round his neck that everyone else used for stashing their phones, he pulled out his cigarettes and a Bic lighter, and lit up.

"That Paco!" Elena smiled. "He can hold his breath underwater for four minutes, but all he wants to do as soon as he hits the surface, is destroy his lungs!"

"Can I tell you my swimming joke?" Napier asked.

"Long as it's not too filthy," said Elena.

"There's a swimming competition for the disabled at the local baths," Napier began. "First up there's this guy who's only got one arm. He dives in, and goes propellering round and round, and never even gets to the other end. Second up goes this guy who's got no arms and only one leg, and he tries to do the butterfly, but he doesn't even get half way before he's swallowed so much chlorine, he has to turn back. Last, there's this disembodied head that's balanced like a cannonball on the edge by the deep end. 'Would someone mind kicking me in to get me started?' It asks.

"The guy with the one good leg kicks him in, going arse over apex in the process himself. Well, this head just sinks straight to the bottom of the deep end, doing nothing. Eventually, people start getting worried it might drown, so they get a net and fish it out and put it back on the side. 'Oh fuck it!' Says the head, 'What a time to get the cramp!'"

"That joke was in execrable taste!" said Paco.

"Nap," whispered Elena, "I just hope to God Bobi didn't hear that. Bobi doesn't have any legs."

Napier Ransom didn't get into the sack with Elena Troy.

Split Focus Diopter

"What about Wally Pfister?" Noah asked.

"What about Wally Pfister?" Indigolin repeated.

"At school in Australia, boss, they taught us never to answer a question with another question."

"Well, without going into the merits of an educational system that turns out people like you, shill, I was wondering what Wally Pfister had to commend him."

"He was available," pointed out Noah.

"I understand that the reason he was available, was because he just walked out of a big budget movie, leaving his producers and cast fuming. It's bad enough having to feed the egos and indulge the temperaments of the actors without having to worry about a director who's also a *prima donna*, shill."

"Yes, boss, but he quit over a matter of artistic integrity and the producers can't sue him, because everyone knows it's like his trade mark: when Wally Pfister directs a movie, the locations are always shot in razor-sharp focus, you know, fully illuminated like a pre-Raphaelite painting. The producer and leading lady, as well as the locations manager were insisting that he shot the set in soft focus, like with half a jar of Vaseline smeared over his lens."

"How come?"

"It appears that when they were shooting on this particular, lesser known Greek island, they all fell in love with the place, and the producer, the leading lady and the location manager all invested in real estate there, and then couldn't bear the idea of the island becoming overrun with tourists who only knew of its existence because Wally Pfister insisted on shooting it in his trade mark high-definition sharp focus. They called upon him to put the movie through a filter to make everything softer, but it couldn't be done, because he's old school, and it was all shot on celluloid, not digital. But even if it could have been done, he wouldn't do it as a matter of principle."

"So he quit in an argument about focus?"

"Correct, as a consequence of which, he himself lost a great deal of money as well as the chance to enhance his reputation by directing this big budget movie."

"Seems like posturing to me, shill. What's the point in falling on his sword over a marginal sideshow that no-one except a focus-puller would have the remotest interest in. Is this Wally a bit woke, Noah?"

"I don't think it's to do with woke, boss. It's like an environmental thing with him. His written essays on the topic in academic journals. He says that directors and cameramen must pay due respect to all their surroundings, not just the actors, and that it's arrogant to shoot the stars in sharp focus and their surroundings out of focus."

"But surely, shill, you have to have one or the other. If the actor's in focus, then whatever else that's in the frame is going to be out of focus. That's how lenses work."

"I think it depends on the depth of field. He wrote a learned tome on something called the split Diopter lens. Cameramen used to use the split Diopter lens all the time, but recently it's fallen into disuse. In the hands of a good cameraman properly directed, the split Diopter enables the director to control his audience and direct them to exactly where he wants them to be. He can literally throw a spotlight on more than one subject in a frame at a time, and that way a good director can get you thinking about the relationship between the multiple subjects. He can convey more information per shot.

"It's not normal in real life to see multiple subjects in focus at different distances, so the cameraman can use the split Diopter to create unease. It's very powerful, but it's hard work setting it up, and modern directors prefer shooting a subject from multiple successive angles, rather than having multiple subjects in the same frame."

"So, it's like Wally's hobby horse?"

"Yeah, any opportunity he gets, he'll climb up on a soap box and treat you to an exegesis on focus. But to be fair to the guy, we're talking about his vocation, his art, and he has strong opinions on it. Anyhow, every cloud has a silver lining, because Wally's thing about soft focus led to him walking out of the project he was currently working on, which means that someone who was going to be tied up for the next eighteen months, happened to be available to direct our film at very short notice. Plus, and wait for this, Wally Pfister has been interviewed on more than one occasion, saying that the thing that he would most like to do in his life, is—wait for it—direct Celia Broadsword."

"Really?"

"Yes, boss. It's like a bucket list thing. You know when they do those interviews? You know when they give you the list: The Book you Wish You'd Written, the Book you Couldn't Finish, the Luminaries You'd Invite to your Fantasy Dinner Party, The Play You Walked Out Of. Well, his answer to the question, The One Thing You Want to Do Before You Die, was *Direct Celia Broadsword.*"

"How come?"

"Unfortunately, the interviewer didn't ask him that supplemental question, so we are just left with the answer he gave. But then he gave another interview, and there was a question along the lines of *The One thing You Most Regret*, and his answer was *Not having directed Celia Broadsword.* Reading between the lines, I'm not a psychiatrist, but I understand his mother died giving birth to him, so maybe he has a thing about older women, MILF's. GILF's, Oedipus complex."

"So we are in a position to make his dreams come true, and ensure he does not lead a completely unfulfilled life by virtue of not having directed Celia Broadsword?"

"Just so long as you let him do it with his backgrounds all in sharp focus, boss."

"Okay, shill. Please explore this with him. Try not to let on that we don't actually have a script to shoot. Let's salami-slice it. Get him on board with the idea of achieving his *desiderata* of working with Celia Broadsword and shooting her against a background of all the focus a man can manage. Let's hope we can get him fully on board before he asks to read the script."

To Hold Infinity in the Palm of Your Hand

From the comfortable cockpit of his Hummingbird Eurocopter, Wallace Pfister was pleased to descry his destination with considerable ease from 2,000 feet up. All the Airstreams were lined up like a wagon train in an old John Wayne movie. Despite his Ray-Bans, they were dazzling him with reflections of the Moroccan sunlight bouncing off the acres of chromium plating and satellite dishes beneath him. And there, anchored slightly apart from the others, he was pleased to see that his own wooden-sided caravan had arrived. He just hoped the piano hadn't fallen over this time.

He made a mental note to check where chrome came from when he landed. Was it some innocuous man-made adornment, or did six-year-old boys have to dig to harvest it from the dirt with no tools other than their fingernails in some toxic mine in the Democratic Republic of Congo?

Since setting out from Battersea, he'd done two refuelling stops in France, two in Spain and one in Morocco. This was the furthest he'd ever flown and he was feeling pleased with himself, albeit weary.

Performing a text book landing in about a million hectares of sand with no obstacles to avoid, had not been challenging. Because he was not a meretricious show-off, he'd put her down at what he considered to be a respectable distance, not calling too much attention to his arrival, at least four hundred yards away from the trailers, kitchens, gardens and movie paraphernalia, even though it meant that he had to carry his luggage further than necessary.

Most of his gear had been shipped out with his Woody-Wagon, but he still needed an overnighter for the stopovers in France and Spain. He cursed himself for having brought a wheelie-bag, instead of his tote bag, because the wheels didn't go round in the sand. He climbed out of the cockpit, carrying his bag in one hand and his battered copy of William Blake's poems in the other.

Despite attempting to make as low profile a landing as was possible in such a noisy means of transport, he was surprised that nobody had emerged from their trailers to greet him. He had thought that someone might show up and at least criticise him for destroying the environment, if not offer to help with his bag. He had heard that the leading man was sulking in his Airstream and the environment of lassitude and pusillanimity had infected the whole crew, dripping down from the top; he'd heard that his predecessor had gone loco, and that they didn't have a workable script. It was as if he'd landed in the aftermath of an electron bomb, where all life had been wiped out and only the tawdry trappings of civilisation remained.

He dumped his bag outside his Woody-Wagon. It was locked and he didn't know who had the keys. He held on to his book, because he didn't want it to get blown away. Despite being in the middle of the desert, unnaturally, there was a fresh breeze, as though he were at the seaside. He called to mind the words of Charles Lamb who had pronounced that the means by which you could distinguish between civilised man and a barbarian was in the way they treated books. He walked along, past Airstream after Airstream, seeing no signs of life. He came up to the kitchen garden where the cook, Aka, had fixed up some irrigation and was attempting to grow courgettes, runner beans, tomatoes and roses, and then he saw her.

He didn't know if she was the only person who'd had the good breeding to welcome the new arrival, or if she'd just stepped out for a smoke. But she was unmistakeable. She was wearing pink Capri pants and a pink shirt with the tails knotted at the bottom, showing some midriff, but not quite a navel. In her hand, she held a pink cigarette packet. She would have looked like one of those fifties pin ups: Kim Novak, Ava Gardner or Sophia Loren, if she'd been topped off with what his French friends would have called *le toque finale,* namely the adornment of a big hat. But that was no hat.

The huge silver beehive looked like she was wearing a nuclear warhead, and when she blew the smoke out, all the tiny smoke particles combined with the spray from the irrigation. Then she stubbed the cigarette, bent down to retrieve the stub and deposit it in a bin, and as she straightened herself up to her full height again, she shook her head, and all the silver hair cascaded like a waterfall. In the droplets and the dancing motes of light, she was prismatised: there was no other word for it. She was like a rainbow. Her face lit up in a big smile, seeing him.

Never in his fifty years had Walter Pfister encountered such presence. Now he fully understood how Celia Broadsword stole every scene she appeared in. There was simply nothing else in nature that compared to her.

Wally had made a few mistakes in his life, but none that he regretted. To misquote Frank Sinatra, *Mistakes, he'd made a few, but then too few to mention.*

It had been a mistake not to finish his university degree. Maybe it would prove to be a mistake to have accepted Tinctorio Indigolin's generous offer to attempt to salvage something out of this cursed film and ludicrous script. He'd not made the mistake of marrying, because his work only brought him into contact with vacuous, air-headed, pretentious, narcissistic, teenyboppers.

But there was no mistaking this apparition of Celia Broadsword in the desert beside the rose gardens and the flowers on the courgettes, her silver hair exploding, and the explosion being reflected in a million droplets from the irrigation spray. Each droplet was one perfect globe enclosing an image of Celia Broadsword turning to water. Each bead held the DNA of an entire woman. It was as though she were minting coins of herself before his very eyes.

'*Three Coins in the Fountain*,' he thought. The 1954 film from the Hollywood in Tiber period that had preceded the Spaghetti western and Hollywood in Ouarzazate periods. That was when they knew how to make proper films, he reminisced. Directed by Jean Negulesco. It had starred Clifton Webb and Dorothy McGuire.

There were visions. There were mirages. There were epiphanies. And there was Celia Broadsword.

For some reason, the words of Sir Winston Churchill came into his head, when that statesman had been asked what role he thought the Soviet Union might play in World War II, and he had said that it was a riddle wrapped in an enigma. But the words were morphed in Wally's head. He was looking at the spectacular Celia Broadsword materialising out of the irrigation mist in a parched desert, and the words that came to his mind were that he was looking at an epiphany wrapped in a mirage.

"I beg your pardon?" She said.

Then Wally realised that he must have spoken the words out loud, and was embarrassed.

When two celebrities who are household names meet up for the first time, there can be an awkward moment. Do they expend words of mere supererogation introducing themselves to one another, when they both know the other already recognises them? Or should they appear so presumptuous and conceited as to skip that step, as though they think they can take it for granted that the other already knows who he or she is? Which is the lesser of the two evils?

Wally simply looked at the vision that he had earlier termed an epiphany wrapped in a mirage and recited some words from the book he held in his hand, but he didn't need to open the book to remember them. It was as though there was a Bluetooth connection from the closed book into his head:

"*To see a World in a Grain of Sand
And a Heaven in a Wild flower…*"

Celia completed the verse:

"*Hold Infinity in the Palm of your Hand
And Eternity in an Hour.*"

"We haven't even been formally introduced," she continued, "but here we are finishing off one another's sentences—" She lit another cigarette from the pink carton. He noticed that the cigarettes she smoked were flat and unfiltered. He didn't think they even made that brand any more.

"—Just like an elderly married couple," said Wally, unwittingly completing her sentence. Then they realised what they'd done, and they both laughed. Then she looked across from Wally to the Hummingbird in the middle distance behind him, and asked:

"Wallace Pfister, are you going to sweep me off my feet?"

Another Desert

Meanwhile in Black Rock Desert, Pershing County, Nevada, USA, the Burning Man Festival was under way. At the theme camp of the New Prometheans, the presiding Ipsissimus, Larry Fairchild (or Firechild as the media often referred to him), was giving instructions to neophytes, proselytes, apostates and renegades alike. All are welcome in his tabernacle, provided they are willing to make the sacrifice.

Fairchild subscribes conspicuously to the anti-consumeristic tenets of the Burning Man. He is wiry and long-haired. He wears nothing except a pair of cotton cargo shorts. The Black Rock sand is blazing hot, but he wears no shoes and expresses no signs of discomfort as he walks up and down, ever the peripatetic philosopher. But, as if the sand isn't already hot enough for him, the time has come for him to ratchet things up to the next level.

They have all enjoyed an excellent barbecue lunch of sustainable foods, but if the so far uninitiated amongst his cult followers thought that they were going to be able pleasantly to digest their cook-out in the sun, they have another think coming. Fairchild makes them upturn the contents of the 30 Weber barbecues onto the sand, so that the white hot charcoal forms a molten track some 20 metres in length. He then has them rake the coals to keep them good and hot. He uses only the best quality Australian briquettes known as Fire Beads. They keep their heat for hours on end.

He then walks up and down alongside the diminutive Phlegethon that his followers have fashioned, and addresses both the members and the aspiring members of his cult, sitting cross-legged on the sand beneath him. He doesn't need any Power Point presentations. He is purely elemental. It's time for the after-dinner speeches. Hundreds of mobile phones are pointed at the master, recording his words and deeds.

"Plato," he begins, "and other contemporaries, such as Xenophon and Aristophanes, have told us how the Greek philosopher, Socrates, never wore shoes, and how he was able to make his body impervious to the elements, so that he wore the same light clothes in summer and the depth of winter. He was known as *the barefoot* philosopher. As am I."

"He fought for his country, as did I. Socrates was regarded as one of the wisest men who ever walked the earth—barefoot every time. He left no writing of his own setting out his philosophy. Our only records of his teachings come down to us from the notes his pupils kept. Same as us. Socrates fought in the Peloponnesian wars. He abjured all form of unnecessary adornment, as do the New Prometheans.

"At the Battle of Potidaea in particular, Socrates was observed by many other members of his army unit, marching for days on end barefoot on sheet ice and sharp rocks. Plato also tells us in his *Dialogues* how Socrates continued this custom after the war, year round, come rain or shine, always barefoot regardless of the snow or ice or rain.

"He was able to do this, because he was in control of his own body. The skin is just a sack of neural transmitters. Socrates was able to turn the transmitters on and off, so that certain sensations were not relayed to the cortex. There is no question that this happened, as we have so many independent witnesses reporting on it.

"All major religions teach us that the body is an irrelevance, a distraction, like a squealing baby, constantly calling out for attention, for feeding, for gratification, and the quest has always been for a way to transcend the demands of the body, to abstract oneself into pure ethereal being, or spirit.

"As one ascends the Echelons of Discipline in the New Prometheans, one passes through many Gates, and one sheds a little more of one's childish skin at each Gate and grows the hide of a mature being. What did Paul tell us in Corinthians? That he had put aside childish things. *When I was a child, I spoke as a child, I understood as a child, I thought as a child; but when I became a man, I put away childish things.*

"What Socrates transcended in snow and ice, the New Prometheans transcend in fire. There is no difference between the ice that burns and the fire that burns."

Fairchild raised his right fist above his head and repeated: "In fire! For in Fire we Live!"

All the others seated on the sand echoed his rallying cry: "In Fire we Live!"

"And For Fire we Live!"

"For Fire!" They repeated.

With that, barefoot, he proceeded to saunter from one end of the burning cinder track to the other. He did so at an unhurried pace, and appeared to suffer no trauma. He then turned round and repeated the demonstration in the other direction, whilst continuing his monologue:

"Those of you who wish to ascend to the level of Ipsissimus, may follow in my footsteps. But you must be utterly without fear or doubt. If you entertain the least doubt, the fire will burn you, the fire will cripple you, and you will never complete your journey to become Ipsissimi."

Designed to Fail

Agent Elena Troy called Agent Anatole Frank. He answered with the usual greeting: "Bvsh Ho!"

"Hi Anatole. How's the weather in London?"

"It's raining stair rods, Elena. How's sunny Spain?"

"It's sunny."

"What can I do for you?"

"I met a creep yesterday, and his name and face rings a bell, but I can't place him. I wondered if you could run some searches for me."

"I thought you were supposed to be doing your community service for the environment, not working."

"Well, I'm not sure it is working, Anatole. It's just the guy leaves a really nasty taste in your mouth."

"OK. What's his name?"

"Napier Ransom."

"Would he be about forty years old?"

"Yes, you know him already?"

"I very much doubt there could be two people called Napier Ransom. Don't even need to look him up. Could've been before your time, because you're younger than me. He ran what was basically a hedge fund in New Bond Street, Mayfair, but it was dressed up to look like an investment bank. Christ's sake, why can't people get it through their heads that you don't do your banking in New Bond Street! It was called Overtake Finance Limited. Point was they only lent money to ailing companies, and their product was all in their security paperwork.

"So typically there would be a company suffering some cash flow crisis, but with decent underlying assets. Overtake's interest rates were very high, but if you missed a payment, default interest rates kicked in that were simply eye-watering.

"The Court, in a case that I'm sure you will have heard of when I remind you, decided that Overtake's product was designed to fail. The judge borrowed that phrase from the language of planned obsolescence and said that Overtake was designed to fail, because once you went in through their front door, there was no way out, because to exit, you had to pay a monumental termination payment, which the borrowers never had, so Overtake then stepped in under their security documents and just helped themselves to your company, and the judge found that this was their *modus operandi* and where they actually wanted to end up.

"In other words, being a bank was simply a front for their real activities that consisted of divesting their customers of their livelihoods. Overtake took all manner of personal guarantees and debentures, but they made their real money from the iniquitous termination fees, with myriad events of default being defined as constituting a Termination Event, triggering a termination fee.

"In the good old days, such paperwork would have been chucked out by the Court as amounting to an illegal penalty clause. But all that changed in 2015 with a case known as *ParkingEye*. That case made the normal prohibition against the enforcement of penalty clauses much less clear and operators like Ransom had a field day. Anyway, in the case I'm referring you to, the Claimant couldn't get home on penalty clauses when Overtake attempted to steal his bathroom fittings company, but he did get home on unconscionable bargain with the judge giving this ruling about how it was 'designed to fail'.

"Designed to fail then became a very famous catch phrase. But what was really catchy, so that it grabbed all the headlines in the papers, was the name of the bathroom company Overtake was trying to shred. If not for the name of the company, the case would probably have gone unnoticed and Ransom would have carried on stealing people's companies."

"What was the name of the bathroom company, Anatole?"

"Shitler Toilets Limited!"

"Shitler Toilets?"

"Yes, and their strapline was '*The Lav that Dare not Speak its Name*'. After Oscar Wilde."

"Yeah, I get the allusion to Oscar Wilde. And yeah, this Napier guy is a shit of the first order. Do we know what he's doing now?"

"Well, after he lost the case, he did what every other disgraced English businessman does."

"He fucked off to Dubai?"

"Correct. He runs a specialist insurance company out of Dubai that provides cover for kidnapping and ransoms. But it's an English company, called Metcalfe Insurance Specialists. When I say he runs the company, it's actually run by his younger brother who, strangely enough, seems like a thoroughly decent guy. He does all the actual work, and Napier just put up the seed capital to get the company started. So the brother is the public face of the company, and Napier himself should be hiding his face in shame, but he's too narcissistic for that. The guy's a sociopath, for sure, and could even be a psychopath. He's all over the globe. Napier is just like a playboy.

"Travels round the world, trying to get laid. Follows established routes; you know, Thailand in November; Barbados for Christmas, Verbier in February; Japanese cherry blossom in April; the Byronic Grand Tour of the Mediterranean every summer; that takes him to September, and then the weather's okay in Dubai for the rest of the year."

"Thanks, Anatole. I didn't know all that stuff about Overtake. As you say, it may have been before I started taking an interest in these things. But I remember the *Lav that Dare not Speak its Nam*e headlines, and there must have been photos of him linked to the headline. That's what I was dredging up from my memory. And is his insurance product any better than his banking track record?"

"We don't know. Looking at their accounts, as I now am, they've never paid out. But that could be because there hasn't been a claim yet. I would say, don't touch the guy with a barge pole."

"Anatole, you don't know how appropriate that metaphor is. Thanks for your time. See you in London soon."

The Unsdorfer Twins

Posthumous Unsdorferbaum called his twin brother, Presley Unsdorferbaum. He had considered WhatsApping or Facetiming him, but as each would have been staring at the other's identical face, it seemed a pointless exercise.

"Hi, Posthumous. Long time, no hear," said Presley.

"Did you see the Ten O'clock News tonight?" He asked.

"On which channel, bro?"

"Any channel you like. It's everywhere as well as being viral on social media. The shooting of the Blue Molecule dude."

"Tinctorio Indigolin, Poss, no, I didn't catch that piece. I'm out of the country."

"No great loss to society."

"Are you referring to me, or the Blue Molecule dude?"

"The Blue Dude, Presley."

"Then it is probably not a great loss to society, Posthumous for several reasons. Probably not."

"The reason I'm calling you at this time, Presley," continued Posthumous, "is that if you had caught that piece on the news, they've just kindly given us a geo-tag for that cunt, Mortimer, our triplet. We might even be nearing the end of our quest to find the ball sack and kill him properly this time."

"How come?"

"Well, the anchor woman, Millicent Marcuson, had interviewed the Blue Dude the day before he was assassinated, and they released the interview, which was very brief, as it seems the man was in a hurry to wrap up the interview and go off and get himself shot. They padded out the time they had obviously allotted to what was supposed to be a longer interview by doing a little retrospective of all the things the Dude had been up to.

"They said that he had purchased the rights to a four-picture deal that they were shooting at the Atlas Film Studios in Ouarzazate which is apparently somewhere in the Sahara Desert, and that right now the whole cast was in mourning. Then they switched to a reporter on location at the shoot, which had come to a standstill for some reason unconnected with the assassination, and she interviewed our brother, who is the star of the film. He was cowering in the door frame of his Airstream caravan, and the interviewer asked him if he would like to say a few words about the late Tinctorio Indigolin, and you know what he said?"

"What did that cretinous cunt say?"

"He said he was too sad to step out of his caravan, so they'd have to excuse him. He said it was as if the film had a curse on it, that one thing after another kept going wrong, and now it was in the lap of the gods if the film was ever going to be made at all. He said that he didn't know if he was ever going to leave Ouarzazate, and then he added that he didn't even know if he was ever going to leave the very caravan whose doorway he was standing in. So we know exactly where he is, and he doesn't seem to have any plans to leave there any time soon."

"Well, I never," was all that Presley could say.

"And I've found us some cheap flights to Morocco," Posthumous continued. "You and I are going to Ouarzazate and teach the shit a lesson he won't forget."

"I'm afraid I'm ahead of you there, Posthumous."

"How so, Pres?"

"I'm already here and on the case, and I'm here with Tinctorio Indigolin."

"The dead dude?"

"Confirmed, but he's very much alive. We're sharing a Riyadh at La Mamounia for a couple of nights, and then we're headed out to Ouarzazate."

"But I've just seen him shot dead on the Ten O'clock News. Dead men don't get up and walk."

"Posthumous, this Blue Molecule Dude is full of surprises. Let's just hope that next time we put our brother down, he fucking stays down this time, and don't hop up again like the Blue Dude did."

"Presley, I'm on my way to help you. This is a two-handed blood-letting I wouldn't miss for all the tea in China. How could you have been so selfish as to think of painting me out of that masterpiece?"

"Posthumous, I don't give a flying fuck if you finish the matricidal ball sack or if I finish him. But, by hook or by crook, no ifs, no buts; we are going to finish off that old Fee-fi-fo-fum Unsdorferbum good and proper this time."

Agent Elena Troy's Exegesis on Immaterial Assets

"Welcome back, Elena. How was your holiday?"

"Loved every minute of it, Anatole. God, it's shit to be back!"

"While you were away, swimming, did you manage to work out how come this Blue Molecule guy pays so little tax, Elena?"

"Well, Anatole, I have a kind of skeleton, but I'm still putting skin and flesh on it. The problem, from the Revenue's perspective, is that he operates in fields that are so cutting-edge we haven't even evolved a vocabulary for discussing them properly yet, let alone a framework for taxing them."

"You mean his bitcoins?"

"That's just part of the picture, Anatole. He has tens of millions staked on CFD's, that's Contracts for Difference. As you probably know, the Revenue regards CFD's as just another form of gambling and any profits are non-taxable, because HMRC took the view that it's a mug's game, and if the mug happens to make a profit on one bet, he's going to end up making gigantic losses over the course of a financial year as he places other bets. So there was no point in making CFD's taxable in the hands of the punter, because they always end up losing whatever they started off gaining, and the Revenue yield would never justify the number of additional investigators we'd need to employ to monitor it all. They always end up losing their bets."

"Except our friend."

"Correct. He appears consistently to make profits, even though he sometimes has to do a white-knuckle ride to achieve them. He takes up positions and hangs onto them whilst everything seems to be crashing around his ankles; but, he hangs on in there, with nerves of steel, and they come bouncing back."

"How does he do it?"

"Either he's genuinely found a way to beat the system, or its illegal insider trading. But we haven't been able to prove the latter, as yet. As far as we can see, he has programmed his computers to make the bets, on the basis of what parameters, we don't yet know, so that rather militates against insider trading, because you can't have an insider that's inside a computer. He then takes all these millions of profits and he tends to invest them in NFT's.

"An NFT or Non Fungible Token is in theory, at any rate, a forgery-proof digitised asset that can take the form of entirely immaterial objects such as film rights, artwork or music. The N in NFT distinguishes them from digitalised assets that are Fungible, such as Bitcoin and Ether which are Fungible tokens, exchangeable like paper money. Cryptocurrencies and NFT's originate in blockchain technology."

"And blockchain," interjected Anatole Franck, the conversation at last entering a field to which he felt an ability to contribute, "is a rejection of all central regulatory bodies in favour of decentralisation. It's a hierarchy in which everybody has the same rights and information, so that each member of a group can see everything all the other members can, and thereby police it."

"Just like a WhatsApp group. Everyone has access to the entire blockchain and that is supposed to make it impossible to forge, because a forger would have to manipulate the hash values of a potentially infinite number of copies. That's what gives the blockchain its security."

"So he realises millions and millions of pounds of profits on CFD's and he invests it in NFT's—"

"Which he can exchange, trade, swap for something else, fungible or non-fungible, and we haven't yet evolved a basis for taxing the further millions of profits he makes on that."

"But isn't it profits of a business?"

"Not necessarily, if your business consists of swapping and exchanging. I mean, it's like bubble gum cards or football programmes. Plus, he invests millions and millions in research and development."

"Of his Blue Rif Molecule—"

"As one good example, Anatole, which is going to be tied up for years before we can get an accurate reading on it. Because all the investment is outflowing at this stage, he has no cash flow, so his income isn't income at all. He borrows his money against the security of his NFT's and blockchains. And then he invests the borrowed money in, for example, films, which may or may not get recouped.

"But he does it in packages, so that if some of the films in the package look like they're going to make money, he ensures another one bombs, and because, in order to make such films, you have to go to remote and exotic locations, and stay there for two or three years shooting the film, he has to hedge currency fluctuations by buying a huge pile of local money in the Forex market on day 1, but then he seems to stock pile it instead of using it to pay the local expenses, which is what he took it out for in the first place. Factor in the additional layer that most of this is highly non-transparent because it's occurring through networks of offshore companies, trusts and tax havens and the end result, as they say, is a riddle, wrapped in a mystery, inside an enigma on the face of a Sphinx."

"How you going to crack it?"

"I'm going in-house. Whilst I was swimming, as you put it, in Spain, I completed my successful application to be his in-house accountant for the film he's making."

"So, you're going to be, like a Trojan Horse, Elena?"

"Anatole, always better to be inside the tent pissing out than outside the tent pissing in."

"So you're going in under cover?"

"Yeah, just like Point Break."

"Good film! Wasn't Ray Winstone a hoot?"

"I was referring to the original, not the remake."

"Need me to give you a reference?"

"No thanks, most of the CV, for obvious reasons, was bogus. I mean, some of it was true, like the fact that I qualified as a chartered accountant and my hobbies include scuba diving, that I submitted a dissertation on the Works of John Donne at university, and that I do volunteering work to save the planet. But I left out anything to do with HMRC."

"You don't think HMRC are going to be saving the planet then?"

"Anatole, we can't tax our way out of Armageddon!"

"But you remember the Blue Dude made a speech about saving the planet."

"I do, but he wasn't very specific about how he was going to achieve it."

"He said it was going to be his legacy."

"The problem is, Anatole, none of us get to write our own legacies."

"So, are you going to be reporting for work at Flyover Life Sciences?"

"Sod that for a game of soldiers, Anatole! I'm off to Ouarzazate in Morocco."

"You've just come back from a month in Cadaqués. Some girls have all the luck!"

Aït Benhaddou

"You certainly know how to make a first impression, Wally!"

"Celia, I'm a film director. That's what I'm supposed to do. And remember that I cut my teeth filming advertisements. In an advertisement, you only have moments of air time, so you have to get your audience eating out of the palm of your hand in the first five seconds."

"Is that what you're trying to do with me, darling?"

Celia Broadsword was communicating with her new director, Wally Pfister, through their headsets on the French Hummingbird Eurocopter. Wally was at the controls. He was following the contours of the *Tizi n'Tichka* Pass.

"I can assure you the pleasure's all mine, Celia. It was my lucky day that the rest of the cast were sulking in their trailers when I arrived. I could fly around aimlessly in this thing until it runs out of gas, just listening to your voice over the intercom. It's the most amazing intonation I've ever heard, and coming through these headphones, it's like having a virtual reality headset into your oesophagus."

"Good grief, Walter! What a thought. How come you know how to fly one of these things?"

"Celia, I figured that if that *schmendrick*, Prince Andrew, Duke of York, could learn to fly one, it couldn't be very difficult. It's no different from flying a DJI Mavic Drone, except you sit inside this one, instead of controlling it remotely with your phone. Most of it's visual, so you don't have to be a wiz at instruments. I took a one month intensive course in the South of France, and Bob's your uncle. I think everyone should take the course. Saying you don't know how to fly a helicopter is like saying you don't know how to blow your nose!"

"The views are amazing, Wally. I didn't know a desert could be so interesting. The light is changing all the time. You sure know how to sweep a girl off her feet."

"Celia, some time when I'm not concentrating on this craft, remind me to tell you about the things you do to me, and have been doing to me from since I was old enough to know better. *Swept off your feet* doesn't even begin to describe it."

"Old enough to know better, but still young enough to enjoy it, huh, Wally? If sweeping off your feet doesn't describe it, what does?"

For maybe thirty seconds, no words passed between their headphones. Then Wally said simply: "*Beguiled*."

Celia let the word roll around in her head for a while and then asked: "Where you taking me, Iceman?"

"I'm scoping out for locations for the new script. Right now we're headed for Aït Benhaddou."

"What's that?"

"Well this is the whole point in having me direct a film, Celia. I can 100% guarantee you've seen at least five films shot there, but you wouldn't know it, because as far as I can make out, all film directors and cameramen, apart from me, like to run up gigantic bills on location, and then when they get to the location, they focus on the stars and leave the location out of focus in the background, so there was no point in going to the expense of dragging everybody out there in the first place."

"I know exactly what you mean, Wally. Like that Matera place in Italy. They shoot loads of films there, but you could never tell that's where you are."

"Yeah, they shot the opening sequence of the last Daniel Craig Bond movie there; but for all anybody saw of Matera, they might as well have been in Pinewood."

"Yes, Wally, it's just another part of our general culture of waste, like people ordering expensive food in a Los Angeles restaurant and leaving half of it untouched on their plates. So, tell me about this place."

"Aït Benhaddou? Well, as I say. You'll have seen films shot there on location, but you won't have known it because they'll be all soft-focus in the background. I mean, I get that when they shoot Sherlock Holmes films in the Inner Temple: they've got to pull the focus and spread the sawdust on the ground so you can't see the double yellow lines on the road, and all the modern street furniture; but for Christ's sake! We're in the middle of a desert.

"Nothing's changed at Aït Benhaddou in centuries. You may have seen it recently in Game of Thrones, but dozens of films have been shot there: Gladiator, The Jewel of the Nile, Time Bandits, The Last Temptation of Christ, The Sheltering Sky, Kundun, Prince of Persia. I could go on. It's what's called a *ksar*, a fortified village on the edge of the old trans-Sahara trade routes. It goes back to the Almoravid period and the 11th century. The entire place is built of mud. Any second now, it's going to hove into view."

"Wally, is there any use for the word *hove* apart from things hoving into view?"

"I'm not sure there is, Celia."

"What did you just say? I mean syntactically, darling. *It's going to hove into view*. Is that a future past participle or what?"

"Celia, if anyone had told me this morning that this afternoon I'd be flying the girl of my dreams along the Ounila Valley discussing syntax through the headsets of a 120 Colibri Eurocopter, I wouldn't have believed them. Actually, I believe it's the present tense of the verb *to hove*, meaning to come or go, with the emphasis on coming or going in a floating or soaring sort of way. I think it's pretty well been replaced by *hover*, as in hovercraft, but like I said, I'm old school."

"The hoves and the hove-nots, huh, Wally?"

"Yep, there are the hoves and the hove-nots and then there are the hovellers."

"And what is a hoveller when he's at home, Wally?"

"A hoveller is an unlicensed boatman who sails out to plunder wrecks illegally, usually off the Kentish coast."

"I like the sound of that."

"And do you know the name of his vessel?"

"I'm the weaker vessel, Wally. I wouldn't know about the hoveller's vessel."

"The boat that the hoveller hovels in is also called a hoveller."

"You mean as he hoves into view?"

"Yes, Celia, the vessel that the hoveller hovels in as he hoves into view is known as a hoveller."

"Like those parents with no imagination who give their kids the same forenames as surnames."

"You mean Greeks?"

"I can see it!" She cried. "Good heavens. It's like a giant sandcastle built out of turmeric!"

The red mud towers of the fortified village materialised like a mirage rising from the Painted Desert. "You're quite right, Wally. It's sacrilege to choose a place like this for a location and relegate it to like muzak in the background. It deserves a film in its own right."

"I figured that a star as big as you, Celia, could play alongside Aït Benhaddou without getting upstaged."

He was bringing the chopper down. He got it so close to the city walls that at one point Celia was frightened the rotors were going to blow the whole place away, like the big bad wolf and the three little piglets. After all, it was just mud and straw. He undid his harness, to helped her out of her's and disconnected her headset, opened his door and ran round to help her out of hers, showing her where to put her feet, and where not to. He took her hands in both of his as she descended from the Hummingbird, onto its landing skids with the *ksar* behind them until she was facing him, holding hands, and staring longingly into her eyes, like he was about to launch into an Argentinian Tango. For a moment, she was positive he was about to kiss her. She was old enough to be his mother. But she wouldn't have stopped him.

Blue Phantom

Albanian George had been in the H R Owen showroom in Berkeley Square to take delivery of his new Vantablacked Bentley Bentayga, when he recognised Tinctorio Indigolin from magazine covers and TV interviews. '*You could always count on H R Owen to act as a meeting place for the right sort of individuals,*' George had thought. It didn't matter that Bentley and Rolls Royce were both owned by Volkswagen, a luxury marque established by none other than Adolf Hitler. They were proper brands, and George was a brands-junkie.

George had introduced himself to Indigolin and learned that he was there to spec up his blue Rolls Royce Phantom. The salesman, Rupert, had created a profile for Indigolin and taken his order, but Indigolin would have to take his place in the queue, and wait nine months for his car. First George had tried to persuade Indigolin to buy a Cullinan instead, as that would be more like his Bentayga and therefore a more prudent choice, and without the long waiting list. Indigolin had said he didn't like the look of the Cullinan, that it was too boxy and had no elegance. Indigolin had pointed out that, if he had need of a luxury off-roader, he already had a blue Lamborghini Urus.

Next George had tried to persuade Indigolin that only a mug would wait nine months for something to be delivered. Indigolin had responded that all humankind must be mugs then.

It was at that point that George ceased to regard Indigolin as a like-minded petrolhead, and regarded him instead as a problem to be solved. George would not leave H R Owen, unless he had persuaded Indigolin to his view. Albanian George's next ploy therefore had been to attempt to persuade Indigolin to steal someone else's place in the queue: "There's a fully loaded blue one downstairs!" He exclaimed. "I just saw it with my own eyes."

"That one's been ordered by someone else, Mr George. That's what it's doing downstairs," explained the salesman, Rupert. "The buyer's been waiting nine months for it."

"Well," said George, "what's it cost to break the contract? All property is theft!"

"That particular customer is a highly litigious Mayfair property developer," explained Rupert.

"Scrote!" George exclaimed. "Just put it on my account! When he finds out that it was George Georgiou who broke his contract, no-one litigates with George Georgiou!"

"How come, sir?" Rupert enquired.

"Because George Georgiou specialises in ADR," George informed him.

"ADR?" Rupert enquired.

"Alternative Dispute Resolution," pronounced Albanian George, with the emphasis on *Alternative*. "We don't do Law Courts. Mr George takes what he likes."

And so it came to pass that Tinctorio Indigolin came to purchase the fully loaded blue Phantom in the basement on George Georgiou's account with H R Owen. George paid a quarter mil over the odds to persuade Rupert to let him jump the queue and break the developer's contract. Adding that to the purchase price of the car, Indigolin drove out of the showroom indebted to Albanian George for over three quarters of a million pounds.

Afterwards, George wondered what had come over him. It was just vanity. It wasn't as if he was even possessed of a desire to impress Indigolin. He'd just blown three quarters of a mil trying to impress the car salesman. Am I a fucking homo or what? He asked himself. *Fuck it! Am I even allowed to ask myself that anymore?*

A Teams Call

"Hi Walt. You OK?"

"You're muted, Ti."

"Sorry."

"How far did you get?"

"We're in Marrakesh. Felt I couldn't take my leave without sampling the Sunday Brunch at *La Mamounia*."

"And how was it?"

"Top shelf, Wally! Tip top! In the words of one film director to another: *Historic*. And Mamounia is set within these ochre-coloured mud walls covered in bougainvillea, and parallel to the walls they have miles of irrigation channels that they've planted up with water-lilies and flags and bulrushes and, wait for it, they're inhabited by millions of frogs. I could watch them all day long. Plus, Walt, we needed to kill some time whilst my driver drives the wheels down from London."

"He's driving your car from London?"

"Yes. France, Spain, and Algeciras: catch the African Queen to Ceuta and drive it through Morocco. Got to arrive in style, Walt! Did my Riyadh in Ouarzazate work out okay?"

"Yep, the girl booked it for you. I haven't had time to go out there and visit personally, but the agents gave me a virtual tour with an Oculus VR headset earlier, and it looks like what you asked for if you prefer not to hang out in another Airstream on location with the rest of us."

"Right now, Walt, I prefer to be behind some reasonably high walls in a house that's a fixture, as opposed to some caravan that someone could attach to a Toyota and drive off into the blue yonder."

"Even if the yonder's blue, Ti?"

"Walt, I have a penchant for blue things, but I'm not completely unquestioning. I mean to say, I wouldn't embrace anything just because it happened to be blue. Dart frogs and moor frogs are blue. I like agapanthus, bluebells, peacocks, emperor butterflies and hump headed wrasses. But the flame on a gas fire is also blue, and I wouldn't stick my head in it just because it was my favourite colour."

"It sounds as if you're in your element, Ti. And the Riyadh should be ok, because on my virtual tour of the garden I observed that it was enclosed behind nine foot high walls, and that there was a very fine, very blue jacaranda tree; and there's a reflecting pool full of bullfrogs."

"OK, Walt. True to your reputation, you grabbed my interest in the first few seconds."

"With frogs. Sorry was that a low ball?"

"Not at all. I'm listening carefully," said Indigolin. "You've been on the set for a whole day, Wally. What's the score?"

"The score is we don't have a workable script, Ti."

Changing the subject: "And have we got to the bottom of what's eating Colman Hunt?"

"Ti, the thing about Colman Hunt is that he's screwed up. He was a childhood star. They're always damaged goods. HBO made a teaser-trailer with this streaming pilot called *King Ferdinand's Book of Hours*, all about Ferdinand of Castile and Isabella of Aragon and the Unification of the Iberian Peninsula. Shot in amazing locations. Plenty of battles, on land and water. There were weddings, funerals, dismemberments. The camera was permanently panning from depucillations to decapitations, from the high seas to the Siege of Granada, but also piracy, plotting and scheming, slave-trading, sodomy, incest, inbreeding, rape, burnings, brandings, buggery, crucifixions and torture, not to mention the Spanish Inquisition, and all captured in ultra-high definition and Dolby sound.

"It was like *The Game of Thrones* years before there was any *Game of Thrones*. Ticked all the right boxes for cultural diversity, because there were plenty of parts for ethnic minorities, dwarves, sub-normals, amputees and Moors. Colman Hunt, straight out of Corona acting school in Chiswick High Road, with no qualifications to his name other than a climactic Caliban in the school play, and a flaccid Henry IV Part II at Questors, successfully auditioned for the part of the young Ferdinand, and was not so much catapulted as positively trebucheted to tinsel town."

"Right, and Isabella of Castile was played by Celia Broadsword."

"That's right, Ti."

"The chick that sounds like a deeper version of Eartha Kitt?"

"I'd say that's a fair description of her voice, but I'm not sure we'd call her a chick anymore. She's like a mature woman."

"Chicken, poultry, doesn't matter to me if she's boiling fowl, I understand she has a huge fan base."

"True, starting with me."

"And, despite all the rape, incest and sodomy in *King Ferdinand's Book of Hours*, she was one of the few cast members who managed to keep her kit on throughout three seasons, much to the disappointment of same fans."

"Correct again, Ti."

"But all that's about to change."

"As soon as the scriptwriters tell us what she's supposed to do."

"Well, we know what she's supposed to do, Walter. She's supposed to get undressed. She doesn't need a scriptwriter to tell her how to do that. The scene is totally irrelevant to anything else, so I suggest we get that scene in the can first of all, because it doesn't need to be germane to whatever ends up getting written in the script."

"That makes sense, Ti."

"The other thing we can be getting on with is the Brunswick Holt cameo with the great big hat. You know our sponsors want that, and that is also entirely self-contained, regardless of what ends up getting written in the script. Plus Holt's agent would only give us one day in Holt's busy schedule, so we have to shoot that scene next week come hell or high water anyway."

"Tell me about it, Ti! Holt's contract specifies that he's got to have a bigger Airstream than anybody else on set, as a result of which, even though he's only going to occupy forty-five seconds at the most of screen time, and can only be on set for one day, we had to hire the bloody wagon for three months, because there was no other way we could get our hands on it. Anyway, getting back to *King Ferdinand's Book of Hours,* no-one really expected the series to take off outside of Spain and Portugal, but it went viral, as they say, and, due to the way they portrayed the Moors, it even went down a bomb in the Arab world."

The thought crossed Indigolin's mind that if Albanian George had been present, a sentence like that couldn't be completed without the appendage—*are we even allowed to say that anymore?* But Indigolin kept that to himself whilst Wally Pfister rambled on.

"So, Ti, the scriptwriters had to rush another episode out and another and another, and episodes melted into series and series melted into seasons. It was the talk of the town in every territory from Berkeley Square to Beijing. They spent eight years shooting it on location, by which time Colman who was a tender eighteen when it started was now twenty-six years of age. But the public still hadn't had enough, so there had to be a second season. That took a year to write and they then started the shooting, which hit union troubles and went on for years and years. This was a prequel, so the studio had to young Colman up digitally.

"Season Two took another eight years, so with time off in between for writing and shooting and marrying his leading lady, Colman's now thirty-five years old. Then the public wanted a sequel, so the producers delivered on that, by which time Colman's hit his half century. Yes, he's fifty years of age, and barely left the set since he was eighteen. Ferdinand of Castile died at the age of fifty-one. Then, of course, Colman had to go and get a divorce from his leading lady."

"Sounds expensive."

"Actually, no, because they grew up on the same set, Ti. The cast are like his only family. So she got rich as he got rich. They both left the marriage with what they brought into it. Maybe they left it a little wiser. Not cutting edge, but no sharp edges either. And no children. I'd say he's worth north of US $100m."

"Do we think the marriage was consummated?"

"God knows. What you've got to understand about these theatrical types, Ti, is that getting spliced is just the acquisition of another accessory for them, like buying a Spanish Water Dog, or a Cockapoo or a pangolin, or going down to Starbucks to buy a cup of coffee. It's just a commodity. *King Ferdinand's Book of Hours* was his life. He doesn't even know anything else. Colman's now a worldwide superstar, but basically he's been institutionalised for nearly half a century and when he came out, he didn't know if his arse was drilled or bored. He speaks fluent Castilian Spanish, as a result of spending so many years on location in Southern Spain, but he can't remember any of his lines anymore. He's a mumbling moron.

"His agent gets him some cameos in crap soaps, but no-one can look at him without seeing King Ferdinand, until you, Mr Molecule, decided to cast him as the lead in this tax loss film of yours, where all he has to do is sit in his Airstream while his body double gets thrown out of a few windows."

"We'll see what the new scriptwriter has to say about that, Wally."

Indigolin noted from the top of his screen that the conference had gone on for thirty minutes now, and felt it was time to wrap it up. He raised his hand to wave goodbye by way of sign-off on the remote call. Wally noticed his handsome wristwatch.

"Snap!" Wallace Pfister said, tapping his own wrist and holding up his blue-faced Breitling Super Chronomat in front of the camera. "Why did you chose Breitling?"

Indigolin looked down at his own blue-faced Breitling Super Ocean Heritage chronometer. "Because only gangsters wear Hublots," was his answer.

"Seriously?" Wally said.

"You go first," replied Indigolin.

"Once I'd learned to fly," began Wally, "I figured I needed a pilot's wristwatch, you know, like John Travolta. Then when people ask me about my Breitling, I would get the chance to explain that I bought it, because it's elegant enough to be worn off duty, but sturdy enough to wear in the cockpit. That way you can discreetly let slip that you happen to be a pilot without, you know, having to take the chopper everywhere and land it on people's front lawns."

"And has anyone ever asked you about your Breitling?"

"To tell you the truth, until this conversation that we're having right now, no."

"And, may I remind you, Mr Pfister, that the only reason why we are having this conversation right now is, not because I asked you about your Breitling, but because you asked me about mine."

"*Touché*!"

"But surely the Breitling association with aircraft is only for fixed wing aircraft? I mean, the bezel's got a slide rule and means of calculating longitude and latitude and all manner of nonsense you can't possibly need in a helicopter."

"Oh God, now you're going technical on me, Ti! Your turn"

"Oh, I'm on now, am I? OK. The reasons to own a Breitling Super Ocean Heritage chronometer are three," began Indigolin. "Firstly, it's blue and blue is my colour. Secondly, I am a very keen member of the sub-aquatic community, and it's certified down to a depth of two hundred metres. Thirdly, it's the most ecologically friendly and environmental watch that money can buy. They're the only luxury watch manufacturer that offers a digital passport based on blockchain technology."

"I didn't realise you were such an environmentalist, Ti."

"We have to pay regards to our planet and the legacy we leave to our children. Whether it's beneath the sea, or above the skies, it's all part of the same planet, and it's our job to look after it. We're not owners. We're just leaseholders, custodians for the next generation. As they say, *There is no Planet B*."

Wally Pfister found himself a bit tongue-tied. Indigolin was a self-publicist of the first order. He'd even monetised his own murder. But maybe Wally had been looking at him through the wrong spectacles all this time. Where Wally had seen a man obsessed with blockchain and NFT's, he'd assumed this was because he was a faddist with more money than taste. But after listening to Indigolin's little sermon on chronometers, a speech that, as Indigolin had pointed out, Indigolin had not attempted to initiate himself and which Wally had tastelessly attempted to draw him into, it occurred to him that he was precisely the opposite of a faddist with more money than taste.

Tinctorio Indigolin was a man deeply concerned with preserving the environment and the planet, and that is why he chose to possess the things that he did possess in formats that didn't threaten it, such as NFT's and blockchain. Wally was going to have to reassess Indigolin.

The Tao of Ying and Yang

By day, Wally sported his Breitling. At night time, Wally removed it and loaded the chronometer onto its Wolf Watch Winder, replacing it with an Apple Watch, because the big chronometer was too heavy and uncomfortable at night, and he could read the time in the dark better with the Apple.

Wally's exercise watch woke him up with some gentle haptics to his wrist at 07.00, as he had set it to ensure he caught sunrise in the desert. This morning, as every morning, he would do his Tao exercises. He had made his schedule known generally, so that if anybody else wanted to turn up and join in, they would be welcome.

But if they preferred not to, that would also be fine. He was experienced in leading others through his routine. If no-one else turned up, he would do his Tao on his own. Bare-chested and bare-footed, the sand not having yet been warmed by the sun, wearing only his exercise pants, with his mat rolled up under his arm, he marched out into the desert.

He was pleasantly surprised to observe a small number of the crew, including Patrick Oculus, Elena Troy, Edgar Ash, Noah, Mohammed and others falling in behind him. There was no sign of Celia. He didn't know if this was because she liked to lie in, or if she preferred not to do her exercises in a group. He wasn't surprised to be joined by the likes of Oculus or Ash, because they would give any fad a whirl for five minutes, if only so that they would be able to denounce it authoritatively afterwards when rubbishing it to third parties, but he didn't think they'd have any staying power. He had no expectation to see them back again tomorrow. He noted that Elena and Noah, who were effectively management, rather than crew, had come along, which he regarded as inclusive and promising. Elena certainly looked pretty trim.

He found a level space, and, facing the distant Atlas Mountains over which the sun was just beginning to appear, changing the colour of the desert from ash grey to what Celia had called turmeric, he led the group in his usual routine.

He initiated some warm-ups to start with, explaining what he was doing as he went along: Foot and Ankle Flexing to prime the major meridians from hips to head; Abdominal Rubs, to smooth the night's weight from the colon; deep abdominal breathing to exorcise the nocturnal zombie; followed by Abdominal Lifts, the Cobra, the Plough, the Pylon, Double Team Back Bends, Dip Splits, the Pendulum and Shoulder Rolls.

Then he announced that he was going to wind it down with some deep breathing exercises: *Chee:* compression breaths interspersed with Deep Bellow; Alternate Nostril Exercises, the breathing known as Grand Celestial Tour, and finally Great Tai-Chi Circle Breaths.

Wrapping up, he said he hoped everyone felt a little bit better for that and ready to start the day. The sun was now warming their faces. If truth be told, they were indeed all feeling pretty good, and pleased with themselves. They were indeed ready to start the day, but the day wasn't ready for them, because there was no script to shoot.

Wally announced that he'd be doing a short evening set in the same place at seven pm if anyone cared to join him, and that if anybody wanted to do any Inner Gate Points, Valley of Harmony Points or Meridians, he was always happy to provide one-on-one guidance throughout the day.

He then rolled up his mat and marched back to his Woodie-Wagon for a shower.

"What did you make of that?" Edgar Ash asked Oculus.

"I'd say we could be headed for a war of the cults, Eddie. He's going to give us New Prometheans a run for our money."

"How do you think you're going to get the upper hand?"

"Ask him to do his exercises in the middle of the day when the sand's burning hot!" Paddy joked. "And what did you make of it all, Eddie?"

"What do I make of it? If the director's going to be doing this every morning and evening, and, what did he call them? Impromptu Gate Meridians and Harmony Points to order, how are we ever going to get this fucking film shot?"

The following morning, when Wally arrived, there were at least fifty people waiting for his class to start, including, he was delighted to see, none other than Celia Broadsword in a pink leotard. She looked fabulous. There wasn't an inch of slack on her.

"OK," he said, once he had spread his mat out on the sand to the right of Celia Broadsword, "Everyone pair up with the person on your left who will be your partner. We'll warm up with a Tao exercise we call Pushing Mountains. This feels clunky first time, but by the end of the week, you will feel the energy channels stretching from your shoulders to the tips of your fingers, and no-one who does this every day has ever been known to suffer a heart attack. We start out in what we call the Horse Stance, and now reach out to your partner."

Once again, he was holding hands with Celia Broadsword, and once again, despite thirty years of Dip Splits, Pylons and Forward Bends having endowed him with the legs of a Roman centurion, he felt himself going weak at the knees. Their fingers touched just like Michelangelo's God Creating Adam on the roof of the Sistine Chapel, at the very moment the sun crept over the Atlas. He felt warmed by her. He felt they were two beings of infinite promise frescoed in the sand.

The thought crossed his mind: *this is what it must feel like to hold Infinity in the palm of your hand.*

A Tour of Atlas Corporation Studios, Ouarzazate

Wally was enjoying the sensation of being a passenger with someone else doing the driving for a change, even if the experience only lasted twenty minutes. He was also highly impressed with Celia's ability to handle the 4WD across sand dunes and desert. A lot of women, he figured, could drive a Range Rover up and down the Kings Road, but they weren't in Chelsea. They were in the middle of a desert. There was no tarmac, only sand, sand and more sand. Before setting off, Celia had checked they had off-road tyres, let the right amount of air out of those tyres and was now mashing all the off-road gears and cresting sand dunes like a Dubai drayman.

Celia had made films at the Atlas Corporation Studios in Ouarzazate before, but Wally hadn't, so she had offered to give him a guided tour. While driving expertly, she explained that Ouarzazate was the world's largest film studios until Ramoji Film City in Hyderabad, India came on line in 2006. As they approached their destination, it was clear that the line between the studio and the Sahara Desert was a blurred one.

Monolithic decaying sets and properties from sets littered the wasteland like Ozymandias' feet.

"The thing is," she explained to him, "they don't seem to dismantle anything. Because land prices are so miniscule in the Sahara Desert, the studio can make more money by leaving all the junk out there as a tourist attraction. It's like the Forbidden Palace, Aswan and Tibet had all been hurled into one giant landfill together with half of the Old Testament and a large stable of flame-red Ferraris."

And she was absolutely correct. There were red Ferraris parked in the Valley of the Kings. But the Ferraris, like everything else there, were fake.

"It's like a Bible made of Styrofoam!" He exclaimed.

Parking up, they walked through the main gates between two gigantic statues of the Egyptian god, Anubis. Two diminutive doormen standing in the shadow of the monolithic gatekeepers, were dressed as medieval knights in chain mail.

They recognised her and said, "Greetings, Miss Broadsword!" as they opened the gates for the couple.

"In between filming," she explained, "you can buy tickets and go on a guided tour. It's a major tourist attraction. But as we've booked the studio out for our film, there's no tourists allowed in at the moment, because everything about our film is top secret and has to be kept under wraps."

"Little do they know that it's a top secret to the cast and director as well, and we have no flipping idea what we're doing here ourselves! Anyway, the bottom line is that I can give you a private tour, Wally. Welcome to the Hollywood of Morocco."

They proceeded through a polystyrene Bethlehem, past some Islamic funerary architecture, into a courtyard ringing with the sound of clashing steel where gladiators were practising a swordfight, down the Suez Canal, through Abu Simbel, across a Necropolis, past the Sacred Barque of Amun floating on the Sacred Lake of Luxor beside the seventh and eighth Pylons of Karnak. All along the way anachronisms were scattered across the landscape: burnt-out aeroplane fuselages in Golgotha, a wrecked McLaren Softail embedded in the side of the Siq in the Nabatean City of Petra.

The artificial Badlands were not uninhabited: they were teeming like an anthill with stuntmen and women, carpenters, extras, riders, going about their daily business, so that at one waypoint you could think you had stumbled into the Senate House in Ancient Rome, where the assassination of Julius Caesar was underway; at another, expert horsemen were galloping through narrow canyons, not simply riding on horseback, but riding underneath the horses, sideways, backwards, and revolving around their steeds like Cossacks. Then, at the end of the Canyon, there was a gigantic Statue of Liberty. And then, after that, they were on another planet in a distant galaxy far, far away.

"As you walk through the studios," she explained, "it's as though you're walking through both time and space, different countries in different ages, progressing through places that never existed as well as history that happened. It's a very weird sensation."

"You're telling me," he exclaimed. "It's quite disorientating, isn't it?"

"It is disorientating, Wally. It doesn't hold true of the older generation, but they say that the younger generation of Berber tribesmen, who live in the desert here, that is to say, the generation that gleans its history and current affairs from films, phones and the Internet, no longer understands the difference between historical fact and fantasy."

"That is quite a worry."

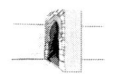

"And it could also be an artistic opportunity, Wally. As you can see," Celia continued, "enormous sets have been built to represent biblical Jerusalem or the Egypt of the Pharaohs, but the owners just leave the sets intact so that they can rent them out again to smaller productions that can make their own films within the same sets financed by the bigger budget productions. It's quite egalitarian, really."

"It would be a good idea if we actually had a script, Celia!" He winced.

They had ducked out of the intense sunlight of a medieval marketplace and into some narrow tunnel held up by pillars covered in hieroglyphics where one stuntman dressed as an Almoravid knight lit a firebrand from a burning brazier and set fire to the other stuntman who then proceeded to hurtle from pillar to pillar aflame and in apparent agony before rolling around in the sand and finally extinguishing himself.

"Arsonist?" Wally asked.

"New Promethean!" Celia replied.

Celia smiled; but this time, Wally didn't get her joke.

They emerged from the smoke-filled tunnel, and suddenly there they were, in the Courtyard of the Twelve Marble Lions in Boabdil's Alhambra.

"This set brings back so many happy memories, Wally!" She said.

Ring Tones

Tinctorio Indigolin, Presley Unsdorfer and Noah were enjoying a bottle of Moroccan *Domaine de la Zouina Volubilia Gris* accompanied by some garlic and rosemary flatbreads with olives and Za'atar humus, around the decorative, reflective bassin in the Riyadh inside the gardens of La Mamounia. Dinner would be brought in by room service shortly, and Indigolin was savouring the first croakings of the frogs on the reflecting bassin.

Indigolin was seriously beginning to wonder if something was wrong with him, because everybody else he came into contact with, including these two jokers, Noah and Presley, spent all their time trying to outstare the screens on their phones. It would be hard to imagine a more tranquil, paradisiacal setting than this microcosm Garden of Eden that he was sharing with his two insensitive travelling comrades. The temperature was balmy, with no humidity. The very air was perfumed with spices and night-scented stocks. The frogs were singing to him. But the only thing his hobnobbers wanted to do was peer into their phones.

"Do you think I should change my ring tone?" Presley asked.

"To what?" Noah queried.

"So it croaks like these frogs," said Presley, wondering to himself how long it would be before he got to croak his twin brother, Mortimer.

"Why do you want your phone to pretend it's a frog, shill?" Indigolin asked.

"Don't know," muttered Presley.

"Frogs deserve our respect," Pronounced Indigolin. As none of the company seemed competent to develop that strand of conversation, Indigolin developed it for them himself. "You remember the Chernobyl disaster?"

"Sure," said Noah, "the nuclear power plant in Ukraine."

"It suffered a catastrophic accident in April 1986 when the core melted down. Twenty years later the uranium levels were still off the chart and Geiger counters were sent spinning. Obviously all the humans who used to live in the vicinity abandoned the area, but the wildlife didn't have the requisite knowledge to make such lifestyle choices, so they stayed put. What is interesting is that the Chernobyl green frog population had turned into black frogs within ten years."

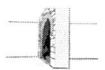

"Sounds like one of those Roald Dahl stories," joked Presley. "Green frogs that turn black!"

"They turned black as part of their necessary evolution," explained Indigolin. "The black pigment is better able to repel radiation and it enabled them to survive. Exactly the same phenomenon was observed following the Fukushima disaster in Japan in 2011. Within ten years, the green frogs had all turned black."

"So it's just like black skin pigmentation or dark clothes are better able to protect humans from solar radiation," offered Noah.

"Yes, Noah. The principle's the same, but the reason it is of interest to me is because it shows that frogs were able to make evolutionary changes that would normally take millions of years, within a decade. A frog's skin is water-permeable, absorbent. We can use frogs as a litmus strip. In a degraded environment, a frog will begin to darken in appearance."

"Like a reverse Michael Jackson effect?" Presley offered.

"If that metaphor helps you better to understand the phenomenon, Presley, yes."

"Your driver's just rung in, boss," said Noah.

"How far down's he got?" Indigolin asked.

"He said he's just passed Casablanca."

"Casablanca! Doesn't it just evoke amazing memories? Fancy creating a film as good as that! I'm going to get all the cast to watch that film. Is there somewhere we can set up a big screen, Noah?"

"Sure, we're in the middle of a desert, boss. Nil humidity. And nil frogs, I'm afraid! We can just put up a big white sheet between two palm trees and project the film one night. The audience, consisting of the members of the cast, can sprawl out on steamers under the stars and listen to the soundtrack on Bluetooth headsets. It's the sort of project our cook, Aka, loves doing. I'll have a word with her."

"Casablanca under the stars, with a glass of *Volubilia Gris* in our hands!" Indigolin added. "I'm up for that! Help build some *esprit de corps*."

"Respectfully, good idea!" Presley put in. "Sounds like some *esprit de corps* is just what's needed with my bastard of a brother refusing to come out of his trailer."

"Moderate your language, Presley. I'm afraid you won't have a trailer. You'll be hanging out with me in my Riyadh, as I've got to smuggle you on and off set, so that you and your brother are never both in the same place at the same time.

We'll get you one of those Djellaba things with a big hood, so we can spirit you around and just remove the Djellaba and the hood as necessary."

"Get me a big red hood, Mr Indigolin, like the dwarf in *Don't Look Now*!"

"Or the big bad wolf in Red Riding Hood," added Noah.

"Does the wolf have a red hood?" Indigolin queried.

"I thought he did in the Disney cartoon, boss, but now you mention it, I'm not so sure. I wouldn't bet the ranch on it."

"What do you want me to do first, Mr Indigolin?" Presley asked.

"We're going straight into the nude scene with Celia Broadsword. Get that over and done with before anyone comes up with some reason for not doing it. She does a dance of the seven veils in a tent; you kiss her breasts, and whatever else happens after that is left to the audience's imagination. Think you can manage that?"

"All day long. What else?"

"Next up," explained Noah, "is the Brunswick Holt cameo, but that's just Celia, Brunswick Holt and a messenger who delivers a letter."

"When do I get to meet my brother, Noah?"

"Never, we hope," said Indigolin. "The idea is to keep the two of you separate."

"Boss," said Noah, looking at his Google Maps, "if your driver's passed Casablanca, it's going to take him about eight hours to get to Ouarzazate."

"What! In my 200 mph off-roader?"

"Boss, the speed limits in Morocco are 60 kilometres per hour in built up areas, 100 kilometres per hour on the expressways and 120 kilometres per hour on the AutoRoutes. But there aren't any AutoRoutes or expressways, so the speed limit's effectively 60 kilometres per hour everywhere, but even if it was more, the state of the roads is so shit you'd be struggling to go much faster than that anyway."

"Hell!" Indigolin said.

"So, if the only thing keeping us here is waiting for your car to arrive, we could cut out of here in about four hours' time and then it's a four-hour drive from here to Ouarzazate, so you and your driver will be arriving there about the same time."

"Well, he's got to come via Marrakesh anyway, right, because there's only one road, the A3?"

"Looking at Google Maps, I'd say you're right, boss."

"Well, Noah, can you arrange to deposit the hire car at the front desk, and have my driver meet us here, and we'll all go down in the Urus together. Then we can dump young Unsdorfer here off at the Riyadh, and you and I can get things organised on set."

"Yep, the Riyadh's only a ten minute drive from the set."

"This is going to be the highest mileage Lamborghini that ever came out the factory doors at Sant Agata Bolognese!" Indigolin remarked. "We should have entered it for the Dakar Rally whilst we're about it!"

"Emilia Romagna!" Presley cried by way of a toast, and they clinked their glasses just as room service rang the bell.

A Jineta Sword

Celia Broadsword's arms were raised behind her head as she removed the ornamental Jineta sword from her beehive and her hair spilled down like a silver cataract across her shoulders and breasts. She laid the bauble in the silver jewellery tray on the dressing table inside her modest Airstream. She smiled at the memory of Wally's uncommercial attempts to haggle with the Berber metalworker in the Aït Benhaddou souk.

She had dragged him into the souk, because she said she wanted him to help her choose seven different coloured semi-pellucid scarves for her dance of the seven veils. Wally found the suggestion inexplicably sexy, knowing what role those scarves were going to play. It was as though she had asked him to accompany her to La Perla to help her try on lingerie.

"Isn't the material wonderful, Wally!" She cried. "I'm going to choose the seven different colours of the rainbow for my dance. I've never seen fabric like this outside of Fortuny's. Do you think it's real or counterfeit, like that guy selling the ersatz Louis Vuitton bags over there? Do you know Fortuny, Wally?"

"No, Celia."

"He's the Spanish designer that did all his best work in Venice. He was born in Granada, so I started taking an interest in him when I was shooting the Ferdinand and Isabella series there. Fortuny used to dress stage sets for Wagner. I mean in person: him to Wagner; but then he decided he wanted to dress beautiful ladies instead. Fortuny was born in Granada, but he set up a factory in the Giudecca Island in Venice's archipelago when the Giudecca was still a ghetto.

"He started manufacturing these totally amazing garments out of clingy, crinkled crepe, all sinuous and erotic. You know, to this day, no-one has ever set foot inside that factory to find out how he does it, except his family and his employees. We're taking seven different colour ways, Wally. Which one would you like to come off last?"

"I think the yellow one, Celia. It's practically transparent anyway."

"Yellow means you're coming back."

"Yes, like tying a yellow ribbon round the old oak tree in the American lyric."

"When you see this come off, you'll be coming back for more, Wally. I promise you!"

"Celia, I've never had a hard-on doing the shopping before!"

"Honey, just think of me as your Personal Shopper, a Very Personal Shopper! You can have Tina Turner as your Private Dancer and I'll be your Personal Shopper."

After she had bartered for seven diaphanous scarves in different colours, Wally had decided that he wanted to go into the adjoining booth to haggle for a pair of slippers, the same kind that Edgar Ash padded around in. Having bought the babouches for the asking price (which seemed gravely to disappoint the slipper salesman), they drifted into the next hole in the wall, which was a metalworker's shop. There, the salesman had pressed this Jineta sword upon him. Of course it wasn't a real Jineta sword, but the blue Berber man had insisted it was.

Come to think of it, most likely the salesman wasn't a real Berber or really blue at all. He'd probably lacquered himself with Druid wizard's woad touch-up paint.

Anyway, the shopkeeper had been adamant that Wally was holding in his hands nothing less than a genuine Nasrid weapon in miniature. He had sung the praises of the double-edged blade with the blood gutter displaying the two four-pointed stars that identified it as a Nasrid dynasty weapon from the 15th century, for sure, the engravings consisting of mixed metals: lead, copper and silver, which, he had informed Wally was achieved by a technique known as *niello*, that no-one had used since the15th century, so it must be genuine.

They'd marvelled at the spherical pommel and hollow quillon, and when Celia had asked what she was supposed to do with it, the salesman had checked with Wally if it was okay to approach *Madam* as he insisted on calling her. Wally had said it was okay, whilst making a mental note to keep him on a pretty short leash, and the guy had gone round the back of her and inserted the little dagger into her hairdo, pinning the whole silver confection in place. Viewed from behind, it looked like a candy floss on a stick.

The shopkeeper had clapped his hands and declared in French: "*Le toque finale!*"

Wally had told her she looked more fabulous than ever. The shopkeeper agreed. The Jineta had been removed from her hairdo and reverentially handed back to the shopkeeper. Wally had requested Celia to withdraw from the metalworker's shop, no bigger than a doorway in the wall, whilst he discussed the price with the vendor.

Before condescending to name the price, the vendor decided to add value to the item by explaining that it was a perfectly scaled-down reproduction of Sultan Boabdil's own dagger, the original of which is to be found in the museum in Toledo. The vendor assured him that he had spent many days and nights working on it, forgetting that moments earlier he had assured them it was a genuine relic dating from the 15th century.

The salesman asked if it was a gift. When Wally explained it was indeed a gift for the woman waiting outside the doorway, the shopkeeper insisted it was a wedding gift. Despite his efforts to dissuade him from this premonition, the best he and Wally would agree to settle on was that it was an engagement gift. Having given him this information in the belief that the shopkeeper was going to gift-wrap the little dagger, the shopkeeper did not gift-wrap the dagger after all. He put it in a black bin liner and handed it over to Wally unceremoniously.

Wally pressed him for a price. The man said it was his wedding gift to the couple. He wouldn't hear of accepting money. Wally regretted having been so indiscreet and pressed the man to name his price. This was met by vigorous shaking of the head. The vendor would not hear of it. Resigned, embarrassed, Wally turned to walk out of the shop, whereupon the man called him back, haranguing him, gesticulating and screaming that Wally was attempting to steal from him, that he was in the process of making off with the fruits of this poor man's labour. The shopkeeper threatened to call the police if he left without paying.

The upshot was that Wally had paid the Blue Man the asking price, but in dollars, not dirhams. When the metalworker had said one hundred, Wally assumed he meant dollars, whereas the Blue Man meant dirhams, so Wally had both failed miserably to carry out a meaningful haggle, and had then grossly inflated the price by virtue of misunderstanding the mysteries of currency exchange. But Celia loved the gift, and he had walked his fiancée out of the souk, proud to have her on one arm, clutching the black bin bag in his free hand. They had concluded that the bauble must have magical properties, because no other vendor in the souk hassled them as they exited its labyrinthine alleyways, heading back to the copter. They decided it was talismanic like Dr Strange's amulet.

Film people paid each other extravagant compliments so freely that the currency was wholly debased, but when Wally had told her she looked even more fabulous than ever, it didn't sound like an exaggeration. This guy meant it. She had told him how the day had been unplanned, unexpected and unsurpassed, and he had told her in that case it was a very good job that she had a souvenir so that she could remember it every time she let her hair down.

She threw herself back on the bed and was asleep in forty seconds. Her dreams were inhabited by blue men armed with daggers.

The Agency Accountant

"Noah, did you know that you're losing a fortune on Forex?" Elena Troy peered into her PC, frowned at the figures, and shook her head.

Noah, Presley, Indigolin and Indigolin's driver had arrived at the producer's rented Riyadh mid-afternoon. Indigolin had chosen his quarters and Presley's room, introduced himself to his staff and then taken a tour of the kitchen, after which he declared himself not satisfied with the culinary arrangements, and told the chef to throw out all the meat. He had then taken himself food shopping in the Urus. Although he had intended to drive out to location that evening, he had changed his plans in light of the need to go to the supermarket, and announced that he'd join Noah on set in the morning.

Presley had retired to his suite, not least because he was under strict instructions from Indigolin to keep a low profile. That left Noah and Elena Troy staring at the spreadsheet on Elena's computer.

"We're shooting three films back-to-back here in Ouarzazate, Elena. Most of the stuff we pay for in dollars or euros, but a lot of it's local, so as we figured we're going to be here paying out the potatoes for at least two years before we see any returns, rather than fuss with volatile exchange-rate fluctuations, Mr Indigolin decided to buy up two years' worth of dirhams at a fixed rate on day one, and he calls them off when he needs them."

"Yes, Noah, but he bought them at the height of the market and they've been going down ever since, and he seems to be warehousing them, not paying them out. Look at this. His production company's getting sued by loads of outfits that haven't been paid."

"Well, I'm sure he's hedged them off against something or other somewhere further down the line, miss. You know he has all these blockchain positions?"

"And he also has a lot of exposure on Contracts for Differences. Are you telling me that, as a fact, he has hedged everything, or just making an intelligent guess?"

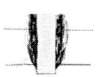

"Ms Troy, none of us gets to see the whole picture. We're like a bunch of guys working on the Ford production line. Every one of us is labouring on a different panel or component. No-one gets to see the assembled whole, the finished article, except Mr Indigolin."

"What if there is no finished article? Suppose it's all some gigantic work-in-progress?" "How am I supposed to audit this when there's no audit trail to follow?"

"It's a Delaware company. Doesn't need auditing. With all due respect, Elena, I don't know why the agency sent us an FCA like yourself. I mean, you're over-qualified. All we needed was a book-keeper. Someone else will allocate the stuff later on."

She raised her eyebrow. "Are you serious?" She asked him. "You've got Aka Akinyola as your cook and you call me over-qualified."

"I can see where you're coming from, but Aka is kind of vocational. You're different. You're a professional."

"Noah, I read English Lit at Cambridge, and did my Tripos dissertation on John Donne, so, unless I wanted to teach, I had to get myself a proper qualification after."

"If you'd already made up your mind that you didn't want to teach, why read English Lit at Cambridge in the first place, Elena?"

"Noah, I wouldn't have missed it for the world. They were the three best years of my life. Living inside all that amazing architecture, as if I was a Tudor princess; being punted down the Backs by a handsome hunk; tea at Rupert Brooke's Grantchester Tea Rooms; breakfast at Fitzbillie's the bakers, and reading all those brilliant books. It just makes me appreciate everything else in life so much better. It's as if I didn't have the vocabulary to understand the world I inhabit until I'd done that. Doors of perception, you know?"

"Well, I believe a number of Tudor princesses had their heads chopped off. The Australian curriculum is very similar to the UK curriculum, and, of course, we speak the same language. So with Australian qualifications, the recruitment door is open to you, not only in Australia, Canada and New Zealand—(what we used to call the Commonwealth Countries)—plus, of course, UK."

"So, what did you read in Oz?"

"I flunked out. I did three years surfing and shagging; sounds similar but less subtle to what you described doing in a punt down the Backs."

"So, no Doors of Perception for you."

"No, Elena. In Australia, it's all shithouse doors!"

"Yes, one thing all the Aussie's I've known shared in common is they weren't noted for their subtlety. I mean, the Yanks gave us Shock and Awe, the Spaniards gave us *L'Age d'Or*, and the Aussies gave us Shithouse Door."

"Talking shit house doors with you is a real education and an eye-opener, Elena!"

"But, with no qualifications, how did you end up as Tinctorio Indigolin's right hand man?"

"Two reasons. Firstly, there's one thing that everyone can read, no matter what language they speak, and that's a balance sheet; secondly, Mr Indigolin is actually very interested in surfing."

"The Blue Dude surfs?"

"Well, I don't actually know if he personally surfs or not; but he's hooked up on anything marine. You know, most billionaires when they buy a megayacht, they commission Sunseeker to build them a bespoke gin palace with a boot on the back that opens up to reveal all the boys toys: Kawasaki jet skis, e Foil Electric Surf Boards, inflatable slides and climbing frames, banana boats…"

"So what's Indigolin got in his boot?"

"First of all, his boat is like scientific, you know, not ostentatious. But to answer your question, he's got a Triton submarine in the boot."

"Wow! They're made by Aston Martin, aren't they?"

"Yeah. With a top speed of five knots, it might not sound much like an Aston Martin, but the interior's all carbon fibre and hand-stitched leather."

"After that informative exegesis about shit house doors, getting back to work, Noah: can you help me on these printing costs?"

"What printing costs are those Elena?"

"Here!" She pointed with her cursor. "Printing costs."

"What about them, Elena?"

"What about them, Noah? They're larger than the gross national product of some countries. Who the hell has printing costs in hundreds of millions of dollars? What exactly is it he's printing?"

"Bitcoins?"

"According to my limited understanding of the subject, you mine bitcoins. You don't print them out. That's the whole point. The printing costs I'm looking at here are all done in the offshore company called Deep Blue Rif. Does that name mean anything to you?"

"No, Elena. I'm only on the films side."
"So you can't actually help me on the printing costs?"
"There's only one thing I can assure you about the printing costs, Elena."
"What's that?"
"He ain't printing out money!"

Bvsh Ho

Agent Anatole Franck saw Agent Elena Troy's credentials flash up from his contacts list as his phone rang out. He accepted her call.

"Bvsh Ho." He said. "How can I help you?"

"Ah, London calling, eh?"

"You're ringing me, Elena. How's the weather in Maroc?"

"Too hot in the day and too cold at night. How's the weather at Bvsh Ho?"

Elena heard a palpable pause at the other end of the line, which meant that Anatole was vaping. He wasn't supposed to vape at Bvsh Ho, but then again, he wasn't supposed to be there at all.

Bush House in the Aldwych was completed in 1925, the work of a wealthy American industrialist. At that time, it was the most expensive building in the world. The south-west wing of Bush House is now occupied by the most senior enforcement officers in Her Majesty's Revenue & Customs. They weren't supposed to still be there. The accommodation was far too expensive. It was hard to justify blowing all that rent for civil servants who could discharge their duties just as efficiently from a lower overhead environment such as Slough or even Dundee, and preferred working from home in any case. HMRC was supposed to have completed its exit from Bush House and relocation in 2020, and as far as the outside world, and indeed, most of the other officers in HMRC were concerned, that had happened.

In fact, the most senior officers had never left at all. HMRC were running two sets of books to conceal their presence, and the astronomical rent was being paid by confiscated POCA receipts that never touched the sides as they went down. Those mandarins that remained in Bush House regarded themselves as the successors to the British Secret Service.

After all, MI6 had blown its cover years ago, and the public had witnessed the spectacle of its highly visible headquarters on Vauxhall Bridge being blown to pieces in every Bond film for the last 10 years. They'd been blown up by Blofeld; they'd been blown up by SMERSH; they'd been blown up by SPECTRE. By contrast, the HMRC special agents in Bush House remained completely undercover and unaccountable, concealing their identity by doing precisely all the things they busted anybody else for doing.

The name of the building was engraved onto the neo-classical entablature across its tall Roman columns, as was the fashion at the time, in Roman letters. After all, if you're going to have Roman columns holding up your edifice, you might as well throw in the Roman alphabet as well. So the inscription on the entablature said BVSH HOUSE.

In order to make their communications with one another as incomprehensible and coded as possible, should anyone chance to intercept them, all the agents referred to their secret headquarters as 'Bvsh Ho', as though they were paid up members of some black underworld drugging and pimping fraternity. They pronounced *Bvsh* as *Bvush*, because otherwise it would be unpronounceable; and they pronounced *Ho*, not like *Westward Ho!* But like a rapper would refer to his whore. *Bvush Hor*.

"Pissing down with rain, as usual, Agent Troy," replied Franck.

"What flavour are you vaping this morning?" She asked him.

"Harissa rose with cumin, apple and cinnamon," he informed her. "Have you solved the riddle of the sands yet?" He enquired.

"I'm exploring the theory that Indigolin could be laundering money."

"Whose money?"

"Well, whose indeed, Anatole?"

"90% of money is laundered within families."

"And the other 10% in nail bars and car washes, I know. I've binge-watched *Breaking Bad* and *Ozark*!"

"It's usually dynastic. The simplest way to launder money is to put the proceeds in your wife's name, then your children's, and so on."

"Indigolin doesn't have a wife or any children. It's not your classic kind of film scheme, Anatole. I mean, it's definitely a scam, but I haven't been able to figure out how he pulls it off yet, or who the victims are."

"Might be happening right under your nose, Elena, like the story about the labourer on the building site who leaves every evening pushing a wheelbarrow with a tarp concealing its contents. The boss sees this going on for six nights and on the seventh night he confronts the guy. He pulls back the tarp, but there's nothing underneath it. "Ok," the boss says, "amnesty. I know you're stealing from me, but I can't figure out what you're stealing." The labourer replies: "Wheelbarrows."

"Very funny, Anatole. Look, this is a kind of long firm fraud. I mean, look at that blue liquid of his, the molecule that passes through flesh and bone. What's he call it?"

"Rif."

"Reef?"

"No, Rif. He's taken in hundreds of millions in investment, but it's a private company, so none of the legislation applicable to prospectuses is engaged. He says it's patented, but he hasn't published a patent, because he says he wants to keep the formula secret. Can you even have such a thing as a patent that isn't public?"

"Because its application is as a delivery mechanism for pharmaceuticals, it's wrapped up in a licensing and testing regime which is going to take years and years before he has to show his hand, if you'll excuse the pun. Same thing with the films; he could've just shot one, but he decided to shoot three more back-to-back, so it's a two to three year project and then they've got to be released and distributed. So it's maybe a five year cycle before we can tell if any of them are recouped."

"So he's got a molecule that's highly cash-positive, because he's already taken in millions before it's been launched versus a highly negative cash flow on his other projects."

"Correct. When I was speaking with Noah Nguyen, his bag carrier, earlier, I said it was all like a work-in-progress, and I think I may have hit the nail on the head. You know the story of Odysseus' wife, Penelope? How she kept all the suitors waiting until she'd finished her tapestry, and every night she'd unpick it and then start weaving it again in the morning? Well, in Ouarzazate, every night before they retire to their beds, the scriptwriters tear up everything they've written, and they start again from scratch with a new script the next day."

"What you mean to say is that Indigolin makes his money for as long as he can keep all those plates spinning, and then he has to find an exit before they all come crashing down?"

"Exactly, Anatole, and until that point when everything comes crashing down, we may not get a chance to hammer him."

"Because he won't have done anything wrong? That thing with the molecule has to be a scam. It's impossible on every level. I've spoken to the best chemists, to medics. It just can't happen."

"Unless it's a miracle. Suppose, just suppose Jesus was amongst us today performing miracles. Turning the water into wine; healing the paralysed at

Bethesda; feeding the 5,000; making the blind man see; walking on water; curing the royal official's son at Capernaum. What's the other one?"

"How about the resurrection, Elena? Are you referring to the fact that the guy was shot dead at point blank range, all recorded on social media, and is now walking around in our midst?"

"Right. They've not found the murder weapon, the perp or the victim, but twenty million people have downloaded his execution."

"And his shares went through the roof."

"Yep, until they got suspended. Anatole, what if Jesus wasn't doing these things for enlightenment or devotional reasons."

"You mean, like he was doing it to attract investment?"

"Interesting theory, Anatole, but isn't the idea of Jesus of Nazareth as Influencer just a tad heretical? Right now Mr Indigolin and his pal, Noah, seem to be spending a lot of time staring at their devices and scratching their heads like they can't understand where all their money's gone. Cash flow seems to be a real problem for them this week. Any ideas what's going down?"

"Yes," said Anatole, removing his big glasses so he could see more clearly, and wiping them on his necktie. He'd been staring at his screen for so long, his eyes were killing him. He'd sprayed dry eye drops into his itching peepers, but the only result had been that his eyelashes had operated as paint brushes, spreading the greasy scum all over the insides of his spectacles, so he couldn't see through the lenses properly. "I think I can help you there."

Elena Troy heard a baritone huff of air punctuate her partner's sentence.

"Anatole, are you cleaning your specs on your tie again?"

"How can you tell?"

"I heard you huffing on the lenses, Anatole."

"You certainly know me, Elena. But turning to the subject of your enquiry, you know how Indigolin has this acquisitive streak. Can't restrain himself from buying up everything in sight, right?"

"Yes, he's quite old fashioned like that. I mean, the days when punters could be persuaded to go to one place for all their needs, whether its groceries, professional services or whatever, I thought they passed in the seventies."

"Not with our friend, Tinctorio Indigolin. Elena, are you ready for this?"

"Take me there, Anatole."

"It appears that the chump went out and acquired his own NOMAD."

"Indigolin Industries PLC bought its own NOMAD? I don't believe it!"

"So now his shares are higher than they've ever been, but they're suspended, and he can't do anything with them. He can't do any deals until he gets it all sorted out."

"Sounds like a nice PI claim. Who are his lawyers?"

"That's the thing, El. Ti's quite loyal, so even though the requirements of his business had completely outgrown the guy's abilities, for his corporate work, Ti still instructed someone he'd known from school by the name of Barnaby Challenger."

"There's a name to conjure with!" Elena remarked. "He must have been destined to argue."

"Come lockdown," continued Anatole, "this Challenger starts working from home doing his Zoom calls against a fake background of law books and spurious framed diplomas. Then he got arrested, charged, tried and found guilty of—wait for it—money laundering offences, and he was sentenced to four years in Ford Open Prison. It turns out that he never informed his clients or his regulator that he was doing shovel, so to all intents and purposes, he just carried on working from home in Ford against the same fake background. He conducted hearings and trials remotely when he was actually serving out his sentence in the penitentiary. He carried on sending out chunky invoices every month from clink.

"The net result is that Challenger was extremely negligent over this NOMAD advice, and has cost Ti a fortune, but Challenger's professional indemnity insurance isn't responsive to it, because, for one, you can't insure yourself against your own fraudulent acts, and, for two, because he couldn't benefit from solicitors' professional indemnity insurance because he'd been struck off the Roll, so he wasn't a solicitor any more. So Mr Indigolin has a theoretical legal claim against his old school mate who is at Her Majesty's Pleasure in the Hampshire slammer, and who has now had his stay there extended because he got another nine months for impersonating a solicitor, which is a criminal offence under the Solicitors Act 1974."

"But, surely, despite his other faults, he is a solicitor?"

"Nope. The definition of a solicitor in the Solicitors Act is that he has to be on the Roll."

"So, if he's struck off the Roll—"

"He ceases to be a solicitor. If he'd called himself something generic, such as a lawyer, he would've been okay; but he called himself a solicitor. Now Indigolin needs another solicitor to dig him out of the shithole that Mr Challenger pushed him into when he went and acquired his own NOMAD."

"So he's really shot himself in the foot this time!"

"Wow! His foot at the very least! A self-harmer with high esteem! That's one for the books!"

"Everything about this guy is one for the books!"

"Yep, someday someone should write a book about him."

RPG-7

That Wallace Fegan should make a life for himself in films was destined from the manner of his conception. His Catholic mother, Kelly Fegan, had been raped by a high-ranking Provo in the IRA during the early eighties. He had shoved an RPG-7 into her mouth whilst he violated her below.

His lieutenant, who had been filming the action on his 35mm camera, swapped places, whilst the Provo took his turn at the camera. Years later, someone had digitised the sequence. By some route, it had ended up on the Internet, and this was Wallace's only memory of his mother, who had died giving birth to her rapist's child. Someone (he assumed one of the rapists), after Wally had achieved fame, had emailed him a link captioned simply *I thought you might like to meet your mother. Signed Your Father.* The faces of her violators still haunted him. He could not get them out of his head.

A North London Jewish philanthropist family known as Pfister had adopted Wallace Fegan at the orphanage. Wally had studied photography at technical college and began his career filming and directing Guinness advertisements to much critical approval. A string of big budget blockbusters had followed all meeting with considerable critical acclaim and respectable box office takes.

No-one was as surprised and delighted as Wallace was when an ambassador from Tinctorio Indigolin approached him and invited him to take the helm in substitution for the outgoing director who had finally despaired of trying to make sense of the final quarter of his 4-picture-deal. He was surprised as the talk was that Indigolin was not a man who was interested in making a decent film with a decent director.

He was delighted because he had lusted with undivided and unfulfilled passion after Celia Broadsword since she first donned the Portuguese crown as Queen Isabella of Castile in *King Ferdinand's Book of Hours*. Wally used to have posters of her up on his bedroom wall as a teenager. Now he was destined to direct her. In the nude.

His only regret was that his birth mother was not alive to witness his success.

HMRC Rewrite European History

The first anyone knew of Tinctorio Indigolin's arrival on set was when he appeared at dawn for Wally Pfister's Tao session in the desert. He was standing on his blue legume mat next to Elena Troy and both of them were already in the abdominal breathing position known as Plucking Stars.

"Ti," exclaimed Wally, "this is an honour! And I see Elena has already started showing you the ropes."

"Oh, I didn't have to show him any ropes," answered Elena Troy.

"I am particularly interested in deep breathing exercises," explained Indigolin. "I like free diving. I can hold my breath in very cold water for five minutes. I would like to be able to hold it for ten. Do you think that's possible?"

"It depends on whether you still want to be alive when they fish you out!" answered Wally.

"When Harry Houdini did his escape from under the frozen Detroit River," Elena pointed out, "he had to hold his breath underwater for eight minutes. If he could do that in freezing conditions, I don't see why ten minutes in tepid water shouldn't be possible."

"Why did he have to hold his breath underwater for eight minutes, Elena?" Wally asked.

"For the stunt, he was manacled and chained, and then they sawed a round hole in the ice on the frozen river, just big enough for him to slip through. Then they chucked him through the hole. Under the ice, with a bit of wriggling, it didn't take him long to get out of his chains and manacles, but then he realised that with all that wriggling and taking into account the strong current of the river, he'd managed to stray a long way from his only point of exit, which was the circular hole they'd cut in the ice.

"The sole way out was the way he'd come in, but he was unable to find his way back to the hole. It was a toss-up whether he was going to perish from hypothermia or drowning. It took him eight minutes to locate the hole, fighting his way back against the current."

"Wow!" Wally said.

"Maybe that was part of the routine and supposed to happen," observed Indigolin.

"Oh!" Wally cried. "One showman judging another!"

"More Shaman than showman!" Pat Oculus said, a New Promethean Shaman himself.

"All I'm saying," explained Indigolin, "is that there's always a thin layer of air that's trapped between the top of the water and the bottom of the ice. He could have been breathing that all the time and not holding his breath at all."

"Oh, ye of little faith!" Elena pronounced, closing the topic.

After the Tao exercises, Indigolin asked for Ti and Wally to meet him and Noah Nguyen over working breakfast to discuss the future of their project. As they walked towards Aka's Umbrella Bar, Elena said, "I didn't know you were interested in diving, Mr Indigolin. It seems we share an interest."

"I know, Ms Troy," he replied. "I read your CV. I can assure you we share more than one interest."

They ate Beghrir semolina pancakes with local honey, a breakfast that had been personally specified to Aka Akinyola, the chef, by Wally Pfister who had devised breakfast, lunch and dinner menus for those who wanted to consider a Tao dietary regime in conjunction with the rest of Wally's programme. Wally advised that the honey would ensure that no-one would suffer from hay fever so long as they consumed the local honey from Aka's hives.

Exactly why anyone would suffer from hay fever in the middle of a desert was uncertain; but the pancakes with honey certainly tasted good. Having consumed the breakfast, they were free to pick at fruit and drink their coffee, but no milk or sugar was allowed.

They were each staring at the same spreadsheet, but each of them was looking at it on his or her own tablet. This exercise had to be carried out outdoors at breakfast, because once the sun rose higher in the sky, no-one would be able to read due to the reflections on their screens. Elena Troy went first:

"Anyone looking at these figures would think you're *trying* to lose money."

"Ms Troy," explained the director, Wally Pfister, "nothing could be farther from my intentions. The trouble is, I've got a leading man who won't come out of his trailer. Even these wonderful Beghrir pancakes don't tempt him out!"

"I'll tell you how to get him out," volunteered Troy.

"Don't tell me," said Pfister, "set fire to his Airstream?"

"Go on," said Indigolin. He was sat next to Elena with his tablet on a brass-cornered campaign table. He was paying half attention to the discussions, but she noticed he was also giving a lot of thought to whatever was on his screen. He kept a 2 TB DataTraveler USB stick in the jacket pocket of his blue legume whatsit, and she'd already noticed that he never seemed to use the tablet's internal storage, but kept his information on external drives.

She couldn't tell if this was for ease of access so he could move seamlessly from one device to another, or because whatever he had on the USB stick was too sensitive to store on the PC. She could see from looking over his shoulder that he was reviewing something very complicated and that it was an exceedingly large file, but there was just too much of it for her to begin to figure out what the hell it was. She wondered how she could get her hands on the USB stick, and whether or not it was encrypted.

When Indigolin's mouse hadn't moved for a few seconds, the wallpaper on his screen turned on. She recognised the wallpaper as an underwater photograph of the sinkhole known as The Great Blue Hole in the centre of the Lighthouse Reef in Belize. She had dived many of the world's most famous dives, but she hadn't had the opportunity or resources to explore the reefs of the Lighthouse Atoll yet.

She hadn't dived those cenotes or the other cenotes awaiting her in the Yucatan Peninsula; but she was confident it was just a matter of time before she did. She had assumed Indigolin had downloaded somebody else's image, or maybe it was one of those screensavers that Microsoft thrust upon you, whether you wanted them or not. But then she remembered his remark about the two of them sharing an interest in diving, and how he had just confessed that he wanted to learn how to hold his breath for ten minutes.

The thought crossed her mind that he could have taken the photograph himself. After all, everything in the photograph was blue. From what she understood, he would have had to dive to a depth of more than 100 metres to get the shot that was on his computer. Could he have held his breath that long?

Agent Troy smoothed down her skirt and began: "Stop wasting your time trying to shoot a Scandi Noir in the Sahara, and get your scriptwriters working on a sequel to *King Ferdinand's Book of Hours*. Hunt won't be able to resist donning Foxy Ferdinand's crown once again, but if he shows any signs of resistance, tell him you're casting his stunt double, Paddy Oculus, in his place. No-one can tell them apart and you can DeepFake him anyway. That should do the trick."

Wally Pfister was shaking his head: "That won't work. Ferdinand was dead by the age of fifty."

"Wally," said Indigolin, "historical accuracy never troubled the streamers before. You could do it like The Man in the High Tower."

"That was the series written on the premise the Nazis won the war," reflected Pfister.

"Yes, it raked in a lot of money," explained Troy. "Just get your scriptwriters to rewrite history on the premise that the Moors never got expelled from Spain."

"What I like about the way she constructs her sentences," observed Wally Pfister, "is the little preposition *Just* that she kicks them off with. So the scriptwriters *just* rewrite all of European history on the premise the Moors never got expelled from Spain!"

"I think she may have something," Indigolin said to Pfister. "Instead of Catholicism, Spain is Islamic. Intriguing idea. Also enables me to find a use for all the unemployed Arabs we seem to be surrounded by."

"And spend some of your dirhams you bought at the top of the market," added Elena Troy.

"We'll need some historical perspective on this if we're going to rewrite history," observed Pfister, researching details on his laptop. Seems like there's an academic expert at Cambridge University known as Elizabeth Drayson, wrote, *"The Moor's Last Stand: the life of Boabdil, Muslim King of Granada."*

"Let's put her on the books as our Advisor on Historical Accuracy," announced Tinctorio. "Muhammed."

"Yes, boss," said one of the lads to whom Indigolin had just generically referred as unemployed Arabs.

"Get Ms Drayson's contact details and see if we can fix up a Zoom conference with her."

"Yes, boss."

"Elena's idea makes quite a lot of sense actually," announced Pfister still staring into his device, "Because the Moors originated right here."

"What, in your tablet?" Indigolin queried.

"No, geographically, almost where we're sitting right now." explained Elena. "They were nomadic Berbers from the ancient Roman province of Mauretania, which was situated precisely here." She pointed at his feet. "Mauretania equals Moors, get it? Mooretania. But apparently the term Moor got bastardised to denote anyone with dark skin; you know, Blackamoor, Othello, the Moor of Venice. The Moors ruled Southern Spain for eight centuries until they got chucked out by *los Reyes*."

"*Los who?*" Indigolin asked.

"*Los Reyes*. The Christian monarchs, Ferdinand and Isabella," explained Troy. "The King and Queen we've been talking about for the last fifteen minutes."

The stars of our *Book of Hours*. But under Moorish rule, Spain had flourished culturally and economically. They had cobbled roads, irrigation, medicine, street lighting, at a time when the rest of Europe was ridden with disease and pestilence. London had highways of ordure, and the sewage solution consisted of tossing the contents of your pot out the window. The Moors had proper underground sewers and hot and cold running water. They were brilliant architects, outstanding astronomers and mathematicians. They enacted codes of laws that continue to shape European society to this day. The Moors got stuff done."

"That's really fascinating, Elena," said Indigolin. "I mean, I knew about 1492 and Columbus sailing the ocean blue, but in the west we've been educated to look upon the Unification of the Iberian Peninsula from the Catholic perspective, as a good thing."

"It was a bad thing, Mr Indigolin. What you mustn't do is look at fifteenth and sixteenth century history through the lens of where the Muslims ended up in the twentieth century, with jihadists, fundamentalists, mad Ayatollahs and decent women getting stoned to death for not wearing their hijabs straight enough. In the fifteenth century, there were Muslim female surgeons operating from within the Alhambra. The Muslims were the Enlightenment. Once the Catholics took over, medicine went into decline, building and sanitation fell over the cliff, and the Catholics were the first extremists, not the Muslims."

"Of course!" Indigolin cried. "The Inquisition!"

"Precisely, from the Inquisition down to the Spanish Civil War. Centuries of using religion as a means of oppression and control, and, of course, if you're going to do that, you've got to keep science under the jackboot of Catholicism in order to keep the people as ignorant as possible."

"So we're going to give our viewers a peek into a what-if world, where the Moors never got thrown out of Europe in 1492, right Elena? Can your scriptwriters work with that, Wally?" Indigolin asked.

"Ti, it's a great idea, but we don't have the rights to do another *Ferdinand's Book of Hours*."

"Rights don't come into the picture, Wally," explained Troy. "No-one has any rights over history; but anyway, we're rewriting history, and certainly no-one has any proprietary rights in that."

"So, Wally, for the second time," asked Indigolin, "can your scriptwriters work with that?"

"With some historical guidance from an academic, such as Ms Drayson, I believe so, Ti."

"And we're going to make a big part for Ferdinand to tempt Colman Hunt out of his caravan," Indigolin continued. "How do you see Ferdinand ending up under Moorish rule, Wally?"

"Quite honestly? With his head on a pole, but that's not going to get Hunt out of his caravan, is it?"

"Correct," said Indigolin.

"Ok, let's say they keep Ferdinand on as a puppet king." Suggested Elena.

"Don't think Colman will like the epithet 'puppet'," Wally pointed out.

"Alright, we'll call him a client king, like the Romans had," corrected Elena. "Client as a euphemism for Puppet."

"So, the way you sell this to Colman Hunt," began Indigolin, just thinking out loud, "I mean, apart from him being the star and all, is that this is a part for a proper, mature thespian. He's going to have to do some acting for a change. You know, Ferdinand's going to wrestle with his conscience.

"Does he prolong his life by renouncing Christianity only to get cast out of heaven when he dies, or does he have his head chopped off now and get welcomed into the afterlife prematurely? Is it better to be untimely decapitated and get to see Holy Jesus straight off, or to convert to Islam, keep your head and your title, but never be united with your God on Judgment Day?"

"But Judgment Day," pointed out Wally, "is when every part of your dead being has to reassemble itself."

"Yes," said Elena. "John Donne wrote about it in his poem, The Relic. Donne ties a bracelet of his lover's hair round his wrist, so that, at Judgment Day, he can be assured of being reunited with her, because she'll have to seek him out to find that missing part of herself when their bodies are reassembled."

"And eventually," developed Pfister, "the message that we get across in this screenplay is that all religions are one, and there's only one God, whether you call him Allah or Yahweh. It's an all-inclusive thing, so we can play it all round the world, like Guy Ritchie's *Aladdin*."

"Good thinking, Wally" said Ti. "Multicultural, all-inclusive. That's what the investors like to hear. Lots of parts for Arab actors."

"And Moors."

"And what do you think this infidel client king does in our story?"

"He could invade Italy and France."

"Yes, all Europe worshipping Mohammed!" Indigolin exclaimed. "No Doge's Palace in Venice. Slap-up Great Mosque in St Mark's Square instead! But they can keep the Triumphal Quadriga, the Four Bronze Horses on St Mark's Cathedral, because they were plundered from Constantinople in the first place.

Only Great Britain keeps its nerve and holds back the rip-tide of infidel invaders. Clutching our stolen Elgin marbles close to our chests, we drive the Moors back into the English Channel!"

"Don't you think that's a little jingoistic, Mr Indigolin?" Elena asked.

"By Jingo, I do!" Indigolin cried.

"Jingo Unchained," pronounced Wally.

"You know, Elena," Indigolin began. "Noah mentioned to me that he thought you were over-qualified for the job you're doing."

"It has its perks," she replied.

"You mean, if you like sand?" Indigolin pressed.

"Wall-to-wall sunshine, Hollywood royalty, yummy pancakes."

"But seriously, Elena; it's not just the fact that you're a chartered accountant when we only needed a book-keeper. You seem versed in John Donne, Harry Houdini, European history. You're a real—what's the feminine version of an *uomo universale?*"

"Mr Indigolin, I suffer from imposter syndrome. I suppose I've come quite a long way in my life, but, you know, I'm always looking over my shoulder. I just never believe it's for real. I'm always worried that someone is going to call me out."

"Elena," he confided. "I too suffer from imposter syndrome. But that is because I am an imposter! I really don't deserve any of the blessings that life has bestowed on me. When I was on my way up the greasy pole, I always had that knotted feeling in my gut that I was being silently judged by those around me, and sooner or later, someone was going to put me down.

"And, if truth be told, they did put me down for a great many things, but, strangely enough, not for not being what I wasn't, which was the one thing I was frightened of. Whilst I was still a teenager, I believed that the only way out of imposter syndrome is that you have to transcend it. You have to put yourself in an unassailable position, so that you are the boss; you are the guy calling the shots. I had to get to a place where I didn't have to look up to anyone else. But you know what?"

"What?"

"It just made it worse, because the higher up you climb, the further you have to fall; the more ignominious your eventual calamity will be when it happens."

"As the immortal Bob Dylan said," put in Elena, "you have to serve somebody. It may be the Devil; it may be the Lord, but you're gonna have to serve somebody."

"Which was the finer poet, Elena?" Indigolin asked, "Donne or Dylan?"

"Seriously," she said, "I'm really going to have to think about that one."

Mohammed bustled in, dragging a big monitor through the sand attached to an electrical source via an extension cable. "Boss, we got Elizabeth Drayson on Zoom."

"Ms Drayson!" Indigolin boomed. "Welcome to the team."

"You're muted, Mr Indigolin."

"Ms Drayson, welcome to the team. Can you hear me now?"

"How can I help you, Mr Indigolin?"

"This Ferdinand and Isabella. They have any kids?"

"Oh yes, you may even have heard of one of them: Catherine of Aragon."

"As in Henry VIII?" He said, incredulous.

"Yes."

"Small world, huh? This is taking shape, eh Wally?"

"What was the name of the Moorish king that got expelled from Granada, Ms Drayson?"

"Boabdil el Chico, known as Mohammed XI."

"Family?" Ti asked.

Drayson continued: "Very powerful mother, Aisha Al-Hurra, usually known under her Spanish name as Aixa. You must have come across what she is supposed to have said to Boabdil after he got expelled from the city of Granada, the city that he used to call his Paradise. He looked back at its ramparts and burst into tears for its loss. His mother admonished him, saying *Now cry like a girl for what you failed to defend like a man*."

"Wow! Strong female part!" Wally pronounced.

"Boabdil's wife was called Morayma," Drayson resumed. "The last Sultana of Granada, legendary beauty and intelligence, but relied on astrologers too much. Children: Yusuf and Ahmed. Yusuf died at the age of five; very sad, but Ahmed survived. Before his kidnapping, Ahmed had lived his whole life in Spain. He didn't know a word of Arabic, but spoke high Castellano Spanish. I believe there may be people claiming to be descendants of Boabdil alive to this day."

"Let's say," mused Pfister, "this Ahmed marries Catherine of Aragon."

"What?" exclaimed Drayson, clearly horrified by this aberration.

"It's taking shape," said Indigolin. "Ms Drayson, any other famous names present in 1492, when the Moors got chucked out of Granada?"

"Oh yes indeed. Christopher Columbus was present when Boabdil surrendered by kissing the hand of Queen Isabella."

"But of course!" Pfister squealed. "As in *1492, when Columbus sailed the ocean blue!*"

"Christopher Bloody Columbus!" Indigolin clapped his hands in delight. "And blue, blue, blue oceans! Wally, we've got everything. Get your bards to put something down on paper and we'll push the first scene under Hunt's door. He's going to come running out of that Airstream like it *was* on fire!"

"And one final thought for you whilst your legal department is getting my consultancy contract drafted," added Ms Drayson. "You could say that all the world's current problems between Islam and the west can be traced back to that one day in January 1492 when the Catholic monarchs expelled the Moors from Spain."

Wally looked to Indigolin. Indigolin looked to Elena. Their eyes were glazing over at the significance of what they had just learned.

The Relic

When the two of them were alone, Tinctorio Indigolin asked Elena Troy:

"Elena, could you take me through that John Donne poem that you mentioned? I rather liked the sound of it."

"The Relic?" She said. "Of course. Let me recite it, and then I can explain it:

When my grave is broke up again
Some second guest to entertain
(For graves have learned that woman-head,
To be more than one abed),
And he that digs it spies
A bracelet of bright hair about the bone,
Will he not let us alone,
And think that there a loving couple lies
Who thought that this device might be some way
To make their souls at that last, busy day,
Meet at this grave, and make a little stay?

"That's the first stanza," she said.

"You just did that from memory," he commented, impressed.

"Of course, Mr Indigolin. I don't have my books with me."

"You're going to have to explain it," he confessed. "I can follow Shakespeare, but this is like another language to me. I recognise all the individual words, but—"

"Ok. As I said earlier, at a time when the east had proper sewers and plumbing, the west was still emptying its excrement onto the public highway. Unsurprisingly, they suffered from periodic plagues and early mortality. As a result the burial grounds and plague pits were overflowing, and the practise of digging up graves and rendering their present occupants homeless in order to make room for new incumbents became prevalent. It was like fly-tipping cadavers.

"So this is where his poem begins, with someone digging up the poet's grave to stuff another body in, at which point they see that he has this bracelet of bright hair (that is to say, blonde hair), wrapped round what is now his wrist bone. So Donne has set this poem at a time in the future when the poet is already decomposing in his grave, at which point there is an attempt to exhume him."

"And this is a love poem! Good grief!"

"We know that the bone in question would be his wrist, because in a much earlier poem, *The Funeral*, we learn how Donne wrapped the hair round his ulna at his own funeral in preparation for Resurrection or Judgment Day, as we were just calling it. He's channelling an earlier poem."

"Jesus, Elena! All that was contained in twelve words!"

"Yes, Mr Indigolin. Then he makes a little throwaway joke about girls pretending to be virgins when they're not, with a play-on-words between woman-head and maidenhead. In those times, if a girl wasn't a virgin when she came to be married, she wouldn't marry well, so they all had to pretend to be virgins, and he's saying that some women have lost their maidenheads on more than one occasion.

"Then, it's really as I explained earlier: the gravedigger that he is contemplating at this future time when he gets disinterred, sees what would be a customary love-token, a lock of his lover's hair, tied round Donne's wrist; but our imaginary gravedigger here in fact is a very imaginative and percipient gravedigger, because he concludes that he is looking at a smart device whereby Donne and his lover can exploit the mystery of the Resurrection.

"Because at the Resurrection, every atom of everybody has to come together and be reassembled. So the two of them are going to have to be reunited after death, because his lover is going to have to hunt him down to find and claim that missing lock of her hair."

"So the last busy day is the Resurrection?"

"Yes, it would be a very busy day indeed if everyone is racing around trying to find every atom of themselves, wouldn't it?"

"Elena, I'm just fascinated how he turns death and disinterment into the metaphors of a love story; at how he approaches his subject on the premise that he, the author, is already dead, but has written this back story before dying, so to speak."

"And he actually did that very thing, Mr Indigolin. These Songs and Sonnets were written when he was younger. But in later life, he was Dean of St Pauls' Cathedral, from whose pulpit he delivered his own funeral speech, wrapped in a winding cloth."

"Heavens! It's like three dimensional chess! I'd like to aim for something like that in this film we're attempting to write, you know. I appreciate that we've got this nude scene embedded into its fabric, and this product endorsement for a big hat; but it should be perfectly possible to do all that and still have the audience leave the cinema lost in thought."

"Mr Indigolin, you are a very demanding employer! I don't think anyone apart from Donne has ever taken the lineaments of the charnel house and used them to weave love stories."

"Well, that is precisely what we are going to do, Ms Troy."

"You want to do the other verses now, or leave them for another time, Mr Indigolin?"

"I think I'd like to digest what I've learned today before my next lesson, thank you, Elena. Let's make this a daily thing. Can we set aside twenty minutes each day? One poem, one verse, whatever?"

"I can, Mr Indigolin, but do you have the time?"

"Emphatically, Elena!"

He made to go, but then he turned round and recited the verse, word perfect, back to her. She was left wondering whether he had a photographic memory, or whether he had in fact known the poem before. After all, hadn't he just admitted to her that he was an imposter.

But so had she. And she was.

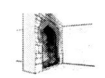

Frogs

"Boss," said Noah. "I've been watching a podcast of that Millicent Marcuson woman doing an interview with you."

"Yeah, Noah, and how was I?"

"Was it true, all that stuff you were saying about frogs?"

"Being the essential component of the first battery, that's Top Shelf, Noah. Tip top!"

"No, I meant about the porosity of their skins and them being like barometers."

"Nature's a funny thing, Noah. I mean why have a reptile like a frog whose skin isn't even waterproof? You know the only thing in the natural world that's more illogical than a frog?"

"No, boss."

"An anchovy. You ever done any cooking with anchovies?"

"No boss."

"Well I have."

"I heard you were a *cordon bleu* cook, boss."

"Yes. It was blue, so I had to go for it. We use anchovies in sauces, such as *putanesca*, that's Italian for 'prostitute's sauce'. I also use them with rosemary, instead of salt, in roast lamb, and in *broccoli conchiglie*, which is a River Café recipe. Peter Langan's speciality at Langan's Brasserie in the sixties (apart from getting blind drunk and throwing up on his paying customers) was spinach soufflé with anchovy sauce. The point about an anchovy is that when you cook with it, it dissolves. What bloody use is a fish that dissolves? We're right up there in chocolate teapot territory, shill!"

"You know quite a lot about cooking, boss. I heard the first thing you did when you arrived at the Riyadh was throw all the food out."

"Correct, Noah. With the right ingredients, you can do anything. You know, I was in Beijing at the time the autocratic government bulldozed the Hutong districts."

"Hutong?"

"They were like slums where the poor people lived. China was just beginning to make its mark on the world stage, and they didn't want overseas visitors seeing their ghettos. So they demolished them and made millions of people homeless overnight. But the people who lived in those shanty towns, loved them. They had few basic amenities, but they were part of a community."

"So where is this going, boss?"

"What I'm saying, Noah, is that tyrants and autocrats, despots and pariah states, they come and go, but their cuisine goes on forever."

"I see how you've brought it back to your subject, boss."

"And that is why the Russian State is irredeemable. It has an autocratic government, but cannot be saved by its food. Unless you call eating foetus harvested from sturgeons washed down with potato vodka, fine dining. It has nothing to offer."

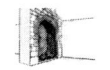

Baby Grand

"I figured this one had to be yours, Wally."

He removed the bins from his head that had prevented him from hearing her gentle knock, and turned to face her.

"How come?"

"Well, maybe because I'm probably the only person on set old enough to remember what a 1940 Pontiac Torpedo Woodie-Wagon looked like."

"I remember, but that's because my dad drove one. I mean who the hell first came up with the idea of adding wooden panelling to a station wagon, so as to make it look like a mock-Tudor house? What'll they think of next? Stone-cladding an Airstream?"

"That could make it a tad heavy for towing around, Wally. I think the idea was that people were supposed to use it for driving into the Great Unknown, smoking Marlboro cigarettes like cowboys and having an Iron John weekend at one with nature. Okay if I smoke in here, Wally?"

He dug out an ashtray and passed it to her.

She paced up and down inside his caravan, taking all the details in. "Walter Pfister," she said, "this is like an English gentleman's club in here."

"How many English gentlemen's clubs you been in, Celia?"

"You've even got a darts board on the wall. Mind if I have a go?"

"Be my guest."

Holding his gaze with hers, she lifted her hands behind her head and extracted the Nasrid dagger hair fastener that he'd bought her in the souk.

"You've seen *180,* darling?"

"I've seen all of your films, Celia."

She crossed the wagon with her back to its door that was opposite the dart board. She tossed the Jineta effortlessly into the bull's eye.

"Up until now," said Wally, "I had assumed that someone else threw those darts for you in *180.*"

"Nope, Wally, I throw my own darts with my own hands. I play my own piano, and Colman Hunt walked through the fire himself in *Ordeal by Fire*."

"I thought that making my Airstream homely and oak-panelled would be a good joke, Celia, and bring a smile to people's faces. Trouble is, sense of humour is a very subjective thing and a lot of people seem to think I customised the Airstream this way, because that's my personal taste, as a result of which they feel nothing but contempt for me. I guess some of it is my personal taste. You know, I'm old school. I just adore nostalgia."

"It brought a smile to my face, darling. I mean, it's non-aggressive; it's homely. A girl could get into this trailer feeling safe."

"You mean, like a gingerbread house?"

"No, I mean that she knows she's not going to be assaulted by some Rohypnol-wielding rapist. And look, the theme continues on the inside. I mean—oak panelling! As I said this is more like, say, the Reform Club or the Traveller's Club in Pall Mall, than a trailer. A place where the men can retire to after dinner to discuss serious topics like strip clubs and cigars, whilst the women get out their sewing samplers or exchange frivolities with one another. How in Mercy's name did you get the baby grand in here?"

"You can see it fits."

"Of course, it fits once it's in here, like a ship in a bottle fits in the bottle. But I mean, how did you get it in here in the first place? Is this a trailer or a Tardis?"

"Oh, that! We took a can opener to the roof, block and tackled it in, and then soldered the roof back on afterwards."

"Seriously?"

"Yup; before that I had an upright Steinway. We managed to get that through the door easily enough, but when the trailer was going down the motorway, it kept falling over; so the upright piano was more like a drunk piano."

"Do you mind?"

"Be my guest."

Celia sat at the piano stool, placed the ashtray on the music rack, and began playing. When she sat down, her wraparound linen skirt gaped open almost to the top of her thighs, but she didn't seem to feel the need to do anything about it. She was just so comfortable in her own skin, so unselfconscious.

"I'm very pleased you decided not to get it in white, darling."

"Yeah, it did come in white, but I restrained my inner Liberace! Needed it to match the panelling."

Wally loved the way her back was ramrod straight, not like all the young girls he'd seen who addressed the piano with the posture of osteoporosis. He had heard the tune she was playing before, but it wasn't until she started singing that he fully made the connection. When he heard her singing voice, he realised just what Indigolin had meant when he had said she was like Eartha Kitt.

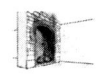

"*The piano has been drinking, not me, not me, not me.*"

She sang all the lyrics of the Tom Waites' song, accompanying herself faultlessly on the baby grand, but her voice, incredibly, was huskier than Tom Waites himself. She was a cross between The Velvet Underground's Nico and Marlene Dietrich, and it dawned on Wally that she was practically Marlene Dietrich's contemporary. He came up and stood beside her stool. Then when it came to the verse about the box office, he joined in, with his hands on her shoulders. They sang a duet together:

"*And the box office is drooling, and the bar stools are on fire
And the newspapers were fooling, and the ashtrays have retired...*"

And at the end, they both sang, "*Not me, not me, not me.*" And then he bent round and he kissed her on the lips.

"I wasn't expecting that," she declared.

"I told you, Celia, I'm old school. You do something to me. You always have, since I was an adolescent. And now standing here with my arms on your shoulders, I feel like an adolescent again, as if my whole head's exploding with hormones. I felt the same way when I was holding hands with you by the helicopter, when I helped you down. I couldn't believe it.

"You make me go weak at the knees. In fact, tell you the truth, my head's spinning so much right now, if I didn't have my hands on your shoulders, using you like a kind of human Zimmer frame, I'd probably be falling over before your very eyes!

"It's bad enough when I see one of your films, and I promise you I've seen every one of them. But you being here in the flesh. Celia Broadsword in Wally's Woodie-Wagon! Sorry, it was all just too much for me. Sensory overload. Are we okay? I mean, I'm not like that Harvey Weinstein guy, am I?"

"Nor Woody Allen either!" She laughed. "I'm old enough to be your grandmother, darling."

"I wouldn't have it any other way, Celia. Forget about the missing years. Let's just take it a day at a time."

"I guess that you wouldn't exactly be the youngest piece of arm candy I've stepped out with in my time, Wally."

"I don't want to be your accessory, Celia. I want us to be an item."

"I repeat, I'm old enough to be your grandmother!"

"Celia, you know I've been practising Tao for about 30 years. Age and longevity are irrelevant. I'm sorry, but this is very important to me, so I'm going to have to give you a bit of a lecture."

"Is it going to be a long lecture, darling, because if it is, I'll light another cigarette and you can pour me a drink?"

"Are you a Scotch woman or a gin and tonic woman?" He asked.

"What do you think, Wally?"

He poured her a Chivas on the rocks, whilst she lit one of her oval Passing Clouds. She turned round from the piano, so she was facing him, paying attention.

"In the Bible," he commenced.

"Jesus!" She interrupted. "If we're starting in biblical times, this is going to be a long night!"

"In the Bible," he persevered, "we're told people routinely lived to 150 years and more."

"But that's the Bible, honey!"

"The point about the Bible, Celia, is that it goes to great lengths to seek to make us believe the events actually happened. It has multiple narrators for authenticity's sake. You heard Indigolin talking about blockchain. Well the Bible uses multiple narrators as a way of policing one another's honesty. I mean, they can't all be lying, can they?"

"Bible as blockchain. Keep going, honey."

"And it drops real historical figures into a timeline we can verify from other credible sources, such as Josephus and the Roman historians."

"OK."

"Why would it go to such lengths to make us believe the events really happened, and then torpedo the very credibility they have gone to such lengths to achieve, by saying something completely preposterous, such as that people were living to the age of 150?"

"So you're approaching the Bible as a documentary or history book?"

"What has undermined western longevity is the coming together of people in large cities. In New York City, for instance, more than sixty tonnes of harmful airborne particles rain down on each square mile of the City every month. These days, the west makes a big deal about how much life quality and expectancy has improved.

"But in fact the opposite is true. Longevity has been declining since biblical times. What the west have recently become very good at is intervention. We can prolong life expectancy by intervention. But if you put aside intervention, and just look at how old people are on average before they die of old age, it's getting younger all the time.

"I'm going to show you Tao exercises that will prolong life. There's no reason why we both shouldn't be pretty fit and spry and what's more, sexually active, in fifty years' time. The fact, Ms Broadsword, that you happen to have stolen the march on me by thirty-five years, if we were to take a snapshot of where we are today, is utterly irrelevant, because we still have the rest of our lives before us. Doesn't matter how long it takes: this one's about the journey, not the destination."

"Well that's really good, Wally. The time it took listening to that little lecture has certainly aged me by several years. What does your Tao of Ying and Yang have to say about smoking cigarettes?"

"That's something we're going to have to work on, Celia. Tao can inform all aspects of your life, from the way you breathe, to the way you eat; you can even attain good health and longevity just by making love the right way."

She lifted her face and kissed him back.

"I'm old school too. Instead of proselytising, Wally, if you really want us to be an item, why don't you start off old school by writing me a love letter?"

Gazelle D'or

Indigolin drove himself to Gazelle d'Or in Taroudant. He figured there couldn't be more than a dozen roads between Ouarzazate and Taroudant for him to get lost on, and it was always an hilarious experience to get behind the wheel of the Lamborghini Urus. Everywhere he went, urchins appeared out of nowhere, even if he was miles away from any sign of habitation. Some of the kids just gesticulated madly at the first car they'd seen that wasn't a Toyota pick-up. For others, the hand was up the other way, begging.

With the help of Elizabeth Drayson, Elena Troy, Wally Pfister and John Donne, they now had a route map of the film. It was going to take the scriptwriters a few days to get something down on paper. He might as well head out to Taroudant for some shooting.

He roared past the terracotta walled city of Taroudant and arrived at the more diminutive terracotta walled oasis that is the hotel known as La Gazelle d'Or, where he'd booked himself in for a couple of day's dove shooting. The manager on the front desk took his bags to his suite, looking out on stunningly manicured, mature gardens and water gardens, much the same as he'd enjoyed at La Mamounia, but on a smaller scale.

As far as the eye could see there were acres of green grass, but towards the end of the gardens, the green grass wore a cloak of blue, where some of the petals had fallen from a magnificent jacaranda tree that must have been hundreds of years old. A woman was exercising a thoroughbred horse on the lawn. He felt a tinge of melancholy that he didn't have a partner to share the experience with.

You'd think a man like him would be a very eligible bachelor. He wasn't minded to find his women by swiping right. He didn't go to clubs or bars. He didn't believe in dating his own employees.

So where was he supposed to find a soul mate? That agency accountant looked hot. She was fiercely intelligent, well read, and judging by her CV on the job application, they both shared an interest in the environment and scuba diving.

They even had Metaphysical Poetry to fall back on now. Maybe he could invite her back to the Riyadh one night for dinner. See how things progressed.

"I see you've booked the dove shooting," the manager said. "Would you like us to look after your guns for you?"

"I figured they'd be alright in the back of the Urus until we arrived at the shoot," Indigolin replied.

"You don't take your car to the shoot, Mr Indigolin," the manager replied. "We take you in the eight-seater minibus. You go in a group with other hunters who have also booked. Today they are mostly French, but there is one other Englishman, Mr Napier Ransom…"

"What time are we on parade in the morning?" Indigolin enquired.

"The doves are roosting birds, sir. We shoot them in the morning and again in the evening, so the shoot bus will be leaving from reception in about thirty minutes time for the evening shoot, and then the journey there will take another thirty minutes. Then in the morning, the shoot bus leaves here at 4.00 am."

"4.00 AM?"

"Yes, sir, as I explained, they are roosting birds, not driven birds, and that is when they roost."

"I tell you what, I think I'll give the morning shoot a miss, if it's all the same with you, and I'll do the evening shoot tonight, get up an appetite for what I have no doubt will be a very historic dinner that I am greatly looking forward to after my long drive."

"The shoot bus will be leaving from reception in thirty minutes then, sir," he repeated.

"Is there any particular attire? In England we tend to dress up in tweeds."

"I think you will find that very hot, sir. I recommend sturdy boots in case of snakes. But apart from that, jeans and a T-shirt and sun screen are fine. Oh, and some padding for your shoulder."

Indigolin gave him the car keys to fetch the guns from the trunk, and asked him to make him up a cool box to go with a half-case of champagne and some champagne flutes. After two days of being polite and humouring Wally Pfister with his diet of sub-acid fruits, buckwheat kernels, honey, nuts, no lactose dairy and sushi, he was looking forward to a proper dinner.

Twenty-five minutes later, Tinctorio Indigolin strode into reception in a blue legume suit, the Nehru collar on which was his only concession towards casual dress. But he did have blue Dr Marten boots on his feet, as advised. The driver of the mini-van was proudly buffing up the alloys with a flourish of his chamois leather. He was wearing Ray-Bans, but he had pushed them up onto the top of his head so as to concentrate more vigorously on these final preparations that would, no doubt, be rewarded with gratuities from all his passengers.

Indigolin checked in the back of the bus that the manager had loaded the cool box of Bolly that he had requested. The French men were already in the minibus in animated conversation that seemed to involve a lot of hand gestures. A tall guy in blue jeans, a baseball cap worn backwards and a tee-shirt with '*Too Drunk To Fuck*' written across his chest, was standing beside the bus.

"Napier Ransom!" He introduced himself, and thrust a business card into Indigolin's hand. Indigolin didn't know people still used business cards to exchange contact information, as opposed to phones.

"Thank you," he said, and of the card: "How quaint."

"Oh, I mean," said Napier, "if you don't do business cards, you can always roll it up and use it for very high-class roach material. We're in Morocco now. When in Rome, eh? It's like the Wild West here!"

The business card gave the title of Ransom's business 'Metcalfe Insurance Specialists'.

"Tinctorio Indigolin," said Indigolin.

"No need to introduce yourself to me. Everyone knows you. You're the Blue Molecule guy!"

After a 30 minute commute, they emerged from the vehicle. During the drive, Napier had insisted on talking shop non-stop, although this was generally considered very bad form on a shooting party. Indigolin was relieved to escape from the confines of the shoot bus: the guy's aftershave was turning his stomach, and Indigolin was seriously concerned that it might scare the doves off. It appeared that the field of insurance that the man specialised in was Kidnap & Ransom Insurance. He was very proud of the fact that he'd taken in tens of millions of pounds in premiums, and never paid out a penny on a claim.

"When it rains," he laughed, "we take the umbrella away! We're like the Wild West!"

Exiting the vehicle, Napier got into an argument with the shootmaster about the fact that they didn't have any loaders, and he was expected to carry his own guns. The shootmaster explained that he didn't have very far to walk, and, as he didn't have a loader, he only needed one gun.

The party were immediately set upon by a pack of teenage boys. Despite the advice from the manager to bring sturdy boots, the luckiest of the boys had flip flops; the others were bare-footed. They wore old track suit bottoms and vests that looked as though they had themselves been used for target practice.

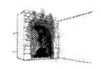

Not one of them had any ear defenders. In fact, a large proportion of them seemed to be missing ears. Most of them had a great many teeth missing, and some were also missing eyes as well as ears, or parts of ears, such as the lobes. *Sans teeth, sans eyes, sans taste, sans everything.* They were pulling at Napier's arms and clothes and crying, "Here boss! Here boss!"

"What the fuck do these midgets want?" Napier demanded, shaking them off.

"They don't use dogs in Morocco," explained Indigolin. "They're bird boys. They pick up your birds for you."

"I used to have a dog," informed Napier. "I called him Andrew, which was the name of my ex-wife's father. I called him Andrew because he was another castrated mongrel!"

"What became of your dog?" Indigolin asked.

"I lost him," said Napier.

"As I say," resumed Indigolin, "the bird boys pick up your birds for you. But you must be careful, because they also encourage you to shoot at themselves, because they get better tips that way."

"No shit! How much for an eye?" Napier asked, quite seriously.

The shootmaster, who had overheard the exchange said, "One must negotiate with the family, sir, but I would say about 500 US."

"Fuck me!" Napier cried, "is that all?"

The team took turns to pick their bird boys, each member having four or five bird boys to himself. Napier's first choice was a scrawny wretch with only one ear, whom he promptly named Vincent. He then told Vincent to pick four of his mates to accompany him.

Napier was further dismayed to learn that no-one was drawing for pegs and there was no champagne to drink before they set off. After all, the sun was below the yard arm, and if he'd still been back at the hotel he'd be onto his second Cosmopolitan by now, or maybe a Negroni.

"I have some champagne, if you'd like," offered Indigolin. He got the cool box out the back. There were six bottles and six glasses inside, which was as much as they could fit in having regard to the trunk space all the guns and cartridges took up.

"I don't mind if I do," said Napier, cracking open a bottle and wasting half of it, spraying it around like he was a Formula 1 driver on the podium, before guzzling a neckful straight out of the bottle, and offering it to Indigolin. Indigolin didn't want to put his mouth where the other man's mouth had been and told him politely that he'd wait until after the first drive.

"They don't drink alcohol in Morocco," Indigolin added, "although it's illegal, as a derogation, we're allowed to drink it in hotels. If we are drinking it outside of a licensed hotel, it's best to be as inconspicuous about it as possible."

"Fuck that!" Napier said and swigged from the bottle again.

The shootmaster placed them at intervals of a mere five yards apart in the dust bowl that was apparently where they were to stand all evening, pricking at doves. The topography was totally flat, ochre earth, punctuated only by Argan trees, watermelons cultivated under plastic, and telegraph poles. If the hunters had expected undulating landscape with towering mountains and plunging ravines where the birds would be launching themselves from stratospheric escarpments, they would be disappointed. Napier was complaining again, because he had to carry both his gun and his cartridge case with two heavy slabs of 12-bore cartridges. Indigolin was bemused at why he hadn't just carried one slab to his peg, and gone back to the minibus for the other if necessary. He was hardly likely to shoot the whole slab on the first drive.

There was no safety talk, no request not to kill ground game, and no instruction to avoid social media in case the 'Anti's' found out where the event was taking place and blockaded it. No horn sounded to mark the beginning or end of the session.

There were simply shouts of 'Here, sir! Here, sir!' as the bird boys drew the guns' attention to any passing bird, even if it was walking on the ground, balancing on the telegraph wires or indeed standing on the head of another bird boy, as Indigolin had warned Ransom. The guns popped away. Indigolin was gravely disappointed. There was no sport. The birds were flying far too low.

By contrast, Napier wanted to kill everything, although thankfully, he hadn't fulfilled his *desideratum* yet of puncturing a bird boy. Spent shot from Napier's Beretta Giubellis rained down on Indigolin's head. Fortunately he had brought his blue legume cap.

After twenty minutes or so, there seemed to be a consensus that it was thirsty work and time for a drink. Napier retired to the shoot bus and opened another bottle of Indigolin's champagne without asking, having left the half empty one out of the cool box in the sun, so that it was now flat, warm, soupy and undrinkable. This time they used glasses.

The case of champagne rested on the tail gate of the minibus. Indigolin noticed that Napier had a particular way of pouring out the fizz. He would grab the bottle and fill the other man's glass first. He would make an expansive gesture of filling it to the brim quickly, before filling his own.

But of course, when the bubbles died down in the other man's glass, there was only half a glass there. He would then continue to fill his own glass to the top, so that when the bubbles subsided, he had, by contrast, a full glass. But he wouldn't release the bottle. He would then take a big glug out of his own glass, and re-charge his own glass to the brim, and only then would he let go of the bottle and put it down on the tailgate.

"It's like the Wild West here!" Napier repeated himself. Indigolin didn't understand the man. They were in the Middle East.

Just then a shepherd came into the dust bowl with his flock of sheep.

"You didn't seem to be going for them, Tincto!" Napier pronounced, devising a foreshortening of Indigolin's first name that Indigolin regarded as rather over-familiar.

"It wasn't like shooting," explained Indigolin. "It was more of a bayonet job. Some of them were extremely low. I'd have been at risk of shooting you, or one of the Frenchmen, or the bird boys. I mean we're shooting in 360 degrees. It's not safe when they're flying so low."

"No Health & Safety here! It's a fucking third-world country. I told you it was like the Wild West! This is the most unwoke shoot I've ever been on!"

Napier seemed quite light-headed on a few glasses of champagne.

"You were pillow-casing them!" Indigolin declared. This was a critical assessment, referring to a member of the team who was shooting so low that the shot birds were reduced to the exploded contents of a feather pillowcase. But Ransom showed no sign of understanding that his shooting etiquette was being condemned.

A goatherd came into the dust bowl where they were shooting. The goats proceeded to climb the Argan trees to get at their fruit. On one tree, Indigolin noted, there seemed to be no less than four goats, the goats with their cloven hooves, having managed to reach a height far greater than most of the doves, despite the addition of wings, had managed to attain.

"Plus!" Napier complained, "they're not fucking doves at all! They're pigeons! I paid for doves!"

"I think they use the terms interchangeably," reassured Indigolin.

Then the watermelon man came into the dust bowl, accompanied by his shoeless son, a lad of perhaps four summers, and they started pulling back the black plastic bin liners under which the melons were maturing and checking for melon spider.

The shoot master gave them a five minute warning. Time to return to the killing fields.

"Hold this!" Napier ordered Indigolin, passing his glass to him so that Indigolin held a champagne flute in each hand. Without moving further, Napier whipped his junk out and began micturating copiously onto the buffed alloys of the shoot bus. When he observed that Indigolin was staring at him in amazement at his behaviour, he laughed and cried out, "*Eau Savage!*" referring to his own piss. Having made some room, he thanked Indigolin, grabbed his glass from his hand and downed the rest before stumping off in the direction of his peg. Indigolin didn't know where to look.

It was time for another drive, although, if truth be told, these were not drives. The un-driven birds just dribbled overhead of their own accord and at their own pace. '*Un-driven wild birds, such as grouse,*' Indigolin thought, '*could be extremely challenging, jinking around unpredictably and accelerating faster than his Lamborghini.*' But pricking at these doves was about as satisfying as shooting pigeons in Trafalgar Square. The birds were just too hot to fly. They were more like oven-ready.

Now that the melon father and son were also in the dust bowl at close quarters to the guns, the obstacles were greater than ever. What with all the bird boys and the Frenchmen squabbling with one another, and the melon father and son, the goatherd and the stratospheric goats in the Argan trees, the shepherd and his flock—things were taking a turn for the dangerous. Then Napier, standing to Indigolin's right (having noticed that Indigolin wasn't shooting at the pigeons himself because they were too low to be good sport) decided to start stealing Indigolin's birds to his left.

Shooting crossing birds was extremely bad form, but Napier figured that he'd paid for them and they were just going to waste. However, this made things even more dangerous for Indigolin, with a drunken homicidal maniac standing beside him, trying to kill Indigolin's birds by shooting across him. Worse still, every time Napier shot one of Indigolin's birds, Napier insisted on shouting out, "*Wiped your eye!*"

Indigolin instructed him in firm tones to stop shooting across him. There was then a bang and a scream: Napier had shot a bird boy to Indigolin's left. Indigolin had the distinct impression that Napier had done this on purpose, out of boredom, after Indigolin had forbidden him from shooting his pigeons.

Fortunately, the wound was not fatal.

"How much for an ear?" Napier enquired, who saw no reason to stop shooting and continued doing so whilst all the others had downed guns and were tending to the stricken bird boy. "Got to be less than an eye!" Napier chuckled. Then he shot right across Indigolin again and cried out his ridiculous refrain: "Wiped your eye!"

Having shot sufficient doves, the shootmaster then announced the shoot was over, presumably wanting to call it a day before Napier shot anybody else. He told everybody first in French then in English that the hotel management would negotiate with the wounded bird boy's family, and tell Napier what the damage was over dinner.

Because Indigolin was polite, he found he was unable to shake off his new found friend. After propping up the bar at Gazelle d'Or with several pints of Guinness and Kir Royals, Napier asked if he could share a table with Indigolin, being the only other Englishman there, although, the term Napier used was not Englishman, but 'white man', and Indigolin felt unable to decline without being point blank rude.

Once again he regretted not having had any more amenable escort to bring with him, such as the fragrant Elena Troy. He did however decide that he would indeed get up at 4 a.m. the following morning, but not to shoot any more doves: to leave the hotel. Nap was still wearing the same champagne-sprayed, offensive tee-shirt from the dove shoot.

Despite not having otherwise freshened up, he appeared to have replenished his noxious aftershave. Indigolin thought about asking what brand it was so that he could make a point of avoiding it, but didn't want the guy to get the wrong idea. Indigolin himself never used cologne or aftershave, but he did moisturise with the aid of his own delivery mechanism.

"I see you haven't changed for dinner," observed Indigolin; but the mild reprobation appeared to have no effect. Nap's inebriated brain didn't process this as a criticism, or even sarcasm; just an observation, possibly an observation of a positive nature, because neither had Indigolin changed.

At the bar, Indigolin had learned that Napier had been 'doing Spain', trying to get off with girls posing as a scuba diver and environmentalist, and had now come to Morocco for some dove shooting, but found shooting bird boys was much better sport. Napier had informed him that he improved his chances by spiking the girls' drinks with something he called a 'leg-spreader', adding gratuitously and noisily:

"But one of them didn't even have any fucking legs to spread! They'd been bitten off by a fucking shark, and she got around on a 40 mph Seabob electric sea scooter. Only came out of the water to charge the thing up every couple of hours! Fuck me! That was the saltiest cunt I've ever tasted! Have you ever fucked an amputee, Tincto?"

Gazelle d'Or was an oasis indeed, but in the company of a crashing bore like Napier Ransom, it was a death sentence. They left the bar where the man was playing the piano. The dinner tables, beautifully dressed with clean linen, brass chargers, cut glass and candles, were set outside amongst lanterns in the gardens. Their walk to their table took them past the ornamental ponds and channels where Indigolin proceeded to listen for frogs. As though he was a conductor and they were members of his orchestra, right then the frogs began croaking.

"I am fascinated by frogs," remarked Indigolin.

"I only know one joke about fish," slurred Napier.

"But a frog is not a fish, Mr Ransom."

A beautiful Arab girl, her hair respectfully encased in a head scarf, had arrived and was standing by to take their order.

"What's fishier than an anchovy?" Ransom asked.

Indigolin look at him blankly, not knowing what he was talking about.

"An anchovy's cunt!" Napier cried out, so loudly that people on other tables could hear the drunken bore, who now exploded into laughter himself at his inane punch line.

"Mr Ransom, that was in execrable taste," Indigolin stage-whispered, "and within earshot of this young lady. And what's more, it wasn't remotely humorous!"

Just then the front desk manager arrived. Indigolin hoped he was coming to throw Ransom out of the hotel. But he was simply coming to report on the negotiations with the family of the shot bird boy.

"The best we have been able to negotiate for the loss of the ear is 36,000 dirhams, Mr Ransom."

"What's that in real money?"

"About three thousand pounds sterling, Sir."

"Tell him."

"Tell who, Sir?"

Napier, nodding his head fiercely in the direction of his dining companion: "Him! Mr Indigolin. He shot the little bastard. It was on his side."

"Kindly move me to another table," asked Indigolin. "Put the bird boy's tip on my bill. I'll be leaving early in the morning."

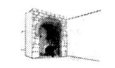

Ambiguity

Despite being a popular celebrity (or maybe because she was a popular celebrity), Celia Broadsword understood the fact that most men didn't find her the easiest of women to approach. This was not the result of any inherent lack of approachability on her part, but rather because of their preconceived perception of what they might be up against. On the occasions when a man plucked up enough fortitude against rejection to ask her for a date, they deliberately couched their words in ambiguity, so that, if rejection ensued, they could deny ever having made the approach in the first place, say that she must have misunderstood their intentions, that actually, they had simply been asking her something quite innocuous, such as whether she preferred M & M's to Jelly Beans. She had heard it called accountable deniability, but weasel words would do just as well.

However, this Wally Pfister had really nailed his colours to the mast and his heart to his sleeve. He'd come straight out with it. No turning back and no hiding place for him. He'd said he was old school, and it seemed he really was. He'd leapfrogged the usual stages of going on a date or out to dinner, or even having recreational, uncommitted sex, and announced that he wanted to be in a relationship with her. He'd cut out all the middlemen, as well as his escape route if she told him to get lost.

From one perspective, it was refreshingly direct and simple. From another perspective, she had reservations that he could just be a gay wanting to splice himself to a mature diva. After all, what dyed-in-the-wool homosexual wouldn't want to marry Judy Garland? She would have to check out his sexuality before the relationship got any deeper.

A Berber on a Bicycle

The moon slipped behind a cloud.

Colman Hunt was sleeping in his chromium caravan. He retired early every night and slept with the night lights on so he could find his way to the bathroom.

In the balmy blackness, the scriptwriters, who had received instructions to work round the clock until they had a screenplay to deliver, had set up a campaign table on the sand, and were brainstorming by the light of a hurricane lamp. They were seated on folding chairs, one on each side of the table, resembling tiles in a game of Mah Jong. The lamp attracted an almost infinite number of bugs. Where had they all come from? Where had they all been hiding before they lit the lamp?

Badiss Slimani was a twelve-year-old Berber. Despite living a nomadic existence with his family in the desert, he had been well educated and read and wrote flawless English. He was one of Tinctorio Indigolin's fourteen million followers, and he had watched the assassination of the cryptocurrency king on his phone, and the Millicent Marcuson documentary, followed by the interview with the exasperated Colman Hunt, expressing his opinion that the film was doomed never to be made.

Having noted that the film that the crew were failing to get into the can was being shot around Ouarzazate, he had pedalled his bicycle across the desert in the hope of acquiring some autographs or other memorabilia from the actors, stationed in the Sahara, maybe even a selfie.

The blue-robed boy, lay his cycle down noiselessly in the sand and let himself into the Airstream where Colman Hunt lay sleeping. On Hunt's counter, a large scrapbook lay open to a photo of Colman Hunt, his double, Paddy Oculus, and two more doubles of Colman Hunt. They were all dressed in black suits with white shirts and black ties.

The boy had seen all Colman's films, but he did not know what to make of this multiple image, as though Hunt was standing between parallel mirrors throwing endless reflections of himself. Pulling out his phone from the pocket inside his blue Djellaba, he took a photo of the photo, to study more closely later.

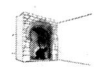

Then, not wanting to see the spine of the heavy scrapbook damaged by being left open all night in this fashion, he closed the book carefully.

He left Hunt's caravan, and crept around the Airstream encampment, drawn like a moth, to the light from the hurricane lamp where the scriptwriters were gathered. The shadows from the light were so profound that it was easy for him to creep up unobserved to within earshot. He lay down on the sand on his tummy, pushed his large spectacles back up to the top of his nose, and overheard their conversation.

"So," ventured Ray Peckett, who had been the head scriptwriter for the previous three seasons of *Ferdinand and Isabella's Book of Hours*, "we start with an establishing shot from the mountain outside Granada, where Boabdil and his mother are looking back with remorse at the city they have lost. Boabdil brushes a tear from his cheek. His mother, Aixa, speaks the famous line: 'Now you cry like a boy for what you failed to defend like a man.' Then we do the titles."

Don Reardon, another of the writers, made a note on his device. "Then," he continued, "we go into flashback. The character known simply as The Traitor, hands the keys of Granada over to Christopher Columbus, camped outside the walled city, and Columbus and his men enter Granada through a minor gate under cover of darkness."

"They steal into the bedchamber of Catherine of Aragon. Columbus clamps his hand over her mouth, and they kidnap her," Peckett continued.

The twelve-year-old boy pinched himself. What rubbish was this, he wondered to himself.

The third screenwriter interrupted. "Did any of this actually happen?" He asked.

"Poetic licence," answered the fourth. "We've been told we can give free rein to our fantasies."

"Cut to Boabdil's bedchamber," announced Peckett. "King Ferdinand throws open the door. Boabdil and his wife are in bed. Of course, the bed is covered in animal pelts and there are flaming sconces on the walls. At this point, Boabdil pushes the wife out of the bed for her own safety, and she's naked, so we'll have the first nudity within the first sixty seconds of the movie."

"Starting out as we mean to go on," said the third man.

"She's naked," clarified the third man, "save for some transparent yellow scarf thing or veil that slips onto the bed as she runs for safety into the *en suite*."

"Undoubtedly," agreed the fourth.

"Boabdil jumps out of bed," said Peckett, continuing the narrative. "He's about to have a sword fight, so he can't be sleeping in the buff. We'll have him wearing some of those harem pants that Paddy Oculus likes to wear on set. But apart from that he'll be bare chested and bare-footed."

"Whilst the camera's been panning on the naked lady slipping into the *en suite* bathroom out of harm's way," interjected Don, "by the time the camera's panned back to Boabdil he has a sword in his hand."

"Not any old sword!" Ray Peckett cried. "It's a curved scimitar."

"And," continued the fourth man, "Boabdil grabs the yellow scarf from the end of the bed and he throws it in the air."

"Colman Hunt, as the aged Ferdinand, takes a swipe at the scarf in mid-air with his broadsword, and fails to rupture it in the slightest," announced Don.

"Then," continued the fourth man, "Ferdinand picks the scarf up from the terracotta tiles and throws it back up in the air."

"As it's fluttering down," enthused Peckett, "Boabdil cleaves it effortlessly in two with his trusty scimitar!"

"And then," concluded Don, "Ferdinand raises his sword and brings it down with huge force, splitting Boabdil's bed asunder!"

"Yes, the entire bed is in two pieces."

"And cut!"

"Hang on!" exclaimed the fourth writer. "What does Catherine of Aragon wear in bed?"

The Berber boy was completely horrified by the mishmash he was overhearing. He had taken on board the fact that the writers had been granted a fool's licence to throw authenticity to the winds, but surely they could come up with a better story than this? Stunned, lost in his own thoughts, he slipped away, retrieved his bicycle and pedalled off into the night.

Death in Venice

"You know, Wally, there's an exception to your rule."

"All the best rules have exceptions, Celia. Which of my rules are you intending to break today?"

"The rule that all other directors apart from Wally Pfister ship the cast out on location at vast expense only to shoot the location in soft focus, so that no-one viewing the movie would even know it had been shot there."

"And what is the exception to that rule, Celia?"

"Venice."

He thought for a moment. She could see the Rolodex in his eyes flicking through all the films that had been shot in La Serenissima. Meanwhile Celia continued:

"*Don't Look Now,* Johnny Depp's *The Tourist, The Wings of the Dove, The Comfort of Strangers, Indiana Jones and the Last Crusade,* Fellini's *Casanova, Brideshead Revisited,* Gary Gray's remake of *The Italian Job.* Even James Bond: as we said yesterday: when they take the cast to Matera in *No Time to Die,* it's unrecognisable that they're in Matera, but when they go to Venice in *Casino Royale,* it's shot in dazzling detail and sharp focus. Roger Moore's Bond also went there in *Moonraker*."

"Ah yes, the hover-gondola! Now we have the hoves and the hove-nots, the hovelling hordes of hovellers in their hovellers as well as a hover-hoveller on a gondola!" Wally took a moment to recover from that alliterative tongue-twister and then added: "Sean Connery's Bond also visited briefly in *From Russia with Love*."

"*Spiderman: Far From Home*. Wallace, I could go on all night."

"Let me give you the answer that explains your exception, Celia. All the other ancient cities that we have discussed, when they are featured in films, are masquerading as somewhere else. So typically, when the viewer is taken to Matera or Aït Benhaddou, for argument's sake, it's important to conceal the true identity of the location, because the viewers are going to be asked to believe that they're really in the Bible or on the planet of Tatooine. In these examples, the true identity of the locations has to be disguised, because the locations are either passing themselves off as somewhere different, or as their genuine locations, but in another era. Soft focus facilitates that dissimulation. It is simply another facet of the disguise. However, there is no other city that is anything like Venice, and Venice remains exactly as she was in the time of the Doges, so there is nothing that needs changing or requires artefact. So if a film is shot in Venice, Venice is always the co-star, and the director also does it to suck up to Venice in the hope of scooping a Golden Lion at the Venice Film Festival."

"That's a very interesting theory, darling. Not least because of the fact that Venice was the city where they invented the Masquerade, but you tell me it's the only city that fails to masquerade. But how do you explain away Visconti's *Death in Venice*. That was all shot in soft focus."

"I will answer that question in three ways, Ms Broadsword. Firstly, the clue's in the title. If the title announces that the location is Venice, you don't have to shove that up the audience's nose any more with scenes shot in sharp focus: the cat's already out of the bag. Secondly, I would say that particular film isn't actually in soft focus at all: it's just saturated with light, because that's a thing about Venice, which attracts it to artists: it has amazing, architectural light.

"Thirdly, and finally, Death in Venice wasn't shot in Venice. It was shot at Hotel des Bains on Venice Lido. To say that Venice Lido is the same as Venice is like saying that Bermondsey is the same as Berkeley Square, just because they're both in London. They're chalk and cheese."

"Wally, do you ever find yourself lost for words?"

"Only when I try to write a love letter good enough for you, Celia."

"I'll just have to try harder to motivate you, Wally, won't I?"

She lifted his hand onto her left breast and kissed him long on the lips. Once again, he experienced that weakness at the knees. He didn't know what it was this woman did to him, but he couldn't get enough of it. Every time, she reduced him to adolescence.

An Email from a Law Firm

Millicent Marcuson's Outlook showed her that an email from Bird & Bird had just arrived in her Inbox. It warned her: *You don't often receive emails from this source.* 'Good job too,' she thought. The fewer legal letters she received, the better.

"What is it?" asked Ynes, the cameraman.

"Legal letter from an outfit called Bird & Bird," Millicent informed him.

"High flyers, huh?" joked the cameraman. He held up his phone for her. "According to their website, they're specialist Intellectual Property Lawyers," he informed her.

"It's the link to the Triumvirate Interview," she announced. "You remember, Indigolin promised us if we sat on the evidence that he wasn't dead for a day or two that he'd share this clip with us? Seems like he's been as good as his word. The covering letter says that I am free to watch this for personal research and educational purposes, but to publish it any further in any medium whatsoever, in whole or in part, would be contumelious and lead to an application to imprison me for contempt of court."

"Charming!" He commiserated.

"It also says that I am not to construe the fact that they have supplied me with this link as a waiver of privilege or a waiver of the benefit of the Gagging Order."

"That it?"

"Well, there's a load more warnings about Norwich Pharmacal orders and CPR 81.2, and there's a Penal Notice attached. In fact there's so many public health warnings on the letter, it's practically radioactive!"

"Maybe it's been dipped in polonium as well as vitriol!" Ynes quipped.

"Ynes, I think the general drift is that this isn't supposed to go any further than my laptop."

"Shall we then?" He said.

Millicent pressed the link beneath the notice that read *You have been sent large files*. A password was emailed to her by Mimecast, which she cut and pasted into the dialogue box and the large file download began.

A Sonnet with 13 Lines

He pushed the folded paper under the door of Celia's Airstream just after midnight. He'd wanted to put something down about how fantastic she looked for her years, or the summer-autumn of their age gap, but all those drafts went in the bin, because he decided the last thing she wanted reminding of was how ancient she was, and if that's what she thought he saw in her, then she wasn't going to see anything in him. He'd already made her sit through his Taoist exegesis on longevity. Eventually he had just made a kind of half-rhyming Almanac of some of the stuff they had shared and laughed about, their dreams and aspirations, what they had in common.

Because he was old school, he knew he had to write it in green ink.

He had pulled the top leaves off his succulent house plant and put them in the coffee grinder. He had then mashed up the resultant green pulp with a pestle and mortar until he had a thick paste. He'd cut the paste with his gin and tonic lemons to stop the dye discolouring to brown. He'd put half a teaspoonful of salt and a splash of vinegar in until he got the right, green, runny consistency, and then decanted the ink into a wine glass. He'd used a wooden toothpick as his pen, careful not to make any blobs.

After a couple of practice runs, he went live on his best headed notepaper. When it was dry enough, he folded it carefully over and wrote her name on the outside. Talking of Venice, as they had done with such animation yesterday, he had a wax seal set he'd purchased at Buffetti's. He dripped the melted wax onto the join at the back of the envelope, and pressed his initials down with the wooden handled stamp.

Then he'd inspected his wax-sealed envelope and wondered to himself whether she would think what he'd written on the sheet of paper within was the true, the genuine Venice, or simply Venice Lido, a dim reflection of the real thing. Whether she'd drink it in as champagne or as ginger beer; ginger beer that still had the fizz and the sparkle, but didn't quite cut it anymore.

If that didn't do it, nothing would.

Celia was a light sleeper. She heard the paper slide under her door and she saw the light from Wally's torch receding as he padded on the cool sand back to his own caravan. She slipped out of bed, lit a candle and retrieved the missive. She picked up the Jineta that she had removed from her headdress before retiring to sleep and used it to break the wax seal carefully, uncrimped the note and pressed it flat. Inside the envelope she saw there was a handwritten poem, also in green ink on headed notepaper. The handwriting was old school, like copperplate.

She sat down at her dressing table to give it the attention it deserved and to aid her concentration, she lit a Passing Cloud cigarette and a second candle with the same match and unfolded Wally's note. The note was creased in half with *To My Darling Celia* written on the outside. It was written in green ink on best Basildon Bond stationary headed, "From the Desk of Walter Pfister."

The first thought that went through her head was *Where the hell had he found the green ink in the middle of the Sahara Desert?*

She took a drag on her cigarette and read it, laughing to herself at the title:

13 LINE SONNET: THE EXCEPTION TO EVERY RULE

I used words before
But never understood what they were for
Until You asked me to set them down
And I've had young girls before
But never known this rapport
Before Celia Broadsword took me down
At the Danielli or the Gritti or the Excelsior
I'll win You the Golden Lion and the Palm D'Or
The glittering prizes, the jewel in the Crown
If You'll just release me from this tug-of-war
This cowardice of the twice kissed
This Death in Venice, film on a spool
Be it town or gown or old, old school
You are the exception to every rule.

Celia Broadsword slept in the nude. She read the poem several times. Then she counted the lines. It had 14, not 13 lines. It brought a smile to her lips. She was flattered by the way he capitalised the Y in You, as though he were addressing a deity. She was still smiling as she brushed her teeth and slipped on a kimono. It wasn't too late to pay her troubadour a visit. He'd earned it.

Catafalque

Under a *nom de plume*, Mr Webb was the author of a book entitled *An Illustrated History of Catafalques*. A lot of research and much of the dark soul of Hugh Webb himself had gone into its writing, and he had been gravely disappointed at the utter lack of interest when he had hawked his authoritative tome around the London literary market for 2 years without it stimulating a scintilla of interest.

"Let's face it," one putative agent who declined to represent the book for Webb, explained. "99% of the population don't even know what a catafalque is."

"It's a raised bier or box used to support the casket, coffin or body of a dead person during the funeral ceremony." Webb explained.

"Yes, you and I know that," the putative agent replied. "but we're the 1%"

"No," said Webb. "That's the Hell's Angels you're thinking of."

The putative agent didn't get it.

Not to be beaten, Webb self-published it. Despite his visiting many bookshops and literary festivals, and offering to provide the Prosecco himself whilst he signed the copies on Meet-the-Author days, fame and fortune continued to elude him. That was until the death of Queen Elizabeth II. After that momentous occasion, suddenly, 99% of the population knew what a catafalque was and wanted to know more. Now the publishers competed for Webb's business, and he had to update the work for a 2nd and 3rd edition, including photographs of the royal lying in state, and the last procession down the Mall behind a gun carriage.

His agent, Manny Wallenberger, had sadly passed away and never lived to share in this success; but nor did he share in the royalties. It was a curious thing that a man could kill some people for a living, but experience genuine remorse and grief at the passing of others. He had stood in a line for eighteen hours to pay his respects to the late Queen Elizabeth II.

If anyone had a rare first edition of *An Illustrated History of Catafalques*, Thomas Sotherans, the antiquarian booksellers in Sackville Street off Piccadilly, were offering a five figure sum.

Somehow, an ex-terrorist and assassin had managed to create a respectable cover story for himself, but not too far removed from his favourite subject, Death.

Billet Doux

Celia stepped up into Wally's Woodie-Wagon. This time she didn't bother knocking softly. She felt she owned the place. Clutching her paper with the Venetian wax seal broken in her left hand, she swept round the space running her fingers across the wooden surfaces like a homeowner looking to criticise her agency cleaner. She glanced from him to the letter and then back to him. He was in his boxer shorts about to get into bed. She was naked under a silk kimono.

The trailer was illuminated only by the candle on his baby grand, throwing deep shadows on the collection of objects inside. She saw the squeezed lemon, the violated house plant and the wine glass of Chartreuse ink. She saw the sheaf of papers where he had laboured at getting the right effect with his viridescent stain before he was ready to commit.

"You're looking me up and down," he said.

"Sorry," she said. She sat herself down on the piano stool and began playing, and then that amazing baritone voice overlaid the lyrics:

> *"Love letters straight from your heart*
> *Keep us near while apart*
> *I'm not alone in the night*
> *When I can have all the love you write."*

She allowed him a French kiss, but when he put his hand on her breast, she gently dislodged it and asked him: "Wally, don't you think you're pushing the envelope on your *billet doux* a little too hastily?"

"But last time, you put it there yourself!" He reminded her.

"Yes, but last time, I was wearing a bra. This time, there's nothing under the silk kimono."

"We're adults, Celia. If we both know where this is headed, why take the ring road?"

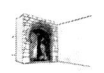

"Because maybe I might find a little detour all the more intriguing. Maybe I'd like to take the scenic route, Wally, and still arrive at the same destination."

"You're just amazing, Celia! How can a diva who was leading lady to Laurence Olivier and Marlon Brando still be so fresh? Do you take HRT?"

"I never liked messing with my hormones, Wally."

"Don't it get a little dry down there sometimes, Celia?"

"Baby, if you want to post that parcel, you're going to have to lick the stamps yourself."

"That's a scenic route I'd very much like to take, Celia."

"Do they have a name for that in the dictionary of the Tao of Ying and Yang?"

"As a matter of fact, they do. It's known as Sipping the Vast Spring."

"So prosaic, Wally. You got any more *lingua franca* on your tongue other than just the basic *billet doux*?"

"Genuinely, Celia, when I was a teenager the orthodontist was going to cut a couple of inches off the end of my tongue, because it kept pushing my teeth forward. You see, my tongue was too big to fit in my mouth."

"Like the baby grand in here. Okay. And did he?"

"As it so happened, he didn't, but not because he gave a toss about amputating my tongue or mutilating me for his personal gain. My parents, remember those of the Pontiac Woodie-Wagon? They took a second opinion, and the other guy said the tongue would just grow back, but even longer, because the tongue's just a muscle."

"They cut anything else off you, Pfister?"

"You know how optimistic we Jews are, Celia. We cut a few inches off our dicks before we even know how long they're going to be. But then after that, it was all bits and pieces, like a death of a thousand cuts."

"Yes, they used to chop things off routinely, for the sake of it, didn't they? Appendices, tonsils."

"Sure, there weren't any children in my class at primary school who hadn't undergone major surgery before they sat their eleven-pluses."

"I remember. Kids these days don't know how lucky they are. They've never had a general anaesthetic, so any opportunity they get, they just want to get shit-faced. Do you remember, when we used to go to the dentist, they gassed us to put us under?"

"I may be old school, but I'm not old enough to remember that one, Celia. I got injections in the gums. Anyway, the dentist didn't get my tongue."

"And what can you do with that tongue of yours, Wally?"

"I can do this." He touched his nose with his tongue.

"Nice party trick, Wally! You got any more where that came from?"

"Certainly. Has the route been scenic enough for you now, Celia? Can I Sip from the Vast Spring?"

She stepped out of her robe and lay down on his bed.

To His Mistress Going to Bed

"He what?" queried Ray Peckett.

"He asked me if we could put John Donne into the script," explained Don, the second senior screenwriter. "He wants him to be in a scene with Christopher Columbus."

"Did Christopher Columbus ever meet with John Donne?" asked Peckett.

"Not unless you subscribe to the director's theory that everybody lives to one hundred and fifty plus years of age," confided Don.

"So, it's a complete anachronism?"

"Well the script is replete with anachronisms," shrugged Don. "It would just be another one."

"Indigolin never said anything about this to me," mused Peckett.

"I think he thought he could sort of get it through the back door with me more easily than if he broached this delicate subject with you, Ray. You know that agency accountant woman has him doing homework, studying John Donne, and he wanted to sort of weave this in as a private joke between the two of them, hidden within the film. The Metaphysical Poets, just like the surrealists, were noted for making connections between completely unconnected things, and he is trying to show her that he has made the connection between John Donne and Christopher Columbus discovering America. Are we going to do it?" Don asked.

"What else have we got to lose?" Peckett enquired rhetorically. "What is the connection anyway?"

"Damned if I know," answered Don.

Licence my roving hands, and let them go
Before, behind, between, above, below.
O my America! My new-found-land,
My kingdom, safeliest when with one man mann'd,
My mine of precious stones. My Empirie,
How blest am I in this discovering thee.

"We got any elephants in this script, Ray?"

"Not yet, Don. Why do you ask?"

"I was just thinking about the John Donne quote about the elephant. You know *Nature's great masterpiece, an Elephant. The only harmless great thing.*"

"Yes, I see where you're coming from, Don," Ray Peckett said. "There's a lot of awareness of bullying."

"But here's a big, harmless vegetarian."

"And you could say that Indigolin himself was a great thing. I don't mean in stature, but in his undoubted achievements. But he's very modest about it. He's not all shouty or in your face."

"Exactly!"

"But I'm afraid we don't have any parts for elephants in this script, Don."

Preserving the Environment in a V12 Off-Roader

Indigolin had returned from his disappointing dove shoot at Taroudant and was taking a coffee with his director.

"Ti, explain one thing to me. If you have such impeccable green credentials, how do you justify a Lamborghini Urus?"

"Wally, the V12 engine is quite thirsty if driven around town, but on a run in the countryside, I get thirty miles to the gallon and it has very low emissions. If any manufacturer offered an electric, long range off-road alternative, I would have to consider it very carefully. I attempt to be responsible, and I am also very actively involved in putting content back into the planet. But there is a happy medium between putting something back, on the one hand, and being a fanatical zealot, on the other."

"So, by putting back, do you mean that, like every time you drive it you plant some trees or something?"

"Wally, I am involved in something along those lines, but the carbon trading process that you described is now evolved to a callous, commercial industry as toxic as any of the emissions it purports to counter-balance. So let's just say that I'm doing my own thing, and when it's ready and I roll it out in Mahé, I think you will better understand me."

After Yoga

"Good morning, Ms Broadsword."

"Good morning. I'm afraid you have the better of me. I don't know your name."

"I'm Elena Troy."

"Are you an actress, Elena?"

Elena noted the diva's deliberate non-use of the gender-neutral address, and it pleased her.

"No, Ms Broadsword. I'm here to help Mr Indigolin fix his books."

"Mr Indigolin has two sets of books, Elena. Books of account, and storybooks; and from what I understand, they're both badly in need of fixing."

"I'm an accountant."

"Isn't that what the boring people in Monty Python used to say?"

"Accountancy Shanty in *Meaning of Life*."

"Accountant pirates; accountant lion-tamers."

"You know, Ms Broadsword, Monty Python turned a whole generation off the idea of training to become accountants, so the boring few of us who persevered despite the reach of the Pythons, were a scarce commodity, and able to command much higher rewards than we could ever have dreamt of. Every night when I say my prayers, I include one for Cleese, Palin, Gillam, Jones and Idle."

"Is that a figure of speech, or do you really say your prayers, Elena?"

"It's not a figure of speech. I'm a Roman Catholic, Ms Broadsword."

"I'm not a believer, but, having acted the part of the most Catholic Queen most of my adult life, as I grow older, I find I am more and more attracted towards all the pomp and pageantry. The whole idea of Rome, the Vatican City, the Swiss Guard. I mean to say, I don't believe in any of the things Catholics believe in, but I adore the outward way in which they express their beliefs."

"And the fact that the things they chose to believe in are wholly unbelievable!"

"I heard you're teaching Tinctorio Indigolin English, Miss Troy."

"Well, not exactly English, but a facet of English literature. We're doing

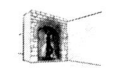

John Donne together. Did you read English at university?"

"Unfortunately not, Elena. I qualified for Cambridge, but my family didn't have enough money to educate the boys as well as the girls, so I had to forego that opportunity."

"I never understood those choices. The males have physical strength. There's plenty of jobs for people with physical strength. Education should be the privilege of the weaker sex."

"If my father had been a woman, Elena, I'm sure he would have agreed with you."

"What would your father think about you doing a full frontal scene in a movie, Ms Broadsword?"

She laughed. "Despite the fact that you're the Catholic, not me, I think he would have sent me to a nunnery."

"In the Ophelia sense?"

"Nunnery being Elizabethan slang for a brothel, yes, that sense as well!!"

"You know, the latest scholarly wisdom is that Ophelia was suffering from PTSD."

"God help us! Why does every generation always have to bend everything and everyone to their own experiences?"

"Isn't that precisely how writers like Shakespeare continue to be relevant, Ms Broadsword?"

"And, I suppose, sex never goes out of fashion."

"Do you think it was wrong for Mr Indigolin to ask you to do that scene?"

"Good heavens, no, Elena. That scene's nothing to do with Mr Indigolin. He just bought the project from the previous guy, and inherited the obligation to pay me US$5m for doing it, an obligation that he met."

"Do you think it's empowering?"

"For God's sake! Why is it that every time a woman does something because she's getting paid a lot of money for doing it, she feels the need to try to rationalise it on the basis that it is somehow empowering? It's just a callous commercial transaction. *Do I think it's empowering?"* She mimicked. "What I think is that men are going to toss themselves off, Elena! That's what I think. But being given US $5M for providing the material, especially at my age, that *is* empowering! Finally, Hugh Hefner can whack himself off to someone his own age!"

Oscietra

"To what do I owe this honour?" Celia Broadsword was in the director's Airstream, seated side by side to him at the narrow teak table with the brass corners. In front of them, Wally Pfister had just set down a 250 gram tin of Oscietra caviar with all the trimmings, and he was now busying himself splashing neat vodka onto the rocks.

"Hope you like it, Celia. I asked Ti to pick it up and bring it over with him on his PJ."

"Doesn't he want it for himself, darling?"

"Turns out he doesn't approve of caviar, or vodka, or anything Russian. He says they're irredeemable. But I'm not clear if it's their politics or their cuisine he disapproves of."

"Honey! You've got the blinis and the sour cream and everything!"

"No point in doing things by halves, Celia. When I was a pimply adolescent, I used to have posters of you up on my bedsit walls. Never in my wettest, wildest fantasies did I imagine that one day I'd be directing you in a big budget movie, that one day you'd be sat right next to me, sharing caviar and vodka in my Airstream. Now tell me, is everything all right for you? I mean, I appreciate that things aren't ideal being in the middle of nowhere here, with no spa or proper hairdressers. Is there anything I can do to make anything a bit better for you?"

"Well, Wally, if anyone had told me thirty years ago that at the grand old age of eighty-five, directors would be asking me to do sex scenes, I would have felt, how can I put this? a bit equivocal, but having to perform those scenes with someone I divorced twenty years ago, and having to pretend I'm enjoying it, that's going to stretch my acting abilities to the limit."

"You've been paid an extra five million dollars for that twenty second scene."

"It's going to challenge Colman too, because twenty seconds was fifteen seconds longer than he ever managed during our marriage."

"And the reason you're being paid all that money is because there's a huge demand for that. You give other women confidence and you give the right sort of men the hots."

"Really, Wally? Would you consider yourself the right sort of man?"

"Celia, I promise you, I've got a hard-on right now just talking about it."

Under the narrow table, she placed her heavily be-ringed fingers proprietorially over his crotch. "So you do!" She wondered.

"To reiterate what I said earlier," he continued, "if anyone had told me twenty years ago that the screen goddess, Celia Broadsword, would have my cock in her hand one day, I'd have said that could never happen even in my wildest dreams; but here we are, and here we are. The cinema-going public aren't interested in silly little girls taking their kit off. If they want that they've got the Internet.

"They want to see a proper, grown-up diva taking the picklock to fantasies buried so deep in their psyches, they never imagined could be released, fantasies they've been having about that very woman for decades, and now, she's finally going to uncork the interminable balls-ache they've nursed all their adult lives. Yes, yes, yes; it's gonna be mega. The Genii is coming out of the lamp! I'm just so sorry that it has to be with your ex."

"Why are you so sorry?" She still hadn't released his cock.

"Tell you the truth? I'm just really sorry it isn't with me."

"You know, so am I," she said. "You're the director. You can do what you want. Why don't you get your scriptwriters to do something about it?"

"Tell me," Pfister probed. "I once read that Colman Hunt threatened to kill a guy he thought had been sleeping with you. Was that true?"

"It was worse than true," she confided. "First, there was no question of the guy actually *sleeping* with me. Just looking at me in a funny way was enough to set Colman off, and secondly, he didn't *threaten* to kill the guy, he *attempted* to. Attempted murder! He shot him with the Portuguese duelling pistols that we had on set. At point blank range. In the face. Fortunately, he had no idea how to fire the things properly because Paddy Oculus always did all that sort of stuff for him. But the other guy still had to have his eyebrows tattooed back on after and lost half an ear.

"Studio sorted the guy out financially and he signed an NDA. I don't think it was supposed to be a lesson so much for the guy as a kind of vicarious lesson for me. Colman's the most jealous man I've ever come across in my entire life. He was criminally possessive with me. He couldn't have me himself; he just never rose to the occasion; he bats for the other side; but it didn't prevent him from doing everything in his power to make sure no-one else could have me either. And he's thoughtless of the consequences.

"The fact that he could have spent the rest of his life behind bars never crossed his mind. Since the time he was a child star, he's lived virtually all his life on set. There was nothing he could screw up that the studio couldn't fix for him. It never occurred to him that they wouldn't be able to sort out a murder, if he'd actually been able to fire the piece properly."

"Well, I hear what you say, Celia, but I'm afraid it's just not going in down there."

She squeezed harder. "No, they've got a mind of their own, haven't they?" She kissed him full on the lips, and placed his hand on her breast.

"Do the scene with me, Wally. Go on."

"Celia, I'd be very happy to do a dress rehearsal with you right now, but I don't want any false pretences. Me doing the scene for the film would be out of the question."

"How come? We all know the script's not even been written yet."

"For the simple reason that I don't bear any physical resemblance whatsoever to your ex. How about you do the scene with his stunt double, Paddy Oculus?"

"Oculus is a bigger girl's blouse than Hunt is. If I'm shooting a nude scene at eighty-five, it's going to have to be perfect."

"That's why I'm directing it, Celia."

"That just makes it worse."

"How come?"

"Because everyone knows Wally Pfister doesn't shoot in soft focus."

"Oops!"

"Even if Paddy could steel himself to do the scene, Colman would attempt to murder him after."

"You know, Celia, an idea is forming in my head. I heard Colman's got an identical twin? As far as I know, the twin's straight. If we shoot the scene with the twin, you're not telling me that Colman would try to murder his own twin now, are you?"

"No, but I happen to know for a fact that the twin would definitely try to murder Col, because it's all happened before."

"But that isn't your worry. Let's suppose, just for argument's sake, they do murder each other? Not your problem, is it? From what I hear, they're like two cheeks of the same arse."

"Actually, Wally, this particular arse has three cheeks."

Horizontal Pin Stripes

Indigolin was constantly jiggling about like a fidget. Just looking at him in that crazy blue legume outfit made Pfister perspire. As Indigolin moved, the facets of his suit caught the light, and it became apparent to Pfister that this wasn't just another common or garden electric blue suit. There was a kind of luminous green horizontal hoop running through it, but the green thread was so fine, it couldn't have been woven in. The only way Indigolin could have attained something so fine and so dazzlingly bright was if the pattern for the suit had been etched out by the coherent light of an industrial laser.

In the background, Noah was manhandling a huge orange pig-skin container from off the back of the pick-up he'd driven in on. The pig-skin container looked like it might be housing a sea mine or a barrage balloon.

As Indigolin moved and gesticulated, it was as if his legume blue suit was complicit in all his movements, emphasising them, winking at you, giving you the eye, as Celia would have put it. There was something lizard-like about the green LEDs, the lines were, how should one put this? Reptiliniar. Damn the man! He couldn't even get dressed without donning controversy.

"Mightn't you be more comfortable in something a little lighter, Ti?"

Wally Pfister, dressed in cargo shorts, sandals and a Richard III tee-shirt with *'And thus I clothe my naked villainy'* stencilled on it, gazed at Indigolin in his two piece legume suit, and overheated just looking at him. It was forty degrees in the desert.

"I'm cool, thanks, Wally. In fact, I'm as cool as a cucumber. If I was any cooler, I'd be sinking the Titanic. The hotter it gets, the cooler I am. My suits are made from highly technical material, so the more of me it covers up, the lower it takes my temperature. You've heard of shot silk, right?"

"Uh huh."

"Well, my suits are shot with a filamental fine stripe of super coolant, same as we put in the heat retardant panels on the space shuttle so it doesn't burn up on re-entry. It's a technical ice vest, like drivers wear when they're trying to get a thousand miles to the gallon out of their cars by not turning on the air conditioning when it's fifty degrees outside. What you've got to understand is that my Blue Molecule is just a delivery mechanism for other stuff, and right now it's delivering refrigerant. The more I jiggle around, agitating it, the colder it gets. I'm like a heat pump in reverse.

"*A propos* of which," added Indigolin, "Noah, do you have the hat box to hand?"

"I do, boss!" Noah cried, continuing to drag the orange pig-skin monstrosity off the back of his pick-up.

Indigolin crossed over to the hat box, and unclicked the three brass fasteners, unlocking its contents. Sheathed inside in the burgundy crushed velvet-lined receptacle was the largest turban Wally had ever seen. But it was in Indigolin's legume blue technical fabric.

"Don't you think it's on the large side?" Wally asked.

"Gotta keep a cool head, man!" Tinctorio joked. "It's made from my molecule. The bigger it is, the cooler Brunswick Holt's got to be. It also has certain other hidden properties that Brunswick Holt doesn't need to know about; but I'll share them with you after.

"Brunswick Holt's wearing this turban in the Courtyard of the Twelve Marble Lions when he delivers the Sultan's letter to Celia. Special request from our sponsors," explained Indigolin.

"When are we due to go to the Courtyard of the Twelve Lions, Ti? That's in the Alhambra."

"We're not going to Spain, Wally. You do it all on the green screen and we'll add The Jungle Book in once we're back in Soho."

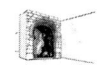

Nomad

"Stop making a storm in a tea cup, Noah."

"Boss, I'm not exaggerating. We can't even pay the staff."

"Noah, it's only the 20th of the month. None of the staff are due to be paid yet. We'll have this sorted before the end of the month."

"I just don't get why you went out and did it without discussing it with anyone, Mr Indigolin."

"Noah, ever since I was a kid, I wanted to own my own bank. You know what all my aunts and uncles used to buy me on birthdays and Christmas? Money boxes. I had locked tin boxes, cars with slots on top, piggies, cows, jars, policemen with holes in their helmets. I had them all lined up on the bookshelf in my bedroom.

"You know there's Harley Street where all the doctors live and Carnaby Street where everything cool in clothing used to be. Well I had Moneybox Street. But that was when I was a lad, but now I'm a man, I put aside childish things, and decided to acquire my own bank."

"I can see the temptation, boss. But there must be lots of banks out there. Why did you have to acquire the company's own bankers and get our shares suspended?"

"What do the mountaineers say? Because it was there. Noah, when the shares come back on the market in a day or two, I promise you, they'll be trading at stratospheric levels. You know what's the USP about Indigolin Industries? That none of the funds trust us. No pension fund would ever dream of entrusting their clients' monies to us.

"Only dangerous people, risk takers, chancers, inveterate gamblers put their money with us, and that's how I like it. If the day comes that we go mainstream and the likes of Aviva and Zurich want to place their funds with Flyover Life Sciences, I'll pull the shutters down, because Tinctorio Indigolin's trademark is that he is the last outpost remaining of the untamed and the restless. We're edgy.

Dogs have fleas, dealers have addicts, Aman Hotels have their Aman junkies. We have Investors that are Indigolinally Inclined. I, I, I, that's 3i's, right!"

"Yeah, I get it!"

"When I started up in business, my money wasn't good enough for a lot of people. They wouldn't deal with me without proof of funds." For emphasis, he made quotation marks with his fingers around *proof of funds*.

"Proof of funds, or a banker's draft, or a personal guarantee from somebody else, somebody of substance. Anybody who wasn't Tinctorio Indigolin! Noah, as soon as the shares are un-suspended, I can write my own banker's drafts like other people write cheques. I myself will be what they call *cleared funds*. I'll be able to walk into any casino in the world and cash my own chips.

"You remember how they used to qualify our accounts? Shattering performance, year after year; but the auditors would always include some sniping, gratuitous solvency qualification in the Notes to the Accounts or in the Auditor's Report; you know: *'Reliant upon the continued support of their bankers.'* "*The accounts have been prepared on a going concern basis, because the director, Mr Indigolin, has assured us, they aren't mechula."* Well bollocks to all that! I've just bought the bank!"

"And your shares are suspended, boss."

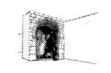

A Symbiotic Relationship

Inside Wally's Woodie-Wagon, Celia saw he had separate, colour-coded recycling bins for his different sorts of rubbish.

"You're a bit of a climate activist on the quiet, aren't you, Wally?"

"How so, Celia?"

"I mean, the Woodie-Wagon thing, your fascination with living a simpler life, like a Berber nomad."

"It's nothing. All it takes is for each one of us to do a little bit. Having a rowdy, opinionated 0.01% of the population go totally over the top isn't going to make any impact whatsoever. We've all got to make some small contribution of our own; we have to crowd-fund the planet."

"But you keep that to yourself most of the time, Wally. You hide your light under a bushel, don't you?"

"Celia, if I get up on a soap box and tub-thump about being greener, people are going to say I'm a hypocrite because I fly a helicopter, so I just try to do my own little piece."

"And is it hypocritical to fly around in a helicopter, Wally?"

"Celia, it's not as though it's my primary means of transport. As you know, I rise at dawn and I do my yoga. Most of the time I walk or jog around from place to place if it's not too far, and if it's further, I take my bike; but I don't go for a pointless run on a cinder track round some urban park every morning for the specific purpose of getting my exercise. I get my exercise as a normal by-product of being a human being. The helicopter thing just takes us back to our discussion about hovellers."

"You mean the hove's and hove not's?"

"Precisely; for a lot of noisy people, it's considered a sin to earn more money than a nurse or a teacher. If you've got a helicopter, *ergo* you must feel that you're entitled and be a bad guy. But I don't happen to feel entitled. I'm really very grateful for all of the advantages I have been afforded in my life, whether it's searching out locations in a helicopter or getting to direct a film starring Celia Broadsword, or, dare I say it, the privilege of making love to her.

"However, with a few notable exceptions, like that Thunberg woman, most people's primary mode of transport involves an internal combustion engine in some shape or form, even if they don't own their own. Once you allow for that, you have to allow for tankers, huge container boats, Indigolin's private jet and my chopper."

"How come, Wally?"

"Because they are simply different stations within the fractionating tower. Do you know what a fractionating tower is, Celia?"

"I'm afraid I don't, but I think you're about to tell me, Wally."

"When you pump the crude oil out of the ground, it has to be refined before it's any use, and that takes place within the refinery. I'm sure you've seen refineries when your plane comes in to land at Dubai. In the refinery, there's a great big column known as a fractionating tower or some writers call it a fractionating column. Think of it like a lift shaft with a lift that stops at lots of different floors.

"On each floor, there is a great big tray or bucket. The buckets collect all the different by-products of the refining process. The top bucket is dedicated to the petroleum that runs your car. The petroleum is the *crème de la crème* of the refining process; but the lower down the hierarchy you get, the cruder the by-products, so that, down the very bottom of the tower, let's say at the mezzanine level, the buckets are full of sludge and bunker fuel.

"But that's the very stuff that my chopper and Indigolin's PJ run on, and it's that sludge, unusable for anything else, that the cruise ships run on and the tankers that travel round the world delivering the black gold. You can't put it back in the ground. What I'm trying to say, Celia, is that it's a mutual relationship.

"As long as we're going to want to continue using the stuff in the top floors of the lift shaft, we're going to be producing the stuff that ends up in the bottom floors as well, because one is an unavoidable by-product of the other, and there's no environmentally friendly way you can dispose of the stuff at the bottom of the lift shaft, except that people like me and Indigolin are getting rid of it by burning it in our engines."

"So you're saying it's like a symbiotic relationship."

"Yeah, like that bird that cleans the teeth of the crocodile."

"The plover."

Wally paused to take stock of this. Underneath the façade of froth and frivolity, *femme fatale* and fandango that Celia Broadsword chose to project, there was a whole untapped world of wisdom, discernment, percipience and intuition that a better man than he could spend a lifetime unravelling. Eventually, he just said:

"Celia, you know the name for everything."

"Wally, don't you remember I played Cleopatra?"

"Of course, you did."

"And I think the crocodile is the most obscene life-form on the planet that makes no contribution to anything else, and I wouldn't even have one as a handbag."

"You were an amazing Cleopatra," he recalled. "Age cannot wither you. Celia, do you think that Colman can pull off this King Ferdinand thing one more time, or is he past it? I'm worried about this inchoate screenplay, you know."

"Wally, I'm remembering that horrible review he got for the last series. The critic who took that quote from Eugene Field and turned it around."

"Huh, Eugene Field?"

"The critic said that Colman Hunt played the King all series as though he was expecting someone else to play the Ace."

"Pure vitriol. But let's face it, even with this new script, it's not very original. Hasn't Antonio Banderas already done it as a mini-series?"

"Wally, you know there's only one reason anybody's going to come and see this film."

Fires in the Desert

Edgar Ash, Mohammed, and Pat Oculus were sharing a smoke on the steps of Ash's Bowlus Road Chief Aluminium Trailer with Agent Troy sipping a glass of pomegranate juice. There was no light pollution and the sky's canopy was awash with a million stars. Edgar Ash could actually name a great many of the stars and constellations above their heads, as he'd had to learn them for a part a few months back when he was playing Nicolaus Copernicus in a series that was intended to reposition Poland. Nowadays it was a nation of plumbers, but in the sixteenth century it had bred polymaths and astronomers such as Copernicus.

However, Ash was worried he might sound corny, and that Elena might think he was hitting on her if he initiated a discussion about the firmament. As well as the countless pinpricks of light above them, Ash became aware of a great many lights twinkling in the desert in front of him. But there wasn't supposed to be anything else out there. That's why they called it The Last Great Empty Space.

"What are those lights over there?" He asked.

"Look like fires to me," said Oculus.

"How can you have fires in a desert?" Ash queried.

"Clearly, you never heard about The Devil's Cigarette Lighter," said Pat. "I doubled for the guy playing Red Adair. That's what I call an action movie!"

"Could be," ventured Elena Troy, seeking to be more constructive and also move the conversation on from the usual narcissism, "that we're observing some atmospheric phenomenon; you know, like Marfa lights. We could just be looking at light refracted from our own Airstreams when the hot desert starts cooling down at night and the light waves get bent."

"Marfa lights. They like Marlboro Lites?" Pat asked.

"Didn't the Stones sing about them?" Ash offered.

"Sure," said Agent Troy, "*No Spare Parts* on the *Some Girls* album."

"But the fires seem to be moving," persisted Ash.

"Let's tap up Mohammed for some local knowledge," suggested Pat Oculus. "Mohammed."

"Yes, boss."

"What are we looking at over there?"

"Berber camp fires, boss," said Mohammed.

"What are they doing?"

"They live in the desert, boss. That's what they supposed to do. Nomadic tribes. Caravanserai. You know, *Keep on trucking!*"

"But I've seen the fires every day this week, Mohammed," said Ash. "Why would Berbers be camping here and not moving on?"

They seemed to have plumbed the depths of Mohammed's knowledge of Berbers, because he did not answer. Elena got the impression it was a class thing, as though Mohammed regarded the Berbers as a caste below his own, about which he did not wish to admit to more than a passing knowledge. Just enough for a footnote in a tourist guidebook, but not wanting to admit he could write a whole chapter.

"There's Tarquin Stamp, the A & E guy over there," observed Troy. "Why don't we ask him?"

"Accident & Emergency?" Oculus queried.

"No. He's the Authenticity and Ethnicity Consultant. We couldn't get a licence to film here without taking him onto the payroll."

"Oh, I get it. More dirhams for the local boys. Hey, Tarquin!" Ash called out. "Why don't you come and join us?"

Stamp stumbled over in his denim jeans and cowboy boots. "How can I help you?" He enquired.

"We were wondering about those fires in the desert," said Ash.

"Just Berbers," said Stamp. "Nothing to worry about."

"But what do they do?"

"Berbers?" Stamp mused. "They're as old as civilisation. They're very good guides, the only people on earth that can plot a route across the desert by day or by night. They take their bearings from the stars, like sailors do. The Sahara Desert is bigger than the whole continent of Australia, and it's almost entirely featureless, and what features you may see here today will get blown away by tomorrow, and most of it's not accessible to your satnav. The Berbers are the only living beings that can find their way across it. They still drive their camel caravan trails hundreds and hundreds of miles."

"What do they live on?"

"This desert covers tens of thousands of square miles; it used to be grassland and woodland. The Berbers used to be arable farmers, but their animals ate up all the grass; that and climate change; all that's left now is this desert. But the

Berbers continue to follow the ancient routes. It's a nomadic patriarchal society. All the tribal heads claim direct descent from the prophet Mohammed; the women weave the blue clothes, which is all they wear.

"In the desert sand storms, they draw their blue scarves up around their faces for protection and their skins get stained with the blue dye, which is how come they're also known as the Blue Men of the Desert. They know where every watering hole is, every oasis, which ones are for real, and which ones are mirages, which ones you can find dates growing, and which dates you should swipe left because they'll poison you. They are good at carpentry, weaving, leather work, and metal work. They take the end products to the souks and sell them. Those slippers you're wearing, you haggled for them in the souk, right?"

"Correct."

"Well, they could've been made by Berbers, but more likely came from a factory in China that's helping to make the Berbers extinct."

"Are they safe?"

"We talking about the slippers now, or the Berbers?"

"Berbers, silly!"

"Berbers like anybody else," said Stamp. "They have their good days and they have their bad days."

"Do they steal?" Oculus asked.

"It's said they're so light-fingered, they could give you a shave in your sleep without waking you."

"Fuck me!"

"But there must be hundreds of them out there!" Pat exclaimed. "What's to stop them attacking us and carrying Colman or Celia off for huge ransoms?"

"Hey, what about me?" Ash asked.

"I think that, after some initial discomfort, they'd be okay," said Agent Troy.

"How come?"

"I could tell you, but then I'd have to kill you," joked Troy.

"Seriously," persisted Ash.

"When I was going through the books, I read the K & R policy," explained Elena Troy.

"And what's that when it's at home?" Ash asked.

"Kidnap and Ransom insurance," said Troy. "It's a product that's out there, but doesn't often get talked about for the specific reason that if you do talk about it, it vitiates the policy."

"Meaning?"

"If the kidnappers know you're carrying millions of dollars of K & R cover, the price goes up when they negotiate for the release of the hostages. The policy requires the insured not to admit any such insurance exists, or that cancels the insurance. The insurance underwriters have specialist negotiators who take the situation over and do the negotiating with the kidnappers."

"Wow!" said Oculus. "I've learned two sets of acronym in the space of two minutes. Now I know about A & E and K & R. I didn't know such things existed."

"Best keep it that way," said Troy, especially because, if anybody's going to get kidnapped round here, it had better be the understudy, not the real deal.

Turntable

In the Woodie-Wagon, Wally extracted an Eartha Kitt LP from its sleeve and put it on the turntable. He was listening to her rendition of *C'est si bon* and reading the sleeve notes, which contained a quotation from the singer:

"It's all about falling in love with yourself, and sharing that love with someone who appreciates you, rather than looking for love to compensate for a self-love deficit."

He thought she was way ahead of her time. Then he read:

"Truth is a theory that is constantly being disproved. Only lies, it seems, go on forever."

Then:

"I am learning all the time. The tombstone will be my diploma."

By a process that he was unsure of, Celia had slipped into his caravan and was reading the sleeve notes over his shoulder. He twisted his head round to look at her.
"She also appeared in a number of decent films," Celia began.
"Some good, some bad, and some ugly," pronounced Walter.
"Orson Wells called her the most exciting woman in the world."
"Yes, said Wally, and at a time when he had the likes of Sophia Loren, Marilyn Monroe and Audrey Hepburn to compare her to. But he chose Eartha Kitt."
"He did."
"Celia, do you think that huskies have husky voices?"
"I think the adjective comes from husks, Wally, as in dried up like a husk; like a dry cough."

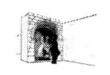

"I see."

"Trust you to have vinyl, Wally. In this caravan, where space is such a premium, only you would have a baby grand and a turntable, when you could have a docking station for your telephone."

"I'm old school, Celia. Listening to music isn't something I do in the background whilst I'm driving the car, or commuting on the train, doing the housework, or because I feel that I need a little something extra to put you in the right mood. It's a holistic experience that includes admiring the cover art, reading the sleeve notes, withdrawing the recording from its envelope and holding the disc up to the light, checking for any scratches or finger marks, watching the way the light bounces off the grooves.

"I am fascinated by the process that goes into bringing this product to the market, just the same as if I buy a book, I want to go into a bookstore in Tottenham Court Road or Hay on Wye or wherever, and I want to pick up the book and handle it. I want to see what images they decided to put on the cover, smell the ink, look at the choice of paper stock they decided to print it on, and run my fingers over it to get the texture and the weight. All this is as important a part of the experience to me as sitting down and reading it. If anything, the reading is actually an anti-climax after so much of a build-up. You know, I could never do an audio book. For me, consuming an artistic product has to engage as many of our five senses as possible. In the same way, I wouldn't do an audio book, I wouldn't play my music on an iPod."

"But you're making a movie for streaming?"

"That's what we thought when another director started this project; but I'm moving away from that idea. I am now leaning in favour of a proper theatrical release."

"Just as soon as we get a proper script, honey."

"It's not that I'm saying there's anything intrinsically wrong with streamed films. They have some great content. It's just that, for me, the process all fits within an evolving continuum, no single stage of which I could bear to dispense with. If I go to see a film, the process typically begins with me standing on some platform on the London Underground and inter-acting with a poster.

"Then I get all hyped-up by the word-of-mouth or the whisper campaign and the reviews. I like to stand in line at the playhouse, waiting to buy my ticket; then I take my seat and watch all the adverts and the trailers for the next films coming up or the films that are playing at the other cinemas within the same auditorium. Then the lights come back on for a while so that people can buy some more popcorn or take a leak, and then follows that amazing, quintessential moment when the lights dim for the second time, and you know that it's about to start. You know where the world's best picture house is, Celia?"

"Not yet, honey, but you're about to tell me."

"The Vernissage in Zermatt."

"What's so special about that?"

"The film posters are propped up outside in the snow. You go in through a modest door, and you have to go down a spiral staircase of seasoned wood that you just know has been locally sourced from the ski slopes. You enter a bar area with a roaring fireplace suspended in a glass box. From the bar, you can see the adverts and trailers playing on the screen by looking through, like, storm windows, opening to the cinema pit below the bar. You continue down the spiral staircase to the auditorium.

"There, you make yourself comfy in a leather sofa or armchair. You've got a table with a lit candle in front of you where your dinner's going to be served. The girl comes and takes your order for dinner and drinks. At this point, the front of the auditorium is a wooden-floored disco from the night before. There are huge chandeliers hanging down. "Then, once you're seated and sipping your bottle of wine, the chandeliers swing away, like the opening of *The Phantom of the Opera*; the remaining armchairs are pushed into the seating area in front of you, and the credits start rolling at the same time as the storm windows from the bar upstairs close electronically, stopping the people in the bar from getting a free movie for the price of a Pilsner; but also completely sound-proofing everything. You have your first course and main course watching the film. Then there's a break when they bring your desert and opportunity for more drinks. Presumably, that is when the projectionist changes the reels. The Dolby sound there is just amazing, and the food's pretty damned good too."

"And how was the ski-ing, Wally?"

"No idea, honey. I only go there for the picture house. It brings a shiver all down my spine, just the same as you do, Celia."

"You're a complicated individual, Mr Pfister. I guess you know what's coming next. When you take a girl out on a date, when you get her in the sack, is that an anti-climax to some process that began playing out in your head much earlier? Where does the process begin with you?"

"Celia, honey, in your case, I would say that we are looking at a process that started about 35 or 40 years ago and is only now just coming to maturity. And no, it is anything but an anti-climax. It's what Nietzsche would have called a glorious affirmation of self."

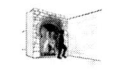

A Nocturnal Visit

By the light of an almost full moon, the twelve-year-old Berber boy pedalled the bicycle two sizes too small for him away from the desert fires of his bivouac towards the twinkling lights of the film crew's Airstream encampment. Dismounting, he leaned his bike noiselessly up against the side of Colman Hunt's caravan, and rearranged his large spectacles that had fallen down his nose during the bumpy ride. The light-fingered intruder didn't intend to steal anything, just help himself to some souvenirs of no financial value, relic-like objects that he could associate with the gods of the silver screen through whose hands they had passed.

Colman Hunt saw no need to lock the outer door of his trailer, but if he had, the boy would have picked the lock with ease. He crept inside and pressed the door closed behind him. Despite the fact that he was now in his seventies, Hunt never killed all the lights, whether he was staying in the Airstream, in a hotel suite, or one of his homes.

As he'd grown older, and his prostrate had grown larger, leading to nocturnal wanderings in the direction of the bathroom, this habit had come to make more sense. However, there had never been a time when he hadn't slept with a night light of some description. The truth was that the great Colman Hunt who had played every hero from Achilles to Alexander the Great, was scared of the dark.

Inside the caravan, the door to Colman's sleeping quarters was slightly ajar and through the chink the lad could hear Colman snuffling in his sleep, like an animal. The boy stroked the peach fuzz that was just starting to sprout on his chin, and contemplated his surroundings. He was pleased to note that the large scrapbook that he had inspected and filmed last night, remained firmly closed on the counter.

For a while, he marvelled at the collection of all Hunt's awards and trophies, displayed in glass cabinets. He took a photo of them, being careful to check that the flash was disabled, so as not to wake up the owner of the glittering prizes.

On the desk in front of him sat the first twenty-odd pages of the new screenplay the scriptwriters had churned out. Taking care not to make a noise pulling the chair out from under the desk, the boy sat down and began reading the script by the illumination of Hunt's safety lighting. It was a very poor piece of writing.

Picking up a red biro from Hunt's desktop blotter set bearing the name of the five star hotel Hunt had borrowed it from, the boy scored through the title, and began methodically rewriting the screenplay. About forty-five minutes later, having completed the edit, he wiped his bottom on the old cover page, left that page on Colman's desk, and crept back through the outer door, having removed nothing except the rewritten script and a glass paperweight from the desk.

He descended the metal stairs from the caravan onto the sand, balanced the edited pages on the bottom step of Hunt's Airstream, and used the paperweight to ensure the rewritten papers didn't blow away in the night. Then he retrieved his bicycle, hitched up his blue Djellaba to raise his right leg over the crossbar, and pedalled off into the moonlight.

Shit Happens

The morning after the sighting of the Marfa lights, Patrick Oculus entered Colman's Airstream, bearing a breakfast tray laden with a Styrofoam cup of coffee, freshly squeezed pomegranate juice, and a croissant from Aka's hospitality tent, for his buddy's breakfast, as he did every morning. Despite enjoying increasingly more infrequent carnal relations, the two of them didn't enjoy spending the night together, because Oculus snored like a rhinoceros, and furthermore because the configuration of Hunt's Airstream would only permit sufficient space for a single bed.

Hunt had specified so many glass cabinets to house all his movie memorabilia and trophies, that the manufacturers couldn't shoehorn a double bed in there as well. Colman Hunt picked up the first page of his new script to ask Paddy's opinion of it, and was troubled to find someone had wiped his arse on it.

"Is this your shit on the script, Paddy?" He asked.

Patrick inspected the soiled page and replied: "I wish it was. I haven't had a decent movement since we came to fucking Morocco."

"Oh, Morocco Bound, huh?"

"It's the script that's shit, Colman."

"Where's the rest of it gone?" Hunt asked.

"Only that page was there, Colman," Pat replied.

When Paddy opened the door of the trailer to dump the dirty page in the bin outside, he noticed a small sheaf of over-written pages stacked to the side of the bottom step waiting for him, weighted down by a glass paperweight that he recognised from Colman's desk. He must have missed them when he came in, because he couldn't see over the top of the breakfast tray he'd been carrying.

Taking the small bundle of pages back into the Airstream, he presented them to Colman as though he was the postman delivering his mail in the morning. Colman looked it over. It was the script that he'd listlessly flicked through the previous evening, but it had been very heavily annotated in red biro, in fact the red biro that he noticed was now missing from his blotter set. The cover page had been removed, and that was the page that his mysterious editor had wiped his bum on. The top page now was the title page.

The old title had been struck out and replaced with a new title:

Bab al-Mahruq, or the Gate of the Burnt One

Colman licked his index finger and turned the page. From the off, this was the most stunning script he'd ever read. The first scene was shot in the Courtyard of the Twelve Lions in the Alhambra.

Virtually every syllable of the screenplay had been crossed out and in the double-spacing between the lines and down the margins, the editor had substituted new characters, new dialogue, new locations, and new instructions for the actors. In red biro, right down to the edges of the pages, typographer's symbols were clustered: →, ↙↕↔↘, directing the reader to numerous riders written at the top or the bottom or the back of the page cross-referenced by the corresponding arrow. The rewritten script was an immeasurable improvement on what had gone before. In fact, he mused, it was a dramatic improvement, and he was using the word *dramatic* in its literal sense. This was a script he could really engage with and emote to.

Colman was visibly crestfallen when the story ended abruptly after the first twenty-odd pages. He was at a loss to understand how or why or by whom these pages had come into being. He had been afforded a Pisgah glimpse into the script of the film that he should be making, as opposed to the crap that he was lending his name to, but it was just an incomplete shard, a teaser.

He wrote down the words *Bab al-Mahruq* on a Post-it note, and rolled them round on his tongue like he was already learning his lines.

As the next night fell, from the Berber camp opposite, the pudgy, bespectacled twelve-year-old boy, wrapped in blue robes, once again furiously pedalled a pushbike sized for an eight-year-old. The tyres were deflated to cope with the sandy terrain. By the time he reached Colman Hunt's Airstream, it was pitch dark. He didn't knock on the door, but like a phantasmagorical newspaper boy, he deposited a bundle tied in string and containing the next twenty pages. Then he pedalled off on his undersized bike.

When Paddy Oculus arrived at Colman's trailer the next morning, carrying Colman's breakfast from Aka Akinyola's chow tent on a tray, there, perched on Colman's doorstep sat the next bundle of pages. He picked them up and placed them on the tray with the breakfast as though it was Colman's morning mail or newspaper. He took the breakfast and the fresh delivery of pages in to Colman.

Seeing the package in the now familiar red scrawl, Colman's fingers were trembling in appetency to get his hands on them, to find out what happened next, or more to the point, find out what the great Colman Hunt was going to do or say next. He'd heard of riddles wrapped in enigmas, but this had been a cliff-hanger ending *in medias res*. The first twenty pages hadn't even broken at the end of a sentence. But the pages that had just been delivered were completely consecutive, finishing off the sentence from the previous night, and starting the next one seamlessly.

Colman got his hole punch and a treasury tag and clipped the first and second set of pages together. He decided to read the whole thing again from the beginning.

The cover page said:

Bab al-Mahruq or
The Gate of the Burnt One

And beneath that:

Starring Colman Hunt
'So far so good,' he thought. He licked his fingers and turned the page.

DRAMATIS PERSONÆ

King Ferdinand II of Aragon	*COLMAN HUNT*
Queen Isabella of Aragon	*CELIA BROADSWORD*
Catherine of Aragon	*TBC*
Christopher Columbus	*Edgar Ash*
Boabdil el Chico, Muhammed XI of Granada	*Aderfi Benjelloun*
Morayma, his beautiful wife	*TBC*
Aixa, his powerful mother	*TBC*
Yusuf, 1st son to Boabdil & Morayma (dies aged 5)	*TBC*
Ahmed, 2nd son	*Badiss Slimani*

The dramatic person of John Donne in the cast list had been struck through in red biro.

Who the hell was Aderfi Benjelloun? He wondered. Who was this Slimy Badass? Must be the guy who wiped his bum on the previous script.

Colman licked his fingers and turned the page again. The subsequent page read

Exterior. A clear night with no light pollution. The Patio of the Twelve Marble Lions in the Alhambra. A torch boy hands a scroll to King Ferdinand of Aragon. King Ferdinand looks up at the stars.

KING FERDINAND: *In chapters of fire*
                                  Across the charcoal dome
                                  God's finger wrote
                                  Deus imperat astris.
                                  "God Rules the Stars."

Colman Hunt raised his eyes from the edited screenplay and said to himself: "Wow! Wow! And Wow!"

When Colman Hunt reads his lines, he reads them aloud but under his breath, owning them. As he read them, the hairs on his toupee stood up with excitement. He couldn't remember when he'd last felt like this. He was hooked on the poetry of his own lines. Even though he only understood about ten percent of the words that the anonymous author had put into his mouth, the lines read like poetry.

"Paddy!" He called out. "What's a *Triumphal Quadriga*?"

Oculus Googled it on his phone and told Colman that was what the four huge bronze horses outside St Mark's Cathedral in Venice were known as. Oculus continued reading from his Wikipedia, "It says the horses were stolen at the sack of Constantinople in 1204."

"And what's *Giza*?"

Paddy dutifully Googled that also. "It's not a what. It's a where," he explained. "It's the city in Egypt on the west bank of the Nile where the pyramids are."

"Oh, that makes sense now," Colman reflected. "I'm telling this torch boy that I'm going to build a pyramid of human skulls that will dwarf Giza."

"What's a torch boy?"

"I think a load of them run along beside my chariot at night time."

"And where does the *Quadriga* fit in, Col?"

"We seem to be engaged in a meaningful discussion about important stuff that's been looted, stolen. I mean, heritage stuff that should be given back."

"Like the Elgin marbles."

"Just so."

"I get it about the Elgin marbles, Colman, because they're just sitting in a museum. But St Mark's Cathedral is going to look kind of unfinished without those horses."

"Queen Isabella doesn't go in for the pyramid of skulls." Colman continued *précising* the pages. "She wants me to build my legacy with works of art. She says to me: *'Don't be ignoble, my liege. I'll have your finest artisans build you bronze horses bigger than the Triumphal Quadriga.'* Paddy, can you hear it? The words have a rhythm, as though they're sprung. *Big-ger than the trium-phal Quad-riga.* It's almost as if the bronze horses are stamping out the rhythm themselves with their hooves!"

"You're right!" Oculus cried. "*Build you bronze horses.* It's an iambic pentameter."

"You don't think that sounds woke?*"*

"It's woke, but it works, you know. Like Ozymandias' feet."

"No, I mean that word: *ignoble*. It's got a ring to it. Never really thought about *ignoble* before. And get this: after that I say *I'll ride in triumph through Persepolis*. That's got a ring to it too. Blow me down, it scans. It's all in iambic pentameters, like Shakespeare! Paddy, this is just getting better and better."

"I think it's Marlowe, Colman, not Shakespeare."

"Same difference, Paddy! Same guy!"

But then the substituted script came to an abrupt end, once again in the middle of a sentence.

Colman continued to read the teaser lying on his day bed like he was already trying to memorise his lines, He read them until he fell asleep. In his dreams, a voice in his ear kept urging him: *Don't be ignoble, my liege*, and he dreamt that he was having a discussion with his artisans about whether one needed planning permission to build a pyramid of human skulls. But he just shrugged it all off and replied: *I'll ride in triumph through Persepolis.*

At five o clock the next morning, just before sunrise, the furious pedalling newspaper boy delivered the next knuckle-biting instalment. After reading this, Colman decided to keep watch all night to find out where these pages were coming from. That was when the pages stopped coming. It was as if their unknown author was telling him, you had to believe in fairies. He had not believed. Colman had gone in search of objective empiricism, and now the pages had dried up.

But from that night forward, the boy delivered the pages to the Woodie-Wagon of Walter Pfister instead.

An Unexpected Visit

Colman Hunt knocked on the door of Wally's Woody-Wagon.

"Colman!" Wally cried with genuine pleasure and surprise. "Blow me down with a feather! You've left your trailer. To what do we owe this honour?"

"Thought I'd like to ride my Quadriga in triumph through Persepolis today." Colman said.

"What's a Quadriga, Colman? Sounds like the sort of Lambretta Tamburlaine the Great may have used."

Colman Hunt neither understood Wally's allusion, nor was he minded to embark upon a debate with him.

"Read this!" Was all he said.

Colman handed the first 60 pages of manuscript to Wally and asked him not to show it to anyone else and to meet up again as soon as he'd had a chance to read it. Wally noted to himself that they were clearly the prequel to the twenty pages he had received, and amended by the same editor in red biro.

Wally opened the first page to the *dramatis personae*. "Well, at least he's cut John Donne out!" He said approvingly.

"Yes," remarked Hunt. "But he's replaced him with a reference to a painting by Salvador Dali."

Then Hunt stumped off back to his own bus.

Wally looked at the sixty pages. He fast-forwarded to the very end, and noted that the twenty pages that had been deposited on the steps of his Woody-Wagon were indeed consecutive. The writing and the conceit were both very good indeed, although it wasn't easy to read as the author used every inch of the paper, above the lines, in between the lines, down the margins and all over the backs of the pages, like paper was a very precious commodity, which, concluded Wally, it was indeed.

However, it would be a lot easier to follow if he had his head scriptwriter, Ray Peckett, transcribe it, typed up in the conventional manner. Peckett would be pissed, because it was his script that the anonymous Bard had edited to oblivion. But Wally's job was to get a film in the can, not to worry about the hurt feelings or failings of his incompetent scriptwriters.

Rigmarole

Wally had the newly-printed pages curled up in his fist. He had the manuscript in his left hand and his phone in his right. Whoever the author was, he seemed to know more stuff than Wally did, because Wally was constantly having to check references on his phone. And every time he did so he found that the anonymous author had got it right and knew more about his subject matter than Wally did.

"This is completely amazing!" He declared.

"How so, honey?" Celia enquired.

Ignoring Colman Hunt's injunction to share the script with no-one else (an injunction that Wally considered Hunt had no authority to impose, as the script was not his property), Pfister was reviewing it with Celia Broadsword.

"Whoever the author of this script is, he is very specific about how and where he wants things done. On one level, it's very sophisticated; on another, it's the opposite. I don't know if you've read any Middle English romantic verse, Celia; but in *Gawain and The Green Knight*, for instance, the story's operating at a very high, even spiritual level on the one hand, but on the other hand, the anonymous author likes to break everything down into unnecessary components.

"So he can't just tell you that the knight gets on his horse. He has to tell you how he lifts his leg up, and what sort of shoes and trousers he is wearing; and how he puts one foot in the stirrup and then he transfers his weight and slings his leg across the horse's back, and all the rest. The author who is rewriting this screenplay is a bit like that.

"Most of it is on a biblical level; it's transcendent; but then he goes into very precise detail, about exactly where everything happened and who was present, and what they were all wearing, as though he's seeking corroboration all the time, despite the fact that we know from history that most of what he's saying never happened."

"It never happened?"

"I'm not talking about Gawain now. I'm talking about this mysterious script. It starts off with what did happen, but then he launches into what never happened.

But he does it so seamlessly, he has you thinking it must have happened, or it ought to have happened."

"That's what a good script is supposed to do, honey. You shouldn't be able to see the joins. The scriptwriter should have you eating out of his hand."

"And he does it so much better than our own scriptwriters. The premise is that Moorish Granada never fell to the Spaniards in 1492. You see, the Granada region of Spain, which was known as the Islamic State of Granada, and was ruled out of the Alhambra Palace there, and which the Moors called Al-Andalus—Andalucía, right?—that had been held by the Moors for eight centuries, and all that ended in 1492 when Ferdinand and Isabela took it back. Eight hundred years of Moorish rule in Spain ended on that day."

"Wally, I know all this. It's been my life for the last three decades!"

"Sorry, Celia. The premise of this guy's script is that Ferdinand and Isabela *failed* to take it back, and in reprisal, Boabdil went on to conquer the rest of Spain, I mean, apart from Andalucía; he conquers all of Spain and then the rest of Europe as well, giving us—"

"The Islamic State of Europe. Dear God, Wally!"

They stared at one another in wonderment.

"What are you thinking, Celia?" He asked after maybe thirty seconds of silence.

"I'm thinking about Bertrand Russell's dictum," she said. "That the point of philosophy is to start with something so simple as not to seem worth stating, and to end with something so paradoxical that no-one will believe it."

"Exactly," breathed Wally, once again in awe of her ability to link seemingly unconnected things in an almost surreal fashion.

"So this script," Wally continued, "is like *The Man in the High* Tower, the premise for which was that the Third Reich weren't defeated in 1945, and that we were all living under Nazi rule throughout the 20th century. But the way this guy tells the story, you really believe it, because he's so confident and firm and specific about everything, that I have to keep pinching myself and checking that we're not inhabiting an Islamic state after all.

"And there's no room for manoeuvre about any of the locations he specifies, where all these events are unfolding. I've never even heard of them, but I've been checking them on my phone as I go along, and they all exist, and they will be stunning locations to film. I mean look at this!"

He tapped the script. "This is a scene taking place inside a library within the Alhambra. But the author doesn't want to do the simple thing which would, of course, be to use the Alhambra. Oh no! That would be too straightforward. He says that the scene has to be shot in the *Biblioteca de Peralada*. Have you ever even heard of the *Biblioteca de Peralada*?"

"I've heard of Peralada. That's the Catalan wine region that makes the fizzy Cava, like the Spanish version of Prosecco but a little more Brut. I've also played golf there."

"I didn't even know you played golf, Celia. I just keep finding out more and more hidden facets to your personality. So your repertoire extends beyond dart-throwing!"

"I've played golf in Peralada, Wally, and I've been to their summer music festival. But I haven't heard of a library there. No, Wally."

"Well, neither had I. But look here." He held up the images of the *Biblioteca de Peralada* on his cellphone.

"It's jaw-dropping," she said. "Take me there!"

"I'm going to Celia! I'm going to. It says there are eighty thousand volumes in there. But get this. They're all different versions of the same book: Cervantes' *Don Quixote*. What does it mean? Who populates a library with the same book eighty thousand times over?"

She didn't answer.

"And here!" He was furiously tapping another page. "Queen Isabella is listening to a music concert when someone brings her some important news. The author specifies the music that she's listening to, which is *Pavane for a Dead Infanta*, and it says the location for this concert has to be the *Palau de Musica Catalana* in Barcelona. So again, I check it out, and it's another amazing location that I never knew existed. Look at this! Look at the modernist stained glass; look at the winged horses leaping out of the ceiling! I can't believe it!"

"But he's specified a location that didn't come into existence until four centuries after the events in the script," observed Celia, reading from the footnotes underneath the Getty images on Wally's phone.

"I know. I'm trying to figure it. Furthermore, it didn't escape my attention that the music that he says she has to be playing, *Pavane for a Dead Infanta*, isn't going to be written by Ravel until about four hundred years after the date on which she is playing it.

"Also, why is he going for Catalan locations all the time when Ferdinand is from Aragon and Isabella is from Castile? Is he trying to tell us something? Is he disowning parts of Spain? Is it *Independencia?* He's taken the character of John Donne out of the script. He should never have been there in the first place. But he's replaced him with a painting by Salvador Dali: *La Découverte de l'Amerique par Christophe Colomb.*"

"Christopher Columbus Discovers America," she translated. "He's replaced a seventeenth century poet with a twentieth century artist in a screenplay about the fifteenth century?"

"Yes, but I think the important thing for him is that Dali is a Catalan artist. That's the key. And look at this scene: he says it has to be shot at *El Monasterio de San Pedro de Rodes.* Again, it's in Catalonia! It turns out some of the scenes for the Sean Connery film of Umberto Eco's *The Name of the Rose* were shot there, but I never knew it."

"Must have shot those scenes in soft focus!" She teased.

"But it gets better, Celia: he insists that this scene is at *Montserrat Monastery*, and you know what's so special about that, Celia?"

"You mean apart from the fact that it's in Catalonia?"

"Yes."

"It's the home of *La Moreneta.*"

Once again, he was floored by the breadth and detail of her knowledge, but he didn't want to show it, because it might seem patronising, so he just continued. "Exactly! The Black Madonna! But the writer uses the Black Madonna as a metaphor to unite the east and the west. Islamic Spain has a black mother for Jesus, and historically she probably was black."

"You have to remember," Celia pointed out, "that Islamic Spain was very light touch. We mustn't confuse it with the mad Mullahs that came much later. If there ever had been an Islamic State of Europe, it would undoubtedly have been a very good space to be living in, for women as well as men."

"I guess that's part of the reason why he's making it all so inclusive. Once you enter the logic of this guy's world, illogical things begin to seem quite logical. In fact, you start to think that all this time you've been looking at everything the wrong way round, that his screenplay is the real world, and everything else, everything you were taught at school, has been propaganda."

"Alice in Wonderland."

"Precisely! I mean to say, once you accept the basic, outrageous premise, once you go down that wormhole with the writer, everything else makes sense. This is just too amazing! But, Celia, honey, I'm talking too much: you already know my thoughts about locations and bringing them to the forefront, not having them skulking in the background, all out of focus. I really adore these places he's taking me to, not to mention the words he's putting into the actor's mouths, including yours."

"He might be a woman, Wally."

Pfister was reduced to stabbing his forefinger repeatedly at the furled up paper.

"You know what that is, Wally?"

He didn't answer in words, but looked her up and down.

"I don't know how much you know about Middle English verse, Wally," she said, mimicking his earlier unintentional put-down, "but that thing that you have in your hand is what they used to call a ragmanroll."

"Huh?"

"The writing used to be on parchment or rags, and it was all rolled up. In Chaucer's *Pardoner's Tale*, the Pardoner has one in his saddlebag with all of his Indulgences that he's trying to sell, written down on it. It was rolled up writing on rags. Pretty much what our script was until the elves started improving it for us in the night. It's known as a ragmanroll, and it's where we get the word rigmarole from."

"Celia, if I've been talking down to you unintentionally, believe me, it was not intentional. I'm really sorry."

"You will be, Wally. You will be. I take it that you never saw my *Wife of Bath*?"

"I've seen all of your movies, Celia; but I never heard of the Wife of Bath."

"It wasn't a movie, Wally. It was on stage in the theatre. But someone did make a bootleg movie of it. The studio got an injunction to restrain publication of the bootleg, but apparently there are five copies in circulation that change hands for obscene amounts of money."

"Celia, between you and this script, I feel like I've learned more today than I've learned in the last couple of years. Yeah, you're right."

"About what, Wally?"

"About it being written by a woman."

Wally was trying to pay attention to Celia, but he was still discovering new material in the screenplay.

"I mean." He continued, " he specifies what sort of flowers are in the vase on the table; and he (or she) has matched the flowers with the seasons. For instance, here, he is referring to a yellow wildflower that he calls *immortales*, and the scene has to be shot at the Cap de Creus peninsula in April. So I've been researching it, and it seems that this peninsula (which is, of course, in Catalonia), is just a riot embroidered with these *immortales* in spring. It turns the whole Pyrenees yellow. The wild flowers are locally known as *immortales or aeternals*, because the locals pick them and hang them upside down and they keep their pronounced yellow colour for ever. He (or she) takes such an interest in what the women as well as the men have to be wearing. No grown man would be interested in those sorts of details."

"So he has to be a woman—"

"Or a child."

The Gate of the Burnt One

Colman followed up on the script by visiting the official website of Montserrat Monastery. The location, atop a mountain consisting of monolithic rock formations the likes of which he'd never seen in Europe before, was utterly breath-taking. The rocks looked like they belonged in the Seychelles. According to TripAdvisor, you had to park your car in the car park and ascend in a funicular rising five metres a second to the dizzying heights of the Monastery itself, in which the Black Madonna was immured.

But then Colman pressed the link to the Montserrat Monastery official website, where he was hijacked by all the other attractions on offer there: not only could he make a supplication to the Black Virgin by remotely buying a candle for €2.50, but he could endow an entire chantry chapel on line, just like in the Middle Ages, and the monks living in the Monastery there would say prayers for the immortal soul of Colman Hunt in perpetuity. It was as though nothing had changed in the last five hundred years.

Then he pressed the tab for The Monks, and a drop-down menu appeared, headed by *How to Become a Monk*. He hadn't entertained becoming a monk before, but now that it was presented to him as a possibility that he could opt into so easily on line with the click of a mouse, he considered the various plus points.

After all, being an Ipsissimus in the New Prometheans, he was already half way to spirituality. He was celibate, well, homosexual, but becoming less active with each passing hour. One day, he figured, the plumbing would just pack up forever, and it would all come to an end.

What do they say in the Scottish play? *The mere lees is left this vault to brag of.* It would be like that. The plumbing would pack up and all that would be left would be the interminable dripping tap in the night, as his prostrate grew larger and larger, until he was just one gigantic, leaking prostate.

He was a vegetarian. He neither drank nor smoked. He'd already enjoyed everything material that anyone could ask for during his long and generally healthy life, and he could do without any of it. For the last two months, he'd led a monastic life: the only time he'd even set foot outside of his caravan was when he delivered the pages of the new script to Wally Pfister.

Also, it would be a way of disappearing from both the glare of publicity and in particular, his murderous brothers. It was the logical progression from sulking in his Airstream. He would refine himself out of existence.

He filled in the online form behind the *How to Become a Monk* dialogue box, inserted his name, address, email, and confirmed that he was happy to receive occasional promotional and marketing material from the Monastery. He clicked the *I'm not a Robot* button, and correctly identified the four tiles that didn't have monks in them. Then he hit *Send*, and looked forward to hearing back from some monks.

When the knock came on his door, Colman couldn't believe the monks had arrived that quickly. He answered the door, and Aka Akinyola was standing in the doorway bearing his lunch.

"Char-grilled salmon," she said, "with a herb crust on a bed of wild rocket from the kitchen garden."

"Where's my usual man, Paddy?" Colman asked gracelessly, referring obliquely to the customary means by which his meals made their way to his caravan.

"In make-up," came the reply.

Colman thought he'd try something out on her. He recited:

"In chapters of fire
Across the charcoal dome
God's finger wrote
Deus imperat astris.
'God Rules the Stars.'"

Aka continued to stand in his doorway, offering him his lunch.

"Well?" He asked. "What do you think?"

"Anything to do with charcoal gets a ten from me," she said. Then she added: "What sort of charcoal is it, anyway?"

Meanwhile, Wally Pfister had finally got round to Googling 'chromium' to check out whether it was man-made or mined. He found out that it was an element, with symbol Cr. He learned that it was about the most abundant element on earth, and located in rocks, commonly getting spewed out in volcanic magma.

But when it was harvested from the earth, its occurrence didn't seem to be in places with very good human rights records: Russia, Turkey, Kazakhstan, South Africa.

He was very pleased that he had his Woody-Wagon. He didn't like the idea of chrome, but as it was the main ingredient in stainless steel, he wasn't likely to manage to live his life without it, he thought, as he put away his stainless steel knife and fork after washing them up in his stainless steel sink.

When Paddy next came into Colman's trailer with his phone in his hand, Colman had a Google request of his own:

"And by the way, Paddy, can you Google this for me and tell me what the fuck it means?" He handed him the Post-it on which he'd transcribed the title, *Bab al-Mahruq*.

"It's the sub-heading underneath the title of the script, Colman," Oculus pointed out.

"I can see that for myself, Pat. But does it mean something?"

When Paddy had first started understudying for Hunt as his stunt double, he had been selected because there was indeed a resemblance, but the two of them had been together for so long now that the likeness had deepened, in the way that owners of dogs start resembling their pets. Pat was fond of Hunt, and it was a long term relationship that wasn't likely to come to an end for any reason that Oculus could think of, but there were things about Hunt that really irritated him, such as the way that Hunt used Oculus as his frontal lobe and could never be arsed to do a Google search of anything for himself.

Hunt could send emails, and he knew how to consult his social media accounts and check that he had lots of Likes and subscribers. He read his reviews, and he printed them all out, good or bad, and stuck them in his big scrapbooks; he did his Instagram religiously and liked to swipe through his photo collection, and even knew how to subscribe to more space on the Cloud when he kept filling it up. But anything resembling research (unless it was research about himself), he'd delegate to his understudy.

Oculus obediently typed the words into his browser. It offered him Babylon, Babington House and Baba's share price, before he got a direct hit on *Bab al-Mahruq*. As he read it, he got a warm feeling in his tummy, and was now pleased that Colman Hunt used him as his frontal lobe, because otherwise he'd never have known about *Bab al-Mahruq*.

"Col," he mused, not taking his eyes off his device. "This is totally, fucking, off the chart, spinning Geiger counter clickety-click-amazing!"

"What you got, buddy?" Colman asked.

"If you put *the Gate of the Burnt One* into Google, you come up with nothing at all. Squat. Not a single hit. That suggests that no-one in the western world has ever taken an interest in it. But if you put *Bab al-Mahruq* into Google Translate and translate it from the Moroccan, it gives you *the Gate of the Burnt One*. So they're one and the same thing, but, as I say, you'll find nothing under its English name. But if you put *Bab al-Mahruq* into the search engine and search for that instead, just look at all this."

He tilted his screen towards Colman. The screen was populated with line after line of references to *Bab al-Mahruq*, serried ranks of them, row after row and arrows to further web pages at the foot of each screen.

"It's like it's something that the west has entirely missed, that is huge in the east." Observed Pat. He handed his device to Colman, who read it out loud.

"It means the Gate of the Burnt One," Colman Hunt read. "It's an actual gate, in Fez, Morocco. It says here that it used to be called the Gate of Justice, because they used to impale decapitated heads on the Gate, a charming practice which continued down to the twentieth century! Blow me! But back in 1203 a Wazzani rebel had done something so bad (it doesn't say here precisely what), that decapitation was considered insufficient to express the disapproval of his conduct by the authorities; so this Wazzani rebel was burnt alive at the Gate of Justice. But look here! They changed its name to the Gate of the Burnt One after the cremated Wazzani rebel walked out of the fire unscathed."

The two New Prometheans stared at one another in disbelief.

"You know," continued Oculus, after a few moment's silence, "there are supposed to be places on earth that have profound telluristic characteristics."

"You mean, like ley lines?"

"Yes, Colman. Ley lines connect triangles of paranormal activity. Don't you think that this Gate of the Burnt One might be some kind of milestone in a telluric map?"

"Where the natural powers of an Ipsissimus might be magnified?"

"Like when Magneto puts on his helmet?"

"If you like, Colman. Let's suppose this Wazzani was some kind of Shaman to begin with, but his gifts are multiplied on the site of a significant hub in the ley line network."

"Such as Stonehenge."

"Or Tudela in Cap de Creus, which just happens to be another one of the waypoints in this very script. And if I click the blue link to Wazzani and follow that up, it says a Wazzani is an inhabitant of Ouazzane in Northern Morocco. It says this Ouazzane is the holiest place in Morocco. Wow! Fancy that, the holiest

213

place we've never even heard of! It says it's a place of pilgrimage, not just for Moroccans, but for Jews as well. Get this, the Jews make a hajj to this Ouazzane place to venerate Moroccan saints entombed there. It's like a contradiction in terms."

"So this rebel from Ouazzane," said Paddy, taking over the thread, "this Wazzani, he leaves this mystical place of pilgrimage; he travels to Fez where he does something so bad that beheading isn't good enough for him. So they burn him alive at the Gate of Justice. And he walks straight out of the fire."

"After which," continued Colman, "the Gate was renamed the Gate of the Burnt One. Paddy, I think that you and I, as the only known representatives of the cult of the New Prometheans in the vicinity, may have to pay a visit to this very special place."

"Not just any old visit, Col: a hajj."

"Right, Pat. I'm finally going to leave this fucking caravan! I'll tell you something. This new script is kind of inspirational. When I read it, I knew that I had to go on a pilgrimage to the Monastery of Monserrat. Now I've asked you about *Bab al-Mahruq*, which is the title of the script, and we find that we both need to go on an odyssey to the Gate of the Burnt One."

"Yeah, Col. Like farewell Iliad, welcome Odyssey!"

"A fiery, new beginning!"

"Colman, remember it was me that introduced you to the New Prometheans. This is a special interest for me. As soon as we get a break from this movie, we're going there. Can't be that far from Ouarzazate. Col, I just keep doing the same thing, because I can't believe it. You know, when you have that belief that, once your computer has given you an answer you don't like, if you ask it again, you may get a different answer."

"Yeah, Paddy, but you never do."

"Correct, I keep typing *Bab al-Mahruq* into the browser, and it takes you straight there, to the Gate in Fez. But no matter how many times I type in the English version, the Gate of the Burnt One, there isn't a single citation. How can something that is as significant as that to the east, be totally insignificant to the west?"

"Paddy, in six months' time, you put *the Gate of the Burnt One* into your browser, it's going to say: *See under Colman Hunt!*"

The Director's Cut

"What's that?" Celia asked him.

Wally was sat inside his Woodie-Wagon in front of what looked like one of those giant reel to reel tape recorders that were supposed to make you think high tech in old spy movies. He was cranking the handle, and the spool was going round, advancing the medium.

"It's a film editor, Celia. You never seen one before?"

"Maybe in ancient history class. Or that book by Neil McGregor."

"What's that?"

"The History of the World in 100 Objects. Wally, no-one does it that way anymore."

"You just assumed we were shooting digital?"

"Well, doesn't everybody?"

"Told you, Celia, I'm old school. I feel more in touch with the editing process this way, rather than having a mouse and some German editing software coming between me and the medium. It's more precise. I can advance it a fraction of a millimetre at a time, get the cuts in the exact frame I want them. We can stripe the M & E in later."

"Where do you even manage to find this old film stock?"

"Jesus Christ, Celia! No-one ever asked me how I managed to find a 1962 Facel Vega Facellia Convertible, or the 1964 Gordon Keeble GKI; or how I had them both restored to perfect working order before I filmed them on the road in *Sixties Driver*. Those were pretty challenging resources to find. But you just want to know where I buy my film stock. Celia, did I ever ask you where you buy your cigarettes, a brand of cigarettes, I should add, that they stopped manufacturing before I was even born?"

"*Touché!*" She declared.

"For crying out loud. I'm making a film starring the great Celia Broadsword. You didn't expect me to shoot it on my iPhone, did you?"

The tapes in his big spools were studded with protruding Post-it notes, like a porcupine, or a paper version of the Iron Maiden, as favoured by the Spanish Inquisition.

"What do all the different coloured Post-its mean, Wally?" She asked.

"They serve as reminders for me. The red ones mean I'm going to make a cut just there. The blue ones mean I need to move that scene. Green denotes where I'm likely to move it to. Purple means I need to find another scene to interpose, because it's calling out for something that's presently missing."

"What about yellow?"

"Yellow means I'm going to come back to that place."

"Wally, this is so primitive. It's like a film made by a caveman!"

"Yeah, Celia, I know. Old school. But this caveman makes good films."

Ossuary

"I give up, Ynes!"

Millicent Marcuson had watched the 25 minute Panorama segment on her PC four times now, and was none the wiser as to why Tinctorio Indigolin didn't want members of the public to see the triumvirate documentary.

"It's very interesting," she informed him, "but completely unexceptional. I mean, the injunction must have been a very expensive remedy. It was defended by the BBC and it went all the way up to the Supreme Court, but always behind closed doors."

"*In camera*, as I believe it's known" remarked the cameraman.

"I just don't get what it was he was trying to keep from the rest of us."

"Unless it's all just a publicity stunt to make you think there's something there when actually there isn't," hazarded Ynes.

"Like the Emperor's New Clothes?" Millicent pursued.

"Yes, Shall we watch together?" Ynes asked.

"Well, I've watched it four times. Why not five times?" Was all she said.

She dragged the red spot at the bottom of her screen to the beginning and they watched together. The interview told the story of Tinctorio Indigolin and his two partners in a marine biology venture. Indigolin was the powerhouse behind the business, and the other two were clearly hangers-on. They had become involved at the outset, latching themselves onto Indigolin's rising star when Indigolin needed investment, and he had been obliged to share his equity with them.

He had then supported the two, who received huge annual dividends of many multiples their original stakes in return for doing nothing year after year. Eventually Indigolin had got fed up with being the milk jug and just walked away from the business and established a competing business doing the same thing, but without the two hangers-on. The two hangers-on and the old business had promptly injuncted Indigolin for breach of fiduciary duties, breach of shareholders' agreement, making a secret profit, and breaches of various other alleged duties, express and implied.

The result was that Indigolin simply walked away from the marine biology company and reinvented himself as a doyen of cryptocurrencies, as a gambler in Contracts for Differences, as an investor in NFTs, and, most recently as the Blue Molecule Man. But, as Millicent had observed, the Panorama documentary itself was unexceptional. There was no apparent reason why Indigolin would have felt it was imperative to stop access to the broadcast.

"Unless," said Ynes, "he's still at it."

"At what?"

"If he's still carrying on a competing marine biology business in breach of the injunction and doesn't want to draw his former partners' attention to it."

"Don't you think, if he was doing that, they'd have found out without a Panorama documentary?"

"I guess so," said Ynes. "Are you willing to watch it a sixth time?"

"OK, but never again."

"Let's make it bigger, so your cameraman's eagle eye can take in all the details."

"I'll put it on the 48" monitor!" Millicent offered.

"Let's do Screen Mirror on the 100" TV," said Ynes, starting the Search for devices. "There we go."

In silence, the two of them watched the interview again on the giant screen. Millicent had watched it so many times, she felt she could do the interview herself. She had all of the questions and all of the answers off pat. There was Indigolin sitting in front of his butcher's block desk with his tablet on it, and his omnipresent DataTraveler embedded in the USB slot. He was sat in his office under the Westway Flyover, with his vivarium of swaying fronds and bouncing frogs behind him.

"There!" Ynes cried, stopping the film at the point where the interviewer's cameraman had taken in some footage of the rainforest behind Indigolin's desk, and was now circling back from behind Indigolin to resume face-to-face. "The screensaver on his computer!"

"What about the screensaver?" Millicent asked.

Ynes wound it back a few seconds, captured it in a screenshot, and then stretched the screensaver as big as he could. Like many screensavers, it was just playing random photographs from Indigolin's C-drive. Foreign holidays, award ceremonies, beaches, friends, flash cars.

"There!" Ynes exclaimed again. He drew Millicent's attention to the screenshot that he had taken just as the playback of the screensaver had changed from a McLaren P1 hypercar to a strange, white, fossilised mass.

"What is it?" Millicent enquired.

"It's bones," said the cameraman. "Like you'd see in a mass grave. Thousands upon thousands of bones. Remains. Let's say his lawyers come up with some specious reason to do with his business affairs that gets him the super-injunction and the gagging order, but what he's actually concerned about is the possibility of anybody seeing that one-second image on his screensaver. It's not an image that Bill Gates put there.

"The screensaver is just dragging across random photos from the Favourites in his C-drive. A normal person might have their summer holidays, their dog, or their grandchildren. This guy keeps photos of remains in his Favourites!"

"Je-sus, Ynes. Do we think that Indigolin had anything to do with how all those bones came to be in the same place?"

"Well, presumably he has some connection with them, or he wouldn't have a photo of them on his C-drive."

"Are they human remains?"

"You can't tell," said Ynes. "There's so many of them that there's no reference point to compare their size to. I just can't say."

"But I know a pathologist who can," said Millicent. "Forward the screenshot of the bones to my phone, please, Ynes."

Pretzel Logic

He watched with undisguised admiration as she unfastened the Jineta sword at the back of her head, which was the last remaining thing she was wearing. He had noticed before that when Celia undressed for him, she removed all of her jewellery also. The striptease was comprehensive. He deduced that, at the age of eighty-five, she must still have all her own teeth, or she would presumably have removed them also. Her gorgeous silver hair briefly illuminated the Airstream like a Roman Fountain firework before tumbling down around her shoulders and partially obscuring her front.

"Why'd you do that, Celia? I can't see your breasts anymore."

"Wally, don't get me wrong, I'm really attached to the little present you bought me in the souk. I'll always treasure it; but when I lie down for the missionary position, the goddamn thing sticks right into the back of my skull."

"Then why don't you get on top of me, cowgirl style, honey?"

"For the simple reason, I'm too fucking old, Walter; I'd need a double hip replacement; but even when I was younger, I was no fucking cow girl!"

"But that's what I love about you, Celia; you're a proper GILF. The way your tits just lie like that on your tummy, in repose. All the curves are so soft. In my dreams, I see all my favourite bits of you converging a little more each day—"

"You mean they're all going south?"

"No, no, no. I mean like a perfect equilateral triangle, where I've filed all of my Favourites in one place, what the ancient Greeks called The Golden Ratio. In my dreams, I want to be able to suck both your nipples and your clit at the same time."

"Well, dream on Wally and wake me up when you can suck your own dick."

"How's this?" He said. To Celia's amazement, he was rocking himself forward on the axis of his hips, a little more pretzeled with each pitch, until with one final lunge he had his plunger in his own muzzle, first just the tip, then, after a further oscillation or two, the shaft, until he was fellating himself.

"Now I've seen everything!" Was all she said. "Is there a name for that position in the Karma Sutra?"

He mumbled something incomprehensible.

"What's that, Wally?" She asked.

He let his Popsicle plop out of his chops. "It's not *Karma Sutra*, Celia! It's called advanced yoga, but I'm not a blooming ventriloquist! Don't try to hold a conversation with me at the same time!"

"Men are so pants at multi-tasking! Where did you learn to do that?"

"I had no idea I still could do it, Celia. I used to be able to do it when I was a teenager."

"Other teenagers who want to do a party trick learn how to pull the tablecloth off the table leaving all the plates and glasses intact, but you decided to pull your own pudding. And can you make yourself come like that?"

"Mmm."

"In your own mouth?"

"Nothing goes to waste in the Tao of Yin and Yang, Celia."

"Go on then, Wally. Let me see you do it, and then I'll try and do what you want me to do."

He proceeded to finish himself off.

"That really is the dog's bollocks!" Celia pronounced. With his eyes staring so far up his own arse, he hadn't even noticed her taking the video on her phone.

She was getting careless in her infatuation with Wally Pfister. She'd let him take her to bed without the usual formality of signing an NDA first. The video she'd just shot would be better insurance than any NDA.

Day Off

Edgar Ash was on set early the next morning. He liked to get into his overpoweringly hot costume of crushed velvet with the huge ruff round his neck before the sun got too scorching. There was nobody else on set. *'That was odd,'* he thought. One could usually count on the lighting guys being there ahead of time, setting their stuff up, or the scriptwriters rewriting the scene at the last minute: they liked to let the actors know that they were important *ganzamachas* too. A scriptwriter could diminish you with a keystroke. Shit! There wasn't even a thermos of coffee or a nice cool flagon of pomegranate juice in sight. The place had gone to the fucking dogs.

Just then Pat Oculus walked past, showing off, barefoot, as per.

"Hey, Paddy!" He called out.

"What's up Ed? Why you in costume?"

"We're supposed to be shooting the big *Sos d'o Rei Catolicos* scene this morning. You know, Zaragoza comes to Ouarzazate. Where is everybody?"

"Haven't you heard? We've all got a day off."

"How come?"

"Director's done his back in. Apparently he's doubled over, can't straighten up. We're waiting for the chiropractor to arrive from Casablanca."

"How'd he do that to himself?"

"Says he has no idea."

Printers

Indigolin came to visit Wally in his sick bed. He had a bottle of something that Wally assumed was champagne wrapped up in brown paper under his arm. Wally was propped up in his Woodie-Wagon reading his William Blake compendium. Celia was also there, playing the baby grand softly.

"What's that tune you're playing?" He asked Celia.

"It's called *Pavane for a Dead Infanta*," she informed him. "It came up in conversation the other day."

"I came to visit your patient," Indigolin said to Celia.

"That's very kind of you," said Celia.

"What happened?"

Wally didn't look up from his Blake book, so Celia answered for him: "Over-ambitious advanced yoga position."

Wally frowned and pretended to carry on reading.

"Mind telling me the name of this position, so that I can make a point of avoiding it?" Indigolin asked.

After a moment, Celia ad-libbed. She had always been good at impromptu: "The Caduceus," she nodded.

"The serpent that eats its own tail," observed Wally, incredulous at her improvisation.

"I never heard of any such position in yoga," remarked Indigolin. "But I'm familiar with Caduceus as an ecosystem for buying, selling and minting NFT's"

"There are more things in heaven and earth, Horatio," was all she said.

In the interests of diversity and inclusion, Indigolin sought to bring Wally more into the conversation: "What you reading, Wally?"

"Blake's Marriage of Heaven and Hell. You read any Blake, Ti?"

"Only the kiddies stuff: Songs of Innocence & Experience, you know. Elena's trying to get me up to speed with John Donne."

"John Donne is too much up his own arse! You know? *Look at me, how clever I am* stuff!" Wally declared. "You should get a load of this." He read:

"*I was in a Printing House in Hell and saw the method by which knowledge is transmitted from generation to generation. In the first Chamber, there was a Dragon Man cleaning away the rubbish from a cave's mouth: within a number of Dragons were hollowing the cave.*"

"*In the second Chamber was a viper, folding round the rock and the cave, and others adorning it with gold, silver and precious stones.*"

"*In the third Chamber was an eagle with wings and feathers of air; he caused the inside of the cave to be infinite. Around were numbers of eagle-like men, who built palaces in the immense cliffs.*"

"*In the fourth Chamber were lions of flaming fire, raging around and melting the metals into living fluids.*"

"*In the fifth Chamber were unnamed Forms, which cast the metals into the expanse.*"

"*There they were received by men who occupied the sixth Chamber, and took the form of Books and were arranged in Libraries.*"

"Sounds like Game of Thrones meets Plato's Parable of the Cave," declared Indigolin.

"How prosaic the dull men appear after all the scintillating animals and birds!" remarked Celia, still playing softly on Wally's baby grand. "They're just librarians!"

"You've got to remember that Blake was a Printer," explained Pfister. "printing out these illuminated manuscripts. He had to write everything back to front in negative, etched into copper plates, and then pour the molten metal into the moulds. These days, any amateur wannabe can buy a cheap PC with a word-processing package bundled in and start composing his *magnum opus*. But for Blake, it was a burning, balls-aching, back-breaking physical process carried on inside a furnace. Here he is describing the infernal process by which he creates the very book I'm reading. Do you like reading, Ti?" Wally asked.

"I like nature books."

"No, I mean, fiction?"

"If it's fiction, I like to read that guy who invented the anti-super hero called The Printer."

"That would be Philip G Cohen in '*Infiniti*'."

"Yes, that dude."

"He had a Printer who printed out Dragons," noted Celia, suddenly stopping her piano playing and dwelling on the symmetry. "Or was it Devils? I'll have to read it again."

"It merits re-reading," observed Wally. "Damn fine book!"

"Seems like all our Printers are on the same page then," concluded Indigolin. "You want me to take your yoga class for you tomorrow?"

"Are you able to?" Wally asked.

"Well, obviously, I'm not as advanced as you were, that is until you became over-advanced. And look where it got you! But the class is only doing some rudimentary warm-ups and breathing exercise. Basically, it's just a way of getting them out of bed. I'd be happy to lead them in that. No Caduceus though."

"Ti, if I'm not fully recovered by tomorrow, that would be really nice of you."

"The crew need something to get up for in the mornings. I'll be there, and maybe you will too. In the meantime, I wish you a quick and complete recovery."

"I'll be there!" Celia cried.

"Oh!" Indigolin said. "I almost forgot. I brought your friend something to aid his recovery." He passed the bottle wrapped in brown paper to Celia, who unwrapped it.

"Lucozade!" She cried in amazement.

"When I was poorly, my mummy always used to feed me on a diet of Lucozade and Heinz chicken noodle soup," explained Indigolin.

"Not in the same cup, I hope," said Celia.

"Where did you manage to find Lucozade?" Wally asked.

"There's a big Carrefour in town," explained Indigolin. "I do my food shopping there."

"You do your own food shopping?" Celia queried. "I thought you had staff at the Riyadh."

"Yeah, I do have, but I like to do my own groceries shopping. Don't want to find they've been buying the meat at one of those fly-blown dysentery dives by the road side. Some of us, Wally," he added, "are very fussy about what we put in our mouths."

He gave Pfister a knowing look before he left his Woodie-Wagon. *'He couldn't possibly know the truth,'* thought Wally. Could he? Celia instinctively patted her pants pocket to check her phone with the insurance video was still in there and locked. It hadn't left her possession. *'Caduceus, my fanny!'* She thought to herself.

Deep Fake

During his convalescence Wally experimented with EbSynth and FaceApp.

These were Deep Fake video editing programs that enabled him to manipulate digital film stock in a number of ways. The way he was manipulating it just now was that he had dragged the photo he'd taken of Celia's face into the program and was now waiting for the program to age her, so he could see what she was going to look like in five years' time. The program seemed to take an eternity mixing it all down before outputting it. The program was so slow, it would have been just as quick to allow the ageing process to take its own course.

When the program had finally completed its work, he wondered if he'd bought a dud program. He couldn't see any discernible difference. So he ran it again, this time instructing the program to age her ten years. This took even longer, but when the program finally fulfilled its mission, the changes were still almost imperceptible: a few laugh lines around her eyes and mouth, but the cheekbones still high and taut, no slack in the neck, no extra chins, no jowls.

It was unbelievable. He could only conclude that the program was recognising the source photo as the image of a much younger woman. Normally, you'd expect a smoker's skin to age quicker: a puckering around the lips, making the mouth look meaner. But there was no trace of any such hallmarks of time.

Sempiternal, changeless. Like Ursula Andress in the film of Rider Haggard's novel, *She*. He went back viewing old footage of her in films ten years ago, and there was no change there either. It was as though she'd hit a certain age and then just stopped getting any older.

He studied the Deep Fake where he'd aged her ten years more carefully. The very fine smoker's lines around her mouth had disappeared. On set, she'd cover them with make-up, but he'd seen her without make-up too. Did this mean that in the future she was destined to give up smoking, or did it mean that she was going to start using Botox or filler?

Then he realised just how ridiculous this line of thinking was. He was merely fooling around with a predictive editing program, an upmarket version of Photo Booth that came bundled with all the other free Apps on your telephone. For Christ's sake! It wasn't *The Picture of Dorian Gray*!

Then he stood back and asked himself why he was even carrying out this exercise. The answer was unequivocal. He had very serious feelings for this woman. He was wondering what it would be like to share the next ten years with her, waking up to that vision every morning. He concluded he felt very good about this. Then he felt faintly ashamed of himself for delving into this line of inquiry.

Like asking your fiancé to take a DNA test to make sure the embryo she was carrying belonged to you before you agreed to marry her. Disgusted with himself for entertaining such unworthy thoughts, before seriously considering getting into a proper relationship with a woman a quarter of a century older than himself, he jumped up from his desk and at the same time heard his back give an almighty crack.

At first, he thought he'd done himself some irreversible damage, but after a few experimental stretches and curls, he realised that he'd just cured his back ache. Wally Pfister was back in action. And he was a man with a mission. Or indeed, more than one mission. Shooting and yoga classes would resume tomorrow morning.

Indigolin had instructed Wally that, if he was match fit, he had to get the $5M sex scene in the can the very next morning. Wally had asked him how he was supposed to film the sex scene when Colman Hunt was so reluctant to leave his caravan. Indigolin had told Wally just to get everything set up with Celia Broadsword, and he, Tinctorio Indigolin, would make sure that Colman Hunt was on set on time. Wally regarded the problems with Colman as insuperable, but he was playing along with it. Let the Blue Molecule guy learn from his own mistakes.

Hannibal

Whether to provide Wally with diversion during his indisposition, or whether to sidestep Hunt who had lain in wait for the scriptwriter one night, the twelve-year-old cyclist delivered the next overnight instalment onto Wally's doorstep, where Celia found it in the morning and brought it in for him to read.

"Ha!" He suddenly cried out loud.

"Huh, honey?" Celia queried.

"Do you think those gladiators you showed me at Atlas Film Studios know how to do a testudo?"

"What is it, Wally? Sounds like a dance they do in the Pyrenees."

"You're thinking of Tarantella, darling. You know: *Do you remember an inn, Miranda?* Nope, a testudo is the name for the tortoise or turtle the soldiers used to make with their shields, to protect themselves from missiles being hurled from above, during siege warfare."

"Course they do, Wally. It's like basic Roman primer. They cut their teeth on it at Atlas."

"Good, because there's one here in the siege of Alhama, in the pages of script just delivered. And in my mind's eye, I can see just how I want to do it. They're going to form the testudo like they're doing a ballet."

"So maybe I wasn't so far out with Tarantella after all, honey."

"I knew it!" He exclaimed, going back to the manuscript pages. "I knew it. When they were in the Monastery at Monserrat with the Black Virgin in the last instalment, that's Barcelona. It's a stone's throw from the French border, and here they are invading France, and my God, Celia, they're doing it in style. Like Hannibal, they're crossing the mountains (except this time it's the Pyrenees. instead of the Alps), in winter, on brightly coloured howdahs atop elephants. What a scene! The endless stream of black Moors in the white snow, enthroned upon elephants, marching across the border. Do you know how to ride an elephant, Celia?"

"I thought you said they were all Moors, Wally."

"Yes, but it says that they put the captured Catholics and their king and queen in the vanguard, so that the enemy seem to expend their energy fighting against themselves, and then Boabdil and his Moors bring up the rear in fantastic armour. The elephants are dressed up like film stars themselves, and they're followed by a camel caravan 2 kilometres long carrying the provisions. When he mentioned the Monastery san Pedro de Rodes in the last instalment, that's the very mountain pass they're going to take from Spain into France.

"Celia, I'm imagining that procession of slate grey elephants and black Moors snaking by that magnificent ruin of a Monastery playing out on a gigantic cinema screen in the blinding white snow. I'll film it from way up high with my drone. You're going to look dazzling. I repeat, do you know how to ride an elephant?"

"Darling, I was married to a dinosaur for years. An elephant will be child's play! Just tell me, Wally, do you want me to ride the jumbo cowgirl or will you be offended if I do it side-saddle?"

"Celia, you are going to be sitting on top of the tusker in a howdah and you're going to have an experienced driver and, I promise you, the pachyderm is going to be comprehensively insured!"

Shooting the US 5M Sex Scene

Although they only had the first eighty pages of an unfinished script as yet, it was generally understood in the Jane Austen sense of being a truth universally acknowledged, that the US $5M sex scene was entirely gratuitous, so the fact that it would not necessarily have any causative, artistic or logical connection with anything else that might eventually make its way into the film, via the phantasmagorical screenwriter, was not a reason for not getting that bit of the film into the can right away.

It bemused Wally that, despite the fact that the very reason for shooting such scenes was to ensure that as many millions of people as possible saw them, as few people as possible had to be allowed onto the set when they were being created. So the lighting guys had already done their tests, and left; the scene dressers had already dressed the scene, and left. Wally was going to shoot the scene himself as well as direct it. In view of her past relationship as Colman's wife, Celia had said she didn't need an intimacy co-ordinator. Her make-up artist had already done his work on her, and left.

So, in the unlikely event that Colman Hunt actually made an appearance, there would just be the three of them: Celia, Celia's new lover, Wally, and Celia's old husband, Colman. What had the late Princess Di said? *There are three of us in this marriage.* Everybody on set would already have had the pleasure of seeing Celia in the buff, so hopefully that would make her more relaxed.

The one thing that, in the absence of a finished script, everyone subscribed to, was the idea that the scene had to be shot in a kind of Moorish way. Whether it was in Moorish Spain or Moorish Morocco, the set was going to look like Colonel Muammar Gaddafi's travelling tent. The location manager had reviewed with Wally and Celia lots of photographs from 2009 when Gaddafi had gotten his fingers burnt for erecting his Bedouin tent in a no-camping area of Manhattan.

They had reproduced all the camel-logo'd swaggings, the extravagant fabrics, the brass lanterns, hangings, drapings, Arab carpets, crenelated endcaps, the animal pelt throws, the filigree Orion finials and fluted poles, the gold rings and holdbacks, the tieback hooks, the yard braided bead tassel fringes, the fabric pom poms, and the opulently upholstered *chaise longue* where the scene would be consummated.

Wally and Celia had been amazed at the life story of Gaddafi's tent: the constant stream of visitors beating a path to its metaphorical door: the Venezuelan President, Hugo Chávez, the English Prime Minister, Tony Blair, the European Union Foreign Policy Chief, Javier Solana; and, of course, the tent had ended up, inevitably, in Donald Trump's back garden. This was glamping *in excellsis*.

Wally had involved Celia in equipping the tent. Together they had weaved their way through ever-narrowing passages in the souks, and she had picked out all her props for herself: every lamp and candlestick, selecting the patterns of the fabrics, the silks, the satins, the chiffons, and, of course, the Fortuny crinkled crepes—and she had told the set-builders where to put everything, so that she would be completely comfortable doing the scene.

She had then practised it with Wally, plotting waypoints where she would pause and remove each veil before ending up on the couch. He had helped her select the semi-pellucid scarves in the souk the day he'd bought her the Jineta hair pin.

So the idea was that Celia would do a dance of the seven veils, flitting around between all the hangings and swaggings and sexy chiffon drapes to the accompaniment of some pentatonic Amazigh oboe Music of the Maghreb, transitioning between the saturated illumination of the desert sunlight and the deep shadows cast by the large zinc, floor-standing Moroccan sconces, superimposed onto which would be the splashes from the hanging multi-coloured star glass tea-light lanterns, as if Wally had painted tinted highlights onto each frame by hand.

Against this background, the leading lady would bob and weave, shedding veils in time to the music, and making her way to the *chaise longue* where Colman Hunt, unable to restrain himself a moment longer, would throw back the huge hood on his Djellaba, lift up the hem, and take her by force. Precisely why any of this was happening, the scriptwriters would have to justify later.

For privacy, the tent had not been set up near the Airstreams, nor in the Ouarzazate studio, but was a genuine Bedouin tent erected in the middle of nowhere in the Sahara Desert, about a mile's drive from the Airstream encampment. Wally had driven Celia there and got his gear out of the car.

Celia was practising her pirouettes and working out just where she was going to remove each veil *en route* to the *denouement* on the divan, with neither of them seriously expecting the leading man to make an appearance, when, to everyone's surprise, they heard the roar of Tinctorio Indigolin's Lamborghini Urus approaching their tent from across the desert, followed by Indigolin's head appearing in the opening of the pavilion. Having ascertained that Celia was respectable and that it was okay for him to come in, he then entered the tent, resplendent in his blue legume suit (single-breasted on this occasion) with Presley Unsdorfer masquerading as Colman Hunt in a hooded blue Djellaba in tow.

"Looks like the Grand Bazaar in here!" Was all Indigolin said.

Presley lowered the capacious hood on the Djellaba for long enough for everyone to be convinced that Indigolin had indeed winkled the reclusive Colman Hunt from out of his Airstream, and then raised it again before anyone took too close a look.

Wally had thought he was going to have to ask Indigolin to leave, but, like a perfect gentleman, he just said that he'd look back in about half an hour to pick Colman Hunt up, and then they heard the huge baritone bang as the 12 cylinders of his off-road Lamborghini burst into life again and drove away.

The actors were professionals. They knew what they were supposed to do. Wally scrolled through his phone's menu until he found the Playlist entitled Music of the Maghreb, selected it, asked his performers to take it in their own time and let the camera roll.

Celia managed to combine grace and poise with brute sex appeal. What was making her performance so arresting was that she was clearly playing to the camera, wielded by her boyfriend, so that every veil shed was shed for his pleasure, not the pleasure of the shadow in the Djellaba who was supposed to benefit from it. Dear God, she was beautiful!

Up until now, each time she had disrobed for him, Wally had been so close to her, he had admired individually all the constituent parts, but now he realised that this was the first time, in broad daylight, he'd stepped back and taken in the whole assembly together. It was faultless. Having removed all of her veils, she seemed in no hurry to cross the pavilion to the *chaise longue*, and it became apparent to Wally, she was prolonging the moment for his personal enjoyment. Colman Hunt was just an onlooker, an extra in a fantasy she was enacting for her boyfriend.

Eventually, she was supine on the divan, and the Jineta dagger was the last item she removed, her silver hair spilling onto the sofa. Presley, in his Djellaba trampled across the yards of carpets, rugs and dhurries. First he knelt beside her, and lifted his hood, kissing her on the forehead and then breasts and stomach. Then he got onto the sofa and lifted his hem. Then there was a gasp from Celia, whether of ecstasy or pain, or shock, it was impossible to say, before Wally said to them and to himself: *"And Cut!"*

A Case of Mistaken Identity

Before Celia could say anything they heard the roar of Indigolin's 200 miles per hour Chelsea tractor, returning to the scene of the crime. Then Indigolin thrust his head back into the tent opening, said, "OK, Colman, let's go." And Colman and Indigolin had evaporated in Indigolin's getaway car.

Celia grabbed a handful of her scarves from the souk and wrapped them around her nakedness.

"Wally," she said, "take me to Colman's Airstream now."

"But he's in the Urus with Indigolin?" Pfister queried.

"Just do what I say, please, Wally, and make sure you get there before they do."

The two of them jumped into Wally's studio Macan. Overtaking Indigolin was easy because although the Urus had 700 more brake horse power than the Macan, the Urus was still shod in its Knightsbridge boots whereas Wally had put sand tyres on the Macan. Wally gave Indigolin a wide berth, not least because his vehicle was slithering all over the place, as if he was driving on an ice rink. Wally overtook the Lamborghini in a spray of sand that caused the automatic windscreen wipers on the Urus to deploy themselves.

Arriving at their destination, Celia jumped out of the passenger seat clinging a fistful of piebald scarves to her breasts and hammered on the door of Hunt's Airstream. A bleary eyed Colman Hunt answered it. Wally's mouth fell open in disbelief. They had just overtaken Hunt, seated in the passenger seat of Indigolin's Urus, but here he was, answering the door.

When You've Eliminated All Which Is Impossible, Whatever Remains, However Improbable, Must Be the Truth

At first, Wallace Pfister had been too dumbfounded at what had happened to even speak. But, on the ensuing drive out to Tinctorio Indigolin's Riyadh just outside Ouarzazate, he had built up quite a head of steam. Celia had called the meeting and suggested it take place there, away from all the rubberneckers and gossips on set. Her privacy having been invaded already once today, she saw no need to rehearse it before the rest of the cast and crew.

Wallace Pfister was not by inclination a violent man, but as he drove Celia closer and closer to their rendezvous at the producer's Riyadh, he found himself harbouring murderous thoughts when he considered what had just befallen his beloved, and, worst of all, upon his own watch.

"If it wasn't Colman, who was it?" He demanded rhetorically.

"Self-evidently, it must have been Presley. As Sherlock Holmes says: *'when you've eliminated all which is impossible, whatever remains, however improbable, must be the truth'*"

"You seem to be taking this very Stoically, Celia."

"I'm not taking anything anyhow, Wally," she explained. "I'm still coming to terms with it. I'm not one of those #MeToo's."

Inside, Indigolin's housekeeper brought them a tray of dates, salted almonds and mint teas, and then glided noiselessly away in his robes and slippers, leaving them in the courtyard with the reflecting ornamental bassin and the tinkling fountains. To pre-empt her boyfriend getting them thrown out of the Riyadh before the meeting had even started, Celia began the dialogue as soon as the producer joined them.

"So, Mr Indigolin," she began formally. "There we were doffing our caps to you because you had miraculously managed to winkle Colman Hunt out of his Airstream, when in fact you'd done nothing of the sort. For my part, you had me fooled, but for your part, it was completely pre-meditated. You knew entirely what you were doing."

"I knew what I was doing, Celia, but I had no idea Presley would do what he did. That was definitely not in the script."

"So, it was Presley, was it?" Wally said.

"Calm down, Wally!" She said. "I'm still processing this."

"What's there to process?" Wally demanded. "You signed a contract to do a simulated sex scene with your flaccid-dicked ex-husband, and you ended up being penetrated by a third party. There's a word for that, and the word is 'Rape'!"

"There's another word for that, Wally," interrupted Indigolin. "Well, three words actually 'Breach of Contract'."

"What!" Wally sputtered. "What's he mean?"

"He means," Explained Celia, calmly, "that I haven't done the scene I was supposed to do, with Colman Hunt, so I'm the one who's in the wrong here."

"Well, whose fault was that?" Wally demanded. "Indigolin was the one who brought Presley Unsdorfer to the party, literally. He chauffeured him to the scene of the crime and then drove the getaway car afterwards, trying to get him back under whatever stone he'd crawled out from before anyone was any the wiser!"

Indigolin was painfully aware of the fact that Presley was not yet inside the Riyadh. Presley had asked to be dumped off at the Ibis Hotel in Ouarzazate, so that he could get a drink after his Oscar-worthy performance, the Ibis being the other hotel in Ouarzazate, where the crew and support cast weren't staying, so no-one there should mistake him for Colman Hunt.

Presley had said he'd make his own way back to the Riyadh after, and Indigolin hadn't objected, because he had no further use for Presley and would be sending him back to London in the morning anyway.

If Presley was to come marching through the front door now, no doubt the worse for alcohol, and attempt to join in the conversation, the scene would be even more ugly and uncomfortable than it already was. Indigolin's strategy had been to be apologetic and conciliatory to Celia, but when her chivalrous boyfriend had decided he wanted to curry her favour by taking greater offence at what had happened than she herself was taking, Indigolin altered his strategy, deciding to go on the offensive with his Breach of Contract allegation.

After all, he'd paid US $5M for her to do a nude scene with Colman Hunt, not some unknown lookalike. His interruption seemed to have worked. Wally Pfister was an artistic type. He made great films. But he couldn't negotiate his way out of a paper bag. He couldn't even buy a pair of slippers in the souk without being ripped off. Indigolin had taken control, and Celia had put Wally back in his box. Now maybe they could start to discuss matters reasonably and make some progress.

"Celia," began Indigolin, then realising that it was her boyfriend who was more in need of being pacified, "Wally. I know two wrongs don't make a right, but the reason Celia got raped was because I was being blackmailed."

"Huh?" An open-mouthed and incredulous Wallace Pfister barked.

"This Presley Unsdorfer guy came to my offices in West London. He says that, because we've got Paddy Oculus working as Colman's understudy, he, Presley Unsdorfer, had been culturally and fraternally misappropriated, because we shouldn't have hired an outsider when Presley is Colman's natural double. He said that either I put him into the film in place of Paddy or he was going to get an injunction to stop us ever making the film and issue so many sets of proceedings that I wouldn't be able to see the sun for writs.

"He said that I would find that I'd paid US $5M upfront for a scene that never got shot in a film that never got released. So, yes, I agreed to find a place for him on the set. Then when we had this problem with Colman refusing to step out of his caravan, and the whole crew twiddling their thumbs at a cost to me, I should add, of hundreds of thousands of dollars a day, I very stupidly thought that we could at least get the sex scene in the can utilising the services of Presley, because (a) it would be some kind of progress; (b) it was the only scene we could do regardless of the fact that we didn't have a script (c) it would serve Colman right, and (d) I didn't think anyone would be any the wiser, except maybe later on at some point, Colman, and, as I say, it would serve him right.

"With the benefit of hindsight, I am sorry to the bottom of my blue legume shoes, but how was I supposed to have any idea that he'd go the whole hog? It was supposed to be simulated!"

"I can't believe you brought the twin onto the set!" Celia mused. "It's just unbelievable. You know Presley's already attempted to murder Colman once?"

"I knew nothing of the sort, Celia. How would I know that? He was just a guy who came to me with a grievance in one hand and a proposition in the other; and, to be entirely fair to me, maybe I wasn't running on all six cylinders at the time he turned up, because a couple of hours earlier I'd been shot!"

"Even I didn't know that!" Wally cried.

"That I'd been shot?"

"No," said Wally. "That Presley had tried to murder Colman."

Celia just stared at her shoes. Finally, she said: "And here's me worrying about me when we should be worried about Colman. Seriously, guys, if Presley gets within striking distance of Colman, no ifs, no buts, he'll try to kill him again."

"I appreciate I've screwed up big time," began Indigolin, switching his approach to conciliatory, "but it seems I have done one thing right. Because it was essential that no-one realised that Presley wasn't Colman, I've made sure that the two of them are always physically nowhere near one another."

"So are you expecting us to give you credit for that, Indigolin?" Wally barked.

"Not at all, Wally. I'm just trying to look at the positives. We don't have to worry about Presley getting near enough to Colman to kill him."

"So where is he now?" Celia asked, looking around the walled courtyard.

"Well, actually he's staying here with me where I can keep an eye on him," explained Indigolin. "You know what they say about keeping your enemy close to you."

"He's here now?" Celia asked, incredulous.

"Well, not quite," began Indigolin, suddenly appreciating that, in light of the recent revelation from Celia, there was an ongoing need to keep Presley away from Colman. "Not at this precise minute, no, because he stopped off for a beer in town." .

"Where do we go from here?" Wally asked, not caring a hoot about whether Presley murdered Colman and wanting to bring the dialogue back to Celia. After all wasn't an actual rape worse than a possible attempted murder?

"Look everybody," began Celia, "I'm afraid that now we know it was Presley, the situation is a lot more complicated than either of you appreciate, and now isn't the right time or place to go into it. But the first thing you need to do, Tinctorio, is get Presley off the set and out of Morocco before he does anything worse than what he's already done. I'm not talking about me. I'm thinking about Colman. What's done is done; but I am very worried about what potentially remains undone."

"That shouldn't be too difficult, Celia," Indigolin began. "He's assaulted, battered and raped my leading lady. He can stick his fraternal misappropriation suit up his woke writ-pusher's keister. He's over-stepped the boundary and common decency. I'll have him shipped straight back to London as soon as I set eyes on him."

"For the future," continued Celia. "I see no benefit in shooting the bloody scene again. We'll use the one we've done. I didn't go through all that for nothing, and I'm not going through it again with his fucking brother!"

The Tailor of Gloucester

Driving back from the Riyadh, Celia made it clear that the topic of her rape was closed, so Wally tried to lighten the mood and change the subject.

"Did you clock that suit of his, baby?"

"Yes, Wally." Celia replied. "Cool threads."

"Cool indeed! Apparently it's made by microscopic robots. The weave is so wispy it would make perfect PPE for the next pandemic. Nothing man-made can weave so fine a thread."

"Calls to mind that Beatrix Potter story of the tailor who saves the mice from his cat, Simpkin."

"Uh huh, the mice make the clothes for the tailor's customers, don't they?"

"Correct, and you know what happens in the end?"

"The tailor becomes as rich as Croesus."

"Correct."

"Celia, honey, can I ask you a question?"

She raised an eyebrow.

"You ever use Botox?"

"Wally, you know what happens to people who use bovine fillers?"

"Tell, me, honey."

"They end up resembling Minotaurs."

"Celia, the way your mind does the connections, it's really labyrinthine."

Vertigo

When Colman Hunt woke up that morning, the roof of his Airstream was revolving. For a moment, he thought he must still be in his hotel suite in Casablanca. When the crew and actors had first arrived in Morocco, under the first director, Wally Pfister's predecessor, the guy who'd gone native on Moroccan weed, that guy had put him up at Rick's Café to acclimatise him to Morocco and its historical back-catalogue of movie provenance, even though Casablanca had actually been shot in Warner Bros' studio in Burbank.

Colman's mind went back to the circulating ceiling fan in his hotel suite, which is what he thought he must be looking at now, until he remembered he was in his Airstream, and his Airstream didn't have a ceiling fan: it was his caravan that was spinning. Do they have earthquakes, as well as fires, in the desert, he wondered?

He closed his eyes, but everything continued to revolve. He put his head to one side, and he felt like he was sliding off the edge of the earth, and there was nothing he could do to stop it. He felt that if he stayed in that bed a moment longer, he was never going to get out of bed again, so he planted his feet firmly on the ground and stood up, only to be overcome by a sensation of falling backwards. Then he did fall backwards, catching his head on the corner of the ice-maker before he hit the deck.

Dr Abbas responded to the callout and arrived on set driving a white Fiat Panda with green Caduceus medical logo stickers on the doors. Elena Troy saw his van arrive and tut-tutted and shook her head. Tinctorio Indigolin, standing beside her enquired why she was tut-tutting and shaking her head.

"It's the Caduceus stickers on the doctor's car," she said. "I guess it's like one of my *Eats Shoots and Leaves* hang-ups. Doesn't everyone have pet hates? One of mine is the Caduceus. The Caduceus is the symbol of Hermes, the patron god of thieves and liars. It has nothing to do with doctors, but millions of doctors and apothecaries around the world stupidly adopted the symbol mistakenly believing it has some association with medicine.

"The correct symbol they should be using is The Rod of Asclepius, which has only one coiled serpent, and that serpent doesn't have any wings. Like so many other bad things, this misuse seems to have started in the US in the 1850s when the Caduceus was added to the chevrons of US Army hospital stewards and then after World War 1, the US Navy adopted it for its Hospital Corps."

"Isn't the Caduceus also the serpent that eats its own tail?" Indigolin asked.

"No," replied Elena. "You're thinking of Ouroboros. Ouroboros is a symbol of eternal cyclical renewal: sloughing of skin; birth, life, death, rebirth."

"Hmm," scoffed Indigolin. "Complicated! I should have stuck with John Donne and the Metaphysical Poets!"

"And that this place may thoroughly be thought
True Paradise, I have the Serpent brought."

Elena quoted from Donne's only poem featuring a snake.

After he had come round, Dr Abbas, shone his pen torch into Hunt's eyes, and then turned the light off and asked Hunt to follow the path of the pen as it arced from left to right, then right to left, then from middle and getting closer, until it touched him impertinently on his nose. Colman Hunt experienced an out-of-body sensation, imagining himself to be a cinema screen staring into the light from the projector. He recognised the film that was being projected onto him as Casablanca.

"Head wounds always look worse than they are," said Dr Abbas. "All the blood vessels congregate there." He seemed to pause momentarily after the word *congregate*, as though he was inviting applause for using such a long word in a language that was foreign to him; but none came, so he continued. "You'll be fine. Has the dizziness gone now?"

"It comes and goes," explained Hunt. "If I lift my head up and turn to the left, I'm okay. But if I lift it up and turn it to the right, I feel like I'm going to fall over backwards. If I lift my arm up to get that scrapbook off that shelf up there, that's just dandy; but if I move my head to look at what I'm doing with my arm, I get that sensation of falling backwards again. I feel like I'm high a lot of the time, but I neither smoke, nor drink."

"It's vertigo," pronounced Dr Abbas.

"You mean, like the Hitchcock film?" Colman enquired.

"No, like Benign Paroxysmal Positional Vertigo," informed Abbas. "You see, you have these very special small stones…"

"You mean, like Thanos in *Avengers Endgame*?"

"No, sir, the stones are inside your ear, and your body interprets the position of the stones to orientate itself. The stones can become dislodged, and this affects your balance. This is what's happened to you, sir."

"How did I dislodge them?"

"It's incredibly common. We really don't know. Since the pandemic, with everybody suffering life style changes, we find it's become more prevalent, because people who used to have a fixed routine—getting up at a particular time, running to catch the train, or going up an escalator at the station—they all started working from home, and the stones were getting dislodged more frequently. It's nothing to be alarmed about. I'm going to prescribe you some Buccastem. If you feel it coming on again, you put them under your tongue and let them dissolve. Don't chew or swallow them. I'm also going to show you an exercise that you can do right here, which is called Epley Manoeuvre."

"So, I could've got this vertigo, because I haven't left my Airstream in so long?"

"That seems as good an explanation as any, sir."

"Is there anything else I need to do?"

"Yes, if you please, sir. An autograph for my wife."

"Will I be okay to go on a hajj?"

"Why should you want to go on a hajj, sir?"

"It's a long story," Hunt informed the doctor, whilst signing a photograph of himself.

Elephantine

"This just gets better and better, Celia!" Wally exclaimed.

"What's happening now?"

"The writer's backtracked, so this is before they cross the Pyrenees and invade France. Of course, they had to get the elephants from Africa into Spain before they could take them to France, didn't they? The writer's realised that detail, so he's written this amazing scene when the elephants are crossing the Straits of Gibraltar. You remember the elephants are wearing armour, and they have flags and ribbons blowing down their sides, howdahs, ropes, chains, the whole nine yards.

"Well, he's got twenty gigantic barges crossing from Morocco to Spain with a dozen elephants on the deck of each barge. Not only does he put amazing words into the mouths of the actors, but his sense of the visually overpowering, is also quite unique. The thing is, Celia, I can already see just how I'm going to film it. It is going to look amazing."

"African Savanna or African Forest, Wally?"

"Huh?"

"I'm assuming that, in order to be authentic, you're not going to use Asian elephants, honey, but there are two types of African elephant to choose from."

"What's the difference, Celia?"

"Well, they both have huge ears, but the Savanna's about three time the size of the Forest elephant."

"Celia, I think I'm going to have to see a man about some elephants."

"You know where to find the right guy?"

"Honey, I am the man who knew where to go to have an Airstream converted into a Woodie-Wagon. You're addressing the guy who sourced a 1962 Facel Vega Facellia Convertible, and the 1964 Gordon Keeble GKI, single handed, remember?"

"How could I forget when you're so repetitive? But, Wally, it doesn't follow from any of what you just said that you know squat about elephants. Where are you going to start?"

"Where you took me, Celia. I'm going to ask at the Atlas Film Studios. They must be awash with elephants there."

"Yes, Wally. What was it Henry T Ford said? Any sort of Leviathan you want, as long as it's grey."

Phoenix

Albanian George sat across the desk in the office of his countryman, Nomikos Phœnix, in Welbeck Street. Nomikos Phœnix was going through the motions of taking it all in and nodding his head like one of those dogs on a dashboard. Nomikos Phœnix was an insolvency practitioner who hadn't passed any exams, because he'd been practising as an insolvency practitioner before they passed the 1986 regulations requiring insolvency practitioners to be licensed.

It was an unusual instance of the cowboys pulling up the ladder. They persuaded the legislature to agree that if you already purported to be an insolvency practitioner prior to 1986, then you were an insolvency practitioner. But anyone who came along after 1986 and wanted to call himself an insolvency practitioner, had to pass a load of exams, none of which Nomikos Phœnix, had had to sit. He practised under the title, Phœnix Legal Consultancy, and he got a lot of referrals from the solicitor's practise of Barnaby Challenger.

When Nomikos was growing up, his little brother, Drakus Phœnix, couldn't pronounce his name properly and used to call him Noddy. The name had stuck, and it fitted him, because, when he sat across the desk from you, taking instructions, he would nod fiercely, indicating his apparent complete concentration, although this was just so much theatre, and after he'd pretended to listen to you for an hour, he'd sell you the one-size-fits-all solution that he'd intended to offload on his client before he walked through the door.

Because everyone else called Nomikos Phœnix, Noddy, Albanian George insisted on calling him Big Ears. And it was true: he did have big ears, although his mouth was bigger. One thing that could be said about Albanian George was that he was a good listener. His dad had told him that the reason why we have two ears and one mouth is so that we can listen twice as often as we speak.

Also, George found that when he did speak, he was prone to malapropisms. He couldn't get by without speaking at all, but he could get by as a man of few words, and he found that this also enhanced the image he liked to project of himself as being a hard guy.

Noddy didn't mind being called Big Ears by Albanian George, because in the Noddy stories Big Ears is the wisest resident of Toyland.

George's dad had also taught him that if you wanted to find a bent professional, they were all located north of Oxford Street on the Baron Howard de Walden Estate. His dad used to call the area bounded by New Cavendish Street, Welbeck Street and Wimpole Street as *The Bent Triangle*. Every unprincipled professional was drawn to the Bent Triangle as though it were a lodestone attracting the brass nameplates of mountebanks.

As an adjunct to burying insolvent companies before they had to account to HMRC for the VAT they had collected on all the goods they hadn't paid for, George sold his clients off-the-shelf companies. He figured that, obviously, having just burnt their way through one limited company, they would be needing another. All of his off-the-shelf companies were known as Phœnix and then a sequential number. He was now up to Phœnix 2300 Limited.

After enquiring what he could do for him today, George had begun:

"Big Ears—fuck it, am I even allowed to call you that anymore? I've received a letter from The Department of Business, Innovation and Skills."

He put the letter on Noddy's desk. Noddy proceeded to read it.

"For Pete's sake, George!" He exclaimed after reading the letter. "When we send you the company kit for the Phœnix company, you get a nice company seal; you get the Memorandum and Articles of Association; you get a Minute Book, and you get an oven-ready resolution to change the name of the company to something more customised to your requirements, a resolution that you are supposed to have passed at a duly convened meeting of the Board, which we know never happened, but you're supposed to go through the motions and file the resolution changing its name with Companies House. I take it that you never passed and filed that resolution?"

"Didn't read down that far, Big Ears."

"This is all about s.216 of the Companies Act, George. You know what that is? Of course you don't. It's what they call the Phœnix company provisions, and when I call my companies Phœnix This, Phœnix That, and Phœnix the Other, it's like a play on words, see. Because Phœnix is my name, but it's also a type of company. A Phœnix company is a company that rises from the ashes of a previous company that the directors burn. So, in your case, I sold you Phœnix 2036 Limited, which you used to perpetrate some carousel frauds on HMRC before we put it to bed. I then sold you Phœnix 2224 Limited which you used to do the same thing. You were supposed to change the name of that company also, and that company was then supposed to get struck off and fade into oblivion. What happened to it?"

"Unpaid creditor wound it up, Big Ears. Thought we could allow the creditor to go to the expense of putting the company to bed, instead of having to muck around with waiting for it to get struck off."

"The problem we have, George, is all down to you not changing the names. If the first company goes into liquidation, they let you get away with it once, but if you have two horses go down whilst you're in the saddle, you get banned from the jockeys club, and if the second company trades with a name similar to the first company, the second company loses the benefit of limited liability."

"So, what's it mean to lose the benefit of limited liability, Big Ears?"

"George, it means that you are personally liable for all of the debts of the company you just burnt."

"Fucking Aida, Big Ears! What we going to do?"

"We're going to have to bring it back from the dead like Lazarus, George. We're going to have to apply to restore the Company to the Register, just so we can kill it off properly this time. This is not going to be simple, George."

"If it was simple, I wouldn't need to come to you, would I, Big Ears?"

"And to answer your original question, they don't call him Big Ears anymore. The publishers deemed that was offensive and might encourage other little bleeders with body image problems to have low self-esteem, so he's now called Mr Squeakie."

"How bad is that?"

"You know we have a professional compatriot over the road in New Cavendish Street by the name of Andrew Panayotis, and everyone calls him Andy Pandy? I like to look on the bright side, George. I'd rather be a Mr Big Ears or a Mr Squeakie, than named after some fucking marionette that lives in a picnic basket."

"So where do we start, Big Ears? Sorry. Are we even allowed to say that anymore? Where do we start, Mr Squeakie?"

"This is complicated, George. You're going to have to leave this with me."

What Noddy meant was he didn't know how to do it himself, but he was going to put a call through to Barnaby Challenger as soon as George had left, seeking legal advice.

"When you say it's complicated," began George. "What you're saying is, it's going to be expensive."

"Not as expensive as paying all of the debts of a company that was only incorporated for the purpose of not paying any its debts, George. Fuck me! This is one really takes the biscuit!"

"Well, I'd better go and earn some money then, hadn't I, Big Ears?"

Albanian George got his phone out of his pocket and touched an app on his screen.

"You calling in some debtors?" Noddy asked.

"I will do, Big Ears; but first of all, I need to pre-cool the Bentayga. Then I'm going to get into it and phone a dude who owes me a lot of money."

He opened the Vantablacked Bentayga app on his phone and started the pre-cool. Then he showed himself out of the offices of Phœnix Legal Consultancy, headed towards where he'd parked his car in the Bent Triangle. He might as well have parked it in the Bermuda Triangle, because when he got to the parking space where he'd left it, it had disappeared. But when he pressed his key fob to unlock it, it's lights flashed on, enabling him to find his near-invisible car.

A Piece of Advice

"Any day now, shill."

Tinctorio Indigolin was responding to Albanian George's phone call, or more precisely the call from Albanian George's car, which had its own phone number and YouTube channel.

"No, dude," Albanian George responded. "You don't get to tell me when you repay my loan. I tell you how it is."

"You're earning a good rate of interest, George. Let it run for a few days. I tell you what. Didn't you lose a lot of money in the OneCoin crypto scam? I've been playing Find the Lady, and, instead of giving me a hard time, I can reliably tell you where the missing Crypto Queen is hanging out."

"You know the whereabouts of Ruja Ignatova?"

"I certainly do, and as a sweetener, I can share them with you. Then you can get on her case instead of mine for a few days. How about that?"

"And what the fuck am I supposed to do with Ruja Ignatova?"

"You want my advice, George. Go back to Bulgaria."

George didn't get the famous film quote. He thought Indigolin was speaking literally. "I'm not from fucking Bulgaria, dude! I'm an Athenian. What you doing now?"

"What am I doing now, shill? I'm going to the movies, that's what I'm doing. So long, shill."

Albanian George stared his phone down. There had ceased to be anyone else on the call. Despite the Vantablacked Bentayga's pre-cool, he had a good head of steam on him now.

The Omnibus

Nomikos Phœnix put a Teams call through to Barnaby Challenger. Challenger checked his upper half was dressed and turned on his background of law books and fake certificates.

"Law Offices of Barnaby Challenger," he announced.

"Barney, it's Nomikos Phœnix here."

"Good day, Mr Phœnix."

"I think we've got a problem on our hands with George Georgiou. He failed to change the name of one of our companies and now it's been compulsorily wound up."

"That means that an independent liquidator is going to be able to take a look at the structure, Mr Phœnix. That is a concern."

"I know, because the structure goes all the way to the top."

"To Omnibus."

"A liquidator can call for the files of the director's professional advisers. He can call Albanian George in for examination on oath. They can subpoena him duces tecum with all his documents."

"We can't have Headco exposed to scrutiny in this way, Mr Phœnix. And Albanian George is a loose cannon. We can't risk him being cross-examined by anyone competent. I think this is a job for Hugh Webb."

"But does George even know about what goes on in Omnibus?"

"The problem with someone like Albanian George, Mr Phœnix, is that even though he probably knows fuck all, he won't be able to resist the temptation to pretend otherwise, and that could be just as dangerous as the real thing."

Moulin Rouge

"What in the name of everything that's Holy is that, Walter?"

Celia was gesticulating at the gigantic, jewelled elephant that had arrived on set. The electricians were attempting to connect it.

"Don't worry," he said, "It's only a temporary elephant. Whilst we wait for the real ones to get here."

"I thought you were going to CGI them, Wally."

"Walter Pfister doesn't do CGI. Everyone knows that."

"But where did you find it?"

"Atlas Film Studios. It's the elephant Nicole Kidman seduces Ewan McGregor in."

"Of course, in Baz Luhrman's 2001 film of Moulin Rouge! But I didn't know that was shot at Atlas."

"I don't think it was, Celia, but you know what they say, how Atlas Film Studios is like an elephant's graveyard for film props. It seems it ended up here. They offered me a choice of this elephant from Moulin Rouge, or the Elephant of the Bastille from Les Miserables."

"Of course, le Gavroche hides inside it, doesn't he?"

"Correct, it's the urchin's shelter; but the Les Mis elephant was seventy-eight foot tall and it didn't light up. When the electricians get this wired, it's going to set the desert ablaze!"

"Don't be silly, honey. There's no fires in the desert!"

Another Urchin

His too-small bicycle leaning against the wall of Colman Hunt's trailer, the Berber boy, from his place of concealment, pushed his big spectacles back to the top of his nose and surveyed the army of electricians going to work on the huge mechanical elephant.

"Oh no!" he whispered under his breath. "Oh no, oh no!"

Casablanca

Celia let herself in to Wally's Woodie-Wagon. She recognised the tune he was playing on his upright piano.

"How appropriate!" She purred.

Coming up behind him, she kissed him on the top of his head, put her arms on his shoulders and joined in with that velvety, baritone voice of hers:

"A kiss is still a kiss…."

Then he joined with her in the duet:

*"You and me beneath the stars
Rocky moonlight in your arms
Magic the movie in my Chevrolet…"*

Through to:

"I love you more and more each day, as time goes by."

As the last note faded away, Celia resisted the temptation to ask him to play it again. Wally closed the lid on his baby grand, and looked her in the eye.

"Shall we?" He enquired.

They kicked off their shoes, and arm in arm, they descended the steps from his caravan and padded across the sand, away from the crash and the blur of the Airstream encampment, headed towards Aka's kitchen garden where he had first seen the epiphany of Celia in the irrigation spray. With the exception of stay-at-home Colman, everybody else was already there, recumbent on the cushioned, wooden steamers that Aka had spread out in the desert in front of the outdoor screen.

"No Chevrolet, honey?" She asked.

"No drive-in, baby." he responded.

"We'll just have to make do with these," he said, finding the on/off switch for her Bluetooth headset and helping her on with it. She stretched out on the steamer. He pushed his lounger closer towards hers. Then, he scurried off towards

Aka's chow tent, and re-emerged with two boxes of popcorn. He presented her with one of them, turned his own headset on, and, under the canopy of stars, untainted by light pollution up to the moment Mohammed flicked the switch on the projector, they lay back as the opening credits for Casablanca rolled by on the makeshift outdoor cinema.

An Outage

Considerately, the electricians waited until the closing credits for Casablanca, before throwing the switch.

For a couple of seconds the huge elephant burst into a million fairy lights like a Christmas tree colossus, in advance of an almighty bang followed by the profoundest and most palpable darkness, indicating that they had probably blown every fuse in the Sahara. The darkness was primeval, Biblical, the same darkness that must have been on the face of the earth In the Beginning.

People cried out and scrambled, falling over one another whilst Aka Akinyola lit candles and searched for torches.

"Maybe you should have bought the one from Les Mis that didn't light up!" Celia told her boyfriend.

In the far-off distance, the Marfa lights from the Berber camp twinkled and seemed to tease them with a light they could not reach.

Gallantly, navigating by the dim light of his Apple Watch, Wally attempted to guide his leading lady to her caravan.

"What is that watch face?" she asked him.

Wally showed it to her.

"You used me as your Home Watch Face!" she cried. "How loyal!"

"I'm your director, Celia, so just follow me. I don't want you falling over anything. I'd never forgive myself. Just keep talking, so I know you're there."

"Do you want me to talk about elephants, Wally?"

"Baby, I don't care what you talk about, just as long as you keep talking."

"Okay. Here goes from your little Scheherazade: *A blonde wakes up in bed one morning with a throbbing hangover. She turns over and, good grief, there's a full size elephant with a trunk and everything in bed beside her. 'What are you doing here?' she asks. 'You mean you don't remember?' asks the elephant ruefully. '...how we met at the disco. We had dance after dance.' 'I spent the night dancing with an elephant?' she says. 'Then we went on,' the elephant continues.*

We went to an all-night joint for mojitos. You must have had eight or ten.' 'I spent the night sinking mojitos with a pachyderm!' she exclaims. 'Then you invited me back to your place,' says the elephant, continuing his narrative. 'We kissed. You undressed. We had amazing sex.' 'Fuck me!' cries the blonde. 'I had sex with an elephant! I must have been tight!' 'Hmmmmmmm,' says the elephant."

Marfa Lights

Colman Hunt could swear he could hear the soundtrack of Casablanca playing somewhere, and that was what had woken him; but that was impossible. What was happening to him? This morning he'd woken up thinking he could see the revolving roof fan from the film spinning above his head; earlier, when the doctor had shone his pen torch into his eyes, he had thought he was the screen on which the movie was playing, and now he had woken up in the night, thinking he could hear the soundtrack. Clearly he'd been in this godforsaken country too fucking long. He looked at the luminous dial of his watch. It was only nine-thirty pm. He hadn't been asleep more than ten minutes.

Someone, somewhere must have written a joke about a guy who thinks he's a cinema screen. Like the guy who thinks he's a pair of curtains. *Just pull yourself together*.

Colman could practically write the joke for himself:

Doctor, doctor, I think I'm a projector.
No, you're just having a light bulb moment.

Naked, clutching the first sixty pages of his script under his arm, the pages that he had been learning before he dozed off, Colman Hunt rose up from his recumbent position too quickly and the vertigo hit him like a truck. But now that he had a name for it, he felt that the spinning feeling was perfectly normal and not something he should be worrying about.

He remembered a joke about that.

This guy walks into a bar. He orders a pint. He drinks the pint, then he climbs up on the bar, unzips his fly, and pisses all over the other customers, ending up pissing in the ear of the barman.

"That's a nasty problem you've got there," says the barman. "I recommend you see a psychiatrist."

A month later the guy returns to the bar and orders another pint of beer.
"Did you see the psychiatrist?" checks the barman before serving him.
"Sure," says the guy.
The barman serves him. The guy downs his pint. Then he jumps back onto the bar and pisses all over the customers and into the ear of the barman.
"I thought you said you'd been to see a psychiatrist about that?" asks the barman.
"Yeah," says the guy. "I'm not embarrassed when I do it anymore!"

Chuckling to himself, Colman opened the door of his Airstream to sniff the night air and count the stars, and what confronted him must have been a mirage, because he saw the distant fires burning in the desert, but either the night air or his vertigo diffracted the light waves, so that he believed the desert right outside his trailer was on fire.

"It's time," he muttered under his breath. "*Ekpyrosis.*"

With his inchoate script of *the Gate of the Burnt One* under his arm, rolled up like it was his yoga mat, gingerly, Colman Hunt descended the steps from his trailer onto the sand. He felt no pain. In fact, he believed he was walking on air: meditate, dedicate, levitate, he told himself.

Confidently, he strode off, naked, into the night in the direction of the twinkling Berber fires burning in the Sahara.

The Threatened Assassin

Presley Unsdorfer decided it would be a good end to a great day if he stopped by Colman's trailer on the way back from the Ibis, and inform him (as was the case) that he'd just had the pleasure of shooting the gratuitous sex scene with his brother's ex-wife, and that there had been no Intimacy Coordinators to get in the way, so he'd decided to go the whole hog and fuck her on set. Just to wind his brother up further, he'd embellish the story a bit, and tell him (as was not the case) that the tent had been packed out, that the whole crew had been on hand when they shot the scene, and that his brother would be able to review the out-takes on TikTok, months before the film's official theatrical release.

Having consumed a gutload of alcohol at the Ibis, Presley had purchased himself a Leatherman knife in the hotel shop, and decided to pay his brother, Colman, a visit from which he wouldn't recover. He'd taken a petit yellow taxi as close as he could to the place where all the Airstreams were parked, and stumbled the rest of his way on foot from the point where the road ran out. He'd torment his brother first of all with the news about the carnal relations with his ex, before sticking him with the knife.

He observed that they had put up a makeshift screen between a pair of palm trees, and a lot of people were recumbent on wooden steamers watching an old black and white film, but he couldn't hear the sound, as it was being transmitted into the headsets of the audience. That also meant nobody could hear him, but he didn't exactly make a lot of noise in the sand anyway.

He found the door to Colman's Airstream ajar with all the good air-conditioning leeching out into the desert and going to waste. The windows were wringing wet with condensation. In an age of streaming, Colman's old CD player was booming out the Stones' *Some Girls* album, but no-one was there to hear it. On the table was the CD's jacket, next to a Deluxe 4 Disc Set of Freddie Mercury & Montserrat Caballé's *Barcelona* Special Edition. '*Fucking gay boy music!*' He thought to himself.

The lights were burning, but nobody was home. '*Could be a good metaphor for Colman's brain,*' Presley thought to himself. There were signs of very recent occupation, but there was no sign of his brother. Having checked that he wasn't in the john, he noticed a big scrapbook open on the galley kitchen counter, and was contemplating a photo of himself, his two identical brothers, Celia Broadsword and Paddy Oculus, the four of them in black suits, staring down at their shoes. He remembered that the photo had been taken at his father's funeral.

The frozen image acted like a link embedded in a webpage, transporting him straight into what happened next, right after the photo had been taken. He'd almost opened up his brother's chest with his Stanley knife, before that old queen, Oculus, had stilled his hand with the shiv in it. My God, Presley recollected, for a limp-wristed faggot, the guy had a grip of iron.

So intent was his reminiscence, and so loud was the Stones' music playing on Colman's CD player, that he failed to notice his other brother, Posthumous, creeping up and duck-taping his mouth from behind before chloroforming him expertly with a wet cloth to the nostrils. Believing he had just overpowered Colman, Posthumous fireman-lifted the supine form of Presley, out of the trailer, down the steps, dumped him in the loading bay of his Toyota pick-up, and drove clean off the set.

Ouroboros

"Did you drink the Lucozade?" Celia asked Wally, who was now able to stand, walk and bend forwards and backwards but not sideways. After his initial dramatic improvement, spending one and three quarters of an hour lying on a wooden steamer watching the movie had brought on a minor relapse.

"It's just a load of sugar!" Wally complained. "Why would anyone want to drink that? It's supposed to be an energy drink. Don't know how it came to have medicinal overtones. It's like getting Red Bull on the NHS."

"But it was a nice thought of Ti's. Can you just picture him, wheeling his shopping trolley up and down the aisles of Carrefour in his blue legume suit?"

"Just like one of those performing pets on Instagram. But I do get his point about the butchers. Have you seen what passes for a butchers in Morocco?"

"Yep, just as he said, an unhygienic hole in the wall where butterflied carcases dripping blood are spatchcocked out in the blazing sun beneath a blanket of flies. It's more like one of those punishments in a TV Reality Game Show than a shop. There's no refrigeration, no glass counter; nothing. The meat must be half cooked before it leaves the establishment."

"We'd better make a note to check that our cook, Aka, gets her meat from Carrefour and not the drive-by butcher."

Just then there was a knock on the door of Wally's Woodie-Wagon and Indigolin strode in with a bunch of cut agapanthus for the recovering patient.

"I came to enquire as to the health of our Ouroboros of Ouarzazate," he said.

"And who is he when he's at home?" Wally asked.

"I am reliably informed that he is the advanced yoga position that you should seek to avoid," explained Indigolin, "and that the Caduceus has received a very bad press for several centuries."

Man Down

Wally sent Pat Oculus to Colman's trailer to enquire discreetly whether or not Colman had had a chance to peruse the latest instalment of the new script and to let him know what he thought of it, now it had all been printed out properly. Paddy reported back that Colman Hunt was missing, the script starring Colman Hunt was also missing, and none of Colman Hunt's clothing seemed to be missing. He also reported there were signs of a struggle in his trailer.

Mohammed was deputed to conduct a caravan to caravan search, but no-one had seen Colman recently. The last person to see him had been Dr Abbas. His ex-wife, Celia, was supposed to have seen him, but she'd received an unexpected and unwanted visit from his brother, Presley, instead.

It was Elena Troy who first articulated what most of them must have been fearing, namely that someone may have kidnapped the star. Although they hadn't yet received any ransom note, the Kidnap & Ransom policy required any possibility of a kidnapping to be notified at the earliest possible opportunity failing which the policy could be vitiated, so Elena sent a formal notification to the K & R insurers.

They logged the call and asked for photographs of Colman Hunt to begin with. Elena felt that she was being triaged with stock footage requests. Everyone knew what Colman Hunt looked like. What was the point in calling for a photograph?

Elena also deputed Mohammed to visit the Ouarzazate police station and make a report of the suspected crime. She assumed the policy would require that also, and she assumed (as proved to be the case) that doing so would involve a lot of queuing up and hanging around, which she had no intention of doing herself. She was pleased to note that the *Sûreté Nacionale* didn't offer an option of going on line, filling out endless reams of poorly interactive forms and then ticking a box that would enable you to receive a *We're sorry to hear you've been a victim of crime* missive. It looked like the *Sûreté Nacionale* were old school, same as Wally and Celia liked to say they were.

Two Men Down

Having discovered that he'd shot the $5M sex scene with the wrong sibling, and managed to record the rape of his own soul mate in the process, Wally now discovered that both the rapist, Presley, as well as his brother, Colman, had both gone missing. The current working hypothesis was that Colman must have been kidnapped, but what had become of Presley? '*Maybe,*' thought *Wally,* '*following the $5M sex scene, he had simply ejaculated himself into extinction.*'

Wally had called Indigolin to enquire if Presley had eventually turned up at the Riyadh. After all, he had said he was going to the Ibis for a beer; why not a lost weekend, after which he might limp back to the Riyadh? Some drunks spoke in euphemisms, so stopping off for a beer could be litotes for disappearing on a bender for several days. However, it appeared that he'd never come back after his detour to the Ibis.

Having completed his form-filling at the *Sûreté Nacionale,* Mohammed had next been asked by Elena to go to the bar in the Ibis and make enquiries there, but being a devout Muslim, he declined on ethical grounds. So Elena Troy thought she had better volunteer for this mission herself. She had shown the barman some stock images of Colman Hunt off the Internet and the barman had confirmed that Colman Hunt had been there drinking heavily and smoking until about 11.00 pm (which confirmed to her that the guy in the Ibis that the barman was describing was actually Presley, because Colman Hunt famously neither drank nor smoked).

At about 11.00 pm, the man who the barman thought was Colman Hunt had then had the barman phone for a petit yellow cab for him. Subsequent enquiries with the cab company revealed that the taxi driver had driven the man they thought was Colman Hunt back in the direction of the Airstreams until the tarmac road ran out, at which point Mr Hunt had said that he wanted some air and had got out of the cab a few hundred metres shy of the set.

Then the trail went cold on both the real Colman Hunt and his fraternally misappropriated brother. There was some closed circuit TV, but (a) all the cameras were in the wrong places, and (b) they weren't infra-red, so they were near useless at night time.

In discussions with Elena Troy and Wally, Indigolin concluded that the guy who had been doing all the drinking at the bar in the Ibis must indeed have been Presley, because going to the Ibis for a beer was what Presley had said he was going to do, and Indigolin offered up the hypothesis that Presley must have kidnapped Colman. Wally thought that a fanciful hypothesis, given that Presley had arrived in Indigolin's car and had no means of transport for himself. It would be rather difficult to kidnap someone in the middle of the Sahara desert and then hail for a taxi to make one's getaway.

Wally Pfister convinced himself that the way he could be helpful and aid the enquiry into the disappearance of Colman and Presley, was to review the footage he'd shot of Presley just before he disappeared. Rewinding the scene, which Celia and Indigolin had agreed they would use, because Celia had refused to put herself through it all again with the right brother, and therefore trying to work out how best to edit it, whilst at the same time searching the footage for clues, he replayed it again and again.

After he'd done this about twenty times, he realised that the emotion he was experiencing was jealousy. His feelings on this subject were highly confused, because watching the scene infuriated him whilst at the same time giving him a raging hard-on. The culmination, which he himself couldn't have predicted if anyone else had told him this story, was that he had joined the Kleenex Club whilst looking at images of someone else raping the woman he suddenly realised he was in love with.

Afterwards he felt so ashamed of the depths the scene had made him plumb that he resolved to destroy the footage, US $5M, or not.

Scrapbook

"The K & R guys want to know if we've got any photographs of him."

"Photographs of Colman Hunt? Everyone knows what Colman Hunt looks like. He's all over the Internet."

"Wally," explained Elena, "the K & R guys want to put some images up on the Internet; help in the search. All of the images we know about belong to the studio from which Mr Indigolin bought the rights to make the four-picture deal. The studio wouldn't let us use any of them unless we paid for a copyright licence. So we need to find some images that don't belong to the studio. Some images that belong to Colman Hunt himself."

After a short silence, Oculus piped up: "He's got a scrapbook. You know. All actors of a certain age still keep a scrapbook. Everything's in there, from his *schnickling*, to his bar mitzvah, all three weddings, stills from every film, and every write-up he's ever had, even if it was pure vitriol. If the name Colman Hunt appeared, out would come the pinking shears, and in the book it would go. It's in his Airstream."

"Shall we?"

The meeting adjourned to Colman's chromium caravan. Pat found the book with ease, given that it was a coffee table book larger than a coffee table, and, indeed, it was still open on the kitchen counter, where Presley had been perusing it before Posthumous had crept up behind him and abducted him. There was Colman Hunt photographed with every leading lady of the last thirty years, with a few politicians, shooting bears in the Carpathians with King Juan Carlos, shooting the breeze with the Pope in the Vatican City, and on set in a great many locations, but mainly in Southern Spain for the King Ferdinand series.

But Elena was transfixed by the wedding photograph, the scrapbook already being opened on the coffee table to that very page. Impeccable in their charcoal suits, they were standing on the steps outside a village church. Celia Broadsword, as befitted a 2nd marriage, was not wearing white. There were no other close family members. Just Celia and four carbon copies of Colman Hunt.

Wally scanned the photo with his phone. It was the same photo the twelve-year-old cyclist had snapped with his phone.

"There's four of them!" Elena whispered.

"No. One of them's me," explained Oculus. "And that's Colman, with his arm round Celia."

"But that still leaves two more of him!" Elena protested.

"That's right, Elena," explained Pat. "It's not twins. They're identical triplets, but you never see them together. They both hate Colman."

"You'd better begin at the beginning," said Elena Troy.

"The beginning is the conception of Colman Hunt. The one thing Colman inherited from his father," began Oculus, "was that his father also shot blanks. So Colman's mother underwent a number of courses of fertility treatment with some other dude's sperm. She bore identical triplets and died in the process."

An Arse with Three Cheeks

Wally Pfister reached for his phone on the bedside table. Celia Broadsword instinctively pulled the sheet up over her breasts in case he was intending to photograph them. The going rate for that privilege had been set at US $5M.

Wally was bathed in a glow of contentment. He'd never had sex as good as that before. He felt as though he'd started pouring himself into Celia Broadsword about an hour ago and forgotten to say *when*.

"You know what I like about you, Celia?" He asked. Celia raised an eyebrow, inviting him to expand.

"No tats. No stupid piercings. No ghastly killing fields of stubble, concealing suppurating boils from ingrowing hair follicles where the razor took a wrong turn. It's a proper Full English down there."

"I don't think I've heard it referred to as that before!" She said.

"What I'm trying to say, what I like about you, Celia, is you're old school."

"You mean, just old."

Having activated his phone with his thumb, Wally opened the scan he'd taken of the wedding photograph from Colman's scrapbook and showed it to her.

"Recognise anybody?" He asked.

"I recognise *everybody*," she purred, enlarging the photo on the touchscreen with her thumb and forefinger. "Mind if I smoke, Wally?"

Although he didn't smoke himself, Pfister lit one of her Passing Clouds up for her and passed it across the bed. Then, like the perfect gentleman he was, he placed the ashtray on his bare chest for her greater convenience.

"You know what really pisses me off, Wally?" She asked, inhaling the smoke.

"No, Celia. What really pisses you off?"

"Actors acting smoking."

"What do you mean?"

"I mean there must be plenty of actors who smoke. Why do so many directors have to cast so many non-smokers in smoking parts so that we can see their pathetic attempts at—" She made a quotation mark gesture with her fingers,

—"*Acting smoking*". None of them are any good at it. They don't inhale. Why do we have to watch them acting smoking instead of just smoking for real?"

"Celia, you're beginning to sound like Indigolin's description of that brother of Colman's, Presley. The guy who raped you."

"Thanks for reminding me, Wally. I'm still working out how I'm going to deal with it."

"According to Indigolin, he bluffed his way onto the set by saying that he was going to sue us all for fraternal misappropriation or something, because Paddy Oculus was employed as Colman's stunt double, when Colman had a genuine identical brother in Presley, who should have been offered first dibs for the job as stunt double. That's how Presley ended up in Gaddafi's tent with you. And now you're beginning to sound like Presley, going on about smoking misappropriation or whatever."

She drew on her Passing Cloud and glared at him, so he kept talking.

"So you think the smoking and acting fraternity need to rise up and assert themselves?" He was going to add something along the lines of: *Before they die of lung cancer*—but he thought better of it in the circumstances and decided to change the subject.

"Celia, what's your take on all this misappropriation thing anyway? Fraternal, cultural, sexual."

"It's the philosophy of a slave religion practised by narcissists, Wally. Same as gender reassignment or saying you self-identify as a member of the opposite sex. It's just another form of self-centred egotism. If you love women, then the thing to do about it, is go out and find the right one and keep her close to you for the rest of your life.

"What you don't do is you don't attempt to turn yourself into her, as though there are no valid experiences in this world unless you personally experience them all yourself through yourself, and to the exclusion of anybody else. It's just the logical extension of all this Instagramisation. Nobody wants to believe you've done it unless you've filmed it and stuck it up there on social media. Everybody feeling the need to live the metaphor, turn it into a reality and personalise it. What's the word they use? *Claim* it. That just betrays a complete lack of imagination.

"It's a rejection of society, an attempt to contain all of society in oneself, and it all coincided with the time when everyone was working from home due to the Covid pandemic, so they didn't have a lot of choice. They became self-centred stationary hubs in relation to which the outside world was, as Indigolin puts it, merely a delivery mechanism; but now we're talking about deliveries from Amazon and Deliveroo and dark kitchens in Battersea, and not in the Indigolin sense of delivering some kind of valuable payload to the crucial place.

"They wanted to make themselves microcosms and be self-complete in everything, so it made sense to be epicene then. But that was all during the pandemic when they didn't have any choice. But now they do have the choice, they should make better choices."

"What you're really saying, Celia, is that they're all a bunch of wankers."

"Wally, I couldn't have put it better!"

"What's the back story of the triplets?" He asked.

"None of them likes to talk about it," she began. "If I'm going to do some pillow talk, you've got to swear to me, it stays in here."

"Course!"

"On your children's lives."

"That serious?"

"That serious, and still more serious some, Wally."

"OK, Celia, I swear. On their lives"

"How many children you have, Wally."

"None, Celia, and I've never been wed."

Before commencing, she took a deep drag and tapped the ash into the receptacle on Wally's chest. "Their father was a Classics teacher, madly in love with his wife, but they couldn't conceive naturally, so she took repeated courses of fertility treatment until she got herself pregnant with triplets. At the birth, the father was present. His name was Morgan Unsdorferbaum. The birth was not straightforward. The three of them were coiled round the umbilical like that ancient sculpture of Laocoön and his sons wrapped up in the giant serpents."

"Or a Caduceus?"

"Or an Ouroboros, as we now know. Anyhow, the first little boy popped out of his mummy easy enough. The second one sprang out together with most of his mother's innards which he was grasping in his little fist, killing her in the process; the third one was a C-section after she was dead. The father, Morgan, called the one that preceded his wife's demise, Presley Unsdorferbaum, the PRE signifying *before* the death. He called the one that killed her, Mortimer Unsdorferbaum, because he delivered the mortal blow. He called the one they ripped out after she was dead, Posthumous, of course.

"Morgan blamed Mortimer for the loss of his beloved wife. It didn't manifest itself at first as he had his hands full with the triplets, but once they were of school age, Morgan indoctrinated all three of them, so that Morty was consumed by guilt, thinking he'd murdered his own mother, and the other two were awash with hatred for their matricidal sibling.

"It appeared that, in addition to the psychological warfare, Morgan also descended to physical violence in which Posthumous and Presley were encouraged to participate, so that they came to regard beating the shit out of their brother whenever they had the opportunity, as perfectly normal behaviour.

"Social services took Mortimer away after neighbours found strange marks all over him, suggesting the boy had been exposed to prolonged sessions of some kind of torture. Mort was fostered. Morgan, the father, underwent psychiatric sessions, but it transpired that he held no mortal grudges against the remaining triplets; he just couldn't forgive the one that had murdered his wife.

"So, social services let him keep Presley and Posthumous. That didn't stop him brainwashing the pair of them, so that they ended up on the same page as he was, the father and the two remaining sons, all pathologically hating their brother for killing their mother.

"As I said, Mortimer had to be put out to foster and the foster parents' surname was Hunt, and when they sent him off to Corona acting school (because that was the only thing the kid was any good at), Mortimer Unsdorferbaum assumed the stage name of Colman Hunt, from the Laocoön coils: Coiled Man: Colman; get it? He'd had the story of how his mother's umbilical had been wrapped all round him and how he'd killed her drilled into him so many times by his father and triplets that he'd come to think of himself as the Coiled Man."

"But if they all hate each other, why did they agree to come to the wedding?" Pfister asked, referring to the photograph from the scrapbook that he'd scanned into his phone.

"It's not a wedding," explained Celia. "You're looking at a photograph of Morgan's funeral. Colman turned up with me and Pat to pay his respects. Right after someone took that photo, Presley and Posthumous tried to murder Mortimer, and they would have succeeded if Pat hadn't saved his life. When I say *murder* I use the word advisedly, because it was completely pre-meditated.

"They'd issued the invitation to their brother to attend his father's funeral, ostensibly a long awaited act of family reconciliation, but in fact they had come equipped with brass knuckles and a Stanley knife. That's how Col got the circular scar on his chest. Presley had intended to rip his heart out and eat it, but Paddy pulled the knife off him whilst it was still at the stage of a surface wound, before it went mortal."

"So the story about Colman Hunt sustaining that injury when he was rehearsing the sword fight in the first series of King Ferdinand's Book of Hours, is rubbish?"

"Course it's rubbish. Oculus stood in for him in the swordfight, and Mort was never even in the first series."

"Bloody hell, Celia. And are these two still bent on killing their brother?"

"Does Rose Kennedy have a black dress, Wally?"

"Jesus Christ! Why isn't Presley in jail?"

"He was, but there were mitigating circumstances. He did seven years shovel. But that's another story"

"Does anyone else know about this?"

"Only Oculus, Col and me, and of course, Presley and Posthumous. It never went public. It was a juvenile Family Court sitting in private. Didn't hit the papers. Colman came up with the duelling scar story when he had to take his shirt off in one of his scenes, but that was years later. I think everyone assumed the scar had been painted on by the make-up department, but it's for real."

"Heavens! Can anyone tell these guys apart?"

"Far as I know, nobody can except me. Until you get their clothes off and play Find the Scar, they're identical."

"Jesus, Celia!"

"But you know the creepiest aspect of this whole thing, Wally? When Presley stabbed Mortimer, Mortimer bore the scar, but it was Presley and Posthumous who bled. They were in agony for weeks, but the bleeding was all internal."

"If the bleeding was internal, how did anybody know they were bleeding?"

"In the end, it always finds its way out, through the eyes. Both of them looked like Gloucester in Shakespeare's King Lear, blood bubbling out of their eyeholes and making tracks all down their faces. It was really scary, honey."

With finality, she stubbed the Passing Cloud out in the ashtray on her boyfriend's chest.

Organogram

"What on earth is that, Mr Indigolin?"

Elena was referring to the complex tree that appeared printed on Indigolin's yoga mat when he unrolled it that morning.

"I believe it's called an organogram," Indigolin informed her. "It was Noah's idea. The corporate tree for my group of companies has become so complicated that it's difficult to view it and navigate it on your computer screen, so Noah decided we might as well print it out like a carpet and unroll it. Trouble is, by the time he had printed it out, it was already out of date.

"You know, every time we want something legal done, the lawyers call for the organogram, and then they need to know who the ultimate owners of all these offshore companies, owned by other companies, are; and by the time we've managed to provide them with all that information, whatever the crisis was that we consulted them for in the first place, has passed on. God help us if we ever need an urgent injunction. Whatever it was, we were seeking to restrain would have happened before the lawyers could get their file open."

"It's like one of those Russian dolls. Is that how you came to acquire your own NOMAD and get your shares suspended?"

"Too right, Elena. I was badly advised by an old friend, but I got impatient waiting for the solicitors to do all their KYC that they say they have to do so that they can establish that I'm not a member of Hamas. Eventually, I just went out and acquired the NOMAD myself. And then AIM suspended my shares. I mean, for heaven sake! How does sending your lawyer a copy of your driving licence and a utility bill prove you're not a terrorist?"

"But they're not suspended anymore?"

"No, Elena. We got the transaction approved, so now I own my own bank. The share price went through the roof, and I've offloaded a handful of shares and paid all my debts, or my company's debts, as Noah would have it. Noah is very strong on the distinction between individuals and limited companies."

"And what do all the different colours in the organogram mean?" She asked.

Noah answered: "The green ones are Panamanian companies; the yellow ones are Delaware companies; the red ones are BVI companies; the pink ones aren't companies at all; they're trusts; the blue ones are UK companies; and the greyed out ones are companies I want to let go, but the boss won't let me."

"No Vaduz Stiftungs then?" Elena asked.

"No," said Indigolin. "I was advised that if we used any Liechtenstein Foundations, that was as good as asking HMRC to start an investigation."

"Why do you want to let the greyed out companies go?" She asked Noah.

"Because," explained Noah, "those are the trading companies holding all the debt, and we can let them go without paying any of the debt, whilst the holding companies further up the tree hold all the assets and carry on, free of debt."

"Unfortunately for Noah," put in Indigolin, "I happen to be very attached to those companies and the name Blue Rif. Letting any of them go down would be bad for my brand, shill."

"Well, no-one has to know, boss. Just before we put the company into liquidation we pass a resolution to change its name to Shitgrade Limited or something. There's a guy called Big Ears in Welbeck Street does this sort of thing for his clients on an industrial scale. All that the outside world sees is that a company called Shitgrade has gone to the ropes. At the same time, we incorporate Blue Rif (2025) Limited, which trades as Blue Rif. It's seamless."

"It's seamless and also pointless," declared Indigolin. "I just don't want to be associated with anything that's shit, and I regard shitting on your creditors as the height of shit. Excuse my French, Elena."

"Would you let me simplify it for you, Mr Indigolin?" Elena asked.

"How come?" Indigolin enquired.

"I mean, as you say, this is a great structure if you intend to shit on your creditors, Mr Indigolin. But if you don't intend to do that, what's the point of it all?"

"Elena, I kinda like all the serried ranks of companies. I just love the organogram. Gives me lots of *sturm und drang*."

"No, Mr Indigolin. It's all so yesterday, like those people who used to have about a hundred different phone lines listed on their headed paper because they thought it made them look like they were bigger than they really were. Or do you remember those professional partnerships who used to have the names of every partner written on their letterheads, so that there was no space left on the sheet to write the actual letters, because the page consisted entirely of phone numbers and partners?"

"I remember that fondly, Elena! In those days I could get my lawyers to open up a file for me without proving I wasn't a member of Hamas. But I still couldn't get them to handle my legal arguments, because they spent all their time arguing with one another about which order their names should appear in on the letterhead!"

"Mr Indigolin, if you're, say, a property developer, then I accept that you need a separate SPV for each asset. But you don't need a corporate structure like this. I could reduce this to ten companies max, and save you millions in audit fees."

"Most of the foreign ones don't need audits," put in Noah.

"OK, Noah; but you still have to pay the offshore professional stooge directors ludicrous fees to sit on your board. Even if the company's only in Jersey, it's money down the pan."

"OK, Elena," said Indigolin. "Do it for me. Noah, give the lady whatever she needs."

"Hey, everybody!" Noah cried. "We could be looking at a very famous yoga mat. Last time you'll hear of some of these companies! This mat could be headed for Fiona Bruce and the BBC's *Antiques Roadshow*."

"Yeah, shill," said Indigolin, "like its burnt-out owner!"

Quiz Master

"The Mississippi!" George shouted before the onscreen contestants could get a word in edgeways. He grabbed a fistful of salted peanuts from the dish on the occasional table to his left, tilted back his head whilst making a funnel with his hand, and poured the nuts into his open mouth.

"The Missouri," ventured the captain from Trinity College, Dublin.

"No," said Paxman. "The Missouri is the longest, but the answer I was looking for—"

"Mississippi!" George exclaimed again, washing the peanuts down with a slug of Grouse. Although there were more expensive Scotches, he could have bought, George favoured the Famous Grouse, as he believed this is what the likes of Guy Ritchie would surely drink on his shoot at Ashcombe, although Ashcombe is in fact a pheasant and partridge shoot and not a grouse moor at all. Guy Ritchie, to Albanian George's mind, represented the perfect synthesis of English country gentleman and gangster. Also, there was no point in buying expensive Scotch when George was only going to drown it in Diet Coke.

"—is Mississippi," declared Paxman. "The Mississippi is the widest river in the USA."

George made a scoffing noise that was both self-congratulatory whilst also epitomising the sound of the constant conveyor belt of salted peanuts clunking down his neck, like a death rattle oiled by alcohol. As he did so he glanced sideways at his wife, making sure she had heard his correct answer.

"Still on the topic of rivers," continued Paxman, "what is the longest river in the United Kingdom?"

"The Thames," pronounced Mrs George, looking to her husband for approval.

"No, it's the Severn," answered George, talking to the television, not to his wife.

"The Thames," buzzed the contestant from Trinity College, Dublin.

"No," corrected Paxman. "It is in fact the Severn."

Again, the scoffing noise and the peanut rattle. Then a glug from his Waterford crystal tumbler.

Mrs George had no idea that the program she was watching with her husband was not this week's quiz show, but a recording Albanian George had made of last week's show, where he had already conned the answers. He did this every week. George's motivation was not to mislead his wife into believing that he was smarter than was the case. His motivation was to belittle her, to make her feel small and insignificant compared to him.

The smallness and the insignificance were simply the first two milestones he had to coax her past on the road to low self-esteem. Once he had led her to that destination, she would do whatever else he told her to do. But he had to get those foundation stones in place first.

"You're smarter than Paxman!" Mrs George flattered her husband.

"Yeah, but the best one of all was Hughie Green," responded George.

"That could be a question in itself," pronounced Mrs George, playing up to him. "Who was the cleverest ever quiz master?"

"Jimmy Saville," answered George.

Mrs George stared blankly back at him.

"Just look what he got away with," explained George.

A Dance of Seven Veils

Celia now only had the yellow scarf next to her skin. The other six scarves were resting where she had discarded them one after another. Rubbing between his thumb and forefinger the scarf that she had deposited in his lap, Wally reflected that Celia had been quite correct: there was indeed something sensuous about that clingy crepe Fortuny material. He could smell her perfume on the scarves, and the scent grew stronger as each shed layer clung closer to the woman cocooned inside. He recognised the perfume: *La Dolce Vita* by Christian Dior. Other women he'd come across had worn it, but every woman combined it with her own scent and made it unique, especially Celia.

"I knew I had to do the dance again, honey," she said, "and not let that little shit, Presley, get the better of me; not let him poison the well, so that he succeeded in giving me a hang-up about my own nice things. And…" she did a little twirl for him. "since poor Wally here is off games until he's made a complete recovery, I thought you might like to watch."

The yellow veil came off. She was naked. But not naked enough, apparently. She removed the Tahiti pearl necklace and matching drop earrings, and put them in a saucer by his editing table. Then, she reached up to the back of her hair for the seven inch Jineta. She tossed the yellow scarf up and sliced it in two in mid-air with the little blade, so that one scarf went up, but two scarves came down.

"Darling," he said hoarsely, bending down to retrieve the cut cordons from the floor, "I get the allusion. I've seen many versions of that scene in every Crusades film that's ever been made starting with Cecil B DeMille's. But I've never seen it done in the nude before!"

"Don't think Celia Broadsword," she instructed. "Think Celia Scimitar!"

"Scimitar Productions was the name of the late Michael Winner's film company," Wally remarked.

"Die hard!" She punned, her gaze dropping to his groin.

"No, honey. Winner was the *Death Wish* franchise. The five *Die Hard movies* had five different directors, the only common strand being Bruce Willis' character. John McClane."

"Don't be so literal, darling. It was a pun. And the five *Die Hard* films didn't have five different directors, because the first and the third both had the same director, John McTiernan."

He marvelled at her. Where did she get it all from, he wondered; presumably an entire life spent in films.

He lifted the two shreds of the yellow veil to his face and savoured the perfume. "I think I must have wasted my youth shooting Guinness adverts, when I could have been doing Silk Cut ads," he said.

"Well, Wally," she said, putting herself to rest on his lap. "feels like you've been doing the shopping again! What are we going to do with this?"

She tied one half of the divided ribbon in a knot round the Jineta and re-inserted it at the back of her hairdo, so that the ribbon hung down like a pigtail. "Now, I wonder what are we going to do with your half?" She asked.

OpenSea

"How are you getting on?" Agent Anatole enquired.

"Well, Anatole," Elena replied. "I'm doing well in one sense. We've got an open book relationship now. I've been given access to all of his corporate structures and offshore trusts, completely transparent, because he's entrusted me to lop a few limbs off his corporate tree and generally make his organisation simpler. But I haven't found anything wrong with any of it.

"Do you think we could be barking up the wrong corporate tree, Anatole? Tinctorio Indigolin actually seems like quite a nice guy. Huge charitable donations, marine conservation projects, protector of the environment; he's trying to grow back amputated limbs for war veterans, people who trod on mines—"

"He wouldn't be a very good con man if he didn't take you in, would he now? All con men seem like really nice guys until you get to know them properly. Please don't tell me you're getting the hots for your mark, Elena. We're supposed to be professionals here."

Changing the subject, she said: "There are multiple references to something called OpenSea in his books of account, Anatole. Does OpenSea mean anything to you?" Elena Troy was standing in the desert apart from the rest of the crew so she wouldn't be overheard. She'd stayed on after morning yoga, contemplating the Atlas Mountains. She heard a sucking noise at the other end of the line, which she recognised as the sound of her colleague's vaping pen, whilst he considered her question.

"Isn't his yacht called OpenSea?"

"Probably. I don't know, Anatole; but the entries can't relate to his yacht. That's all accounted for in a Panamanian corporation."

"OK. So it's just like everybody else's boat, flying under a flag of convenience."

"Right, so what else can OpenSea mean?"

"You mean, over and above what open sea means to everyone else?"

"It's just a hunch, Anatole. But, you know how his name's been linked to marine biology projects and undersea conservation projects. Didn't he even have a two man yellow submarine that pops up out of a toy box on the back of his yacht?"

"No, that was the Beatles!"

"And, as you know, I share an interest in marine biology. So, when I saw the name OpenSea appearing in his accounts on so many occasions, and we're talking about sizeable transactions, not nickels and dimes, I wondered if it was some kind of code word and that is where I should be drilling deeper."

"You're a conservationist and a marine biologist, but you want to go drilling in the sea? Why don't you just go fracking in the Peak National Park, Elena?"

"Anatole, could you just stop jerking me around for five minutes and answer my question?"

"OpenSea. It's like a company name, yes?"

"Yes, like it's a company name."

"Is it OpenSea all one word but with a capital S in the middle."

"You've got it."

"It's a peer-to-peer digital marketplace for trading bitcoins, NFT's and crypto-collectibles. Exactly what one would expect to find in the books of Tinctorio Indigolin."

"So, OpenSea is completely innocuous?"

"Yes, like eBay, except its turnover is increasing by 12000% per annum."

"It couldn't be put to some illegitimate use?"

"Elena, it's impossible to think of anything legitimate that, at some time or another, by some devious, creative, criminal mind, hasn't been put to illegitimate use, including venerable institutions such as the Church and Marriage. But, assuming some criminal mastermind isn't going to traduce it from its original intentions, OpenSea is a kosher bourse."

"OK, Anatole. I guess it all stands to reason. If he was doing something wrong, a cute cookie like Indigolin wouldn't have been so readily receptive to the idea of opening up all his books to a complete stranger, like me. No, if he's doing something wrong, the answer's got to be on the DataTraveler he always carries with him. I've got to get my hands on that."

"We done now, Elena?"

"Only thing that remains is to congratulate you, Lord Torriano."

"Huh, what are you talking about, Elena?"

"I heard you were taking early retirement from the Civil Service and a knighthood."

"Well, that would be very welcome, but no-one's mentioned it to me."

"You're a poor agent, Agent Anatole. You don't even know what's going on in your own life."

The New Prometheans

"Does Colman Hunt believe in anything?"

Wally put the question to Celia. Wally had just finished making love to her. The chiropractor had made him feel like a new man. Making love to Celia was an amazing experience (certainly an improvement on fellating himself) but it was so good, he couldn't believe it was true, and his disbelief, was ruining the experience for him. His lust feasted upon her naked body, but his reason kept asking him *Has she had work done?* Lust and Reason. Like his good and evil angels whispering in his ears. He'd had sex with plenty of women, but Celia was the first time he'd felt like he was making love.

"Sure he does. He's a New Promethean."

"What the heck is a New Promethean?"

"Haven't you seen him do his party piece with the red hot ploughshares?"

"To tell you the truth, Celia, I've seen Colman Hunt doing a lot of overshare, but not so much in the way of ploughshare; no I haven't."

"Wally, are you telling me you never saw Colman Hunt in *Ordeal by Fire*?"

"'Course I saw Colman Hunt in *Ordeal by Fire*. No-one's not seen *Ordeal by Fire*. Wait, Celia. Are you telling me that scene was for real?"

"Hundred percent! He walks on the red hot coals with his bare feet. His head is actually on fire when he's leading them out of the Maze!"

"Blow me! I assumed the scene was photo-shopped!"

"Wally, they didn't have photo-shop in those days! You know, the ordeal by fire used to be a way of testing women for adultery. The appropriately-named Cunigunde of Luxembourg proved her innocence by walking over hot ploughshares."

"Is that what the New Prometheans do, Celia?"

"It's a millennial thing, Wally. A cult. Like Mormons, except you get to keep your money in your pocket. Paddy got him into it. You know how impressionable we thespians are. We're so god-damned impressionable that we all call ourselves thespians, instead of actors, despite none of us knowing what the hell a thespian is. It was a way of Colman sublimating some of the deep-rooted guilt his father had drilled into his skull. Colman saw Paddy doing the hot coals thing, and he's like *Whoa! How the hell do you do that?*

"And afterwards, he's inspecting the soles of Paddy's feet with a magnifying glass. So Paddy explains to him that with dedication, meditation and medication, anyone can do it. By the time you're doing the walking on hot coals thing, you're very high up in their hierarchy, the grade known as an Ipsissimus."

"Do they have a special day that they celebrate, Celia, like Easter of Christmas?"

"They do indeed. St Joan's Day."

"Like St Joan of Arc?"

"No, Wally. It's a man's name in Spanish. St Juan, as in the famous Byronic Lothario, Don Juan. It's St John the Baptist's Day, and in Spain it's a fire festival. They throw everything that's flammable onto gigantic pyres and set them alight: if they've got nothing else to set fire to, they rip the doors off their own houses and the tyres off their own tractors and toss them on the bonfire. You must have seen it, when they do that thing burning the great big effigies."

"I've seen it on TV. I haven't seen it live. It used to be *papier maché* people like Nero had their effigies set alight, but now it's more likely to be Donald Trump."

"Correct. Or Vladamir Putin."

"Burning's too good for him."

"He's burning in hell anyway. St Joan's was originally a pagan festival for the summer solstice, but when the Catholics put their mark on pagan Spain they shifted the festival backwards a couple of days to their nearest Saint's Day which was St John's, which is how come they have a pagan fire festival on St John's Day instead of celebrating the rebirth of the pagan sun.

"It's known as syncretism—the process by which one religion absorbs the iconography of another. Anyway, the New Prometheans go totally mad that day: everything's ablaze, and the Ipsissimus people are walking along these beds of burning coals, showing the more junior acolytes how it's done; but also, if there's any new-borns, they pass them hand to hand across the fire, like to harden them up."

"Like New Borns and New Burns, huh? How do you get to be an Ipsissimus, Celia?"

"I don't know all the ins and outs, Wally. Colman said that you reach a point where you arrive at a Gate. Most people will be daunted and they won't pass through the Gate. Those who do, and come out on the other side, attain the level of Ipsissimus."

"Is this a physical Gate or some sort of spiritual Gate?"

"Like I said, I don't know all the ins and outs. But if you see a man walking barefoot over burning ploughshares, you'll know that he's attained a very high status in this New Prometheans thing, and been through the Gate."

"Or, if you see a woman doing it, that she's adulterous, like Cunigunde—"

"—Wasn't."

"But in *Ordeal by Fire*, the whole cast did it."

"That's the weirdest bit of it, Wally. The scene where Colman is at the front of the queue, like the Pied Piper, and he makes them all join hands, and he says *Tread exactly where I tread*, and this undulating human conga line follows in his footsteps, placing their bare feet in the fire, taking their time about it, and one by one, Colman delivers them all from the intestines of that inferno. He was able to transfer whatever ability he had developed himself onto the others. It actually happened."

"I'm going to have to watch it again. I must have seen it twenty years ago. Celia, I've read that when shamans do tricks like that, it takes its toll on them and they're weakened and sick for ages afterwards."

"Correct. But Mortimer was fine. It was Presley and Posthumous who were sick as mice for weeks after that stunt."

"You're going to have to explain that one to me, Celia, baby."

"Wally, promise me this doesn't go any farther than this wooden caravan of yours."

"On a stack of Bibles, honey."

"It's probably the biggest cover-up in Hollywood. I mean Babylon is full of cover-ups, but this one takes the Toucan. There was a complete failure by the crew and the SFX team to observe any of the most basic health and safety guidelines when they were shooting that movie, which, incidentally, wasn't called *Ordeal by Fire* at that stage. Explosives were stored in open kegs next to highly inflammable liquids and substances; there were jerry cans of petrol and accelerants strewn all over the place with nothing more than screwed-up newspaper for stoppers.

"They had generous helpings of gunpowder just lying around in paper cups with no lids; live rounds of ammo were mixed up with blanks; none of the props, including the firearms were registered or accounted for or kept in locked cabinets.

The Stunt Co-ordinator was a drunk junkie who couldn't take anything seriously: the schmecker used to lay out parallel lines of cocaine and gunpowder on a glass table, before snorting the cocktail up his nostrils; and the crew members just used to help themselves to guns and play target practise in between takes.

"Of course, the inevitable happened. The film wasn't originally called *Ordeal by Fire*. It was called *Maze Games*, and they were shooting a scene from above looking down into this elaborate maze. The carpenters had constructed the maze so as to make it look like huge boulders and rocks, but, of course, it was all wood and painted polystyrene. Colman's character was like the leader of these slaves who are forced to participate in Roman-style games: like Norman Jewison's Rollerball, but ten years earlier.

"The slaves are all dumped blindfold in the centre of the maze, and then the blindfolds are taken off and they have to find their way out of the maze in a certain period of time. If they don't beat the clock, things start getting a little more interesting. That is to say that, section by section, the maze bursts into flames, each time diminishing the paths by which they might get out. All the slaves are bare-footed in Spartacus-style loin cloths, and I have to say, Colman was well ripped in those days.

"In between takes one of the slaves lights a cigarette and suddenly the entire structure is ablaze. The temperature in there was like the surface of the sun, and they're all bang in the middle of the maze when this happens. At first, the actors thought it was part of the special effects and someone was just testing it and was then going to flick a switch and turn it all off again; but after a few seconds, the heat and the smoke were unbearable, and they're racing around in circles trying to get out of the inferno; but the whole point is that there's only one path that will lead them out.

"Logically, no-one should have escaped alive. But what happened was that Colman rounded them all up, made them join hands and then, in like a giant conga line, he threaded his way, the only way, through all that smoke and fire and collapsing disintegrating carpentry and popping polystyrene, with all those—I can only call them *disciples*—following him blindly, and without putting a foot wrong, without missing a step. With his head and shoulders all wreathed in fire like a halo, he led them out of the maze and to safety. The cameras recorded it all and the whole sequence lasted some ten minutes, during all of which time, beyond a shadow of doubt, Colman was on fire.

"The title of the film was changed to *Ordeal by Fire*, and the scriptwriters re-wrote the entire film to showcase that one scene. Everyone involved had to sign

NDA's; if it ever got out what had actually happened, no-one associated with that project would ever be insurable or bankable or work in films again."

"Jesus, Celia!"

"But the damnedest thing of all, Wally: Colman was covered in smuts and his hair was white with ash, but apart from the dirt, there wasn't a mark on him; but his two brothers who weren't even in the same country, let alone on the set, suffered third degree burns on their chests and arms. They underwent years of skin grafting."

"A lot of people have said for a long time that that scene, shot in those days when special effects were in their infancy, set the bar for everything else that came after, but I had no idea that was because it was for real."

"Every frame of it, Wally."

"I'm lost for words, Celia."

"Well, I'm not Wally. You know when I just said that the damnedest thing of all was that Mortimer walked through the fire, but Posthumous and Presley needed skin grafts?"

"Yep."

"Well, actually, that wasn't the damnedest thing of all."

"Is this my cue to say *Celia, mine, What was the damnedest thing of all?*"

"The damnedest thing of all was that the brothers didn't have enough of their own good skin left for the grafts."

"Oh my God! I think I see where this is going."

"—So they had to use Mortimer's. They took the skin off Colman's arse to do the skin grafting on his brothers. And that just made this crossover thing, this transference from Mortimer to his two brothers worse than ever. They started off sharing the same womb, but they ended up sharing the same skin. For Posthumous and Presley, it was the worst thing that could've happened to them. Like they were imprisoned inside the skin of the person they hated most in the whole damned world."

"So when you described the triplets to me as *an Arse with Three Cheeks*, you were being quite literal."

"I was. They're like three sausages sewn up and sizzling in the same skin."

"But, in between walking on hot coals, what do New Prometheans believe, Celia?"

"Honey, they believe in *Ekpyrosis*. The periodic destruction of the universe by fire. And when it happens, so they believe, only the New Prometheans are going to walk out of the fire. Everyone else will be toast. Everything is cleansed, and the New Prometheans inherit the earth."

"Old wine in new bottles, huh? I guess with all this global warming—"

"Correct; they think their hour is almost upon them. Whilst all the woke vegans wet themselves every time someone measures an iceberg with a Vernier gauge micrometer and announces it's become imperceptibly smaller, the New Prometheans are happy as clams at high water, because they see it as the harbinger of *Ekpyrosis*."

"Celia, your ex is as mad as a cut snake."

"Wally, I've come across plenty of pricks in my time, but Colman's the whole cactus!"

The Plot Thickens

After making love again, Celia lit another Passing Cloud. It was getting so that the interior of Wally's Woodie-Wagon not only resembled a gentleman's club in appearance, but was beginning to smell like one too.

"What would you like to do now?" Wally asked.

"I could use some more of that Cunigunde of Luxembourg, you sweet-tongued charmer! I didn't want to be presumptuous, but I did come over in the black lacy La Perlas that you like."

"And why isn't that presumptuous, Celia?"

"Because left to my own devices, I wouldn't be wearing *any* underwear, Wally."

"Celia, you are one sexy octogenarian!"

"Old enough to know better, but still young enough to enjoy it," she purred.

"But you didn't finish telling me the story," Wally pointed out. "In fact, just when it was getting interesting, you said that part of it was 'Another Story'."

"Oh, I've got to sing for my supper now, have I, lover?"

"It's either that or a dance of the seven veils."

"Well, I told you the story, but not the whole story: only one facet of it."

"So now you're going to show me another facet, eh? You're like the tale-weaver in the Arabian Nights, Scheherazade, aren't you?"

"Or you could just say that having me is like having your very own *Book of Hours*."

"Is the W in *Hours* silent, Celia?"

"No, funny boy, but the W in Swordfight is. I think we'd got up to that, hadn't we?"

"And Presley going to prison for seven years for attempted murder."

"Right. What I didn't explain is that Morty (that's Colman, remember) has had his Jewish guilt for his mother's death rammed into him by his father and two brothers for so long, that he felt it was his own fault that his brother, Presley, tried to murder him. So he took the rap. They swapped places, so that when

Presley was tried for attempted murder, the guy that was standing in the dock was Morty."

"And Morty ended up serving seven years?"

"Yep. At this point, Mortimer, now known as Colman Hunt, had landed the part of King Ferdinand in the first epoch-making series of *King Ferdinand's Book of Hours*. But the actor who played Ferdinand in the second series was none other than Presley Unsdorferbaum."

"So, Colman served seven years inside Wormwood Scrubs……"

"For his own attempted murder, right."

"I'm dumbfounded!"

"And everything might even have ended up okay if the State had played its part fair; but unfortunately, as is so often the case, the State was the biggest problem. In the Scrubs, pretty boy, Mortimer—"

"That's Colman, right?"

"Right. Matinee idol, Mortimer, was raped up every orifice for seven years by guys of every race and denomination, save for some time off for good behaviour. Not surprisingly he came out firing blanks, and had acquired a taste for buggery. However, the positive was that whilst he was in prison, Colman was at least safe from his two murderous brothers."

"So when we say Colman was always institutionalised, that's correct, but we just got the institutions wrong."

"Correct."

"Hang on! Isn't that the period when he married you."

"Right on. Turned out, I married Presley. But Colman's name was on the certificate."

"While Colman was in the Scrubs…"

"Serving out Presley's sentence—"

"For trying to murder himself."

"But didn't you notice the absence of the scar and the skin grafts and realise you hadn't married Colman?"

"No, because the marriage was never consummated. I never saw him with his clothes off."

"And when did the penny drop for you?"

"Not until Colman came out of prison and turned up on his own doorstep with no house keys."

"And how was that?"

"Well, as I say, Presley had never laid a finger on me anyway, and then when his brother came out of prison and took his place, the marriage remained unconsummated for three years, despite me trying, due to what they'd done to him in the Scrubs, and then I got a divorce to escape from that family. By now, we were onto the third series of *The Book of Hours*, and in the third series the part of King Ferdinand was indeed resumed by Colman Hunt, and the whole cast was shipped straight out to location in Granada before Presley tried to murder him again, whereupon Presley went straight back onto the herring queue."

"You mean, Presley was unemployed."

"Yes, Presley lost his job, which was technically Colman's job, because Colman came out of the penitentiary and kind of segued seamlessly into the next series. Viewed from Presley's perspective it was just like a death of a thousand cuts. He'd attempted to murder his brother at his father's funeral, and ended up bleeding out himself; then he'd tasted fame and fortune, and in theory if not in practise, been the wife of one of Hollywood's most famous actresses for seven years. Then he found himself back on the rock and roll."

"Dole?"

"Right. Unemployed."

"And what's Posthumous doing all this time?"

"You'd better ask your little Scheherazade tomorrow," she said, stubbing out the cigarette. "Time to make love to me, Wally."

"Celia, you're insatiable!"

"That's because I had ten years off for good behaviour during my sham marriage, and now I want to make up for it, darling!"

"Celia, I'm going to have your tongue dipped in gold!"

"And, Wally, the way you use yours, I'm going to have that tipped in gold too, or maybe platinum to match the hair down there."

"You're very lucky it's still there, Celia."

"What do you mean, honey?"

"When I was a teenager, I had this overbite, and I looked like Goofy. I was all hung up about it and my parents wanted me to be perfect. So they had me booked into this orthodontist who was going to cut the tip off my tongue."

"Wally, that's barbaric!"

"—So that it would stop pushing my teeth forward. But then they got a second opinion, and it appears that other parents have done this, and what happens is that the tongue simply grows back again, like a gecko's tail. So the teenagers endure unspeakable agony, and then the humiliation of not being able to talk properly to their classmates for a year—whilst all the time it's simply growing back again. But worse, because by the time that happens, their teeth are fixed and then they can't be corrected by conventional means, so they have to stay Goofy for ever, because they missed the window of opportunity when they could have fixed it conventionally with a brace."

"Wally, I've no idea where all this comes from, but thank God, they didn't muck around with any bit of you, especially your tongue."

"Enough of my tongue, Celia. What about yours? You're the most amazing story-teller in Christendom. I could listen to you for ever. Did anyone ever tell you that you have the most sensuous voice in films?"

"Yes, Marlon Brando, Anthony Hopkins, Sammy Davis Junior, Michael Gambon. Even Kenneth Williams said I was better than Fenella Fielding. I put it down to two things, Wally. Firstly, it's the English accent; the American accent is so coarse and grating; secondly, I have to smoke at least 30 a day."

"How come you let them dub you when you're so fluent, so mellifluent yourself?"

"Wally, I've been translated into so many languages, dubbed, subtitled, I never worried about it. The foreigners all like it dubbed; the English, because they like to think that they are in-te-llec-tuals are the only ones who prefer sub-titles, but as I'm speaking in English, the problem never arose. I'm old school, like before the talkies. I'm just happy to do the expressions and the real acting. If they wanted to put sub-titles on or dub me, I wouldn't give a tinker's cuss, you know. As long as my face is onscreen, that gets me the royalties and repeat fees."

"Celia, that's all very interesting about how they dub you, but may I say, you're still the best French kisser I've ever come across. Come here with that amazing tongue!"

"Don't get me started, Wally."

Teaser Trailer Trash

The next morning, after yoga, it was pretty much like business as usual. The leading man, Colman Hunt, who had been refusing to come out of his trailer for weeks, had now disappeared altogether, simply turning his living metaphor into a reality in the same way that Celia Broadsword had observed all sallow, self-centred narcissists did these days, but in his case, maybe with more sinister overtones. The working hypothesis was that he'd been kidnapped, and Elena had submitted a report to the K & R guys, and she was waiting to hear back from them.

But in the great scheme of things, to all intents and purposes, Colman Hunt had ceased to be a participant in this project some time ago and Indigolin wanted to drive it forward whether or not he had a leading man. Elena had filed a missing person's report with the local police, because she assumed that overlooking something as basic as that would vitiate the K & R policy, and Noah had been deputed to ensure that the kidnapping of Colman Hunt on set reached the world's media, so as to fan the flames of the fans' publicity machine.

Having generated this interest in their non-existent film, the script for which (*Inshallah!*) was being delivered in batches each night by a mysterious author who was not under contract, but was certainly under the radar, Tinctorio Indigolin pushed home his advantage by pressurising Wally Pfister to shoot the teaser-trailer for King Ferdinand's Endgame, because Indigolin had already claimed the social media handles and wanted to get his whisper campaign going to big up the new series with all haste. He rationalised that he couldn't keep all Colman's fans waiting whilst Colman was sulking in his tent or kidnapped.

Elena negotiated for the rights to some twenty seconds of screen time of Colman Hunt's face from the previous series. Pfister then interspersed these cuts with various dramatic scenes of Celia Broadsword doing stuff in the desert along with some stuntmen mashing one another up at the Atlas Film Studios, and some CGI barges of elephants. He edited the trailer and put it up on social media the same day. The following day it had received more than a million likes. More viral than virile, he said to Elena Troy.

Elena Troy, who had become a confidante and sounding-board for Indigolin, was concerned about the legality of using the sex scene. Indigolin told her (as was the case) that the studio had in fact taken legal advice on using Presley to stand in for Colman, and the gravamen of that advice was that Colman couldn't do anything about it, because he had already colluded with Presley when the two of them had conspired to mislead the public when Presley had stood in for Colman during the entire second series of King Ferdinand's Book of Hours (generally reckoned to be the best series of all) whilst Colman was serving out his brother's time in the Scrubs, as a result of which, Colman would now be left without remedy by virtue of something known as the legal doctrines of waiver and estoppel. He informed Elena that he had come by this information at a very high level and it was all ring-fenced by NDAs, and mustn't go any further, but legally they were watertight.

Elena had said that wasn't what she had been referring to when she had questioned the legality. She said she didn't give a toss about the teaser trailer. She was referring to the rape.

The Smile on the Face of the Sphinx

"The other weird thing," Celia purred as though she was having a conversation with each of Pfister's chest hairs individually, "is that Mortimer has this X-Men thing. You know how Professor Xavier can find other mutants? Well Colman has like Google Maps for his brothers.

"When they were tiny, they used to play hide and seek, but no matter where Presley and Posthumous hid themselves—I don't just mean around the house, I mean maybe on a neighbour's property ten miles away—Morty could find them with his eyes closed. And as he approached them, he used to do this chanting thing: *Fee-fi-fo-fum, I smell the blood of an Unsdorferbaum! Be he alive or be he dead, I'll grind his bones to make my bread.* That's why they dropped the *Baum* tag in Unsdorferbaum, to stop Morty rhyming with it; so the other two of the triplets are now plain Unsdorfers; but that didn't stop him knowing where they were. He has like a lodestone in his head."

"Good job the opposite doesn't also hold true, Celia."

"Huh?"

"You said the other two are permanently wired to 'Kill Morty Mode'; so it's a good job Morty can find them, but not *vice versa*."

"Correct, Wally. Good point."

"But having a lodestone in his head, doesn't explain how he was able to get out of that maze alive."

"Wally, at various points in our lives, we have to admit to ourselves that there are certain things for which there is simply no rational explanation. I mean, the explanation for him not burning to death in that inferno is that he's a New Promethean. But that's not really a rational explanation; it's just the explaining away of one irrational thing by reference to another. I can just about buy that if someone dedicates himself to learning how to walk through fire, it's a social skill that he has acquired by dedication and self-discipline and practice; but it doesn't explain how he was able to transfer the skill to the rest of the cast in that maze."

"A riddle, wrapped in a mystery, inside an enigma, huh?"

"Yes, and then packed inside a conundrum-filled condom and stuffed up the bum of a Sphinx, like a suppository, darling!"

"Well, that would certainly explain the smile on the face of the Sphinx, Celia!"

"Where does that one come from, Wally?"

"Wow! Where that one comes from is one for the books! Walter Pfister finally knows something that Celia Broadsword doesn't! It's a limerick:

The amorous urge of the camel
Is greater than anyone thinks
After many long months in the desert
He yearns to make love to the Sphinx

You want me to go on, Celia?"

"We've come this far, Wally!"

"*But the Sphinx's capacious vagina*
Is clogged with the sands of the Nile
Which accounts for the hump on the camel
And the Sphinx's inscrutable smile."

"Elena's got Indigolin learning John Donne and you dish me up this doggerel, darling?"

"Sorry, Celia."

"The fact that Morty is a New Promethean is like a rhetorical answer, but it's not an explanation of how he survived. As to how he found his way out of the maze, as I say, he could do this *Fee-fi-fo-fum* thing and find things; but that's not an answer either, because his brothers weren't there. It's just another question for which we're never going to have an answer. The fact is, we just have to accept that there are things in this universe that we are not supposed to understand, whether it's what happened and what was recorded in *The Maze* before they re-titled it, or the Blue Dude's molecule passing through living flesh, or the same

Blue Dude being shot at point blank range and walking away from it. There are more things in heaven and earth, Wally."

"One of those being the effect you have on me, Celia Broadsword. Every time you open your mouth, you enchant me. You are the most stunning person I have ever met!"

Tamazight

Colman smelt the encampment a long time before he reached it: a cocktail of camel dung, kif, Casa Sport cigarettes and unwashed bed linen. Beckoned by the twinkling fires, it wasn't until he was almost amongst the Berbers that his step faltered and he became conscious of his nakedness. By the adumbral indistinction of the firelight, he made out a group of a dozen or fifteen men in blue robes, recumbent on ornate tasselled cushions with chainette fringe trims, scattered on the sand around the fire pit.

A number of earthenware tagines were planted around the outer edges of the fire, and every now and then, someone would grab one of the bell-shaped lids with an insulating glove, and ladle out some of the contents onto his plate. In another nearby fire pit, stood a tripod from which an iron teapot was suspended from a chain.

The diners' features were partly obscured by the blue robes wrapped round their faces, but from the depths of the shadows etched into their wrinkles, Colman guessed the men were aged from teenagers to old men. Apart from one anachronism, they could have been a painting by Alma-Tadema.

The anachronism was that they were all playing with their mobile phones. The one with his back to Colman was watching *Suits* on Netflix. The instalment was just coming to an end and the viewer was being offered the chance to watch the next episode, when he dabbed the pause button and turned round as though he had been aware of Colman's presence all the time and just waiting for him to be within earshot. He said: "Welcome!" and then he said, "maybe we'd better get you some clothes."

"Who are you?" Colman asked.

"I am Aderfi and we are Tuareg," said the viewer.

"But you speak English?" Colman puzzled.

"Only the women speak Tifinagh these days, my friend. They use it for their letters to their lovers, because they know we can't be bothered to learn a dead language. The women pretend they are keeping our traditions alive, but they are simply maintaining communications with their paramours. They WhatsApp them in Tamazight and Tifinagh. Fortunately, the women are taking their dinner inside the tent over there. As the men of the family, we are responsible for maintaining the Berber tradition of hospitality, especially to strangers, so, again, welcome, and sit by our fire."

A chubby boy, probably no more than twelve years old, came up to Colman. He was pushing a bicycle that seemed a few sizes too small for him. In between the handlebars, a wicker basket was mounted. In the basket was a bundle of blue rags. He pushed the big frames of his spectacles back up to the top of his nose and said: "Try these, mister."

"And then perhaps you'd care to join us for some pigeon bastilla?" The first said. "As we're Berbers, we have to live up to our reputation for hospitality. Not to do so would be—" he seemed to be searching for the right word, "Iconoclastic."

"Where does a Berber get a word like that from?" Colman asked. "Not sure I know what it means myself."

"We aren't all shepherds and carpenters," explained Aderfi. "The community also supports other disciplines and even professions. I, for example, am studying to be a human rights lawyer. I alternate three months at university and three months in the desert. That way we maintain our sense of civic community and don't lose track of the old ways and customs."

"Don't see how that works."

"No different from the Inner Temple in London where they keep term by eating a specified numbers of dinners in the Great Hall."

Colman wrapped the blue robes around himself gratefully and approached the incandescent gathering. Aderfi gestured for him to sit down on one of the cushions, which he did, and another man passed him a blue crackle-glazed earthenware plate.

Aderfi spooned out some of the pigeon in filo pastry onto Colman's dish. Someone else tore him off some flatbread to dip in the rich, creamy sauce. It tasted good. Colman was suddenly aware of the fact that he hadn't eaten since Paddy had brought him breakfast, but was that this morning or yesterday? He'd lost track. The cream sauce had been spiked with nutmeg and spinach; the filo pastry was dusted in egg and crisped up in the fire. Somehow, chow always tasted better under the stars round a bonfire.

Aderfi continued:

"My name is Aderfi Benjelloun. Aderfi, in our language that we can't be arsed to speak anymore, symbolises freedom and independence. That old guy over there is the head of the tribe, and his name is Amastan which means Protector.

This is my brother, Aghiles."

"Like Achilles?"

"Don't know. It means like a lion. Aghiles is studying to be a surveyor. Just think of the possibilities, a land surveyor who can navigate the vast Sahara Desert guided only by the stars! And now we have our very own Hollywood star, how you say? *In House*. It's the combination of tradition and cutting-edge science or professionalism that are our hallmarks—that and traditional Tuareg hospitality. The little one who gave you the clothes just now is called Badiss Slimani. Many of our kings were known as Badiss, the most famous being Badiss Hammadit; but we call the little guy Badass, for fun."

Aderfi Benjelloun. Badiss Slimani. Colman had come across these names somewhere or other quite recently, but he couldn't quite make the connection. His long term memory was fine, but his short and medium term memory tended to let him down, even before this vertigo thing had started. He liked to read all his lines off the auto-cue. The only lines that he couldn't get out of his head right now were the ones about riding in triumph through Persepolis, and the chapters of fire across the charcoal dome.

Badiss, was wearing a blue tea towel on his head, and large headphones on top of the tea towel, securing it in place. He had spectacles that seemed much too big for him, and was leaning proprietorially on a bicycle that seemed much too small for him with virtually no air in the tyres. Hearing his name mentioned, he removed the headphones. Colman could make out the tinny music that was playing inside them.

It was one of his favourites: Freddie Mercury and Montserrat Caballé's *Guide me Home* from the Barcelona album, made at a time when Freddie was trying to get himself recognised as a serious musician by associating himself with the Spanish diva. Colman snapped out of his little vertiginous reverie when Badiss pinged his bike bell and piped up: "Volkswagen even named a four wheel drive after us!"

Then, when Colman stared blankly back, the lad added: "Tuareg."

"Shall I introduce myself?" Colman asked.

"We all know who you are," laughed Badiss. "You're Colman Hunt."

"Yep," affirmed Aderfi, "earlier on we were watching the teaser-trailer they've just put out for King Ferdinand's Endgame."

"Well that's mighty strange," announced Colman, gesticulating towards the rigmarole under his arm, the only item the naked man had brought with him across the desert. "I've got the script right here, but I sure as hell don't remember shooting no teaser-trailer."

Smoking

"If this film is as good as those Guinness adverts you did, Wally, it's going to be mega. How did you manage to get some of those shots in that Evolution of Man thing?"

"Thing is, Celia, I never forget a face. You know, a lot of people say that; but with me it's gospel. They could hire me out to the Feds for a facial recognition camera. Once I've seen it, I can't forget it. The face can be worked on; it can grow old; it can grow a beard or side whiskers or a handlebar moustache, but I never forget it, and it was just like an ejaculation, if you'll forgive me. For the Evolution of Man thing, I just spewed out thousands of faces and joined them all together, and it happened to come at a time when everyone was into multi-ethnicity and the inclusive society populated by children of mixed race, so the end result of the omnipresent face, blending western and eastern physiognomy, just seemed to be of its time."

"You're really talented, Wally."

"You know," Wally said to Celia. "This doesn't have to be a casual thing."

"What are you saying, Wally?"

"I'm saying that we really click, Celia. This doesn't have to be like a holiday romance."

"Wally, are you crazy? I'm more than a quarter of a century older than you are."

"Doesn't put me off one tiny bit. Promise you, Celia, it doesn't matter. I feel like I've had to wait twenty years for the best ten minutes of my life. In fact, it thrills the socks off me, Celia. You said this was the best sex you'd ever had."

"I did, but that was about the sex."

"Well, I want to share a secret with you, Celia. It's also the best sex I've ever had with anybody, including myself and my Caduceus. But it's not just a sex thing. You embody all the values I hold most dear. You're old school. I just love you to pieces, Celia Broadsword."

"So, you want us to get spliced?"

"One condition, Celia. You've got to give up smoking."

She produced her omnipresent pack of Passing Clouds from her clutch bag and tapped the cigarette on the pack before lighting it. Wally couldn't tell if she was doing this as an aid to her concentration whilst she seriously considered his proposition of marriage, or out of contrariness to demonstrate that he didn't have a hope, or if she was just anxious to smoke as many last cigarettes as possible before she gave up and accepted his condition.

"Wallace Pfister," she began, blowing a long banner of smoke into his face. "You do not ask for my hand in marriage and then stick conditions on it. Or that's going to be yet another question for which you're never going to get an answer. Not a positive one, any road. Maybe if it was me who was asking you, then you could put conditions on it; but you can't stick conditions on your own unsolicited proposal. Wally, I've told you: the smoking, it's my voice, but it's not as if I haven't tried counselling, chewing gum, patches, cold turkey. Sorry, it's not going to happen. Better carry on enjoying the sex, with me, or with yourself, but I'm not giving up smoking."

"Celia, you know what they say? Never make an important decision without sleeping on it overnight. A lot of problems that seemed insurmountable the day before evaporate after a good night's kelp. Will you at least do that?"

"Of course I'll do that, Wally. I've got to get my beauty sleep, haven't I?"

"And Celia, what the heck are those Passing Cloud things that you smoke anyway? I googled them and the manufacturers (who don't even exist anymore, by the way) stopped making them forty or fifty years ago."

"I know, Wally. When I heard that they were planning on doing that, I went out and bought hundreds of thousands to last me the rest of my life."

"But don't they have, like, a Best By or a Use By Date, or something?"

"What are you telling me, Wally? That if I smoke out-of-date cigarettes it could be bad for my health?"

Excel

Whilst Colman Hunt's features were burnished by the light of the camp fire in the desert, Tinctorio Indigolin's face and the face of his amanuensis, Noah, were illuminated by the same Excel spreadsheet on Indigolin's laptop. He had his DataTraveler inserted in the USB port.

"You know, Noah," said Ti, "we've just made a very big, very silly, schoolboy mistake. The sort of thing we'd never have done if that Elena Troy had been running this side of our accounts, but needless to say, we can't have an outside agency accountant looking at this side of our books."

"I'm sorry, boss, I didn't notice either. I should have realised there were other Tabs under the first spreadsheet."

"Yeah, we're keeping too many plates spinning. All the CFD's were in the other Tabs."

"Yes, boss, we've taken in the investments on the Blue Molecule thing; we've blown some on NFT artwork and boys' toys, but the bulk of it is in these two positions on the Contracts for Differences."

"They've taken much longer to liquidate than we expected, but we can't dump them now or there'll be all hell to pay. We've got to keep the positions open."

"And buy more."

"Indeed, and buy more. We have to spend our way out of this. Who was it who said *You can spend yourself poor, but you can't save yourself rich?*"

"Noah, you're looking at a broke billionaire."

"Not broke, boss, just illiquid."

"Yeah, it's just a cash flow thing, like on a spreadsheet. Double entry book-keeping. Put something in one column, take it out of another. We need to find a few million in the next few days if we're going to keep these positions open. We can't go back to the investors so soon. The NHS has already blown its budget. Can't tap them up for any more in this fiscal. We've borrowed on 20% coupons from all our friends. I don't see where else we can go, Noah."

"Boss, we're going to have to kidnap our leading lady."

"Celia Broadsword?"

"The same."

"Noah, we can't get involved in anything like that. It's criminal."

"Boss, it's a crime with no victim. Elena found out that we've got a watertight policy of Kidnap and Ransom insurance. Let's use it."

Noah saw his boss' brain chewing on that detail.

"With whom?" Indigolin asked.

Noah made some clicks on his computer, and then announced: "Metcalfe Insurance Specialists Limited of London."

Indigolin dug into the jacket pocket of his blue legume suit with the Nehru collar and retrieved the roach material business card that been foisted upon him by the ill-smelling bore at *Gazelle d'Or*.

"Snap!" He said, studying the card, and then showing it to Noah. Normally, Tinctorio Indigolin fired back immediate answers, but Noah could see he was having to ponder this question, before he stared Noah in the eye and said: "As long as Celia doesn't come to any harm, you know, I could even be up for this. Tip top!"

"Boss, she's still very bankable, and, as I say, we've got the K & R insurance. I didn't even know about it, because the previous owners took it out, but the agency girl found out about it when she was doing her audit."

"Elena Troy?"

"Yeah, Elena. We just need to go through the motions of a kidnapping, put on a show, nothing unpleasant for her or us or insurers. What we'll do is just spirit her off some place and blame it on the Mocro Mafia."

"They have a Mafia in Morocco, Noah?"

"Yes, boss, several, but the one that does all the drugs and kidnapping is known as the Mocro Mafia. There's also a Morocco Jewish Mafia, but that's generally considered to be part of the Israeli Mafia. We give out that she's been kidnapped by the Mocro Mafia, find someone to act as her minder, keep her out of the way for a few nights, and he can set up some Gmail accounts to issue ransom demands to us.

"We can use our bitcoin accounts to receive the ransom anonymously, and we'll have her back on set in no time at all. If we play this right, she won't even know that she's supposed to have been kidnapped. We can book her into a spa for the weekend or something."

"But the K & R guys will want to waste time negotiating. Take too long."

"No, I found this mad Provo on the Dark Web. He's an assassin, but you'd think he was a fucking film star. He's got a website listing all his trophies; he's got an agent and everything. Look!"

Noah fired up a stand-alone PC, because he didn't want to leave a history of his visits to the Dark Web on his boss's regular PC, and showed Indigolin an image of the white-haired hitman on LinkedIn.

"What's his name?" Indigolin asked.

"Mr Hugh Webb. He's got all these testimonials from satisfied clients who he's done kidnappings for, suitably anonymised, of course. This site I'm sharing with you is like the Debretts of the Dark Web."

"Or in this guy's case Who's Hugh?"

"Very good, boss!"

"If they're anonymised, how do we know he's not just written the testimonials himself?"

"There's no need. The guy is a brand. We can use him as like a crossroads for the insurance people. He does the dirty work for which he gets paid *per diems*, and we bank the ransom."

"Does he take bitcoins?"

"He won't take anything else. Boss, all I know, he's as mad as fuck. If the K & R guys try to drag it out, once they find out that Mr Webb is involved and he's going to start slicing bits off Celia Broadsword and posting them, they should put the pedal to the metal."

"Do you mean 'posting' in the accounting sense, or 'posting' like the Getty kid's ear?"

"Yes, the Getty sense; but not her ear, too visible for the close-ups; well not to start with anyway, because we need something that don't show. I'd start with her tongue. All her films are dubbed anyway. That should loosen things up."

Indigolin looked visibly alarmed. "Noah, I just explained to you that there are personal reasons why I am attracted to your proposition, which are not to do with me gaining money, but to do with this particular insurer losing it, but Celia must not come to any harm. She just lies low for a few days. No tongues, no ears, nothing like that. Won't hear of it. Verstehen, shill?"

"OK, boss. We take it one step at a time. First, I get this Mr Webb guy out here."

"Yes. We salami-slice it. Sorry, Noah, bad choice of words. Just so long as nobody gets hurt except the shareholders in Metcalfe Insurance Specialists."

Mint Tea

"Aderfi," said Colman, seeking the man's attention.

"Mr Hunt?"

"May I inform you that was the finest meal I've had in all the weeks I've been here in Morocco."

"Mr Hunt, the food always tastes better when it's been marinated in good company and taken in the open, round the fire pit, beneath the stars *with* the star. You know, we Berbers are famous for our hospitality. One must always welcome a stranger in the desert."

"Indeed, good company does make good food taste better—" added Colman politely.

"Yes," said Aderfi. "Male company. The women are apart over there, messaging their boyfriends. We men are free to pour mint tea from a great height and discuss weighty matters, such as politics…"

"And the films of Colman Hunt!" Badiss piped up.

"Yes indeed," added Aderfi, "Mr Hunt's special subject will be—*The Life & Times of Colman Hunt.*"

Badiss distributed expresso-sized glass cups with handles. Aderfi, wearing an industrial-rated oven glove, had removed the iron teapot from the chain beneath the tripod, and now circulated, pouring its content into the expresso cups. Colman held his cup out at arms' length, whilst Aderfi, as promised, poured mint tea into it from a great height. Colman observed that Aderfi was exceedingly tall and good looking, and had no problem in pouring the mint tea from a lofty height.

"*As-shay al Magrebi bib-nana*," pronounced Aderfi.

"Berber tea," explained Badiss.

"We make it with spearmint leaves, sugar, boiling water, and we add secret herbs, depending on the time of year. I pour it from a great height so as to aerate it and also keep the tea leaves in the pot instead of in your teacup," explained Aderfi.

"And what would those secret herbs consist of, Mr Aderfi?" Colman asked.

"Mr Bond," parodied Badiss, "I could tell you, but then I would have to kill you."

General laughter ensued round the fire, and Colman flicked Badiss' shoulder.

Colman had a good warm feeling radiating out from the pit of his stomach and illuminating the rest of his constitution; he also had a mild, inchoate tumescence which made him glad he had accepted the offer of the blue rags to cover his nakedness. Lying back on the pillows accentuated Aderfi's stature. He was stick thin and must have been at least six foot four.

Such of his face as was visible beneath the blue robes, revealed olive coloured skin and a parallel nose and forehead, like a Roman emperor's head on a coin, Mortimer thought. His movements, pouring the tea, were balletic and non-self-conscious. His dark feet, protruding from the bottom of his Dishdash, were shod in open-toed leather sandals, and Colman noted that his first toe was longer than his big toe, the same as Michelangelo's David.

There was a bruise of peach fuzz above his upper lip: he was at the age that Homer describes in the Iliad as most beautiful in a man, just when the beard is beginning to grow. Colman found himself wondering if Aderfi wore any underwear beneath his robe.

"You know," pronounced Colman, "in the *chiaroscuro and sfumatzo* of the camp light, at a stretch, one might almost say you were good looking."

Aderfi paused in his pouring of the tea to question: "Sorry, Mr Hunt, who is Chiara Shura and Fumata?"

"Young man," informed Colman, "they are terms from Italianate Renaissance art, describing the shadows, the interplay of the light and the dark; but these days they are used a lot more to describe the way sets are lit in films. Scenes illuminated by a single incendiary light source are of great interest to me, because I am a New Promethean."

"What is New Promethean, Mr Hunt?"

"We are a brethren who share knowledge beyond the common man. We believe in the periodic destruction of the Universe by Fire."

"All things come to an end, Mr Hunt."

In his mind, as Aderfi flitted from recumbent diner to diner distributing tea, Colman thought of the heads of emperors, the toes of statues, Ozymandias' feet, the illumination of The Night Watchmen, but when he opened his mouth to speak the words that came out were: "Aderfi, you know who you remind me of?"

"Who, Mr Hunt?"

"Casper the Friendly Ghost."

"I get it!" Badiss cried, twigging that Hunt was referring to the way his very tall, very slim companion's robe swayed as he moved, pouring the tea.

Around the fire the Berbers poked one another in the ribs and explained the joke. It went round the circle like a relay until everyone was smiling, sipping tea and drawing on their kif reefers.

"Mr Hunt," said Aderfi, "you like to smoke some kif, locally sourced, line-caught, hand-picked by ecologically certified Jewish drug dealers, members of the Israeli Mafia?"

"Young man, as a New Promethean, I neither smoke nor drink alcohol. When I used to act in the theatre, I drank heavily, but when I became a New Promethean, I put aside those childish things"

"We don't drink alcohol neither, mister," piped up Badiss, "but we are allowed to smoke kif."

Mortimer tapped the rolled up papyrus in his left hand. "You know what this is, Aderfi?"

"Paper with writing, sir."

"Yes, indeed, but this isn't just any old writing. What you are looking at here is an oven-ready script for the new King Ferdinand movie with Ferdinand playing alongside Boabdil. There's a decent part in here could have been written for you. Do you want to be in the movies? Come and sit on my knee here and we'll read it together. You can play the part of my cup-bearer, my Ganymede, my Patroclus."

Aghilles whispered in his brother's ear: "Are you thinking what I'm thinking, Aderfi?"

"Yes, brother. Colman Hunt wants to embugger me."

"*Wakha! Wakha! La! La! La!*" Aghilles murmured. "Of course he wants to embugger you! Everyone wants to sodomise Aderfi! He wouldn't be natural if he didn't want to Socratise my little brother! *La! La! Shoukran!* I'm thinking how much ransom we could get for Colman Hunt."

"For King Ferdinand? A King's ransom, brother." Then aloud to Mortimer. "Sorry, Mr Hunt, we speak fluent English, but none of us can write or read it, except young Badass here. Have to sit on your knee another time."

Young Badiss approached Colman Hunt and said: "There's no Patroclus or Ganymede in the script. The part of Boabdil was already written for Aderfi. It says so in the *Dramatis Personæ*."

Colman was trying to compute that piece of information from the mouth of the boy. His brain couldn't process it. He felt the vertigo coming back.

Hunt made to stir himself. "I've accepted enough of your legendary hospitality, gentlemen. If it's okay, I'll have my runner return these blue robes to you in the morning."

"First," says Aderfi, "you tell us some war stories, because it is impolite not to consume at least three cups of tea; then in exchange, I may tell you some secret ingredients that go into the mint tea. Now we do *The Life & Times of Colman Hunt*. You're the celebrity and I'm—who shall I be, how you say, Chat Show Host—Jonathan Ross, male Oprah, David Frost, Simon Dee."

Mortimer propped himself up on one elbow and addressed the group of blue veiled faces glimmering in the firelight.

"I guess I've always tended to play warrior kings and knights in armour. As soon as I was out of my baby-grows I was wearing chain mail. Always done medieval, not swords and sandals. Before I was discovered by Hollywood, I used to tread the boards, and I did a lot of Shakespeare. In England, all the best actors cut their teeth on Shakespeare.

"In those days, before they built the South Bank (ghastly cement and concrete carbuncle that it is), the RSC (that's the Royal Shakespeare Company), used to be based on a corner of the Aldwych. The Aldwych is quite Moorish actually, because it's a crescent-shaped street off the Strand. The Strand is now a major thoroughfare from Trafalgar Square to Fleet Street and Covent Garden, and it's built on top of the Fleet, which is one of London's many subterranean rivers, and in Shakespeare's time the Fleet, from which Fleet Street takes its name, was an open sewer.

"I was being directed by the legendary Trevor Nunn. In those days, I used to drink heavily, that is before I discovered the New Prometheans and renounced the demon alcohol. The Aldwych was the last remaining London theatre that still had a backstage bar for the actors, and we used to get sozzled before we came on and try to make one another fluff our lines. We played our parts half cut every night. For some parts, it didn't matter. If you were, say, acting in a play by Edward Albee or Tennessee Williams, it was a positive advantage.

"Anyway, I remember I was King Henry IV, in Henry IV Parts 1, 2 and 3, and I had to be in this suit of armour all night long. It took them half an hour to get me into it, and a can opener and another half an hour to get me out of it. I'd been drinking Black and Tans with Stanley Baker in the backstage bar; must have sunk at least eight pints each, and suddenly it dawned on me that I'm bursting for a piss, and there's no interval, and I'm on stage all the time for the next two Acts. You know what I did?"

Mortimer looks from face to face in the firelight. Just like in the good old days when he performed live. Before his career deliquesced into this endless streaming cycle, he used to have his live audience eating out of the palm of his hand.

"I thought to myself, no-one's going to notice in this suit of armour. I'll just piss myself inside the chain mail and carry on with my lines."

His audience didn't understand every word, but they understood enough to respond with cries of laughter and gasps of incredulity. They sat open-mouthed, waiting to learn what happened next. Some of them were filming this little symposium on their phones. One was using a GoPro.

"Now, I'm going to have to do the naming of the parts with you, because you may not know about this. The piece of armour that goes round your pelvis is known as the Faulds, easy to remember, because it folds around your hips. The bit that protects your knees is called the Poleyn. The piece that protects your shins is called the Grieves, and the shoes are called Sabatons. Lovely word."

Colman inwardly marvelled to himself at the fact that he couldn't remember what he'd been doing yesterday, or whether or not he'd had any breakfast today, but he could remember all this irrelevant shit from half a century ago about items of clothing they stopped wearing five hundred years ago.

"Anyway, I'm striding up and down, belting out my lines, with this minor cataract pissing from the top to the bottom of my Faulds, down my Poleyn and Grieves and exiting via my squelching Sabatons. Within a few minutes, the whole stage is awash so that Shrewsbury is looking more like Passchendaele.

"But the thing is, Trevor Nunn had crayoned all these different colour chalk marks on the stage, signifying where the actors were supposed to stand for their parts, and each actor was represented by a different colour chalk, and I somehow managed to wash them all out, or more precisely blend them all into one multi-coloured smudge. Everybody ended up in the wrong places, and then Joan of Navarre skidded arse over apex and they had to bring down the safety curtain as the pee was dripping into the orchestra pit…"

Colman was clearly intending to make a move, and return to his Airstream but Aghilles initiated a new line of conversation.

"Mr Hunt, Mr Hunt, which would be the best of all your leading ladies?"

"Achilles, seeing as how I was married to all of them at one time or another, that is not a polite enquiry, but, as hindsight is an amazing thing, I would say that Celia Broadsword was particularly prominent in my affections, because she was silken of tongue and also, despite the fact that she knew all the worthless things I was pissing our money away on, she never once asked me what they cost."

"Mr Hunt, maybe she already knew all the answers off the Internet, and didn't need to ask you?"

"Well, boys, it's been a historic night, but I guess I'd better be getting back to my own bunk."

"But we promised to tell you the secret ingredient we put into our mint tea if you told us your tales first."

"So you did. Let's have it then. Out with it."

"Pennyroyal."

"Pennyroyal. What's that?"

"It's a herb that grows in the desert."

"Well, I never. Pretty word. Pennyroyal. Maybe John Travolta should've said that instead of *Burger Royale* in Pulp Fiction. Boys, it's been a pleasure!"

"No, no, Mr Hunt," said Aderfi. "You must enjoy the legendary Berber hospitality all night long. You stay here. A night under the stars *with* the star. No mosquitos in the desert. You enjoy. We insist."

"Things to do, places to be," began Colman, rising from the tasselled pillows on the sand, but then the vertigo hit him like a truck, and all the stars in the firmament that Aderfi had just mentioned were suddenly spinning round in the vast empty quarter in his skull where his eyeballs ended and before his brain began. He fell back onto the cushion, and seemed to experience what the medieval poets had termed the music of the spheres, as the stars revolved, performing private orbits that only he could bear witness to.

Then, it appeared to him, in chapters of fire across the charcoal dome: the whole night sky was spinning like the spinning ceiling fan in Casablanca that he'd dreamt about—was it last night or another night? When the theme music had been playing in his head. Then he made the connection that the very same fan morphed from the helicopter rotor blades at the beginning of *Apocalypse Now* to the soundtrack of Jim Morrison singing *The End*. And then everything else joined up: where he had heard the Arabs' names before. Aderfi Benjelloun. Badiss Slimani. But nothing made any sense. How had these two dimensional people from his *Dramatis Personæ* walked right out of the pages of his script?"

"Maybe you're right," he said, collapsing onto his back, "it would be impolite not to accept your generous hospitality. I kind of like the idea of the night under the stars *with* the star." Then he passed out.

Kasbah Toubkal

The plus point about Kasbah Toubkal (into which lofty hotel hideaway Posthumous had already booked himself a room where he intended to keep his brother, Mortimer aka Colman Hunt, immured for as long as it took to get a decent ransom negotiation underway), was that the so-called 'reception' for this backpacker's hotel was an open stall wedged between a fly-blown butcher's counter and an Internet café in the high street of the village of Imlil, with the hotel itself being situated 1820 metres above the reception stall atop Morocco's highest mountain in the High Atlas range, Mount Toubkal. The greatest marvel about Kasbah Toubkal was how they managed to get the building materials up the mountain to build it in the first place.

The remote reception setup meant that Posthumous wouldn't have to worry about smuggling any inert bodies into the hotel, past the prying eyes of some officious concierge or busybody Front of House Manager. The minus point was that, Kasbah Toubkal being situated 1820 metres up Morocco's highest mountain, Posthumous had to dump the pick-up at reception in Imlil high street and complete the last 1820 near vertical metres on foot, or on the back of a donkey.

When Posthumous opened the boot of his Toyota, the captive he believed to be Colman, was still out cold. Posthumous had manoeuvred him into a Dolce & Gabbana suit carrier and zipped him up in it. When Posthumous asked the flunky to assist him manhandling the suit carrier out of the car and onto the back of the donkey, the suit carrier was so heavy that it took both of them to complete the operation.

"What kind of suit you got in that suit carrier, mister?" The flunky asked, wiping his perspiring brow on the sleeve of his Dishdash.

"Suit of armour, son!" Posthumous quipped. "Don't you know? We're shooting Knights of the Ream at Ouarzazate!"

Posthumous then removed his suitcase from the boot. He didn't know how long he was going to be holed up at Toubkal, and he'd figured that he and his brother, being the same size, would have to share a few changes of underwear whilst he administered mortification to him by degrees, before he finally killed him. Then he chuckled at his own Freudian slip: bringing Morty to mortification.

Maybe he'd get hold of his other triplet, Presley, and they could take it in turns to torment Morty. He'd go up the mountain fast asleep on the back of a donkey in the suit carrier, and the same guy could come down the mountain on the back of the same donkey, dead in the same body bag. Then they'd just dump the bag with all the other roadside garbage they seemed to prefer here to landfill.

Finally, Posthumous took the two panniers out of the trunk and passed them to the flunky to load onto the donkey. They contained twelve litre bottles of Raki, which wouldn't have been his tipple of choice, but they didn't have anything better at the gas station where he'd stopped off along the way for a slash and a coffee. Toubkal was a dry hotel, run by practising Muslims, and that was definitely not one of its plus points; Posthumous didn't fancy going an indeterminate length of time with no alcohol, although he figured he could always go native and smoke some weed.

The management didn't serve any alcoholic beverages, but if you wanted to bring your own, pour it yourself, drink it yourself, and take the empties away with you yourself and dispose of them yourself off their premises, firstly, they wouldn't stop you, and secondly, they wouldn't charge you any corkage.

That almost amounted to a plus point, or it would have been if he'd had the presence of mind to acquire anything more drinkable than the paint stripper he'd bought in the gas station. Truth was, he'd spent too long deliberating over the right amount of chloroform to administer to his triplet, and not enough time perusing the Wine List.

Maybe, he thought, he could slit his brother's throat, and hang him with a meat hook through his foot, upside down in the Hammam above the drain, where the heat would make his blood nice and runny, and it could all go down the sump. Then when his triplet was well and truly exsanguinated, he'd trash all the empties by the roadside: the spent flagons of Raki, and the hollow sack of skin and shit that used to be his hated brother. Or he could slice him up into unrecognisable portions and have him hanging up in the camel butchers with the other unrecognisable cuts of meat.

The donkey, now fully loaded with two sorts of contraband (namely the stupefied sibling and the stupefying aqua vitae), the flunky set off up the mountain, leading the mangy beast by a greasy rope, with Posthumous trudging along behind. The donkey paused periodically either to bray at Posthumous or take a dump in his direction. It took forty minutes to make the ascent to the hotel, and the flunky didn't get a tip, even though he attempted to hang the suit carrier up in the wardrobe, but the weight had broken the coat rail, so Posthumous had told him just to lay it out on the bed.

Posthumous was pooped. He felt like he'd scaled Everest.

Posthumous found the fact that his hotel room had turf on the roof real authentic and rustic; but it was only once he got his phone out that he realised that there was no Wi-Fi and no mobile signal. He ransacked Settings on his phone to no avail. How could he have been so stupid? This is why the dropshit donkey had been laughing at him! Posthumous unzipped the Dolce & Gabbana suit carrier just enough to reach inside and pluck out Colman's phone from his pants pocket, which he opened with his own face, because the facial recognition program in the phone was the same as everybody else: it couldn't tell them apart.

But there was no signal on Colman's phone's network either. Posthumous was going to have to conduct the ransom negotiations from the Internet café in the high street next to the fly-blown butcher's stall. There was no Uber to call, and no road for Uber to drive on if there had been. He was going to have to phone for a donkey, except there was no signal for the phone. Fuck, fuck and fuck! He was going to have to go back down the fucking mountain same way as he'd come up. But first of all, he sure as hell needed some Raki. He stuffed both phones in his cargo pants and upended the first flagon of fire water.

Rodrigo

"Did you have time to read *The Perfume*, Mr Indigolin?"

"I did, Elena, and I didn't understand a word of it."

"And did you read the selections from 1001 Arabian Nights?"

"I've read the passages that you recommended, but I'm still at a loss to understand how the Moors got into Spain in the first place."

Indigolin was addressing Elena Troy after morning yoga.

"It's an interesting question, Mr Indigolin, and I'm afraid the answer is the usual answer: men not being able to keep their junk in their trousers."

"You are a singular tutor, Elena. *Men not being able to keep their junk in their trousers.* Is that a set text?"

"It certainly ought to be! I didn't find the answer in any of the history books, but there was a footnote in a 1997 travel guide on Historical Paradors I came upon on eBay. It's said that Rodrigo, the Visigoth king of Spain, who ruled for only one year, raped the daughter of Don Julián, the governor of Ceuta. The outraged father-in-law took his revenge by allowing the Moors to disembark in Spain."

"Simple as that?"

"You'd be surprised if you knew how many of the most momentous events in history flowed from that same simple cause."

"Guys doing their thinking with their dicks instead of their brains?"

"I'm afraid so."

"And do we believe she really was raped?"

"That is also an interesting question, because it could well have been consensual, a secret liaison that was discovered. You have to understand—certainly, if you want to understand John Donne's poetry, you have to understand—that any sex outside marriage would be ruinous for a high-born woman. Don Julián could have been found out. Maybe the governor's daughter fell pregnant.

"She would have felt morally obliged to accuse Rodrigo of a rape even if it never happened, because in those days, for a nobleman, being a rapist was just like being one of the lads, and wouldn't close any doors to the ravisher, except, maybe, the door to his victim's parents, whereas, for a woman, having sex outside of marriage, was disastrous. She was spoiled goods. Her parents would never be able to marry her off well. Interestingly, not only did it not close any doors for Rodrigo, but he is very famous for opening a door."

"So a long and bloody war starts because Don Julián can't marry his daughter well?"

"What is also strange is that the daughter's name seems to have been Florinda la Cava."

"As in the Catalan fizzy wine?"

"Nowadays, yes, but in those days a Cava was a whore."

"So was she known as a whore before or after her abduction?"

"It's all pretty obscure, Mr Indigolin. The story appears in William Rowley's tragedy *All's Lost by Lust*. More fascinatingly, Rodrigo also features in Nights 272 and 273 of the *1001 Arabian Nights*. Rodrigo opens a secret door in his castle that had been sealed up by the previous kings. Inside he finds paintings of Moors and a note addressed to him, telling him that if the secret room is ever unsealed, the city of Toledo will be sacked by the very Moors in the paintings. And that is precisely what happened."

"Like the picture of Dorian Gray."

"As re-told by Scheherazade, yes"

"And all history gets turned on its head, because Rodrigo couldn't keep it in his codpiece. It's so arbitrary, isn't it?"

"Arbitrary serendickity."

He scrutinised his tutor's expression, seeking to go behind that play on words, but Elena had gone into Sphinx-like mode.

She continued: "All down through the ages: raping of women, raping of countries; most of history's problems start out with someone taking something that doesn't belong to him, starting with our oldest ever epic poem by Homer."

"The Odyssey?"

"No, the Iliad. It tells the story of how the Trojan prince, Paris, ravished the wife of King Menelaus of Sparta, and the long and bloody Trojan War that ensued as a consequence. It's strange. Rape is such a vile word. But when we use the word *ravished*, you know, there's a part of me that longs to be ravished."

"Elena, it has to be more than nomenclature."

"In terms of dictionary definitions, there's no difference."

"Elena, you're wasted as an accountant. The way you traduce language, you should go into politics!"

"One word refers to something completely despicable, but the other carries a kind of complicity with it. No sane woman would ask to be raped, but she might dream of being ravished. The notion of being ravished implies that absolutely wonderful things are done to her, but without her having to demean herself by consenting to any of it. It's the ultimate in unaccountable deniability."

"She keeps her legs open, but her fingers crossed."

"You could look at it that way."

"Being serious for a moment," he began. "putting behind us possible rapes that may have occurred two thousand years ago, and looking at my own situation in the present tense, you know about our Celia and Presley."

"I'm afraid I do."

"How do you think I should I deal with it?"

"It may not be that it's you who should be dealing with it at all. But in my book someone has to pay a heavy price for that. What happened was firmly in the category of rape and not ravishment."

"Celia doesn't want to go to the police,"

"That's not what I was referring to. Sometimes you have to take things into your own hands if you want results, Mr Indigolin."

Death Hath Ten Thousand Several Doors

In his time, Hugh Webb had kneecapped numerous traitors; he had tarred-and-feathered any number of miscreants whom the Vigilance Committee had referred to him for correction. He had committed rape. He had committed incest. In his home village outside Belfast, the definition of a virgin was a girl who could run faster than her brother. He had been a dab hand with a cat-o'-nine-tails, even though he wasn't of a naval family.

He couldn't even begin to put a figure to all the whippings, knifings, slashings, lashings and casual vanilla maimings and dismemberments he had either discharged personally or officiated over during what he referred to affectionately as his military service, or, euphemistically as 'the troubles'. He'd shot at many people and been shot at a few times himself. Indeed, very recently, during what should have been a routine job on the Blue Molecule Man, he had somehow managed to put a bullet in his own gut.

Anyone who knew him would have said that Rough Hugh was fearless. But one thing terrified Mr Webb: flying. Sat in the Business Class of the British Airways flight to Casablanca, he alternated between his offensive pint of Black and Tan, and his patriotic chaser of Jameson's Irish whisky, imbibing the Dutch courage whilst he thumbed through the Dorling Kindersley Guide to Morocco that he had picked up at the airport. To keep his mind off the fact that he was trapped inside a noisy metal condom hurtling through the atmosphere at 30,000 feet, he kept his wits sharp by calling to mind famous literary allusions to death and murder.

Because of his fear of flying, he seldom took a foreign holiday. If he needed to go to Ireland on business, he drove to Holyhead or Liverpool and put his car on the ferry. In the same way that people with dogs used them as an excuse for not flying, Webb used his gun collection as his excuse. There was no way he could take his guns on a commercial flight, and he didn't like being separated from them. He loved curating and admiring his collection.

He never left the house without at least one of them concealed about his person. He felt naked on the flight without one; but obviously, trying to smuggle a gun onboard a commercial jet was out of the question. Also, the job didn't call for a gun. He was to look after Celia Broadsword for a few days, make sure she had everything she needed except her liberty. He thought he could handle an eighty-five-year-old woman without a weapon.

He'd seen every one of Celia Broadsword's films, and he had them all on DVD in a boxed set. He had the boxed set in his hand luggage, where he'd normally have packed a firearm of some description, and he was very much looking forward to spending some quality time with her going through her Catalogue Raisonné together. The boxed set was stowed directly above his head in the overhead locker like his guardian angel. It was far too precious to Hugh Webb to consign it to the hold.

Looking after elderly ladies wasn't quite his normal line of work: kidnapping them would have been, but this was playacting a kidnap. However, the job had two USPs that he could not resist, even if it meant putting himself through hell for four hours on the aeroplane. Firstly, the opportunity to have the diva all to himself for as long as the job lasted. Secondly, his employer was the Blue Molecule dude.

Therefore, as soon as he'd been paid by the Dude for babysitting the leading lady, he'd find a way to bump off the Blue Dude and then collect the rest of his wad from Albanian George. He hadn't yet worked out what weapon he was going to use to dispatch Indigolin, or maybe he'd do it with his bare hands, as he had done once or twice in his checkered past.

He was sure that they must sell weapons of some description in Morocco, or something he could make a weapon out of. He was resourceful enough to make a killing engine out of many everyday objects. If he couldn't lay his hands on a proper gat or a roscoe, he'd use a flintlock, a fireball or a howitzer. If push came to shove, he could dispatch him with a wire coat hanger, but it wouldn't be a very dignified way to check out. Didn't really matter. Death hath ten thousand several Gates.

Because Hughie Webb was travelling in Business Class on his own, he'd managed to get himself into the front row of seats. As he was frightened to look out the window, he was sat in the aisle seat. The advantage of this row of seats was that they had a lot more leg room and he'd be first off the plane when it landed. He didn't want to prolong the experience a second longer than necessary. But there were disadvantages, some patent, others latent.

The patent disadvantage was that you didn't get to have your own tray folding out the back of the seat in front of you, because there was only the emergency door and a bulkhead with a baby bassinet in front of you. This meant that the fairy air steward had to humiliate him by fishing his tray out of the arm rest, breaking his varnished nails in the process. That had got the two of them off to a bad start.

The latent disadvantage of this seat was that Webb didn't just watch Celia Broadsword films. He also liked war films and commando raids. He knew from *Raid on Entebbe* that if anyone attempted to hijack the plane, then Mossad, or their Moroccan equivalent, ran up the wing and stove-piped the emergency door in, so that the passenger seated where he was seated, would be killed by the weight of the door crushing him as the commandos effected their entry.

'But, let's face it,' he thought, '*the only person on the flight likely to hijack it was Hugh Webb himself.*'

Yes, thinking of his quotations about death and killing, and commandos kicking in doors, certainly helped take his mind off the interminable flight. The worst bit had been the take-off. Noisily, the plane had climbed and climbed, and then, suddenly, the engine noise had just stopped, as if the engines had packed up and the aircraft was going to fall out of the sky. But it seemed it was supposed to do that, because no-one else appeared to mind, and the plane kept going.

It was only once that had happened, that the flight attendant came round and Webb was able to order himself the Black and Tan. Alarmingly, at that point, the captain had emerged from the locked cockpit, and dived into the john before any of the paying passengers could relieve themselves, leaving Webb to wonder who the fuck was flying the plane.

The BA flight attendant was a cross-dresser. He'd obviously started out as a man, but he was wearing nail varnish, lipstick and pearl earrings with a matching bracelet and necklace. What depths had British Airways sunk to, Webb asked himself? They had started out with an illogical, but ruthlessly enforced dress policy, so that perfectly respectable young ladies got the sack if their little gold crucifixes worn round the neck were on show; but now they had gone completely to the other extreme, saying that male flight attendants could wear skirts and lipsticks, and anybody who didn't have a visible tattoo had better go and work for another airline.

When Mr Webb had asked for a Black and Tan, the hobble-de-hoy had told him that wasn't respectful and to call it a Half and Half, and Webb had replied: "What, like you?" The attendant had frowned at him, as though he was a recalcitrant child. The attendant's badge said his name was Eamon, but Webb couldn't imagine anyone looking less like an Eamon.

John Webster had many great quotes about death.

I know death hath ten thousand several doors
For men to take their exits, and 'tis found
They go on such strange, geometrical hinges
You may open them both ways...

The steward hadn't liked that quip about being a Half and Half, neither One Thing nor the Other. He obviously went on his own strange, geometrical hinges, so that you could open him both ways. People had been cross-dressing since time immemorial, but Webb didn't see why he had to be served by the likes of one:

Tell me, gentle, hobble-de-hoy. Art thou girl or art thou boy?

He had to accept a drink from the attendant, out of necessity. Not because he was thirsty, but because it calmed his nerves. But he wasn't going to accept any food served from that hand. He didn't know where he'd been. The creature was wearing a pearl necklace that Webb had seen in the High Life duty free magazine. How did the whole quote go? Bosola is threatening the Duchess of Malfi with killing and she just shrugs him off fearlessly. Then he says:

BOSOLA   Yet, methinks
            The manner of your death should much afflict you
            This cord should terrify you
DUCHESS *Not a whit*
            What would it pleasure me to have my throat cut
           With diamonds? Or to be smothered
           With cassia? Or to be shot to death with pearls?
           I know death hath ten thousand several doors

Eamon reappeared. Webb wondered what Eamon was hoping to get up to in Morocco. Filthy bastard! Still fretting at the nail that Webb had caused him to snap, getting his tray out from the arm rest, Eamon plonked a pint glass down on Webb's tray. Then he came back with a can of Guinness, which he opened with his already-broken finger nail before placing that on the tray too. Then he returned to the galley and came back again with two diminutive bottles of champagne, the tops of which he unscrewed, before placing them on Webb's tray also.

"So, you trust me to mix my own drink, but you don't trust me to open the fucking bottles myself!" Webb said to Eamon.

Eamon went back into the galley and came back, holding up to Webb an A4 size laminated card, which had something printed on it in bold letters about the people working here having a right to be respected and not abused.

"If you want to be respected," barked Webb, "don't go round looking like a stupid cunt!"

Just then the captain exited the toilet. *Exitus mortis*. And a passenger slipstreamed in behind him.

"He didn't come from Business Class!" Webb complained, referring to the slipstreamed passenger. "He's just sneaked round the curtain from Economy, because you were busy fetching your stupid sign, instead of paying attention! He has no fucking right—"

Eamon had dropped down onto one knee in order to whisper quietly but firmly into Webb's ear, so that the other passengers didn't hear: "If you don't shut up your foul mouth, at all, I'll have you arrested as soon as we land, you old dinosaur."

"You can do that?" Webb asked, in awe.

"Most certainly," said Eamon.

Webb looked at him with renewed respect.

Be absolute for death. He loved that phrase although he couldn't remember which of Shakespeare's plays it came from. Generally, life had been good to Rough Hugh; but at times like this he regretted not having stayed on to finish his English literature Tripos. He had flunked out of Trinity College, Dublin in the second year and enrolled in the IRA.

The Revenger's Tragedy by Cyril Tourneur: now that was a play that had everything: murders, rape, poisoning, incest, a beheading:

Whose head's that then?
Villain, I'll brain thee with it…
Ay, master, he's slain; look how his brains drop out on's nose
Oh, one incestuous kiss picks open hell!

It was a crying shame that *The Revenger's Tragedy* was so seldom staged. Maybe once every ten years. Webb would travel from one end of the country to the other to see it. Then there was *The Atheist's Tragedy*. Webb had read that, but had never heard of it being staged anywhere. *Antonio's Revenge* by Marston never got an airing. *The Changeling* was staged from time to time. As was *The Spanish Tragedy*, but that was only because some idiots thought Shakespeare had had a hand in writing it.

Webb tried to keep his mind occupied by composing a jingle. If it was good enough, he could put it on his website, or it could play whilst punters phoning in to his call centre in India were waiting for their calls to be answered.

Your call is valuable to us
If you want someone thrown under a bus;
Should you need to bid an enemy adieu,
You are fifth in the queue.
With your dying breath
Coûte que coûte
Be absolute
For death.

He was quite pleased with that; especially the casual insertion of the French phrase that gave his jingle added sophistication; but the problem was he wasn't entirely certain how one pronounced *Coûte que coûte*, and whether or not it did indeed rhyme with absolute. Anyway, it had passed the time and taken his mind off the humiliation of barrelling through the atmosphere in a huge metal cannula with a bunch of morons off on their 'holiday of a lifetime'.

Mr Webb believed in fate. There must be more than two hundred people hermetically buckled into this flying cigar tube with him, he thought. All it needed was for the number for just one of them to be up, and all of their fates would likewise be sealed. If the bloke in Row 26 seat B, or the very guy who had slipped past the curtain in Economy to take an unpaid-for, upgraded urination in the Business Class passenger's toilet to Webb's chagrin mere moments ago, was destined to die in a plane crash today, then he would have to bring all his fellow passengers down with him. Webb was willing to be absolute for everyone else's death, except his own.

The plane's PA system made a bong. Eamon sat down on his dicky seat and spoke through the address system telling the wayfarers that the captain had lit up the fasten seat belts sign that meant they were going to land in fifteen minutes, so all the incontinent people in the toilets had to get back in their seats and strap themselves in now.

'*Well,*' Webb thought to himself, he had managed to pass the time and exorcise his fears by running through his catechisms of quotations and picking on the hobble-de-hoy steward. Then he thought to himself: couldn't the fucking captain have waited and had his piss on dry land without doing his business in the Business Class passengers' toilet?

He had heard of people wanting to hit the ground running, but this man wanted to hit the ground pissing. He was obviously checked into some sybaritic hotel in Morocco, and didn't want to waste his own time on a toilet break. It was the first rule of the downtrodden proletariat: always take a leak in governor's time, not your own.

The captain had hair as white as Webb's. They were both of an age. The captain had been in that jakes for so long while the plane was flying itself, he must have a prostate problem. Probably the sort of man who could piss himself into next Tuesday, but still not feel he'd knocked all the drops off the end. Webb wondered if the captain was headed for an amorous assignation with Eamon in Marrakesh. He wouldn't be surprised in the least.

When a man grows old
And his balls grow cold,
And the tip of his tool turns blue
And the hole in the middle refuses to piddle,
I'd say he was fucked wouldn't you?

The plane landed with an almighty crash whilst all the trolleys that Eamon had failed to secure correctly went careering down the aisles. Hugh Webb gripped the sides of his seat as the captain braked with a heavy boot.

It's always a cunt that bears the brunt,
But the shooting's not so bad.

As the plane skidded to a halt, and as Webb braced himself for the commandos to kick the door into his chest, Webb played his catchy jingle over and over in his head.

Be absolute for death.

The Man in the Suit Carrier Comes Round

When Presley had eventually come round, bound hand and feet in the room with the turf roof in Kasbah Toubkal, Posthumous was enjoying some room service. He had considered room service the more prudent dining option, given that he intended to wash every mouthful down with Raki, which the staff would find offensive, and further, given that he needed to be present when his brother woke up, but he didn't have any idea when that was going to be.

Because he hadn't used chloroform before, and had decided to err on the side of extravagance, rather than have his victim wake up before check-in time. Posthumous was tucking in to a pigeon tagine that passed for poultry when he saw movement inside the suit carrier laid out on the bed. He wiped his mouth with a napkin, balanced his fork on the side of the bowl, and unzipped his prisoner.

Presley stared up at him in disbelief.

"I guess you must be hungry, Morty. You've been out for at least 20 hours. Now tell me this, you old *fee-fi-fo-fum*, if I take the ball gag out of your mouth, Morty, are you going to start screaming, in which case I am going to have to chloroform you all over again, or are you going to be civilised, in which case I may be inclined to shave a little off this very fine Trafalgar Square Pigeon and share it with you, before I begin shaving bits off you?"

His brother's eyes had darted from side to side, and there had been some grunts from beneath the ball gag. But no unequivocal reply.

"Let me try this again, Morty. I realise that it was inconsiderate of me to phrase that question in the alternative when you only have the ability to answer by either nodding or shaking your head. Let me rephrase this. First off, would you care for some chowder?"

A nod.

"If I remove the gag, will you put your mouth to good use and eat said chowder and not get lippy with me?"

Another nod.

"Because if you don't, am I going to have to put you out cold again, brother?"

A pronounced shake of the head.

"OK, let's do this then."

Posthumous had removed the gag. His brother couldn't speak at first his mouth was so dry. He was completely devoid of saliva. He couldn't even swallow, let alone scream. Posthumous poured him a tumbler full of Raki, and lifted it to his lips. Presley thought the clear liquid was water. He swallowed a big dose before he realised his gullet was burning and he sprayed the rest of his mouthful out, pebble-dashing the room and soaking his brother.

"Fucking hell!" Posthumous shrieked. "Now I smell like a giant aniseed ball! What you do that for, Colman?" Posthumous wiped the firewater off his forehead and out of his smarting eyes with his napkin.

"Not Colman, you stupid cunt! If I was a New Promethean I'd be able to swallow fucking fire water, wouldn't I?"

"But then again, Colman Hunt, being a New Promethean and all, doesn't drink alcohol, does he? So you not drinking my Raki is just what Morty would do in the circumstances."

"Well why don't you undo my shirt and check, Posthumous?"

Even in hot climates, such as they were in at present, Posthumous and Presley had been advised to wear long sleeved shirts, because if all the delicate plastic surgery they had undergone on their chests and arms was exposed to the sun, the pain could be excruciating.

Posthumous undid his brother's shirt and saw the two-tone skin on Presley's chest, the pale parchment-like porthole in the middle, like Iron Man's power source, surrounded by the papery, semi-pellucid tissue left from all the skin grafting following Colman's little escapade all those years ago in *Ordeal by Fire*. Colman had been paid a lot of money for shooting the *Ordeal;* but the Ordeal had been undergone by Presley and Posthumous.

Posthumous undid his own shirt to reveal his torso maculated by the identical skin grafting.

"Snap!" Presley said.

By way of final check, Posthumous pulled Presley's confiscated phone out of his pants pocket, and switched it on with his identical face. Then he went into Settings; then he went into the sub-menu marked General, then he went into the sub-sub menu marked About, and he saw that under Name, it said *Presley's iPhone.*

"Oh shit!" Posthumous had cursed. "I think we have a case of mistaken identity. So sorry bro, so sorry. Here!"

He sat his brother up on the bed, and diluted the clear Raki with water from the tap, whereupon it turned milky white, and, cutting open the ties on his brother's hands and legs, gave him a drink.

"Is it okay to drink the water out of the tap, Posthumous?" his triplet enquired meekly.

"This Raki will kill any bacteria, bro. You could safely drink the water out the toilet bowl once you'd added this stuff to it. Don't worry about a thing."

Presley had downed the tumbler and then began rubbing the sore spots on his arms and legs where the cable ties had cut in. "I think you've got some explaining to do," was all he said.

"Yeah," replied Posthumous. "How about you have a few mouthfuls of this chicken tagine with me, get your energy back, and then we'll go and have a good old chinwag in the Hammam?"

Beyond Good and Evil

"Don't knock it if you haven't tried it!" Indigolin said to Elena Troy. He was referring to his aperitivo of Blue Curacao and champagne. Outside Aka's chow tent on the set, the chef had set out some glass tables and wooden chairs under a forest of parasols in Heineken livery, and Indigolin was sat at one of the tables, mixing cocktails.

Elena had joined him at the counter to watch the sun go down behind the terracotta-hued sand dunes. He prepared one of his special drinks for her. He took a chilled highball snifter from a cold bag and placed it on the glass table. With a very sharp mandolin, he peeled the zest from a green lime, some of which he left in the goblet, some of which he curled round the rim.

Opening an ice bucket, he clinked an unfrosted, perfectly clear ice cube into the glass using hallmarked silver tongs, and then splashed blue curacao in, followed by the same quantity of lychee liqueur, and then topped it up as a long drink with champagne, and passed it to her.

"I've never seen ice as clear as that," she said.

"You've obviously never dived in the pack ice of the Arctic Ocean beneath the light of the midnight sun, swimming along the floe edge known as The Line of Life, watching a polar bear trying to outstare you, whilst standing on the glacier above you!" He remarked.

It was impossible for her to determine if he was incredibly worldly and romantic, or simply a preposterous bullshit merchant. She wasn't entirely sure that he wasn't quoting from *Eskimo Nell*. Was he saying that he had done any of these things, or done all of them together and at the same time?

"Sounds as if you've been diving off the side of a Fox's glacier mint!" She quipped. "Also sounds too cold and too expensive for the likes of me; but I've dived Iceland," she countered.

"Seriously, I bought the cook some new water filters from Germany for the fridge," he smiled. "She didn't realise that you're supposed to replace them from time to time. Like putting salt in your dishwasher. Most people just put the soap tablets in; some put the rinse-aid for the glasses, but few remember the salt."

"Oh yes, like putting petrol in your car, but never changing the oil."

"Now that the cars are all going electric, they don't need oil anymore."

"Of course," she mused. "No internal combustion engine to lubricate."

"I do her an injustice," Indigolin conceded. "She's not really a cook. She's a Michelin-starred chef, and I presume that when she was running her famous restaurant in LA, Aka would have had underlings to change the water filters in her fridges."

Then, raising his glass, he called: "*A ta santé!*"

He toasted her. She noted that he used the familiar *ta*, rather than the more formal *votre*. She wasn't quite sure whether she should be flattered or worried about this, or maybe he just didn't know any better. Why was everybody so over-familiar these days? No sooner had Elena been introduced to anybody than they were contriving ways to foreshorten her name.

The usual result, El, sounded like some caveman's grunt; Ellie was childish. She'd even been called Len. Everything on the Internet was *Regards, Kind Regards, Warmest Regards*. When people signed off *Yours Faithfully* on behalf of a company, they inserted their personal names. She was sick of stupid memes and Emojis and unnecessary responses and replies to SMS texts and WhatsApp messages that made it impossible ever to finish a conversation.

As though he had read her mind, he said:

"Should I have said, *A votre santé?*"

She was stunned.

"The truth is," he continued. "I never know how well you need to know someone before the *votre* matures into a *ta* or a *tu*. I mean, if you're a family member, it's obvious. That's black and white. But at work, there are more grey situations."

"Whereas you would prefer them all to be blue situations?"

He smiled graciously. "You're a consultant," he continued, "but we are working together at close quarters on a long term project. Is there some guidance in Debretts or something?"

"I think," she began, "Debretts is more about how you address people correctly, I mean verbally, or letter writing. If you're introduced to an Earl or a Viscount or a Judge's wife, or you're writing a letter to a German Baron, or whatever."

"So, it won't help me in my predicament?"

"I tell you what!" She said.

She got up from her chair, went round to his, clinked glasses with him, and kissed him on the cheek.

"Cheers!" She said. "I think that if we're kissing on the cheek, we can use *tu* and *ta*!"

"I've been upgraded!" He smiled.

"Another way round," she continued, "would be to use the Moroccan form of Cheers, which is *Bssaha*!"

"*Bssaha*!" He repeated.

"Yes, I think it's short for *Bssaha! Lay i âtik ssaha*!" She wrote it with her finger in the condensation on the glass table where the cold highball glasses had been.

"You know," he said. "I think that must be the first time I've seen a circumflex on top of an a. But thank you so much for the upgrade and also for the kiss. Do you think this *Bssaha* is related to *Bacio* or *Beso,* which are the words for Kiss in Italian and Spanish?"

"I dare say they are," she said, coming to the conclusion that she had underestimated this guy. It was entirely possible, she now realised, that he had indeed been contemplating the pack ice of the Arctic Ocean beneath the light of the midnight sun, swimming along the floe edge known as The Line of Life watching a polar bear standing on the glacier above him, and the only part of his story that was untrue was the bit about buying new water filters for the fridge in Germany.

He was really quite urbane and sophisticated. She didn't know any other billionaires, but she had assumed they would all be monomaniac narcissistic brutes focussed on nothing except the pursuit of more money. Had he really dived the Antarctic Ocean? If she didn't have a job to do for Bvsh Ho, she could get to like him.

Sipping her drink, she said, "It tastes as good as it looks. But has it made my lips go blue?"

"I'm afraid not," he replied. "I think that if you want blue lips like a true Goth, it's hemlock you need to drink. Like Socrates."

"Ah, yes," she said. "We owe a cock to Asclepius."

He looked straight into her eyes for a second, trying to verify whether she was just quoting Plato, or propositioning him.

"You're staring at me like your polar bear!" She smiled.

As he couldn't tell one way or the other, if she was giving him the come-on, or engaging in Socratic dialectic, he felt it safer to continue the conversation along purely Platonic lines.

"Indeed," he responded. "Socrates' last words, as spoken to his disciple, Crito. Asclepius was the god of good health, and sacrificing a cock to Asclepius was the usual way of thanking him for a recovery from illness."

Now it was her turn to be kept guessing. Was he completing her sentence, or talking in *doubles entendres*? She couldn't tell if he had been acting dumb when he had told her he didn't understand Donne, given the level of unexpected knowledge he was now displaying. Had he just been positioning himself for some extra-curricular classes with her that he didn't actually need? Or, if she was looking for an innocent explanation, it could be that he'd read classics or philosophy, but not poetry. She decided to continue to play him along.

"So Socrates' words mean that he was cured of the disease of life and not frightened at the prospect of his death by the Athenian State forcing him to drink the hemlock."

"But, Elena, if my drink did make your lips go blue, I wouldn't mind at all, because it's my favourite colour and I name my companies after it."

She was aware of the fact that he had sensed the conversation straying into uncharted territories, and he had very quickly brought it back to mundane small talk.

"I love to sit here and watch the sun disappearing behind that sand dune," he confided. "Having attended Wally's sunrise salutation yoga classes, I now know which mountain the sun rises over and which sand dune it sets upon. Don't you think that the aperitivo is a wonderful institution, because it's pure unalloyed pleasure, a drink that has no pretensions about itself? It's not passing itself off as being an accompaniment for your dinner, like red wine with meat or white wine with fish. It's just a drink in its own right; what Nietzsche would have called a glorious affirmation of self."

"My word! Moroccan, Spanish, Italian, French, Plato, and now Nietzsche. You get around don't you?"

"I get around, just like the Beach Boys! Have you read 'Beyond Good and Evil'?"

"As a matter of fact, I have, Mr Indigolin."

"Please, now that we are on kissing terms, on the cheek at least, call me Ti."

"I don't like foreshortening people's names; but I'll call you Tinctorio. I mean, it's a fantastic name. Why brush it under the carpet?"

"Then perhaps you can help me with a little dilemma on the horns of Good and Evil that is troubling me. Suppose one does something illegal, but with the best possible motives, something that is illegal, but not necessarily morally wrong."

"Does anybody get hurt?" She enquired.

"Only someone who deserves to be hurt," he answered. "and he is only hurt financially, not physically. But he needs punishing, and the financial harm will be inconvenient, but not irrecoverable."

"You're going to kick him in the balance sheet, but not the balls?"

"I couldn't have put it better myself, Elena."

"You mean, it's like if someone decides to become a vigilante, because that's the only way an important job that the authorities won't do, is going to get done?"

"Possibly. Let's say an individual has acted culpably, but it is a moral culpability, a form of culpability that is below the legal radar, a form of culpability for which the law offers no remedies."

"As in *De Minimis non curat lex*?"

"Remind me to tell you my limerick about that concept later. No, it's not that it's *de minimis*; it's just not a wrong that the law addresses; so at law, unless the vigilante takes matters into his own hands, the perpetrator would remain unpunished."

"So you're saying, Tinctorio, that it's incumbent on you to mete out the punishment, because otherwise the perpetrator gets away with it."

"Correct."

"But the only reason that he gets away with it, is because legally, technically, he isn't doing anything wrong. But when you punish him, you do something wrong. You commit a crime."

"That is what's troubling me, Elena."

"The problem is that when we get into areas that aren't recognised as crimes, we stray into matters of personal taste and censorship, highly subjective areas."

"Well, indeed. Let's suppose we have laws against hate crimes or racism, but they don't protect a woman from misogyny, because the laws are framed to provide protection to members of a race as opposed to a gender."

"So in your example, the woman would take the law into her own hands."

"Yes."

"Tinctorio, it may surprise you, but I'm all for that. The only thing I'd say is to be proportionate in your response, and don't forget that what you're doing is illegal, so you could get into trouble for doing it. But I personally wouldn't leave something that needs doing undone, just because I might get into trouble for doing it. I should add that I'm a Catholic, so I'd confess it, get a few Hail Marys and be done with it."

"Elena, that is excellent advice. Except for the confession and the Hail Mary's, which are not appropriate to me because I am not a Roman Catholic, I shall follow your wise counsel. If I get myself into a little trouble, will you be my advocate and stand up for me? Will you explain that I conducted myself as I did with only the best intentions and motives and that it is, as you said, *de minimis?* Will you act as priestess for my confession?"

"Tinctorio, I will be pleased to hear your confession, and, in keeping with the Sacrament of Penance and Reconciliation, I will ask God for your forgiveness. But please remember that, whilst this may have the effect of saving your eternal soul from damnation in the hereafter, it won't necessarily keep you out of jail in the here and now."

"Elena," he replied. "I always take the long view."

She clinked his glass, before emptying hers and smiling said, "*Bssaha!*"

"*Bssaha! Lay i âtik ssaha!*" He replied, emptying his own glass.

"You learn very quickly!" She remarked.

"Not at all, Elena," he replied. "It's written on your leg."

She looked down, shocked. The last rays of the sun were passing through the words she had etched with her finger into the condensation on the glass table and they had cast a shadow on her tanned and toned leg, a shadow that stencilled *Bssaha! Lay i âtik ssaha.*

He noticed that there were extremely fine golden hairs on her thigh. He had to fight back the urge to stroke them. They were like the ciliae on the stem of a plant. He wanted to show her how well he had conned his Donne by making some reference to *gold to aerie thinness beat*, but he realised it would be wholly inappropriate.

They both stood up quite abruptly. The dissolving stencil slid off her leg and swiftly regrouped itself so that it was now imprinted on the sand.

"The sun has quite gone down behind his favourite dune now," he declared. "But I hope to see you in the morning for yoga when he rises behind that particularly fine mountain over there."

He set off to leave her.

"You asked me to remind you," she began.

He stopped in his tracks and turned back round to face her.

"About the limerick," she completed.

"Ah yes," he said, and then:

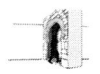

"There was a young man called Rex
Who had a very small sex.
When charged with exposure
He said with composure
'De minimus non curat lex'."

She laughed out loud, cleanly and sincerely, and turned on her heel.

As she made her way back to the Berber Hotel, she wondered whether he had just made her his confessor or his confederate. Had he been flirting with her on a very high level? Polar Bears, Nietzsche! Cocks to Asclepius!—but she had set that hare running herself, and he had just followed it.

Her thigh was still tingling from when he had pointed out to her the letters tattooed there, the Arabic words on her leg that translated as some kind of a kiss administered high up on her thigh. That had been quite witty of him. But she had written the letters, and he had simply made use of the materials she had given him. If he had been flirting, she thought she quite liked it. He was a contradiction in terms.

She suppressed a chuckle at the thought that she gave him John Donne Holy sonnets, and he gave her a limerick about a man with a small penis. For some reason, she couldn't get the end of Donne's Holy Sonnet out of her head:

for I Except you enthral me, never shall be free
Nor ever chaste, except you ravish me.

Laocoön

Wally was sitting at his editing desk with the two great spools to his right and his left like his good and evil angels. He was knee deep in discarded celluloid. It coiled around his legs in springs.

"You know who you remind me of?" Celia asked.

"Who?"

"The marble statue of Laocoön in the Vatican Museum."

"Ah, yes, when the huge serpents come out of the sea and entwine Laocoön and his family. I presume you're referring to all this material wrapped round my ankles, Celia?"

"Yes, as in Dickens, when Scrooge wakes up on Christmas morning and Dickens says he's making a perfect Laocoön of himself trying to put his socks on. That's what you look like, Wally."

"I guess it would have been too much to hope for that you were comparing me to the noble marble statue, as opposed to a guy getting tangled up in his own socks."

"A guy getting tangled up in his own socks, is so much like Winston Churchill's image of the man standing in a bucket trying to pull himself up by the handle."

"Yep, height of pointlessness, Celia."

"Did you know, it's the origin of the expression, *Beware of Greeks Bearing Gifts*?"

"No, I didn't Celia."

"Laocoön was a Trojan priest. He told the Trojans not to let the wooden horse inside the walls."

"As in *Beware of Greeks bearing gifts*?"

"The same. But then these giant serpents came out of the sea and wrapped Laocoön and his sons in their coils and choked them all to death. This was interpreted by the superstitious Trojans as a punishment imposed by the gods upon Laocoön for fomenting dissent about the horse."

"No Article 10 of the European Convention on Human Rights in Ilium, eh, Celia?"

"I don't think they told Homer about that, Wally. So the Trojans opened the gates to the wooden horse, and the rest, if not history, is certainly the stuff of legend."

"Ah yes, baby, where does legend end and history begin? King Arthur, Jesus, the Bible, the Iliad. They all feature real settings and real people, which the authors use as a base; but then the ancient bards start adding gods and goddesses into the cocktail."

"And one hundred and fifty-year-old people, Wally!"

"It's the stuff our films are made of."

"Have you read Lessing's Laocoön?"

"No, Celia."

"It's a very readable essay on aestheticism. He bases it on the statue of Laocoön, because that's an image that most people will have seen. I mean, if you're trying to communicate with people, there's no point in using a metaphor that no-one's heard of. What he says is that the reason the Laocoön image is so powerful is because the sculptor depicts Laocoön before his arm is fully extended.

"If the arm were fully extended, the image would become static, but because poor, struggling Laocoön is still trying to extend his arm, against the suffocating force of all the coiling serpents, the image has huge kinetic energy, and that's what makes it so compelling. And it has always seemed to me that is something we must bear in mind when we, as actors and directors, craft our own images, Wally."

"Babes, when someone has even a casual conversation with you, they should really be awarded some kind of diploma, like a university degree in Practical Celia. I mean, you just slip in here unannounced and we cover the Iliad, the Bible, and Lessing on Laocoön, but somehow, the catalyst for all this started with Eartha Kitt!"

"Yes, it's a bit like Proust dipping his cake in his coffee, isn't it, Wally?"

"Proust, Laocoön, Eartha Kitt, Lessing. Celia, you've got such a range!"

"William Blake."

"Huh?"

"I didn't miss your reference to the Ancient Bard, Wally."

"Blow me down! Where did you acquire all this stuff, Celia? Did you read it at University?"

"I never went to University, Wally. I did A levels in Art, Ancient History and English, and I won a scholarship to Girton College, Cambridge to read English, but my parents couldn't afford for me to spend the next three years not contributing any income to the household, so I wasn't able to go up to Cambridge; but of course, my two brothers were. Then a talent scout spotted me, and, if you recall, I became the Camay Soap girl on ITV adverts; then I was the teenage daughter in the Bisto Gravy Family; then I got onto the silver screen with Pearl & Dean, remember them?"

"Poop-poop, poop-poop, poop-poop! The theme song's officially known as *Asteroid*, but everyone just goes poop-poop, poop-poop, poop-poop!"

"I was the girl who got the Milk Tray delivered to her."

"Did you ever do the Girl that Things Happen To After a Badedas Bath, or the Cadbury's Milk Flake Girl?"

"No, Wally, because first my parents and then, once I got an agent, my agent, would never let me do anything smutty. But now look at me? My parents and my agent have passed away, and I'm doing full frontal sex scenes."

"Not any more, Celia."

"What do you mean, *Not any more*, Wally. What's happened to it?"

"I'm sitting in it, Celia."

"You mean all that tape wrapped round your legs, Wally?"

"I've cut the scene, Celia."

"Jesus Christ, Wally. What's Indigolin going to do to us when he finds out? He paid US $5M for it."

Hammam

The two brothers had sat on the stone settle in the Hammam, naked, ladling lashings of steaming water over one another and catching up on lost time. Posthumous had explained his plan to kidnap their hated triplet, Mortimer Unsdorfer AKA Colman Hunt, and ransom him to the studio. Presley thought it was a great plan. There was only one thing wrong with it, he had said. Posthumous had not kidnapped Colman Hunt.

The problem wasn't with the plan. The problem was with the execution; but they both had to agree that it had to be a million to one chance that Presley was going to be there, in Colman's caravan, at the very moment that Posthumous came to chloroform Mortimer and put him in the loading bay of his truck`.

So that was the path by which the two brothers had come to be sitting on the bench in the Hammam inside Morocco's most altitudinous inn. If truth be told, after his pigeon tagine and an hour and a half exfoliating his remaining, non-grafted skin with black soap, Presley had turned to his brother, and illuminated him with those famous Unsdorfer eyes that could light you up like a New Promethean, and he'd said:

"Posthumous, brother, thanks for bringing me here. You know, I kind of like this place. I mean, I'm not a spa guy, but this primeval thing: the scalding pales, the buckets overflowing with water heated to just the Goldilocks temperature, the steam coming up from real fires lit under the floor, the solemn charnel house atmosphere and the echoes of our words bouncing off the dripping ceiling, plus the fact that we've got the place all to ourselves, this is proper manly."

"Cave-manly?"

"That too. I'm really chilling out now. I feel my inner nomad trying to break out of my chest. I feel like I've been re-born as a Berber tribesman."

"Well, Presley, we don't have to be anywhere else. It is not what I would call an expensive joint, and this Hammam, they're not even charging us for it. Comes with the room. They seem to regard it as a basic necessity."

"Like having a Corby trouser press or a Goblin Teasmaid in the room?"

"Or an exceedingly long shoe horn in the hotel cupboard. By the way, we can't hang our clothes up, because you broke the hanging rail in the wardrobe. Another story. But, if we're staying on, can you do me one favour?"

"Sure. What is it?"

"Will you make the next trip down the mountain? Go into the Internet café and download the news, and see if you can score us some decent alcohol to drink. Sinking this Raki, breakfast, noon and dinner, my liver's beginning to feel like Portnoy's Complaint, and my legs are like jelly from all the trips up and down the fucking mountain I've already made."

"OK, Posthumous, just so long as you tell me one thing truthfully."

"What's that?"

"Was that really chicken in that stew?"

"Close."

"Boiling fowl?"

"Close."

"Pigeon?"

"Close."

"What's close to pigeon?"

"Dove."

And so it came to pass that, after a hearty breakfast on the outside terrace, gazing at the view partially obscured by the low altitude clouds, Presley had set off down Mount Toubkal.

After being bound be hands and feet in the suit carrier for so long, it felt great to have his legs pumping blood again, even if the air was too thin to get any good oxygen into his brain. He followed the irrigation trenches down from the peak, through the drizzly clouds, past the stone houses of the Berber Gheghaia tribe, until he emerged into bright sunlight. The journey through the cloud base had left his clothes damp, and now the warming sun was burning steam off his shirt, as though he was the Fantastic Four's Human Torch extinguishing himself after another heroic mission.

He found his way to the village centred around the hostel run by the Club Alpin Français offering rooms for 30 dirhams a night, the price of a cup of coffee, which price included the use of the hostel's kitchens to cook your own meals. He proceeded to the Internet café next to the butcher's fly-blown stall and the hotel's check-in. He had downloaded all the news and emails and messages on both of their phones, and having failed to find anywhere selling alcohol, had trudged back up the cordillera.

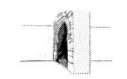

Once he had scaled the eminence, he discovered his brother, sitting in a broken chair, smoking some kif he'd scored from a member of the hotel kitchen staff. Posthumous saw that he'd come back empty-handed. Exhaling smoke, and passing the joint to his brother, he said:

"I take it that the penurious and destitute nature of your disposition means that you didn't manage to find anything for us to drink?"

"I went to both the supermarkets, and, so far as I could get by in French, the whole village is dry. The guy said you can only get booze in the hotels. But you seem to have checked yourself into Morocco's only hotel where that is not the case. Also, I couldn't think of anything else to cut the Arak with to make it taste better. I mean the only thing that goes in it is water. Dr Peppers or Coke, would make it taste even worse."

"So, your mission was a complete failure, Presley?"

"I wouldn't call it a complete failure, brother. I've updated our phones with the day's news."

"And just what is the burning news of the moment, Presley? What did the editor hold the front page for?"

"The news that they are holding the front page for, brother Posthumous, is that matinee idol, star of stage and silver screen, Colman Hunt, has disappeared and not been seen by anyone for more than 48 hours. They think he's been kidnapped."

"That doesn't make any sense, Presley."

"Well, it kinda does, Posthumous. I went in to Morty's caravan with a knife, intending to stick him, but he wasn't there. If the reason why Mortimer wasn't in his caravan—when you went in there looking for him, and you found me there instead and mistook me for him, and kidnapped me—was because someone else had already kidnapped him before I walked in—then that makes perfect sense."

"Right. So we could still act out my plan. We could still demand the ransom," exclaimed Posthumous. "Colman's missing. People think he's been kidnapped. We call for the ransom. No-one's to know we ain't got him."

"Long as the people who've really kidnapped him don't get there first"

"Even if they do, how's anybody except Colman going to know who the right guy is?"

"They may have to pay two ransoms," observed Presley.

"Or we may have to go and make the real kidnappers think they've grabbed the wrong triplet," offered Posthumous.

"Well there is a whole world of possibilities to conjure with, but I have only one thing to say to you, Posthumous."

"What's that, brother?"

"When the time comes to send the ransom demand, it's your turn to make the next trip down to town."

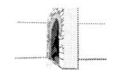

Work Done

Wally Pfister was sharing a Blue Curacao and Cava with Indigolin in Wally's Woodie-Wagon. If Wally had known that Elena's Curacao had been cut with champagne, whilst Wally only qualified for Cava, he might have felt a little sore.

"So how are you getting on with your leading lady?" Tinctorio asked him. "Not too temperamental for your liking?"

"Tell you the truth, Ti, she's bloody amazing. We're working in an industry where actresses used to be all washed up by their late twenties; but she breaks all the rules. I'm just observing her all the time trying to figure out if she's had any work done or not."

"Well, Wally, if she hasn't already, I think she's about to. Would you excuse us now?"

Indigolin made his way out of Wally's gentleman's club, past the dartboard on his oak-panelled wall, and down the steps. He shambled off across the sands to keep his rendezvous with Noah and the mad Irishman Noah had found on the Internet. To ensure privacy, they conducted the meeting in the back of Noah's car, with Noah getting neck ache from sitting in the driver's seat and constantly twisting round.

"Mr Webb?" Indigolin checked with the newcomer.

"At your service, Mr Indigolin."

"You know me, shill?"

"I'm a supporter of Westway Life Sciences, sir."

"You got shares, shill? They're going up."

"No, I've got no shares, but I'm a supporter."

"In what way, Mr Webb?"

"When John Laing & Sons were building the Westway motorway in the late sixties, in those days, before we joined the EEC and the Poles stole our jobs, all the navvies working in construction were Irish. As a paid up member of the IRA, I immured a number of my casualties in the pre-stressed concrete stanchions that are now holding up the roof of your headquarters, Mr Indigolin. There are so many of my load-bearing corpses in the construction of the Westway, I like to think that I am a supporter in my modest way."

"Got it, so you're a supporter in a literal sense. Charming credentials, Mr Webb! I thought that was an urban myth; but we won't be needing any of that for this assignment. We're going to be running two sets of books here. Think you can handle that?"

"Only form of book-keeping I've ever understood, sir."

"We're going to be running two sets of books, one for the insurers, who think they're going to be the recipients of prime slices of Celia Broadsword if they don't quicken their step, and another for everybody else (including Ms Broadsword), where you are just Ms Broadsword's minder for a couple of days."

"And which book reflects the genuine position, Mr Indigolin?"

"The book that says you are looking after Ms Broadsword, as if you were some kind of Victorian lady's companion, and not a silver hair on her head is to be harmed, Mr Webb."

"So, the job doesn't call for me to cut bits off Ms Broadsword if the negotiations with the insurers flounder?" The white-haired assassin enquired. "It's just that your colleague here, Dr No, mentioned the possibility of cutting off the end of her tongue *in extremis*, but still as a possibility."

Indigolin waited until Noah next turned round from his position in the front seat of the car and then frowned at him pointedly. Dr No was a good name for him though. Indigolin continued:

"The fact is, Mr Webb, I am 100% confident that I could put Ms Broadsword in my BioDome, smear her in cell-regenerative muck and grow her tongue back again within a month; but if I'm going to carry out that kind of experiment, it's an experiment that morally I feel I should carry out on myself first."

"There's a name for people who carry out experiments like that, Mr Indigolin."

"And what name is that, Mr Webb?"

"Nazis."

"Mr Webb, that is a facetious answer. Many famous and distinguished scientists have had to conduct their experiments on themselves, not least because the experiments were too dangerous to carry out on a third party. At least, five of them, to my knowledge, have been awarded Nobel laureates as a result. I could name Tom Friede, who exposed himself to lethal snakebites, Daniel Zagury's who tested his AIDS vaccine on himself and Max von Pettenkoffer who deliberately infected himself with a huge shot of cholera so he could attempt to cure it.

"At the other end of the spectrum, there was Constantin Levaditi, who was researching a cure for syphilis, but instead of shagging like a rabbit in an attempt to contract it, he injected himself with spirochete from syphilitic rabbits. If ever there was an error of judgment on the part of a medical practitioner, surely that was one. Then there were Shaughnessy and Levinson, two guys attempting to find a cure for dysentery. They injected themselves with a vaccine that had previously only been used on mice, despite the fact that all the mice who had received the vaccine had died of it.

"Mr Webb, we are using you, because when insurers hear your name, they are going to know that Ms Broadsword is in mortal danger, and there isn't a minute to spare. That's how we want to play it for insurers. But in true life, she is not in any danger whatsoever. You're going to be such a perfect gentleman that she's going to need counselling to wean her off Stockholm syndrome once it's all over. Verstehen?"

"Yeah, I get you. No worries. I must be her greatest fan, anyway. I'll cosset her but make out I'm cudgelling her."

"That's the Dunkirk spirit, Mr Webb. Tip top! You're going to be like the god Janus. Multi-tasking, two faced. Two sets of books. Think you can manage that?"

"Yes. No."

"Very funny! Tip top Shelf, shill!"

"But why?"

"You asking me But Why? What did Alfred Lord Tennyson say? *'Ours is not to reason why, ours is but to do and die.'* But, so that you can have a better understanding of your mission, we're playing a prank upon the shitgibbon who happens to own the company that's insured the studio against the eventuality of Celia Broadsword being kidnapped. They have to pay the ransom. I want to hurt him in his pocket, or as a very attractive accountant paraphrased it for me very recently: we kick him in his balance sheet, but not his bollocks. Ms Broadsword, the famous diva, is the honey in the trap. So insurers need to believe that horrible things are about to happen to her if they don't pay up, but nothing bad must actually befall her. Verstehen?"

"Two sets of books. No worries."

"Tip top!" Indigolin said to Webb. Then to Noah: "Okay with you, Dr No?"

Tongue Lashing

"Boss."

"Yes, Dr No?" Tinctorio Indigolin stared straight into his amanuensis' eyes. "I was wondering why you had to put unpleasant ideas into that Webb guy's head that we wanted to cut Celia's tongue out."

"I've been reading a medical book; well, it's not so much a medical book, as research for all the maimings and killings we've gotta do in the 4th series, King Ferdinand's Endgame. I guess you could say, it's a medical book but by 14th century standards."

"And what conclusions have you come to, Noah?"

"Well, it seems that the tongue's just a muscle. If you rip the whole thing out and cauterise it, then it won't come back, least, not in our lifetimes; but if you just cut a couple of inches off the tip, it all grows back again."

"Remarkable! How many more people are going to tell me about that today? No BioDome involved? Doesn't make sense."

"That's what I thought. 'Cos at first blush it sounds like you chop an arm off and it just grows back on, and that makes no sense, 'cos we know that don't happen. So I looked into it, and it's occurring all over the world to this very day. Kids who have tongues that are too long and are pushing their teeth out of shape; as an alternative to braces, they have an operation to cut a couple of inches off their tongues to stop that happening, and you know what happens?"

"It grows back? Wally's already told me."

"It grows straight fucking back again and, after enduring excruciating pain and talking funny for a couple of years, they're right back where they started."

"Mr Goofy?"

"Yeah, Mr Goofy, pushing their crooked teeth out of their mouths. If it was their dicks that were having inches chopped off—"

"They'd be Jewish?"

"No, I'm saying that if they were doing this to other parts of their body, the Daily Mail would be saying it was FGM or some form of sinister gender reassignment before the kids are old enough to make their own lifestyle choices. But as it's ostensibly orthodontics, no-one's actually noticed that they've been hacking pieces off unwitting kids for years in the name of vanity."

"There has to be an opening here for my Blue Molecule, Noah."

"Yes, boss. Grow your own tongue back, like those Sea Monkeys they had in the seventies, you remember? Just add water and the monkeys grow out of thin air and a starter pack."

"Yeah, should've been the answer to all the world's food problems; *grow your own edible monkeys*; but instead they marketed it as a kid's novelty. Noah, this could be brilliant!"

"Boss, just suppose we really let the mad Irishman cut our leading lady's tongue off. The K & R guys pay the ransom. We receive the payoff, because Mr Webb's working for us behind the scenes. But he chops just the optimum amount off so it grows back again, and it grows back with the accelerant of your Blue Rif Molecule, so the molecule gets all the credit and publicity, the share price goes up, and then we can dump as much on the market as is prudent; meantime, we've earned the gratitude of our leading lady whom we're going to dub and subtitle anyway, whilst she grows her tongue back."

"How are we supposed to earn her gratitude for chopping her tongue off, shill?"

"Well, first 'cos she doesn't know it was us behind it all, but second, because we make it grow back in record time. The film goes out on schedule despite the leading lady being mutilated during its shooting. It's going to be *mega*!"

"Top shelf, Noah. Sounds like you've come up with one of those gifts that keep on giving, apart from the fact that I said that we weren't going anywhere near there! Noah, I've already unintentionally been responsible for the poor woman being raped. I would rather jump up the eye of my own dick and sound my urethra with a crowbar, than cause Celia Broadsword any discomfort whatsoever. Do I make myself clear as the driven snow, Noah?"

"Yes, Mr Indigolin."

"Noah, where do you find out all this shit?"

"This particular piece of shit, Wally Pfister told me. His parents were going to do it to him, but they got a second opinion and relented."

"Ok, Noah. Very interesting. Topic closed. Tip top! Any questions?"

"Actually, boss, yes, I do have one question. How come we're not allowed to use the N-word or the P-word, but it's okay to refer to mad Irishmen and yids?"

"Simple, Noah. It's because the Irish and the yids don't cultivate that immense sense of victimhood that the P-'s and the N-'s have made it their life's work to attain. They just get on with it, like you and I do. You get it, Noah?"

"Tip top!"

"Are you taking the piss out of me by any chance, Noah?"

"Wouldn't dare, boss."

"Because if you are, or if any harm comes to Celia, just remember what the mad Irishman called you."

"Dr No?"

"Dr No. In the story, he has no hands, remember? He fooled around with radiation, and he had to have his hands replaced by crude bionic dukes. Remember also that I said that I believe that morally, its incumbent upon scientists to carry out their experiments on themselves before they unleash them on an unsuspecting public?"

"Where's this going, boss?"

"If you're so interested in discovering whether amputated body parts can grow back on under my BioDome and with the help of my Blue Molecule, why don't you give me a hand?"

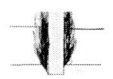

Anfa

"If you'll excuse us," said Aderfi. "We're going to go over there for a smoke."

Aderfi rose from the fireside, and went off to the perimeter of the compound, accompanied by a skinny Tuareg with eyes like a rat who Colman had learned was called Gwafa. The brother, Aghilles came with them.

Out of Colman's earshot, Aderfi offered a Moroccan Marquise from his pack to Gwafa, put another between his own lips, and the men cupped their hands round the flame from the Zippo to light them.

"Are you thinking what I'm thinking?" Aghilles asked.

"100%, I am," answered Gwafa. "We demonstrate our famous Berber hospitality by kidnapping Colman Hunt and get a nice ransom off the studio."

Scheherazade

"Then what happened?" Pfister asked.

"They say that prison toughens you up," Celia said. "It certainly did that for Morty. He learned how to street fight in there, and he learned how to defend himself. If Presley was to come at him again with a Stanley knife, he'd probably be able to disarm him now. He deliberately got himself into a lot of knife fights in the Scrubs. He says that in a knife fight, you've got to reconcile yourself to getting cut. If you try to avoid it, you're never going to win.

"You have to allow yourself to get cut to get close enough to disarm the assailant, so it's counterintuitive. The one thing you must never do in a knife fight is try to avoid the knife. And whilst he was learning all this, he got stabbed a few times. But no vital organs. I asked him what it feels like being stabbed, and he said it didn't feel like being stabbed at all. Apparently, it feels like someone's hit you with a shillelagh.

"But the craziest thing of all is that when Colman gets stabbed, it's his brothers that bleed. When they were small and his dad used to clip Colman round the ear, it was the two brothers whose heads would be spinning, and then, years later, when Presley stabbed Morty with the Stanley knife, Morty got a big scar, as we know, but Presley needed twenty stitches."

"Jeez! No wonder he's obsessed with cultural misappropriation!"

"Anyway, by the time he was ready for his parole, he'd become like a Sensai in there, because he'd completely mastered the art of self-defence, and it didn't matter what weapon you came at him with, he'd disarm you in a trice, because he knew no fear. It was all defensive. Colman would never attack anyone; but if anyone attacked him, he could deal with it. He never tried to get away from the weapon; always confronted it head on.

"What with that, and his New Prometheans thing, walking on fire, when he'd done his time and was up for parole, the other inmates were in denial. They couldn't hack it without him. The inmates had a whip round for a lawyer's fees and they mounted a legal objection to Morty's parole application, because they couldn't bear the idea of serving out their time in there without him."

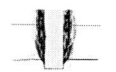

"And was the objection successful?"

"Of course not, but when their objections were not sustained, four of them committed suicide the same week Morty walked out through the Gate, and there were more failed suicides."

"How'd they manage to commit suicide in prison?"

"They swallowed hot coals from the fire."

"But what is a coal fire doing in a prison?"

"It was the wardens, Wally. They were on strike in December, because the government had announced that no essential workers were going to receive a Christmas bonus. The exercise yard was under a foot of snow, and the inmates had built a snowman. The wardens had a picket line in the exercise yard, and they were warming themselves up around a brazier they had lit in a metal bucket. First, they let one of the inmates help himself to an unlit coal from the sack for the snowman's nose. Then the same guy thrust his hand into the fire, plucked out four live ones and passed them round as if they were marshmallows."

"…And they ate them like marshmallows? Jesus!"

Wally reached over to the ashtray he kept on his bedside table for Celia and planted it on his rock of a chest.

"What's that for?" She asked.

"You always like to smoke after."

"Darling," she said. "I've quit."

He let that sink in for a while.

"So, we're going to be an item?" He checked.

"Yes, darling, we're going to be an item."

"And Celia, if we're exchanging vows and recounting stories about New Prometheans, I've got a confession to make to you."

She stared him straight in the face.

"I've just set fire to your tits."

"Huh?"

"Well, as you know, they were on the cutting room floor anyway. Before some smart Alec picks up all the pieces and tries to reconstitute them, I've cremated the nude scene. Don't ask me to explain it. It was just too painful."

"You don't have to explain it, Wally. We can do another one for your own private consumption. This one, you can have tits and everything else."

"And it won't cost me five million dollars?"

"Not unless you want a divorce! And Wally, one final confession. God, I feel like fucking Rousseau!"

"Share it."

"The stuff about my age the studio puts out. It's not true."

"It's not true. You mean you're older, or you're younger?"

"Wally, work it out for yourself. You've seen me playing alongside Kirk Douglas, Samantha Eggar, Fernando Rey and Yul Bryner."

"So, when the studio says you're in your seventies, and I assume that means that you're really in your eighties…?"

"Maybe I'm in my nineties, but you said it didn't make any difference."

"Well, it does, Celia. It does. It just keeps getting better. You're blooming amazing!"

"And who are you to say?"

"I am Spartacus!"

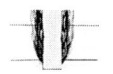

Brunswick Holt's Airstream

Brunswick Holt was only slated to occupy thirty seconds of film time. Allowing for make-up and re-takes, he was only expected to be on set for a couple of hours.

But because Brunswick Holt was Brunswick Holt, his agent wouldn't permit his imprimatur to be added to the credits, unless he had a bigger Airstream than anyone else. That bit of pettiness was actually written into his contract. And because everyone's Airstream was expected to be customised in some way, his people covered the walls in posters from Holt's own films, so as to make the star feel at home.

But these were very special posters. They had been signed by Holt personally at the time of each film's release. So the studio had spent hundreds of thousands of dollars in acquiring original signed memorabilia of old Brunswick Holt films, when they could just have run them off anew on a printer, asked Holt to sign them, and framed them, for a few cents.

The Lady's Dressing Room

Wally was studying the storyboard for the upcoming scene in the Courtyard of the Twelve Marble Lions, the new opening that had been delivered by the unknown scriptwriter. He desperately needed to get some perspective because in a script where a lot of the key scenes shouted at the viewer, competing for attention, this scene was very subtle and emotional, and the setting in the Courtyard of the Lions was stunning.

But the one jarring note that was completely out of place was the gigantic, Indigolin trade mark blue legume turban that Boabdil's messenger would be wearing when he delivered the letter to Queen Isabella of Castile. In a James Bond film, there would be merchandising: the cars, the wrist watches, the clothes. But in an Indigolin film, it was all self-promotion of the producer's Blue Molecule.

Hadn't anyone even explained to Tinctorio Indigolin that legumes were usually green? The guy just made his own language up, or traduced the decent language that was served up in front of him. Come to think of it, there was a greenish tinge to the blue turban, lizard-like, as though the huge hat was woven out of chameleon skins.

This was the only scene in the entire film that Indigolin had decided to put his stamp on. In the same way that Alfred Hitchcock always had a cameo appearance for himself in his films, Indigolin had asked for a part for John Donne, the Metaphysical poet, to be written in to the script, and the rumour was that Indigolin was going to play it himself. But the unknown screenwriter had redacted it with a stroke of his red biro. When Elena Troy had been told what had happened, quoting the Metaphysical poet's reflection on the bad consequences of his marriage to Anne, she'd just laughed and said: "*John Donne; Anne Donne, Undone.*"

Indigolin had cast none other than Brunswick Holt as the messenger. Brunswick Holt was probably currently the most bankable star in Hollywood. He dwarfed Colman Hunt. But Indigolin had blacked him up (which was obviously going to go down badly amongst the cultural misappropiationists in itself) and put him in a cartoon turban for a 30 second appearance, when Brunswick Holt and his gigantic hat were going to steal a very important scene in which Wally really wanted Celia to shine through.

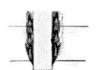

Somehow he was going to have to shoot the scene so that Celia came out on top, despite the box office star in the towering turban vying for the audience's attention. Worse still, no-one actually spoke in this take. Boabdil's messenger delivers the letter on a silver platter. Isabella splits the Sultan's seal and slits the envelope open; we see her read the letter to herself, and then her eyes have to explain its contents to the viewers. No-one says a word. How was she supposed to convey all these subtleties silently to the camera, whilst facing a black-and-white-minstrel in a gigantic hat? If it was Wally, he wouldn't even be able to keep a straight face.

Wally personally thought Brunswick was a bit hammy, but the public adored him.

Wally wanted to write the world's most amazing love poem for Celia, and put that in the envelope. So that when she slit the envelope, she would indeed be pleasantly surprised, and reading the contents of her envelope would bring a genuine Quixotic smile to her lips. Hardly any acting involved on her part at all. That was what Wally wanted; but, as he sat in his Woodie-Wagon staring at countless images of her, the words just wouldn't come. She left him tongue-tied.

He went online for inspiration. His poem had to be the greatest paean to a mature woman ever framed. He first went to his William Blake poems for inspiration, but the thing about Blake was he'd never written any love poetry. Given the role that John Donne had until recently almost played in the film, he read and re-read John Donne's *The Autumnal*, but found it frankly patronising; the old woman who was its subject was clearly Donne's patron, rather than the true object of his affection; it took all Donne's considerable conceit and ingenuity to try to come up with something nice to say about the old harridan.

It's what you get if you pay for it, he thought. He had recourse to Jonathan Swift's *The Lady's Dressing Room*. He'd found that amusing as a kid, but re-reading it as an adult, he found it cruel and misogynistic, although its subject did happen to be called Celia. He liked the last lilting line: *Celia, Celia, Celia*...but didn't like the last word.

His mind drifted off to George Kaczender's twelfth feature film. Jeez! People took the piss out of his name, Walter Pfister, but fancy being called George Kaczender! What was a Kaczender anyway? A shitten arse. Then the offensive Swift poem surfaced again, like a turd that won't flush: Celia, Celia, Celia. Kaczender had directed Vizinczey's novel, *In Praise of Older Women.* Just like in his Isabella and Ferdinand film, there was a sex scene with an older woman, but Karen Black, who played Maya, was only in her thirties. But when the film premiered in 1978, a woman was definitely finished by her thirties, so this was trailblazing.

In Praise of Older Women was cutting edge, that a woman could still be so attractive in her superannuation. The insensitive censor demanded the removal of the thirty-five second sex scene with Karen Black. But that was the entire point of the film! Nonetheless, Kaczender was able to show the uncut version at the Toronto International Film Festival, and despite an underground train strike preventing most people getting there and the torrential rain that doused the huge queues of the people who had made it despite that obstacle, the Elgin Theatre in Toronto was mobbed by curious fans wanting to see this unknown novelty, a woman in her thirties disrobing and having some soft-focus sex.

But then Joan Collins had filmed those novels of her sister's books, *The Bitch* and what was the other one called? *The Stud*. When she was in her fifties. And not to forget Ann Bancroft in *The Graduate*, both the film and the subsequent stage version. But Celia, Celia, Celia, she really upped the whole game to the next level.

Just like in the westerns when the gunslingers are playing poker and one gunslinger pushes a huge stack of chips onto the table, and then our hero say *I'll see you*. And he matches the stack. And then our hero adds: *And I'll raise you!* And he pushes another stack twice as big onto the table, before the shooting starts. That was Celia. She'd see off all the other women. But then she always raised any game she played to another level.

Tomorrow, they were back on set in the Courtyard of the Twelve Marble Lions. Well, that's what they called it anyway; but rather than go to the trouble of shooting it in the Alhambra, where they could have the benefit of the actual courtyard still standing there in all its glory from the actual period, Indigolin had told them to CGI it. To be fair to Tinctorio, it was quite a novel idea.

Hitherto, film makers had CGI'd the humans, because it was all the actors and extras who were expensive and temperamental and wanted repeat fees and mollycoddling, whereas the scenery was pretty well for free; but Indigolin had said it made more sense to use the real humans and CGI the location after. In Morocco, according to Indigolin, you could get all the bodies you wanted.

"A dirham a dozen," were his actual words. So tomorrow they were actually shooting in the courtyard of the big green screen, and later they were going to drop the real actors into the CGI Courtyard of the Twelve Marble Lions back at Framestore in Soho. Wally just hoped that Celia and the others could get into the

spirit of it, acting in front of the green screen and trying to imagine they were in the lion courtyard, alongside a bloke in a gigantic *titfa*.

Celia was familiar with the courtyard from the previous King Ferdinand series, but Wally had ensured that all the cast had visited the virtual courtyard on YouTube: *El Patio de los Leones, Nasrid Palaces, Alhambra, Granada, Espagne.*

He remembered how Celia had confessed to him in bed that *El Patio de los Leones* was one of her favourite places in the whole world: replete with memories, shining in its symmetry. She had told him how she used to stay in the *Parador San Francisco* and wander round the Alhambra and that courtyard in particular, after all the tourists had gone back to their restaurants and hotels for the night. She could drift from courtyard to courtyard, walled garden to walled garden, in between the towering hedges of neatly-clipped ewe, through Gate after Gate, as though she was Boabdil's Queen, Moraima.

As though she owned the place. For the upcoming scene, he knew that Celia could just close her eyes for a moment, and she'd be there, in that courtyard. The green screen would not be a factor for her. But could she shake that absurd oversized *titfa* out of her head and keep a straight face in front of Holt's cartoon turban? The script said that, after she'd slitted the wax seal and read the contents of the envelope, she had to smile 'Quixotically'. How, he wondered, did Don Quixote smile? He was known as *El caballero de la triste figura.* 'The Knight with the sad face'.

How does a knight with a sad face smile, especially when he's a woman? What were the constituent characteristics of Don Quixote? He was idealistic, romantic, unworldly, lofty, impractical, but very, very loveable. She had to conjure it all up in a smile.

When Wally had given them the virtual tour of the courtyard on YouTube, the cast had marvelled at the symmetry of the filigree columns of carved yeseria, the light domed roof, and then that Fountain of the Twelve Marble Lions bang in the centre, hewn out of Macael marble, pillaged from the palace of the Jewish Vizier, Yusuf Ibn Nagrela.

Sounded like *Hava Nagila*! History repeating itself. Jews having their gear stolen from them all down through the ages. It was the way their cultural influence disseminated itself: through straightforward theft, never mind cultural misappropriation. A courtyard of purloined lions.

When Wally had got this film in the can, and before Celia had to do the dull rounds promoting the damn thing, he was going to take her to the Alhambra. He'd worked it all out. They were going to stay at the Parador San Francisco, the hotel she'd mentioned, which was the only hotel actually inside the precinct of the

Alhambra, so they could stroll arm in arm through the Alhambra's marble streets and ewe hedges after all the tourists had gone home, just as she'd described it to him.

They could marvel at its every nook and cranny from daybreak, dipping their *churros* in their cups of hot chocolate at breakfast, and in the evenings, as they drunk a brace of *San Miguels* or an iced *Jerez* with plates of *tapas*. Because they were staying inside the Alhambra Palace, they'd beat all the queues, and he was going to stand with her alone and do the Instagram-able thing, there in *El Patio de los Leones*. No green screen. The real thing. He wondered whether she would be wearing one of her lovely sun dresses, or if he'd have her in full costume from the film, maybe the embroidered gold number they wore for the scene he was about to shoot.

What the heavens was he going to do about Brunswick Holt and his gigantic turban? It was as if the scene had been written by the guys from Charlie Hebdo.

He wondered if they could get a licence to marry in the Alhambra.

'But then,' he thought to himself, *'the Alhambra Palace just sounded like every seedy provincial theatre or picture house.'* The sort of venue where decrepit stand-ups come to die on stage or get pelted with rotten fruit after a pantomime crammed with dubious *double-entendres*. The Doncaster Alhambra! The Wolverhampton Alhambra! It was no different to a trip to Dignitas. She had him all tied up in knots!

Anyway, getting back to reality, tomorrow they were shooting in the courtyard of the Great Big Green Screen, and it was the scene when the turbaned messenger from Boabdil brings Celia, playing Isabella, a letter on a silver tray. She reads it. We can't see what's in it, but the expression on her face has to say it all for the audience. Quixotically. It has to be an inscrutable, but intriguing smile, that begins in her eyes before it illuminates her whole face and just brushes her lips, curling up for a moment. Celia was a real professional, but could she do it in front of a green screen?

He had decided that there was not going to be any blank piece of paper with typographer's drivel etched onto it. He was going to write the letter and put it in the envelope himself, the letter that Brunswick Holt, as the messenger, delivered to her. It wasn't going to be another film property. It was going to be a real letter from Wally to Celia, and its contents were going to elicit that smile from her, whether it was Quixotic like Don Quixote or enigmatic like the Mona Lisa: he was going to draw it out.

What was it she'd said about him having to lick the envelope himself or get the stamps sticky? He was going to write a letter or a poem, dedicated to her, and when she read it for the first time on set, expecting a sheaf of typographer's tripe or glyph-setter's gobbledegook, his poem was going to generate exactly the expression that he needed for the scene. To Hell with *In Praise of Older Women, The Autumnal, and The Lady's Closet*!

He was going to write a cross between doggerel and the divine, something that combined the sublime with the ridiculous, with half rhymes that didn't quite rhyme, metres that were all wrong, and lines that didn't scan. A poem that tilted at windmills. And she was going to read it, and the look on her face would transport them out of the fake green screen in the desert in Ouarzazate, and they would be in the real magical Courtyard of the Twelve Marble Lions together. Just him, and his Celia, Celia, Celia.

Economics

"What happens to all the money in the world?" Elena asked Indigolin.

"In what way?" He clarified.

"I mean, hardly anyone uses money these days."

"I guess, it must all end up in the banks then," replied Indigolin.

"Yes, but what do the banks do with it? It's a commodity no-one wants any more. Lots of businesses refuse to accept it. It's a dirty word. Money's had its heyday."

"And when the economy's shot to pieces, the government rolls out quantitative easing."

"—which is a fancy euphemism for printing more money. But, since no-one wants to use it in the first place, how does making more of it improve the economy?"

"Good point, Elena. And why didn't they just trickle out some of the trillions that must be sitting in bank vaults, doing nothing, instead of printing more of what they're already stockpiling?"

"We'll have to ask those guys who wrote *Freakonomics*. You know, how come drug dealers always live with their mums?"

"Is it time for my John Donne quote of the day, Elena?"

"Let me think. Okay. Commit this to your memory and think about it, Tinctorio:

Whoever loves, if he do not propose
The right true end of love, he's one that goes
To sea for nothing but to make him sick!"

She smiled and threw her handbag over her shoulder in what might even have been a come-hither kind of way, and left Indigolin alone beneath a Heineken umbrella outside Aka's chow tent. Indigolin repeated the words in his head and analysed them. Maybe, he thought, he was over-analysing them; or was Elena Troy giving him the come-on? Maybe her gesture with the handbag was less come-hither and more come hotter. This seemed more subtle than owing a cock to Asclepius, but it seemed like another route to the same destination.

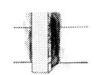

Celia Quits

They were gathered in the Courtyard of the Twelve Marble Lions. At least, that's what it said in the script, but there were no physical lions in evidence. Celia Broadsword, as Queen Isabella, was in full costume, namely a stunningly embroidered square cut cloth of gold dress, white yarmulke, worn more raffishly than respectfully, and a double-strand gold necklace with a huge pendent ruby and pearl cabochon. Celia's dresser had dressed her from the portrait of Isabella of Castile dating from 1490 hanging in the Prado in Madrid. The cameras were running and the director, Wally Pfister, was identifiable by the fact that he was sitting in a director's chair with Walter Pfister stencilled on the back.

The messenger, a cameo modestly played by none other than the renowned Brunswick Holt, wearing a huge blue legume turban befitting his seniority, presented Queen Isabella with a letter on a silver platter, the envelope bearing the wax seal of Boabdil. After allowing the camera sufficient time to graze upon the Sultan's seal, Celia took the letter from the silver tray, plucking it up with her be-ringed fingers.

Then she did something that wasn't in the script. She detached the ornamental Jineta from the back of her head, and the silver cascade that had transfixed Wally so many times, came tumbling down. She used the Jineta as a letter opener, first breaking the wax seal and then slitting the sleeve open. Wally was on high alert, because his girlfriend had just gone completely off piste.

There was nothing in the shooting script about her pulling the Nasrid dagger out of her beehive and using that to open the envelope. But it was certainly a nice touch. Reading the contents of the letter to herself, a smile of pure, unalloyed intrigue began to enlighten her eyes, before it played along the edges of her lips, just as Wally had prayed for.

Celia Quits

By Walter Pfister

In this world of cheap glamour and false bits,
And ditzy chicks putting on the Ritz,
Art house films hijacked by industrialists
Of scripts with serpentine twists
Cannibalised by New Prometheans and a non-fungible enigmatist
Who never studied English lit,
Where a woman's worth is measured by the size of her tits
And she's on the scrapheap by the age of 36,
Only one woman stands out from all the counterfeits,
As exquisite, sempiternal, infinite,
Celia, my only, only ever, always,
Celia, Celia, Celia, quits.

She folded the paper and re-inserted it in the envelope. Playfully, she took aim with the stiletto, and to the messenger's shock, unscripted, threw it overarm from a metre away, safely impaling itself in the dart board of his huge hat. The entire crew could hear Brunswick Holt exhaling in relief. He had been positive he was going to lose an eye, at the very least.

It was exactly the facial expression Wally had been looking for. Celia Broadsword had triumphed against all odds and against Indigolin's attempts to sabotage his own film with an absurd turban. She had completely stolen the scene. Wally had caught both the Mona Lisa-like smile he'd been looking for on Isabella's lips, and the sheer, genuine terror in the face of Brunswick Holt who was certain he was about to be exoculated.

For his mere thirty seconds of screen time (thirty seconds that had undoubtedly taken ten years off his life), Celia Broadsword had upstaged the great Brunswick Holt.

Of course! That's what a Quixotic smile would look like: the smile on the face of the Mona Lisa. And Walter Pfister had just captured it on celluloid.

"And cut!" Wally said.

He'd almost said *And quit*.

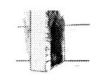

El Zogoibi

"You're muted, Mr Indigolin."

Tinctorio Indigolin and Ray Peckett, the head scriptwriter, were consulting Elizabeth Drayson again over a Zoom call. Peckett unmuted his boss. It was Peckett's job to take the raw material the anonymous scriptwriter delivered and give it a conventional appearance so the actors would be able to work with it.

"We were wanting to know what happened to Boabdil after he surrendered the keys to Granada, Ms Drayson," Peckett explained.

"Little is known of Boabdil after he handed over the keys to Granada. We don't know for sure when he died or where he is buried," Ms Drayson began. "During his lifetime he was nicknamed Boabdil el Chico, for his youth; but after he lost Granada, the soubriquet, Boabdil el Zogoibi stuck—the Unlucky One. Because, in truth, he was unlucky. All his life his uncle had been plotting to overthrow him, so Boabdil had to fight wars with his own people as well as the Spanish.

"At the end, in the Siege of Granada, Boabdil was hugely outnumbered. His allies from Morocco never turned up to relieve him; but I think the most important thing of all was that Ferdinand had kidnapped Boabdil's son.

"Kidnapping was the norm in those days. In the Hollywood epic films, we see the king leading his men into battle on horseback, always wearing the finest armour and riding the finest steed, and we think how much braver the leaders were in those days, going out of their way to draw so much attention to themselves, compared to our leaders these days, conducting proxy wars from the comfort of arm chairs in cabinet offices. The kings or sultans always wore the brightest colours and the most expensive armour, broadcasting their royalty.

"But it wasn't quite like that. The fact was that no-one was going to kill a monarch intentionally, because they were worth so much more by way of ransom. Therefore it was important that the monarch was distinguishable from the rest of the rout by his splendid accessories: every item of a monarch's armour was branded, customised, personalised and high fashion. Boabdil wore a helmet in the shape of a pomegranate, which was the symbol of Granada, and, of course, the Greek symbol of the afterlife. The monarch had to stand out from his expendable troops to ensure he wasn't killed unintentionally in battle like the rest of them. If the tide turned against his side, he would be kidnapped and ransomed instead."

"So when Nelson famously calls for his red jacket—" began Indigolin.

"That's because he thought he was about to be defeated, not because he was impervious to fear," completed Drayson.

"You were telling us about Boabdil's children," Indigolin prompted.

"Boabdil had two sons, Ahmed and Yusuf, and a daughter, Aixa."

"I thought Aixa was his mother's name," interrupted Indigolin.

"Correct, Mr Indigolin. Aixa was the name of Boabdil's mother, and that name was also shared by Boabdil's daughter, and indeed, Boabdil's sister. Ferdinand kidnapped Boabdil's elder son, Ahmed, and held him hostage for years but without ransoming him. Eventually, after Yusuf was born, Ferdinand agreed to swap one son for the other, so the new-born, Yusuf, was held hostage and Ahmed was released. So Boabdil had one son, who was now a complete stranger, returned to him in exchange for giving up the other son to whom he would become a complete stranger.

"It was barbaric. Ferdinand held Yusuf hostage for nine years and the ransom he demanded was the keys of Granada. However, the original surrender deal would have seen Boabdil remain *in situ* as a client king with some dignity for himself and his family, and permission for his people to continue their Muslim religions, traditions and language.

"However, as soon as the keys were handed over, Ferdinand reneged on every single promise, and Boabdil became a fugitive and disappeared into oblivion. He was despised by his own people for throwing away eight centuries of Muslim rule in Spain. He is the only Emir whose date of death or even place or means of death remain a mystery."

"So where did he go?" asked Don, the second scriptwriter.

"We believe he lived the rest of his life in exile," explained Drayson. "Most of the time he was exiled in Spain. It was as if he had become an embarrassment to his own people, so he had to stay in Spain after having given up the Jewel in the Spanish Crown that he and his ancestors had created and treasured. As an exile in Spain, he was an eleemosynary, which is to say, one dependant on gratuitous alms, from his enemy, Ferdinand.

"Eventually the money that Ferdinand drip-fed him seems to have dried up. Boabdil handed over the keys in January 1492, but by December that year, Ferdinand had been attacked and gravely wounded by a madman in Barcelona.

Ferdinand was then distracted by problems in his home base of Aragon, and lost interest in Boabdil. Boabdil's beloved wife, Moraima, died in August 1493, the year after the surrender.

"Boabdil then seemed to get kicked around from pillar to post until there was no succour for him anywhere in Spain, and he ended up eking out an obscure existence for himself in Fez in Morocco. Having become an outcast and impoverished in Spain, he had no choice other than to go back to Morocco, but there he had to live in total obscurity, as he was an object of shame in his home country for what he'd given up. Ferdinand had been presented with a choice: his city or his son, and he had made the wrong choice."

"And what happened to the son?" Indigolin asked.

"It's believed there are still descendants living somewhere in Morocco," she informed them.

"Can we make something out of this?" Indigolin asked Ray.

"Boss, it's a history lesson, but it ain't no movie," Ray answered.

Frock Horror

Celia was wearing a knee length dress the colour of coral held up by spaghetti straps on her tanned shoulders. Not dried spaghetti. What the food critics these days called artisan spaghetti. In fact, it was too fine to be spaghetti at all. Wally was trying to remember the name of that very thin pasta: *like gold to airy thinness beat*, as Elena would have quoted from Donne. It came to him: Angel Hair Pasta, and Celia was the angel.

"May I?" He asked.

She had no idea what the question referred to. It was as if he was offering to pour the tea. Nonetheless, she didn't say no; so he went ahead and slid one of the Angel Hair strips off her shoulder. She wasn't wearing a bra. Her left breast slipped out. She heard his sharp intake of breath. It was the sound of unarticulated admiration.

"What?" She asked.

"Your areola," he began. "and the nipple," he continued.

"What's this, Wally? The naming of the parts?"

"They're exactly the same colour as your frock, Celia."

She hadn't heard anyone calling a dress a frock since she was at high school. She smiled: "Well, Wally," she said, "why don't you kiss them and see how many shades darker you can make them go?"

"Pass me your phone, please," he requested.

She was surprised that he appeared to be turning down an invitation like that, but she fished her phone out of her bag and handed it over to him as asked.

"Open it up, please."

She wasn't sure that she'd been in a situation quite like this before, but in the nearest situations that she had been that resembled this one most, she didn't remember that the thing she was asked to open up was her phone. She held it up to her face and it unlocked.

He took a picture of her. He satisfied himself that it was a good photo, and then he handed the phone back to her.

"Wally, why have you put a picture of my tits on my phone? If I wanted to do that, I could do it myself."

"I thought it was more respectful that way, Celia. So that you'd always know that you were in control, and not worrying that I might be posting it up on the wall or showing it off to the jocks in the locker room. If I want to look at it, I'll have to ask you nicely."

"Walter Pfister, why do you want to look at a photo of my tits when you can look at the real things as often as you want?"

"Because the way your tits look today is different from the way they looked yesterday and will be different from how they're going to look tomorrow. Every memory is unique. It's like Zeno's parable of the river. You never enter the same river twice."

"Or the same woman, it seems, Wally!"

"Yes I do, Celia. But it's never the same."

Coil

George had barely driven his new Vantablacked Bentayga one hundred metres from his house in Mayfair's Hays Mews, headed in the direction of Berkeley Square, when a warning light flashed up on the instrument cluster and an alarm beeped. The yellow warning light told him to check the vehicle into the Bentley workshop and not drive it.

Using the car's own SIM card on which the salesman, Rupert had stored the showroom as a Favourite, George put a call through to HR Owen. Rupert recognised the Bentley's SIM and took the call.

"How can I help you, Mr George?"

"Morning Rupert. The car's telling me I mustn't drive it and it wants to be towed to the workshop."

"Where are you, sir?"

"I'm right outside your fucking showroom! Can't you see me?"

"Don't forget, you specified an invisible car, Mr George. Can you open the passenger door? Then I'll be able to see you when the interior lights come on."

George tried to open the door, but it was locked.

"No," he said. "It's locked itself."

"I wouldn't worry, Mr George. Mechanically, nothing ever goes wrong with these cars. Any fault, it's always with the electronics, some of which we have to buy in from other suppliers. The coil on this vehicle is very temperamental."

"I didn't know the fucking car even came fitted with a contraceptive! Did you charge me for that?"

"Just turn everything off, Mr George. It will start getting very hot, because of the paint job. Wait fifteen seconds and then turn everything back on. It should be okay."

"What? Like a computer?"

"Like re-starting your computer. Precisely. I promise you, the problem will be electronic, not mechanical."

George hung up. He switched everything off. Within seconds, with the A/C not running, the temperature inside became oppressive. He counted fifteen seconds out loud, like they'd taught him at school: *One little second, two little seconds, three little seconds…* Then he counted out five more just for luck. Then he prodded the red START button and the car roared back into life. The warning light had gone off.

The A/C was powering on, destroying the planet. The warning light didn't come back on when he put her into gear. He concluded the remaining two hundred and fifty metres of his journey to Annabel's without further incident. Of course, he could just have walked from Hays Mews to Annabel's, but that wouldn't be arriving in style.

Annabel's car jockey put his top hat on the passenger seat and performed the valet parking service expected by the likes of George. As there were no spaces in Berkeley Square, he ended up parking it outside George's house in Hays Mews.

Set Your Turban to Stun, Mr Spock

"I'll get it, honey," said Celia Broadsword. She had been playing the piano in Wally's Woodie-Wagon when they heard a light knock on his door. Opening the door, revealed Tinctorio Indigolin. He was wearing Brunswick Holt's gigantic turban, and prodding icons on an iPad in his hand. Holt would be half way back to California by now.

"Ti," she said.

"Celia," he replied, "I thought I might find you here. I heard that you were inspirational in the Big Hat scene." He looked beyond her at the dart board on the far wall behind her head.

"Are you coming in?" She asked.

"I'd love to, darling, but the *titfa* won't go through the door."

"You could remove it," she suggested.

"After the demonstration," was all he said, and then, "please step down, out of the wagon."

She climbed down the three steps and was on the sand in her mules. "Is Mr Pfister within?" He enquired.

"Wally!" She called out.

Wally Pfister's smiling face appeared in the doorway.

"He had better step down also," advised Indigolin. Wally descended the three steps and stood beside her. Indigolin took several paces backwards, away from them and continued prodding icons on the touchscreen of his device.

"Now, Celia, could I ask you to repeat the dagger-throwing scene you executed so exquisitely with Brunswick Holt earlier. Take the little stiletto hatpin and throw it at my turban like you did on set with Brunswick Holt."

She approached Indigolin in his ridiculous hat and withdrew the hat pin from the folds of his turban. She retraced her steps a few paces and drew her right arm back, before hurling the dart in the direction of Indigolin's preposterous stovepipe. It was within millimetres of connecting when it was repelled violently, whistling back past her and Wally's heads, and embedding itself in the dartboard on the far side of his trailer's interior.

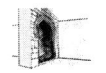

"Bullseye!" Indigolin said, congratulating himself.

"How did that happen?" Celia asked.

"It's the minute pin stripes in the weave of the legume cloth in the turban," Indigolin explained. "I can set their electromagnetic filaments, and I can reverse their polarity with this controller. I can also use this slider to control how strong I enable the electromagnetism. I had set my turban, as Captain Kirk says of his phaser in Star Trek, to *Stun*. Of course, I could have dialled in more deadly force, but that could have been dangerous. Don't you wonder," continued Indigolin, "what the crew's phasers had been set to before Captain Kirk ordered they be set to stun?"

"But the dart could have ended up in her skull!" Wally exclaimed, suddenly concerned that Indigolin's party piece could have played out very badly. "You could have taken her eye out!"

"That's why I insisted you both came down from the trailer," explained Indigolin, "so that the trajectory I had selected would ensure it went over her head, and not in her head. We can't go around impaling our leading lady now, can we?"

"Can you do any other tricks with your ten-gallon turban?" Celia asked.

"For sure, I can," responded Indigolin. "As I say, the secret is in the minute pin stripes in the toque. 'Just like That', as Tommy Cooper would have said. It's the same weave as the blue legume double-breasted jacket I was wearing when I was shot. The bullet hit me with stunning velocity and I was really winded by the impact, but the suit rejected the bullet, in the same way that one's body might reject an unwelcome organ transplant. It hurled it straight back at my attacker with such force, he may well have killed himself, for all I know.

"The greater the force on impact, the greater the repelling force, as energy is always preserved in a collision. Basic Newtonian physics. Just think of kitting out an army in my blue legume uniform. The enemy would immolate themselves, wave upon wave, like Whitewalkers, because all their artillery force would be aimed straight back at themselves. It would be the perfect encapsulation of the pointlessness of war. They get all dressed up, go out on the battlefield, and shoot themselves! Just like that Chalsey Wilder poem about Two Dead Men. Might as well have stayed at home! Tip top! Mega! But never mind all that!" He cried. "Look at this!"

He was stabbing the icons on his control screen again. "By enabling the filaments, I can match the magnetic pull of the earth's gravitational field. And then," he stroked a slider bar on his screen, "by turning it up a tad, I can reverse the gravitational field, like so."

They watched in amazement. Tinctorio Indigolin, in his gigantic headpiece was no longer subject to gravity. He had levitated and was hovering one metre off the sand. However, not a grain of sand was displaced, as would have been the case if the means by which Indigolin had elevated himself were mechanical. As he had declared, he had moved himself by some magnetic force harnessed in the hat.

"I didn't tell Mr Holt about these little optional extras!" Indigolin joked. "In the future," he confided to his audience, "everyone's going to get around like this!"

Then, making a backward swipe across the monitor with four fingers, still smiling like the Cheshire Cat, he floated noiselessly off into the distance, powered by his prodigious pillbox.

"What do you make of that?" Celia asked Wally.

"Bah! Homburg!" Was Wally's reply.

"Do you know the poem he was talking about?" She asked him.

"Of course I do, Celia. Elena is good for John Donne and I'm good for nonsense like *The Smile on the Face of the Sphinx* and Chalsey Wilder limericks."

"So what was he talking about, lover?"

"One fine day in the middle of the night
Two dead boys got up to fight
Back to back they faced each other
Drew their swords and shot one another."

"That Blue Dude!" She exclaimed. "Impossibilities are his stock-in-trade!"

The Battle of Algeciras

"But why did Boabdil lose in 1492?"

"You're muted, Mr Indigolin."

Tinctorio Indigolin unmuted himself on the Zoom call with his historical accuracy consultant, Elizabeth Drayson, and repeated himself: "Why did Boabdil lose in 1492?"

"Well," she advised, "it was pretty much a done deal that he would lose. It had all been sewn up nine years earlier. What our esteemed former Prime Minister, Boris Johnson, would have called an 'oven-ready surrender'. Boabdil had suffered a humiliating defeat at the Battle of Lucena, when he had been kidnapped by Ferdinand's forces. In order to ransom himself, Ferdinand took in exchange Boabdil's new-born son. The deal was done that day nine years earlier so that the only way Boabdil was going to get his son back was by surrendering Granada in exchange.

"Boabdil tried to bargain and bluff his way out of the deal for the next nine years by attempting to call in favours from the contacts who should have been his natural supporters from North Africa. But unfortunately for him, Morocco at that time had degenerated into a fragmented country ruled by cabals of corrupt Emirs and bent viziers, who were too preoccupied with their own self-interest to lend him a hand. Plus, even if they had wanted to, Ferdinand had put a naval blockade across the Straits of Gibraltar, which was the only feasible route that any aid could have taken to reach Spain from North Africa.

"Boabdil found himself holed up in the Alhambra, insulated in the most literal sense from both his supposed African allies and the rest of Spain. Granada had become an island, and Boabdil had become a bad case of what we call *Man in the Branch Office Syndrome*. You know, the man in the branch office always thinks that his partners in the head office are plotting against him, denying him support, that the accounts team based in head office are issued with instructions to feed him misleading management information, and so on. The writing had been written on the wall from the time Ferdinand kidnapped Boabdil's son. It just took nine years before Boabdil finally despaired of finding any other way out."

"Thanks for your time, Elizabeth," Indigolin said, ending the call with a friendly wave of his hand, and hoping to himself that his own kidnapping plans didn't take nine years to come to fruition.

Wally Pfister came into the room and slapped the next twenty pages from the 12-year-old scriptwriting prodigy down on the glass table.

"What do you think?" He asked.

Indigolin picked up the sheaf.

The Battle of Algeciras is fought out at sea in the Straits of Gibraltar when Boabdil's navy smashes King Ferdinand's blockade, using their new weapon, the Lateen rigged boat.

Next scene: back in the Patio of the Twelve Marble Lions, Alhambra Palace

QUEEN MORAYMA (wife of Boabdil, speaking to Isabel): Did you seriously believe that I would exchange for the return of my son, this city of Granada and all the thousands of precious souls within it, that I would throw away the last 800 years of history as well as the limitless future?

QUEEN ISABEL: You have no choice, Queen. You're outnumbered three to one.

QUEEN MORAYMA: Look again.

Enter the Emirs of Tangiers, Fez, Rabat and Agadir.

EMIR OF FEZ (to Boabdil) My lord, please excuse our tardiness. Slack winds and Ferdinand's blockade delayed our crossing momentarily, but we have cut the Spanish navy to shreds and their crews lie with their weapons and men of war at the bottom of the Straits of Gibraltar. King Ferdinand, your puny army is surrounded by three armies of our own. We have deep-throated bronze canons and fierce fighters ready to serve King Boabdil.

BOABDIL: King Ferdinand, your choice and the choice of the rest of Europe is very stark: either you all become Mozarabs, or you are burnt at the stake.

QUEEN ISABEL:(to her husband) A Mozarab is a Christian living under Arab rule, my Lord.

EMIR OF RABAT: And adhering to Arab beliefs. They must pray in the mosque, not the church.

EMIR OF AGADIR: They follow the Crescent, not the Cross.

EMIR OF FEZ: And the men must all be circumcised.

"What do you think?" Wally repeated.

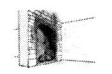

"I think," said Indigolin, "that we can dispense with the services of our historical accuracy consultant."

Pfister laughed.

"I'm deadly serious, Wally. You know, there used to be a saying that history is written by the victors, and I think that until the twenty first century that held true. But these days, history is written by the losers. We're living in an epoch of victims. Nowadays, in the Age of the Internet, anybody can write history, and, since the winners tend to be the movers and the shakers, they're all busy moving and shaking, so, these days, it's the underdogs who are writing up the records."

"Wasn't that why Elon Musk wanted to buy up Twitter?"

"Just so. To command the wildfire of wrong opinions. I was watching a BBC programme on thrilling cities the other night. The narrator was sauntering down past Check Point Charlie, where the Berlin Wall used to be, but now it's all cute boutiques, edgy nightclubs, specialist food shops, and the narrator was blathering on about how inhumane the Berlin Wall was, and what a wicked and terrible thing it was to divide people from their families, and so forth.

"Nobody saw fit to mention the reason they put the blasted wall up in the first place. They're airbrushing that out of the history books. We don't know who is writing this script for us, but, as far as I'm concerned, his version of history is as good as anybody else's, and a damn sight more watchable!"

An Abundance of Caution

"As I think some of you may already have guessed, I very much regret that Presley never returned to the Riyadh after he stopped off for a beer at the Ibis."

Indigolin lowered his gaze, rather than look Celia in the eye.

"Celia, I wanted personally to give you the bad tidings before you had to ask me if I'd kicked him off the set yet."

Indigolin was clearly embarrassed to be giving Celia this news. He delivered it at the conclusion of the morning's yoga session. Also within hearing were Elena Troy and Wally.

"And, as you also know Colman's gone missing." continued Elena. "but," she added, "you may not have put the two together as yet."

Celia noted that Elena had become a near-constant companion for Indigolin. She had started out as an over-qualified agency book-keeper. She had graduated to some kind of Metaphysical Poets Lifestyle Guru for the billionaire; and now she had segued seamlessly into being his go-to person for almost anything. *'Noah Nguyen was going to have to watch his step,'* she thought, *'or he'd be out of a job.'*

"So," continued Indigolin, "putting the two and two together, and hoping that we have erroneously come up with five, the working hypothesis is that Presley has kidnapped Colman."

"Kidnapped?" Celia queried, incredulous of her own ears.

"Kidnapping we can deal with by throwing money at it," began Indigolin.

"It may not even have to be our own money," continued Elena. "It may be an insured peril."

"But why do we think it's a kidnapping?" continued Celia. "Historically, Presley has demonstrated a propensity to attempt to murder his brother. This is like a dog returning to its vomit. He's tried it before and he'll try it again. This leopard won't change his spots. Presley's a killer. What's the logic for thinking he'd draw the line at kidnapping him?"

"Elena's filed a report with the police," said Indigolin. "When it was just Colman missing, they weren't very interested, because he'd not been missing for long enough. But now that two of them have gone missing, perhaps they'll take it more seriously, especially with one of them being a celebrity."

"The border police have been notified," explained Elena. "and I've filed a notification with the K & R insurers, because it says that you have to do this at the earliest possible opportunity. So even if there's doubt as to whether or not he actually has been kidnapped, it's best to put in a protective notification, as they say *ex abundanti caetulla*."

"Ex what?" Wally asked.

"It means 'out of an abundance of caution'," explained Elena. "So even if he's just been in the john for longer than usual, we play it on the safe side and make an early protective notification, because not to do so might void the cover."

"Now two of the triplets have gone missing," observed Wally. "It should make the job easier for the Moroccan police, because they've only got to remember one face."

"So speaks Wally Pfister," said Celia, "the man with the photographic memory for faces! Let's just hope that when Colman turns up he's still got his face on the right way round!"

The Mosque de Notre Dame de Paris

Scene: inside the Mosque de Notre Dame de Paris

King Charles VII of France, known as 'the Affable' kneels on his prayer mat as the Muezzin calls the faithful to evening prayers.

Boabdil enters with the Habsburg Holy Mozarab Puppet Emperor Maximilian, and his wife, Anne of Brittany, after Boabdil has dissolved her wedding to Charles VII as bigamous and given her hand to his client Emperor, Maximilian. Boabdil is accompanied by builders and an architect who proceed to unfurl A3 size plans.

Zoom in to plans showing elaborate series of red and white stone horseshoe-shaped arches, similar to the Mosque in Cordoba.

BOABDIL to architect: If we remove the two steeples, will it all fall down?

ARCHITECT: No, your Highness, I can support the superstructure during the alterations.

BOABDIL: And replace them with two ribbed domes.

ARCHITECT: If it please your Lordship, why not twin minarets for the Muezzin where the bell towers now stand, and one huge dome above the hypostyle supported by multiple horseshoe-shaped arches?

BOABDIL: And where do you think we should put the Quadriga I removed from St Mark's Basilica when my armies sacked Italy?

ARCHITECT: When we've removed the main stained glass rose window, the horses will look as though they were made for there, your Lordship. Do you want me to remove the Old Testament Kings?

BOABDIL: Not one jot. Let the Old Testament Kings remain where they stand, but have the stonemason continue the lineage with likenesses of the Nasrid Kings:

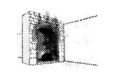

	we shall have statues of Nasr, Mohammed, Yusuf, Isma'Ili, and all the other Yusuf's and Mohammeds in a line until you come to Boabdil. Be sure to make each Nasrid at least a foot taller than the Old Testament Kings.
ARCHITECT:	(sycophantically) My Lord, they would not be proper likenesses done any other way.
BOABDIL:	And sit me on my favourite horse, Aliatar.
ARCHITECT:	And should the masons depict the faces on the Nasrid Kings, my Lord?
BOABDIL:	Yes, for this was a Christian cathedral before they saw the error of their ways.
EMPEROR MAXIMILIAN:	My Lord, Notre Dame, means Our Lady. We cannot have the Mosque named after the Mother of Christ.
ARCHITECT:	Henceforth, it will be known as The Mosque of Mohammed XI.

Suffragette

Celia looked at the girl on set. She certainly seemed to present an argument for the need for a dress code in Aka Akinyole's Umbrella Bar. She was what *Hello* magazine would describe as an aspiring starlet. She was wearing a micro-skirt, barely larger than a belt. From behind, you could see the T of her thong sticking out of the top. She had a sleeveless blouse, where the sleeve holes were so wide, you could see her entire breasts when she stood sideways on.

"Look at that, Wally," Celia said. "Did suffragettes padlock themselves to parliament's railings and go on hunger strikes? Did they throw themselves under the King's Horses at Epsom Derby, just so some tart would be free a hundred years later to walk around with her tits and tush hanging out in public? What did those women sacrifice themselves for?"

"I guess for a veto on men saying that they were asking for it."

"When that's exactly what they are doing," Celia pointed out. "And if she actually gets what she's asking for (which is the only way she's going to get started in films), once she's got her foot on the ladder, she'll attempt to finish her ascent to the top rung by denouncing the poor *shmuck* who put her there."

"Excuse me, Celia, are you turning into an apologist for Harvey Weinstein?"

"Of course not. It just pisses me off, Wally. We all act as bimboes when it suits us, and I just don't think it's right for the bimboes to claim they were exploited ten years later, after they've reaped the rewards."

"The question one has to ask, honey, is whose benefit is it for? I mean, I'm the director of this film, and, as you would imagine, she has no effect whatsoever on me. Mr Indigolin is the producer, and I don't think she would have any effect on him either. So unless she thinks she's going to make her debut into the world of films by getting into the pants of the Gaffer or the Grips or the guy who fetches the coffees from Aka's hospitality tent, I think her charms, such as they are, are destined to be wasted on this particular set. There used to be a gratuitous sex scene, but that was with a proper woman, and not a bimbo, and that scene no longer exists. We're not making that sort of a film any more. We're making history."

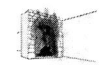

"Well, Wally, we're certainly rewriting history!"

"Have you seen the latest?" He asked. "It's as if it was commissioned by someone like me who believes that human beings can live for ever."

"Show me!" She said.

He did better than show her. He read it out to her:

"Decay was never heard of
Until the King of Kings, Pharaoh, Sun, Moon and Stars,
Set his throne upon the burning sands,
And dared the desert to wet his feet."

"It's beautiful!" She declared. "It could be a prequel to Ozymandias."

The Mosque of St Paul's, City of London

Indigolin came into Wally's Woodie-Wagon with the storyboard.

"What do you have there, Ti?" Wally asked him.

"The artists have done a storyboard of St Paul's Cathedral after it's become a Mosque, like our anonymous scriptwriter requires. And I'll tell you something. I think it's quite an improvement."

Wally took a look. "It's exactly like the Great Mosque in Cordoba. All the red and white horseshoe arches," he said.

"Yes, Wally, it's exactly the same principle. In Cordoba, the Moors 'sympathetically restored' an earlier Catholic cathedral. But what they actually did, was they just stuck a dirty great mosque inside the cathedral's frame. Here, we're going to do the same thing with St Paul's Cathedral, but the cool thing about St Paul's is it's already got a bloody great dome!"

"But the uncool thing is Sir Christopher Wren didn't finish building St Paul's until 1710, by which time Boabdil would be more than 200 years old."

"Well, that's what happens when you sack your historical accuracy consultant, Wally!"

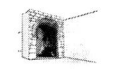

Argan Oil

"Not shooting today, Ms Broadsword?"

"No, Noah. Our secret scriptwriter has to catch up, so we have a day off."

"Ms Broadsword, if you need any of those Argan products for your hair, Mr Indigolin's driver is just leaving for the Argan Farm."

"Noah, how did you know I use Argan products?"

"I'm a follower."

"But only women follow my cosmetic tips, Noah."

"Ma'am, anything I can use that keeps me looking as good as you, I'll buy it."

"Where is the Argan Farm, Noah?"

"Didn't you know? Mr Indigolin bought an Argan Farm and factory down near Taroudant. He's planning to mix it up with his Blue Molecule delivery mechanism, and he'll have his Argan reaching parts of your body that other Argans can't reach. Seriously, if you hop in with the driver, and select what products you want, we can mix them up back here with the Blue Rif Molecule, just like a Smoothie, and it'll penetrate straight to where you need it.

"You know, if you just rub Argan oil into your skin, or Argan shampoo into your scalp, it doesn't do any good. It just sits on the surface of your skin, attracting fruit flies; but if we use the Blue Molecule delivery mechanism, it will penetrate right to the hair follicles and stimulate them. Put that in your blog."

"Where's the driver?"

"In the Range Rover over there; you can't see him 'cos the windows are blacked out, way Mr Indigolin likes it, but he's sitting in there. You can have a stopover at Gazelle d'Or and do some spa there, if you like, because the spa at the Argan Farm isn't operational yet. Gazelle d'Or has lovely gardens, but the famous pianist, Adam Stevenson, who also seemed to run the place, passed away in 2017. Not the same without him."

"OK, ask the driver to wait up 5 minutes and I'll be there. What's the driver called?"

"Mr Hugh Webb."

"Have I seen Mr Webb around before?"

"Don't think so. He's not the driver who drove the Urus from London. This one drives the Range Rover. Mr Indigolin just decided he wanted a more mature driver. Got sick and tired of juvenile hotheads throwing him all over the back seats doing Lewis Hamilton impersonations. This one's got white hair and everything. Look, there he goes now."

They watched as the driver's door opened, and a tall, dark suited man with a crown of white hair emerged, took out a cigarette from a silver case and lit it. He had a pure white pony tail, like a geriatric rock star.

"Well, as long as he's only got white hair and not a white stick! Tell him I'll be along in 5 minutes, please, Noah."

Celia stopped by Wally's Woodie-Wagon to let him know she'd gone off set, but he was off set himself, interviewing a man about some elephants and some large barges to pose them on. She removed her half of the cut yellow veil and draped it over his desk, so he'd know what she meant. What had he told her? Yellow means *I'll be back.*

Holt's Writ

Brunswick Holt had starred in so many man of action films, from caveman to gladiator, from corsair to cavalier, from foot soldier to Marvel mutant. The only thing all his parts had in common was that he only ever played heroes.

Which is why it seemed so out of character when the writ arrived from Holt's lawyers complaining that Brunswick Holt's mental health had been deleteriously affected by an unscripted incident of bodkin throwing at his turban during the shooting of the film that now went by the name of *the Gate of the Burnt One*.

The brash, swaggering brute, Brunswick Holt, was claiming, through his Machiavellian Tennessee lawyers, that he had lost his mojo and was never going to be able to work again. He wanted a jury trial in Nashville.

Indigolin said he couldn't even bear to look at the document covered in coats of arms and button seals. He gave it to Elena and asked her to deal with it.

The Argan Farm

Several times along the journey, Celia attempted to engage the driver in conversation. She was tempted to tug at his white ponytail to get his attention, as though it was a bell rope; but all the man wanted to talk about was her films. It had been quite flattering for the first hour, but now she was fed up with talking about herself, and it just made her feel ancient.

She had managed to get as far as his name, which she had established was Hugh Webb. In truth, she had already absorbed that much from her conversation with Noah, but she had now independently corroborated it.

"Hugh, as in Hugh Grant," she had said.

"Hugh, as in Hughie Green!" He had joked.

That was a name from the distant past, she thought. *"Double your Money,"* she said, correctly placing the deceased quiz inquisitor.

"And *Opportunity Knocks*," Webb supplemented. "He's buried in Golders Green Crematorium," Webb added needlessly. Mr Webb was fascinated with crematoria as well as catafalques and columbaria. He could go on Brain of Britain, answering questions about North London burial grounds. He could tell you every famous person that was buried in Highgate Cemetery. He could also name all of the deceased that were holding up the Westway Flyover.

Apart from divulging his name, his fascination with her films, and his knowledge of the last resting places of deceased television personalities, he didn't seem interested in anything else, and the conversation had faltered.

Exasperated, about thirty kilometres outside of Taroudant, she tapped him on the shoulder and told him that Noah had said they were stopping at Gazelle d'Or for lunch. He said *No problem, missy*, and they pulled in to this oasis of calm just as an English shooting party was returning from the morning session with the roosting doves. Mr Webb acted very protective of her, like he was a bodyguard saving her from the paparazzi.

When one member of the shooting party recognised her and asked for a selfie, Mr Webb refused on her behalf, although, left to her own devices, she would have agreed. Leaving Mr Webb with the car in the turning circle outside the hotel, she proceeded into the reception area and introduced herself to the Front of House Manager, whose badge proclaimed he was called Muhammed, just like everybody else.

"You need no introduction, madam," he said. "Everyone knows Celia Broadsword."

Celia smiled and asked him if it would be okay to take a swim in the pool as long as she ordered a light lunch. Muhammed said they would be honoured, and walked her through the gardens to a terracotta-tiled outside seating area with informal tables round the pool under the shade of the date trees; not the formal seating area where Indigolin had taken his dinner with the boor the other evening. Muhammed sat her at a table and gave her the lunch menu and the Wine List. He also showed her where she could get changed and help herself to towels.

A waiter, also called Muhammed, wearing a brown Dishdash and a red toque took her food and beverage order, and humbly asked her if he could take a selfie with her for the wife. In stark contrast to Mr Webb's aggressive and proprietorial refusal, she said that of course he could and entered into the spirit, as though she had known Muhammed all her life. She waited for the glass of sauvignon Blanc to arrive, took a sip, and then slipped off to get changed.

She had the pool all to herself. The water temperature was just Goldilocks: not too hot and not too cold, but just right. She did a number of lengths of the pool. Having one's own luxury Airstream with all mod cons was one thing, she mused as she swam up and down the pool, alternating between breast stroke, crawl and back stroke; but they had been in the middle of the desert for more than a month now, and it suddenly dawned on her that access to a *piscine* was not so much a luxury as a bare necessity in these temperatures, a necessity that the support staff they had put up at the Berber Hotel would be enjoying every morning and every evening, whereas the stars, who 'wanted to be alone', and consequently lived in mobile trailers, had not enjoyed in weeks.

Returning from her swim, her hair wrapped in a towel somewhat smaller than Brunswick Holt's turban, she finished the white wine, nibbled a mouthful of her salad, left more than enough money on the table to cover whatever it came to, and then made her way back to the car with her hair still wet.

She presented herself back at the Range Rover. Mr Webb was practising his Three Card Monté on the bonnet. Seeing her, approaching, he compressed the cards back into their pack, and offered her a Lucky Strike.

"No thanks," she said. "I've quit."

They then drove on to the Argan Farm. The only signposting was a small plaque inscribed 'BLUE RIF'. Neither of them noticed the blue-robed charcoal burner on the edge of the forest. The driver turned off the main road and followed a bougainvillea-lined avenue for some way. The layout of the Argan Farm was similar to the *Gazelle d'Or*. Everything was enclosed by terracotta walls about 3 metres high, and there was an impressive blue gate with a large iron lock to which Mr Webb had the key. He proceeded to unfasten the gate, through which they drove. He then got out of the car and locked the gate again behind him.

"Don't want any of the goats escaping," he told her.

Suddenly she was aware of a super-abundance of goats, but no sign of any goat herds. "The place hasn't fully opened yet, ma'am," Mr Webb explained. "Soft opening's next week."

Celia was amazed to see the goats in herds climbing up into the trees, to reach the precious Argan nuts. The Argan trees were festooned with goats, hanging like baubles on a Christmas tree, so that you would think the fruit the trees bore was in fact goats, not Argans at all.

"Oh look!" She cried, reading what was written on the Today's Specials Board. They're offering a tasting of Argan Oils.

Mr Webb pulled in beside the Activity Centre, and remarked: "Ma'am, if you knew where that stuff comes from, you wouldn't rub it on your skin, let alone eat it."

Then he opened the car door for her and stood by the car whilst she went into the Argan Farm.

She wouldn't come out again anytime soon.

The Book of Andrew

The sands of the Empty Quarter are reddish brown in hue due to the presence of cooling magma known as feldspar. But the magma had cooled down hundreds of thousands of years ago. These days, there was nothing cool in the Empty Quarter, unless you could find your way to an oasis.

It took Andrew two days to make his way to Liwa Oasis in Abu Dhabi. There he found water and shade. But nothing to eat. He was almost a stone lighter after his journey across the desert. Then he turned round and set off back in the inhospitable direction from which he had come. This time, trotting near the edge of the motorway, he developed a taste for roadkill. He also found that scorpions were nutritious and juicy sources of sustenance. He fell in with a pack of feral dogs.

They opted him into their fraternity, and at nights, they hunted together for cape hares and oryx. One night the pack brought down a gazelle and began a feast that lasted two whole days. The feral dogs showed him how to lick the condensation from cooling stones as the sun rose. He developed a penchant for the taste of warm blood.

His appearance was quite different from the days when he had been man's best friend in Dubai. The dark ridge along his back was still there, but his rib cage now protruded through his belly. His claws were long and uncut. His eyes were wild and rabid. Even his teeth had grown more pointed and sharper. When he stood up on his hind legs, he was almost six foot tall. He could tear apart a striped hyena, unaided. The striped hyena were the only beasts in the Empty Quarter that ever picked a fight with the feral dog pack.

Having honed his survival skills over a period of several weeks, Andrew then left the pack and set off alone, continuing to re-tread the path that had brought him there. He traversed Star Dunes in the shape of pyramids, rising to 250 metres. He crossed the Domal Dunes that occupied the centre of the desert. He made his way across infinite sand sheets that moved and reformed like waves.

Eventually he arrived at the feldspar salt flats that marked the outer boundaries of the Empty Quarter. Then he followed along the edge of the road, sleeping by day and hunting and scavenging and journeying in the cool of the night. He had covered two hundred kilometres before he saw the lights of Dubai spread out, resembling charms from a giant bracelet dropped in the desert, crowned by the jewel of the Burj Khalifa, like a giant Jineta, piercing the night sky.

Celia Makes a Counter-Offer

Celia Broadsword had selected a range of Argan products in the shop and placed them in a strong bag-for-life with *BLUE RIF ARGAN FARM* printed on it above a stencilled representation of a very happy looking goat with a kif cigarette hanging out the side of its mouth. She made a mental note to have a quiet word with Indigolin about the questionable judgment of the marketing company he was using.

After all, the market he was seeking to appeal to consisted of family groups of western tourists with young children in tow, with maybe a smattering of local Moroccan Islamists blended in, not Rastafarian Bob Marley wannabe's from Ethiopia, worshipping the Emperor Haile Selassie, and wanting to get mullahed on cheap Moroccan kif.

Having established that there were no staff in the farm shop, and having established that there was no mechanism by which she could pay for the products as yet, because the Argan Farm was still awaiting its soft opening next week, and having further established that Mr Indigolin would be very annoyed if he was to discover that Ms Broadsword had been charged for the products anyway, she returned to the Range Rover, climbed into the back seat, ready to return to Ouarzazate, and was surprised when Mr Webb didn't respond like a regular chauffeur would, by climbing into the front seat and turning the key to start the engine.

Instead, Mr Webb opened up the tailgate of the Range Rover and began unloading cold bags and other kit and taking them into the reception of the hotel area of the Argan Farm.

Eventually, she tired of waiting and climbed down out of the car and went round to the back of it, where she found Mr Webb sitting on the tailgate of the Range Rover with his feet dangling down, enjoying a cigarette. At least, she thought, his face looked more sensible than the stoned goat on the bag-for-life.

She had asked him when he was planning to drive her back to the set, and it was at this point that he respectfully informed her that his instructions were that they would be staying at the Argan Farm for the foreseeable future, until the insurance company paid her ransom, a ransom, she noted, that happened to coincide with the sum that Mr Indigolin had paid her to get her kit off.

"Am I under house arrest, Mr Webb?" She asked.

"Ma'am, it's just that it wasn't safe anymore on that film set. Important people keep disappearing."

"And now I've become one of them!"

"It's for your own good, Miss Broadsword."

"Are you telling me that Mr Pfister knows about this 'arrangement'?"

"He doesn't know anything about it, ma'am. It comes right from the top. But it's only temporary and I'll take good care of you until it's all boxed up."

"Remind me again, how much is the ransom that you're demanding?" Celia asked Mr Webb.

"I'm not the party who's doing the demanding, ma'am. I'm just a *del credere* agent. I understand that the ransom demand is for US $5M."

"Well, I can pay you more than $5M to let me go."

"You got that sort of money?"

"Petty cash. Lend me a phone and it will be in your Swiss bank account in the click of a mouse."

"That is very generous of you, Miss Broadsword, but I can't take your money, even if it was $10M."

"And why is that?"

"Because I've got my reputation to consider."

"What happens if I'm past my sell-by date and don't fetch $5M?"

"I wouldn't worry about that, ma'am."

"Well, I do happen to worry about that."

"In that eventuality, I'm supposed to escalate, you know: show them we mean business."

"And how exactly would you propose to escalate, Mr Webb?"

"I'm supposed to cut bits off you and send them."

"Any bits in particular?"

"Your tongue."

"Dear God, my tongue! Who came up with that one?"

"My employer."

"And you're going to do it for real?"

"Course not. Start cutting off pieces of Celia Broadsword? You were my poster girl since I was old enough to know real class when I see it."

"So how are we going to play this, Mr Webb?"

"If push comes to shove, I'll send them someone else's tongue."

"Who else?"

"Maybe an animal, one of those fucking goats."

"They won't buy that."

"Well, maybe I'll cut out my own tongue. But your pretty label is staying in your minikin mouth, miss. No ifs; no buts! If I have to, I'll pay the fucking ransom myself."

"Don't you think that's taking Stockholm syndrome a little too far, Mr Webb?"

FERDINAND:	And women like that part, which, like the lamprey Hath never a bone in it
DUCHESS:	Fie, sir!
FERDINAND:	Nay, I mean the tongue…

Just then Mr Webb was abruptly woken from his *Duchess of Malfi* reverie by his phone ringing and vibrating in his pants pocket. He was surprised as he didn't think there was any net here. If his phone had network, then so would her's, so he was going to have to confiscate it. Before he took his call, he spoke to Celia. "Sorry, ma'am. I didn't think there was any reception here. But as it seems there is, I'm going to have to borrow your phone. You know, like when you go into a museum or something."

She handed it over. He stuffed the confiscated device into his pants pocket and then said, "Excuse me," as he walked out of earshot to take the call.

"Mr Webb!"

It was Albanian George's voice.

"Good evening, Mr George. Sorry, my phone didn't recognise the call was from you, or I would've picked up quicker."

"Mr Webb, my Vantablacked Bentayga has its own SIM card and its own YouTube channel. I'm phoning you from the car on the car's telephone number. Put it in your Favourites for next time. This isn't me you're talking to. It's my car."

"Right. And what does the car want to say to me?"

Having heard the foreign ring tone, Albanian George asked: "Where are you, Mr Webb. It's midday here."

"I'm in the middle of the Sahara Desert, Mr George."

"I suppose you know why I'm ringing you."

"I didn't think you were ringing me."

"Huh?"

"I thought your car was ringing me."

"Very good. You know why my car is ringing you, Mr Webb?"

"Same reason I haven't been round to collect my money, Mr George. Job's not finished."

"But you've had half your money."

"No, sir. You lost that money fair and square at Three Card Monté. You still owe me all my money, and I haven't been in to collect it, because I haven't finished the job."

"Mr Webb, don't be faecetious with me. I don't know why I waste my fucking time with a spastic like you. I've got these Romany types—Fuck it! Am I even allowed to call them that these days? I've got these pikey travelling twins. I call them Tweedledum and Tweedledee: one of them restrains the mark, while the other one does urethral soundings with a brown Tasmanian tree snake. Those guys get proper results for me."

"Mr George, you asked me to kill the guy, not leave him with a burning sensation when he takes a piss."

"Never mind all that! I also know this cross-dressing narcissistic nigger who'll do things to you, using nothing but his own body, things so disgusting that you'll feel so unclean afterwards, that you'll scrub your own skin off. You won't stop until you've flayed yourself alive. Am I even allowed to call them that these days?"

"Far as I can tell, it's okay for one nigger to call another nigger a nigger; but if anyone who isn't a nigger calls a nigger a nigger the nigger will feign offence!"

"I hired you to put someone down. If anybody's Adam and Eavesdropping on this call, don't matter we're not minding our P's and our Q's, 'cos it's not me doing the talking; it's my car. You know who owns Bentley?"

"Huh?"

Putting on a German accent: "Wokeswagon!" He laughed. "Get it? Volkswagen."

Mr Webb thought that Albanian George didn't know how to be authoritative. If he was trying to put the frighteners on Webb, he shouldn't be telling him bad jokes. The joke didn't even make any sense.

"I also remember you telling me, Mr Webb, all about figures of speech and how when you put someone down he stays down. But when you put Tinctorio Indigolin down, he bounced straight back up again and walked off like a fucking Jack in the Box, and the only result I've noticed is that when Hugh Webb puts a man down, the man's company's stock goes up. In fact, it's gone through the fucking roof.

"If I'd invested the money I paid the assassin with the assassin's target instead, the debt the target owed me (which caused me to hire the assassin in the first place) would have paid itself off five times over and I'd be licking my own face by now like the Cheddar cat in Alice in Wonderland. What the fuck happened?"

"Far as I can tell, something that hasn't happened since biblical times. A dead man got up and walked away. But I'm on his case. That's what I'm doing in the Sahara. His production company is shooting a film out here. I know exactly where he is, and when the time is right, I'll be knocking on your door for the balance of my fee."

Webb didn't mention the fact that the slug had ended up in his own stomach. He was still in denial over that detail. But in the Moroccan heat, when he sweated, at the point where his shirt went into the top of his trousers, he experienced a painful, itchy reaction as though he'd been smeared in honey and anointed with fire ants; and that reaction served to remind him of the slug that he'd extracted with the shellfish utensils. He'd stopped wearing a belt to keep his trousers up, as it was too uncomfortable. He'd taken to wearing red braces like a barrow-boy banker.

"You followed him all the fucking way to the Sahara? Are you sure you ain't intending to sub-contract my job to some queer-bashing Arab minger? Fuck it! Am I even allowed to say that these days?"

"I'm a professional, Mr George. Got my reputation to think of. When I put a man down, he's supposed to stay down."

"So you keep telling me. But the opposite seems to happen in practice. Does he know you're following him?"

"He thinks I'm working for him, but I've got my own agenda."

"What's he doing in the Sahara?"

"We're all on set. Like I said, his production company is shooting a film here."

"What's it about?"

"The USP is that an eighty-five-year-old woman strips off for a sex scene."

"Already been done by that cake woman, Mary Berry, in Monster Ball."

"I think you may be thinking of Halle Berry, Mr George."

"If you're all on set, doesn't he recognise you from last time you failed to kill him?"

"When I shot him, I was wearing a disguise."

"What kind of disguise?"

"It's a long story for another time, Mr George, but I was disguised as Tinctorio Indigolin. I was disguised as my mark."

"You mean like a Seduce-us."

"Huh?"

"You know, Seduce-us. The snake that eats its own tail. Mirror-image."

"I think you mean an Ouroboros, boss."

"Yeah, right. I'm the robber boss. You remember that, Mr Webb. This time, do me a favour and do the job properly. Do it decisively, determinatively. What did the Bard say? *Be absolute for death.* Sorry, is that quotation too Araldite for you? I want something *pour discourager les outré*, if you get me. I want a fucking conflagration with that thieving yiddisher oven-dodger, Tinctorio Indigolin, in the middle of it. A Viking funeral! Shit! Are we even allowed to call them Vikings these days? Have you been to a Viking funeral, Mr Webb?"

"No, Mr George, I never get invited anywhere."

"I want to see him change colour from blue to red. Fuck it! Has anyone even understood why the dude is obsessed with the colour blue?"

"Well I have a personal theory, Mr George. Porphyrophobia is a morbid fear of the colour purple. This could be what led Indigolin towards blue as a compromise. He eschewed purple because of its association with tyrants. The Alban kings used to wear purple. Under the Roman Republic the colour was outlawed. But Julius Caesar revived the fashion and was promptly assassinated. He was wearing the purple robes of the tyrant when they stabbed him on the steps."

"So, you're saying that if he'd gone to the toga party in his blue sheet instead of his purple sheet, he might have lived to tell the tale, like Tinctorio Indigolin?"

"It's just an idea that I was working on for the next edition of my book on catafalques. We've also added a whole chapter on columbaria."

"And who the blazes is he when he's at home, a Columbian drug lord, like Pablo Escoffier?"

"No, Mr George, it's a building, a structure consisting of niches or pigeon holes. A dovecote for the dead. You can either use the niches for storing funerary urns of the cremated, or in a Catholic columbaria, they just slide the whole dead body into the niche, like in a mortuary. Then they put a cap or a cover on the niche. People usually think the space contains ashes of the dead, but that's not necessarily the case. You're looking at floor to ceiling horizontally stacked skeletons."

"Always a gruesome eye-opener chatting with you, Mr George. Just burn the Blue Dude, ok? I don't care if it's his ashes or his bones that end up in Columbine, but I want to see him burn. Burn like the Crazy World of Arthur Brown. Make him do the whole fucking rainbow for me. Am I even allowed to refer to rainbows these days if I'm not a homo?

"I want to see him go Snap Crackle and Pop like fucking Rice Krispies. I want him to burst like a bubo! I want to see him pop like popcorn, sizzle like a sausage. I want to see 4K footage of the man melting before my fucking eyes, just like the Man from the House of Ruby Wax. Burn him and show me the evidence on your phone."

"I'm gonna need a burner phone then!" Webb quipped; but George's car had already hung up on him and terminated the call.

If the footage of the firestorm was good enough, thought Mr Webb, *he could put it up on his own website.* Maybe re-name the website, *Be Absolute for Death.* Had a ring to it. A kind of finality. Time to change his ring tone.

He still couldn't remember which of Shakespeare's plays that quotation came from. At first, it had been playing on his mind all day long, but he couldn't find a pigeon hole for the quotation, or should he say a columbarium? Then he had decided to put it out of his mind and not think about it at all, in the belief it would naturally slot into place without him having to do anything; but that hadn't worked either.

How would his life have played out, he speculated, if he had stayed on at Trinity College, Dublin, instead of following the vocational course of becoming an assassin? It was strange how one fell into these things. His parents had been upstanding pillars of the community, but they never discussed politics with him.

Neither he nor they had ever subscribed to a newspaper. His introduction to Sin Fein had been through James Joyce's novel, *Ulysses*, being a compulsory text on his English literature module. Time and again Joyce returns to the theme of The Phœnix Park Murders. Bloom discusses them with Daedalus at the busman's shelter in Chapter 16. When teenage Webb had read about the character known as James Skin-the-Goat Fitzharris, the Invincible, Rough Hugh had identified with both the character and the name, and from that time he himself began planning to join the Invincibles.

Skin-the-Goat Fitzharris and his Invincibles had brutally murdered Lord Cavendish and his under-Secretary, Thomas Burke in Phœnix Park. Fitzharris had driven the getaway car. Joyce seemed fascinated by those assassinations and returned to the theme of the Phœnix Park Murders, again and again: in The Lotus Eater chapter; in the Æolus chapter. The murders were like a spot Joyce couldn't help picking at.

Despite never having read a newspaper or heard a wireless broadcast or owned a television, Webb had become infatuated with the Invincibles, and their Fenian followers, the IRA, through the compulsory text of his English course. And this, despite the fact that *Ulysses* was not even English literature. It was Irish. It was a reworking of the Greek epic, set in Dublin and written by an exiled Paddy, travelling between Trieste, Zürich and Paris. But it had changed the course of Hugh Webb's life. Without *Ulysses*, he would probably have evolved into a headmaster in some parochial, rain-driven village school near Derry.

One thing was for sure: he wouldn't have had the pleasure of spending quality time in North Africa with the incomparable Celia Broadsword.

'*There is a divinity that shapes our ends*,' he thought. '*Rough Hugh them how we will.*'

The next call Mr Webb put through was to Mr Indigolin.

"Yes," answered Indigolin.

"I was calling to let you know there's good network here. I've got three bars and there's Wi-Fi too. I wasn't expecting there to be any net here. There's nothing for miles around, but then suddenly, once you're inside the big gate of the Argan Farm, there's really good net."

"I know. I had it put in. The Argan Farm's supposed to be a visitor attraction, learning centre, farm shop, activity hotel. No point in all the tourists making the pilgrimage to the Argan Farm and taking selfies if they can't put them straight up on Instagram and spread the word to other potential punters."

"I see."

"Also, as it so happens, you're going to need the Wi-Fi, Mr Webb, because you've got to set yourself up an untraceable Gmail account and send me a ransom demand for the return of my leading lady, so that I can pass that on to the K & R insurers. You get the money. You take your fee; but here's the Top Shelf bit: the insurers won't pay a kidnapper, because it's insurance against a loss you have to suffer first; so I have to pay the ransom, and then they reimburse me after."

"So you are going to demand US $5M from me in cryptocurrency. Has to be cryptocurrency, Verstehen? I happen to be sitting on a stash of bum bitcoins that

I unwisely paid $5 mil for, which are now only worth a couple of hundred thou. Swings and roundabouts, shill. Ups and downs. I've enjoyed other positions that have increased by 12,000%; so I can't complain about this one, especially as I've found a use for it. We unload the negative tokens on you for the ransom. You use them to pay your fees; I assume you're ok with £200K for two days' work?"

"Don't think we ever agreed on a fee, did we? As I remember it, we were okay with discussing criminal activities such as kidnapping and maiming and glossectomy; but we were too refined to talk about the dirty subject of money. So I pay you US $5 mils worth of cryptocurrency that now no longer happens to be worth 5 mil, and Metcalfe Insurance Specialists then reimburse me with US $5 mil of real money. Now that's what I call alchemy! Everybody's face gets washed! Does that sound Top Shelf to you?"

"Yes, Mr Indigolin. Top shelf."

"But only so long as not one hair on her head is harmed. Remember?"

"Yes, I remember. Two sets of books. What's the password for the Wi-Fi, Mr Indigolin?"

"Goat."

"Is that upper case or lower case, Mr Indigolin?"

"It's just fucking Goat. Slice and dice it how you like, shill."

"That's not a very strong password, Mr Indigolin. Don't you think you should put your birthday and a special character such as # or @ in, or a lower case underlining?"

"Mr Webb, I'm running an Argan Farm and a petting zoo, not GCHQ!"

Having taken the stuff he needed out of the car, Mr Webb parked it under cover, considering that there couldn't be that many Range Rovers in Morocco, and remembering that her boyfriend piloted his own chopper. It would be too easy to spot the car from the air.

Mr Webb put Goat into his various devices. Then he took the rest of the food and drink supplies in the big cold box from the Range Rover and unloaded them into the catering size fridges in the kitchens. The farm stretched to some 80 hectares and was surrounded by a continuous three metre high wall of sun-dried adobe bricks rendered in mud, sand and straw. It was a style of wall typical of Morocco, not really high enough to repel enemy invaders, but more than sufficient for privacy.

Within the walls, there were countless Argan trees, spaced equidistantly apart, and in between the Argans, there were cacti and dates as well as a lot of other exotic flora and fauna the names of which he didn't know. There were beautiful rose gardens with the High Atlas Mountains in the far distance. Visitors were encouraged to tour the farm following a specific boardwalk route marked out between low box hedges.

The route started at the Visitors Centre where they could watch films about goats and Argans and also the cold pressing of olives and grapes. Armed with this knowledge visitors could hire audio visual guides and ramble through the box hedged route through cultivated Argan groves, olive groves and vineyards, taking in some rose gardens and cactus gardens along the way, and dodging the spray from the irrigation vaporisers that soaked everything every thirty minutes or so, until they ended up at a souvenir shop where they could buy all manner of Argan products, olive oils, wine, soap, candles, cacti and fridge magnets in the shape of goats. It was intended that there would be some sort of cafeteria area here also, but nothing had gone live yet.

At the back-of-house area, where the rubbish was emptied and the broken-down plants were dragged for compost, there was what Mr Webb at first assumed was some kind of tented encampment and toilet block, where the seasonal workers would bed down, comprising about forty tents, spaced well apart from one another.

However, as he got closer, he realised these must be what they called Glamping: the pavilions were appointed with every conceivable luxury. Some even had their own plunge pools or hot tubs. This was the five star accommodation for the paying guests, not the workers. Seeing the tents spread out before you, you could think you were on the Field of the Cloth of Gold with Henry VIII of England and Francis I of France. He liked that comparison and made a mental note to repeat it to his captive audience, and impress her with the depth of his knowledge. He thought the scene resembled a film set for some medieval jousting tournament.

Further back, there was a more permanent concrete structure, and Mr Webb now realised it was in that concrete honeycomb that the workers would bed down when the place went live, because there weren't any villages near enough for a commute.

He roamed amongst the pavilions, deciding which one would be his and which one would be Celia's. One thing he knew for sure: they'd be right next to one another. He didn't know how long they'd be staying, but he felt like he'd won the lottery: being paid two hundred K to spend his quality time with Celia Broadsword!

Having verified that everything was secure and that she could run, but she couldn't hide for long, Mr Webb went back to his charge.

"Ma'am, I've checked out the compound and it's all secure. There are no trees close enough to the walls that you could climb, unless you wanted to try doing yourself an injury, scaling a prickly cactus, and it's a nine foot drop on the other side. The ramparts surround the whole compound and I've locked the gate."

"They're not ramparts, Mr Webb. They're known as *pisé* walls. They originated in the design of harems. They're nine foot high, because that's considered sufficient to preserve modesty; they're not intended to repel an enemy invasion."

"How do you know all this stuff, ma'am?"

"I've played the part for most of my adult life, Mr Webb. I've read up on it."

"Well, the bottom line is that you're free to come and go as you please, just don't try to leave the farm. I don't intend to tie you up or restrict your movements unless I have to."

"Can I have my phone?"

"I'm afraid not. I've turned it off."

"What are we supposed to be doing here?"

"Waiting—until someone pays your ransom."

"And how am I supposed to occupy myself in the meantime?"

"There's the Visitor Centre. You can feed the goats. I can show you the sleeping and washing facilities. I'm afraid the spa isn't functioning yet. But there's private plunge pools by our bivouacs, you know, the ones that filter and clean themselves using solar panels, because they don't smell of chlorine. I mention this because I know you have your swimming costume with you from *Gazelle d'Or*. We can play cards. I can teach you how to do Find the Lady. There's a DVD player, but no DVD's, but I've got my own DVD's in the car. Complete boxed set of Celia Broadsword. Never go anywhere without 'em, ma'am."

"Which one are we going to watch first?"

"I thought we might start with *the Wife of Bath*."

"*The Wife of Bath*. I've never seen that myself."

"Like me, it isn't supposed to exist. But it does."

"What are we supposed to eat?"

"I brought plenty of supplies in the car and I've stowed them in the big fridges in the kitchens, so we can microwave them when we want. Plus I've got meat and poultry; good stuff from Carrefour, not the roadside dysentery vendors; and there's proper ceramic barbecues; and I've found lump wood charcoal."

"Lump wood? Our location chef, Aka Akinyola, wouldn't touch it if her life depended on it. She insists on burning her own charcoal."

"Normally, I'm a perfectionist, like this lady you mention, but we're going to have to make do with lump wood, 'cos that's what's in the bags. As I was explaining, they've got ceramic Egg barbecues that cost thousands of dollars and have proper thermostats. There's even a Josper Oven. I can do a cook-out for us under the stars."

"How romantic! I can see you're really going to enjoy your time here, Mr Webb," she said sarcastically.

"Well, actually I think I am. I'm sorry if you haven't got better company or the right sort of charcoal. But you couldn't have more attentive company. I'm sorry if we got you here under false pretences. But now you're here, I'm going to look after you, like you were staying at Dromoland Castle."

"Do you mean Dreamland Castle, Mr Webb?"

"No, ma'am. Dromoland. If you're looking for malapropisms, you need to speak with one of my employers. You won't find them here with Hugh Webb. Dromoland Castle is Ireland's finest 5 star *Relais Chateaux* castle and golf course. And I was just saying that I'm going to look after you just as good as if you were staying there. I've got fine French wine. I want to make your stay here as pleasant as I can.

"We can eat together, or if you're going to prove troublesome, I can lock you in your room, but I'd rather we just sit down as a couple and have TV dinners and barbecues and watch the box set. Never dreamt I'd be watching the entire canon of Celia Broadsword with none other than Celia Broadsword sitting beside me."

"I'm afraid that prospect holds far less attraction for me than it does for you, Mr Webb, and I really hope that we won't be staying here long enough to watch the complete works. Is there anything to read?"

"Yes, ma'am. In the Visitors Centre. But as far as I can see, it's all educational stuff. No works of fiction."

"And what are the sleeping arrangements, Mr Webb?"

"We've got like ultra-luxury his and her's en suite wigwams, ma'am. I was just touring them and thinking to myself that, all spread out like that, as far as the eye can see, that's what the Field of the Cloth of Gold must have looked like when the English and French kings met up at Balinghem in France."

"Mr Webb, in the sixteenth century, although Balinghem was on French soil, it was considered part of England, the same way that Ceuta in Morocco is part of Spain."

Mr Webb was dumbstruck. This lady was so much more than just an ageless pin-up.

"Well, Mr Webb," she continued. "I guess I'd better orientate myself before it gets any darker."

She strode off towards the Visitors Centre. Mr Webb returned to the back of the house and proceeded to drag out one of the ceramic Egg barbecues he'd found there. There was good dry charcoal, even if it wasn't the sort of charcoal that A-listers prescribed for their cook-outs, and there was accelerant to light it with.

There was petrol. There was citrus plant food, cactus food and enough other fertilisers for him to make a dirty bomb, if he was so minded; but he'd been told to burn the Blue Dude, not blow him to smithereens. He wondered if Mr Indigolin would complain if he set fire to him with proprietary lump wood charcoal instead of burning his own charcoal in a bespoke fashion, like Celia recommended.

BOSOLA. Yet, methinks,
The manner of your death should much afflict you:
This cord should terrify you.
DUCHESS. Not a whit:
What would it pleasure me to have my throat cut
With diamonds? or to be smothered
With cassia? Or to be shot to death with pearls?
I know death hath ten thousand several doors

Smithereens. That was a nice word; one of the few words the English had condescended to import from the Irish: the Irish version was smidirins, meaning small fragments. That's what the scientists in their white lab coats got up to in the great Hadron Collider at CERN. They fed big particles into it and smashed them up into smidirins. Big science: small particles. Big Bang!

There was a shed with all sorts of farm implements, but nothing he figured, that his charge, Celia Broadsword, could do too much damage with. There was diesel fuel and a tractor. But, best of all, he found an XM42 flamethrower. It never ceased to amaze him that you could pretend to be a farmer and just buy one of these on the Internet, purportedly for agricultural purposes. No forms to fill in. No permits. No proof of age.

You just added petrol and the thing spat out a twenty metre stream of ignited gasoline. Albanian George had asked for a conflagration. In his mind's eye, Mr Webb imagined the inferno when he torched all those tepees. All he needed now was a pretext to get Indigolin out to the Argan Farm after he'd stashed Celia somewhere nice and safe. Give him a nice, warm welcome.

Celia found a book of Flora and Fauna in the Visitors Centre. She took it with her and strolled the gardens, identifying all the different varieties of pomegranate, almond and date trees, and many species of cacti. As the sun went down, solar powered LED lights winked on and lit her way. She checked out the washing facilities and was pleased to find there were normal flushing WC's in the pavilions and she didn't have to squat over a hole in the ground.

The mattresses and bedding were still wrapped up in cellophane and had never been used. The gardens and varieties of plants and shrubs she'd never seen before, were simply amazing. She'd forgotten how many natural, green things she'd been missing in the middle of a barren desert for so many months.

Mr Webb was a pushover. She hadn't been brought here of her own free will, but everything had been taken out of her hands, so she might as well see what she could learn from her surroundings during her enforced sojourn, and leave here a better informed person than she had been when she arrived. Make the most of it, just like Don Quixote would have done. She'd get Mr Webb to pour her a gin and tonic now the sun had gone down, and if he wanted to do the cooking and washing up, that was fine with her. An image of Mr Webb with his white pony tail, standing at the kitchen sink with a pinafore and yellow Marigolds flashed through her mind, and brought a smile to her face.

She cast her mind back to the late Sir Roger Moore in *Live and Let Die*, and told herself she was really lucky that she'd been brought to an Argan Farm. After all, it could have been a Crocodile Farm.

Mr Webb surveyed the contents of his boxed set and wondered which one he'd kick off with. He had hinted to her that it was to be *The Wife of Bath*. Dangle the forbidden fruit in front of her first, had been his reasoning; but he was concerned that she might disapprove because it was bootleg, a breach of intellectual property.

Then he reasoned with himself. Although he was trying to make her stay as nice as possible, he had kidnapped this film star. And he was planning on cremating the Blue Molecule dude. But here he was worrying himself sick about breach of copyright! Having made his DVD selections, he went to do some more unboxing.

Mr Webb got the XM42 flamethrower out of its carton. Like everything else here, it didn't appear to have ever been used. It had been waiting for Mr Webb's touch to summon it to life. Like the genie of the Lamp. All shod in iridescent stainless steel with a painted shark motive down the side. It looked like a ray gun soldered together by a redneck. He primed the pilot torch with butane, checked that the gasoline bottle was full, and turned it on.

It made a hissing noise like a dragon expelling air, until he pressed the red button, and then it spat out a continuous ribbon of flames like Wonder Woman's lasso, and nothing would stop it unless he took his finger off the trigger or ran out of gas. There was no way that genie was going back in the lamp! He wouldn't have any trouble getting the barbecue alight, he thought.

That kid came to mind who had about a gazillion followers on YouTube, the one who did all the posts of himself unboxing toys. He'd made a million before he started primary school. Maybe, thought Mr Webb, he could upload posts of himself unboxing weapons: Galil SAR, Skorpion VZ, Mosin-Nagant, Jackhammer MK3A1, Groza, Shipka, Dragunov—it was like a catechism to him; kept his old brain pin sharp and avoided Alzheimer's. He'd get lots of Likes from cunts like Vladamir Putin.

He'd had to work out his priorities in light of the possibly conflicted position he found himself in. First of all he needed to collect his fee from Indigolin via the insurers for kidnapping the lady and cash up the bitcoins for some proper money. Then cremate Indigolin and collect the balance of his fee from Albanian George, as soon as he'd uploaded the footage to YouTube. He imagined YouTube had all sorts of sophisticated algorithms so they wouldn't let you put an under-age girl or an erect cock up there, but the algorithms wouldn't worry about a man being set on fire.

He needed Albanian George to get it clear in his head, that the half of his fee that he'd paid so far, was not in fact any of his fee, but a lost bet on Three Card Monté, so that Albanian George still owed him all of the fee. It might take a while to get that through his employer's malaproprismic skull; but that was a conversation that it would be easier to conduct face to face when George was staring down the muzzle of Webb's gun. He'd conjured with doing it the other way round, killing Indigolin first, but then he only got paid once.

Talking of YouTube, he put *The Crazy World of Arthur Brown* into Search, and it came straight up: two minutes forty-three seconds of Arthur Brown performing *Fire* live. The man's head was on fire, just like when Colman Hunt led all those people out of the maze in that film. Albanian George would get what he asked for in spades.

What a card that Albanian George was! He was perfectly comfortable discussing murdering his fellow human beings, burning them alive, shooting them in a hail of bullets, or inserting Tasmanian tree snakes up the eyes of their willies. But he was very worried about minding his P's and Q's. That was his heterodoxy: that was the fardel he had to bear: that he was a woke psychopath, a hamster on his own euphemism treadmill.

You're gonna burn!
You're gonna burn!

Damn Albanian Bloody George! He'd given him The Crazy World of Arthur Brown on the brain now.
Still it made a change from being absolute for death.

You've fought hard and you saved and earned
But all of it's going to burn

The Triplet's Ransom Note

Presley needed a drink after a kif-fuelled stumble all the way down Toubkal to the village of Imlil, but there was nothing stronger on offer than local beer. First he ordered himself a Spéciale Flag; then he ordered himself a Casablanca, and decided he couldn't tell the fucking difference between them, so in future he'd just buy whichever was the cheapest.

Enjoying his beer in the Internet café, he fired up Posthumous' laptop, got the Wi-Fi password from the proprietor and set up a Gmail account known as ***abduct@snatch.ma.*** He then set about writing his ransom demand. He was surprised at how difficult the task was. The problem was establishing the right tone. It had to sound sufficiently menacing for the reader to take it seriously, but not so much over the top that it would be dismissed as some kind of Varsity prank. It needed to speak with the voice of authority.

Also, since they didn't actually have Colman, or even know where he was, it was best to keep the note short, because the more details he embroidered, the more likely he was to trip himself up with his own verbosity. When he'd been in conference with his Queen's Counsel before Mortimer had decided to take the rap for his own attempted murder, his brief had explained to him that was how most witnesses got caught out under cross-examination. Instead of just answering the question, bad liars always go on to elaborate, driven by a desire to make what they know is a falsehood sound more convincing. It just does the opposite and they end up hoist on their own petards. There were elephant traps everywhere.

As you can see, we have Colman Hunt, he began typing.

He uploaded the photo they'd taken of Posthumous this morning holding up a copy of today's *Aujourd'hui le Maroc* newspaper, and made sure the date was in focus, and the background was generic and untraceable. He chuckled to see that Posthumous was holding the newspaper open at the page that carried the article captioned *Colman Hunt est Disparu!*—accompanied by a photo of the eponymous Colman Hunt. The effect of the photo within the photo was like one of those Russian dolls. He re-read what he'd written:

As you can see, we have Colman Hunt. See attached photo of him with a copy of today's Aujourd'hui.

Then Presley wasn't sure if that was bilingual repetition, like *See attached photo of him with a copy of today's Today.* Sounded stupid. The whole fucking idea of attaching the photo was so that the reader could see for himself that he was holding up a copy of today's *Aujourd'hui*. People always thought more of what you'd written, if you let them figure things out for themselves. Then again, a picture, as they say, tells a thousand words, so why say anything at all?

They could see for themselves that this was Colman holding up today's paper. With the benefit of hindsight, he should have set his phone up for time lapse when he'd taken the photo, then he could have wrapped a balaclava round his face and had his brother kneel on the floor with his hands behind his back, whilst brandishing a gigantic jihadist sword, Damocles-fashion above his head.

But if his hands were behind his back, how was he going to hold up the *Aujourd'hui le Maroc*? Who would have thought these things could be so complex? Were there Kidnap Planners, who could offer guidance, just like they had Wedding Planners, he wondered? Was there etiquette to follow? The tone was so important. It wasn't just a question of getting the grammar right or the spelling correct. Anyone reading this had to realise straight away that the guy who had written this, meant business.

As you can see, we have Colman Hunt, he typed again.

As you can see, he continued, *he is intact.* Then he crossed out *intact*. Sounded like some Arab father promoting his daughter in an arranged marriage. *As you can see, she is intact*, accompanied presumably by a photograph shot with a gynaecological camera. He redacted *intact* and substituted *whole*.

As you can see, he is whole.
If we don't get your agreement to pay us US $5M within the next 48 hours, the next photo you receive will be of an incomplete Colman Hunt.

No, that didn't sound right.

If we don't get your agreement to pay us US $5M within the next 48 hours, Colman Hunt will not be whole in the next photo you receive.

That still didn't sound right. It didn't sound right because he wasn't comparing apples with applies, because he was playing off *whole* against *complete*. But both adjectives needed to correspond. But if he wrote *As you can see, he is complete*; that sounded ridiculous.

He was attempting to draw a distinction between a Colman Hunt who at present had all his limbs, eyes, ears, fingers, whatever, and one who didn't. But the problem went beyond just the wording. Where am I going with this? Presley asked himself. If he and Posthumous actually had Colman Hunt, it wouldn't be a problem; they'd just start slicing bits off him and taking photos, because he was going to end up dead anyway. They could even have a short video of the day's *Aujourd'hui le Maroc* newspaper, and open up the paper and there'd be a bloody ear inside, or a finger, and then an updated photo of Colman with the corresponding bodily part missing.

But the problem was they didn't actually have Colman. So if Presley made this threat, to start lopping bits of Mortimer, and if he didn't get a positive uptake in 48 hours, either Posthumous or himself was going to have to sacrifice an ear or an eye, in order to escalate to the next stage without losing credibility. He could just hear his brother, Posthumous, now: *I didn't tell you to write a fucking ransom note saying you were going to chop Colman's fingers off in the next 48 hours, did I?* So it would be Presley's own fingers being hacked off, for sure.

And, being realistic, who was going to pay $5M for a cunt like Colman? If he was indeed worth US $5M complete, surely, as they chopped bits off, and there was less and less of him to negotiate the release of, the price would have to go down. By the time they'd reduced him to a limbless torso with a head, how much was anyone going to pay for that? It was a sliding scale that slid the wrong way. Rather than start off with a demand that was so big as to dishearten the studio into making any reasonable sort of a counter-offer, better to set his sights lower to start with, so that the studio had some traction. Ask for £1m, so the studio could revert with £250K and then they could shake hands on half a bar. If he kicked straight off with $5M, the studio would feel there was no point insulting him by making a counter-offer at £250K. They'd just sit back and wait for bits of Colman Hunt to arrive in the post. Plus Presley didn't even know how to send a parcel in Morocco. Did they have Amazon? Could he send across a severed arm or a leg by Uber Eats or Deliveroo without setting up an account first?

He tried again:

As you can see, we are looking after Colman Hunt well. So far.
If you want to see him alive again, just hit Reply and we'll tell you how the ransom of £1M is to be paid.

That would have to do. He dug out of his jeans pocket the Post-it on which he had written Wally and Indigolin's email addresses, and entered them. Then he wondered if he should put *Regards* at the end, or not send any Regards. Since the email was anonymous, who would it be that would be sending his Regards? He decided to throw etiquette to the winds and hit Send.

He finished the beer, and thought he'd get a couple more for the trek back up the mountain.

"Which is cheapest?" He asked. "Spéciale Flag or Casablanca?"

"They're both the same price," came the answer.

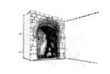

The Dynamic *Status Quo*

Colman Hunt awoke naturally in the morning. He was delighted when he realised that, despite his enlarged prostrate and three cups of mint tea, he hadn't needed to get up in the night.

After a pleasant sojourn under the stars with the star, Colman Hunt was ready to get back to the set, but found he was expected to be the recipient of further Tuareg hospitality. When he told them enough was enough, Aderfi and Aghilles explained that, if he wasn't willing to remain, he was going to have to stay against his will until the studio made a contribution towards their university fees.

"How," he asked, "is kidnapping me supposed to be compatible with studying human rights and surveying?"

Aderfi replied. "We didn't kidnap you, Mr Hunt. You came here of your own free will."

"Yes, but the situation's changed."

"Mr Justice Hoffman (as he then was)," explained Aderfi, "dealt with that, coincidentally in a case concerning the film, Highlander."

"Sean Connery?"

"—And Christopher Lambert. Lot of spin-offs, but the first one was best. There was a great deal of litigation over its release, reported in *Cannon Films v Films Rover International*. 1986"

"The Go-Go Boys."

"That's right, Golan and Globus. The Italian distributors wanted to release the film in Italy in August, but the Go-Go Boys wanted a Christmas blockbuster release, especially as in those days the Italian cinemas didn't tend to have aircon, so Italian viewers seldom went to the cinemas in August. Too hot."

"What's this got to do with the price of fish?"

"We're getting there, Mr Hunt. In order to stop the threatened release, Cannon needed an injunction, and it came on before Mr Justice Hoffman (as he then was), and Canon's solicitor was the celebrated Mr Philip G Cohen."

"The guy they call the Rottweiler?"

"You've got it. Now, injunctions are normally all about preserving the *status quo*, but Mr Justice Hoffman—"

"—as he then was, yah, yah yah."

"Came up with the idea of a dynamic *status quo*, that is to say, a *status quo* that is constantly changing and evolving, but it's still the *status quo*. Status quos don't have to be static, see?"

"And where is all this going, son?"

"I think what he's saying," put in Aghilles, "is that you may have come here of your own free will, but now you're staying on as our guest. It's the staying aspect that is the *status quo*, not your frame of mind. Because you aren't going anywhere until we get paid. We didn't kidnap you. You came to dinner. You were, how shall I put this? Lost property. We find you. We didn't kidnap you. But when we hand you in, we get a reward."

"So this is it, is it? This is what it's come to? The great Colman Hunt is reduced to an item of lost property? I'll make a solemn oath not to eat until I've built a pyramid of all your miserable Arab skulls."

"Don't you think that's a bit ignoble, my liege?"

Colman looked down. It was Badiss, in his blue Dishdash, astride his push bike quoting Colman's own lines to him. From the rewritten *Gate of the Burnt One*.

Colman instinctively clutched for his rolled-up script, but realised it wasn't in his hand anymore. He could have sworn he'd used it as a pillow when he went to sleep last night. Then he dimly recollected that he'd started making connections in his head just before sleep overcame him.

"Where's my lines?" He shouted.

"Sorry," Mr Hunt said Aderfi. "Badass here doesn't get much spare time to write them all down, because he has to do all his family chores as well. He just catching up on the scriptwriting."

"Here's your script, Mr Hunt. Can't wait to see it on Netflix!" Badiss passed up the pages from the basket on his handlebars, but Aderfi intercepted it. He opened it up and began turning the pages.

"Let me take a look at this for you, Mr Hunt," Aderfi said. The script appeared to have grown much fatter than it had been when Colman had last read it. But how could that be?

"As long as I get it back in one piece," replied Mortimer.

"Shall we ride in triumph through Persepolis, Mr Hunt?" Badiss asked.

"What you talking about, son?"

"What he means," said Aderfi, "is just look at what you've got and what we've got. You've got the house in Mulholland Drive; the Manhattan mansion overlooking Central Park; you've got the ski lodge in Zermatt; you've got the *pied a terre* near Harrods. We admire you, Mr Hunt; we love you. But just look at the way we live here, under the stars and under tarpaulins, sharing our quarters with the livestock. You and us. The word for that is bifurcation. And do you know when that bifurcation started?"

"Hell, no."

"In 1492, when King Ferdinand married Queen Isabella, and the Moors got kicked out of Granada."

"Of course. Of course. I just never put it together."

"There's always been the haves and the have not's. But January 1492 is when the west finally separated from the east, when the west raped the east and drove it out. Mr Hunt, compared to you, we have nothing. But that didn't stop us sharing everything we have with you."

"Well, I guess you did make me very welcome, son."

"And it's not as if we're doing nothing for the money, Mr Hunt. We have already made a valuable contribution, and will continue so to do."

"How come, son?"

"Who do you think has been rewriting your script for you every night?" was all his captor said. "We stopped delivering it when you started looking out for it, but then we delivered it to Mr Pfister instead, and we have the rest of it all here. It's finished: *The Gate of the Burnt One*."

"You wrote that?" Hunt exclaimed, genuinely astonished. The question was addressed to Aderfi.

"No, Mr Hunt. *He* did," was all Aderfi said, cocking his thumb in the direction of the twelve-year-old, Badiss, on his shrunken bicycle. "And then he delivered it each night to your door on his pedal bike. Until you started trying to lie in wait for him and ambush him, and then he delivered it to Mr Pfister instead. Isn't that worth some form of reward? Isn't there a price for that?"

Now Colman Hunt was genuinely lost for words. It was as though he had fallen down some wormhole into a parallel world were nothing made sense any more. He'd thought that those references to ignoble and *my liege* must have come about because the Berbers had been reading his script. The reality was just beginning to sink in: they had written it.

Whereas the finest scriptwriters in the world had been grappling unsuccessfully with the subject matter for months, a twelve-year-old nomad on a pushbike four sizes too small for him, had cracked it, and he had created an upside down world where Boabdil won the Siege of Granada, where the Moors never got booted out of Spain, and where they went on to subjugate the rest of Europe, so that, in the present day, Europe was the Islamic State of Europe. Of course, it was a fairy story, but the way the kid told it, it read like it was history. A big part of him wanted to help these people write that history.

"Badiss!" Colman cried, seeking to authenticate the story, "tell me, where is the first scene set in your script?"

"El Patio de los Leones, Mr Hunt. In the Courtyard of the Twelve Marble Lions in the Alhambra."

Colman Hunt's jaw dropped in disbelief. It stayed like that for thirty seconds that felt like thirty minutes whilst he took all this in. The fact was that once you had gone down that wormhole, and entered that seemingly impossible parallel world that Badiss depicted and he himself encapsulated, everything else seemed to be quite reasonable and made sense.

"Well, if I was to go along with this, and I'm not saying I will, but if I was to play along with it…How do you think you're going to get away with this heist?"

"We hope you're going to help us, sir. It's not coming out of your pocket. The studio pays up."

"But unless you're planning on killing me, I'll be able to identify you."

"No, you won't, sir. We're just some more blue men. Thousands of us, all the same. We just evaporate. What did you say earlier?" Aderfi asked, "Like Casper, the friendly ghost. We disappear."

Holy Sonnet; John Donne

Celia had watched *The Wife of Bath*, *180* and *Ordeal by Fire*, back-to-back on the big screen in Mr Webb's tent, having to listen as Mr Webb repeatedly hit the Pause button on the remote, whilst he explained all the best bits of her own films to her, and told her what was coming up next. He was quite ready to insert another DVD, but Celia suggested they take a break. She thought it absurd when he sought to entice her into his pavilion with the promise of a flat screen TV. Why did hotels still boast about such peripherals? Only people as ancient as Celia Broadsword even knew that TVs that weren't flat had ever existed.

She took the envelope from her handbag and read Wally's sonnet to herself. Once again, just as in the big turban scene with Brunswick Holt, that Quixotic smile played round her lips and she tried to supress it, lest her captor thought she was having a good time.

"Do you know any poems, Mr Webb?" She enquired.

Mr Webb knew a lot of poems, because he had made a point to commit them to memory, so as to keep his mind sharp. But they were all about death and dying. He'd put a lot of them up on his website. He cast around for one that didn't sound too gloomy. Then he cleared his throat and recited to her in his Dublin brogue:

Death, be not proud, though some have called thee
Mighty and dreadful, for thou art not so;
For those whom thou think'st thou dost overthrow
Die not, poor Death, nor yet canst thou kill me.
From rest and sleep, which but thy pictures be,
Much pleasure; then from thee much more must flow
And soonest our best men with thee do go,
Rest of their bones, and soul's delivery.
Thou art slave to fate, chance, kings, and desperate men,
And dost with poison, war and sickness dwell,
And poppy or charms can make us sleep as well,

And better than thy stroke; why swell'st thou then?
One short sleep past, we wake eternally
And death shall be no more; Death, thou shalt die.

"You've got a good reading voice." She remarked. "You could do voice-overs for *Peaky Blinders*."

CCTV

When Celia failed to show up for her usual rendezvous with Wally, Wally was concerned for his own sake. She'd draped the yellow veil over his work desk, which he interpreted as meaning that, like Arnold Schwarzenegger, she'd be back. The scarf smelled of her skin, and he loved it. It was a good job that she'd removed all the veils before that brute, Presley, set upon her, or the veil would have been contaminated and he wouldn't be able to bear to touch it. But as it was, it remained unsullied and sensual.

When Celia failed to show up for his early morning yoga session or on set the next day also, he became concerned for her sake. After asking everyone on location and ascertaining that no-one knew where she'd gone, he became alarmed that he had lost his leading man and leading lady in the space of the same week. After all this waiting, he finally had the makings of a crackling script, but now his principal actors had evaporated. At this rate, there was a serious possibility that the mysterious scriptwriter could outstrip the shooting schedule.

He called for the security company to give him all the CCTV footage, and laboriously watched it until he saw Celia climbing into the Range Rover with the blacked-out windows. Then he rewound it to the point when the driver, hidden inside, got out for a smoke. He didn't know the name of the old white-haired rocker pressed into the chauffeur's outfit with the ponytail sticking out the back of his peaked cap, but for reasons that weren't clear to him as yet, his face struck a chord.

That's what everybody said about Wally Pfister: that he never forgot a face. Well, this face, temporarily, he had forgotten, but he hadn't forgotten that it meant something to him. He decided that if he got on with something else, it would come to him in its own time.

Whoever the face belonged to, the important question for now was what was the guy doing on set, and why had Celia climbed into the back seat of his car?

The Moroccan police were no help. Elena had got them involved when Colman had disappeared, but they clearly hadn't taken it seriously. Now Wally attempted to get them engaged with his own missing person, but, no matter how famous she was, she hadn't been missing for long enough. Also, it didn't help that both she and her ex-husband had gone missing around the same time.

Where Wally saw two kidnappings, the Moroccan Sûreté Nationale, who, let's not forget, had been trained by the French, saw *un liaison amoreuse*. Wally knew that it was preposterous to imagine that Celia, who had just found true love with him, would decide to elope with her loopy ex, but he didn't think that he had the right to go public on their own relationship as yet, because going public was a joint decision they both had to make, and he'd been too busy enjoying the relationship, to discuss its finer points with her, such as when they would put the bans up.

Wally wondered if they had private dicks in Morocco. He could think of English and American literary detectives. He could think of French and Scandinavian literary detectives. There were medieval detectives such as William of Baskerville in the Umberto Eco book. There were Chinese detectives. There was the guy who solved the problem of the Murders in Edgar Allan Poe's Rue Morgue, thought to be the first literary detective ever, even before Sherlock Holmes. There was Harry Hole, Miss Marple, Philip Marlowe, Hercule Poirot, even Father Brown. But he couldn't think of a single Moroccan detective, not if he had to save his life. Or Celia's.

There was no CCTV outside the set. Just miles of featureless desert. But Wally found Elena Troy miraculously resourceful. She pointed out to him, correctly, that there were only 4 or 5 major roads in all of Morocco. They simply had to travel them, stop in all the petrol stations, restaurants and hotels, ask the right questions, and sooner or later, someone must have seen her. She was a celebrity for heaven's sake!

Remains

"Are they human remains?"

The question was posed by Millicent Marcuson to the Chief Medical Examiner at the Royal College of Pathology at Alie Street in London's East End. They were looking at the screenshot of the Golgotha of bones that Millicent Marcuson's cameraman, Ynes, had printed out as a 10 x 8 from the Panorama Triumvirate interview that she had faithfully promised Tinctorio Indigolin she wouldn't share with anyone else in the universe. Here she was showing it to a pathologist. She looked up, as though apprehensive that one of the high-flying lawyers from Bird & Bird could be circling above her, vulture-like.

"Definitely not!" The pathologist pronounced.

"Then who do the bones belong to?"

"I would say that they are fish bones, Miss Marcuson," said the Examiner.

"Fish bones!" Millicent repeated, wondering why Indigolin would want to have fish bones as his screensaver.

"It's bleached coral," he continued. "It's a cross-section of a dead coral reef."

"Why do coral reefs die?" Millicent asked.

"I'm a pathologist, not a marine biologist, Ms Marcuson; but my understanding is that they are under constant attack from a variety of predators: climate change, rubbish in the oceans, overfishing, pollution, unsustainable coastal developments, to name but a few."

"Can dead coral reefs be brought back to life?" Millicent asked.

"As I stated, Ms Marcuson, I'm a pathologist. I can usually tell you what cause has taken life from the living. It is beyond my art to tell you how the dead can be brought back to life."

First You Kill Yourself; Then You Bury Yourself

"So, how are you going to carry out the negotiation without them knowing who you are?" Colman asked.

"We're not carrying out any negotiations," explained Aderfi. "We're delegating that job to you. We're staying here, and you're going to walk across that desert, going out the same way you came in, and deliver your own ransom demand."

"It's called delegation," added Aghilles.

"But this time, you won't be in the buff," said Aderfi. "We're going to give you something to wear. You're going to deliver your own ransom note in person, on foot."

"Just like in the good old days, huh?"

"First we put this on you."

"Fuck's that?"

"Superdry gilet, boss," said Aghilles.

"With modifications," added Aderfi. "Superdry Suicide Vest, boss. We find it's easier to put this on first and the handcuffs after."

"What the cuffs for?"

"You may be tempted to remove it otherwise."

"And why would I want to do a thing like that?"

"Because it's a nitro-glycerine gilet. Each of those tubes that's normally filled with eider-down is packed with enough explosive to reduce you to the same consistency as this sand whilst opening up a huge sink hole in the desert. You seen Dune? What happens is that basically you blow yourself to bits and then neatly bury your own remains in the crater you leave behind. Full turnkey service, boss."

They pulled the gilet over his head, on top of his blue robes, fastened it at the rear, and then cable-tied his hands behind his back. Then Aderfi clicked something on the front and a small LED started flashing green.

"What's that mean?" Colman asked.

"It means it's activated," explained Aghilles. "Whilst it's flashing green, you're okay. Any funny business, or try to take it off, and it flashes red for five seconds before detonating. Then you and anyone within about ten metres of you will be confetti scattered across the Sahara."

"Yeah, yeah, wedded bits, for better for hearse, I get it. I remember, and my corpse conveniently self-digs a trench and incarcerates itself, full turnkey service. How do you plan to set it off?"

"We're not planning to set it off. We're hoping it all goes smoothly, Mr Colman. But if we do have to set it off—" Aderfi produced his phone from his Dishdash. "Got the app right here on my home screen. See? emails, Texts, FaceTime, WhatsApp, Music, Banking, Bombs."

"How much am I supposed to ask 'em for?"

"You ask for a cool US $1M."

"Fuck that, son! That's chickenfeed. I don't want to be reading in Variety that Colman Hunt was ransomed and the studio got him back for an ignominious mil!"

Then Colman turned to his new twelve-year-old friend and nudged him on the arm. "That would be a bit ignoble, my liege, wouldn't it?"

They both chuckled in a fashion that could only be described as complicit.

"I'm asking for ten mil or you can fucking well detonate me now," Colman Hunt pronounced.

"You know what you remind me of, Mr Hunt?" Aderfi asked.

"No, son."

"The fabled parrot at the auction who bids against himself."

"I don't know that fucking fable, and I don't want to."

"Will you agree to compromise on US $5M, Mr Hunt?" It was Aghilles putting the question.

"I'm not paying it, but, with some reservations, I'll agree to go that low when I'm asking for it, son. How they supposed to get the money to you?"

"First trip, you just ask for it. We'll work out the inside leg measurements once they've agreed."

"So, that it?"

"Not quite, King Ferdinand. Last of all, we have to put your crown on." Aghilles was passed a plastic headpiece by Badass, who was too short to anoint Colman Hunt himself.

"What the fuck sort of a crown is that?" Colman asked.

"Badass here is keen cyclist. He's been on two foreign exchange swaps, one with an English student in London and one with a Spanish student in Barcelona. Badass was pampered by middle class professional families, firstly in a stucco villa in Herne Hill for three months, then in a luxury apartment in fashionable *Paseig de la Gracia* for three months whilst the exchanged sons lived with us under a tarpaulin with sheep and goats.

"Nowadays, Badass has to make do with letting most of the air out of his tyres and cycling around on the sand; but when he was living in Herne Hill, the family bought him his own bicycle, and his favourite pastime was to cycle down to Halfords in Brixton and look at all the accessories and gadgets he could get for his bicycle, if he only had any money. Anyway, this is his Halfords cycle helmet, which is going to serve as your crown; adjustable, see, and lightweight for your added comfort."

He placed the helmet on Colman's head and fastened it under his chin, and gave it a rap on the dome with his knuckles for good measure.

"On top, we have head-mounted camera in the shape of Samsung phone with extra long-life battery pack and 64 gig SIM card. We'll be watching everything you say and do." Aghilles pressed the red button; Hunt heard the phone's video camera beep once."

"Okay," said Aderfi. "We have light, actions, sound. You're on, Mr Hunt. The stage is yours."

"Well, I'd better put my best foot forward and get moving then before the extended life in your Duracell bunny packs up," said Hunt, making to start his journey.

"Hang on!" Cried Aghilles. "He's got no shoes."

"Sorry, Mr Hunt," put in Aderfi. "Sand's blazing hot; we're going to lend you some trainers, but we should have let you put them on before we cuffed you. Going to be tricky now."

"Don't need no fucking trainers, son. I'm a New Promethean."

"Do you have any questions, Mr Hunt?" called out Aderfi after him.

"Yes," barked Colman Hunt over his shoulder as he walked away. "Which version of Dune? David Lynch's 1984 version or Villeneuve's 2021 version?"

"You're the New Promethean, Mr Hunt!" Called out Badiss. "You tell us."

Despite the clock ticking against him, Colman Hunt turned on his heel, and went back to the Berber encampment. He lowered himself to Badiss' height and enquired:

"Just what do you mean by that, son?"

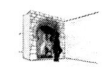

"Wasn't Dune a book about the dangers of Messianic sects, Mr Hunt?"

When Colman continued to look uncomprehendingly into the eyes of his diminutive companion, the companion added: "—Such as the New Prometheans."

Then the penny dropped for Colman Hunt. He got the point, but he couldn't say if it was a good point or not, because he'd only seen the films, not read the book.

And with that Mortimer Unsdorferbaum strode off, barefoot, across the blazing sands of the Sahara, clothed in blue robes, a Superdry Suicide Vest and a Halfords cycle helmet. And as he went, he repeated to himself:

"Decay was never heard of
Until the King of Kings, Pharaoh, Sun, Moon and Stars,
Set his throne upon the burning sands,
And dared the desert to wet his feet."

Once he was safely out of earshot, Aderfi punched his brother playfully on the arm and, with a twinkle in his eye, said: "He fell for it."

"Superdry Suicide Vest! I love it! And the app on your phone. Where'd you get the flashing LED from?"

"Halfords Cycle light."

Deep Fake

Wally Pfister had an uncanny feeling about the image of Mr Webb. The face evoked some distant memory, but he still couldn't fix it.

He made a screenshot from the CCTV camera's video footage of Mr Webb's face when he got out of the Range Rover for a smoke. It wasn't of the best quality but he enhanced it with Moviva Video Enhancer until it was workable. He smiled as the Moviva program booted up: the strapline '*This Changes Everything*' was brilliant given the function of the software. It really did what it said on the tin.

There was something about the face that disturbed him. He dragged the enhanced jpg into his Deep Fake programs, EbSynth and FaceApp, and set it to work. He asked it to wind the clock back. Then he went to bed, leaving the program to do its work. He knew it would take hours to turn the clock back fifty years. He asked the program to set an alarm when it was done.

He was woken at 4.00 in the morning by a persistent pinging. Rubbing his eyes, he remembered he'd asked the editing program to alert him when it was completing its task. He rose and stared into the blue screen of his computer. What he saw froze him in his tracks. The unforgettable ghostly face materialising like the image on the Turin Shroud. There was no doubt about it. He was staring into the cold, compassionless eyes of his mother's rapist.

The Wild West

"It's like the Wild West out here, bro. You've gotta come and join me!"

Napier ("Nap") Ransom had been on at his brother to come to Hong Kong with him for years. Nap had obtained mediocre A-level grades and not progressed to university. Instead he had pursued a career in merchant banking. After putting in some early years with Bankers Trust of America, he had taken a high salary posting to Hong Kong, and once safely installed there, he had attempted to beckon his brother, Kid Ransom, out to the Far East, to keep him company and share in his stratospheric plutocracy.

When the expats were about to get chucked out of Hong Kong by the Chinese, Nap had come back to London and opened a boutique bank known as Overtake Finance, until scandal hit and he made his escape to Dubai, where he bought himself a panoramic penthouse in the Burj Khalifa.

Kid, by contrast, was not interested in making a quick buck, owning the latest Bugatti, or having paid for sex with women whose eyes were not horizontal. He was a steady plodder, writing policies of marine insurance for Chubb from their East London headquarters. Every morning he commuted in to Aldgate East underground station, and when he turned on his computer in Leadenhall Street, emails from his brother with enticing pictures of the dubious charms of the UAE attached, would pop up in his Inbox.

Initially, from his apartment at the top of the Burj Khalifa, Nap would WhatsApp his brother regularly: "Hey, kid brother, Kid. It's like the Wild West out here. You really gotta come and join me!" or "I've got a date for you down the Cyclone Club tonight. If you want to play, you've gotta pay!"

Then, when he relocated from the Burj Khalifa to a house on Deira Island, the Palm, the incessant stream of teaser-trailers continued.

Obligingly, Kid flew out Emirates a few times at Napier's expense, and, standing in front of the floor to ceiling windows in Nap's first abode in the Burj Khalifa, made polite appreciative noises about the smog-hazed vista of lesser

Lilliputian skyscrapers below them and the unremarkable coastline stretching into the distance.

Then, when Nap moved to Deira Island, Kid visited him again and made appreciative noises about how much better it was down there at ground level with the waves of the Arabian Gulf practically lapping at Nap's front door. He looked the other way when regular oil spills washed the tar up on his brother's doorstep, and at the shoals of dead fish that were deposited like sandbanks with the tar, and which were euphemistically referred to as the crimson tide. They ate Shawarma and smoked a shisha pipe in a Lebanese restaurant whilst watching some sashaying musical fountains and even essayed an indoor ski slope.

Unlike his brother, Kid had been to university where he had read English literature, and this enabled him to call to mind Samuel Johnson's words about women preachers: *It's like a dog walking on its hind legs. It is not done well, but you are surprised to find it done at all*. And this was pretty much his verdict on Dubai.

It was just a curiosity. He wasn't interested in taking a ride down to the Cyclone and choosing a hooker for the night. It pissed him off that he could only get a proper drink in a hotel, and even in a hotel you couldn't get a proper draft beer but had to drink fizzy stuff out of a bottle. He wouldn't be joining his brother there on a long term basis any time soon.

Because Kid was fed up with making trips to Dubai, Nap took the risk of returning to London, but steered well clear of his old Mayfair hunting grounds where he had been discredited, and agreed to meet his brother near Aldgate East, where he didn't believe any of his old associates (or victims, as they preferred to call themselves when being interviewed by the tabloids), would be likely to venture. He had come up with a proposition tailored to Kid's skills, and tailored to his own, also, as it involved him pumping in some start-up capital, and his brother doing all the heavy lifting.

And that was how Kid's life had been turned upside down by his brother, Napier, after accepting his invitation to a bibulous four-hour Friday lunch at the Brokers Wine Bar in the Leadenhall Market. "We'll just be re-setting the weekend a bit earlier than usual," Nap had explained.

Over a starter of steak tartare, followed by a 2 kilogram steak cooked blue, Nap had tried to persuade Kid that, even in the Leadenhall Street market, "It's like the Wild West in here."

"Nap, will you stop saying that wherever you go! What the hell has the Brokers Wine Bar got in common with the Wild West?"

Napier appeared genuinely surprised. Kid followed his gaze towards the mass of red meat oozing blood on his plate and just said: "Steak's called a Tomahawk."

They had both laughed. Over Remy Martins, Nap had put his proposition to his kid brother.

"It's already huge in the States and South America. Kidnap and Ransom insurance. I've got the initial equity to get the thing kick-started and we can then get mezzanine finance. Your job will be to lay off the risk with underwriters and write-up the policies of insurance, preferably on terms that are as unresponsive as possible to the risk, so we don't ever have to pay out."

"Well," slurred Kid, "that sounds just like every other policy of insurance, but is there a market for it? I mean, I get it in South America where there are gangs and cartels and there's a lot of kidnapping, so there's a demand, and in America, everyone carries a gun—"

"Yeah, you know something, kid brother?"

"Don't tell me, '*It's like the Wild West out there!*'"

"Right on!" They gave each other a high five.

Most of the other diners had left a couple of hours ago and returned to their desks, but the few stragglers still remaining gave them looks at once both curious and disapproving.

"You know, everything that starts in America comes here," Napier resumed. "What do they say? America sneezes, and we all catch a cold! This is what we do. We start by hooking up with all the biggest theatrical agents, so that every actor requires the producer to take out K & R insurance. If we can just get some big names signed up, you know, the Tom Cruises and Matt Damons of this world, then all the aspiring tarts lower down the food chain will start demanding it too, and soon it will be offered as an optional add-on to everything, just like taking out an extended warranty when you buy your fridge, or paying an extra £15.00 with your car insurance to buy yourself some legal expenses cover.

"You know, Kid, it used to be bankers that pulled all the levers and controlled the world, but now it's insurers. They tell you what car you can drive and how fast you can drive it; they control who you employ, if you can get them underwritten, whether or not they can be directors and be fidelity bonded; what stuff you can have in your house, even how far out of your house the branches of your trees can extend over the highway, whether you can go on holiday, and if you can go on holiday, whether or not you can go skiing or bungee jumping, how many days you can have off sick, and whether or not you can have your haemorrhoids operated on privately or have to spend eighteen months sitting in a rubber ring waiting for your NHS appointment. The whole fucking world is being run by insurers. You can't even take a dump anymore without insurance. So, are you in?"

"Nap, how could I refuse after hearing the longest speech I think you've ever made in your life?"

"It was like it was written in the stars from the time our parents named us: Kid, Nap and Ransom. It's a 50/50 partnership OK? But I have a Chairman's casting vote in the event of deadlock. You do the technical stuff, and I'll sell it and lay off the risk."

Napier had then said that they had to have a name for the nascent partnership. He wanted something that was redolent of Englishness, quintessentially Anglo-Saxon. They had spent the next inebriated forty-five minutes bouncing crappy English-sounding names off one another, most of which, such as Rolls Royce and Bentley, already belonged to Germans. Eventually, Kid had come up with 'Metcalfe'.

Neither of them quite knew where the name had come from, or why it sounded particularly English, but they both agreed that there would be absolutely nothing out of place in having a butler by the name of Metcalfe in one's stately home. And thus was born Metcalfe Insurance Specialists. And the insurance they specialised in was Kidnap & Ransom Insurance.

As his brother had said, the product proved a great success and now every budding starlet required her agent to have it written into her contract.

That had all happened five years ago. In the present day, Kid Ransom was rocking, raising and lowering himself on the balls of his feet, whilst cracking his knuckles, as he always did when he was turning something difficult over in his mind. For five years, they'd been taking money in and writing crap policies of insurance. He'd just put the phone down on their first real claim. He didn't have the faintest idea where to begin.

Three Card Monté

Celia failed to find the lady for the twelfth successive time.

"Well, this is great fun, isn't it?" Mr Webb beamed.

"I'm having a plankton of a time!" Celia replied.

Webb had set up a campaign table outside their tents where he attempted to impress her with his sleight of hand at Find the Lady. As far as the eye could see all the conical tents stretched out, like beehives or those Trulli dwellings in Puglia. What was the collective noun for a huge number of beehives, she wondered?

"They call it glamping, ma'am," he had informed her, referring to the five star luxury tents that made up the premier accommodation at the Argan Farm.

"Good grief!" She had exclaimed. "Do families really scrimp and save all year round so that they can condemn themselves to spending their vacations in oubliettes like these?"

Webb didn't know what an oubliette was, but he understood it was not intended to be complimentary.

"It's what people want these days," he explained. "They want to think that they're closer to nature in a yurt, but they've still got all the luxury of a chateau."

"It's not a chateau!" She exclaimed. "It's just a conical caravan park!"

"But when you're inside on your Egyptian cotton sheets and goose down pillows, you'll forget it's just a glorified tent."

"*Je n'oubliet rien!*" She punned.

Detective Benyaacoub Bencheckroun

Wally was seated in the office of Benyaacoub Bencheckroun, the private investigator he had found in Google. He had been astonished by the sheer number of private investigators that were listed in every city of Morocco. In Ouarzazate alone, there must have been one sleuth for every sixth member of the population. There were hundreds of investigators with names beginning with A, such as Abbas or Abdelbaki, Ali, Atik or Aziz; but Wally had passed them over, in the same way that he would ignore the listing of a plumber known as AAA Plumbers, or the like, knowing that they had arrived at that name, simply to ascend to the top by alphabet, rather than merit.

He had got as far as the B's, but then the remaining alphabetically-listed serried ranks of gumshoes had defeated him and he had got no further than Benyaacoub Bencheckroun.

This Bencheckroun was like an amalgam of many literary detectives. His office with his name stencilled on a glass and wooden door, was straight out of Raymond Chandler. He had a moustache, like Poirot, and sucked on a Meerschaum pipe, like Holmes. Wally wouldn't have been in the least surprised if he had produced a violin.

By way of small talk, Wally had begun: "You know, Benny, can I call you Benny? When I was doing a bit of private detective work for myself, that is, searching for private detectives, I was amazed at how many private detectives there were *per capita* relative to the population of Morocco. I mean, why do Moroccans need so many detectives?"

"You know," replied Bencheckroun, after sucking on his pipe thoughtfully, "in Morocco, the ratio of private detectives to other people is higher than in London or New York City."

"How come?"

"The fact is that Moroccan males are all obsessed with the morbid belief that their wives are being unfaithful to them."

"And are they?"

"Well, strangely enough, they are. In order to detect that, I first had to learn dead Arab languages, because the wives communicate with their lovers exclusively in dead languages known as *Tamazight* and *Tifinagh*."

"Holy cow! That would be like conducting a love affair in Latin."

"Precisely! Their cover story is that, like dutiful wives, they are keeping these traditional languages that are part of their birth right and their children's birth rights alive, but in fact they are just carrying on with their paramours."

"But some men must speak these dead languages you mention, or they wouldn't be able to carry on the dialogue with the women."

"Indeed, they learn the languages professionally, as I had to."

"Professionally?"

"The only males who would seek skills in *Tamazight* and *Tifinagh* are, how do you say? Gigolos."

"Gigolos?"

"But these gigolos are paid for by the husbands, not the wives."

"I don't understand."

"So that they can discover evidence of their suspected infidelity."

"That the husband has precipitated himself via an *agent provocateur*?"

"It is no coincidence that so much of the language of adultery is French, Mr Pfister."

"And, when you discover that your employers' wives are being unfaithful, what happens to the wives? Do they get divorced?"

"Morocco has a very low divorce rate. But it has a very high incidence of female mortality. But the male officials (whose wives are also unfaithful), and whose job it is to maintain these statistics, do not break them down."

"What do you mean, they don't break them down?"

"They are listed by sex, but they are not further sub-divided, for instance, by age. So no distinction is drawn between an infant mortality and the death of a grown woman or mother. This enables them to promote the heresy that the high female death rate reflects a patriarchal society where the fathers kill their infant female offspring, disappointed that their wives have failed to produce a male heir who can get to work and help them pay the bills. When actually, incidences of infant mortality are very rare, and the statistics in fact reflect husbands murdering their adulterous wives."

"But if you know that is the destination of all your detecting, that once you've filed your report with your employer, an innocent woman is going to be killed, aren't you troubled by that?"

"The adulterous woman is not innocent. Adultery is illegal under Article 491–493 of the Moroccan Penal Code."

"Good grief!"

Wally had come to the conclusion that he couldn't possibly retain a man with so low an opinion of the fairer sex. If Benyaacoub Bencheckroun was remotely representative of the thousands of other detectives that he had Googled, if all the flatfoots this country turned out were simply Moroccan misogynists, employed by other Moroccan misogynists, Wally would have to make his own enquiries.

The Art of the Deal

"Well, how hard can it be?" Nap had asked him.

Kid was at Metcalfe's office in Aldgate, watching the sleet dribble down the window. Napier was Face Timing him from North Island in the Seychelles. Kid could see palm trees and huge granite boulders in the background, but no giant tortoises.

"About as hard as it comes," was Kid's answer. "Our policies say that the insured has to let us do the negotiating or it vitiates the policy. How do I negotiate with kidnappers? It calls for special skills, psychological profiling, patience that I don't have. I don't know where to begin, Nap, and suppose they kidnap me as well?"

"Brother, there has to be one of those *How to* videos that someone's put up there on YouTube."

"How To negotiate with Terrorists and Extortionists on YouTube?"

"No, no, no. If it's terrorists, that's the best thing that can happen to us, because it's illegal to provide insurance that pays ransom to terrorists, so we're off the hook. Unless, of course, they're Somali pirates, who, for some reason are an exception to the rule, so that even though they have known links to the terrorist organisation, al-Shabaab, for some reason that don't count, and you're allowed to pay huge ransoms to Somali pirates."

"Nap, since this incident went down in the middle of the Sahara Desert, I doubt that we're dealing with Somali pirates."

"That's the trouble, weak and corrupt governments and disputed territories breed favourable conditions for kidnappers. If you can't find anything on YouTube, I suggest you get your arse out there and pick up one of those motivational books in the airport terminal."

"Napier, do you really imagine that WH Smiths at Heathrow Terminal 3 is going to be stocking books on how to negotiate with kidnappers?"

"No, no, no, it doesn't have to be that specific, Kid. You're not seeing the wood for the trees. You just need one of those management-speak-guru books about how to negotiate. Negotiating with kidnappers is no different to negotiating with a trade union or anybody else.

"I will concede that if you're negotiating with *terrorists*, things can get more complicated, because they may have a whole cocktail of motives, ideologies: political, hegemonic; but we ain't going to carry out any negotiations with terrorists, because our insurance isn't responsive to that. Assuming the kidnappers aren't terrorists, they want the same thing as everybody else: money. So all you've got to do is agree the lowest price for the commodity."

And that was how Kid Ransom came to be sitting in the Club class section of BA's flight BA2666 to Marrakesh, reading Donald Trump's *The Art of the Deal*.

Discretion

To begin with Wally had inherited a leading man who wouldn't come out of his trailer. So initially he hadn't been able to get much filming done for that reason. He'd been able to shoot the stand-alone set piece for the sponsors with the big turban; but where had that got him? He'd promptly got his production company sued by Brunswick Holt as a result. He'd been able to shoot the other stand-alone set piece in the absence of the leading man, that is to say the gratuitous sex scene, unintentionally using the leading man's brother as his stand-in, and he'd got his leading lady and fiancée raped in the process, and then irretrievably and premeditatedly deleted the scene his producer had paid US$5m for.

They had also not been able to get much shooting done, because they didn't have a workable script to shoot to. But then, just as an amazing script had mysteriously began to materialise, as it were from the sands of the desert itself, a script so good that it enticed the recalcitrant leading man out of his trailer, the leading man had disappeared, presumed kidnapped.

Then his leading lady had also disappeared. He felt as though he had presided over her kidnap as well as her rape.

Well, Mr Pfister, he heard his inner cliché saying to himself. It just doesn't look like it's your lucky day!

Each day, more pages of the amazing script were delivered in the dead of night by an unknown and uncredited hand; but Wally was now reduced to having no stars with whom to enact the story, so the film was on hold again, and he couldn't even use the identical twin to stand in for Colman Hunt anymore, because he too had mysteriously disappeared.

As a result, after morning sunrise salutation yoga each day, Wally found that he had a lot of time on his hands, and he drove up and down the few highways in Morocco, thrusting his telephone with a photo of his fiancée into the face of anyone he came into contact with, and stopping especially at gas stations, hotels and restaurants. Eventually he found his way to *La Gazelle d'Or*. He parked up and walked into reception, and showed the photo to Muhammed.

"I don't suppose you've seen this lady recently?" He asked.

"Only in the films and on TV, sir," lied Muhammed.

Wally took a stroll round the grounds. He came across the other Muhammed, the waiter, at the casual dining area round the pool and asked him the same question and again elicited a negative answer.

However, Muhammed, the waiter, was serving the English guy who had spotted Celia, returning from his early morning dove shoot, the guy who had asked for a selfie and been denied one by Mr Webb. This guy corrected Muhammed.

"How the hell can you say that?" He asked. "She was here just the other day and you were falling over yourself to take selfies with her." Then to Wally, "He's lying." Then to Muhammed, "Give me your phone!"

Without waiting, the guy took the phone out of Muhammed's hand. As it was already unlocked, he was able to open the photos and find the series of dated selfies that Muhammed had taken. He showed them to Wally. Wally took the phone, and, without asking permission from the mendacious waiter, emailed all the photos to himself, so that he knew the time and the date when she had been there. Then he gave the phone back to Muhammed.

"Why did you lie to me?" He asked.

"I'm sorry, sir, but we have strict instructions never to divulge who has been staying here. We have to be discreet. Many men are here with ladies who aren't their wives. Many ladies are here with men who aren't their husbands. When asked, we always deny everyone was here."

It was just like the misogynistic Moroccan detective had told him. Everybody in Morocco was committing adultery.

"That can't do much good for your occupancy rates!" remarked the guy who had been refused the selfie.

"And where did she go after she left?" Wally asked.

"I don't know," replied Muhammed truthfully.

Wally thanked the stranger for his timely intervention and walked back to reception.

Encountering the other Muhammed, he asked him the same question: "Why did you lie to me? Your waiter's got a phone full of photos of Celia Broadsword taken here just the other day."

"I'm very sorry, sir, but it is a rule in the hospitality sector not to disclose the details of who comes here. Also in the case of celebrities, such as Ms Broadsword, there is the added dimension that celebrities very much value their privacy, and would be most offended if they thought we were violating it, so as to use them, as it were, to endorse our product. They pay to stay here, but if we were then to use them as unpaid brand ambassadors, that would not be respectful."

"And do you know where she went when she left?" Wally asked.

"Yes, sir. She got back into the car that had brought her here. She arrived. She had a swim. She ate her lunch, and she got back in the car."

"She took a swim?" Wally was incredulous.

"Yes, sir. Her hair was still wet when she left."

"And she got into the car willingly?"

"Most certainly, sir. A black Range Rover."

"Did anyone take the licence plate of the Range Rover?"

"We would normally do that if it might prove necessary for us to move the car or ask for it to be moved, but her chauffeur stayed with the car at all times, so it wasn't necessary."

"The guy you describe as her chauffeur," ventured Wally, calling up on his phone the photo he'd cut from the CCTV footage, "is this him?"

Muhammed looked at the grainy image of the tall, elderly man with white hair and the pony tail.

"Certainly, sir."

"And do you know where they were headed?"

"Sorry. No idea, sir. Is anything wrong?"

"I just wish I knew, Muhammed. I just wish I knew."

The footage just kept replaying in Wally's head, the same way as the footage of her rape by Presley Unsdorfer had before he had exorcised it by cutting it and burning it. But this time it was the CCTV footage of her walking willingly towards the tall white-haired man in the dark suit; how he stubbed his cigarette out as she approached, and held the car door open for her as she climbed into the back. Maybe, he thought, she had fallen for someone more her own age.

But that someone was the man in the link that he'd been sent years ago: *I thought you might like to meet your mother. Signed Your Father.*

Gmail

Elena, Indigolin, Wally and Kid Ransom stared into the blank desert as if for inspiration.

For a moment, there was a complete absence of any sound. The silence was profound and lasted maybe thirty seconds with everyone locked within their own thoughts, and was then broken by simultaneous alarms on both Wally's and Indigolin's phones. Wally read his message out loud.

"It's a ransom demand from Celia's kidnapper," he announced. "He wants US $5M, or he's going to perform a glossectomy on her."

"Snap!" Indigolin said. "I've got the same message."

"What's a glossectomy?" Kid asked.

"It's a surgical tongue removal," explained Elena. "Ugh!"

"Where's the email come from?" Kid asked.

"It's weird," said Wally.

"The email address is, and I quote," informed Indigolin, "*BeAbsoluteforDeath.com*."

"It's a quote from Measure for Measure," noted Elena.

"*BeAbsoluteforDeath.com*," repeated Indigolin. "Upper case B. Upper. Case A. Upper case D."

"BAD," mused Elena.

"How does he want the money paid?" Kid asked.

"Bitcoins to be transferred to an untraceable cryptocurrency account," read Indigolin.

"How long have we got before he starts chopping bits off her?" Elena asked.

"It just says *forthwith*," said both Indigolin and Wally together.

Evidently, Mr Webb was more skilled at composing his ransom demands than Presley Unsdorfer.

How did this woman always get his emotions so entangled, Wally asked himself? They had just received a ransom note from someone who was self-evidently a homicidal madman, threatening to saw pieces of his girlfriend off, and the sensation that should be washing down over him right now was horror. But the sensation that he found he was actually experiencing was relief that she hadn't run off with another man.

Colman Hunt Negotiates His Own Ransom

Patrick Oculus, bare-footed on the hot sand, walked up and joined the group.

"How do you know something's going to be happening soon?" Elena Troy asked him.

"Because I received a WhatsApp from an unidentifiable number telling me that Colman had been kidnapped and that the demands of the kidnappers would be made known to me at about midday today," replied Oculus.

"So," said Elena. "It looks like it's going to be *Game On* for you soon, Mr Ransom."

Kid, Elena and Oculus were still loitering outside Aka Akinyola's hospitality tent staring at Aka assembling her charcoal into neat cones on her sundry barbecues. It was not a productive use of time, but there wasn't anything else for them to do, as they couldn't make any progress on the film that had brought them all together in the middle of the Sahara. Beyond Aka's charcoal arrangements, spread the desert, terminating in the High Atlas Mountains. Kid was not relishing the next step.

Aka lit the first barbecue, preparing for lunch. As the heat radiated off the Weber, the undulating horizon began to shimmer.

Indigolin came out of the hospitality tent with a coffee in a Styrofoam cup, saw everybody staring at the same point on the horizon, and focussed his own eyes in that direction. The constantly changing light seemed to play tricks with his vision.

"Wasn't there a very large sand dune over there when we did our yoga this morning?" Indigolin asked Elena.

"Shifting sands," she shrugged off his enquiry.

"To tell you the truth, I'm not looking forward to this one tiny bit, Ms Troy," Kid Ransom confided.

"Well, I've consulted the policy, Mr Ransom, and it says that if you don't handle the situation, the insurance is voided, so, unless Metcalfe are being represented by another negotiator, I'm afraid it's down to you."

"It's a game of give and take like anything else," Indigolin informed them. "You have to make some small concession to get a bigger concession from the kidnappers."

"Mr Indigolin," began Elena, feeling it was only proper that, in company, she should not address him by his first name, as he had invited her to, "We're not talking about Celia Broadsword. In the time it took you to duck inside and get a cappuccino, we've been told a ransom note for Colman Hunt is also on the way."

"When I got shot and sued on the same afternoon, I thought I was having a bad day, but this is turning into what our late Royal Highness called an *annus horribilis!*" He replied.

"The small mercy," responded Elena, "was that she passed away before she had to see the abortion that Netflix made of it."

"Or read his grandson's book," added Elena.

Resuming her advice to Kid: "You have to find some means to earn their trust," offered Elena. "What you need to avoid is confrontation and threats, as that would be counter-productive and could endanger the hostage."

Elena continued burbling advice to him in the background. Kid's mind drifted back to the time when he was going out on his first date. In between splashing lashings of aftershave on himself, his elder brother, Nap Ransom, had embarked upon a litany of unsolicited advice about the quickest way to get his date into the sack, which advice sounded remarkably similar to the way, he now understood, one was supposed to negotiate with a kidnapper.

Aka fired up another of her barbecues. This was the chef's answer to any of life's problems: to try to cook her way out of it.

Kid attempted to refocus into Elena's assessment of the situation. He had no doubt that it was better to follow advice from her than from his brother.

"From what I understand," she continued. "In the early stages, the kidnappers will be seeking to ascertain the market value for their subject. If it was a random opportunistic kidnapping, that stage could be lengthy, because if they pluck a figure out of the air and it's agreed to too quickly, then they'll realise that they must have benchmarked it too low and they'll just jack the price up. But with Colman Hunt, assuming they know who it is they've got their hands on, he's a trophy asset, so they may already have an idea of his worth."

"That means, if they come out with a figure first, I should take my time and manage their expectations down," said Kid.

"Salami-slice it!" Indigolin advised. "Punishment and reward. Use the carrot twice as much as the stick!"

"Less of the salami-slicing, please," interjected Wally.

"I wouldn't be so quick with the punishment aspect," said Elena. "Once it's understood that they want money and we have to give it, and we're just discussing quantum, everybody is on the same page, and we can have a sensible dialogue. But start talking about punishments, and things could turn nasty quickly."

Aka lit a third barbecue. Oculus speculated if she might be a covert New Promethean, like a New Promethean who hadn't come out yet. A covert convert, so to speak.

"They'll want to probe how much their victim is worth," continued Elena, "but the probing will take time, and they may not have time. So if you can offer them a quick deal, speed in itself could be currency that you could negotiate with. A way of adding value."

"Yes," agreed Indigolin, impressed by how savvy his accountant was, "speed is a universally recognised currency. If you want expedition, that comes at a higher price. Speed is added value."

"You seem to know an awful lot about this, Ms Troy," observed Kid. "You ever been in a ransom situation?"

"Yeah, every night when I was small and I wanted some favour off my brothers, Kid."

"What's that?" Oculus enquired. Something had just punctuated the horizon flickering in the heat haze coming off the barbecues.

Kid, whose younger eyes were sharper than Oculus', made out the figure. "Someone's walking towards us." He said.

"Can you make out who it is?" Indigolin asked.

"I can't tell you who it is," said Ransom, "but I would say he's wearing Arab robes. Blue Arab robes."

"Has anyone got any binoculars?" Indigolin asked.

It seemed no-one had, but Elena shot off and came back with a camcorder with a 20 x Optical Zoom lens. She put the viewfinder to her eye, because the glare of the sun was too intense to use the screen, and then she announced: "It's Colman Hunt, but he's wearing a blue Dishdash."

"May I?" Ransom asked.

Elena passed the camcorder to Kid. He put it to his eye, but the magnification was too great for him to zero in on the figure. He had to zoom out first, locate the moving form and then zoom back in again for a closer look.

"God!" Kid explained, "at this magnification, it makes you feel quite sick. I've gone all dizzy."

Indigolin and Troy glanced to one another. Their expressions both seemed to say the same thing: *what kind of a pathetic wimp have we got for our hostage negotiator?*

"Here, let me!" Oculus said, reaching to take the camera from Kid. "It's Colman Hunt, alright," he pronounced. "And he's alone. And I can confirm he's wearing a blue Dishdash. And he's also wearing a suicide vest."

"May I?" Indigolin asked. Ransom passed the camera to Indigolin.

"And he's got a smartphone strapped to his head," observed Indigolin.

A few moments later, the bare-footed Colman Hunt had covered enough ground for them to be able to make out the details with the naked eye.

"If Hunt is indeed wearing a suicide vest," said Elena, "don't you think you had better go and head him off before he gets any closer?" The question was addressed to Kid.

"I mean," she continued, "we don't know where he's been. He could've been radicalised. He belonged to some weird cult as it was. These theatrical types can be very impressionable."

Patrick Oculus didn't like to hear the New Prometheans being dismissed as members of a weird cult, but didn't think the time was right to go all evangelical and attempt to convert Elena.

Elena's little speech was addressed to Kid. Kid saw the logic in what she was saying, but didn't like the idea of walking up to a guy in a suicide vest.

"Well, if he isn't the victim of a kidnap, but is in fact coming here in the guise of a terrorist, then your policy of insurance isn't responsive to that risk, so I'm not so sure about that," Kid replied artfully. "By worldwide convention, we're not allowed to write policies of insurance against terrorists."

Oh, here we go, Elena thought to herself. His brash brother soused in aftershave was the skunk, and this more humble version was the weasel. She made a mental note to herself. The next lesson in John Donne she was going to give to her pupil, Tinctorio Indigolin, was on the poem known as *The Perfume*.

"Well," said Indigolin with finality, "the only way we're going to get clarity, is by someone going out and finding out what his demands are. I'm perfectly happy to go myself. By rights, I should be dead anyway. But as I don't want to do anything to vitiate my insurance cover, can I suggest that you engage with Hunt sufficiently to tell me if this is an insured risk or not? I mean, for heaven's sake, he's only been gone a couple of nights. Even for an impressionable moron like Colman Hunt, it must take longer than that to radicalise someone."

Reluctantly, Kid started walking towards the approaching figure in the blue robes. To the observers, it looked like a scene from a spaghetti western. Eleanor noted the song Wally was humming under his breath was *Do Not Forsake Me, Oh my Darling*.

When they were about twenty metres apart, Kid started to call out to Hunt to hold it there. But he found there was no force in his voice and it wouldn't carry. As a result, the two men continued to walk towards one another until Colman Hunt lifted up both of his hands, and called out: "I think we're close enough to hear one another, and for your own good, I don't recommend you come any closer."

They both stopped in their tracks. Surprisingly, Ransom noticed Hunt had bare feet on the blazing hot sand, but expressed no sign of discomfort.

Remembering his brother's catchphrase, *It's like the Wild West*, Kid attempted to break the ice by saying: "We must look like a scene out of High Noon."

"And may I ask whom I have the pleasure of addressing?" Hunt asked.

"My name's Kid Ransom. I'm the negotiator for the studio," Ransom managed to get out before his voice rose higher than he would have liked.

Hunt found that he was mesmerised by the size of Ransom's Adam's apple. Ransom had a neck as long as a swan's with a very protrusive laryngeal prominence. If William Tell had been on the scene with his crossbow, thought Hunt, he could have shot that apple right out of the man's neck from a hundred paces. A smile flickered around Hunt's lips as he called to mind a joke someone must have told him more than fifty years ago, that the definition of an intellectual was someone who could hear Strauss' William Tell Overture without thinking of *The Lone Ranger*.

That was because *The Lone Ranger* had been such a popular TV series from 1949 to 1957 and the theme music had been The William Tell Overture. Clayton Moore had been just like Colman Hunt in the King Ferdinand series; Moore had played the Lone Ranger, but for just one season, they'd substituted John Hart, in the same way that Presley had understudied for his brother, Colman Hunt, in the second series of King Ferdinand's Book of Hours. No-one had known about Presley standing in for Colman when Colman was in jail serving time for his own attempted murder.

Nor did people know that John Hart was understudying for Clayton Moore, because the whole point about the Lone Ranger was that he wore a stupid mask. But some very observant viewers did notice that Hart wore his mask in a different way, and the conspiracy theories had started. All these inane reminiscences brought a smile to Colman's face at the same time as they annoyed him, because he could so readily remember all this shit from half a century or more ago, but he wouldn't have been able to tell you what colour shirt he had been wearing the day before, or remember his lines. Somehow or other, Mortimer Unsdorfer's mind had travelled half way round the universe, and fifty years in time, all set off by this guy's Adam's apple.

Ransom could put on a hard voice, but his quivering Adam's apple was a sign of weakness and would give him away every time. Kid Ransom misinterpreted Colman's Quixotic smile as being an evil smirk from a radicalised zealot in a suicide vest, and found that his Adam's apple went up and down in an even more pronounced fashion, but no noises were coming out of his voice box. It was the raising and lowering of a ballcock in an empty toilet.

"I'm afraid there ain't going to be any negotiation, son," began Hunt, picking up on the few words that Kid Ransom had managed to speak before his voice let him down. "As you can see, they've got me wired up to a pack of explosives. I've just been sent to tell you what the price is for my release, and my understanding is that it is not negotiable. It's US five mil or nothing.

"I just have to tell you this, and then turn on my heel and go back. It looks like ransom negotiations are going the same shithouse way as everything else: first of all they started making us fill our own cars up with gas, making unpaid petrol pump attendants out of us all; then we had to act as unpaid checkout girls at the supermarket, and turn our food over until we found the barcodes to scan. Now the kidnap victim has to negotiate his own fucking ransom. The whole planet has gone to the dogs!

"Anyway, once you've agreed to pay the ransom, they're going to send me back to you again, and I'll have to discuss the logistics with you, whether you drop it out of Wally's helicopter in some appointed place, or leave it in a litter basket at Grand Central Station, or what-the-fuck. But wherever you leave it, it's gonna have to be five mil. They are filming your response through this phone on my helmet, and if there's any funny business they detonate this thing remotely, whereupon I, for certain, will be blown to buggery, and, for all I know, you will too."

"Who are *they*?" Ransom asked.

"I apprehend that *they* would regard the answer to that question as constituting 'funny business', so if you'll excuse me, I'm going to have to take the 5th on that one, Mr Kid."

"Did they have any other demands, Mr Hunt?"

"Only one. They need paper."

"Paper?"

"Yeah, like printer paper. Go and fetch me a ream now, would you? Last time I looked, there were blocks of paper by the photocopier."

Kid called out some instructions to Oculus, who ran off and reappeared moments later with two reams of printing paper, which he tossed over, not wanting to get too close to Hunt. But, in an unsuccessful attempt to lighten his friend's mood, he did shout out to Colman as he tossed the packs of paper: "Knight of the Ream, huh! Get it?"

But apparently Colman didn't get the punning reference to paper measurements, nor did anybody else. So Oculus was left looking like a moron. The two blocks of printing paper thudded, landing on the hot sand. Hunt gazed down at the twin packs. They were encased in wrappers that said *Complete Office Solutions* followed by *A4 500 PCA009. Premium Plus+Business Paper.* Colman wondered what the point was in having the Plus sign as well as the Plus word. Down the right hand side of each pack it said: *Laser: Copier: Inkjet: Office Printing.* This should keep the budding scriptwriter quiet for a few days, Hunt mused.

Noting that his friend's hands were cable-tied behind his back, Oculus opened the scissors attachment in his Swiss Army Knife, and cut through them.

Colman gratefully rubbed his wrists to restore the circulation, and then he bent down and picked the two blocks of printing paper up, one under each arm. He felt as though he was Moses in blue robes, carrying the Ten Commandments down Mount Sinai, as he turned himself round and balanced the two bricks, preparing to stride off back into the desert.

Charlton Heston had been truly amazing in that film, he reflected. No-one could do or ever had done epics like Cecil B DeMille. What a cast! Yul Bryner was Rameses II; Ann Baxter was Nefertari; a young Vincent Price had been in the cast also, before he started churning out endless Hammer House of Horrors. Edward G Robinson had played Dathan; Yvonne de Carlo as Zipporah; John Derek was Joshua. Wasn't John Derek the guy who kept discovering and marrying gorgeous Swedish blonds? First he brought us Ursula Andress. Then he married Bo Derek, who starred in Ten, as in *I'll give her ten out of ten!*

Charlton Heston had played both Moses and the voice of God coming out of the Burning Bush. That guy had to be one of the first New Prometheans. A Bush that burns, but is never consumed by the fire. Better than a Phœnix. A Phœnix burns, but comes back to life. But the Burning Bush burns, but is never burnt. That pretty well summed up his cult of New Prometheans. Why hadn't Colman Hunt ever been offered a part like that? His second wife had always been on at him, telling him that he liked to play at being God, but how sweet it would sound to pick up the phone to his agent and be told that he was actually going to be cast as God. When the credits rolled at the end:

And Starring Colman Hunt
As God

The scene with the Burning Bush could have been written for him. For heaven's sake!

Come to think of it, that entire chapter of the Bible could have been written for him. Exodus. And getting to play the voice of God too! Moses was made in 1956, but it still crackled as though it had just been unwrapped yesterday. Technicolour. $15m budget even in those days. In today's money that would be like a billion dollars! Actors who spoke their lines properly instead of mumbling everything and throwing away all the great lines like today's heartthrobs.

Well, he thought, *he was too fucking old now.* He'd missed the boat. Unlike Cecil B DeMille who only just caught the boat. Three years after he released the film, he snuffed it. Network television has aired that film on Passover week every year since 1973. In its day, it was the most successful film ever made.

Come to think of it, one of the sources for the Moses film had been the J H Ingraham novel, *Pillar of Fire*, and wasn't that how the film began after they'd got the bullrushes back story out of the way? With Moses leading the Children of Israel out of Egypt. They were guided by a Pillar of Cloud by day and a Pillar of Fire by Night. There was no two ways about it. The Old Testament had definitely been written by a New Promethean.

Colman was clearly getting ready to leave again.

Kid didn't know where to take it from here. Indigolin had said to offer some small concession or other.

"Can I lend you any shoes, Mr Hunt?"

"Thank you for the offer, but my feet are just dandy, son. Now, I'd ask you to talk to whoever it is you have to talk to, and I'm going to walk back to where I came from, before the batteries running this harness wear down and end up doing something horrible to me; and I have no doubt a second meeting will be set up once you've sorted the ransom, and we can discuss all the inside leg measurements at our next little rendezvous. So for now, it's *Ciao*!"

Having made his demands known, Mortimer Unsdorferbaum trudged back towards the unpunctuated place from whence he'd come, carrying a Tablet of the Law under each arm. He hadn't missed the boat. He could still play Moses. According to the Torah, Moses was one hundred and twenty years old when he died, and he still died prematurely, because he never made it to the Promised Land.

By comparison, Colman Hunt was a mere spring chicken. It was just like Wally attempted to preach: in the future, everyone's going to live forever. After his ransom had been paid, and after he'd got this *Gate of the Burnt One* in the can, he was going to make a comeback, a huge revival. Colman made a mental note to have a word with Tinctorio Indigolin about re-making Moses, now that SFX had evolved as far as it had, so that he could part the Red Sea with ease, and turn his rod into a serpent and all that, convincingly.

But for the best scenes, featuring the Pillar of Fire by Night, Burning Bushes, and Burning Hailstorms raining down on Rameses, no special effects would be needed. It would just be Colman communicating with the inferno. This would be Colman Hunt's finest hour since *Ordeal by Fire*.

Social Media

Agent Elena Troy was holding her mobile phone at arm's length. She handed it to Mr Indigolin who was leaning against a camera dolly and in conversation with Wally Pfister, Kid Ransom and Noah.

"You'd better read this, Mr Indigolin," she said. "It came into the generic email of the Accounts Department, *enquiries@knightsoftheream.com* where it was brought to my attention."

Indigolin took the device between thumb and forefinger. In doing so, he was pleased to note that it was a decent smart phone, a good choice of smart phone; but not the latest. Few things pissed him off as much as young people constantly moaning about not having enough funds, whilst they spent all their money on the latest phone as soon as it came to market, not that it would be any different to its predecessor, but just so they could wave it around and have street cred for five minutes before someone snatched it, or Apple replaced it. For Pete's sake, they queued up mindlessly all night long, pissing into milk bottles under blankets, just so they could be first through the traps when Apple opened their doors in the morning.

Then he realised he was speaking to himself within his own head as though he was an old fart. The horrible realisation dawned on him that, although members of the public with whom he interacted, regarded him as an innovative, trail-blazing, thinking-out-of-the-box, inspirational kind of a guy, when left to his own devices, internally, when Tinctorio Indigolin was addressing himself, they conversed in the language of a pair of old farts. Having achieved so much in a comparatively short time and having so many responsibilities weighing down upon him (including the livelihoods of thousands of employees worldwide who relied on him to pay their mortgages each month) had artificially and prematurely aged him.

Not in appearance; he still looked pretty good; but in his mind set. Probably a symptom of spending too much of his time with lawyers, who spoke lawyer-talk and who thought in lawyer think, and never reacted naturally to any stimulus. Here was he admiring Elena's choice of phone and telling himself that she was different from all the other young folk, when she was probably his contemporary. He made a note to check her CV again in HR, but there couldn't be more than a five year age gap between them.

He read the communication that had come from an otherwise unidentifiable email account designated *abduct@snatch.ma*. The wording was laconic. There was a photo beneath. It appeared to depict Colman Hunt holding up yesterday's *Today* newspaper, spread open to a photo of Colman Hunt and a piece on his mysterious disappearance. Indigolin pinched the photo so as to zoom in and out of the subject, and then said: "Well I never."

"What is it?" Wally asked.

"I think it's one of those riddles wrapped in an enigma," said Indigolin.

Wally looked at Ti's face for any sign that Indigolin had somehow managed to read his poems to Celia, but didn't find any. Indigolin continued: "We seem to have a counter-offer in on Colman Hunt. This abductor only seeks £1m."

"Whereas," remarked Elena, "the ransom demand that Colman Hunt just delivered to us himself was for US $5M. What do we make of that?"

"Maybe Colman Hunt needs a better agent," was all Indigolin said.

"Maybe, the abductors have fallen out amongst themselves," observed Kid. "There could be a breakaway group that has kidnapped the hostage from the other kidnappers, but the breakaway group has an imperfect understanding of the subject's worth."

Kid Ransom had found his voice now that the threat in the detonating waistcoat had departed. Elena summed him up in her own head: he was one of those guys who wrote vitriolic emails but was a kitten on the phone. '*Pussy*,' she thought.

"Or maybe," said Indigolin, "we are dealing with two sets of kidnappers, one of whom has Colman Hunt and the other has grabbed one of his brothers. Has anyone seen that arsehole Presley since he went for a beer at the Ibis?"

"The fact is," said Elena, "we don't even know that the guy in the suicide vest and cycle helmet we were talking to just now actually *was* Colman Hunt. It could be one of his triplets, just pretending that he has been kidnapped, so that he can collect a ransom for himself."

"That would be a bad case of identity theft," remarked Indigolin. He then said, "You'll have to excuse me, but I believe I can still catch him up," and he trotted off following Colman Hunt in his suicide Dishdash.

"On this theory," continued Elena, "Presley acts in keeping with his usual *modus operandi*, which is to seek to kill his brother. So somehow or other Presley murders Colman, and, having thus got Colman out of the picture—"

"—he then pretends to be Colman himself," completed Wally, "so as to earn himself a $5M reward for killing his own brother."

"Except he senses something's wrong with his plan," said Elena, "so he suddenly drops the price by more than US $4m. for a quick and dirty deal."

"And if we're stupid enough to pay it," interjected Kid Ransom, "he just delivers himself and fools us it's Colman before running off and giving us the slip further down the line."

"The guy you were talking to just now was Hunt, for sure," pronounced Paddy.

"How can you be so sure?" enquired Kid.

"Because he was able to walk barefoot across the blazing, hot sands with no apparent discomfort," Oculus informed them.

"Presley went for a beer and never came back again," Noah reminded the meeting. "He didn't take any of his things."

"That poses a very interesting conundrum," said Kid. "If we are dealing with two sets of hostage-takers, and one has taken a very valuable asset, but the other has taken a less valuable triplet (and allowing for the fact that all human life is, of course, sacred and has some value), how do we know, when we pay, that we've paid for the right one, and what are we going to do about the other one? Suppose we end up paying the murderer a large ransom in the belief that we're procuring the release of the very person he's already murdered?"

"As far as I know," said Wally, "there's only one person can tell them apart."

"And who is that?" Elena asked.

"Celia Broadsword," pronounced Wally.

San Pedro Manrique, Soria, Spain

Aka Akinyola removed the steaks from the marinade and tossed them onto the barbecue.

"How do you like them?" She asked.

"Burnt," replied Oculus. "You know, Aka," he continued. "I was wondering if you might be, like a closet New Promethean."

"What's that?" She asked, salting the steak and turning it with her tongs.

"We're a sect that walks on fire."

"Anything to do with fire, I've already done it," she answered. She was tossing up a salad of mint, courgette, broad beans and pine nuts in a saffron and yogurt dressing, most of the ingredients having been picked from her own garden that hadn't even existed a month back. Oculus didn't know how she could do it so quickly. She served the steak with the salad.

"No fries?" He queried.

"Wally don't allow fries on the menu," she explained.

"Have to see what Mr Indigolin's got to say about that, Aka. You ever been to the Burning Man Festival?" Oculus enquired.

"Every year without fail."

"You kidding me."

"No, I take my heat sources very seriously. I'm the only chef I know that curates her own charcoal. I mean to say, Paddy, the most important ingredient in cooking is the heat source, but all other chefs leave it to chance. I burn my own charcoal. You want to know if I've visited Burning Man. Paddy, I've done a lot more than that. I'm a doer, not an onlooker. Where I blaze, others trail! I've been an honorary Móndidas."

"What's Móndidas, Aka?"

"At 9 pm on 23 June every year without fail, the villagers of a remote town in Spain known as San Pedro Manrique, build a pyre."

"That's Midsummer's Eve, right, Aka?"

"Right, Patrick. They build the pyre and they use exactly two thousand kilos of wood, and it has to be oak wood. 23rd June is the day before the Feast of St Juan, the Fire Saint. They use oak wood because it catches fire nice and easy and it doesn't burn down in clumps. That is very important. If you want to walk on fire without burning your feet, it's the clumps that you've got to avoid. The fire don't burn you. It's the clumps in the fire."

"At 11.30 pm, the men start raking out the cinders from the oak wood, using special poles called *hoguneros*. They do this to iron out the clumps and lumps and any foreign objects. They sweep them out into a veritable red carpet of glowing embers. Normally, it's forbidden for anyone outside the village to participate, but, as I say, I stayed with them for a few years. I cooked with them. I taught them how to curate fire, and eventually, one Eve of St Juan, they appointed me as honorary Móndidas. The Móndidas are the priestesses.

"Now, although in folklore the Móndidas seem to have originated the ceremony, over time, like so many other things, it got appropriated by the menfolk. So it's the men that do the fire walking these days, and the Móndidas are reduced to handing out *arbujuelos*, which are like gigantic breadsticks that the firewalkers are rewarded with after they've done it.

"Now, the men always carry someone else, piggy-back, usually a woman. Know why?"

"Make it harder?"

"Precisely the opposite. It makes it easier. As I say, it's not the fire that burns you. It's the clumps. Oak wood doesn't form clumps, and it also burns very dry, because it has minimal moisture content. It's the hot water in the burning wood that burns your feet, not the fire. The thermal retention properties of oak wood embers are just perfect if you want to walk on it. The men carry someone on their backs and they stamp in the embers with flat feet, because the extra weight and the stamping are expelling the oxygen from the embers, so they're hardly hot at all. In fact, they're not so much walking on the fire, as stamping it out.

"Anyway, as soon as the trumpet sounded that announces the beginning of the ceremonies, I was first in the queue to do the *Paso Del Fuego*, with my piggy-back passenger on board."

"So you've done the *Paso Del Fuego*?"

"I did it, and I've been back and done it again every year except 2020."

"How come not in 2020?"

"Would you believe it? They cancelled the festival because of Covid. You know, they say that everyone who has done the *Paso Del Fuego* becomes immortal, but they cancelled the fire festival because of the pandemic."

"And do you think you're immortal, Aka?"

"Wally Pfister sure does! Time will tell, Paddy. Time will tell. How's the steak."

"It's beyond historic, Aka!"

L'Heure Bleue

Colman Hunt, unshod, sporting his explosive gillet, had trudged the first five hundred metres of his return trip when he became aware of someone jogging up behind him. The steps in the sand were soundless, but he sensed that old *Fee-fi-fo-fum* thing that made the hairs on the back of his neck stand up when his brothers were nearby, but this time he didn't *Fee-fi-fo-fum smell the blood of an Unsdorferbaum*. When he turned his head, he saw the smiling visage of Tinctorio Indigolin, looking completely incongruous, but also completely cool and unruffled, in one of his blue legume lounge suits in the middle of the Sahara Desert.

His visitor said, "I'm coming with you, Colman."

"I don't recommend that, Mr Indigolin."

"I'll be coming along with or without your endorsement, Colman."

"What for?"

"Thousand reasons, shill. Such as. Nice day for a walk in the desert in my cool threads; do the Marathon de Sables in my blue molecules; shoot the non-existent breeze with my leading man; I can carry one of those blocks of paper for you, share the load. I can observe how you New Prometheans do that cult thing with your non-fungible feet; but mainly because the Chairman of Indigolin Industries inclines to anything blue, and I intend to meet those blue men who held you captive."

Tinctorio Indigolin helped himself to one of the parcels of printing paper from under Colman's elbow. Colman appreciated Indigolin meant well, but, especially when his residual vertigo was factored in, it just upset his equilibrium, and he would have preferred to carry both weights for himself, and at least be balanced. Also, he couldn't while away the walk, pretending he was Moses, coming down from Mount Sinai, bearing the Ten Commandments any more.

"How do you know about any blue men, Mr Indigolin? I never mentioned no blue men."

"Oh, I see, shill. You're concerned about that camera working on your head. Don't want to put your foot in anything by giving something away that you shouldn't. Well, I figured from the way you were dressed that your captors must be the Blue Men of the Desert: Berber tribesmen. They practically dressed you up in their school uniform! Those old Oompa Loompas of the Sahara!"

"They're not Oompa Loompas, Mr Indigolin. They're dangerous men and they told me to come back alone. Aren't you worried that if they set this thing off, we'll *both* be blown to kingdom come?"

"Tell you what, shill. I'll observe social distancing. Jay walking at two metres." He fell back a few paces.

"That might do the trick for you, Mr Indigolin; but how about me?"

"Don't worry, I'll pick up the pieces wherever you leave off. I've got my continuity men on set! Only joking! Come on, Colman, keep walking. One foot in front of the other!"

"Yes, Mr Indigolin, I understand the theory of walking. I just don't like walking into trouble unnecessarily."

"Colman, you won't come to any harm with me looking after you, I promise you. I'm like a lucky charm. You know what everyone says about Tinctorio Indigolin? *'He always makes his partners rich'.*"

"But that's the whole point. Suppose they kidnap you as well?"

"After I've poured my Blue Molecule clean through their blue hides, they'll be eating out of my hand, I assure you. They'll be worshipping me like I was one of those cargo cult gods that drop out from the skies."

"What the fuck's a cargo cult god?"

"It's an Indigolin indigenist millenarian persuasion that believes if they conduct themselves in a particular way, manna from heaven's going to drop on their heads. It started in Melanesia in WW2. The American soldiers and their supplies arrived by airdrop, so the natives thought they were gods that had come down from the skies. They traded with the primitive locals. After the troops departed, the locals mimicked the behaviour of the soldiers in the belief that this would make them return from the heavens and resume trading with them. It's like a Second Coming, but it's all about trade. Anyway, which way are we headed?"

Colman shuffled on and replied: "No idea. Like you said, just putting one foot in front of the other until night falls. Then we'll see their fires and head for them."

"Tell me something, Colman. Instead of meandering aimlessly for a couple of hours, waiting for the sun to sink below the horizon, so that you could spot the fires, why didn't you just wait until it was dark before setting off?"

"Because I figured that if I set off in the heat of the day, everyone would be shut up in their air-conditioned trucks, and I'd be able to do my Walk of Shame solo like I'd been told to without company and without getting blown up."

"You didn't reckon on my blue legume suit keeping me cool, shill, did you?"

"Tell you the truth, I didn't reckon on an explosive gillet neither."

"Thing about these parts, shill, is that the transition between day and night can be almost instantaneous."

Indigolin clapped his hands together for emphasis and Hunt's heart missed a beat, thinking the sudden noise might detonate his waistcoat. "You know what the definition of dusk is? It's the time it takes for the sun to sink eighteen degrees below the horizon, during which period there's still all the reflected and refracted light scattering about, so it's not got totally dark yet; and that time accelerates the closer you get to the equator, because the angle at which the sun descends gets sharper and sharper. So that if you're, let's say, in Scotland, or in Sweden where they have these White Nights—"

"Like the Tony Hackford film starring Isabella Rossellini and Helen Mirren, with the Lionel Richie soundtrack, *'Say You, Say me'*?"

"Colman, you know, there is a life separate from the world of films. I mean, you know, out here there's a real world going on. Anyway, White Nights happens in places like St Petersburg, where they shot the eponymous film you just mentioned, or Sweden, and the point is, the night never gets dark, because the sun's angle is like a parabola in those parts and the inhabitants of those regions are crawling through a perpetual twilight zone. At the equator on the other hand, the sun drops perpendicular as a plum line.

"It's gone from sun shine to coal mine in a second. Photographers and cinematographers, such as our very own Walter Pfister, refer to that time when the sun has dropped below the horizon, but continues to make its presence known by all the reflected and refracted waves, as *L'Heure Bleue*, which is also what the French call it. And *L'Heure Bleue* also happens to be the name of my favourite Relais Chateaux hotel in Essaouria. We ought to check it out. Buy you a mint tea poured from a great height when we get out of this, Colman."

"Mr Indigolin, whilst you've been talking about it, that's just what's been happening."

"What?"

"It's got dark."

"You're right. See how effortlessly you can pass the time with me. Before we know it, we'll be at our destination."

"It's got dark. And there are the fires."

They strode towards the Berber fires like cavemen. The good thing about a dark night in the desert, observed the vertiginous Colman Hunt, was that there were no obstacles for him to trip over.

Wally Receives Another Female Visitor

Elena knocked softly on the door of Wally's Woodie-Wagon. He let her in and asked her what he could do for her. First of all she had to make the usual observations that every visitor made on his or her first visit, about how the place looked like a Pall Mall Gentlemen's Club, and was this the desk where the famous director sat down to do his editing with real cellulose? Wally hurried her along, because he didn't want Celia to turn up unexpectedly from wherever she'd disappeared to and get any funny ideas, such as, that after a mere few hours parted from her, he had started inviting other women into his Woodie-Wagon for hanky-panky. To keep things looking innocent, he asked her not to close the door, even though the idea of his air conditioning seeping out into the desert and destroying the environment, gave him pains in the chest.

"Indigolin doesn't have his own wagon, does he?" She asked.

"No, he likes to stay in hotels."

"Which hotel is he staying at?"

"Well, it's not exactly a hotel, Elena. He's rented himself a Riyadh in Ouarzazate near the Atlas Film Studios, Riyadh Chay, it's called."

Elena figured out that if she was going to find out what was on Indigolin's DataTraveler, now that the Blue Molecule guy had gone trotting off into the desert with Colman Hunt, leaving his Riyadh unattended, this was going to be the best chance she was ever likely to get.

"Why do you ask, Elena?" Wally queried.

"Oh," she exclaimed, and continued, winging it, "I don't like the hotel I'm staying in and thought maybe I could move, but, now you tell me that he's not staying in a hotel, it wouldn't really be appropriate for me to share his Riyadh with him."

"Which hotel are you at?"

"The Berber Hotel."

"What's wrong with the Berber?"

"It's full of extras and two-bit actors with chips on their shoulders 'cos they don't have their own Airstreams," she improvised.

More Nomads

They were now close enough to make out the figures illuminated by the fires. In fact, Colman could even put names to some of them.

"Not too late to turn back, Mr Indigolin."

"That would not be a good idea, Colman."

"How come?"

"Because, headed towards the beacon of those fires, it's like a walk in the park, Sunday school outing. Tip top! But in case you haven't noticed, if we turn round and walk back in the direction we've just come from, it's pitch dark, black as the grave. I'd start off merrily thinking I was walking in a straight line and end up fifty miles in the wrong direction."

"Are there wild animals in the Sahara Desert?" Hunt asked.

"There are animals, such as Rhim Gazelles that have very long, very sharp horns that can do you a mischief. There are wild dogs that will tear you to pieces. They didn't all start out life as wild. Many of them were domesticated, but once a dog gets out of human control by abandonment, it can become co-opted or accepted by other wild dogs, and then it becomes feral itself. You know, it's possible to radicalise animals, as well as humans.

"There are Ruppell's foxes, Scimitar Oryxes whose antlers can cleave you clean in two; and then there are reptiles such as the horned viper, who can also give you the kiss of death." It was Aderfi speaking. He had seen the two men approaching, and had come out of the throng to receive them. "And who's this?" He asked.

"Tinctorio Indigolin at your service, shill." He held out his hand. Aderfi looked unsure what to do, but then clasped it.

"What a handshake!" Indigolin exclaimed. "It's like a vice! And my God, just look at that face! His forehead's exactly parallel with his nose! The blue robes, and he has blue eyes. I've never seen that combination: dark skin, black hair and piercing blue eyes. He's like *Lawrence of Arabia*, but with a real Arab instead of a drunken Paddy!"

"What are you doing here, sir?" Aderfi asked.

"Shill, I am very, very interested in Nomads, in fact, back in London, I've just bought my own. I thought I would accompany my friend here and meet you blue Oompa Loompas of the desert."

"Weren't you frightened we Oompa Loompas might detonate his vest, Mr Indigolin?"

"Never occurred to me for a minute. No self-respecting Berber is going to blow up a $200 Superdry gillet! Shill, I've not been working in films for very long, but it's been long enough for me to be able to tell a prop from the real thing. Want me to put it on?"

"What!" Colman cried. "You mean, this isn't for real? You've had me shitting bricks over a film prop?"

"You didn't really think we'd let you come to any harm, did you, Mr Hunt? We just need the money," said Aderfi.

"Well, I'll tell you what the three of us are going to do," said Indigolin. "I am going to be your spokesman and negotiator-in-chief. Let me do the talking. I am going to get you five million dollars in untraceable bitcoins or other cryptocurrency of your election from the insurance that dare not speak its name; the insurance we're not supposed to tell anybody we've got, and I'm going to pay it to you and you in turn are going to play the part of Boabdil, Mohammed XI of Granada in my upcoming film and mini-series that re-writes European history.

"You'll get your five million dollars. Hollywood gets a new star, and the Metcalfe Insurance Specialists are going to pay for it all. You'll be able to buy that kid over there a bike that fits him. What do you say, shill?"

"Pounds, Mr Indigolin. Not dollars."

Just like Elena Troy had said: they'd try to jack the price up.

"Don't overplay your hand, shill. I mean, as kidnappers you are running seriously short of credibility here. You've got no guns; no getaway cars; you use the hostage as your postman and have him deliver your demands for you; the exploding waistcoat's a dud. For what you have here, which is a very low budget operation, US5 mil for a first picture is iconoclastic; it's mega. You know what people say about Tinctorio Indigolin? He always makes his partners rich. When I first started out talking about my *blue legumes*, they'd write me up in the newspapers and magazines, and the condescending schmendricks would write *'blue legume'* and then they'd put *'sic'* in parenthesis after it. Do you know what that is, shill?"

"Do I know what what is, Mr Indigolin? A schmendrick, a blue legume, a sic, or a shill?"

"*Sic*."

"It's Latin for *Thus*," said Aderfi, " and if it is used with parenthesis around it, as you suggest, it means that they're quoting you exactly as you said it, but they know your usage is erroneous."

"Right on, shill! What it means is *We know better than him! But we're putting it down in the ignorant man's own words in the interests of accurate reporting.* That's what *sic* means with brackets round it! Sanctimonious sacks of gibbonshit! You know there's two places where I just hate to see any brackets. One is round the net assets line in the accounts of any of my companies, and the other is around the word *sic* when I am being quoted! They thought I was trying to say *Blue Lagoon*, but didn't know any better.

"So every time someone did an interview with Tinctorio Indigolin, and they'd write it down, I'd see that every single sentence consisted of more *sics* than any other word. But we are where we are, and now ten years into my meteoric elevation to cargo god, I've re-educated everybody. Nowadays all the kids believe that a legume *has to be blue*. They don't know any better (*Sic*).

"Talking of blue lagoons, they also thought I didn't know how to spell the name of my own company or molecule. So when they wrote about Rif or Blue Rif, there it would be again, that inevitable, condescending *sic* in parenthesis, because they thought I meant Reef, as in Coral Reef, Blue Lagoon. And you know what? That put an idea in my head. But that's a story for another day.

"Now you and I are going to do precisely the same with my new film. Me, because I'm going to make it, and you, because you're going to star in it, alongside Mr Hunt here, of course. The kids don't know proper history anymore. The teachers that should be teaching them to learn from the mistakes of their forebears, are too busy inculcating them with woke ideologies, in between going on strike, persuading them to change sex, and encouraging them to tear down statues of their betters, and push them into the canal. They get their history from Instagram, TikTok and QAnon. By the time I've finished with them, everyone's going to believe that after 1492, the Moors continued to rule Europe."

"That's the trouble with history, Mr Indigolin. It's always written up by the victors. We'll give you a Muslim perspective." It was Aderfi speaking.

"We've got Professor Elizabeth Drayson on board as our consulting scriptwriter and historical accuracy expert."

"We don't need Ms Drayson. Badiss will continue to write your script for you, Mr Indigolin."

"So you're the secret scriptwriters, are you? Top shelf, shill! First rate. Tip top! Where did you learn English?"

"At Charterhouse, sir, but I'm not the scriptwriter. Young Badiss is."

"Course you're not the scriptwriter. You're going to be the star. Olive skin, black hair, blue eyes. How tall are you, shill?"

"Six foot four, sir."

"Tip top and tickety-boo! Your name is going to be up there alongside Colman Hunt and Celia Broadsword. Your name's going to be at the top of the billboard and Brunswick Holt is going to be beneath you. Second fiddle. You'll have your own star in the firmament and another five pointed one in terrazzo and brass on the pavement. Do you fancy Hollywood Boulevard or Vine Street? By the way, shill, what is your name?"

"Aderfi Benjelloun, sir."

"We'll have to fix that!"

"And how do you know we won't kidnap you as well, Mr Indigolin?"

Nodding in the direction of Colman Hunt: "Because if you kidnap me, there won't be anybody to pay you for him, will there? I told you, I'm willing to entertain your request that we give you US5m, but we do it my way."

"Mr Indigolin, with respect, you won't be giving me anything. I'll be providing you the services of my team in return for a retainer."

"What services would those be, Mr Ben Julian?"

Aderfi handed him the over-written pages. Indigolin thumbed through and read the new pages that had been written up by Badiss from where he'd left off. He was impressed. The quality was consistent.

"Is this my script?" He asked.

"You may call it a script if you like, Mr Indigolin. Or you may call it a delivery mechanism."

Indigolin scanned Aderfi's face for signs of sarcasm, or indeed any indication that he was quoting from the Millicent Marcuson interview; but he didn't see any. He read on until he reached the end of the segment Badiss had edited.

"It's top shelf!" He declared. "But it ends on a bit of a cliff-hanger!"

"Well then," said Aderfi, addressing both of them now. "You'd better hand over those two boxes of paper that you've carried all this way, so that we can do something about that, hadn't you?"

Ay de Mi Alhama

Shortly after sunrise, Aderfi came into the tent they had made available to Indigolin and Hunt the night before, following what Indigolin had declared a sumptuous feast. He poured them cups of mint tea, to make up for the lack of any toothpaste in the unscripted visit, and showed them something in his phone called *Ay de Mi Alhama*.

"What's it mean?" Hunt asked.

"It's the title of a very old ballad. They couldn't sing it for centuries. But now they can sing it today. It's the story of the sack of the Spanish city of Alhama."

"Not the Alhambra?"

"No. It was another citadel close to Granada. Ferdinand's general laid siege to it and it was sacked before Granada; but the siege of Alhama was regarded as a kind of terrible prequel to what happened in Granada. The song itself is a kind of prequel to the events covered by your script. The ballad has a fascinating history. After the anonymous poet had written it and after it had been set to music, an Arab law was enacted, upon pain of death, never to sing it, because when the Moors heard the strains and words of this ballad, they were completely overcome with grief and went into mourning.

"Centuries later, your English poet, Byron, seems to have discovered a copy of the ballad written down during his travels, and he translated it into English, or, more correctly, he mistranslated it. It then found its way back into the Arab world through Byron's mistranslation, and it's now been covered by a great many modern bands and singers. By the way, here is the latest, consolidated version of the script for you."

Aderfi handed Hunt Badiss' updated script. "The song is the ballad of the Moorish king who lost Alhama and it leads up to Boabdil losing Granada. It's very haunting. Very sad. I propose we use it as the opening soundtrack for the film. And I propose that it is sung by Celia Broadsword. She has such a deep, sensuous voice. I don't know why she hasn't been asked to sing in any of her films before. This will be a first. *Ay de Mi Alhama* is anonymous. No copyright issues. Here—"

Aderfi called up a version of the ballad on YouTube.

"Here it is being performed by the band, Mediterrenea. It's just as I said. Five hundred years ago, you could have been beheaded for singing this. Now, it's the staple of boy bands, and I think it should be the soundtrack for our film."

Indigolin noted the use of the possessive noun. *The Gate of the Burnt One* was now openly being acknowledged as *our* film. He could see that these guys were going to be a pushover. It might end up costing Metcalfe Insurance Specialists five million dollars, but he was getting a free script and a newly-discovered leading man for gratis, and possibly also the score for the film.

Aderfi pressed the play button on his phone and passed it to Colman. It was three and a half minutes long, and he listened to the end. Then he handed back the phone and said:

"You're right, Aderfi. It's exquisite. It's haunting. It was made for our script. What do the words mean?"

"The last verses translate as:

And as these things the old Moor said
They severed from the trunk his head;
And to the Alhambra's wall with speed
'Twas carried, as the King decreed.
Woe is me, Alhama!

And from the windows o'er the walls
The sable web of mourning falls;
The King weeps as a woman o'er
His loss, for it is much and sore.
Woe is me, Alhama!"

Colman looked down at the updated script in his hand. He turned the pages. The first page of his new script was the *Dramatis Personae*. None of the characters had been redacted, but a number of new names had been added, such as Zoraya. The next page marked the beginning of the shooting script. Virtually every line had been scored through in red and rewritten by Badiss in neat but tiny hand. And every line was an immeasurable improvement on what had been there before.

"I can't believe this!" Hunt cried. "How can you do this? It's amazing. It reads like poetry."

"It's nothing." Aderfi explained. "The kid has just done it from a Moorish point of view. Many of his sources are poetry, as there are many old ballads. His principal source is an anonymous contemporary Arabic chronicle from the fifteenth century known as *The Nubdhat*. The conceit of our script is that Ferdinand and Isabella didn't drive Boabdil out of Granada in January 1492. Instead, our conceit is that Boabdil drove out the Christian Kings and the previous eight hundred years of Spanish hegemony over Spain continued, and then the Moors expanded from their base in Spain and conquered the rest of Europe.

"It's a nice idea, but if the audience are going to swallow it, you have to lay down some foundations so that you achieve what we call *willing suspension of disbelief*. I think that Badiss has achieved that, and now the script speaks with more authority. Also your script lacked a huge opening. You need to grab your viewers from the beginning. We are living in the days of the download. Kids have a very short attention span. If you don't carry them away in the first twenty seconds, they'll switch to another channel. I think we've done that for you now."

"Who's Zoraya?"

"Zoraya? It's Hebrew for *Lamp*. She was the most beautiful and also the most manipulative woman of the time, a Spanish Christian who converted to Islam and with whom Boabdil's father was so infatuated that he completely lost his judgment, and also his wife, Boabdil's mother. The boy's added in some love interest and some plots and scheming for you. Evil Grand Viziers, that sort of thing."

Colman continued to turn the pages. His mouth was open in disbelief as he read the lines and imagined the scenes playing out.

"Listen to this!" He instructed the others, reading his own lines from the script: *"Better to be a camel-driver in the African Sahara than a swineherd in Castile!"*

"He's saying that it's better for the Berbers to have independence, leading simple lives in Africa than mix with the pork-eating Spaniards," explained Aderfi.

"Yes, I get that. But I didn't realise your people played a part in this story."

"The Berbers," explained Aderfi, "have unfortunately been exploited throughout history. They were very religious and very gullible. The thing about zealots is that holy men can turn them on and off like switches with a mere word. The conquest of Andalusia was initiated by Berber tribes from Africa led by Tarik. The Berbers were the first people to accept Islam, and they accepted it with an undivided zeal and loyalty, and they followed orders."

Hunt read on: *El ultimo sospiro de Moro.* "Of course! The Moor's last sigh. That must be where Salman Rushdie got the title of his book from!"

"Correct, Mr Hunt, when Boabdil stood at the spur of the Alpuxarras mountains with his mother, Ayesha, taking a last tearful look at the Paradise he had lost."

"The arms thereon of Aragon they with Castile display
One king comes in triumph—one weeping goes away."

"It's haunting," Colman pronounced.

"Mr Hunt, Mr Indigolin, I told you, we don't expect anything for nothing. I told you we'd make a contribution."

"Well, Aderfi," was all Hunt could say. "I'm just speechless at what you've done, and what the lad, Badiss has achieved, and it's just totally amazing that Celia Broadsword has been in films for more than six decades, but this will be the first time she's ever sung."

Or got her kit off.
Or been kidnapped.
Or been raped.

Ay de Mi Alhama!

Crossbow Purchase

Posthumous haggled with the metalworker in the souk. There were all sorts of weapons, but most of them were for mounting on the wall of your den, rather than lethal combat. He had his eye on a crossbow. Despite having been artificially aged to look like an antique, he figured it could still kill someone.

"What do you reckon?" He asked his brother.

"OK, if you're auditioning for *Game of Thrones*," was Presley's reply.

"Ah yes," mused Posthumous. "The dwarf puts a crossbow bolt through the heart of his own father—"

"Whilst he's sitting on the john," completed Presley.

"What's good for the goose is good for the gander!" Posthumous exclaimed. "So if one can kill one's own father with a crossbow, one should be able to kill one's brother."

Posthumous picked up a dagger. It had a richly decorated pommel and handle, and there was Arabic shit written all up and down each side of the blood gutters. "Wonder what it means?" He asked, holding it up to the light.

"Probably means *Don't touch*!" His brother answered.

"Nasrid Jineta," explained the shopkeeper. "Genuine fifteenth century as used by Sultan Boabdil."

"Shit!" said Posthumous to the shopkeeper. "I didn't know you spoke English."

"It was Charles Dance," grinned the shopkeeper, "sitting on the john."

Posthumous caught the eye of the vendor, looking him up and down. "Like this?" He asked, and he drew his arm holding the dagger back, as if preparing it for an overarm throw.

"No, no," said the shopkeeper. "No spear. No throw. Weapon only good for close combat!" He mimicked a stabbing in contradistinction to a throwing.

"I think," said Presley, "he's saying that if you want to throw a projectile you need to buy one of those pikes." He gestured towards a collection of spears and grisly arrowheads mounted in a wheel pattern on the wall. None of them was short enough to even fit in the pick-up.

"Kind of lacks the element of surprise," said Posthumous. "I think we'll just take the crossbow, mister. Is it accurate?" He asked.

"Not good for a fast moving target, sir. But okay if he's going to be sitting on the john."

"How many bolts it come with?"

The shopkeeper showed him the two bolts that were fitted into the wooden handle.

"Suppose we want four bolts?" Posthumous asked.

"You have to buy two crossbows," answered the shopkeeper.

The Third Crusade

By the light of the camp fire, Colman read the outline out loud.

"The date is 1191; the scene outside the port city of Acre. The setting is the Third Crusade. Richard the Lionheart, Head of the Christian forces, comes face to face with Saladin, Head of the Muslim forces, and the two of them enter into a now famous comparison of whose sword is best.

The scene is set in Saladin's bed chamber.

Taking his broadsword between his two chain-mailed gauntlets, Richard brings the broadsword down with such force that it sunders the huge bedhead and the whole bed collapses in two at their feet.

Not to be undone, Saladin, dressed only in Moorish skirts, unsheathes his scimitar. Just then a slave girl tosses a near-weightless silk yellow handkerchief in some versions, (a yellow silk scarf in others), up into the air. As it drifts slowly down, spinning like a sycamore seed, whilst it is still in mid-air, Saladin slices it cleanly in half with his razor-sharp scimitar."

"Yes," said Colman. "I've finished reading that bit."

"And what do you think?" Badiss asked.

"I think it's three centuries too early," observed Indigolin.

"Doesn't matter, Mr Hunt. We are just looking for constant comparisons between the east and the west, and some of the old ones are still the best. We transpose it, so that you, playing Ferdinand, bear the broadsword, and Boabdil bears the scimitar. And we play the scene out in Europe somewhere, not Acre."

"Where is Acre, anyway?"

"It's lies in what is now known as Israel, Mr Hunt."

"But people will know that it didn't happen, Baddy!"

"Mr Hunt, it never happened anyway. Saladin and Richard's armies fought together, but it's very clear, the two of them never met face to face, let alone engaged in a sword comparison website. It's just a neat east-west metaphor, like the cross and the scimitar. Kids aren't taught proper history these days. No-one will know any the better. After all, the entire conceit of our film is a lie, a lovely lie. Here we are just embroidering the lie a little bit."

"But people will remember seeing that scene in the film, you know, the Rex Harrison film with Virginia Mayo and George Sanders."

"Mr Hunt, that film was made in 1954. No-one who has ever seen it is still alive."

"Careful, son. I am."

"Please, just read the lines I've put in your mouth, Mr Hunt, right after that scene. I'm sure you'll see it my way."

Outside, night time: Ferdinand walking on the battlements.

FERDINAND: *Come, let us march against the powers of heaven,*
             And set black streamers in the firmament,
             To signify the slaughter of the gods.
             In chapters of fire across the charcoal dome
             Shone the words: Deus imperat astris.

Indigolin, who recognised some of the words as having been cannibalised, chuckled and commented: "Something old, something new, something borrowed, something blue!" Placing the emphasis on *Borrowed*.

Colman looked up from his reading.

"Wow!" He said. "Can anyone tell me what it all means?"

"Doesn't matter what it means," said Indigolin. "What matters is what it sounds like, and what it looks like. Aderfi, you're coming back with me, because I want you playing my Boabdil alongside Colman's Ferdinand in this, what did the lad call it?"

"*The Gate of the Burnt One*, sir," said Badiss.

"Right. Baddy, you stay here for the time being please, and keep doing what you do best. Aderfi, you're on the payroll now. I'll recompense the lad with an *honorarium* of $5M for the script, or the ransom, or however you prefer to write it up in your books. *Quantum meruit*, whatever! Aderfi, no more sleeping under gabardines for you. I'm taking you to the Riyadh Chay, and we'll get you suited and booted and introduced to the rest of the cast as the new Jean Reno."

"How are you going to smuggle him onto the set?" Colman asked.

"Don't worry about it, shill. I'm becoming an expert at it. I'll hide him in plain sight. It's what everybody expects of me, a new fad. I go to Atlas Film

Studios one day and come back the next with a new protégé on my arm, like he was a man bag or some sort of an accessory. It's already the middle of the night. We'll wend our way back across the desert. Aderfi's a Berber, so he can show me the way in the dark. Colman will have to stay here until you guys have banked your *Quantum meruit*. I'll bring Aderfi Ben Julian from the Riyadh and onto set tomorrow and show him off after Wally's yoga session. Not so much the Big Sleep; more the Big Reveal."

Fee-Fi-Fo-Fum

Celia had told Wally about that '*Fee-fi-fo-fum*' thing. How Colman had an uncanny ability always to sniff out his brothers. *Suppose,* Wally thought to himself, it was Celia who had been kidnapped by Presley, not Colman. That Presley had kidnapped Colman was simply Indigolin's theory that Indigolin had evolved before anyone realised that Celia had also gone missing. But suppose it was Celia that was Presley's mark. Then Presley would have to come back and neutralise Colman, because otherwise Colman would be able to use his '*Fee-fi-fo-fum*' thing to figure out where Presley was hanging out with Celia.

This theory was superficially attractive; but it didn't fit in with Presley's *modus operandi*, which was to attempt to do away with Colman, rather than use him for financial gain. But what had Kid Ransom said? You couldn't expect people like that to play by the Queensbury Rules. Presley could take the ransom and then murder his brother anyway. Wally tried to put such thoughts out of his head. Colman wasn't Wally's worry. Wally's concern was with Celia.

Wally had given up on the door-to-door enquiries amongst people most of whom spoke little or no English. He had tried playing at being his own detective, thrusting photos of his fiancée under the noses of individuals who thought they were being invited to participate in a game of identifying famous film stars, rather than a missing person's investigation.

After they had correctly said *Celia Broadsword*, they all had their hands out, expecting a monetary reward. He had gone into town and purchased a Moroccan Ordnance Survey map on scale 1/100,000. He had stuck a pin in *La Gazelle d'Or*, which was her last positive sighting, and each day he patrolled the skies in ever increasing concentric circles from that fixed point. What he was looking for was a black Range Rover.

Riyadh Chay

Elena located the Riyadh and parked outside, a little way off. It was ten o clock at night. She had a full moon to help her navigate. The Riyadh was entirely wrapped around with those pisé walls, about nine foot high; not exactly a fortress, but not a doddle to climb over either. The good news was that Elena figured, once she had managed to scale the walls, if the layout was like other Riyadhs she'd visited, it would all be open courtyards and open rooms leading off them, so after the wall, there shouldn't be any locked doors to worry about.

Having walked all around the Riyadh and established that, whilst there was an abundance of trees inside the walled garden, there were no convenient trees outside the walls that she might use to climb into the garden, she went back to the car, parked it as close to the back wall as she could, climbed up on the bonnet, from the bonnet onto the roof, and jumped into the Riyadh, cushioning her tablet to her chest, and rolling with the fall. She figured she'd work out how to get out again when she'd found what she was looking for. Maybe, now that she was in, she could even leave through the front door.

She was in the garden. In front of her was one of those reflecting bassins, not deep enough to swim in, unless you were a fish, just ornamental. It was illuminated by lanterns spaced equidistantly around its edges, and more lanterns illuminated the path leading to the open glazed doors of the house.

For a moment, she felt quite intoxicated: it was the perfume of the garden, as if she'd walked through the wardrobe into a parallel world of olfactory sensation. The heady scent of the night stocks with a high note of verbena, the jasmine and honeysuckle, clinging to the walls. Fig trees, the yellow pom poms of the climbing mimosa, Jerusalem Thorn, Pomegranate, almond trees, cherry trees, splayed roses, the powerful white fragrance of the plant the French call *galants de nuit*.

But most of all (how could she have been as blind as not to have guessed?) the luminous blue of the jacaranda trees dominated the perimeter. As if Tinctorio

Indigolin would stay in a house without that unearthly blue tincture. There was plenty of cover for her in the garden. The stratospheric vertical lines of the palm trees breaking the horizon counterpointed the horizontal planes of the different surfaces of the Riyadh.

The lanterns were candle lanterns. Someone must have lit the candles. Then she saw figures moving in the dim lighting inside the Riyadh. How could she have been so stupid? Tinctorio Indigolin wouldn't rent a house on his own! Of course, he'd have staff! She kept out of sight behind the pseudostems of a clump of banana trees whilst she counted the number of hired hands he had in the Riyadh.

They were wearing white robes with red toques on their heads, and as far as she could make out there were only two of them, both male. Presumably, one was the guy who had lit all the candles in the lanterns, and maybe the other was a cook or housekeeper. Presumably, further people turned up in the morning to clean the house and make the beds; take away his laundry. Did he dry clean his blue legume suits, she wondered, or was it just money he laundered?

She was startled by the strident call of the Muezzin for night time prayers. She turned in the direction of the sound and saw a far-off minaret from whose loudspeaker the recording was playing. Turning her gaze to the illuminated doll's house of the Riyadh, she observed the two staff unroll their prayer mats and prostrate themselves on the kitchen floor, facing the east, and that was the moment she grasped to make her entrance into the house from the west.

The floors and stairs were all marble, so she was able to move around without having to worry about creaking wooden floorboards, but as the sole means of illumination was the light from all the candles, she had to be very careful about which direction she cast her shadow.

There were rooms leading off the reception area, and she crept into the room that Indigolin must be using as his study. The room was furnished in beautiful fruitwood marquetry. His PC was on the table. She pushed the study door to and by the light of her phone opened the desk drawers until she found what she had come for, the DataTraveler. She had been correct in assuming that he wouldn't want to take something as important as that on an impromptu trip into the unknown, accompanying Colman Hunt across the desert.

She snapped open her tablet and booted it up. She had assumed that she wouldn't be able to figure out the password on any PC's Indigolin may have in the Riyadh, although they were bound to be something to do with Blue, so she'd decided that she'd bring her own tablet. But it was taking an inordinate time to boot up. She realised she had absolutely no idea how long night time prayers lasted, after which the two house staff could start prowling around, performing whatever their evening duties were.

Eventually, the tablet booted up, displaying her familiar screensaver of Cenote Angelita in Tulum, the underwater shot she had captured herself at a depth of 30 metres at the point where the hydrogen sulphate layer separated the fresh water and salt water like a phantasmagorical blue cocktail; Something that the present occupier of the Riyadh she had just illegally entered, would very much appreciate, she thought.

She put her password in, waited for the screen to populate itself, shoved the DataTraveler into the USB port of her device, and began copying its contents to her desktop. Fortunately, the stick wasn't encrypted. The green bar started moving across the screen and to her horror an alarm made a very loud ping as an announcement popped up. She'd forgotten to mute the device, but she did so now.

The announcement said that it was going to take about 2 minutes to complete the copying operation. She waited with bated breath bathed in the blue light from her phone and joining in the Muezzin's prayers with a few prayers of her own; but just as the 2 minutes were almost completed, the message corrected itself and announced that it was now going to take another 3 minutes. There was nothing she could do. She turned off the phone to extinguish its light and save the battery, and she waited for the copying to complete.

The prayers had ended, so presumably the staff were moving around the house now. Before she had to wait the full 3 minutes, the display suddenly informed her that it was only going to be about another 90 seconds, and then ten seconds later, that changed to 30 seconds, then 10 seconds, before going back up to 30 seconds again. But eventually the green bar filled the whole box and the copying was completed to her desktop. She closed the tablet, put the Data Traveller back in the drawer, and went to the study door to work out how she was going to make her way out again.

The two men had finished their prayers, and their prayer mats had been shipped away. One man was much taller than the other, at least six foot two, but his toque made him look taller still. They had large daggers hanging from the white rope sashes that served as belts on their robes. She assumed the daggers were primarily ornamental, but they could have other uses.

The whole downstairs of the Riyadh was open plan: there was a huge open courtyard with the other rooms leading off it, but if the staff were working in the kitchen, the kitchen itself was open plan to the dining area that showboated a huge slate table in the middle of the courtyard. She needed to get across the courtyard in order to re-enter the garden.

She ducked back into the study to assess the situation with the window, hoping she might climb up onto the desk and exit through the window; but there was no glazed window. Instead, the light and the breeze came through an open hole decorated with an ornate ironwork screen so that the people inside could see out, but it was difficult for the people outside to see in. She had read that this style of window screen was known as Mashrabiyya, although she referred to them by their less prosaic name of burglar bars. Indigolin's study featured two Mashrabiyya and they were fixed in position. They weren't demountable. They didn't open up like plantation shutters.

The other unfortunate feature of the Mashrabiyya was that there were no curtains for her to hide behind. There were some large items of furniture, but they were all pushed up against the walls, so if she pulled one out to hide behind it, if anyone then entered the study, that the item had been moved would be pretty obvious. There was simply no cover for her. If anyone came into the study, she was fucked. She went back to peer through the crack in the study door.

A ringing sounded out and the tall man produced his mobile phone from a pocket in his white robe and answered it in French: *"Oui, oui!"* And then, "Yes, Mr Indigolin. Of course, Mr Indigolin."

Then he clapped his hands by way of orders to the other man who didn't seem to speak French: *"Yella! Yella!"* and the other guy got busy fetching plates and cutlery and glassware from the kitchen and setting the slate table for two places.

'Shit,' she thought. If Indigolin was on his way back and had a dinner guest with him, she was going to be in for a long and worrisome night.

Through the Mashrabiyya she heard the roar of Indigolin's 12 cylinder Lamborghini Urus approaching and the car doors shutting. At least, she'd concealed her car at the back of the compound.

Now, the familiar figure of Indigolin in his crazy blue legume suit was in the courtyard. He was accompanied by a tall Arab youth in blue robes. Even by the candlelight, she could see he had unnaturally blue eyes.

"Allow me to introduce Aderfi Benjelloun," he said to the staff, "my new Boabdil! Ibrahim, please show him to his room. He can go in the room next to Presley's."

So the big guy was called Ibrahim. Ibrahim went up the staircase followed by the Benjelloun guy. Benjelloun was taller than Ibrahim, and he wasn't even wearing a toque. Everything about the Riyadh was open-plan. Even the staircase was open plan: just stone rungs attached to the side of the wall, not so much as a handrail or bannister to cling to or hide behind.

Indigolin poured himself a large Chivas Regal and came back into the courtyard. Just then there was an almighty commotion, and Indigolin smashed the tumbler down on the slate table and was shouting: "Out! Out! Out!"

The smaller guy came running into the courtyard and started bellowing something in Arabic also and clapping his hands. She didn't know what the problem was, but she grasped the opportunity to get out of the study with her laptop, cross the living space and get through the doors into the garden, where she had cover from the trees. She needed to move quickly before the two tall guys came down from upstairs to join in the commotion.

From behind the trees, she saw what the problem was. A large stork had come down from its nest in the Riyadh's chimneys, and was making a racket flapping its huge wings, trying to hover just high enough above the bassin to get its beak in and make off with the fish without actually getting its feet wet.

Indigolin and the short guy, who was now wielding a broom, did all they could to scare it away, but when it took to the skies, it was bearing a large blue-gold trophy in its beak. At this point, Ibrahim and Benjelloun were back in the courtyard. They must have come down the stairs whilst everybody else, including Elena Troy, was distracted by the stork.

"It's got one of the koi carp, sir!" Ibrahim said.

"Well there goes my deposit!" Indigolin said. And then to Benjelloun: "They're hundreds of years old. Aderfi, can I offer you a drink."

"Just mint tea, please, Mr Indigolin."

They went back from the courtyard to the open living space. Under cover of the darkness, Elena crept round the perimeter wall behind the trees until she found her plantain plantation. That had been easy to slide down, but would be more difficult to climb up. Instead, she made her way round, concealing herself behind carob trees and almond trees, walnuts, willows and date palms and exited via the blue jacaranda tree nearest to where she'd parked the car. She climbed back over the pisé wall onto its roof. She hoped that whatever was copied onto her desktop justified the years she felt she had just taken off her life.

Once back in her room at the Berber Hotel, she used Mimecast to transfer the large file to Agent Anatole Franck back at Bvsh Ho. She couldn't make head or tail of it herself.

When Agent Anatole Franck at Bvsh Ho in London turned on his workstation the next morning, there was an email waiting for him from Elena Troy which said *I'm using Mimecast to share large files*. He clicked on the link, and the program sent him a password. He cut and pasted the password and the download began. It was a huge file, 60GB. For a file that contained no photographs, just hierarchies of letters of the alphabet, numbers, formulae and equations, 60 gigs seemed extraordinarily large.

The Horniman Museum

Still on the topic of large file downloads, Millicent Marcuson continued to pursue the line of enquiry that had begun when her cameraman, Ynes, had spotted the mound of dead bones on Indigolin's screensaver, the mound that had subsequently been identified as bleached coral.

"Fascinating, aren't they?"

The person posing this question was none other than the Deputy Aquatic Curator at the Horniman Museum in South London. She was referring to the seemingly luminous display of barrel jellyfish that Millicent Marcuson was observing behind the reinforced glass of the museum's aquarium. The sight took her back to the meeting when Indigolin had flicked the light switch in his office under the flyover and illuminated his vivarium.

"They're like ballerinas," replied Millicent Marcuson. "I mean, if I went swimming and I found them in the sea, or got stung by one, or found a load of them washed up on the beach, I'd be completely disgusted. But looking at them in an aquarium like this, lit so beautifully, they're simply exquisite, balletic, and elegant. It's as though they were meant to be in captivity, if that doesn't sound too ridiculous."

"Well, I understand where you're coming from. In fact, these ones were indeed all bred in captivity. We grow them here ourselves. It's all done on the premises. We feed them on plankton to get them started, and they're full grown after about 6 months. This species is the Bright Blue from Australia. It has a symbiotic relationship with the algae. The algae feed it and in return it gives the algae a safe place to live."

"And you're the lady in charge of Project Coral."

"I am."

"I wanted to know if you could help me with one question. Is it possible to bring dead coral back to life?"

"Of course it is! Without intervention, such as we're developing here at Project Coral, it's reliably predicted that by 2050, 90% of the world's coral will be dead. You can even grow your own coral. We sell propagator kits in the museum shop, so that children can learn about it. Get them interested in nature early. It's called coral fragging. But what we're doing here in the aquarium is far more advanced. Our team here at the Horniman are world pioneers in the field of in-vitro fertilisation of captive coral reefs. We were the first institution in the world to develop techniques to stimulate coral sexual reproduction."

"My God!" Millicent exclaimed. "I just had no idea that there was any such thing, or that any of this was possible. It just never occurred to me that a coral reef could even have a sex life! Can my producer get in touch with you to see if we can do an awareness-raising sort of a programme on your work?"

"I'd be delighted!"

"And one more question: does the name Tinctorio Indigolin mean anything to you?"

"Of course it does. He's our largest single benefactor. He's donated millions."

"What's his interest?"

"Here at Project Coral, we're focussing on creating synthetic coral in-house to compensate the environment for all the coral that's being bleached by pollutants: we are pioneering techniques for bringing dead coral back to life. But Mr Indigolin's interests go further than that. He doesn't like to go public on it because people might start calling him a Dr Frankenstein or something. But he believes he can regrow amputated limbs using similar techniques. And his initial success with frogs indicates he might be right.

"But there's a lot of work to do bridging the gap between frogs and human beings, if you get my drift. Also, we helped him develop the dye for his Blue Molecule. I mean, the molecule thing is his own, but the colouring isn't natural. We make it from Blue Eagle Eye Zooanthid Coral, so that it's completely harmless when it penetrates the skin, but it's also a living organism."

"With a sex life of its own, as I now know."

"Indeed!"

"So he gets his blue dye from coral!"

"And definitely not from his frogs!"

"How come?"

"The blue dart frog is generally considered the most toxic or poisonous animal on the planet. Proper name: *Dendrobates tinctorius azureus.*"

"Do you have any here, in the aquarium?"

"No, Ms Marcuson, they're far too deadly. But experiments by others tend to show that in captivity, they lose their bright blue colour anyway. They're insectivores and it's thought that the colour and the toxicity come from their diet of insects that have been consuming different poisons from the plants they eat. Generally speaking, if you see anything in nature that's bright blue and isn't a plant, I would give it a very wide berth. Do you have any more questions, Ms Marcuson?"

"Yes, where's the shop? I'd like to buy my son one of those coral fragging kits you mentioned."

Indigolin Debriefed

"They say they want the equivalent of US5m in cryptocurrency or they blow his head off. No if's, no but's. It's the Big Mac or nothing. Tip top!"

Tinctorio Indigolin had planned on rolling out his new protégé, Aderfi Benjoullin, at morning yoga, but he hadn't factored in just how long and tiring the walk back across the desert to Riyadh Chay was, and he had over-slept. He therefore decided to introduce him at sundown drinks that evening outside Aka Akinyola's Umbrella Bar.

There, Indigolin proceeded to show off his new film star, drawing everyone's attention to the colour of his eyes (blue, of course!) and the parallel nature of his forehead and nose.

Indigolin attempted to impart the wisdom that he had acquired from his walk into the desert, only interrupted occasionally by Aderfi who referred to it as *Mr Indigolin's Road to Damascus moment*. He had been gone for thirty-six hours. Kid Ransom, Elena Troy and Noah were gathered round Aka's assortment of fire pits, enjoying the freshly-gathered charcoal in Aka's Umbrella Bar, drinking Casablanca premium lagers straight from the bottles with the green palm trees on the label.

Noah asked his boss if he wanted to join them. Wally hadn't returned yet from his explorations of possible hiding places for Celia. Of course it was all pointless, and he hated flying the chopper after dark; but he'd never have forgiven himself if he felt there was something that he could have done that he hadn't done, or that he might have overlooked an opportunity to achieve some sort of finality.

"Don't like that Casablanca," Indigolin replied in answer to Noah's offer of a beer. "The label looks like it's made from cannabis plants and I don't do drugs. I'll have a Spécial Flag, shill."

Noah went off in search of a Moroccan Spécial Flag beer.

"You're not supposed to do the negotiating, Mr Indigolin. It voids the policy," explained Ransom.

"Who said anything about negotiating, shill? These guys weren't up for a negotiation. As I said. It's Take it or Leave it. I'm just delivering the message so as to save a very weary Colman Hunt having to make another two way march across the Sahara in a suicide vest. The poor guy's on a hair trigger as it is. He's a nervous wreck. One stumble and he could have blown himself to next Tuesday."

"Where did you go?" Elena asked.

"I'll be able to tell you as soon as Noah gets back with that Spécial Flag, Elena. The walk's made me thirsty."

Noah came back with a cool beer. "Don't have no Spécial Flag, boss, but here's a Moroccan Heineken. It's brewed under licence in Fez."

"That'll do, shill." Noah removed the lid and passed it to his boss, who downed the bottle in one, wiped his lips and began his largely mendacious account:

"Well, we must have walked for at least ten miles. Then two guys on quad bikes came over the horizon and bagged our heads up, so we couldn't see where we were being taken to. We had to get on the bikes under gunpoint, and then they drove off for about 30 minutes at speeds I would estimate between 20–30 miles per hour. By the way, we had to get on the bikes backwards so as to further disorientate ourselves; you understand, not hanging on to the drivers, but back to back with them, and hanging onto the grab rail. Very strange sensation!

"Eventually, tired and saddle-sore, we arrive and they take the bags off our heads, and we're in a compound with more than a hundred kidnappers, for sure. They're all living out of tents and lean to's and huddled round fires, just like we are now. Before you ask, I couldn't describe any of them, because they were all wearing blue robes like Colman was, but they've got the robes pulled up over their faces."

"Berbers," pronounced Kid.

"Or kidnappers wanting you to believe they are Berbers," declared Elena. "Can't be very hard to lay your hands on some blue robes."

"—Unless, of course, they happen to be blue legume robes, my dear," qualified Indigolin.

"Then what happened?"

"The guy who was their spokesman, medium height with a funny eye, came up to me and said *Cool threads, man* in a cut-glass English accent, like he'd been to Eton and Harrow. For which compliment I thanked him. He didn't know who

I was, but he asked what I was doing there, as Colman had been told to come alone. I said that I was just there for moral support and along for the ride. They gave me a mint tea for my trouble.

"Having refreshed me, he told me to tell whoever I reported to that if they wanted to see Colman Hunt in one piece again, we'd have to come up with US5m in non-traceable bitcoins, and that figure was up for negotiation, as long as we didn't mind it going up, because it wasn't ever going to be coming down in a month of Sundays. Then he said I could either walk back like Colman in a suicide vest, or I could get bagged up again and they'd give me a lift part of the way on the quadbike, and point me in the right direction, which is the option I took.

"I then did another half hour of dune-bashing with my head in a sick bag before the driver pulled it off and showed me the distant lights of downtown Ouarzazate. I walked the rest of the way to my Riyadh and got some shut-eye. In the morning, I drove past Atlas Film Studios and discovered my new protégée, Aderfi Ben Julian; but we're working on another name for him; and here I am."

"Were they armed?" Kid asked.

"The kidnappers? To the teeth. AK 47's and spare cartridge belts criss-crossed across their chests, Ché Guevara style."

"Was he for real, boss?" Noah asked. "I thought he was just a motivational speaker."

"They also had satellite phones, cell phones with net, and a sophisticated remote detonator device for Colman's gillet."

"Would you recognise the spokesman's voice again, Mr Indigolin?" Kid asked.

"Quite possibly, shill."

"If we put a bag over your head and drove you into the desert, would you know the way again?" Elena asked.

"They wouldn't be there again, Elena. They would just up sticks and disappear. Probably already have. They could move on like the caravan, or they could split up into twenty different cells, and we wouldn't know which one Colman was in."

"We could put the photographic drones up in the morning and take a look," said Noah.

"If you want to get your expensive drones used for target practice, shill."

"Anything else?" Kid queried. "They demand a jumbo jet or pizzas or anything?"

"As a matter of fact they did, shill. They need paper."

"Paper?"

"Writing paper, same as Colman asked for, but Colman couldn't carry enough just by himself."

"To write their ransom demands on?" Kid queried.

"No, shill. He says that they're the guys who are rewriting the script for us, but it's going to come at a cost of US $5M, and Colman Hunt will be returned to us intact, as it were, as a bonus. Their USP was that we're not being asked to pay US $5M for a ransom demand; we're paying for a new script."

"We didn't write a policy of insurance that's responsive to needing to rewrite your script, Mr Indigolin."

"Yeah, yeah! I get all that, shill. It's just their way of putting it. With these Arabs, it's all face-saving. So, rather than steal from us, which is what we all know they're actually doing, they like to pretend they're selling us something that we need in return. We're looking at a kidnapping situation, but they like to package it up as some sort of an arms-length business arrangement. Like when your car's stuck at the traffic lights on Vauxhall Bridge and the Romanian economic migrant, armed with a squeegee and a bucket of brown slops, demands money to clean your windscreen."

"OK. I get it," said Kid. "This isn't an arms-length sale of a script."

"They also said No funny business and no police, or Colman gets executed, and they said that they'd film the execution, and that their film would be watched by more fans than ever watched one of Colman Hunt's serious films."

"Sounds like a very serious film to me," said Elena.

"They said," Indigolin improvised to Elena, "that his acting had shown early promise, but all his mature performances were, how did they put it? Hammed-up juvenilia—but that when they bumped him off for real and filmed it with their phones, that would be the best performance he'd put in since *Ordeal by Fire*. At which point I said that *Ordeal by Fire* wasn't a performance actually, because it was for real. But the bloke with the funny eye poo-poo'd the idea, and said I was off my wheeler-basket."

"So where do we go from here?" asked Noah.

"We let them stew for a day or two," said Kid. "Show them we're in no hurry. You agree anything too quick, the price will just go up. I mean, we're dealing with murderers and pirates. We can't expect them not to renege on any deal we shake on if they think they can slice a better one."

"As long as they don't start slicing bits off Colman in the meantime, shill. Just remember that the studio has an economic interest in Colman Hunt, the same as the insurers do, and if I find that our investment is, how shall we say, diminished, because insurers are dragging their heels trying to get the price down, I'll sue insurers for the diminution in my asset. Mr Hunt was on my books before he came on yours. I expect this to be wrapped up in the next 24 hours."

A Gentlemen's Agreement

Tinctorio Indigolin didn't have his own trailer. He preferred to come and go, sampling 5 star hotels, or rent a Riyadh, rather than be cooped up in some VW camper on steroids. So this afternoon, we find him sitting in the cosy interior of Wally's Woodie-Wagon, wearing a cerulean Gossypium chemise and sipping a long drink of Cava and Blue Curacao by the light of a goose-necked lamp that illuminated hallmarks of homicidal intent towards the wagon's only other occupant.

"You did what?" He repeated.

"I cut it out, Ti. That's what directors do."

"But the bit you cut out, shill, is the *raison d'etre* of the entire film! You get that?"

"Ti, it was maybe the *raison d'etre* of another film. But we're not shooting that film any more. We've got a meaningful movie now, deep, thought-provoking. I'm shooting a proper film. The scene that I cut had no artistic integrity with the movie I'm making."

"Put it back, shill. That's an order."

"I'm afraid I can't do that even if I wanted to."

"Why not? Restore it. Take it out of your deleted items. Go search in your Trash Can and put it back, Wally. Retrieve your *raison d'etre.*"

"Mr Indigolin, I don't do digital. It was celluloid. I cut it, and I burnt it."

"You'll have to shoot it again."

"Celia's contract required her to do it. She's done it. My contract gives me complete artistic hegemony, and I've exercised it. And besides, Celia's disappeared."

"I paid US $5M for that scene, shill."

"I appreciate that, Ti, and I've thought about that. And this is what I'm going to do. I'm going to cut you a cheque now for $5M."

"And why would you do that, shill?"

"Because I'm a reasonable man, Ti, and I have my reputation to think of."

"Shill, I only paid her US $5M, because I was advised the scene would bring me in US $50m at the box office."

"Well, I'll tell you what else I'll do. If the film, as I cut it and shoot it, doesn't bring you in US $50m at the box office in the first 10 days, I'll give you another US $10M on top of the US $5M."

"What about the other US $35m, shill?"

"Ti, I can only give you what I've got. I don't have another US $35m."

"So you're risking everything you have so that the public don't get to see that scene?"

"I guess you could look at it that way."

"She really has cast her spell over you, hasn't she, Wally?"

"I guess you could look at it that way."

"Well give me your hand, shill, and we'll shake on that, because I find it strangely refreshing to stare some genuine emotion in the eye when I'm surrounded by so much tinseltown *tromp l'œiul*, and when I'm wading waist deep in insincerity, sycophancy, hypocrisy and pretence all day long. You're like a breath of fresh air, shill. Top shelf!"

He downed the Blue Curacao and extended his palm, which was grasped by Wally.

WMD

Elena Troy hadn't smoked since she was a student, but she had resumed smoking now as it gave her an excuse to step outside and make her private phone calls. She walked what she considered to be a safe distance from the trailers and put a call through to Agent Franck. The fact was that if she made her calls to Bvsh Ho on set, there was the danger of blowing her cover, but if she tried to make the call any further from the set than the safe distance, there was no net anyway. Taking up smoking gave her an excuse to go that distance.

"Anatole?"

"Hi Elena. How's the weather in the desert today?"

"*Plus ça change*, Anatole. What did you make of the file I sent you?"

"Not a lot I'm afraid. It's written in another language."

"You mean like a foreign language?"

"No, Elena. I mean that it seems to be written in machine code. It's a set of instructions from one machine to a much larger machine for the much larger machine to execute certain functions, perform certain orders that are given to it by the smaller machine, but it's not written in any programming language anyone here has been able to identify."

"You mean Tinctorio Indigolin has evolved his own language?"

"No, the machines have been designed to talk to one another. The first machine will simply be a PC or small computer device. Could just be an iPad or something like that. The small device is giving elaborate and complex instructions to the big device."

"How big are we talking about, Anatole?"

"We're talking about a machine the size of a football pitch, Elena, maybe bigger."

The line went quiet for a while, and Anatole, who was used to people phoning him from difficult locations, thought he'd dropped the call; but it was simply Elena trying to assimilate all the possibilities in her head.

"I'm just wondering where Indigolin would even keep a device that size. When I was going through the accounts, one of his companies, called Deep Blue Rif, has a storage unit of 0.9 hectares. That's a football pitch, isn't it?"

"A football pitch and some, Elena. I'm just Googling here and FIFA says a football pitch should be between 0.62 and 0.82 hectares. Where is this storage unit?"

"It was on Mahé in the Seychelles, Anatole. There isn't anything else I've seen in the books big enough to hide something as big as what you're looking for. But what are we looking for?"

"WMD, Elena."

"Weapons of Mass Destruction? Jeez!"

"A fucking great dirty bomb!"

"But that doesn't make sense, Anatole. In terms of profiling, the guys a billionaire. Why would he want to throw all that away and become a terrorist?"

"Why don't you ask Osama bin Laden that question, Elena? He was a billionaire. The fact is that we've been chasing this Blue Molecule guy down because we think he's laundering money, but, as it happens money laundering and terrorism are normally very comfortable bedfellows. But now that you've mentioned the Seychelles, everything's just moved up a notch."

"How come?"

"Well, the Seychelles are very famous playgrounds of the wealthy. World's finest beaches, clearest turquoise waters (although I hear most of the coral's dead by now), and good health care because the population consists of UHNY individuals. But they are also very famous for not asking too many questions about where those UHNY individuals get their money from. You can buy a US $20m residence with a bag of cash there, and you buy your citizenship in the same transaction."

"A bag of cash, huh, Anatole? Or bitcoins?"

"That would seem to follow."

"So where do we go from here, Anatole?"

"I've passed the file over to MI6. Can you get me the address of that storage unit in the Seychelles?"

"Sure."

A Price Reduction

Posthumous and Presley were sat on the terrace at Kasbah Toubkal. They were drinking mint teas, but when no-one was looking, they cut them with Arak. The effect was like brushing your teeth with 40 proof alcoholic toothpaste.

"Did you read that pamphlet in the room about how long it took them to build this fucking hotel?" Posthumous asked his brother.

"I did, and what's the fucking point? They had to drag all of the materials up here by donkey, just so they could be at the summit of the highest mountain in Morocco, and now they've done it—" He made a gesture taking in his surroundings.

"Now they've done it," continued his brother, Presley, "it's so fucking high up that all you can see is fucking clouds and no fucking views."

"Plus it's freezing cold!" Presley added, wrapping closer around himself the itchy rugs the proprietors had thoughtfully scattered around the terrace for the greater comfort of their customers. "And half the time it's pissing with rain, cos we're so high up that we're like sitting inside a damp, pregnant raincloud. I'd rather be back in the Sahara Desert!"

"I mean, there's the Hammam," continued Posthumous. "But you can only spend so long in the Hammam before you're totally dehydrated, and then, once you've come out, you just feel colder than ever."

"And worst of all," added his brother, "is the total fucking lack of two things."

"Alcohol," said Posthumous.

"And Wi-Fi," said Presley.

"So whose turn is it to walk to the bottom of the fucking mountain and the Internet café?" Posthumous asked.

"We'd better toss for it," said Presley.

"I'll be tails," claimed Posthumous.

Presley flicked a dirham, caught it on the back of his hand and revealed it.

"Which side's heads and which is tails?" Posthumous asked.

"No fucking idea!" Presley said.

"Best of three?" Posthumous offered.

Once it had become apparent that Posthumous had kidnapped Presley and not Colman, they had wondered how long they could maintain the illusion that they actually had Colman. They had decided that, rather than simply abort the abduction, having come this far, they might as well brazen it out and let it run for a while longer; see how it all developed. These things sometimes assumed a momentum of their own.

However, as time was not their friend, they would offer a price reduction for a quick and dirty deal. They were minded to offer a reduction to £0.5m, but, coming down from £1m. to £0.5m, when the other side hadn't yet made any counter-offer, seemed to be lacking in credibility, so they had decided to go in at £0.75m, leaving the studio the option to revert at £0.5m, and then maybe split the difference, whatever that came to. The only detail that remained to be thrashed out was which one of them was going to have to *schlepp* down Mount Toubkal to the Internet café and send off the next email from abduct@snatch.ma. offering the generous reduction.

Presley was annoyed with himself for not taking this possibility into account last time he had made his way to the Internet café at the base of the mountain. When he was there, he could have devised a Voucher with some spurious code, and made it part of the ransom demand, so that now, when they were contemplating a price reduction, he could just follow up with another e mail, to the effect of Got a Voucher?

And then the studio could just click on the voucher and it would say that the voucher could be redeemed for a 25% reduction, but was only valid for today. That would have been a more credible way of communicating the fire sale.

New Kid on the Block

The next time Tinctorio Indigolin drove his Urus from the Riyadh to the set, to take part in the director's sunrise yoga session, he embroidered upon the backstory of his protégé, Aderfi, after the brief teaser-trailer at the Umbrella Bar the night before. He explained to anyone who wanted to listen that Aderfi, his protégé, standing by his side, was the man who was going to play Boabdil, not Boabdil el Chico; not Boabdil el Zogoibi, but Boabdil the First Sultan of the Islamic State of Europe. Indigolin fired the scriptwriters and sent them back to England, saying that he preferred to rely on the services of the absentee twelve-year-old Badiss in their place.

Needless to say, these new acquisitions were not linked in any way to the kidnapping of Colman Hunt. The cover story was that, as his stars kept disappearing, and as it was costing him a fortune keeping everyone on set and not getting any film in the can, he, Tinctorio Indigolin, had taken matters into his own hands, and was effecting local hires that also enabled him to blow some of the dirhams they'd bought at the top of the market.

Indigolin had Brunswick Holt's Airstream sanitised and all the mementos of its distinguished former inhabitant boxed up, and Aderfi was installed there as his new star. Brunswick Holt's former caravan still had nearly three months left to run on its lease, and it had all mod cons. Just as Mr Indigolin had pointed out, an air-conditioned Airstream was a step up from sleeping under a gabardine in the Sahara.

Having thus reshuffled his cabinet, Indigolin went up to Kid Ransom and asked him how he was progressing in having his leading man and lady returned to the set, because he had a film to shoot.

The Umbrella Bar

"Shall we continue this conversation in the Umbrella Bar?"

"The Umbrella Bar?" Indigolin queried. "I mean, I know what you're referring to. I just didn't know it had an official title now."

"The Umbrella Bar," confirmed Wally Pfister. "Our cook, Aka Akinyola—she's Nigerian. She's a no-nonsense, down-to-earth type of lady, so she has us refer to her as *cook* even though she's a fully accredited Michelin-starred chef. She used to run a restaurant in Los Angeles, but she had so many A-listers, stars and assorted celebrities beating a path to her door, she decided to join them. She sold up and reinvented herself as a location chef, so she could immerse herself completely in this world of shallow, narcissistic ephemera.

"I wouldn't blame you if you mistook her for Grace Jones in *A View to a Kill*. Ebony skin; high cheekbones, and she keeps a lot of herself, including her face, wrapped up in blue robes like a Berber. She moves with a poise and self-confidence that's really something else. Is the word for it *gamine*? Although it would never have occurred to you that you could think in the abstract that she was your kind of woman, once you've come face to face with Aka, you start thinking to yourself that it wouldn't really be so bad to spend your days with a girl like that. She gives your preconceptions a reboot."

"Jesus, Wally!" Indigolin exclaimed. "Your's is a really broad church, isn't it? One minute you've got the hots for an 85-year-old diva; the next minute, you're drooling over Bloody Mary in South Pacific! Where does an umbrella fit into all of this?"

"Aka didn't like the actors on set just turning up to her counter for self-service and taking their tagines back to eat in their tents. She tried to create a communal, collegiate destination where people could have water-cooler moments even though we don't have a water-cooler. She believes that everything tastes better if it's cooked in the open over wood. She's got every kind of barbecue you could imagine: Hibachis, Ceramic Eggs, Weber, Mexican firepits, Gaucho

Grill, Argentinian Crucifixion, and she set up all these wooden tables and chairs outside.

"She planted an herb garden, a kitchen garden, a vegetable plot, and a rose garden; she's laid irrigation; but obviously it was still too hot to sit there shooting the breeze, so she invested in these giant Heineken umbrellas. They'd been made for some shoot and were still adorning the Atlas Film Studios. She planted them in the sand and hey presto! You've got the Umbrella Bar. So if anybody has a problem, they go to the Umbrella Bar, have a beer and think it over."

"Well, we've certainly got no shortage of problems, Wally. We'd better repair to the Umbrella Bar."

They had been walking as they talked and, as if on cue, the Umbrella Bar materialised like an oasis in the desert. Edgar Ash was already there, sipping a beer and nursing an unsmoked cigarette, and had caught the end of the conversation. Ash was trying to quit smoking. So he would light a cigarette and then just hold it very still, seeing if he could create a pillar of ash all the way down to the filter without it falling off. Of course he never succeeded.

"She's writing an illustrated book," Ash informed Indigolin and Pfister. "On the Hollywood stars and their weird eating habits, the dishes she's devised for each one of us. You know how we're all faddies and foodies. Like the guy who wants omelettes but only made of eggshells. Then there's the Veganarians."

"A Veganarian?" Indigolin queried.

"Only eats vegans!" Ash joked.

Aka Akinyola came out from her tent wearing blue Moroccan robes. Looking at her, Indigolin understood Wally's description. She certainly didn't conform to his blueprint of the perfect woman, but when you studied her, somehow or other, you did end up thinking this was a pretty good alternative. Even concealed in her blue robes, she exuded sex appeal, but somehow combined that with looking really wholesome. It was like reading the pages of Mrs Beeton's Book of Household Management and finding you'd got a hard-on.

"Mr Indigolin, I presume?" Aka said, a broad smile lighting up her face, which was the only part of her that was visible.

"Aka Akinyola, cook to the stars, I presume?" replied Indigolin. "You're dressed as a Berber."

"I like to blend in. What are you gents needing?" She asked the two needy-looking newcomers.

"I guess we'd better have Heinekens," said Indigolin. "Why so many cook-outs?"

"Each one has different properties," Aka explained. "But the most important ingredient is the right sort of charcoal. The stuff you buy in sacks from the gas station or supermarket is shit. It's all pumped up with additives just like chlorinated chicken is. They bulk it all up before they bag it. They douse it with propellant to make it easy to light, but then, as they're going to be transporting it in big quantities; they douse it again in retardant, to stop it accidentally bursting into flames when it's in the container. That's why, when the customer opens the bag and puts it on the barbecue, it won't light.

"So they have to add firelighters and any inflammable stuff that's to hand, such as polystyrene packaging balls, accelerants, some people even chuck gasoline on. The end result is an oily, chemical film on your cold, shrunken sausage."

"I know that feeling!" Wally exclaimed.

"Too much overshare," pronounced Indigolin.

"So what charcoal do you prefer to use?" Indigolin asked her, at the same time asking himself why he was making inane small talk about charcoal with his employee when he had so many more important things to think about.

"Fresh charcoal, Mr Indigolin. If I've got time, I go down to the edge of the forest and burn my own." she said. "If time's at a premium, or if there's no forest, I'd use Australian Fire Beads."

"Good to know Australia has some use!" Wally said. "Someone had better pass on the good news to Noah!"

"Shit!" Edgar Ash cried as the grey cylinder from the end of his fag fell off into the sand.

"The secret is to use a grill with a lid and apply indirect heat," Aka continued. "You've got to get the coals burning at 300 degrees Celsius, but the last thing you want to do is put your food directly over that furnace."

"Don't tell me," interrupted Indigolin. "I'd have a burnt, shrivelled up sausage."

"Your steak would be leathery and burnt on the outside and uncooked on the inside," Aka explained. "You need to cook it over indirect heat."

"If you do that," Indigolin questioned, "why go to all that trouble finding coals that burn at 300 degrees in the first place?"

"Maybe I'm trying to get a product endorsement from Pat Oculus and Colman Hunt!" She joked.

"Don't get that one," said Indigolin.

"They're members of a sect known as the New Prometheans," Pfister explained. "They go through an initiation ceremony which involves them walking on hot coals."

"No-one in his right mind's walking on my Australian Fire Beads!" declared Aka.

"At what temperature does a human being melt?" Indigolin persevered.

"After about ten minutes at 210 degrees, a human being turns into scrambled egg," Aka informed him.

Silk Threads

Wally and Indigolin were sitting cross-legged on rugs in the desert beside Aderfi, around the campfire. Wally's Airstream would have been more commodious. Aderfi's recently acquired huge hangar, previously but briefly occupied by Brunswick Holt, would have been roomier; but there was something primal about squatting round the spitting fire under a canopy of a million stars woven into an indigo sky devoid of light pollution, and listening to the Berber spin his tales. He was explaining the latest edits phoned in by the twelve-year-old scriptwriter.

Wally was very restless for Celia and wanted to be out searching for her at night time as well as day, but the K & R guy was calling the shots for the next few days, waiting for the price to go down, and Wally didn't feel safe flying the Eurocopter in the dark. Kid Ransom had assured them that nothing bad was going to happen to either of the hostages in these early days when they were just establishing a rapport with the kidnappers, because the objects of their ransom became devalued once they started harming them.

Harm would only ensue as a last resort if the kidnappers thought they were just being jerked around. But they would expect some sort of a negotiation on price as opposed to a downright capitulation. Wally, as the guy who had haggled his way to more than the original asking price when he negotiated the purchase of Celia's hair grip in the souk, realised that he was totally unsuited to the task, and was feeling frustrated by his inability to contribute to the narrative of her rescue.

Thus it was that Wally and Indigolin found they had some downtime to work on the film with their new star and scriptwriter, even though they were temporarily missing the leading man and lady. Aderfi took them through Badiss' script.

"As this is a prequel," Aderfi began, "we start off with actual history before we begin blurring the frontiers between history and fantasy. So the scriptwriter thought you might like to commence with a couple of sieges preceding Boabdil's surrender of Granada—which on our version, of course, never happened."

"If we shoot the sieges of Ronda and Malaga together, you can use the same extras, catapults, ramps, trebuchets, ladders—all the properties you need for siege warfare—back to back. The siege of Ronda speaks for itself: this one is all about the location, because, gentlemen, I assure you, there is no location as stunning as the Gorge of Ronda. It's like the Grand Canyon but with houses all down the sides of the abyss." He called up some current images on his iPhone and shared them.

"Good grief!" Wally said. "You can rent that place on AirBnB!"

"And that place is a Pizza Restaurant," said Aderfi. "If you lean too far out the window, it's a thousand foot drop. Obviously we don't show the modern improvements when we're filming. As I say, Ronda is all about the location, but for Ronda, we're not going to use Ronda. Badiss has specified that we're going to shoot it in the volcanic Garrotxa region, because the screenwriter has specified a Catalonian theming out of sympathy for their exiled government. So everything that should be Southern Spain, we're going to shoot in Catalonia.

"As for Malaga, we have tried to make this into a further metaphor for the east and the west. Malaga was strategically very important as the port through which all of the supplies for the Islamic State of Granada came into Spain. The stars of both Malaga and Ronda are the most Christian monarchs, Ferdinand and Isabella.

"Ibrahim al Jarbi was an Islamic Shaman living in Europe. Disguised as an informant, he deliberately plotted to get himself arrested in order to get close enough to Ferdinand upon pretext of disclosing valuable information about the enemy, so as to kill King Ferdinand with a dagger concealed in his turban. Needless to say, he must insist on revealing this information to no-one except the king in person."

"That sounds very like the premise for Zhang Yimou's *Hero*," said Wally.

"Yes," conceded Aderfi, "with Jet Li. I believe *Hero* was nominated for an Oscar and a Golden Globe as Best Foreign Language Film in 2002. But there the similarity ends, because this actually happened. We haven't reached the turning point yet where our factual account becomes counter-factual. So, as I was saying this penniless Shaman, Ibrahim al Jarbi, evolves a bold plan to deliberately get himself captured in order to get close enough to Ferdinand to throw the lethal dagger concealed in his modest turban."

"You say modest, in contradistinction to the type of turban Brunswick Holt wears?" Wally asked.

"Sorry?" Aderfi queried.

"No, it's me that should be apologising to you. I forget you've been here less than a day, Aderfi. I'll show you the scene later, and then you'll understand what I was referring. Please continue."

"Unfortunately for him, Ferdinand had enjoyed a bibulous lunch and was sleeping off the after effects. I believe the Spaniards call it a siesta. So this Ibrahim was taken to another fine tent where he was supposed to wait until Ferdinand woke up. As this Ibrahim spoke no Castilian, he didn't appreciate that he had been put into a holding pattern, and that he was simply supposed to bide his time in the waiting room. His poor research and poorer language skills led him to mistake the two Spanish nobles he found in the waiting tent for the monarchs, Ferdinand and Isabella.

"The scene, as the scriptwriter tells it, is like a microcosm for East versus West. You see, Ibrahim was so poor, devoid of any possessions apart from the rags he stood in, that when he first caught sight of a well-dressed man and his wife, in a sumptuously decorated tent, he imagined they must surely be the king and queen, because who else could look so fine? Thus he took his concealed dagger out of his turban and proceeded to assassinate Alvaro of Portugal, the son of the mighty Duke of Braganza, and was in the process of murdering his wife, Felipa, imagining them to be Ferdinand and Isabella, as he had never beheld such western luxury and excess before.

"He murdered Alvaro, but was apprehended before he could finish off his wife. The irony is that the debauched western glutton, Ferdinand, slept through the whole massacre. So Ferdinand was spared by virtue of his western decadence, Alvaro of Portugal was murdered for his, and as for Ibrahim al Jarbi…

"After his failed attempt, Ferdinand had this Ibrahim sliced up into collops and the poor, mistaken man's broken body pieces were catapulted over the walls onto the Moors who were besieging Malaga. The Moorish seamstresses on the other side of the walls, recovered every shard of his torn body, assembled it like a jigsaw and sewed it back together with silken threads, washed and cleaned and perfumed it and gave it a decent burial. It is very difficult for the opportunistic, modern western mind to comprehend this level of pointless devotion to a lost cause in the name of giving a proper burial to a sack of mincemeat.

"It is interesting that both the east and the west in their histories always depict the other as being engaged in the pursuit of excess and luxury."

"I like it!" Indigolin pronounced.

"Yes, it does seem to tick all the right boxes," agreed Wally. "Sensational locations, bold strategies, fantastic costumes, luxury, excess, brutal murders, revenge, pathos and pointlessness."

"It's the whole Lexicon," remarked Aderfi. "And that's just the opening scene!"

"And what happened in the end?" Wally asked.

"Malaga?" Aderfi checked. "The besieged Moors inside the walls were reduced to eating donkeys, cats and dogs and even stripping all the trees to eat leaves to stay alive. When the city finally fell, the stench of famine diarrhoea and putrid corpses was so overwhelming that the conquering monarchs were unable to ride in triumph through the city Gate. The process of disinfecting the city took months by which time Ferdinand and Isabella had moved on to their next campaign. So it's like an exercise in utter futility and pointlessness. It's a metaphor for war for you. But as I say, this is just the *mis en scène* to get the audience engaged before we get into the real story. Two minutes, maybe, of screen time; then we stop for the titles and Celia Broadsword singing *Ay Mi Alhama*."

"If we find her," remarked Wally, sadly.

"*Inshallah*, you will find her," pronounced Aderfi.

"Well, I never," said Indigolin. "I've watched every episode of *Ferdinand's Book of Hours*, but I never knew about the siege of Malaga before."

Wally repeated the invocation under his breath. *Inshallah*. He believed that travellers abroad should pray to the local gods. That way the prayers had less far to travel, before the deity answered them. He just hoped that he wouldn't be called upon to get his sewing kit out and start stitching pieces of his girlfriend back together.

The Gate of the Burnt One

"Bab al-Mahruq," said Aderfi.

"Meaning?" Indigolin asked.

"It translates as the Gate of the Burnt One."

Aderfi paused to let that one sink in, before continuing:

"Can you think of another monarch where no-one knows where he's buried? And not just any monarch, but the last Sultan of the Islamic State of Granada; and his resting place remains a mystery. There are a number of theories as to where he lies, but in 2014, it looked as though an international team of experts from many disciplines had found it with the help of georadar. It's a simple cube of a mausoleum beside a spot known as Bab al-Mahruq, in Fez. Bab al-Mahruq translates as the Gate of the Burnt One.

"It used to be called the Gate of Justice, until the authorities set a rebel on fire there, so as to discourage others from following suit, since when it's been known as the Gate of the Burnt One. The mausoleum is nearby and is a modest affair to the extent of being nondescript. The theory that it is Boabdil's tomb gained credibility because the Moorish sources suggested Fez and the georadar showed there were two skeletons down there. It was the custom at the time for deceased of the highest rank to be buried next to a holy man or saint, the idea being that the holy man would help the nobleman on his way to heaven.

"Similar to having enough money to endow a chantry chapel so that the monks could make prayers for you for the rest of their lives, so as to ensure your passage to Paradise."

Aderfi explained how the joint Emirati-Spanish effort to disinter the remains and test the DNA against that of Boabdil's living descendants had been scuppered by the Moroccan's refusal to contribute to the cost.

"But," continued Aderfi, "if we were to do it now, and the cost would be wholly insignificant compared to the budget for the film, think of the publicity this would generate."

"Blue Rif sponsor the discovery of the final resting place and disinterment of the last European Caliph at the same time as they release a film about his Islamic State of Europe." Wally spoke the words and looked across at his sponsor, Indigolin, whose money would have to make the words come true.

"What colour is this gate?" Indigolin asked.

"It's also known as the Blue Gate, sir," Aderfi said.

Indigolin's mind was working. He couldn't find anything about this not to like. "Let's check the site out!" He pronounced. "How do we get there?"

"Bus takes 11 hours," informed Aderfi.

"I'll put you down in an hour and a half," said Wally.

"You okay to fly us?" Indigolin checked.

"Yeah, do me good. Need to keep myself busy while I'm waiting for something positive to happen on the Celia front."

Wally sought out Kid Ransom and told him they were making a day trip, but if there was any news on Celia or Colman, any news at all, to call him and he'd turn the copter straight round.

They landed the chopper at Fes Sai International airport and jumped into a pale sand coloured Grand Taxi, being a Mercedes with plastic bench seats and several hundred thousand miles on the clock. When Wally shoved the piece of paper on which he'd written *Bab al-Mahruq* under the cabby's nose, the cabby had looked at his passengers in disbelief.

Indigolin was cool and comfortable in his blue legume suit. The others squirmed on the shiny plastic bench seat.

"Ask him how far it is," said Indigolin.

Aderfi spoke with the taxi driver and then reported back. "He says it's another 30 minutes, by the medina. It's what we call a *musallah* or hermitage. He says he'll wait for us, because it will be hard to get another taxi for the return trip from there. It's not in a good part of town."

"How does he know how long we're going to be?" Wally asked.

"He says we won't want to hang around there for long," explained Aderfi.

If one wanted to be grandiose, one could call it a ring road, or, if one wanted to be grandiose with a smattering of colonial French, a *Boulevard Perepherique.* But in truth, old Fez was a walled city. Entrance to the old city was effected via a series of Gates, and the road that encircled the Gates in the ramparts was simply the route that the taxi driver had taken.

He brought them to a halt beside the peeling blue paint of the Gate formerly known as the Gate of Justice, now known as Bab al-Mahruq, the Gate of the

Burnt One. Wally, Aderfi and Indigolin jumped out of the taxi and began taking photographs of the Gate on their phones.

"So, this is it, " Wally declared. "The famous Gate of the Burnt One. "

A tour guide who overheard them corrected Wally.

"No, it isn't, " He said simply. "This is Bab Boujeloud, the Blue Gate. Bab Boujeloud is a tourist attraction. Everyone's heard of it. No-one knows about Bab al-Mahruq. "

"Except you, it would seem, " Indigolin observed.

"Tariq Hussain at your humble service, " said the individual. "Until I was made redundant, I was an archaeologist and historian. Now I'm a tour guide and taxi driver. "

"So this blue Gate isn't Bab al-Mahruq? " Aderfi double-checked.

"I'm afraid not, sir. But the good news is that Bab al-Mahruq is the very next Gate along. We can walk there together. Bab al-Mahruq is a modest, unprepossessing wooden Gate with no blue tiles or ornamentation. That's why all the tourists come to Bab Boujeloud to take their selfies instead. "

"Can you show us? " Aderfi asked.

"Please, be my guest. *Yalla yalla.* "

"It means *Let's go,* " Aderfi explained.

They followed behind Tariq Hassan for a distance of about thirty or forty metres until they came to the next Gate. It was a monumental Gate in plain wood with a smaller entrance door cut into it.

"This is Bab al-Mahruq," Tariq announced.

"And what does Bab al-Mahruq mean? " Indigolin queried. "How does it translate into English?"

"Gate of the Burnt, " Tariq informed them.

The small door within the Gate opened and a man in uniform emerged.

"Can we go in?" asked Indigolin.

"Not unless you are Muslims," Tariq replied.

"And do you know anything about the last resting place of Boabdil, the Emir of Granada?" Indigolin persevered.

Tariq Hassan nodded his head in the direction of the opposite side of the *Peripherique.*

Beyond the Gate of the Burnt One, within a walled cemetery on the opposite side of the ring road, stood a cuboid structure, as though the gods had tossed a dice from the sky, and it had come to land there.

The *musallah* was a modest edifice, a honey-coloured stone cube standing on a slightly raised stone plinth with a small fringe of ornamental crenulations topped by a Moorish green dome. Each of the four walls was punctuated by one keyhole-shaped window. The taxi parked up and waited for them. There was no signpost, no indication of any kind that the Emir of the Islamic State of Granada was resting here. On the contrary, as they trod closer, taking care to avoid the broken syringes and rubbish, the smell of stale piss and faeces became overpowering.

Inside the unmarked cube, the space was littered with used condoms, broken glass and more shit. A one-armed beggar in a moth-eaten brown Dishdash extended his good hand for alms. A low wheelbase cat slunk away.

"The problem is," explained Tariq, "that the mausoleum is now inhabited only by stray cats, flea-ridden dogs, beggars, drunks, drug addicts and prostitutes. Can you think of a Christian king who suffered such humiliation?"

"Well," began Indigolin, "didn't they find the remains of Richard III under a Tesco supermarket car park in Leicester?"

"Yes, I read about that," answered Hassan , "and I think the humiliation of Richard III was that it was Tesco's and not a Waitrose supermarket. Richard III was universally reviled; but Boabdil was loved and respected by his people. But seriously, can you believe this to be the final resting place of the last Emir of Granada?"

"So what happened?" Wally asked.

"The archaeological team pinpointed this as the mausoleum of Boabdil el Chico, from references given by the Moorish historian, al-Maqquari, who tells us Boabdil was granted asylum in Fez. The team was principally funded by Mustafa Abdulrahman of Abu Dhabi and curiously enough, a Spanish film maker, Javier Balaguer, who was shooting a film on location in Spain, later released as *The Last Sultan of Granada.*"

"He thought it would be great publicity to associate himself with the project. They got all the necessary permissions from the Moroccan government to do the dig, to disinter the remains and compare them to the DNA of his living relatives, but then the project fell over in Moroccan bureaucracy and a refusal by the Moroccan government to provide any funding. And so, the last Sultan of Spain continues to rot beneath a shit house.

"It would have been, it could have been such a very different world, my friends," continued Tariq Hassan. "According to the historians, Arab as well as European. The Islamic State of Granada was everything Europe is belatedly and unsuccessfully striving to become at the present time: affluent, multicultural, tolerant, sophisticated, and artistic—all of the *desiderata* that were stamped on by the jackboot of Catholicism and the Inquisition. These days, it's all lip service and hypocrisy, platitudes and excuses for imagining new taxes.

"But in those days, for eight centuries it was a reality. You know that when Boabdil signed the peace treaty with Ferdinand and Isabella under which he delivered them the keys to Granada, he carved out terms of tolerance not only for the Moors who had lived and ruled there for eight hundred years, but the Jews also. Just think of that for a moment: an Arab King going to pains to ensure no harm came to his Jewish brethren once he had ceded control to the Catholics. Within eight months, the Christian monarchs had completely reneged on every syllable of the treaty and the Jews were thrown out along with the Muslims.

"Eight hundred years undone in eight months! The planned starvation of multiculturalism has many comparators now, and we can see how society has become much the poorer, for instance, in post-Brexit England. Under the Balfour Declaration the Jews got their homeland of Israel. If not for that Declaration, the Jews would be our bogeymen and terrorists, not Al Quayedah. Our civilisation is so much older than yours. We have progressed from being a pretty infant to a wise grown up. In the west, you are still at the stage of a gawky adolescent."

"My God!" Indigolin said, "this story cries out through all the ages. What do our kids know about 1492? That Columbus sailed the ocean blue. To them, it's just doggerel, a limerick. They have no idea that it was the pivot for all subsequent history. Aderfi, I'm up for it! Finally I've found a use for all those godamned dirhams we purchased at the top of the market. Locate Boabdil and dig him up, and then let's bury him properly in the Courtyard of the Twelve Lions! I'll succeed where the Spanish guy failed."

"But where do we begin?" Wally asked.

"Get Elena Troy onto it," ordered Indigolin. "She gets high on tearing strips off civil servants; she just loves ripping bureaucracy to shreds."

"Please," Indigolin said, extending his hand with two five hundred dirham notes enclosed in it in the direction of Tariq Hassan. Mr Hassan shook his head politely and declined the money.

"As I said," he said. "Be my guest." With dignity, he walked away from them in the direction of the Blue Gate.

"However hard I try," joked Indigolin to Aderfi and Wally, "I can't seem to get shot of any of these confounded dirhams!"

"But, Ti," pointed out Wally, "don't you think that we should make sure that we've actually got a cast and a script before we embark on a project to promote the film we have barely started shooting yet by disinterring its historical protagonist?"

All that Indigolin replied was: "Be absolute for death."

Satellite Phone

Indigolin stepped out into the Sahara and put a call through to Mr Webb on his satellite phone. The phone needed a lot of open sky to get a signal, and this always gave Indigolin an excuse to walk away from the crowd and have a word in private.

"You want me to bring her back?" asked Mr Webb, incredulous. "What am I supposed to tell her?"

"You can tell her the ransom's been paid, and she can get back to work. Is she intact?"

"Can't speak for her hymen, but the rest of her's still there. I've never heard of anyone paying a ransom as quickly as that with no negotiations."

"Mr Webb, this is between you and me, but her boyfriend's paying the US $5M as compensation for a little dispute that we had over artistic integrity concerning a redacted scene, and that's good enough for me. He's also paying overages, but quite frankly it doesn't make any difference, because the scene that he cut has already been hyped up so much that all of her fans are going to pay to see the movie in the expectation that the scene is still in there somewhere. From what the director tells me, they may even get to watch a better movie. I appreciate that the money was supposed to be routed via you, so you could clip your fee, so now I'll have to sort you out myself."

The conversation wasn't proceeding according to Mr Webb's taste. He had been hoping to spend a little more time with the diva before he surrendered her. Also, he needed to get Indigolin out to the Argan Farm and try out his skills with the XM42 flamethrower on him as Albanian George had specified a good conflagration.

"Why don't you play one off against the other, Mr Indigolin?" He asked.

"How, so, shill?"

"I mean, you take the 5 mil ransom money secretly off her boyfriend, but you also collect it off the K & R insurers."

"That did cross my mind, shill, but the fact is, this negotiation is dragging on too long, so, on the one hand, I might get another few mil, but on the other hand, every day we're not shooting's costing me a shed load of money too, so very soon, I'm going to be robbing Peter to pay Paul."

"You don't have to hold out for the full five mil if you've already got it off the boyfriend, Mr Indigolin. You could say that the kidnappers have reduced their claim to 2 or 3 mil, but they have to have it in 48 hours or something nasty happens to her. Give the impression that time has become a factor to them, so they are prepared to make concessions in return for a quick deal.

"Plus, the deal you've done with the boyfriend doesn't enable you to launder any of your bum bitcoins. Anyhow, there's no point getting her back straight away, because you haven't got your leading man that she's supposed to act alongside back yet. So what are you going to do with Queen Isabella when you don't have her King Ferdinand? You'll be about as much fucking use as a one-legged man in an arse-kicking contest!"

"We could give it a whirl."

"Also, Mr Indigolin, when the deal's done, I can't be hanging around to pay the piper. You can come here and pick up Celia; because you'll appreciate I can't be delivering her. When the ransom's paid, I have to disappear. But you can make a grand entrance, striding into the Argan Farm wearing your blue legume boots, and liberate her. I'll leave her in tent 22 where you can find her."

"Ok, you'd better start work on another of your anonymous emails to me, Mr Webb. Price reduction."

"Yeah, getting back to Tesco's motto: *Pile 'em high!*"

"Not sure I like the sound of that!"

"Nothing sinister. It was Tesco's slogan. It refers to cans of groceries, not dead bodies. They reckoned to pile 'em high and sell them cheap."

"Mr Webb, I've lived all of my adult life in England, and I've never set foot in a Tesco's. I come to Morocco, and you're the second person that's told me about them today."

"I suppose you're more of a Waitrose person, Mr Indigolin."

"When I'm in Morocco, Mr Webb, I'm very much a Carrefour person, and so would you be if you saw the alternatives."

"And you'll be able to come to the Argan Farm, and play the hero in Pavilion 22. Make sure someone films the liberation of Celia Broadsword."

"No problem, Mr Webb. We're a film company. I think we can manage that. You can count on me."

"That's what I'm doing, Mr Indigolin."

Bvsh Ho 2

Elena put the WhatsApp video call through to Agent Anatole Franck.

"Bvsh Ho," he answered. "You're looking very bronzed and healthy, Elena."

"Thanks, Anatole. What's the weather doing in London?"

"Persistent drizzle. Not enough to turn the automatic wipers on in your car, but just enough to make it difficult to see through the windscreen."

"You driving?"

"Can't afford to. Fucking mayor's just put the Congestion Charge up again. What have you discovered now, Elena?"

"Anatole, I've been here a month, and I'm discovering less with every passing day. I don't know if it's because our subject has a labyrinthine mind, or if I'm looking in the wrong places, or if he's not doing anything wrong. So far, he seems to be recycling ransom monies, and laundering dirhams to disinter an Emir to compare his DNA to that of his surviving relatives. If you can figure out what he's up to, please let me in on it."

"Shall I call you in, Elena?"

"Not yet, Anatole. I need you to do something for me."

She explained how she needed Anatole to liaise with his counterpart mandarins in the Foreign Office and resurrect the project that Mustafa Abdulrahman of the Emirates and the Spanish film director had started, so that Indigolin and Wally could finish the job off.

"Shouldn't be too difficult," he had said, "if someone has already brought the disinterment paperwork into existence, all we have to do is find it and complete it."

"That's what I figured," she said.

"What time of day is it out there?"

"It's six o clock at night, Anatole."

"You got anything planned for the rest of the evening?"

"As a matter of fact, I have, Anatole. I've just been invited to dinner by Tinctorio Indigolin."

Blow Job

Albanian George had to wipe his eye, he was laughing so much. Someone had sent him a WhatsApp message and video consisting of the 10 worst injuries guys had suffered being given hand jobs, blow jobs and so forth. Of course, John Wayne Bobbitt was right up there at the top. But some of the other injuries were so appalling he laughed until it hurt.

Fuck me! He didn't know that you could actually die of a bad hand job; of course, there were cases of snapped off cocks, todgers stuck in Dysons, bitten off members, girls choking to death. Why did these things always seem to happen in America? He didn't know up until then that it was possible to transmit STDs by a hand job. You could catch gonorrhoea, syphilis or even AIDS, it seemed without penetration.

In Australia, accidents sustained in masturbation were so common that they had coined the term, *Wankidents* to describe them. Presumably, in the Outback, the distances from one's neighbours were so huge that men had to experiment with new and often fatal means of masturbation. The injuries were life-altering.

What had he said to that crazy white-haired Mick? *Be absolute for death.* But when he'd said that, he hadn't even though of all the Wankidents that might carry one off. *Death hath ten thousand several doors:*

Death by Blow Job!

Death by Hand Job!

He rubbed the tears from his eyes so that he could see which of his contacts he wanted to forward his WhatsApp to.

Deep Blue Rif

Indigolin's driver pulled the Urus up outside Riyadh Chay with Agent Elena Troy in the passenger seat, having collected her from the Berber hotel. She had thought about climbing into the back, but the instrumentation in the front looked like the cockpit of a fighter jet, and she didn't want to miss any of the excitement. The dashboard was a riot of colour, but one could select the predominant colour. Of course, the colour that had been selected was blue. She was struggling to understand how the driver could concentrate on the driving with the dashboard representing so much of a distraction. There were so many searchlights; it was like driving a prison break around Piccadilly Circus.

Talking of riots of colour, there were the stunning blue jacaranda trees she remembered from her previous nocturnal visit, poking their indigo heads above the pisé walls. She had been intrigued by the producer's invitation, and hoped that this visit to the Riyadh would be much less stressful than her last. She was wearing a simple linen wraparound dress. She didn't think she'd be climbing any trees on this occasion.

Without even thinking about it, she just realised, that the linen dress was cerulean blue, as though there was no way of getting away from it. Nor did she have to scale any walls. In fact, the driver punched the key code into the finger pad and they made a comparatively conventional entrance through the front Gate this time.

Inside, just as she remembered it, was the breath-taking courtyard with the reflecting bassin. She wondered if there were any koi carp left or if the stork on the chimney pot had consumed them all. The bassin was rectangular and filled with lily pads, although now the sun was going down, the lilies themselves had closed up. The candles in all the lanterns were lit, signposting her way to the slate table. It was set for two.

Viewing the place at dusk as opposed to pitch dark by the light of her mobile phone, she saw that the beautifully-tended gardens were predominantly themed blue, like the famous Jardin Majorelle in Marrakesh. Apart from the jacaranda trees, dropping their blue petals on the lawn, all of the ground cover in the flowerbeds consisted of blue spiderwort and purple hearted Tradescantia. Blue agapanthus raised their heavy heads towards the sun's last position before it had slipped behind the pisé walls.

Flowerpots were cerulean blue. There were blue dolphin statues, a blue tile band around the bassin, and the water that spilled into the bassin where the koi carp shimmered, exited from the mouth of a blue lion's head. She wondered if her host had drawn up a list of blue selection criteria for his lodgings, whether the Riyadh just happened to be cobalt themed, or if Indigolin had given it an azure makeover after moving in, although the latter explanation seemed unlikely, especially after his overheard comment about losing his deposit when the stork made off with the koi carp the other night.

The big guy, Ibrahim, welcomed her respectfully. He still had the huge, curved dagger in his belt. After opening the front door with the code, the driver had left her to fare for herself, and disappeared. After all, she thought, what else was he supposed to do? Introduce her to someone she already knew? She learned the smaller guy was known as Hamas and was a housekeeper, whereas Ibrahim seemed more front of house. There was a female cook, who was presumably brought in for special occasions, such as the present.

Looking back on her love life, such as it was, for some reason she seemed to attract men looking for a cheap date. It was nice, for a change, to be a protagonist within a special occasion.

Indigolin made an appearance from inside the house. In fact, she could swear he came from the study. He hadn't changed for the occasion: it was another blue legume suit. Ibrahim served the two of them with vintage champagne, which was very good. It seemed that if it was vintage, Indigolin restrained himself from splashing Blue Curacao into it. She commented on the amazing variety of exotic trees and especially the jacarandas.

The fruit of the banana tree was hanging down like something in the Garden of Eden that one should be forbidden to eat. The air was heady with the smell of the honeysuckle and jasmine. The stone floor had been washed down with citrus to make sure no mosquitos disturbed them.

He took her by the arm and walked her round the garden, pointing out the different flora and fauna. This close to him, she noticed, he wore no aftershave or cologne. It suddenly dawned on her that, ever since Napier Ransom, she had developed a distrust and a dislike for men who wore colognes. Instead, he picked lemon thyme and peppermint leaves from the garden, bruised the leaves in his hands and passed them to her to sample the aroma. This was a much better, natural experience that banished the demon aftershaves from her psyche.

After they had finished the first bottle of champagne, he asked her if he should open another one. She had said that she didn't think she ought to on an empty stomach, and enquired was he proposing to feed her? She had observed there was cutlery laid out for three courses and a dessert. He said that he was indeed proposing to enjoy supper with her, but he made it a rule never to sit down to supper until he had been invited to do so by his frogs.

She looked at him blankly, not understanding, but then, right on cue, the first tree frog croaked very discreetly. That provoked a reply from another frog, and soon the whole garden was alive with the incessant noise that drowned out the whisperings of the cicadas that had preceded it. She laughed.

"Those are just the tree frogs," he explained. "You know the nursery rhyme about the London Bells?"

"Oranges and lemons?" She asked.

"Exactly! And the Bells of Old Bailey say *When will you pay me?* And then the Great Bell of Bow says *I do not know*."

He puffed himself up and pronounced *I do not know* in his most stentorian tones.

"When the parliament of the proper frogs starts croaking, not the little tree frogs, but the proper ones in that bassin over there, that is like the Great Bell of Bow," he said, "and that will be our dinner gong. They can conduct their debate, whilst we enjoy our first course."

Seconds later, the first burp from the bassin made her laugh again, and soon the whole garden was alive with noises of the night, and, just as he had described, it was as though the two of them were sitting in a parliament of frogs, the amphibians conducting their business in the background.

"Did you know," he began, "that after the nuclear catastrophe at Chernobyl, within 10 years the green frogs there had evolved into black frogs so that they were able to survive the lingering radiation?"

"I believe that theory was discredited," she stated. "The current thinking is that it was the frogs with the darker green pigmentation that were more resilient, and they simply passed their stronger genes on."

Indigolin raised an eyebrow and scanned her face. He had never met anybody who was able to continue a conversation with him about frogs, let alone someone who was able to contradict him. This promised to be a memorable evening, he thought.

The first course arrived: courgette flowers stuffed with ricotta, accompanied by an Albarino white wine. The next course was tartare of langoustine with a *sauce vierge* accompanied by a *Pouilly Fume*. There followed what was known as a *trou normande*, an apple sorbet floating in a tumbler of Calvados, which, he informed her, in Normandy, they served to refresh the palette and burn a hole in your stomach to make room for the next course.

Over the courgette flowers, the langoustine and the *trou normande*, she managed to unlock more of the modest wit that she had sensed she was tapping into in earlier conversations about owing cocks and Asclepius, Nietzsche and John Donne. She found him not only good company, but positively spellbinding. She could understand how he had risen to the position of eminence and success he now enjoyed.

He was incredibly knowledgeable: he knew the name of every species of flora and fauna in the garden; he knew the names of every star and constellation in the night sky above their heads; he was on first name terms with every frog and tree frog in the bassin. But none of this in a boring way. It was as if he was a magic lantern that, once rubbed, delivered just the correct amount of worldly wisdom. He never offered, but he could always answer.

He didn't give her lists or lectures of the names of trees or stars; but if they came up in the conversation, he knew every detail. In particular, he knew the sea. No, that was not the right word. He didn't just know it: he understood it, as much as a mere human being can. Time and again, he steered the conversation back to her sub-aqua experiences, to every dive site and wreck she had swum down to. He never actually attempted to take ownership of the experience by saying that he had also dived there; but he would make throwaway lines, kind of *sotto voce* asides, that made it clear that he also knew every site personally and intimately.

For instance, when she described the joys of night-diving at Kona, Hawaii, he had just said: "Those beautiful manta rays!"—making it clear he knew the inhabitants of that particular site very well and had presumably dived it. When she mentioned Cenote Angelita in Tulum, Mexico, his eyes lit up and he cried out, "The Underwater River!"

When she had mentioned what she considered her most ambitious, if not her deepest dive in Silfra Fissure, Thingvellir National Park in Iceland, he had clapped his hands together and expressed his delight to discover blue grasses growing underwater between the Continental tectonic plates. He managed to say just enough to share each experience with her, without attempting to take over the subject himself.

But most of all, more than natural reefs, the loss and bleaching out of which they both mourned, he seemed particularly interested in the artificial reefs thrown up by sunken wrecks, and he encouraged her to talk about her experiences wreck diving. For instance, when she told him how magical it had been when she had dived the wreck of HMNZS *Waikato* off the Tutukaka Coast of Northland, New Zealand, he had said: "Isn't it just amazing when you see those four and a half inch guns on deck, now encrusted with anemones and hydroids like jewels? Doesn't it call to mind *Those are pearls that were his eyes*?"

Then he had reminded her of the French 75 cocktail ordered by the German officer's mistress, Yvonne, in the film, Casablanca, that they had both watched just a few nights past, a few nights that now seemed months ago. The French 75 drink, he informed her was named after a 75mm French artillery gun, and he suggested that they experiment with their drinks until they had mixed up something worthy to be named after the submerged four and a half inch encrusted guns on the Waikato.

And she had asked him if, when he referred her to *Those are pearls that were his eye*s, he meant in the sense of Shakespeare's Tempest or T S Eliot's fragments. He had given her an amazing smile that lit up his entire face, winked at her and said: "Hieronymo's mad again!"

He presumed nothing. He was not narcissistic or vain. He constantly steered the conversation back to her, and never volunteered anything about himself, his business, his possessions, the work he was doing—unless asked a direct question, which he then answered plainly and honestly, before navigating the conversation back to her, necessarily, but by the most elegant.

Given that she was here, working under cover, as a spy, with a false, constructed past, and given the amount of drink she had already consumed, she was beginning to have doubts about her ability to continue to answer questions about herself. She felt like an iceberg keeping nine-tenths of herself hidden from him. Maybe she should just let him get her in the sack as soon as possible and stop the conversation, pleasant as it was. How was she supposed to get back to the Berber hotel, she wondered? Was the driver going to wait outside all night?

Meanwhile, Indigolin had finally assembled a cocktail which he announced was the very same French 75 that was ordered in Casablanca. He told her it was mixed to a recipe the British soldiers stationed in France during the Great War had created, using London Gin and local champagne; and that he was now adding his secret ingredient, which turned out, of course, to be Blue Curacao, enabling him to name this new cocktail they had created from the base of the French 75, the Blue Waikato. Just as James Bond created a Vesper cocktail for his girlfriend, Tinctorio Indigolin had created the Blue Waikato for Elena. Raising her glass, on cue, she said: "Here's looking at you, kid!"

Gazing into her eyes, he pronounced that Elena did indeed bear an uncanny resemblance to Ingrid Bergman, and, not for the first time, he wondered to himself what she was doing in the back office, poring over the books, when she should be in front of a lens.

After the main course, which was lightly schwarma'd lamb with rosemary potatoes and roasted vegetables paired with a Lebanese red wine from the Bekka Valley, she protested:

"Tinctorio, we've done nothing but talk about me all evening. Don't you think you should tell me a few things about yourself now that we've finished the main course?"

"But there is so little to tell," he shrugged. "I was taught that if you kept your date talking about herself all evening, she was less likely to get bored. What is it you want to know?"

"For a start, how am I getting home?"

"My driver is waiting outside. He doesn't drink alcohol. Whatever the hour, he will be sober as a judge, and at your disposal."

"Why am I here?"

"Because you very kindly accepted my invitation."

"But why did you invite me?"

"Elena, you are very beautiful and very intelligent and I adore your company. But I also invited you out of self-interest. They say that you are over-qualified for the work you are doing on my accounts; but I have more important accounting work I would like your input on. Also, when I read your CV on your job application, I saw that you were a keen scuba diver, which is highly relevant. So am I. But I was going to wait until after the coffee to discuss business."

Ibrahim served the desert. It was a Blue Curacao sorbet paired with Hungarian Tokay. He asked her if she liked it.

"It's delicious!" She said.

"I asked the chef to pair it with the Tokay. It needed to be quite robust to stand up to the palette-numbing sorbet. What do they say in that poem of Robert Browning's? *Up jumped Tokay on our table*'"

"Yes, after his heart had sunk with the Claret Flask."

"See, I said you were intelligent. How many other people would have identified that allusion to someone who is no longer a popular poet? And completed the verse, better still."

"So, Tinctorio, are you saying that you picked this menu yourself and it's not just something your staff dreamt up?"

"I am saying that I picked it, and I specified it, and the recipes are not chosen from a book. They are my own recipes. Also, I paired the wines, and I told the staff what ingredients to buy, and I would indeed have been very happy to buy all the ingredients and cook them for you myself. I am, of course, a *cordon bleu* cook, because, anything that's blue, I have to have it; but if I was to do the cooking, I wouldn't have been able to chat to you beforehand, so I asked the chef to execute it, but all the individual parts of the plan are mine.

"Have you noticed that there is a direct link between the complexity of a nation's dishes and the servitude of its female members? The fact is that Chinese and Indian food cannot be prepared in advance and are very labour-intensive at the last minute, as a result of which the women get stuck with the preparation; and, as a result of that they can't participate in the pre-dinner banter and gossip, or the weightier drinking and philosophising that the men engage in.

"It leads to a two tier society in which women are underducated, and regarded as fit for nothing except cooking, cleaning and child-bearing. By contrast, French, English and Italian cuisine is very simple. You can prepare most of it in advance and keep it warm in the simmering oven of your Aga. As a consequence, western men are willing to assist in the kitchen and women are valued and share a far more equal place in the hierarchy."

"I've never heard that theory before," she said.

"That is because I've never told it to anyone else before," he answered.

"Tell me about this blue thing. What is it about you and blue?" She was conscious of the fact that, without thinking, she had put on blue lacy underwear before leaving the Berber hotel. She wondered if he was going to find out.

"Just a trade mark. It is a colour that occurs so rarely in nature that I identified with it. I mean, on the one hand, blue things in nature are highly unusual, but on the other hand, half of nature is blue: the sea and the sky."

"But the sea's only blue because it reflects the sky!" She pointed out.

"Indeed, but it's what makes those jacaranda trees over there so amazing. Look! It's dark, but it's as if they have little lights switched on. The Blue Curacao. The Blue Rif Molecule, my company, Deep Blue Rif. The blue legume suits…"

Her heart stopped at the reference to the Deep Blue Rif company. She attempted to conceal her momentary hesitation by asking him about the molecule.

"We still have some testing to go," he explained, "but it's the world's smallest molecule. We combine it with other substances as a delivery mechanism. I hope to cure cancer one day, or at least, treat cancer in a comprehensive manner, but before I cure humankind, I have a little debt I wish to repay to the natural world first, and that is why I invited you."

"Can you show me the molecule?" She asked.

"Of course. May I touch you? Will you give me your hand?" For an instant, the thought crossed her mind that he was proposing marriage to her. But the thought was just too ridiculous, and she banished it instantaneously.

He held her outstretched hand, and produced his vial from the pocket of his jacket. Just as he had done at The Royal Society, he decanted six drops into the palm of her hand.

"This will take a minute," he said. "Please excuse me. For the next part of the evening, I need my PC." He was no longer the towering brute force in nature that he had appeared to be up to now; no longer the headmaster giving orders. No, now, she thought, he was like an excited schoolboy, bustling around.

He left her in the garden with the amazing olfactory overload and the parliament of frogs, and the blue reservoir in her palm. And she watched, as the liquid disappeared into her skin, and then saw the droplets forming on her knuckles. Ibrahim brought out three white coffee cups.

"One cup for each of you," he said, "and one cup to catch the Blue Rif!" He placed the third coffee cup under her knuckles just in time to catch the drops as they fell from her hand, having passed clean through it. He then poured the coffee.

Indigolin reappeared with his computer.

"How was that?" He asked whilst the computer booted up.

"I've seen it with my own eyes," was all that she could say. What had just occurred defied any logical explanation. Now she really did feel as if she had been through the door in the back of the wardrobe.

"Because you are highly intelligent," he said, "you will find it difficult to come to terms with what has just happened to you. You know what my motto is at Deep Blue Rif?"

The name of that company again. Why was he teasing her with it?

She shook her head.

"The difficult takes time." He said, "The impossible takes a little longer. That is our motto. Would you mind awfully if I drink this? I find the idea that the liquid has passed entirely through such a singular woman, unspeakably attractive."

"It's drinkable?" She queried.

"Oh yes," he assured her. "The blue colour comes from Blue Eagle Eye Zooanthid Coral. Perfectly natural."

He then drunk the contents of the third coffee cup. For reasons that were unclear to her, fully dressed as she was, she felt as if she had somehow been complicit in the most intimate ceremony any man had ever shared with her. It was as though she had been violated, but in a manner she found deeply sensuous, if such a contradiction was possible. But of course it was possible. It was the stuff of the Dracula legend.

The computer was now live. There had been no password. She needn't have wasted five minutes copying his gigantic file onto her own tablet. She could just have brought her own USB stick along the other night when she had broken into his house uninvited.

Talking of USB sticks, he had his DataTraveler in his hand, the very one whose contents she had covertly copied so recently. He inserted it in the port and clicked it open.

"This," he announced, "is something that I have been working on. I have lots of money, but I am a nobody. I hope that what I am about to show you will be my Nobel Peace Prize, my knighthood. Perhaps I am a little vain after all. You remember I said I wanted to repay a small debt I owed to the natural world before I got to grips with humanity?"

"Yes." She was looking at the screen. Trillions of characters were dripping down like in the Matrix, continually rearranging themselves. "What does it all mean?" She asked.

"In the Seychelles," he began, "on the main island of Mahé—"

She felt a lump form in her throat. It was good that he was doing all the speaking, because she didn't think she would be able to speak if called upon to do so. She could feel her heart beating in her rib cage. Some of it was animal desire; some was sheer terror. He sipped his coffee and continued:

"In the Seychelles, I have built a very large machine. It has taken me years, because it had to obey a complex set of instructions issued to it from this smaller machine." He gestured towards his PC. "Those are the instructions you are looking at now. I wish this to be my legacy to mankind. It has cost me many billions of dollars and I've even had to borrow to make ends meet. Yes, even billionaires have to borrow, Miss Troy. And some of the people I have borrowed from have been more concerned with their own financial wellbeing than the wellbeing of the planet. Indeed, quite recently, you will have read that one of them attempted to have me assassinated by a contract killer.

"I intend to donate this legacy to nature, at cost. I cannot afford to simply give it away, because it has come at too high a price. But I want to donate it at exactly what it has cost me. However, I have no business model for carrying out the calculations so that I sell it to the human race for exactly what it has cost me, not a penny more, not a penny less. But I understand that you are over-qualified as a production accountant, and you may be able to work out the number that I should ask when I make this donation to our planet.

"But what is it that you are donating?" She asked. "What is the huge machine in the Seychelles?"

"I've built the world's largest 3D printer." He explained, "What you are looking at are the instructions that will be sent to that printer."

"And what is it that you are going to print out, Mr Indigolin?"

"From sawdust and cement and seaweed," he answered, "I'm going to print out a coral reef."

Her jaw dropped.

Aftermath

Elena hadn't needed to trouble the driver after all. She'd stayed the night. It had been such a magical evening that ending it by climbing into the back of a car, even a Lamborghini off-roader, and being dropped off at her room in the 3 star Berber hotel back in Ouarzazate would have been too much of an anti-climax.

The short guy had cleared the table, then rode off on his moped. The cook had wiped down all the surfaces and loaded up the dishwasher, which would be emptied in the morning by the short guy when he came back to work. The cook had then got onto her moped and disappeared into the night.

The tall guy, Ibrahim, had checked if they needed anything else, and then the two of them had walked him to the front door, as though they were seeing off the last of their dinner guests, and watched with amusement as the huge guy in his pure white robes, curved dagger, and red toque climbed astride the Lilliputian moped like the Colossus of Rhodes and pop-popped off into the night.

Indigolin had asked Elena if he should call his driver round for her now, and she had said firmly that wouldn't be necessary. Indigolin had shown her to a guest room. Using a guest's washbag that she found by the sink, she had cleaned her teeth and removed her make-up and then by candlelight, made her way in her blue lace underwear into his master suite. Despite the copious quantities, they'd both had to drink, she found him a very attentive and capable, and completely unassuming lover. He hadn't taken anything for granted.

Afterwards she reached for a Kleenex and inspecting it, said: "It's not blue, then?"

"I certainly didn't need any Viagra, Elena!" Was all he said before kissing her good night.

She drifted into sleep to the music of nightjars singing in the trees, their song being carried on the light breeze through the ornate open ironwork of the Mashrabiyya windows. The following morning she awoke in his bed, not hers, not to the nightjars or the parliament of frogs, but to the dawn chorus of leaf warblers and rosy starlings singing their songs right outside the open Mashrabiyya. The light danced through the ironwork in the window lattices and illuminated the complex geometrical patterns in the terracotta Zelliji tilework adorning the walls, of which she noted the predominant colour was blue.

She drifted back to sleep but was awoken an hour later by the recorded nasal shout of the Muezzin calling the faithful to prayer. This time he was awake also, and they made love once more.

Probably the Best Beer in the World

Wally was in Aka Akinyola's Umbrella Bar. He placed the three screenshots of the Range Rover with the blacked-out windows on one of the glass tables, waiting for Aka to bring him a beer. He turned the A4's round and round as though they held the answer. He shuffled them as if he was playing Three Card Monté with them.

Aka came out from the tent and moved the photographs aside so as not to place the condensing stein on them.

"Your next set of wheels?" She asked him.

"No, Aka. I need to find this car. The last anyone or anything saw of Celia, she climbed into this car and then she disappeared."

"It went into the Argan Farm," Aka pronounced.

"What?"

Wally couldn't believe the answer could be so simple. He just hadn't been asking the right questions, or directing the questions at the right person.

"I'd been burning charcoal by the edge of the forest." She said. "I saw that car go into the Argan Farm. I was there for another four hours before the charcoal was cool enough to move. No-one came out again. What the hell can you do in an Argan Farm for four hours?"

Aderfi Has a Brainwave

"There must be other ways to tell them apart other than asking Celia Broadsword," said Kid Ransom.

"What do you mean?" Indigolin asked.

"Well," continued Kid, "we've been focussing on getting a positive visual identification. But there must be other ways we can sort the wheat from the chaff. There must be a question to which only Colman Hunt knows the answer."

"If Colman's the only one who knows the answer, how are we going to know it's the right answer?" Tinctorio tested. "It's no use asking him when his birthday is, because they were all born the same day,"

"We know something that Colman knows, but neither of his brothers know," announced Aderfi. All eyes were on the good looking Berber. "We simply ask each of them where the opening scene of *the Gate of the Burnt One* is shot. The only one of the three brothers who can know the right answer to that, is Colman."

A Price Reduction

Kid Ransom felt that things were going well for him. He'd pretty well followed his brother's advice to just sit on it and things would work themselves out. Today they'd received an email from the unidentifiable Gmail account informing them that the asking price for Celia Broadsword had gone down from US $5M to US $1m, but this was a once-in-a-lifetime concession that had to be paid in 48 hours or it would be withdrawn and the previous price would be reinstated and indeed increased.

Mr Webb had been torn between lowering the price to US $1m, which threatened to bring his pleasant sojourn on the Field of the Cloth of Gold to an end, or hovering it at US $3m, which might protract the negotiation and allow him to watch a few more DVDs with Celia. But, due to the conflicted position that he occupied, he had to balance the mutually exclusive wishes of his two employers, against his own incongruent objectives of getting himself paid by both his client and his victim, whilst procrastinating as long as was feasible, so that he could continue to enjoy the company of his hostage.

Also, Kid Ransom had received another visit from the unshod triplet in the blue robes and the suicide vest, who told them that he was now on offer at the unrepeatable price of US $1m, and he had, without guile or hesitation, come up with the correct answer to Aderfi's riddle namely that the first scene of the Gate of the Burnt One took place in the Courtyard of the Twelve Marble Lions, which Aderfi confirmed was the correct answer.

The email they subsequently received from abduct@snatch.ma had taken a punt with Ouarzazate, as being the right answer, and failed, whereupon Indigolin had hit Reply and typed out: *Presley, the game's up. Get your thieving arse back to the set now and I'll overlook your little indiscretion. If you're not here in 24 hours, I'll report it to the police.* He then hit Send. He could have told Presley to get his thieving arse out of Morocco, but he preferred the intermediary step of getting Presley's arse where he could see it, and he would then be in a position to ensure Presley boarded the plane, rather than have Presley try to blow any more smoke up his own arse.

Kid had checked with Elena and each star's insurance was written under a separate policy and each carried a US $0.5M excess, so the studio were seriously considering paying the whole ransom themselves, rather than lose their no claims bonus. For the first time since he'd boarded BA flight BA2666 to Marrakesh, Kid had a broad smile on his face. His brother would be very proud of him.

Given the $0.5M deductibles on the policies, and given that Indigolin's shares had ceased to be suspended, and since skyrocketed in value, Tinctorio Indigolin said he was fed up with shadow-boxing, and simply paid Colman's ransom in the reduced amount of US $1m, in the manner specified, thereby offloading himself of some of the dubious bitcoins that he had earmarked for Mr Webb and Celia, as these were no longer all needed in light of the price reduction that had likewise been offered for her release.

Indigolin found himself comfortably liquid. As he had envisaged, now that the market was aware of the fact that he had survived an assassination attempt at point blank range by virtue of his blue legume suit, his stock had risen stratospherically amid rumours of a contract to kit out the Armed Forces. He had offloaded a miniscule amount on the market, and paid off his creditors, including Albanian George. The unfortunate situation concerning his acquiring his own NOMAD had been resolved by his having to give a series of undertakings to his regulator and appoint another NOMAD, so his shares were no longer suspended.

Colman Hunt, at last a free man, in his now favoured blue robes shuffled back for his last shuttle from the Berber encampment, but this time without the Superdry suicide vest. Like a see-saw, he was momentarily elated to see his old friends and be reunited with Paddy Oculus, but then thrown into despond when he learned that his ex-wife and leading lady had also been kidnapped.

Wally continued to comb the countryside from his chopper, searching for his loved one. On this occasion, he was accompanied by Aka Akinyola, who was riding shotgun for him. He was low on gas and just getting ready to turn the Eurocopter round and head back after another wasted morning of aerial surveillance, when she said, "Down there! It's the Argan Farm"

He caught sight of what could very well have been a black Range Rover entering a walled compound. The driver seemed to act suspiciously, because, hearing the chopper, he sought to conceal the car under a tarpaulin. Wally decided to descend for a better look.

He landed the helicopter just outside the pisé walls of the Argan Farm. Mr Webb had quickly covered the car and his next priority was to make sure that his captive kept out of sight. There could be no explanation for the visitation by the helicopter that would end well for him. He had seen tourists making balloon flights, but that was in the early morning and at dusk, when the conditions were right.

There was no innocent explanation he could think of for someone circling above the Argan Farm in a chopper at midday. At least, it wasn't a police chopper. He doubted if the Moroccan police force even had such assets.

Webb found Celia and grabbed hold of her from behind. He pressed her snug to the walls, by the rose garden with his hand over her mouth, and told her not to move or make a noise. She assumed the helicopter she'd heard belonged to her lover, but she hadn't been able to get out in the open in time to attract his attention.

Having killed the engine, the better to listen, Wally left Aka in the cockpit and circled the compound on foot, but there was no way in except through the locked Gate. Little did he know that his girlfriend was pressed up on the other side of the low wall separating them. She wasn't more than a metre away.

Then the farm's irrigation system for the rose garden came on. It sprayed right over onto the other side of the wall where Wally was positioned. In the midday sun the spray made mini-rainbows, and suddenly there she was, like a water nymph, reflected in a million tiny water droplets, the image of Celia Broadsword with her unmistakeable silver hair and with a man's hand clasped over her mouth. He needed to come back later with help, maybe with the police, to force an entry. He climbed back into the Eurocopter with Aka and fired up the engine. He took a note of the co-ordinates, so he could tell the police where to come to. He rose up over the compound. He took one last inhalation, not knowing how long is was going to have to last him, filling his lungs with her perfume, like a free diver, and then he threw his half of the diaphanous yellow veil out of the open doorway of the chopper. From her station, pressed up against the other side of the wall, Celia watched it, fluttering down like a snowflake.

Yellow, she remembered, meant that he was coming back.

The Perfume

"Time for another reading from John Donne?" Indigolin enquired of his teacher.

"I noticed that you wear no cologne or aftershave," Elena began.

"I've never found one that smelled right on me," he said.

"Tinctorio, I've never found one that smelled right on any man. They're all rank. Also, I had an unpleasant experience once, diving at Cap de Creus. I shut the guy out from my mind; but I wasn't able to expiate the stink of his aftershave. I think that, even if they cremated the guy, that smell would outlive him. I thought we might study one of Donne's Elegies known as *The Perfume*."

"Okay."

"Up to now, we've been doing his *Songs and Sonnets*. There's also a lot of holy stuff, but in between there are some *Elegies*, and this one's called *The Perfume*. Now that your ear is attuned to the Metaphysical Poets, instead of me reading the poem and translating it to you afterwards, I'm going to explain the structure and read you an extract, and leave you to work it out for yourself. Okay?"

"Top shelf!"

"You remember when we read *The Relic*, I explained that all women in Donne's time needed to maintain the pretence they were virgins?"

"Yes, the maidenhead that was more than one a-bed."

"Exactly. It follows from that that extramarital relationships had to be carried on in the utmost secrecy, and you can assume there were plenty of prying eyes. In this *Elegy* called *The Perfume*, Donne, like the perfect gentleman, conducts himself with the utmost discretion. His mistress has a mother that embraces her, pretending to be affectionate, but actually testing her for any pregnant swellings; the mother offers the daughter all manner of strange fruits and foods to see if she has any longings that would be associated with pregnancy.

"The mother also confesses her own sexual exploits (real or imagined) to her daughter, in the belief that one confidence begets another, so that the daughter will reciprocate by confessing any dalliances of her own. The father bribes the girl's brothers and sisters to shop her. The household has a huge serving man that keeps watch on the girl. But, somehow or other, Donne manages to give them all the slip.

"Donne even teaches his clothes not to rustle and give him away as he creeps around the girl's house at night, where she naturally lives with her parents until she is wed. He avoids every creaking board. But he lets himself down ("self-traitor"). The one detail that he forgot was that he was wearing a loud aftershave that gives him away. I'll begin in the middle. The poem starts out addressed to the girl, and then at the end, it's addressed to the aftershave."

"Got it. Okay. Let's go."

"Though thy immortal mother which doth lie
Still buried in her bed, yet will not die,
Takes this advantage to sleep out daylight,
And watch thy entries, and returns at night,
And when she takes thy hand, and would seem kind,
Doth search what rings, and armlets she can find,
And kissing, notes the colour of thy face,
And, fearing lest thou art swollen, doth thee embrace;
To try if thou long, doth name strange meats,
And notes thy paleness, blushing, sighs and sweats;
And politically will to thee confess
The sins of her own youth's rank lustiness;
Yet love these sorceries did remove, and move
Thee to gull thine own mother for my love,
Thy little brethren, which like fairy sprites
Oft skipped into our chamber, those sweet nights,
And kissed, and ingled on thy father's knee,
Were bribed next day, to tell what they did see;
The grim eight-foot-high-iron-bound serving-man,
That oft names God in oaths, and only then,
He that to bar the first Gate, doth as wide
As the great Rhodian Colossus stride;
Which, if in hell, no other pains there were,
Makes me fear hell, because he must be there;
Though by thy father he were hired to this,
Could never witness any touch or kiss.
But, Oh, too common ill, I brought with me

That which betrayed me to mine enemy;
A loud perfume, which at my entrance cried
Even at thy father's nose, so we were spied.
When, like a tyrant king, that in his bed
Smelt gunpowder, the pale wretch shivered.
Had it been some bad smell, he would have thought
That his own feet, or breath, that smell had wrought…
I taught my silks, their whistling to forbear,
Even my oppressed shoes, dumb and speechless were,
Only, thou bitter sweet, whom I had laid
Next me, traitorously, have betrayed
And unsuspected have invisibly
At once fled unto him, and stayed with me…
Gods, when ye fumed on altars, were pleased well,
Because you were burnt, not that they liked your smell;
All my perfumes, I give most willingly
To embalm thy father's corpse. What? Will he die?"

The Book of Andrew

Meanwhile another former loved-one used his heightened sense of smell to navigate his way to the doorstep of his master's house. There are three Palm Islands in Dubai: Palm Jumeriah, Deira Island and Palm Jebel Ali. The five bedroom house of Napier Ransom was on Deira Island. The Range Rover was on the drive outside.

It was ten o clock at night. Nap was off to the Cyclone, a club the size of a football pitch with a greater concentration of hookers than you'd find in an entire city anywhere else in the world. Periodically, there would be some trouble and the authorities would have to make a desultory gesture at closing the place down on the stated grounds of 'violating Islamic laws and indulging in immoral activities'.

No matter how many times they did this, it always re-opened within a matter of days, although the location changed. It was like a turd that wouldn't flush. Napier had an app on his phone that would tell him where the current location was on a daily basis. Today, it appeared it was on the outskirts of town by the football pitch in an area known as Oud Metha.

Napier was wearing a light tan linen suit with an ostentatious open necked surf shirt, correspondent shoes and a loud aftershave. He picked up the car keys from the shelf in the hall, turned the alarm on with his key fob, opened the front door, and had his throat torn out by a rabid dog.

Burnt Pavilions

Mr Webb had explained to Indigolin that he, Mr Webb, couldn't be personally present for the prisoner exchange. The idea was that Indigolin would drive out to the Argan Farm and redeem Celia, as though she was some sort of pawned item that had been pledged, whilst Mr Webb, the public face of her captor slipped away unobserved.

After his refuelling stop, Wally's helicopter had arrived back on set just as Indigolin was setting off. Wally told Indigolin that he'd discovered where Celia was being held and was going to the police. Indigolin told Wally that they'd just negotiated her terms of release, which didn't include any police involvement, and that he was going to the Argan Farm to set her free right now. He invited Wally to join him for a ride. Wally said it would be quicker for them to take the chopper. So Wally, Colman and Indigolin piled back into the refuelled Eurocopter and took the place of Aka Akinyola.

Mr Webb had informed Indigolin that his trophy would be waiting in Pavilion 22 for him, as it was important for publicity purposes that Indigolin play a part personally in her release; but he had added that there was also something else waiting for him in Pavilion 22 that had to be opened by him personally and no-one else, something that he would find to his advantage.

Of course, there was no truth in this: the USP of Pavilion 22 was simply that it was geographically the pavilion in the middle of all the other pavilions, as it were, the omphalos. So that once Indigolin was within Pavilion 22, his escape route from the conflagration that Mr Webb intended to start by setting all the pavilions ablaze, would be quite impossible. He would be sitting in the very seat of the fire, in the area of severest burning.

Indigolin was piloted to the rendezvous by Wally in his copter. He hadn't been able to persuade Colman not to join them. Colman's quest was driven by dedication to the woman with whom he had made his career, and who had been his wife, albeit he had spent his honeymoon and married life inside Wormwood Scrubs whilst his brother stood in for him. Wally's quest was for the missing leading lady from his film, the woman whose hand he had inchoately asked for as his wife, and who, equally inchoately, seemed to have agreed by the simple expedient of quitting smoking.

Ascending, those seated in the chopper saw the incoming Toyota pick-up with Presley and Posthumous on board. Arriving on set, with neither Indigolin nor Pfister to report to, they resorted to asking Edgar Ash where everybody was, and he informed them that Indigolin, Pfister and Colman had gone to the Argan Farm. After obtaining directions, the brothers jumped straight back into the pick-up.

Albanian George was checking his bank balances online with his telephone app, and was pleasantly surprised to see that Tinctorio Indigolin had repaid him his full debt plus compound interest to the due date plus iniquitous interest, which was default rates, from after the due date. It was just like the Blue Molecule Man had always said. His stock price was going to go through the roof and then he'd dump some of it and repay him. Albanian George didn't want to have blood on his hands unnecessarily. He put a call through to Mr Webb to stand him down.

Wally landed the copter, and Indigolin and Colman disembarked with him. Indigolin had set the combination for the gate to the Argan Farm himself, but he didn't need it as Wally landed within the compound. They traversed the neat avenues of boxed hedge past the Visitors Centre towards Pavilion 22.

The Eurocopter made so much noise coming down that Mr Webb failed to hear his phone ringing when Albanian George attempted to connect with him to call off the contract killing. Albanian George had decided it was prudent not to leave a message and thereby a footprint. He'd try again later. It was Wimbledon week. He took his phone out of his shirt pocket and set the app for his Vantablacked Bentley Bentayga to pre-cool.

He'd get his motor all nice and chilly, and drive round to Annabel's to watch the semi-finals on their big screen. It was a glorious summer's day. They'd open the roof at Wimbledon and the roof at Annabel's too. He'd wear his seersucker jacket and correspondent's shoes. He'd try ringing Mr Webb again from the car's SIM.

Mr Webb had chosen Pavilion 22, because exiting Pavilion 22 necessitated threading one's way through an obstacle course of all the other pavilions, which would by then be ablaze. Webb remembered from his primary school classics lessons that Scylla and Charybdis was the ancient Greek version of a watery obstacle course. He wondered if there was a fiery equivalent.

Not wanting to harm Celia, he had apologetically gagged her and tied her up in the concrete workman's quarters, so that she would be nowhere near the conflagration. Once alone, Celia had managed to get her hands up to her head, remove the ornamental dagger that Wally had bought her and which she used as a hair grip, and she had cut herself free with it and taken out the gag, before reinserting the Jineta in her beehive.

However, she wasn't free for long, because she came to the conclusion that Mr Webb must have tied her up in the workman's block for some sinister reason: maybe he'd gone to fetch something to finish her off with. So she crawled out of the block and into the safety of the pavilion complex where she was astonished to come face to face with her ex-husband, accompanied by Tinctorio Indigolin and Wally Pfister. She had no idea what this motley triumvirate were doing in Pavilion 22, but she was glad to see them.

Presley and Posthumous arrived at the Argan Farm. They found the gate locked and didn't know the combination that opened it, so Posthumous shot the clasp clean off with a bolt from his Marrakesh market crossbow. He then reloaded the weapon with his remaining bolt, and the two of them entered the compound. They followed the boxed pathways, past the parked helicopter, and proceeded towards the ultra-lux wigwams.

Once everybody was sufficiently buried within the tabernacle complex, Mr Webb emerged from hiding with the XM42 flamethrower with the ridiculous smiling shark motif down its side. Mr Webb had noted that Indigolin was accompanied by Hunt and Pfister. Albanian George had only paid for one cremation, but he was going to get three more, like a Baker's Dozen.

Nothing Webb could do about it: the Albanian malapropist had specified an indiscriminate means of execution, so there was going to be some collateral. Mr Webb didn't know that Celia had managed to set herself free and also crawled into the pavilion complex, and that there were actually going to be four more sets of charred remains than paid for, not three, when the ambulance crews sifted through all the ashes.

Mr Webb primed the XM42 and calmed his nerves with the reassuring hiss before pulling the trigger. He took the GoPro Hero Black Edition with the Shorty tripod out of his jacket pocket. He'd bought this bundled with a one year subscription to the Cloud, so that he could deliver on his promise to Albanian George; give him good footage of the conflagration without worrying about sending it from his phone or another traceable device.

He'd just WhatsApp his patron a link to the Cloud and he could watch it with a glass of Ouzo, or whatever the fuck it was a Bubble like that drunk. The GoPro bleeped on and its ready light winked. He propped up the Shorty tripod, adjusted the angle of the viewfinder, selected video and pressed the shutter again. It gave another reassuring beep, and the red recording light came on.

The lasso of lit gasoline leaped out of the barrel of the XM42 like a dragon's breath as he sowed the seeds of destruction from tent to tent. He didn't take his finger off the trigger until all 40 tents were ablaze. Only when he saw that the inferno that he had created was inescapable, pavilions deep, all their serried ranks on fire, did he take his finger off the trigger, wipe it clean of prints, and then chuck the XM42 into the tumult where the remaining gasoline in the chamber exploded with a satisfying thwack.

It was a shame to leave the nice GoPro behind. He'd become kind of fond of it. But it was evidence. He wiped it with a damp lens cloth, to make sure there were no fingerprints, and walked away, leaving it recording and beaming its live content up to the Cloud. Then he headed for the car. He took the concealed Range Rover out from under its covers and disappeared through the gate considerately left open by the incoming Presley and Posthumous, and headed for the airport.

At the airport, he'd just dump the car in the car park, short term or long term car park didn't matter, as he wouldn't be paying the bill to retrieve it. Then he'd be on the flight to Dublin's fair city where the girls are so pretty. He frowned at the acrid air in the Range's Rover's cockpit. His clothes smelled like a Guy Fawkes' night bonfire. He wound down the window. With the window open, he thought he might have a smoke, but there was an oily petrol film on the back of his hands, and he didn't want to finish off all his good work by accidentally setting fire to himself. Go out with a bang! He decided to wait until he'd scrubbed up in the airport lounge toilet. Assuming there was an airport lounge in a third-world country like this.

Presley and Posthumous surveyed the carnage from the safety of the Visitors Centre. They couldn't get any closer as the temperature was like the surface of Venus, and the tents must have been clad in some synthetic shit that was producing choking plumes of black smoke. Nothing could survive in that. Colman and Celia, Indigolin and Wally, were at the very seat of the fire where everything must be hottest. Every now and then there was a small crack or fizz as a television or other appliance exploded in one of the tents.

The brothers decided to squat down as close to the inferno as their grafted skins could bear and go picking through the remains when they were cool enough, make sure their brother was finally laid to rest. They took up their positions on the wooden boardwalk lined with the box hedges, leading up to the burning pavilions. A deafening crack sounded as the main tent pole to pavilion 13 came down, and then they saw something that defied reason.

Hand to hand, like the Pied Piper of Hamelin, Colman Hunt, shoeless and wrapped in blue fustian, was leading a conga line of survivors out of the inferno. First was his ex-wife, Celia Broadsword. She was linked hand-to-hand to Wally Pfister, and Pfister was linked hand-to-hand to Tinctorio Indigolin wearing what appeared to be an un-creased and un-phased legume blue suit. Colman's disciples were placing their feet exactly where he placed his, weaving, bending, arching, and angulating like smouldering snowboarders through the forest of falling canvas and masonry, as he led them unscathed into the clearing where Presley and Posthumous lay in wait.

"Neat trick!" Presley said.

"But it wears off after a few repetitions," said Posthumous, levelling the crossbow at Mortimer's head. "And it was all for nothing, because I'm going to shoot you clean through the cranium anyway, you matricidal moron."

Celia's hand went up to the back of her head where she knew she had the bobbin. She removed the seven inch Jineta dagger and her silver hair tumbled down on her shoulders.

"Don't get any stupid ideas, lady," said Presley. "That's an ornamental Nasrid dagger. It's a close combat weapon. No use for throwing. This crossbow, on the other hand, has a hair trigger. I'll have buried the bolt in Morty's eye socket before you can even think about throwing that toy."

But Celia had no intention of throwing the dagger. Before anyone, including Mortimer, could begin to compute what was going through her head, she had sunk the Jineta into Mortimer's gut with all her strength as Presley and Posthumous doubled over in agony, blood spewing from their mouths, eyes and nostrils. Then a stomach-churning howl went up from Presley when he saw that the bolt from his crossbow with the hair trigger had gone clean through his own shoe, when he had doubled over in pain. The bolt was buried in his foot, nailing him to the boardwalk like a crucifixion.

Then Wally noticed the red flashing light of the GoPro mounted on the Shorty tripod winking at them. "Smile please, everybody!" He said. "You're on Candid Camera!"

Edgar Allen Poe

Never mind the fucking Sahara! It was a glorious summer's day in England, and Albanian George was taking the Vantablacked Bentayga round Berkeley Square to Annabel's to have his lunch and watch the Wimbledon men's semi-finals there on the big screen. He switched off the pre-cooling app with the phone that he'd just used unsuccessfully to attempt to put the call through to Mr Webb, and he turned on the Bentley's own A/C.

He'd only gone two hundred yards when the fucking warning light came on, telling him that if he had any ideas about going to his club to watch the tennis, he'd better think again, because the car wanted to be towed ignominiously back to the factory. He dug his mobile out of his jacket pocket to put a call through to Rupert at HR Owen's.

By now, he had him on speed dial. The phone was dead. He must have used up all the juice on the pre-cool for 20 minutes before he set off. Never mind, the car had its own SIM. Unfortunately, whatever had crashed the rest of the car and lit up the warning light had crashed the car's phone too.

How hard can it be? Albanian George asked himself. When it came to IT, he was a bit of a Luddite, but he thought he could remember the procedure that Rupert had run him through. Turn everything off. Wait fifteen seconds. Five more for luck. Then turn everything back on again. Bingo!

He hit the kill switch and everything turned off. Immediately the light-absorbing Vantablack started making the cabin swelteringly hot. He was already perspiring like a Dresden drayman as he counted the fifteen seconds out. He realised that he couldn't even summon enough breath to count out loud as he had done last time, because now it was the men's semi-final on a swelteringly hot July day. It was as if the paint job on his car was sucking the oxygen out of the atmosphere. It was unnaturally hot, unbearably hot. He wanted to dig his handkerchief out of his pants pocket and wipe his brow.

The sweat was dripping into his eyes and he couldn't see what he was doing properly. He felt like his contact lenses were melting into his eyes and fusing them together. But his seat was pushed so far forward for his favoured driving position that he couldn't reach into his pants pocket and extract his handkerchief. The seat and steering wheel position were stored in his preferences, and the seat wouldn't push back unless he opened the driver door. But the doors had locked themselves.

Fuck the extra five seconds for luck, he decided. He stabbed the START button and stamped on the brake, but nothing happened. He stamped harder and prodded more, at first, probingly and eventually, desperately, but the car was completely lifeless and unresponsive. The temperature was intolerable. He pulled his dead mobile out of his jacket pocket to see if there was enough juice left to put a call through to the emergency services, but there was a warning message showing on that device too. It said TOO HOT in big red letters.

Now George could barely breathe. The air was too superheated to draw into his lungs without scalding him in the chest. He wondered if he was having a heart attack. He certainly had all of the symptoms. Unsuccessfully, he tried to wriggle himself into a position where he could kick out a window or a windscreen or a door; but he didn't have the traction because of his stupid driving position so close to the steering wheel. Also, he simply didn't feel he had the strength anymore. This must be what it felt like to be a spent force, he ruminated.

'Jesus Fucking Christ!' George thought to himself as it dawned on him that he was going to die locked inside this invisible, mobile crematorium right outside H R Owens in Berkeley Square, and no-one would even know he was there. Was it the burning pain or the insignificance of it all that was worst?

'Fuck me!' He thought, and *'Fuck me again! I'm going to be the first person since Shirley Eaton in Goldfinger killed by a fucking paint job!'*

The temperature inside the cabin topped 200 degrees. George's heart contracted and stopped. He was dead.

The last meaningless catches of words and phrases that flitted through his brain as his heart stopped would not have made sense to anyone else:

Death by Blow Job!

Death by Hand Job!

Death by Paint Job!

The temperature continued to rise. Later on when another car inadvertently collided with the Vantablacked Bentayga, attempting to bag what it thought was a coveted, vacant parking space in Berkeley Square, Rupert heard the almighty bang and came out of the showroom. He found the invisible car with his app, and opened the doors easily from the outside. It was as if he'd opened the safety doors on a blast furnace. The interior temperature was hot enough to melt the heat retardant panels on the space shuttle. The wave of heat roared out and burnt his face. Inside the cabin was a nearly liquid mass of loathsome—of detestable putridity that once went by the name of Albanian George, but was now just scrambled eggs.

Consequences

Presley and Posthumous were in such crippling pain for a few hours that Wally and Indigolin were able to restrain them until the officers from the Moroccan National Brigade were on the scene. The felonious Unsdorfers were loaded into the back of a van and taken off for processing. They were subsequently charged with assault with a deadly weapon, attempted kidnap, attempted murder and conspiracy to murder. Subsequently, the two brothers ran a defence in which each denied that it was him who was going to carry out the execution of the sundry felonies. Each one claimed it was the other. In a more liberal jurisdiction, such as England or America, both of them might actually have walked free, because no jury would have been able to convict either beyond a reasonable doubt, as there would always be the lurking suspicion that it might have been the other one.

Fortunately, the Moroccan judge was not persuaded by such woke defences, and he sentenced them both for the same crime. They would do 12 years each in very unpleasant conditions in Tazmamart jail. Tazmamart was a secret prison in the desert that historically had been used for political prisoners, and had a reputation for resorting to illegal methods such as torture. The brothers were sent there purely as a matter of convenience: it was the prison closest to the Argan Farm and Atlas Film Studios.

Apart from the fact that it had resort to illegal methods, nothing else about it resembled a resort.

This time Mortimer let them serve out their own sentences.

With a little help from Elena Troy and a little more help behind the scenes from Bvsh Ho, Wally uploaded the image of Mr Webb that he'd taken off the security camera footage with his sniping tool, when he had climbed out of the Range Rover for a smoke. An all-points went out and Rough Hugh Webb was pulled over by the Border Force at Agadir International airport attempting to board a flight to Dublin.

Evidence from his phone confirmed that he'd been retained to execute Indigolin, and the phone also contained an email confirmation from GoPro

Accounts, thanking him for buying the camera and confirming his one year subscription to the Cloud. If he was making mistakes as careless as that, maybe it really was time for him to jack it in, he thought to himself. Here was a man who wouldn't even take his hit money in an envelope with his own name written on it: he'd gone to so much trouble to use the GoPro instead of a phone to make the recording, because he didn't want anything linking the recording to him, but he'd overlooked the confirmation of purchase that GoPro had emailed to him as it had gone straight into his Junk folder marked *You don't often get messages from this source*.

This led the Moroccan authorities straight to the Cloud, which contained the incriminating footage of arson, kidnapping and attempted murder. Most pointlessly of all, although Webb didn't know it, his patron would never even view the recording the making of which was going to cost Webb his freedom, as he was scrambled eggs in Berkeley Square.

The evidence on his phone confirmed that he had been retained to assassinate Indigolin, but the phone didn't say by whom he had been retained. Nor could the officers from the National Brigade work out who had paid him to abduct Celia Broadsword. According to his banking records, he didn't appear ever to have been paid for it, and the conclusion the authorities came to was that he had abducted her for his own perverse satisfaction: he was clearly a great admirer, potentially, a stalker.

He was apprehended in possession of a boxed set of all her works on Blu-Ray DVD, including bootleg works not available to the public. He was travelling with scant other luggage. The erroneous conclusion that was therefore drawn was that in the matter of her kidnapping, Webb was probably the principal as opposed to an agent.

Mr Webb declined to implicate either of his employers, because he was a professional and had his reputation to think of. However, he was already in his early seventies, and as he was sentenced to a minimum of 15 years for kidnapping, assault, arson, criminal damage to property and attempted murder, his reputation wouldn't be much use to him for some time, and he would probably not be match fit when he came out the other end. Once again, purely as a matter of jurisdictional and administrative convenience, he was weighed off to Tazmamart.

He was also convicted of infringement of copyright in a bootleg recording of *The Wife of Bath*.

They didn't charge him with the rape and murder of Wally's mother, because it was all too long ago and they'd have to exhume her to get the DNA evidence. But Wally felt justice had been done and that he had played an important part in bringing the man who had raped his mother and kidnapped his fiancée to account.

Wally had commented to Celia that Mr Webb's story was proof that smoking was bad for you, because if he hadn't got out from behind the tinted windows of his Range Rover for that one, ill-fated cigarette, he would probably have been back in Dublin by now. Celia had said that she was glad that she had quit, and found that quitting had opened all sorts of new doors to her.

On the other hand, Indigolin's Blue Rif productions did obtain all the necessary licences to exhume the believed remains of Boabdil Il Chico from his ignominious resting place by the Gate of the Burnt One. They matched his DNA to his only surviving descendant. The descendant turned out to be Aderfi Benjelloun.

Although it proved impossible to inter the exhumed Boabdil under the Courtyard of the Twelve Marble Lions in Granada's Alhambra, the remains were reburied with all due formalities and in the pomp and solemnity appropriate to the last Sultan of the Islamic State of Granada, and the footage was viewed in the Islamic east and the infidel west, and Indigolin's stock went up and up, and the film associated with the excavation, entitled *The Gate of the Burnt One*, broke all box office records, re-establishing Colman Hunt and Celia Broadsword as two actors still at the top of their games, and introducing Aderfi Abdallah Muhammed XII, as he was now known, as the glittering new star who stood astride the east and west like a true Colossus. He was quite literally cinematic royalty.

"I told you we could improve on Aderfi Benjelloun, didn't I?" Indigolin teased. "Ben Julian! You're an Arab, but you used to sound like a Yid! Now you sound like bloody royalty: Aderfi Abdallah Muhammed XII."

Nobody could really be surprised that the film smashed all box office records. No film had ever had so much publicity before its release: the kidnapping and ransom of both the leading man and the leading lady, the exhumation of the film's subject; the discovery that that subject's only living descendant was in fact playing the subject in that very film; the miraculous escape from the conflagration, the footage of which had been downloaded from the Cloud and viewed by tens of millions of people; and the betrothal of the leading lady to the director.

Even without any of these considerations, the film would have been assured success due to the fact that the script was corking and the camerawork unparalleled. Unfortunately neither Albanian George, who had commissioned the film of the conflagration, nor Hugh Webb, who had set it, ever viewed either the footage of the miraculous escape from the fire, or the film it was used to promote, because Albanian George was a liquid mass of putrescence, and Mr Webb died of old age in the Moroccan prison.

Mr Webb was allowed one hour a day on the Internet. He spent it working on the 3rd Edition of his Illustrated History of Catafalques. Then it came to him, naturally, when he wasn't trying or thinking about it. He managed to resolve an issue that had been annoying him since he boarded the fateful BA plane to Morocco:

> CLAUDIO: The miserable have no other medicine
> But only hope:
> I have hope to live, and am prepared to die.
> DUKE: Be absolute for death; either death or life
> Shall thereby be the sweeter. Reason thee with life:
> If I do lose thee, I do lose a thing
> That none but fools would keep: a breath thou art
> Servile to all the skyey influences,
> That dost this habitation, where thou keep'st
> Hourly afflict. Merely, thou art death's fool;
> For him thou labour'st by thy flight to shun,
> And yet, run'st towards him still.

Measure for Measure; Act 3 Scene 1

Rough Hugh Webb went to his death absolutely, and in the knowledge that he had finally remembered where the quotation that had been playing in his head for so long, came from.

The film, *The Gate of the Burnt One,* also received additional, unprecedented publicity at its premieres in London and LA. The traditional red carpet was replaced by pyres consisting of precisely 2,000 kilos of oak wood. The embers were then raked out, carefully so that there was no clumping, and then Colman Hunt, Patrick Oculus and Aka Akinyola walked the red carpet of burning cinders barefoot into the picture house. They carried Wally Pfister, Tinctorio Indigolin and Celia Broadsword on their backs, and were careful to stamp heavily on the coals and with flat feet.

Wally had decided that the film had simply become too big to chop up into a mini-series for the streamers, and it required a full theatrical release. *The Gate of the Burnt One* took Oscars for its director, its three leading actors, and its twelve-year-old screenwriter. As Indigolin had predicted, a year after its release, most people believed that the events of the film were true.

The twelve-year-old scriptwriter had rewritten the history of the east and west, and for his efforts he received an Oscar for best scriptwriter, another Oscar for best film in a foreign language, as English was foreign to him, and a third Oscar for most promising new entrant to the world of films. The critics said that only two people had ever written dialogue more crackling than his: William Shakespeare and Elmore Leonard.

Celia Broadsword, in addition to seizing her Oscar for best actress, also received a special lifetime achievement award. She also received a Palm d'Or at the Cannes Film Festival. She also received a Grammy for her husky rendition of the number one theme song, *Ay de Mi Alhama*. It went on to become the most played song worldwide at funerals, knocking Frank Sinatra's *My Way* from the top of the chart.

Celia and Wally were contractually obliged to continue participating in promotional events for the movie for sixty days after its theatrical release, but on the sixty-first day, they put a placeholder in their diaries and the diaries of their close friends: they were getting married.

During the course of her promotional interviews, Celia Broadsword gave a withering vitriolic put down for the feeble, pathetic Brunswick Holt, the likes of which had never been heard of even in the Babylon of Hollywood before. She eloquently compared her own rape, her kidnapping ordeal, near cremation, and stabbing her leading man through the guts with a Nasrid dagger on the one hand, to Holt's puny, sickly, infirm, woke impotence in exaggerating the effects of a little game of dart-throwing by an eighty-five-year-old woman on the other hand. The subsequent postings and re-postings of that interview went so viral that Holt had been humiliated into withdrawing his own inchoate writ and paying the studio's legal costs.

Patio De Los Leones an Exhumation Is Followed by Two Weddings

It isn't lawful to get married in the Alhambra, but Wally and Celia did the next best thing. They stayed in the duplex turret room at the Parador San Francisco, where Celia had been billeted for the shooting of the first two series of *King Ferdinand's Book of Hours*. The Parador is a little old fashioned, but, as Celia and Wally were often heard to say, they were old school themselves. What it sacrificed in modern amenities it recouped in location, as it is the only hotel that is part of the Alhambra and within its walls. At night when the day tourists have had the gates closed on them, the residents of the Parador have the Alhambra and its magnificent gardens all to themselves.

The wedding ceremony and subsequent reception were held within *Carmen de los Chapitiles*, the Nasrid gardens within the *Generalife* and facing the *Albaicin* and *El Sacromonte*, beneath the snow-capped mountains of the Sierra Nevada, which was about as close as one can get to actually being married within the Alhambra. Celia Broadsword was given away to Wally Pfister by Colman Hunt, and Aderfi was Wally's best man. He made a short, but touching speech, remarking that, after so many kidnappings, it was always good to see a disinterment followed by a wedding.

The catering was provided by Aka Akinyola, the charcoal curator.

During the speech from the royal best man, Colman's phone inconsiderately emitted an almighty ping. Wally glowered, because he had addressed the guests beforehand, requesting everyone to turn their phones on to silent at the beginning of the occasion. Undeterred, Colman fished through all the pockets in the unfamiliar morning dress his tailor had supplied for the occasion, and eventually identified the pocket where the offending item was pinging.

As if allowing the device to ping wasn't rude enough, Colman followed through by extracting the phone from his pocket, and then holding it at arm's length to read the message, as he was too vain to put his bifocals on. Having read the message his mouth dropped open. It had been so long since he'd filled in the form for Monserrat, confirmed that he wasn't a robot and hit Send that he'd forgotten all about it.

By now, Wally Pfister had a good head of steam on him.

"Would Mr Hunt like to share with the rest of us the message that he has just received that is so much more important than me getting spliced to his ex-wife?"

"Duh," said Colman, still incredulous, and then, "sure, sure. Hear this, everybody, I've just been admitted to Holy Orders. From this day forward, Colman Hunt is a Cistercian Monk and my new address is El Monasterio de Monserrat, near Barcelona."

Wally had to admit this was important news, so he forgave him and subsequently made a toast to the child prodigy who had chosen to end his career in a manner no less remarkable than he had begun it.

The other child prodigy, Badiss, had been reluctantly pressed into the clothes of a page boy, which, as soon as the reception was over, he couldn't wait to throw off and resume his traditional blue robes. Most of the cast were there as well as Tinctorio Indigolin who insisted on hosting the wedding and providing the wedding ring which featured the largest, bluest Tanzanite ever seen.

"Good grief!" Celia exclaimed when she first caught sight of the blue bauble, "That's what my mother would have called a Bobby Dazzler!"

Brushing off Wally's protestations that the groom normally bought the wedding ring for his fiancée, Indigolin had also bought the couple a fortnight's honeymoon on North Island in the Seychelles, close to Mahé, where his huge printer was busy pumping out a coral reef that was already much-befriended by denizens of the deep.

Of course, the new reef, as printed, was blue, but Indigolin has assured the world it would weather down to the usual colours within a few centuries. Elena Troy was Celia's Maid of Honour. Elena never did find out what Indigolin had done wrong, but she believed that, whatever it was, it had been cancelled out by a lot of things he'd done right.

Badiss wasn't the only one who couldn't wait to get out of his hired suit and back into blue robes. After the ceremony, Colman Hunt returned the rented suit to Moss Bros, and (in common with his screenwriter) resumed the blue robes that he'd taken to wearing ever since the night he'd strode out naked into the desert with his rolled up script under his arm. He continued to wear those blue robes, until the Cistercians at Monserrat gave him a brown habit to replace them with.

Aderfi was offered a great many roles, but he never appeared in another film. He became the poster boy for every Arab spring, but shunned anything political and completely disappeared from the scene. He went back to his nomadic life with the other Blue Men of the Desert.

Elena Troy had proposed to Tinctorio Indigolin at the wedding. After all, it was a leap year. Celia Broadsword had been standing next to the couple and within earshot. Elena reminded him of their dinner at the Riyadh, and before his demonstration with the Blue Rif liquid, how he had asked her if he could take her hand. She'd said it was belated, but the answer was *Yes*, if he'd have her. He'd asked her why she'd waited so long, and she answered: "I couldn't let you slip through my fingers a second time!"

Indigolin had turned from Elena on one side to Celia on his other side and, looking up at her silver hair, said simply, "May I?"

Celia didn't know what he was referring to but politely said, "Of course!"

Indigolin removed the Jineta from Celia's beehive, and with the famous dagger in his hand, posed the same question to Elena: "May I?"

This question elicited the same answer, although Elena was as much in the dark of what Indigolin was asking permission to do as Celia had been. Indigolin used the Jineta to snip a lock of Elena's blond hair. He then returned the faux-Nasrid weapon to Celia, and asked Elena to tie her bracelet of bright hair around his wrist until they could choose some proper rings. She did so. Indigolin later had the hair plaited with strips of leather professionally, and a proper closing mechanism added, and he wore it to his dying day.

Having elicited a positive answer to her proposal, Elena told her fiancé that she'd only marry him if his lawyers drew up a watertight pre-nuptial agreement first, so that he would know she wasn't marrying him for his money. Genuinely, he told her that the thought had never crossed his mind. In the upshot, the agreement never got drafted, and, as time would tell, it was never needed.

Before they published details of the engagement, she told him that there were a few things about her past that she needed to share with him first, as they couldn't embark on married life without being completely honest with one another. She reminded him that she was Catholic and believed in the confessional. He had asked her if there were other men. She had told him that, of course, there had been other men, and she wasn't worried about them and assumed he wasn't either. She had then gone on to fill him in with details of her background and Bvsh Ho.

"I've got a confession to make, Tinctorio."

"Yes, Elena."

"The reason I seem so over-qualified for the job, is because I'm not who I am."

"So who are you really, Elena?"

"I'm an inspector of taxes, Tinctorio."

"You mean you don't go diving and study Metaphysical Poets?"

"Yes, yes, yes. Everything else I've told you is true, but there was one big, dirty lie, and now it's eating me up. I was put here to investigate you?"

"And how do you like me so far?"

"Mr Indigolin, if you asked me to ski down Everest in the nude with a carnation up my arse, I'd do it!"

"Be careful what you wish for, Elena! So the reason why you suffer from imposter syndrome—"

"—is because I am an imposter. Tinctorio, I had to get close to you, but once you let me in and I became so close, I'm afraid I grew to like my subject too much, and ended up falling in love with him. What are you going to do with me?"

"After that confession, Elena, I'd better do the same that you did for me. I am going to prescribe a few Hail Mary's, and a course of protracted and passionate love-making. As you pointed out to me earlier, we sometimes have to do the right things for the wrong reasons, and if, as Nicolo Machiavelli said, the ends do justify the means, look where we've ended up. We're lovers."

"Are we, Tinctorio?"

"I very much hope so, Elena."

"So the hunter has become the prey."

"I prefer to think that both hunter and hunted became domesticated and now prey upon one another."

"Just as long as you don't get too domesticated on me, Mr Indigolin!"

"I'd rather be housebroken than heartbroken, Elena!"

"So that's a yes to my proposal, Tinctorio?"

"Emphatically, Elena."

The photos and footage of Celia and Wally's remarkable wedding were syndicated around the world. There had been other celebrity weddings with huge age gaps, but these had invariably consisted of an aged Lothario or diva getting hitched to a younger air-headed accessory. This wedding was of a completely different order: two highly accomplished professionals, both at the top of their careers, very successful and wealthy in their own fields, getting married because they were totally besotted with one another.

Wally asked Celia how come he'd managed to get this far without having to sign an NDA. It was at this point that she said she had a little confession to make. She showed him the video she had taken on her phone, the video of his advanced yoga position, before she hit the delete button.

The nuptials coincided with the general release of *The Gate of the Burnt One*, and the stunning dagger-throwing scene with Brunswick Holt and his huge blue turban, playing alongside Celia Broadsword, the sequence now made all the more notorious by Holt's widely-publicised and subsequently withdrawn writ.

The media had not failed to link that scene to Celia's subsequent escape from her captor by the remarkable, ballsy and very much out-of-the-box strategy of stabbing an innocent bystander through the gut with the very same weapon; and now, here she was in the wedding photographs syndicated worldwide, wearing the world-famous Jineta dagger in the back of her hairdo.

Wally and Celia formed a charitable company whose objects were to promote living standards in the Arab world and Morocco in particular, by patronising and preserving dying local skills. They funded the metalworker from the souk, and he began making reproductions of the little Jineta on an industrial scale. The seven inch hair accessory became the hottest selling Christmas gift of the year, relegating the usual slew of tacky electronic ephemera to subsequent rankings.

However, the Jineta itself went on to become a symbol of much wider meaning, and members of all sexes, whether or not they wanted to wear one in their hair, wore it as a lapel badge or a brooch. It became the year's most often requested image at tattoo parlours, and the logo was identified with female empowerment. A movement grew up around the ideogram, the movement taking on the name that it was given by the Mail on Sunday newspaper, *#Me3*, evocative of the triplets. *#MeToo* had been all about victimhood. *#Me3* was about making other people the victims, about making the abusers pay the price through one's own decisive actions and deeds, and Celia Broadsword was its figurehead and ambassador.

After all the photos and speeches and curtain calls, the guests had gone their various ways, and Celia and Wally had the Alhambra all to themselves that evening. Hand in hand they stood in the Courtyard of the Twelve Marble Lions as the sun set behind the Sierra Nevada, with not a sound except the tinkling of the fountain.

One hundred and twenty-four intricate white marble columns supported the surrounding galleries to the 35m x 20m courtyard with the Twelve marble lions carrying the wellspring in its centre. It was the name of this Courtyard that had got Colman Hunt released from his captors.

"Well, Wally," Wally's bride said, "in your doggerel 13 line sonnet that had 14 lines, you promised me a Palm d'Or, and now you've given me one."

"Just imagine," Wally mused, "being a Nasrid Emir, such as Boabdil. One of those apartments up there in the gallery would have been where he lived.

Imagine looking out on this very courtyard every morning and walking among its columns in the cool of the evening."

"Yes, Wally, you can see why he wept when he had to leave it."

She was framed by the wellspring and the cataracts from the twelve lion's mouths. Directly behind her silver hair the argent jets from the main fountain in the reservoir carried by the lions bubbled out. She raised her hands and removed the Jineta. Her gorgeous hair sprayed out mirroring the fountain behind her. It was as though she had always been intended to be part of the fountain.

Then he remembered the first day he'd set eyes on Celia, face to face. He'd just climbed out of his Hummingbird Eurocopter, and there she was in the irrigation spray of Aka's kitchen garden in the middle of the Sahara Desert. And he'd told himself that he was looking at an epiphany wrapped in a mirage. And he realised he was always going to think of her that way.

Wally saw a mirror image of her in the globe of a water droplet from the fountain. Then he realised there were millions of duplicates, each suspended droplet capturing an image of her face and the firework of her silver hair at the point where the fire and the water became one; an oasis of calm and beauty in the midst of any desert in the world.

"What were those water nymphs called in Homer's *Iliad*?" He asked her.

"You mean Naiads?" A million Celia's asked him.

"Yes," he said.

"Achilles' mother was one," she added. "Thetis."

Here was Wally Pfister, one of the world's most celebrated film directors, on the most important day of his life, without a camera. But he would never forget that haunting image when there was nothing else in the frame except the face of his wife and its infinite reflections in every airborne water droplet until she became part of the fountain.

Two Epilogues of Fire and Water

Celia and Wally had sent a post card to Indigolin and Elena from their subsequent honeymoon in North Island. Neither Tinctorio nor Elena could remember when someone had last sent them a postcard from their holidays. These days it was all Instagrams or emails or texts with attachments. No-one bought postcards and stamps any more. Except Celia and Walter who were 'old school'.

That no-one purchased post cards anymore was further evident from the fact that the card concerned appeared to have been sitting outside the souvenir shop on a wire rack in the sun for so long that practically all the detail had bleached out and, much to Tinctorio's delight on receiving it, the card was almost entirely blue with no other discernible features. On the back of the card, they thanked him for making the wedding, thanked him for the ring, and, most of all, thanked him for the honeymoon. They said it was like paradise there, and told him that he had to come here with Elena as soon as their schedules allowed.

"Shall we make a trip, my little mermaid?" Indigolin asked his fiancée, alluding to her genuine hobbies and interests that had been listed on her otherwise mendacious forged CV when she applied to work for him. "The diving should be fantastic for you, Elena."

Indigolin's jet had to land at Mahé which was the only island in the archipelago big enough to boast a runway for a jet, and from there they would take the helicopter to North Island. Before leaving Mahé, they stayed a few nights at the Four Seasons. On the second day, Indigolin told her to put her bikini on under her dress. They took some towels and snorkels and masks, and got the hotel to make them a packed lunch, and the taxi took them down to the beach where Deep Blue Rif's gigantic printer was continuing to print out the coral reef. They went in to inspect the artificial atoll at close quarters.

It was already home to hundreds of triggerfish, wrasse, bumpheaded parrotfish, clownfish, yellow-lipped emperor fish, lyre tail groupers, long fin bannerfish, racoon butterfly fish and trumpet fish. Surfacing together, as a spotted eagle ray slipped by, she removed the snorkel from her mouth, and said:

"It's like a Jackson Pollock painting down there!" And then: "Ti, can I ask you a question?"

He removed his own snorkel and said: "As long as it's as sweet as the question you asked when you proposed marriage."

"I can't promise that, Ti."

She made an expansive gesture with her arms half in and half out of the Indian Ocean; a gesture taking in the open wilderness of sea bounded by gigantic granite boulders, and the creeping progress of Indigolin's cay. "Why did you call it The Gate of the Burnt One?" She asked.

Indigolin smiled at his little mermaid and followed her gesture with his eyes.

"You think I should have called it Watergate?" He smiled.

Indigolin was never apprehended by HMRC. He didn't go to jail. He didn't end up in clink, or do shovel or porridge, or get bumped off by Albanian George. But he was given a seat in the House of Lords. Now he was Lord Indigolin, and Elena was his Lady. He turned down the by now *de rigeur* offers to host the Apprentice and to sit inside the Dragon's Den.

Within his monastic cell at El Monasterio de Monserrat, Mortimer Unsdorfer, who had reverted to his true name, received few letters. There was no Wi-Fi except in the library, but he received few emails also. When therefore he found that there was an item of surface mail awaiting him in his pigeon hole that morning, it came as a pleasant surprise. It was a glorious December morning. The sky was a piercing cobalt and his cassocked shadow, as he took the letter into the courtyard garden to read, was attenuated like one of those Giacometti statues.

Sitting on a stone bench, he slit the envelope with his fingernail. A smile creased his face, as he remembered that the last time he'd seen someone slit open a letter was when he had attended the premiere of *The Gate of the Burnt* One, featuring his ex-wife's unscripted dagger-throwing scene with Brunswick Holt. She had broken the wax seal, slit open the envelope, and whatever was written on the paper inside, had lit up her face with an amazing smile, a smile that was a cross between the Mona Lisa and the Sphinx, and maybe even had a little helping of the Cheshire Cat added in, because the smile and her eyes, kept on playing after the scene had finished. It was that unrepeatable facial expression that had been used for the publicity posters when the film was released.

Inside Mortimer's envelope was a note. Apparently, the sender didn't have any letterhead, or maybe didn't even have an address, or perhaps he just didn't know how to write a letter properly. It said simply:

Dear Colman

I went to Fez and I've passed through the Gate of the Burnt One. I had to convince them I was a Muslim. It's all been cleaned up with funds from Blue Rif Enterprises: no more graffiti, no broken bottles or syringes.

As I expected, there are huge telluric forces in play. Col, I don't know how to put this into words, but I felt if anybody would understand, it would be my old friend, my fellow New Promethean, and now a member of Holy Orders! Whatever the forces were, they practically hit me in the chest as soon as I walked into the Gate. When I entered the arch, I was aware of him walking along beside me: the Wazzani rebel, the Burnt One, and guess what?

He told me what it was that he had done, which was why they had to burn him.

Yours
Patrick

The author and his wife at the Gate of the Burnt One

Bab Boujeloud, the Blue Gate

Some examples of Moroccan butchers

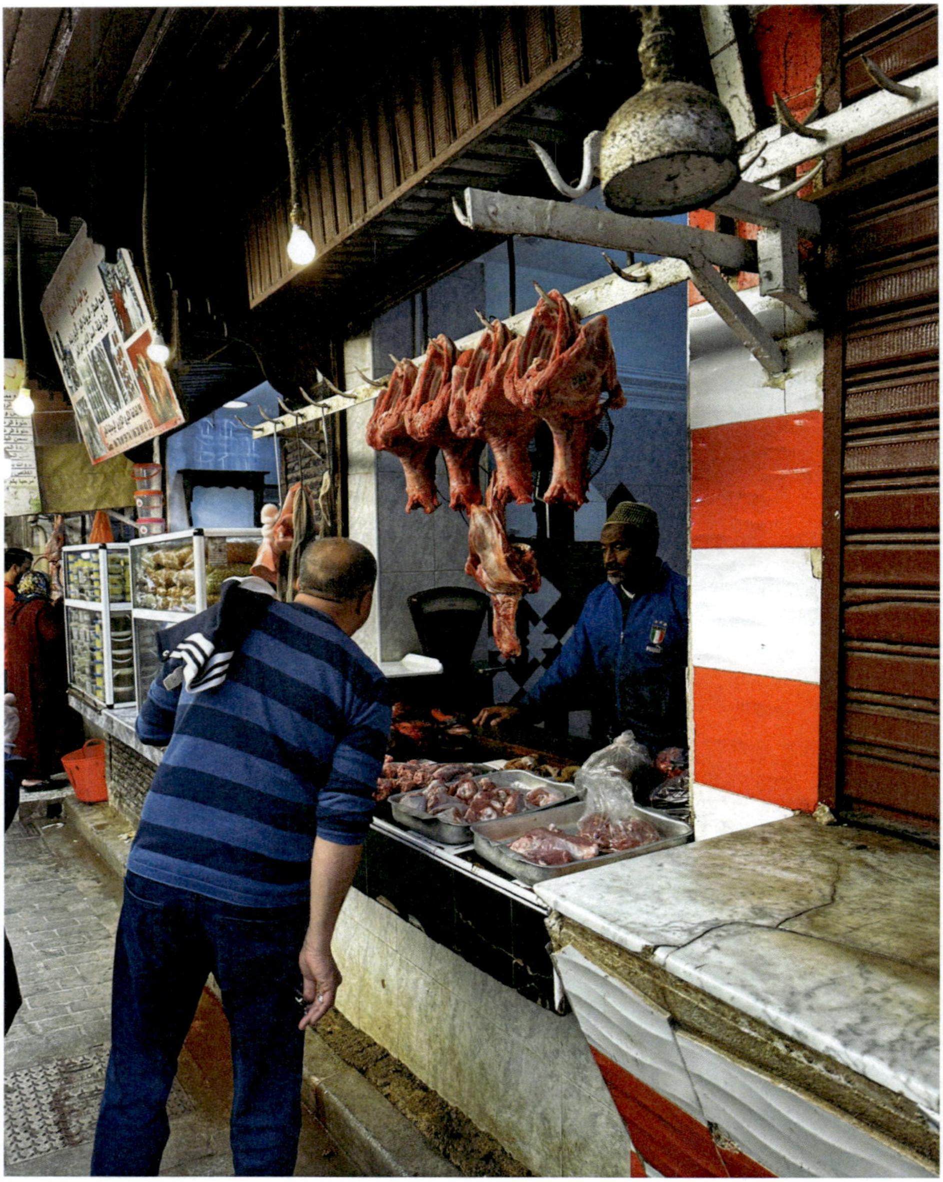

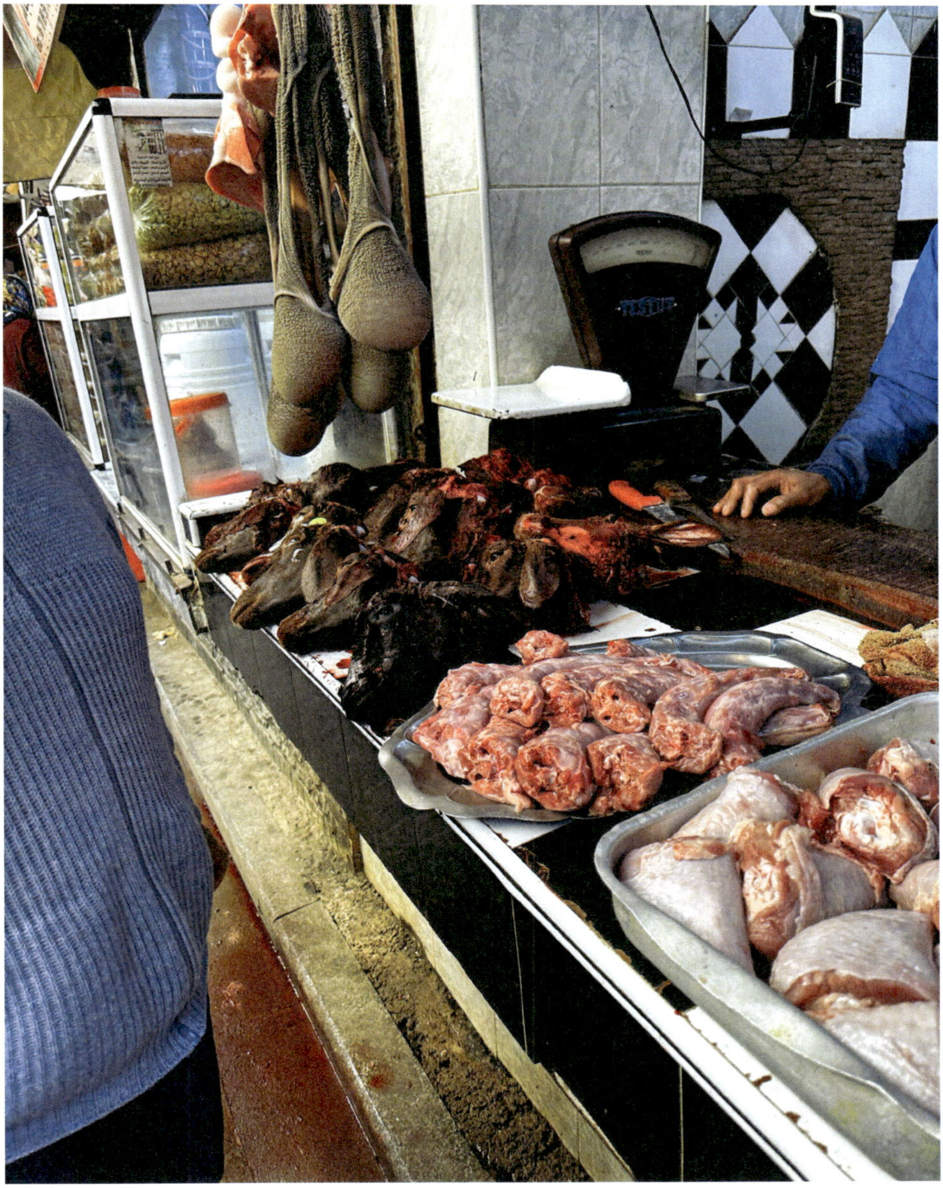

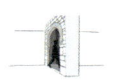

Boabdil's cube. It has now been removed from the wasteland and enclosed within a walled cemetery. Only Muslims are permitted to visit

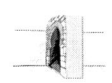

Further Reading

The Moor's Last Stand, Elizabeth Drayson, published by Profile Books
The Story of the Moors in Spain, Stanley Lane-Poole, published by Pantianos Classics.
Paradores históricos, Francisco Ontañón and Juan Eslava Galan, published by Lunwerg Editores, Barcelona.